A SERIES OF UNFORTUNATE MEET CUTES

A ROMANCE ANTHOLOGY

TORI ALVAREZ   RINA DAYNE   MARIA ANN GERMAIN

G.G. GLEASON   KELLY KAY   MARISA MOHI

K. RODRIGUEZ   KATHRYN TRATTNER   MELISSA WILLIAMS

ETERNAL DAYDREAMER PUBLISHING

A Series of Unfortunate Meet Cutes

Cover Design by Maria Ann Green
Formatting by Eternal Daydreamer Publishing, Tori Alvarez

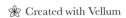 Created with Vellum

A SERIES OF UNFORTUNATE MEET CUTES

HEAT RATING

As you begin reading this romantic anthology, you'll notice at the end of each story blurb there is a specific rating in heart-eyes. While each title in this anthology portrays consensual intimacy, the rating is in place to help give you insight into the steam level of the stories you are about to read–and for your reading pleasure.

We hope you enjoy our collection of uniquely awkward and adorable meet-cutes and fall crazy in love over-and-over again.

Graphic sexual depictions, open door sex and explicit language
Content is recommended for an over-18 audience.

This anthology contains no erotica.

CONTENTS

MI SOL, MY SUN

TORI ALVAREZ

A Fast Lanes series Prequel Novella

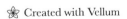 Created with Vellum

ABOUT MI SOL, MY SUN

Subgenre: Contemporary Romance
Trope: Second Chance

Graphic sexual depictions, open door sex and explicit language

BLURB:

Marisol has never felt connected to anyone or any job she has ever had. She has floundered through life dating guys, but never getting serious. Taking jobs, and quitting because none ever speak to her. That is until the blue eyes that hypnotized her in high school walk back into her life.

Eliazar is nursing a broken heart, letting his emotions show on the canvas. To forget his troubles he focuses on his photography business and his art. How can seeing the one girl he thought he hated a lifetime ago, bring light back into his gray world?

MARISOL

MY LAST CHANCE. I'M NOT SURE I BELIEVE IT, BUT I'M ALSO TOO SCARED TO push it. So here I am, a little over a month until opening my dream. But is it my dream? Or is it something I chose on the spur of the moment to appease my father? Or to have a chance of making a living? Whichever it is, I need to stick with it, at least for a few years, before I can go crawling back asking for anything else.

Well, according to my father, this is it. No more handouts. No more chances. No more "finding myself." He gave me my "last" financial help and told me not to come knocking on his door for money again. A hundred thousand for whatever my heart desired, but if I blow it, too bad, so sad. That's it. No more.

I roll my neck, hoping to stretch out the knots that have been forming there each day for the past few months. It all began on that fateful day I decided to quit yet another job. Why is it nothing interests me? I did what I was supposed to. I went to college. Got my degree. And now…now I can't find anything that excites me. Nothing holds my attention. Nothing sparks a desire. I'm a twenty-eight-year-old who has held too many jobs and quit just as many. I almost didn't land the last one because of my work history. It would be a miracle if someone else hired me again. So…my next option, open my own business.

While a cute clothing boutique sounded interesting, I feared it would tank. What if my style didn't resonate? What about all the online shops that would be able to offer better prices with no storefront overhead? I ruled a clothing boutique out very quickly.

Now coffee. Everyone loves coffee, and let's not forget all the influencers who love taking pictures with coffee in hand. And wine. Who doesn't love a glass or two to unwind? My brilliant idea was to merge them together, and Sol y Luna was born. Sol, the sun, to represent the coffee and start of the day and Luna, the moon, to close it out with a delicious vino.

My logo is everything and I spent the money to make sure it was perfect. If I can get influencers taking pictures displaying my logo, it will be a huge win.

A loud crash startles me out of my thoughts.

"Dammit!" one of the construction workers shouts.

I spin around to find him picking up a couple of tools that he dropped. The construction madness is almost done. *Don't lose patience now,* I think to myself.

"Hey, chica!" Natalia's voice brings a smile to my face.

She strides through the door like she owns the world. She has been my saving grace since college. She has climbed the ladder at a marketing firm with her brilliance. She always seems to know how to get people to "need" things.

Her expertise is benefiting me—she has taken on my marketing. A big expense when opening a business, and I'm paying her in cocktails when we hit the town.

"What are you doing here in the middle of the workday?" I ask, grabbing the green smoothie she's handing me.

"Just checking on you." She shrugs her shoulders, taking a sip from her own drink. "Checking on the progress. Dropping off the names of a couple of photographers you can choose from."

"I'm fine. Progress is fine. And just pick someone." I roll my eyes biting on the straw in frustration. I don't even know why I'm frustrated. Argh!

"Right," she drags out the word. "Everyone who is 'fine,'" she air-quotes with one hand, "is doing great."

She places her cup on one of the counters that has yet to be installed and lifts herself up to sit on it.

"Let's start over." She pauses. "How are you really doing?"

I nervously bite the inside of my cheek, scared of opening the floodgates.

"I'm waiting." Her questioning gaze never falters.

"I'm scared, okay? What if this fails? What if this isn't what I want? What if I just placed all my eggs into a losing basket?" The questions that have been playing on repeat in my head for the past couple of weeks are spoken out loud.

"I can only help with the success. I will help you make this place thrive! Seriously," she says with such certainty, smiling. "Now, whether this is what you want…" She shakes her head. "You are the only one who has that answer. You have been floating in life, never wanting to settle. You don't settle for a guy, always dumping him before it becomes too much. You drop jobs. I don't know what you are looking for, but only you can figure that one out."

"Yeah, yeah, yeah…" Those words are sounding very much like the lectures my mom has given me. "So I've heard."

"Don't get mad at me for the truth." She sticks her tongue out, jumping off the counter. "But at least if this place is booming, you'll have money to play at being something else." She winks then laughs.

I flick her off, smiling. She does have a point. As long as this place is profitable, I can do something else if I want.

"Here are the names and websites of the two photographers I recommend. I've worked with both, and they are really good. Very professional and amazing shots. Look over their online portfolios, and text me tomorrow which one you choose. I need to book them."

"I'll look at them tonight when I get home."

"Perfect. Oh, and before I forget, I have an invitation for an art showing Friday. Keep it open. We're going," she says, walking to the door.

"You know I'm not an artsy person," I say to her back.

"I know. But I am, and I get inspiration from it. So you are going with me because you love me." She walks out the door, not waiting on me to answer her.

ELIAZAR

Scanning the blank white walls in front of me, trying to picture which pieces should go where, sounds like an easy task. Instead, I've been standing in the same spot, slowly spinning around the small room I was given to showcase my work. I have dozens of canvases I could display, and my brain has *nothing*!

Every artist has a reason, a purpose for displaying their pieces. They tell a story. Build a reaction. Or simply just evoke some sort of feelings. My latest pieces are doom and gloom. Not the vibe I want to give off. *Hey, I'm depressed. Come be depressed with me.* Nope, those will not be shown.

Walking back to the storeroom, where most of my pieces are waiting on me, I try and stop the never-ending loop of *Why*. Why did she say no? I thought we were good. I thought we were solid. How could I have been so blind to her pulling away? Did I spend too much time behind the lens and not enough time looking at her? Did I do this? I thought we were both chasing the careers we wanted. We were both in a great place. The next logical step was marriage. Or so I thought. I thought surviving a private high school as a scholarship kid was embarrassing enough. Nope, having the girl you love turn down your proposal is embarrassing. The fact that it was being filmed while all our friends watched? That takes the cake.

"Still trying to decide what to do?" Nancy startles me.

7

"I didn't know you were back already." I avoid her question. I don't want the curator to know I have no idea what I'm doing. I was able to get the small space in this exhibition because a friend of a friend pulled in a favor.

"I just walked in," she says nonchalantly. "I moved your pieces around earlier, playing with the colors and ideas."

She steps closer to me, and I notice the house shoes she is wearing, which explains why I didn't hear the clink of her heels against the concrete flooring. She points at the piece in the far-left corner.

"That's happiness. The colors, strokes, pattern…" Her head drops to the side just a tad as she's taken in by the work. After a moment, she continues, "It's abstract, but more. I can see the landscape, the flowers, the brightness of the sun."

It's odd that she mentions a sun when there is no yellow in the piece, but it's there. I know it's there because it was our special place by the lake. A secluded spot near her family's vacation house.

"And then these here." She points to the right. "These feel like you want to tear my heart out and stomp the shit out of it."

She looks at me with inquisitive eyes. She doesn't know me. No one does. Not in this world. I go by a pseudonym. I don't want one of my businesses to affect the other. Not until I know they both are successful. I'm a man behind the camera as Eliazar DeLeon and a broke artist looking for a break as Zar León.

"I'll agree with you on both those interpretations." I don't want to give her anything about why.

"Have you thought of doing a sort of yin-and-yang display? Forget about all this." She waves her finger at several canvases. "They are boring in the grand scheme of shock and awe. This being your first showing, you want to *wow*. Light and dark is how you will achieve that."

Damn! She's right. I was too busy figuring out how to show a piece of everything, I forgot I needed to grab their attention first.

"Thank you!" I tell her, genuinely happy for the first time since getting the news I had this opportunity. "That is what I'll do."

"Good." She pats my shoulder before walking away.

2

MARISOL

DRAGGED TO ANOTHER BORING ART SHOW BY NATALIA, I'M WALKING around aimlessly as she pauses for an ungodly amount of time and admires each canvas. She lives for this crap, and I don't see the significance in any of it. A painting is a painting is a painting, really. Sure, there are different colors and that abstract-versus-real-life stuff, but I don't understand the high price. Pick something that will go with your décor, and be done with it.

I turn the corner into one of the smaller rooms this gallery has and come across a couple of girls talking.

"I don't appreciate this work. It's too dark and morbid. The brush strokes are too harsh. The colors..." One of the girls leaves her sentence hanging when she sees me.

"Don't mind me. I'm just here for the free wine." I say as I lift my wine glass wanting her to know I could care less about the critique she was giving.

I glance around the room and notice the works she was speaking of. Her eyes dart around the room, and she remains quiet. Her friend does the same.

"I'll agree about it being dark." I roll my eyes. "Is it just me or is slapping paint on a canvas and calling it a 'piece,' what they consider art these days?"

The girl who was making the earlier critique quietly laughs. "I would have to agree. Most of it is. There are a few really great artists still around though." She is quick to defend the profession.

"Yeah, sure." I wave my hand around the room. "But this? Is not it."

A male clearing his throat startles me, and I spin around to look into a familiar set of clear blue eyes. Eyes I would admire from afar but never admitted to enjoying.

"Still the mean girl I see," he says evenly.

Caught by surprise and taken back to memories of high school so suddenly, I'm speechless.

"Just like before. Talked all your shit when you thought people weren't looking. Had to keep that sweet prom queen persona going?" He raises a brow with his arms crossed as I stand dumbfounded in front of him.

Before I could think of a reply, he turns and walks away. By the time I get my feet moving, I lose him in the crowd of people mingling around the entrance and bar area. *Ugh! Me and my big mouth! When am I going to learn to just keep my mouth shut when I'm uncomfortable or feel out of place?*

"We aren't leaving yet," Natalia says, grabbing my hand and pulling me behind her.

As she drags me through the room, I scan the area trying to find him. She takes me back to the room I had just vacated.

"Now these are amazing." She's smiling, getting a closer look at each one, then stepping back to admire from a distance. I wish I could look at the world through her eyes. When she sees beauty, she isn't scared to say it. Appreciate it. Cherish it.

"What do you see?" I ask stupefied that all I see is colors mixed on a pulled piece of fabric.

"In this room I see life." She spins slowly. "The good and the bad. The joy and the sorrow. Happiness and anger."

I mimic her slow spin, wanting to see something. Anything.

"These are life. This is how I draw inspiration. In marketing, you have to evoke emotions about the products you are trying to sell. Draw people to them. Convince people they need them." She takes a deep breath and stops in front of a dark piece.

I stand next to her.

"What do you see?" she asks.

I shake my head.

"Well. Just your first impression. Start talking," she encourages.

"Black. I see black." I shrug my shoulders.

"Sure, yes, there's black, but there's more. Look deeper."

I wish I knew what she was talking about. All I see is blobs of paint with no rhyme or reason. "I don't know," I huff, frustrated I don't see what she does.

"See that speck here?" She points at a spot in the painting, one that's free of all the random, colored madness that I can see the weave of the canvas.

I nod.

"That's hope." She points, then waves her hand around the rest of the painting. "This is anger. This is frustration. The colors. The paint left in places, not brushed out in gentle strokes. But here…here in this tiny spot, hope resides. Maybe in all of this pain or anguish or I don't know, but right here, it can start over." I look in awe at my best friend and notice a single tear slide down her cheek.

"This one means something to you?" I ask.

"A story for another day." She shakes her head and wipes the tear gently away, making sure not to ruin her perfect makeup.

A story for another day? I thought I knew all of her secrets.

ELIAZAR

The gallery showing was pretty good. Over the last week, a couple of pieces sold. One of the happier pieces and another that wasn't on show. Someone asked if I had other pieces and came back a few days later so Nancy could show them the work I still had in the back. It's nice to know I evoked something so powerful, they want to live with my work.

I'm packing up my equipment to meet a client. I'm glad I've impressed Natalia from Cedar Lane Marketing, because she's keeping me busy. Not only busy, but well paid too. And that is the reason I agreed to lower my rate as a favor for her. She is helping some friend of hers open a new coffee and wine bar. It's not like the city doesn't have enough of these, but Natalia is insistent this spot will be the place to be.

———

I PARK in front of a warehouse, which has been renovated into a new commercial site. This area of town is exploding with condos and apartments, restaurants, outdoor areas, and shops. It dawns on me why she believes it will be a hit. Not only do the residents in the area frequent these places, but it attracts everyone in the city with the atmosphere and newness. Old meeting new, refurbishing these buildings that have been abandoned for decades. The developer who had this insight was a genius.

Loading the bags of equipment into a wagon for easy transport, I hear, "Hey, Eliazar!"

I turn to see Natalia walking toward me. I wave at her as I place the last bag on top of the mountain of things I brought. I knew I would be taking some shots, but I wasn't sure what kind of light I would be working with or what exactly she had in mind. This job was very spur of the moment, and I had no time to prep the location, prepare for the time of day, or pull together ideas. That's what favors will do. Leave you unprepared.

"I'm so glad you could do this for me!" Natalia smiles. "Don't mind

Marisol. She's a bit frazzled this morning and is a bit testy. She's worried about it succeeding."

My blood runs cold. Did she just say Marisol? That's not a common name. I run into her at the gallery as she is bashing me, yet again, and now... It's just a coincidence, right?

"Uh, yeah, sure." I stumble over my words. I turn away from her to grab the handle of the wagon to compose myself.

My heart is racing with thoughts of her. She was larger than life, walking the halls of St. Anthony Prep. Skirts always rolled up shorter than they should be, and ready to unroll if an administrator said anything. She intimidated most; no one challenged her. Her honey-colored eyes never showed emotion, yet she was charming. Always smiling sweetly when the time called. But never at me. As much as I wanted to be the recipient of her dazzling smile, I was somehow the thorn that ruined her perfectly curated life.

I wish I knew what I did to make her hate me. I wasn't the only scholarship kid on that campus, but I was the only one that drew her ire.

I didn't ask to attend her school. They found me. They invited me. They wanted me. St. Anthony's handed me a full scholarship to attend their prestigious high school if I played baseball. They used me for my pitching arm, not wanting their baseball team to suck yet another year. I played, and I was good. The team won more games once I was on the mound. A pitcher is all they needed. The team was good; they controlled the field. Strike outs were what they were missing.

My fastball and curve ball came naturally. I liked the sport. I just didn't love it enough to make it my life. I would much rather be behind the camera than in front of it.

Natalia is chatting on our short walk to the shop, but my mind is elsewhere. I need to get my head on straight. I'm a man now. Even if it is her, why would I let her unravel me? I'm a different person now. I'm successful. I don't need her approval to survive like I thought I did back then.

Natalia opens the door, holding it open so I can wheel in the wagon. I take a look around, and I'm in love with the aesthetic of the place. Exposed-brick walls and high ceilings. Metal beams overhead, with artistic pendant lights hanging sporadically from them throughout the space. Tables, couches, and chairs fill the area. The white of the counters and cabinets and the light furniture is a nice contrast to the dark, restored warehouse.

"Are you ready?" Natalia yells.

"Ready!" Marisol walks through a swinging door to a back area.

Her eyes immediately come to me, and she stops, her mouth opens slightly, before my name falls from her lips.

"E.A. Sports?" she says, using the nickname the guys gave me in high school.

"Art hater," I respond, tipping my head, not ready to say her name.

"E.A. Sports?" Natalia says trying to get her attention.

Her chest rises and falls before she takes her eyes off me and turns to Natalia. "Uh... How, uh... I'm confused."

"About what?" Natalia walks over to her.

"Why is he here?" She's looking at her friend but waves her hand in my direction.

My old nickname spilling from her lips does something to me. I wasn't sure she would even recognize me after our encounter at the gallery, but she even remembers my name. The twitch in my pants annoys me. She shouldn't still be able to get that reaction from me. It's been years. And I was, am, supposed to hate her.

"This is Eliazar, the photographer." Natalia looks back at me, her brows furrowed in confusion.

A thought comes to mind—Marisol needs my help. Mine. So I guess I have the upper hand here. Finally, the tables have turned in my favor.

"I was E.A. Sports, once upon a time." I flash Natalia a smile and wink.

"Were you now?" A short laugh escapes her lips.

I watch as Marisol narrows her eyes and clenches her jaw.

"It seems like a lifetime ago." I push my shoulders back a fraction. No reason for me to get worked up; I have the power here.

Natalia claps her hands together once and says, "Well then, since it seems you two know each other, let's get to work."

Body rigid and clearly upset, Marisol responds, "Fine."

We spend the next half hour brainstorming ideas. Throughout, Marisol keeps directing her ideas and thoughts to Natalia, refusing to acknowledge my presence. A couple of people, baristas I assume, walk through the door, interrupting our discussion about what content I should capture during the week-long soft opening and then, finally, at the grand opening.

"I want the place to seem approachable. Regular. Fun." Marisol finally looks at me directly pointing at a couple of the baristas that just walked through the door. She begins elaborating on what we were just discussing. "I want some pictures and possibly videos of them working. Showing them making drinks, creating the fun, social-media-worthy latte art. Opening bottles of wine. Talking about the different varietals to make it easier for someone who doesn't know much about wine to order and not feel intimidated."

Her demeanor changes, softens, while she is talking.

"This area was rebuilt to be high-end. Prestigious. But I want my place to attract everyone. Why shouldn't everyone be able to enjoy the amenities of an area? Some parts of town, stores, restaurants, pride themselves on their exclusivity. I want to attract people to this area. It has green areas for relaxation, splash pads for families and kids, a dog park and dog friendly restaurants. It was built to be the 'It' destination, but so far, the traffic isn't here. Why? Because the places that have joined are more worried about their own success than thinking larger. Bringing people in and having them enjoy. Then they will frequent our establishments."

There was a twinkle in her eyes as she gave this long explanation. The hardened persona I came to know so well a lifetime ago fell away, and all that was left was a passionate, beautiful soul.

"I know that we are paying for the photography to go on my website and to get my social media going, but…" She hesitates, nervously biting her lip. "If you're good at videos and editing and more of the interactive content I would like to put out, I would appreciate the help."

The queen of confidence has just asked for help…from the person she tried her hardest to ignore and make miserable years ago. I took this job thinking it was going to be a quick in and out.

As much as I would like to say *hell no*, I don't. "Sure, no problem," leaves my mouth. *Shit, now I'm stuck working with her for several more weeks.*

She still captivates me now as much as she did back then. As much as I hated her, I always wanted to see her. I guess nothing has changed.

3

MARISOL

I was unnerved when I saw E.A. Sports, or I mean, Eliazar, at the gallery. There I was bashing an artist's work, and of course, he would walk in and hear all of it. He now thinks I have no appreciation for their work. I may not understand it, but that doesn't mean I meant to be heartless. Call it a defense mechanism when I'm out of my element. And all I did was give him more ammunition to judge me more than he already does.

When he walked into my shop, I wanted to lose it. I can't believe after all these years, he affected me that way. Pining over someone who thinks less of you is not what I want to do, yet here I am, still fascinated with him.

It was his eyes that drew me in that first day he walked into my classroom. I watched him from afar not wanting to admit I was crushing on him as hard as I was. I wanted him to chase me, but he never did. Instead, he bad-mouthed me. Not sure why, but ... never mind. It is in the past and nothing I can do about that now.

He still looks the same, tall and lean with strong arms and chest, but he's a man now. The boyish good looks are more rugged. His clean-shaven face gave way to a five o'clock shadow. He's not playing ball, but somehow seems bigger, stronger.

I didn't keep up with him after we graduated, even though I wanted to stalk him. I tried, but he wasn't much of a social media guy. His accounts were private, and I *would not* be friend-requesting or following him.

Desperate is not a good look on anyone, especially me. I had a reputation to uphold. I would not be fawning over the guy who…never mind, no reason to think about the why anymore. This is a professional business relationship, and that's the way it will stay. Even if his eyes still pull me in.

I exhale a long breath. After agreeing to help, he had some great ideas to build my content and draw customers in. It was even his idea to have a loyalty card for college students. The mark-up on coffee and wine is enough to offset a loyalty program. It would last one year and only college students with proof of ID would qualify. Bring them in, treat them right, and then they will be repeat customers.

An email notification pops up on my laptop screen as I'm working. It's from E.A.—*Eliazar*. I need to remember to call him Eliazar. That's what he goes by, and I should respect that. High school crush need never be mentioned.

I click on the bubble, which takes me to a folder of some pictures he took of the shop the other day. They are good. Really good. I watched him as he worked. The baristas clearly felt comfortable with his presence, not like they were on show with a camera pointed at them. There were photos I didn't realize he took of me—laughing, smiling, relaxed. All flattering angles that looked natural. If only he saw *me* that way.

I'll see you tomorrow, E is the only thing written in the email with the attachment.

———

I PULL my bag over my shoulder, ready to meet Eliazar for my photoshoot. Me with my merchandise—cups, a few of the barista T-shirts, and wine glasses. Natalia was going to join us, but she texted me at lunch that a new client of hers demanded a meeting today and I would be on my own.

"Marisol!" I hear my name and turn toward Eliazar.

"Hi," I say pleasantly, holding a smile. As much as I want to hold a grudge, I want to be around him. Years away from the hurt he caused. Away from the people I wanted to impress. Matured beyond the insecure girl trying to hide behind popularity.

His eyes are hidden behind a pair of aviators—which is probably better for me. No need to be captivated when it's fruitless.

"I'm here with everything you asked me to bring. What's this idea of yours?"

"Your location is great. The ability to come and go utilizing the outdoor areas, the greens, the splash pads for stay-at-home moms—I want to be able to showcase all of that. But here, I'm able to create a better illusion of what you can get at the explorable district. We'll head back there for more, but I wanted to play with the effect of the openness we've got here."

I wish I could see his eyes, because the enthusiasm in his voice somewhat settles the nerves that have been fluttering in my belly since I woke up.

"Sounds great. How do we start?" I say, wishing I didn't feel as out of place as I do.

"The sun is great right now for human subjects. The cloud cover is our friend." He places the bags he is carrying down on a bench. "What color shirts did you bring?"

I set my bag down next to his and take them out. He holds each one close to my face and scans the area.

"We'll use these two." He drops the others close to my bag. He has chosen a dark heathered gray and a pink one. "Why so many colors?"

"Of shirts?" I ask, making sure I answer the right question.

"Yeah."

"I was thinking I would have the baristas wear certain colors during the morning and day. Then I would have the wine stewards wear others. Kind of a way to break up the day. I'm still not sure about it, but it was a thought. Nat keeps telling me I need to make the decision and stick with it. At least for a few months. See how it's received before I change my mind."

"Still fickle I see." A smirk appears before he turns to look through his bag.

That one word makes my blood boil! What was I thinking? I can't do this. Not with *him*! I'm about to throw the shirts in my bag and walk away when my phone rings. I take it out of my back pocket to see Nat's face on my screen.

"Hey, Nat," I answer, holding the frustration I'm feeling back from her.

"Hey. Just calling to make sure you found Eliazar. I'm hoping to be down there before you leave. I'm trying to wrap up my meeting."

"Yeah, I found him." I roll my eyes at no one, because from the corner of my eye I can see him messing with a camera.

"Great. Okay. Just follow his lead. He's a genius."

"I don't know if I can follow his lead, I may be too fickle and find a new photographer before you get here," I snark.

He laughs beside me. Laughs. Are you kidding me? He actually finds this funny.

"What?" Natalia asks.

"Never mind. I'll see you when you get here."

I hang up the call and place my phone on the bench. I grab the hem of my shirt, pulling it over my head.

"What the hell?" Eliazar says, looking at me wide-eyed.

"I'm changing." I pick up a shirt and slide it on.

"A child could walk by." His brows furrow.

"Yeah, and." I shrug. He thought I was a slut way back when, so might as well keep that persona going. Besides, I have on a sports bra. If he really paid attention, he would have known. Women are running around in these all over the park. He just wants to think the worst of me.

An uncomfortable silence surrounds us. I don't want to fight with him. I just want to finish this and be done. We won't have to see each other again. The next fifty years can be just like the past ten.

ELIAZAR

All I see is Marisol taking off her shirt. I'm stunned. Or more accurately, jealous of the other men that are out here, able to appreciate the view without a history of animosity. All, I'm sure, are ogling her. Who wouldn't? And when she answers, "I'm changing", to my question so casually, I have to scramble to find a reason why she shouldn't other than I'm a jealous bastard who wished he could have gotten a better look instead of averting my eyes out of respect.

Working alongside her is going to be difficult. All I've done is piss her off and we have only been alone for five freaking minutes. I meant the jab about being fickle, but instantly regretted it.

Back in high school, she dated the biggest losers but couldn't waste her time on the guy who had no financial means. They all treated her like crap, sharing everything they did that should have stayed behind closed doors. Whether they told the truth or embellished like teen boys are known to do, no one will ever know but her and the dumbasses.

Not knowing how to bring us back to a healthy working relationship, I decide to just ignore the past couple of minutes and move forward.

"For the first pics, I want you up under that tree." I point to it. It's only a few yards from where we are standing, up a small hill. "You and the coffee cup."

"Does it matter that I didn't bring any coffee for the cup?" Her cheeks redden.

"Not at all. I didn't add that to your list of things to bring. The angles I'll be taking won't show that the cup's empty." I give her a quick wink, hoping to make amends for my earlier jabs.

"Okay. Then tell me how to pose." She takes a few steps away up the hill before turning back to look at me expectantly.

I grab a book and my camera to follow her.

"Sit leaning against the tree." I smile hoping the remainder of our time is pleasant.

"What's with the book?" she asks as she lowers herself to the lush grass. The grass is why I chose this location. It's not a smashed mess, thanks to the hill—this area's no good for group exercise, soccer, or small kids.

"Just a prop. Something to keep you from looking at me...unless I ask you to." My voice drops an octave with the last five words. I didn't mean for it to happen but thinking of her eyes on me... Well, never mind.

"Yeah, okay, sure." She reaches her hand up to grab the book from me.

"Just be casual. Hold the cup, place it down beside you, flip the pages, look in the distance. I'm just going to be working around you. Don't pay attention to me right now."

She bites her bottom lip, glancing my way, and nods.

I watch her for a few moments before I bring the camera up to my eye. Zooming in, I study her. I take a few practice pictures to see how she'll react to me moving around her. She's stiff, uncomfortable, forcing a smile. What can I do to help her relax?

Crouching down by her feet, I glide my hand over her bare shin. "Relax. You're beautiful. Trust me."

A spark hits me as I let my hand linger. Her eyes widen briefly as her gaze follows my hand, then comes up to my face. I nod at her, and she gives me the slightest smile.

"Dream about something happy," I say just above a whisper, bringing the camera back up.

I start moving around again, and after a few seconds, I watch as her shoulders relax, and her face softens. She places the cup down by her legs and holds the book like she's reading. She flips through a few pages. Then she places the closed book on her lap and places the cup on top. She bends her knees and tucks her legs to one side, gripping the cup in both hands. She pretends to drink from the cup, closing her eyes.

My dick twitches thinking about her lips on the cup. Nope. Full stop. Think of something unappealing— stepping in dog crap yesterday should do the trick!

As the minutes pass, she is braver in her movements and poses. Suddenly, she breaks into a full-bellied laugh. I snap a couple more of her head thrown back in reckless abandon before bringing my camera down to figure out what happened.

I follow her gaze and notice a kid on the walkway laying on his back, a skateboard a few feet from him.

"I'm guessing he took a tumble?" I raise a brow, as her laugh subsides.

"Yeah. And before you say how insensitive I am for laughing, I knew he was okay. It wasn't bad. And he raised his arm with a thumbs up for anyone who saw him eat it. That's the funniest part. Like he knew people were watching."

She gently swipes the tears of laughter.

I nod my head, smiling. "For the record, I wasn't going to say you were insensitive."

"Oh." She looks down at her lap.

"Come on." I stand, extending a hand to her.

Another jolt hits me as she places her hand in mine. Time stops, and all I want is the heat that's creeping up my arm to continue. I pull her to standing, and she's so close to me. She glances up, meeting my eyes, but quickly looks down and takes a step back.

"Thanks." She turns away, bending over to pick up the book and cup from the grass.

Awkwardness settles over us. She walks toward the bench where we left our things, and I follow.

"Are we done for today?" she asks as she places her things in her bag.

"I was thinking of taking some shots at your place as the sun goes down." I snap the lens cover on my camera and tuck it away.

"Why would you need to come to my place?" she asks, brows pulled together.

"Get some dusk and night shots as a wine bar."

"Yeah…uh…the wine bar." Pink tinges her cheeks.

"Can we do that today?" I keep the conversation going, not letting her know I noticed her mistake.

"Sure. We need to get all this done. Thank you."

4

MARISOL

I can't believe I thought he wanted to come to *MY* place. The shop should have been my first thought, but of course, my mind went elsewhere when my hand was in his.

I called Natalia before we left the park to let her know we were done and heading to my shop. She decided to head home and get some things done since Eliazar has things under control. I was about to beg her to come anyway, but there's no reason for her to know he still bothers me after ten years. Or that he bothered me at all. Head held high and all that jazz, like I have been doing my whole life.

I look in the rearview mirror, and his Jeep is following closely behind. I have the next few minutes to get my head straight. Maybe he's not really trying to bother me? Maybe I'm being too sensitive. He's a guy. Guys don't hold on to crap from the past like girls. It'll be fine.

The sun has almost set, making way for a purplish glow. It seems more pronounced tonight. I wait at the door for him. Turning the key, I open the door as he walks up and close it behind him, locking it.

"I've been meaning to tell you I really like the business name. Really catchy and unique," he tells me as he places his bag on the main counter.

"Thank you!" How can one compliment, not even directly to me, cause the butterflies in my stomach to go wild? "Sol y Luna. My last chance," I mumble under my breath, thinking of the past few years.

"What was that?" he asks as he pulls a bottle of wine out of the bag.

"Nothing." I don't know why it came out. "You know I have wine here. This is a wine bar." I say trying to pull the attention away from my comment.

My lips pull as I cock a brow.

"Yes, I do know this is a wine bar. But since I didn't see the shelves stocked yet, I wasn't sure if you got your shipment in, or maybe you just weren't keeping it here until the construction was complete." He childishly sticks his tongue out at me. "Besides, an empty wine glass isn't as tempting as a full one."

"My coffee was empty," I say before it dawns on me that the wine glass is see-through, unlike the ceramic mug. "Never mind," I quickly say before he can school me.

His deep laugh vibrates in my chest. "Caught yourself?" he says through his laugh.

"Ha-ha." I roll my eyes at him. "I had a lapse in brain power there." I smile knowing anyone would laugh at that ditz moment.

"Happens to the best of us." He collects himself.

As he begins opening the bottle of red wine, I walk to the storage room to grab a couple of glasses that are still boxed. Looking at all the boxes, more stacked furniture, and randomness I purchased reminds me of all I have to do this week. Construction ended yesterday and now for all the finishing touches.

The moving of furniture breaks me from the doom-filled thoughts of all that needs to be done. I begin opening boxes, looking for the glasses, and by accident, I run into the plastic, stemless travel glasses I will be selling for wine to go. I grab one to show Eliazar and find the box with the regular wine glasses.

Walking back, I notice how he has arranged a table by a corner. It has windows on both sides, and the early evening glow almost looks fake.

"You want to hurry and change into one of the nighttime shirts so we don't lose this light?" he says when he catches me standing and watching him.

I place the glasses down and pull my shirt up to do the quick wardrobe change he requested. When I pull the shirt over my head, I catch him staring at me. He quickly diverts his eyes to the glasses I placed on the counter.

I grab the other shirt, pulling it over my head as I hear his steps coming closer. I tuck it in, fixing myself and fluffing my hair with my hands as he begins to pour the wine. He walks back to the table and places it in the middle. He brings his camera up to his face and begins to snap pictures. He's fluid as he moves around, catching different angles.

"Ready?" He turns to me.

I nod walking to him. "Where do you want me?"

"Stand here." He grabs my hand, and the familiar zing and warmth I felt earlier somehow calms the nerves I'm feeling being here with him.

He places me in the corner, the table slightly to my left.

"Bring the wine glass up, close to your face, but don't drink yet," he directs me as I hear the click of the camera. "Look a smidge more to the right. I want to see a little more of your profile." More clicks of the camera.

Standing here in the quiet of the evening, watching couples walking and enjoying the area, I wish for that type of closeness. Natalia wasn't wrong when she said I didn't commit to anything. I haven't. Nothing and no one have felt right. They didn't fit in my life somehow. They were square pegs, and I'm a round hole.

"Still with me?" Eliazar's deep voice breaks me away from my thoughts.

"Yes. Sorry. So much to do I guess." I smile at him, not wanting to admit my shortcomings.

"Take a couple of sips, then you can take a seat."

The next few minutes, I work at staying in the present with him and not letting my mind wander to places it has no business of going, especially right now.

"And done. The light has left us." He places his camera on the table. "I'm glad we came when we did. Dusk was beautiful tonight."

"Thanks for today. I can't wait to see the pictures." Not knowing what to say, I keep it to our working relationship.

"I'll work on them tomorrow so you can have them by the end of the day. I know Natalia wants the website complete," he answers, grabbing his camera and walking to the counter with his bag. "I'll leave the wine. Enjoy."

Not wanting him to leave so soon, I blurt out, "Why don't you pour yourself a glass and relax for a second?"

He turns to me, and for a brief moment, I think he's going to say, *No thank you*, but instead, "Are you sure?" comes out.

"Yes. Please." Why did I say "please"? Could I sound anymore desperate?

"Okay." He pours wine into the travel glass and brings it to the table, pulling a chair with him.

He takes a drink of his wine, smiling.

I look down at my glass on the table, spinning it between two fingers to aerate the wine. I want him to stay. I want to be able to look at him freely, instead of stolen glances like I did back in high school. I want to get lost in his eyes—clear blueish gray I've never seen on anyone but him.

"Regretting asking me to stay?"

I look up, my heart pounding with him so close, just the two of us with wine. This was a dream of mine, once upon a time.

ELIAZAR

I wonder if she realizes her leg is shaking uncontrollably underneath the table.

"No. Of course not. Uh… Just strange…I guess."

It's odd to see the self-assured, hot girl I remember from school looking uncomfortable. Is it my presence?

"Strange?" I inquire, wanting to know what's going on in that gorgeous head of hers.

"I don't know." She pauses, taking a sip of her wine. "High school seems like a lifetime ago. I didn't keep up with anyone really. So seeing you is…" Her voice drifts off.

I'm surprised she didn't keep up with her friends. "I thought you and your friends were thick as thieves. At least it seemed that way."

"Yeah… It would have, from the outside looking in." She shrugs her shoulders.

"Then tell me how it really was," I ask—the curiosity of what I thought I knew versus what she's insinuating wins out.

She takes a sip of her wine, her leg still bouncing. She shakes her head slowly, licking her lips.

I'm so far removed from the insecure young kid trying to impress the private school kids, but I'm still somewhat angry and hurt by her. And yet, I want to calm her from whatever is making her so jumpy.

I place my hand on her knee of the leg that is shaking.

"Sorry. Bad habit." She sucks her bottom lip into her mouth.

She doesn't push my hand off, doesn't pull away, but instead the tension in her thigh relaxes under my touch.

"Are you going to share how high school really was?" I push.

I gently squeeze her leg then bring it back up to the table, grabbing my glass. Her soft skin in the palm of my hand is more intoxicating than the wine.

"High school was full of pretending to be something you're not… I guess. If I wanted to stay in the good graces of the 'cool kids,'" she air-quotes with her hands, "I had to be who they thought I should be." Her shoulders slump forward as she places her arms on the table.

I'm amazed she's sharing this with me.

"We all did that. Some, I'm sure, more than others." Why she would say she needed to pretend, escapes me. "Why were you pretending if you were a quote, unquote, cool kid?"

"From the outside in, that's what it looked like…but the dynamics inside the circle of girls was different. Not sure if it's the same with guys, but…" She shrugs her shoulders, watching her spinning wine.

"Explain." The difference between what I thought I knew about her and what she's saying now is mind-boggling.

"Paige called the shots. She was the one in control." She looks up, her gaze meeting mine, eyes narrowed. "You had to have known that. You dated her."

"Sure, I dated her, but it was never serious." I take a drink, not understanding where the conversation is going.

"Not serious?" Her voice level increases as her brows furrow.

I shake my head.

"Maybe you didn't think it was, but she had other thoughts about it."

"What do you mean?" I was happy to leave high school. Get away from all the shallowness I was constantly inundated with. I was overjoyed when I could break it off with Paige. I knew she was upset I turned down the offer to play at a D1 college, but playing baseball wasn't my dream. It was just something I was good at.

"You're telling me you really don't know?" Her eyes widen with a hint of a smile.

Shaking my head, I'm willing her to continue.

She busts out laughing, and I'm waiting to figure out why.

"Spit it out already!" I say, happy she seems more comfortable now.

She calms and says, "According to Paige, y'all were the 'It' couple and soon-to-be college power couple. She applied to every school that offered you a baseball scholarship. She researched who needed pitchers and applied to those as well to increase her chances of being at the same school with you. She bragged about how she was going to marry a major league baseball player. So when you chose to go to a small liberal arts school with a D2 program, she was pretty pissed. She wouldn't admit it outright, but I could tell. Then one day she said she decided to break up with you."

Her last sentence catches me off guard; I have to choke down a laugh so I don't spit out the sip of wine I just took.

"What?" She's smiling wide.

"I broke up with her." I pause, letting that sink in. "I knew she wanted to go to a big college. Or at least I thought she did based on all the schools she talked about. We weren't heading in the same direction. I knew this. She never paid enough attention to me really. I thought I was just something to pass the time."

"I guess she was pretending too. Who knew?" she says quietly.

Could everything I thought about Marisol in high school be wrong? I always thought she was the one who was the mean girl.

"Why did you dislike me so much back then?" What have I got to lose by asking?

"I didn't. Not at first, at least." She cocks her head to the side.

"You didn't? But then you did?" I ask, knowing I just heard her clearly.

Her head shakes back and forth.

"If I told you that Paige told me you hated me, what would you say?" I cock a brow, holding my breath.

Her eyes widen, almost comically. "She said something similar to me. She said you called me plain, desperate, and fickle. So I kind of did hate you. But in my defense, it was in response to everything you were saying about me."

"I never said any of that."

"You never called me plain?" She rolls her eyes.

"Never. I said just the opposite. Paige overheard me talking to the guys one day after practice. I was pissed. I can't remember who it was, but they were bragging about what happened behind closed doors with you. I said something about being respectful to the beautiful girl."

Marisol's mouth parts slightly, her eyes never leaving my gaze.

"Later on, Paige made an offhand comment about me being too nice and that I should be wary of who I'm friends with or defend. She said I should be careful because I was a scholarship kid, and everyone thought less of me because of it. Especially you. She talked about how shallow everyone was, but I could see she was also."

"Then why did you date her?" flies from her mouth as soon as I utter the last sentence.

"To pass the time. To have something to do. To at least have an in with the social circle." I shrug. It's not like I'm proud of myself for it. I've come to terms with the disappointment in myself for things I let myself get caught up in back then.

She leans forward, her eyes soften. She doesn't say anything but instead takes a sip. I lean in closer to her, placing my hand on hers. My thumb strokes the back of her hand.

No words. Just a moment of peace. Maybe an understanding of the scared teens we once were. A truce to an imaginary battle we fought for no reason. The glow of the emerging moon adding to her beauty. The sounds of happy people enjoying the spring evening outside in the patio area.

I dreamed of a moment like this ten years ago—just her and I. She flips her hand over below mine, then closes my hand in hers. A simple, G-rated act, but one that holds significance. She leans in, and I follow her. So close I can feel her breath. Just as our lips brush, her phone rings, startling the both of us, and we jump back.

She darts out of her chair to get her phone from the counter. She looks at the screen and swipes, bringing it to her ear.

"Hey. Can I call you back in a sec? We just finished and are packing up... Yeah... It was good... Let me get in the car, and I'll call you back." She looks at me and mouths, 'Natalia.' "Seriously, give me five. Bye." She touches her phone's screen and places it back on the counter.

I stand, grabbing my glass and walking to her. "I should be going. I know she will be calling in five flat if you haven't called her."

Working with Natalia, I know how persistent she can be.

Marisol's lips pull out as she cocks her head slightly to the side. "Okay."

"What do we have to do so you can lock up?" I don't want to leave her to close and lock up by herself.

She looks around and shakes her head.

"Nothing. I'll be back in the morning to start setting up, so it can wait until then." She grabs her purse, bag, and keys from the counter as I grab my mine.

DRIVING HOME, my thoughts are filled with Marisol. The girl who I wished gave me a second glance a decade ago. The one I hoped to kiss. To hold. To protect. Her eyes. Her laugh. Her smile. A crush ten years ago, as strong now as it was then.

As I walk into my townhouse, I notice the picture and stop in my tracks. The last picture. The one that I hadn't parted with since she walked away. For the better part of the past eight months, I've been nursing a broken heart. She was who I woke up thinking about. Who flooded my thoughts day and night.

But since I started working for Marisol, I haven't thought about her once. Somehow, I found my way out of the black hole I was lost in. The sun rose again. *El sol. Mi sol.*

I place my things down and pick up the frame. The picture was of our last vacation to Cancun—tanned and happy, holding each other. I slide the hooks in the back, yanking off the backing. I take the picture out, giving it one last glance before tearing it in half. I place the frame down, then tear the photo again into fourths. Then again, before tossing it in the trash in the kitchen.

I walk upstairs and enter the bedroom I've turned into my studio. An unfinished canvas covered in more gray and black stares back at me. I pull my shirt off and grab several paint tubes.

5

MARISOL

WE KISSED. TECHNICALLY. ALMOST. MAYBE. ALL THE WAY HOME, ALL I COULD think about was how mad I was at Natalia for ruining the moment. But how could she have known? I didn't tell her what happened. I haven't even mentioned the huge crush I had in school. Or the fact that the crush turned to hate along the way. All she knows is that we went to school together. Knew each other. End of story.

Sleep was hard to find. My mind kept racing thinking of what would have happened if Natalia hadn't called. What would his kiss taste like? How heated would it have gotten? Finally, after too many fantasies playing out in my head, I drifted off to only dream about him. His eyes, those blue eyes, were all I saw.

The light of the morning sun woke me. A new day of questions and 'what if' possibilities. Is my high school fantasy going to finally come true? I can't continue wondering about something that may never be, that may have been a mistake, a moment in the past that we got caught up in. I need to dress and make my way into the shop. Lots to do, and the opening is approaching fast.

ONE OF THE managers I have hired comes in to help me figure things out. We are also expecting a couple of the baristas soon. I have hired a few brand-new baristas who need to learn the skill of coffee making. They will be training with Lisa today. And tonight, I will be working with my wine manager and the new hires that will be working the afternoon and evening shifts.

Opening seemed to be so far away, and the days crawled by, but now they are racing, and I'm a little freaked out we won't be ready. As stressed as I feel, there's also exhilaration. I'm doing all this. I'm accomplishing what my parents feared I would fail at. It's not time for celebration, but I'm focused on this. I have never felt this type of determination to do anything before.

The day is filled with moving furniture, unpacking supplies, inventorying everything, and decorating. Even rustic, minimalist décor takes time and attention. Furniture placement took me longer than expected. I wanted to create a flow that would work for both day and evening. It could transition from coffee bar to classic wine bar just based on the beverages on the tables.

I'm unpacking and racking wines in the small climate-controlled room with glass walls I had added. I love the idea of the customers being able to see all the wines. I look out and see Eliazar walking in. How can he make a Henley shirt and jeans look absolutely delicious? I step off the ladder to greet him, wondering why he's here.

As I walk up, he's greeting my manager, and the baristas that are working on learning drinks.

"Hey!" His eyes sparkle as he faces me. "Y'all've done a lot this morning. It looks amazing. I didn't even think to bring my camera today."

"Hi." My lips pull out. "Thanks! We've been busy. I want to make sure we are fully ready for opening. No hiccups if I can help it."

"Well, then, are you ready to look at some pictures? I can send the ones you approve right over to Natalia." He cocks a brow.

"Absolutely. It will give me a chance to get off my feet for a few minutes."

He doesn't try to hide his smile. It's welcoming and warm. He walks over to one of the tables and places his backpack down. I sit on the bench waiting for him. He reaches into his bag, pulling out his laptop, and places it on the table before sitting next to me on the bench. He flips open the screen just as my stomach growls loudly.

"Have you had lunch?" he asks me.

"Nope. Coffee has been my sustenance today." My lips turn down, partly in embarrassment.

He pushes his screen down and says, "This can wait. Let's get you fed, then we can look at pictures." He stands back up.

"You don't have to. I can eat something later. Seriously, it's okay." Excitement pumps through my veins that asked me to lunch, but I know it's probably just him being nice.

"I insist," he stays, standing, wiggling his fingers for me to grab his hand.

I place my hand in his and stand up.

"I'm going to leave my things here," he says to my employees still practicing lattes and coffee art.

My manager nods her head at him.

29

He opens the door and keeps it propped open so I can walk through as he follows behind me.

"We're in luck. You have so much to choose from within walking distance. What do you feel like?" he asks me.

"How about the food court? Several things to choose from, and it's quick, so we can get back to the pictures," I answer. I don't want to hold him for more time than necessary if he has things to do today.

"If that's what you want." He places his hand on the small of my back nudging me to start walking. The thrill of his hand on me sends chill bumps all over.

This area is beautiful in the daytime and has a magical presence at night. There are apartments that surround all the shops and restaurants. We walk, not saying anything for a bit. Just strolling the couple of blocks to the food court where they serve upscale, fast food. It's filled with restaurants that offer ramen, gourmet burgers, rotisserie chicken, pizza, and fun desserts.

"Are you nervous for opening day?" he asks, breaking the silence.

"Yes and no." I shrug my shoulders. "I want the day to be here already, but I'm scared of no one showing up. I've sent out the emails and messages to different bloggers, letting them know we would be open for them to come in and experience the place before the grand opening, but what if none of them are interested? What if no one posts about it?"

"I'm sure they will come." He wraps his arm around my shoulder pulling me into his side, giving me a gentle squeeze as we continue walking, then letting go.

We turn the corner, leaving one of the main complexes and walking out onto a sidewalk with a busy street. He grabs my hand and pulls me in front of him to his left. He quietly and without hesitation placed himself on the street side of the sidewalk. How many men still do that or think about that?

I'm in my head swooning when he says something to me, so I have to ask, "I'm sorry. What?"

"I was just asking how you chose your wines?" he repeats, looking down at me.

"Oh. Yeah. I chose reasonably priced wines in different varieties. I still need to head up to Fredericksburg and pick up more cases I ordered from some vineyards there. I want people to come in. I want easy drinking wines that people enjoy and can afford. A place to meet friends and not have the stuffy wine bar feel some places have."

"That sounds like a good plan."

"I think so too."

. . .

AFTER A QUICK LUNCH and more casual conversation, we are back at my shop scanning the pictures he took yesterday. I can't believe how many he has. I don't remember hearing the click of his camera that many times.

I usually take twenty pictures of myself to find one good one. That's what I was scared of, being the face of Sol y Luna, but somehow Eliazar captured me in the best ways. I like more pictures than not out of the ones he took yesterday.

"There are so many good ones!" I exclaim, surprised. "I really didn't think I would have this many to choose from." I continue scrolling.

"Didn't believe I could take a good picture?" I turn around to look at him leaning back against the bench, his arm draped on the top, with his brow cocked mischievously.

"I had faith in your skills. It's me in front of the camera I was unsure about." I bite my lip, shocked I was so honest.

His eyes narrow, and I can't help but stare into them. "Then you don't see the beauty I do."

He says it with such conviction, anyone would believe those words. I lick my lips as my heart pounds against my chest.

He lifts the hand that had been resting on the back of the bench and places it on my cheek. He rubs his thumb once over my cheekbone then slides it back, cupping my neck. My breath hitches. He leans toward me, and I follow until our lips meet.

His lips are soft but firm against mine. His tongue brushes my lips gently, and I open, deepening the kiss.

The sound of someone clearing their throat reminds me we aren't alone. I pull away, tucking my head into his neck taking a deep breath. I feel his soft chuckle against his chest. I clear my throat before turning around to find Lisa holding a smile tightly.

"Need some alone time?" She smirks at me when I face her.

I know my face has to be beet red, so I just say, "That won't be necessary."

Her lips pull out further, and I know she is suppressing a laugh as she shrugs her shoulders.

"Just needed to let you know that Jamie let me know he's coming in early for the wine tastings. Said something about wanting to talk you about other options."

"Got it. Thanks!" I reply and she turns around to go back to the bar area.

I close my eyes for a second before turning around to face Eliazar, nervous about what's to come. Or not come.

The smug look I see when I open my eyes to look at him eases the knots that had started to form in my stomach. He comes in close to my ear. "We can continue that later." He places a soft kiss to my neck, then says, "But right now, back to the pictures."

He pulls away looking at me, waiting.

I mouth the word "later" to him. He nods, then brings the hand that I have laying on his chest back to the trackpad on his computer.

"Which ones are we going with?" His tone is deeper than usual.

"How about I tell you the ones I don't like and let Natalia choose what's best for the website and socials," I answer since I am in love with so many of them.

"Sounds like a plan."

ELIAZAR

A few texts back and forth throughout the remainder of the day was all I got after that kiss. I would be lying if I said I was okay with the texts, but damn, I wanted to see her. Wanted to continue what we began. But I had a client to meet, and she was working with her wine steward until late.

———

I TEXT Marisol as soon as I wake up.

ME: Good Morning! What do you have going on today?

Marisol: More prep work at the bar. Then heading to Natalia's to finalize my website. Another busy day.

Bummed she's busy, but I understand. She's about to open a business.

Me: Can I see you tomorrow?

Marisol: Are you busy tomorrow?

I'm confused why she's asking if I'm busy.

Me: Not really. Editing pics

Marisol: Want to go pick up wine with me?

Road trip with her? Hell yeah, I do.

Me: Sure.

Marisol: Great! I'll pick up the rental then pick you up. Say 10ish?

Me: Rental?

Marisol: I can't fit all the cases of wine I bought in my car. I rented an SUV

Me: No need. I'll borrow a friend's. Save your money. I'll pick you up. 10ish? Address?

Marisol: Are you sure?

Me: Absolutely.

ALL I HAVE today are a couple of projects to work on. It would be better if I was busy to keep my mind occupied, but all I got is free time. I take my vintage

Jeep into a friend's auto shop so he can change out my oil and I can ask for his Tahoe.

Mateo is under my vehicle letting the oil drain while I sit around watching. His auto shop is busy today. It's not a quick oil change business, but I only trust him with my Jeep. He restored it and will now need to keep it running for me.

"Are you going to tell me why I'm lending you one of my cars?" Mateo says loudly over the sounds of the garage.

"I'm helping a friend. That's all." I don't know why I feel I need to keep things quiet.

"A friend? What friend? I thought I knew all your friends." He chuckles to himself, knowing it has to be about a girl.

I school my face to give nothing away to his teasing, watching all the guys in the shop. The door to the inside waiting area opens, and Damian, the guy Mateo bought this shop with, walks out. He sees me and walks over.

He extends his hand, and we clap hands in greeting.

"Still running smoothly?" Damian asks, looking at my Jeep.

"Yup. Just an oil change," I answer.

"Ask him why he needs to borrow my Tahoe." Mateo exclaims as he begins changing out the filter.

I roll my eyes, knowing he's going to get all his guys involved and continue harassing until I share something. Damian looks in my direction, and another one of their friends, Jaxson, walks up with a goofy grin.

"What are we talking about?" Jaxson inquires.

"Ask the artiste," Mateo says with a fake French accent.

"Fine," I say loudly. "I'm helping an old friend out. She bought cases of wine for her new shop, and I told her I would go with her to the vineyards to pick them up." "Old friend" is a stretch since technically we weren't anything before.

"And where is the old friend from?" Mateo smirks as he drags out the words "old friend."

"High school," I blurt out quickly. I'm a twenty-seven-year-old man getting excited about a damn girl from high school.

"Ah!" Jaxson says, "One of those. Is she the one that got away?"

All the guys laugh, but I notice the look on Mateo's face change after Jaxson's comment. I wonder if he had one of those.

"She was never mine, so she didn't get away." I keep it simple. No reason to get into the craziness that was once upon a time.

"So wine?" Damian continues, letting go of the jabs.

"Yeah. Y'all should check out the coffee and wine bar she's about to open. Sol y Luna at the Heritage Center."

"Oh la la!" Jaxson sings out, as Mateo says, "That's the new swanky part of town. But you are a private school kid." He laughs to himself.

I met Mateo too many years ago, and I told him where I went to school.

I shake my head. "Yes we both were, but she wants her place to attract a wider audience. Look. This is the place." I pull out my phone to show them a couple of the shots I took with my phone the first time I was there.

"Nice." Damian says evenly, nodding his approval.

The guys get back to work, and my conversation continues with Mateo until he's done with my vehicle. I head on home to finish up some of the edits before tomorrow and wait for Mateo to drop off his SUV.

6

MARISOL

I ASKED HIM TO COME WITH ME TO WINE COUNTRY? I REALLY DID THAT! AND now I'm sitting here waiting for him to pick me up. Forget about nervous butterflies in the stomach, I swear there is a flock of birds fighting to escape. While I'm nervous about being with him, there are also flutters of excitement trying to push through.

Looking at him after that kiss, I wanted more. I wanted to get lost in him. It's crazy how a crush from almost ten years ago can slam into you so hard and make you lose your bearings.

A ping on my phone distracts me from my thoughts of Eliazar. I may be using the name he goes by now, but in my head, all I can hear is E.A. Sports. The name the kids gave him as soon as he arrived. The new kid who was going to take the mound and finally bring home the championship again.

The website is looking amazing! I can't wait to show you. It will be up and ready tomorrow. No more shell of a site with just basic info. You will have a kick-ass website to make people want to visit!

I love Natalia's energy. She believes wholeheartedly in everything she does. I wish I had her enthusiasm for life. For me, life has always been dull colors and moving from one thing to the next.

I send her a quick reply. *I can't wait to see it. Thanks for everything. Heading to pick up the last cases of wine and I'll text you when I get back.*

Laters, chica! she replies quickly.

Before I can get lost in more worrying, there's a knock. I take a deep breath and head to the door. I open it, and my stomach drops just a tad. How does he make simple clothes look delicious? His broad chest is stretching the thin fabric of a Henley tee over a pair of black shorts.

"Ready?" He gives me a sexy smile.

"Sure." I hold my lips tight, not wanting to lose my composure.

I turn around to grab my purse from the entrance table as he waits for me.

Walking to his friend's vehicle, my eyes widen a tad in surprise. It is not your typical SUV. It's lifted with a slew of other additions, including grill guards and lights. He opens the passenger-side door, helping me in before going around and jumping in.

I want to say something about the car, but I also don't want to offend. We are just getting back on track, and I'm scared anything I say will come out wrong. He backs out and begins driving, the radio on a country station.

"Are we going to have an hour-long silent trip?" I can hear the teasing in his voice.

"No. Sorry. Your friend's car just took me by surprise. I didn't want to say the wrong thing."

"Wrong thing?"

I shrug, not wanting to bring up my latest faux pas at the art showing.

"I'm sure you were expecting just a regular Tahoe when I mentioned it. This is a little much, and even I can admit that." He turns to look at me with a wide smirk and winks. "I've known Mateo for years now, and he is the one that rebuilt my Jeep. He has a shop in town and would like to only rebuild classics or anything that catches his fancy, but to get the shop growing with business, they are taking on a lot of collision repairs."

"Wow!" I turn slightly to look at him. "I was wondering about your Jeep. I wondered if you did all that work."

"I helped and learned things along the way, but Mateo and his friends at the garage are the auto geniuses."

"His friends at the garage?"

"He and another friend of his from college went in together. They also have a couple of other friends working there. Kinda like a family business."

"How did y'all meet?"

ELIAZAR

Fuck! I walked into this question, and I don't really want to answer it. Answering it brings up *her* again. Just when I'm moving on and not thinking of her. Mateo was wrapped up in my meeting Angela. Crap. I thought of her name. I said I wouldn't...or couldn't think of her name again.

"Sorry. Didn't mean to pry." Marisol's voice is just above a whisper. I barely heard it over the song playing.

"No. I'm sorry." I reach over placing my hand on hers giving it a squeeze.

I guess it's time to talk about it. Even if I wish it would just stay dead and buried.

"Never mind. It's not important anyway." She gives me a tight, forced smile.

I rub my thumb over the back of her hand, loving the feel of it in mine.

"It is…or was important. Before. Not anymore. It just caught me off guard because I didn't want to think about her." I fumble, not sure how to explain.

"Her?" Her brows pull together, and her body tenses.

"My ex," I explain right away. I don't want her to think that there is someone else right now. "I met Mateo through my ex. He was dating one of her friends way back when. They didn't stay together, the friend moved away, and I got to keep Mateo." I smile, glossing over the story.

"Oh" is all she says, but her body is still rigid. She pulls her hand from under mine and scratches her face, then places it on top of her other one.

Her body language is telling me my answer was not sufficient and I'm going to have to explain. Just when I thought I had done a spectacular job of answering without answering.

"It's uh…" I don't know how to begin, but we aren't even halfway to the vineyard, and if I don't bring us back to solid ground, it will be a long, miserable day.

"Don't worry about it. It's fine. It's none of my business anyway." She's still tense but tries to cover it with a forced smile.

"Until recently, I was going through the motions. I guess you can call it heartbroken. Or angry. Or betrayed." I take a deep breath. "I met Angela in college, and we started dating. We stayed together, eventually moved in together. I thought we were on the right path. The next logical step to me was marriage. Especially since we had been together for six years."

With each word that I admit out loud, Marisol listens intently, slowing turning her4 body toward me. I can feel her gaze on the side of my face.

"I had brought it up a couple of times, joking around to get a feel on how she felt. She never said no. She never seemed opposed. I took that as a *I'm waiting* in girl talk. You know, not pressuring the guy and waiting patiently for him to be ready." I pause, knowing there's no going back. I started the story and would have to see it out through the end. I haven't spoken about this out loud to anyone. Everyone in my life knew what happened, and I never had to say anything. This is the first time I'm processing it with someone who doesn't know our history.

"So I bought the ring. I brought in our family and friends to celebrate the occasion. I had it all worked out, or so I thought. I took her to the rooftop bar at the Regency Hotel right before sunset. I reserved a table for apps and drinks. I asked as the sun set in the background. I even had Mateo there filming. Tears sprung to her eyes, and I assumed they were tears of joy. They were tears of sadness. Sadness she had been feeling with me. Trapped in a relationship. I guess it had been building for a couple of years, and she didn't know how to let go of the comfort I provided. She said she wanted to see the world, and now that I wanted to place a ring on her finger, she knew she needed to get away before she resented me. I'm not sure why she would resent me. She didn't even ask if I wanted to see the world with her. It was all what she wanted and somehow, I didn't fit into the picture."

Marisol's eyes bubble with tears as I finally turn to look at her.

"Hey. I'm sorry! I didn't mean to make you cry with my stupid story. I just didn't want you to think there was anything with anyone else. It's just me."

A tear falls free, and I move to swipe it gently with the pad of my thumb. She grabs my hand as I bring it down and envelopes it in both of hers.

"How long ago was this?" Her brows furrow.

"Almost a year ago. It's fine now," I say, not wanting her to think I'm still hung up on Angela. I was until Marisol walked back into my life. Now, life is brighter. The colors around me intense.

"I can't imagine what you went through. And I'm sorry that you had your heart broken."

"It's happened to all of us at one point or another." I try and lighten the mood.

"Not really." She shrugs.

"You have always been the dumpee?" I cock a brow.

"I don't count ending a casual relationship as dumping. I have never had a long-term, committed relationship. No one has ever interested me enough for me to want to continue with them." She pauses for a bit then adds, "I'll admit though, while I feel bad you had to go through that, I'm selfishly happy that you aren't dating anyone right now." A beautiful, devilish grin appears on her face.

My cock twitches at the thought of continuing what we began. "You don't know how happy I am that I'm single right now." I grab one of her hands and bring it up to my mouth, placing a kiss on the back of her hand.

She brings her left leg under her and leans into the center console for the remainder of the way as the conversation continues to flow.

We walk into the tasting room of the first vineyard, and she's greeted by a tall gentleman about our age.

"Eliazar, this is David. He's the winemaker." He extends his hand, and I shake it.

"Are you staying for a glass or just picking up?" he asks her with a sly grin.

Marisol looks to me, so I shrug. "I'm yours for the day. What do you want to do?"

"You want to taste the Chardonnay and rosé I chose?" She bounces on her toes.

"Sure."

She looks to David. "Will you bring us a couple of glasses of the Chardonnay?"

"Of course." His earlier excitement to see her dims.

She leads me towards a door and walks through like she owns the place. Did she date the winemaker? The space is set up with tasting bars around the room and a few small tables. David comes in with a couple of glasses and a bottle. He sets them down on the bar in front of Marisol and pours her glass then mine.

"Enjoy."

He turns to walk back out, and as soon as he is out of hearing range, I whisper close to her ear, "You know he likes you, right?"

I look down as chill bumps appear on her arm.

She looks at me with a crooked smile. "I guessed. But it has never been anything but talking wine." She fills her lungs with air and lets it out slowly. "Come, let's sit for a second."

She moves to one of the small tables, sitting down and swirling her wine.

Why she hasn't dated him eats at me. It's like high school all over again, and all I want is to call her mine.

"Why not the winemaker?" I can't hold my curiosity anymore.

She drops her head, looking at the wine glass as she bites her bottom lip. "Honestly, I may have if I wasn't so focused on the shop. I told you, no one has interested me to get serious with."

"What was your longest relationship?"

"Six months, I think. No one to bring home to meet the parents. And if they did, it was by accident because I needed a plus one for an event. Guys have not been what I thought." My eyes widen at her statement, but she continues, "Or life, I guess. Do you know my job history is just as tragic as my love life?"

I shake my head back and forth, slowly, not wanting to interrupt her story.

"Well, it is." She takes a sip of her wine. "Life has been…boring, I guess. I got my degree, got a job, because that is what you do. But everything seemed dull. Out of focus somehow. Even the guys I dated. Somehow, they seemed more interested in themselves than they did in me."

"How did Sol y Luna come into play?" I ask, wanting her to continue.

"I quit another job, yet again. My dad found out and gave me a chunk of money to 'get my head on straight,'" she air-quotes, "but told me not to come back asking for anything else. To him, I need to settle down and get serious.

39

What he doesn't seem to understand is, I'm trying. I just don't know what's wrong with me. That money he gave me is Sol y Luna. That is why I need it to be successful. I want to be successful. I want to love something as much as you love taking pictures."

Pulling back the curtain on her life is not what I would've thought it would be. All along I thought she had the perfect life. The snob who had it all. In actuality, she was the scared girl once upon a time, just wanting to survive like the rest of us. She has stumbled and is trying to make her mark on the world.

"Thank you," slips from my lips quietly.

"For?" Her chest expands with a deep breath.

"Trusting me." I reach over the table, bringing her hand into mine. "We are all walking through life lost. Some are just better at hiding it than others."

Her lips pull out into a small smile. I take a rather large drink of wine, nervous about my next statement. What have I got to lose except it being weird between us until I finish this job?

"I'm guessing the reason Paige did her best to keep us apart was because she could feel I wasn't as interested in her as maybe she was in me."

Caught off guard, she laughs with wine in her mouth. Once she swallows, she says, "Well that's one hell of an ego." She is still giggling.

I roll my eyes, smirking. "No." I chuckle at her statement. "Because she probably caught my eyes wandering over to someone else."

Her eyes widen. "Who?"

"You." I lick my lips, ready and wanting to taste her again.

"Oh," she drags out, as her hand squirms in mine.

A quiet settles over us, so I take another sip of the wine to break eye contact, and she does the same.

Just as I was about to blurt out something to bring us back to steady ground, she says, "You… uh…"

"Yes," I simply say. "From the first day I saw you in class. You had these big, innocent eyes. Every time you batted your lashes, all the guys would fall over themselves to help you. It was innocent. But you were dating Lance."

"I was! I forgot about that. It lasted all of a couple of months. It was more of a fun summer fling than anything of substance. His talent was on the football field and not in the classroom." She giggles, covering her mouth. "Sorry. That was mean."

"But true." I say, knowing she's so much more now.

"You hooked up with Paige pretty quickly." She cocks a brow.

"I did. But in my defense, I was trying to fit in. You guys had been in school with each other for the past two years."

She bites her lip nervously. "I didn't think about that. I'm sorry."

"No need to be sorry. But when Paige offered me an 'in,' I took it. I didn't want to be the poor kid alone in that school." I take a deep breath, remembering that time.

"I can't imagine how hard that was for you. I was never the new kid. You're right. Some of the people we graduated with I'd known since kinder." She rolls her eyes.

"The innocence and life I saw in you that first day slowly dimmed. I couldn't understand why you dated some of the guys you did. They didn't treat you well and talked lots of shit."

There's a minuscule shake of her head before she drops it. "I figured. I heard about the reputation I earned from Paige," she says just above a whisper.

"We don't have to think about that now. We are way past that place in our lives." I stand up and pull her up with me, enveloping her in my arms. I place a kiss on the top of her head.

"I went about it so wrong back then," she mumbles.

"Went about what wrong?"

"Trying to get your attention."

I let her go and push her shoulders back, but she tucks herself back into my chest. "What do you mean, get my attention?"

"That first day in history, I noticed you too. Your eyes drew me in. Your smile felt inviting. But there was Lance. And Paige kept telling me to stay with the captain of the football team." I feel her chest expand with air. She lets it out, continuing, "Then you were with Paige. I thought if I made myself look like the 'it' girl you would choose me instead of Paige. But all it did was give me a bad reputation for nothing. I didn't sleep with any of those fools, but they sure liked to brag about what they thought we did."

"Look at me." I grab her chin, lifting it.

Her eyes are tear filled.

"We are way past being those dumb kids that thought they knew about life. We are here now. No need to go back to the past now." I brush my lips past hers.

Her hands slide up my chest, landing on my shoulders. "From this moment on." She lifts up on her tiptoes, and her lips meet mine hungrily.

I swipe her lips with my tongue, and the kiss deepens. She's the breath I have been missing. The light that I thought was extinguished. The person to jumpstart my life. Just a few weeks ago I thought I was destined to live in darkness, but seeing her again lit something in me.

7

MARISOL

I can't decide if I'm drunk off a glass of wine or him. As much as I enjoy wine, I want to continue tasting him. We slow it down, composing ourselves before sitting down again. We continue talking and drinking until we finish our wine. A couple of guys help Eliazar load the cases of wine.

Back in the car, he asks, "Where to next?"

"Exit and take a left on the highway. We have more wine to pick up. We've got to stop at four vineyards today."

"Are we planning on tasting all the wines?" He greets me with the sexist smirk.

"Do you want to taste all the wines?" I toss back, teasingly.

"I would actually love to." He exaggerates squinting his eyes, like he's thinking. "But…" He drags the word out.

"But?" I turn my body to face him completely.

"It won't be safe to drive back to the city." He shrugs his shoulders. "Maybe we should find a room in town." His voice suddenly husky.

"I may…be open to finding a room." I roll my eyes and lick my lips, flirting.

"Then it's settled. Let's go taste some wine."

The afternoon was perfect. More flirting, more teasing, more kissing, and always touching. My heart continues to race with excitement, thinking of being with him. After several glasses of wine at the different vineyards, we head into town to find a place that has vacancy at the last minute. There's a quaint motel-slash-bed-and-breakfast I'm hoping has availability. It's the place Natalia and I stayed a couple of nights when we were up here choosing the wine to buy.

He parks the car at the motel, and he quickly jumps out to help me out of the lifted vehicle, as he has done each time we've stopped at a new location. His hand grazing my lower back as he guides me to the door is gentle but oh so incredibly sexy. How is that small gesture making me melt? I'm sure one of the guys in the past had to have done this, but I don't remember. It never made an impression on me the way everything Eliazar does.

He opens the door and lets me walk through, following close behind. The man behind the desk is the owner. I met him on my last visit.

"Hello, Michael!" I announce walking up to him.

"Natalia! Back again?" He greets me with a smile that reaches his eyes.

"Yup. I had to pick up all the wine I purchased." I sit in the chair in front of his desk as Eliazar stands behind me.

"Very nice. But did we lose your reservation?" His smile fades as he looks over a sheet in front of him.

"Oh, no. I didn't think we would be staying the night, but plans changed." I smile as he looks back up at me. "I was just hoping that you may have a room."

"Ah! Yes, this town and all the wine can be intoxicating. And yes, you are in luck. It's a slow week. I have a couple open. I have a king room and a double room. Which would you like?"

I turn to Eliazar, and the storm of want I see in his eyes is all the answer I need.

"The king." I smile innocently. No need for this old man to be subjected to all the dirty thoughts that are floating through my mind right now.

Before I can pull my wallet from my purse, Eliazar is handing Michael a credit card.

"Please charge the room to this card," he says with authority.

We finish checking in and make our way to our room. I step in with a couple of shopping bags. We bought shirts from one of the vineyards and stopped at a Walmart for a few necessities, like toothbrushes and under garments.

Eliazar closes the door, and the energy of the room shifts. I place the bags down on the small side table then turn around.

"I don't want to assume anything, so please tell me what you want." His voice is gravelly as his eyes take me in.

I take the couple of steps back to him, placing my hand on his chest. "I've wanted this for a long time." I slide my hand up to his neck while standing on tippy toes, bringing him down to meet my lips.

43

He brings his body flush with mine, wrapping me in his arms, and I can feel his growing erection. I need to be closer, melt into him. The kiss is desperate, like we are fighting for the air we breathe, but it's each other we so urgently need.

Time stands still or speeds by, I can't tell which. But too soon, he slows us down and places his forehead on mine, taking a deep breath.

"Michael was wrong," he whispers.

"How so?"

"It's not this place that's intoxicating." He places a soft kiss on my forehead letting his lips linger as he breathes me in. "It's you that's intoxicating."

He slowly places kisses on the side of my face. He grabs my ass, lifting me so I wrap my legs around him. He walks us over to the bed and sits down with me straddling him. His hands are rubbing my back and coming up to my neck, where he grabs my hair in a ponytail and pulls it to the side. My head moves with the pressure, and he kisses my neck. My core tightens with the feeling of his bulge under me.

I push into him, my whole body alive. I want to pull him closer into me but push him away because it already feels like so much.

"Stand up." He pushes me away from his body, a storm brewing in his clear, blue eyes.

I lick my lips before pulling my bottom one in. I scooch off him and stand in front of him.

"Take off your top," he says in a low growl.

My heart races in anticipation of his dominance. I grab the hem of my shirt and lift it over my head. He leans forward and runs a finger slowly from my throat down between my breasts to my navel.

"*Qué belleza*," he says so quietly, I barely hear him.

How can two words make me feel like the most gorgeous woman alive? His hungry gaze emboldens me to unbutton my jeans and slowly slide them off then take a step back out of his reach.

I glide my hand over my stomach up to my breast, tucking my hand under the bra cup. I pinch my nipple softly, and it hardens instantly with him watching me. I want to tease him a bit before I give into the burning between my legs.

"Hands to your sides." His voice is husky.

I drop my arms, letting them hang. He grabs the back collar of his shirt sliding it over his head. I watch the muscles of his tanned, well-toned chest contract and relax with each of his movements.

He gets up and comes around me to stand at my back. His breath on my neck makes me shudder in excitement. I turn to look at him.

"Face forward."

My heart skips a beat, and I turn back around. His hands come to my shoulders and slide down my arms with a feather-light touch. He then gathers my hair and places it over my left shoulder. His lips meet the skin on my shoulder as he licks and kisses my neck then down my back. With a quick twist, his fingers unhook my bra, and he slips it down my arms.

His hands slide over my ass to my hips. Hooking his fingers on each side of my panties, he pushes them down. This slow teasing has my senses heightened, and I'm eager for more. My breaths are fast yet deep. His large, strong hands come to my thighs and massage their way up.

As his hands get closer to my warm center, I move and open a little wider, giving him access. He brushes quickly past, leaving a tingling trail in his wake. He moves them to my stomach, gliding up to cup both my breasts. He pulls me back into his chest as his lips connect with my neck.

I roll my hips feeling his hard cock, and wetness pools between my legs. He turns my head and devours my lips. Kisses, licks, soft bites as he continues to caress my breasts and tease my most sensitive spot.

"I want to feel you." Every fiber of my being feels alive. Every sound, color, touch is so much more than I've ever felt before.

"You are more beautiful than my mind could ever have imagined," he says in my ear, then leaves a trail of kisses down my neck to my shoulder.

His hand travels south and separates my folds, dipping into my wet, heated center. A loud moan escapes my lips at his touch. As soon as a finger slides into me, my legs get weak, and I lose my balance. His strong arm still around me steadies me.

"Hmmm, looks like your legs aren't going to hold you up much longer," he whispers as he slides a second finger in me. A few strokes, and he withdraws his hand and wraps it around me, pulling me closer to him again. A few deep breaths, and he lets me go.

"Sit down and open your legs."

I turn around and sit on the side of the bed. His abdominal V leads my gaze to his erection.

"Open your legs," he repeats.

Feeling bold, I say, "Take off your underwear. I want some eye candy too." I lick my lips waiting.

He looks at me for a couple of seconds with hooded eyes before stepping out of them. His large dick stands at attention, and all I feel is a pulsing in my center that I want his cock to relieve.

"Open." His voice is gravelly.

I lie back, propping myself on one bent elbow. I bring one foot up on the bed and widen the other. He's on his knees in an instant, and as soon as he sucks my sensitive nub and slides a couple of fingers in me, I scream in ecstasy. I let myself fall into the bed as I come down from the high.

He trails kisses up my stomach, over my breasts until he reaches my mouth.

"And now for the second act," he informs me.

We scoot up the bed, kissing, caressing, tasting each other. Eliazar is propped up on his elbows on top of me, and his bulging dick teases at my opening as he moves.

"I want you now. All of you," I say as I take him in my hand, leading him to my entrance.

"Not so fast beautiful." His voice still deep but resigned. "I don't have anything on me." His lips continue their assault.

"It's fine. I'm on the pill. Please. I need to feel you." I plead, not wanting to wait.

He eases himself into me slowly. When he's fully in, he kisses me softly then begins to rock in and out of me. It begins slow, then speeds up as our release nears. Too soon, I'm seeing more stars as my whole body comes alive.

ELIAZAR

Tucked into my chest, I can't...or don't want to stop my hand from gliding over her soft skin. Up and down her back, slowly to her side, then back down to the round of her butt. Never in a million years would I have dreamed of this perfection, Marisol in my arms.

"Are you hungry?" Marisol asks, then begins kissing my chest.

"You're going to have to be more specific. If you're asking me for another round, just give me a few more minutes and I'm down." I laugh, assuming that's not what she's talking about.

I feel her body shake with silent giggles. "No. For food, you fiend!" She slaps my chest playfully.

"Oh. Yeah, I could eat." I pull her closer, knowing I need food, but not wanting to separate from her either.

"There's a fun honky-tonk a block away that has good bar food. Wanna walk there?"

"Sure. Come on, let me feed you." I cup her chin, bringing her gaze to mine, then kissing her again.

THE NEXT COUPLE of hours are filled with food, drinks, and a whole lot of flirting and teasing. I've had a hard time keeping my dick soft. I can still smell the sex on us, and it is driving me mad just wanting to slide into her warm, tight center. The way her body responds to every touch is addicting. Kissing her, tasting her, touching her is all I keep doing. I'm addicted to her already.

Back in the room, after a few more orgasms, she's tucked into me with her leg draped over. The marathon sex session we just had was something I've never experienced. Just when I thought we had our last one, a kiss would turn desperate, or a touch would ignite passion. Over and over. Until finally, we both lay spent and her soft breaths are brushing across my chest.

The shadow that was cast over my life has lifted. Marisol has revived me, illuminating my life once again.

"Mi sol," I whisper to myself and kiss her head as she sleeps.

8

MARISOL

Yesterday was amazing, and I still can't believe that it happened. High school obsession turned into the hottest date I've had in ten years. All I wanted was to feel him inside me, again and again and again. His slight dominance was an instant turn on. His teasing and continued foreplay had me on edge all day until...until... I need to get my head on straight and stop daydreaming about yesterday. I have enough to do without spending the whole day in an erotic fantasy. Well, I guess it doesn't have to be a fantasy. Full stop. There I go again!

I need to inventory everything before opening and now that I have all the wine in, that is what my day consists of. Work. Now focus.

As soon as I start entering numbers in my software, a ping of my phone distracts me.

When can I see you again?

Eliazar sent me a text. And the text bubble pops up, letting me know there's another coming.

*I'm trying to work but can't stop thinking about seeing ALL of you. *wink emoji**

I feel the heat come up my neck thinking about his hungry gaze on me.

Tonight too soon?

I don't have time to think whether I'm going too fast, because I want to see him too.

Where and what time?

My breathing picks up thinking about being tucked into his muscular chest again.

My place. Say 6ish

I'll be seeing him again. Tonight. His lips, tongue, strong hands—my breathing picks up and that tickling sensation begins between my legs again. I can't give myself the Big O just by thinking of him, can I? Let's not try that out in my place of business. Numbers. I need my head back on work.

Finally with my mind on numbers and work, I get through the boxes of supplies we have, and I begin the email to send out to the company for the wine lists I need printed. My phone pings again and my heart races thinking it's Eliazar again. I lift my phone to see Natalia's name on my screen.

Lunch?

I need to talk to Nat about what happened, so I quickly respond to meet at our favorite lunch spot.

I walk into our usual sandwich and salad spot and see her sitting with drinks already on the table.

"Hey, chica!" She smiles brightly as I take my seat.

Not being able to hold back any longer I blurt out, "I slept with Eliazar!"

Her eyes widen immediately, and she says, "Okay." She shakes her head and lets out a chuckle. "Tell me more."

I go through our visit to pick up the wines. The conversations, the flirting, and our high school past along with what we learned by talking to each other. I held back the spicy details, because that's just for us, only mentioning we were together, and I would be seeing him again tonight. She listens, never interrupting, letting me tell her everything that I had been holding back.

"You found him!" Natalia exclaims, smiling, when I finish my story.

"What?" I ask, confused.

"The one that you've been looking for! The one that will hold your attention. The one that you will fall for. It's Eliazar." She bounces and shimmies in her seat.

"One date. We've had one date. How can you say that?" I shake my head at her. While I've never felt the *need* to see anyone in my past, that doesn't mean anything. Does it?

"The light in your eyes as you told me about him. The easy way you talk about him. The excitement to see him again. You have never had any of those, and certainly not all three, for one person." She cocks a brow, knowingly.

THE PAST COUPLE of weeks have flown by. I have spent more evenings than not with Eliazar. And as much as I wanted him to stay over last night, he gave me a quick kiss goodbye before heading home. He wanted me to sleep, and sleep isn't what we've been good at lately.

The sound of an alarm wakes me from my slumber. The soft opening is today. I can't believe it is here already. When I began this journey, the days crept by, and I thought this day would never come. But then, the closer it got, the quicker time seemed to go. I stretch my arms up, not really wanting to leave the comfort of my bed but too excited to want to dillydally.

Yesterday was amazing. Eliazar didn't need to spend the whole day at the shop helping me get things in order, but he did. He was testing coffee drinks the new guys were making. He was stacking bottles of wine in the climate-controlled room. He said I didn't need to do manual things because he was here. I could focus my attention on more pressing matters. He's the gentleman I thought he was but never got to experience way back when.

My phone buzzing on the nightstand grabs my attention. I grab it seeing Natalia's name on the screen.

"I'm up," I croak.

"I know you're not a morning person, so I thought I would check on you. Also, because I know you probably couldn't sleep with all the excitement." Her cheery voice sings into my ear.

I clear my throat then respond, "And you are, of course, one hundred percent correct. But I'm getting up now."

"I'll meet you there. Text me when you're on your way. I'll bring breakfast, and you provide the coffee."

"Natalia," I say before she has the chance to hang up.

"Yeah?"

"Thank you. Really. If I haven't said it enough. Thank you. I couldn't have done this without you." Tears collect in my eyes. She's the best friend a girl could ask for.

"You know I got you." A loud kissy smack comes through the phone, which makes me smile. "Just like I know you will be there for me when and if I ever need it."

"Love you. See you in a bit." I say with tears spilling out of my eyes as I finally sit up in bed and tap the phone.

I can't help all the emotions I've been feeling so strongly this past week. My dreary, gray life has turned so much brighter than I ever could imagine.

WALKING UP TO THE SHOP, I see Natalia and Eliazar at the door waiting on me. They are talking and laughing and my heart fills with joy knowing they like each other. Natalia has not liked many of the guys I've dated. But to be fair, I didn't either.

Natalia looks in my direction, noticing me walk up, and waves. Eliazar turns to see me carrying a few bags and rushes to me.

"Here, give me this one." He grabs the strap on my overnight bag before giving me a quick kiss.

"Oh please, she's not a damsel in distress, she can carry those bags," Natalia says loudly while laughing. "You just helped to get a kiss."

He shrugs his shoulders at her and responds smiling, "Maybe you're right, maybe not."

I laugh at their banter, again thankful of their friendship.

"What are all these bags for?" Eliazar asks as Natalia helps pull the keys for the door out of my purse.

I point to the one he's carrying. "That's a change of clothes, shoes, and makeup. It's going to be a long day, and I don't want to leave." Then I tap on the strap of my backpack. "My laptop and, you know, business crap in here."

Natalia unlocks the door, and we walk in. Placing my things down, I say, "Purse and a bag of healthy snacks."

Even without him there, I ended up going to bed late last night because I was scrambling around packing. I wanted to make sure I had everything I needed today. It will be a shorter day than when we have our grand opening, but I know this week, and probably the next, will be full of working out the kinks.

I only advertised to influencers and bloggers to pass along information by word of mouth. All their posts will be the official grand opening date. I wanted business for a couple of weeks but was worried about getting slammed and not being ready. I figured this could be a good test run. Drawback is we don't know how many will show up.

"Let's eat." Natalia says, pulling out breakfast sandwiches from a paper bag.

I grab a sandwich as one of my managers walks in.

"Good morning," he greets me. "I'll start on the coffee."

"Good morning and thank you," I respond. I need some food in my stomach to calm the unsettled nervous nausea.

We sit at a table, and I watch as Natalia and Eliazar begin talking. I can't seem to focus on their words. I take a bite and taste nothing. My chest is tightening, and I can't get enough air in my lungs.

"Mi sol. Look at me. Focus on my voice." I can hear Eliazar, but I can't see him. "It's okay. It's a panic attack. Breathe for me… Slowly, in and out." I feel his hands on my arms. "Good. Now another."

I hadn't realized I had squeezed my eyes tightly shut. I slowly open them to Eliazar's face. His brows are furrowed as he runs his hands up and down my arms. I take another deep breath trying to calm the pounding in my chest.

"Have you had one before?" he asks in a quiet voice.

I shake my head. I just had my first panic attack. I need this to be successful. I want to be successful. I don't want for him to see me as the flighty girl I once was. Or still was, up until I started working on this business.

"Here's a glass of water and a coffee, just the way you like it." My manager places both on the table for me. "Don't worry about anything. Everyone will be here in a few minutes, and we got it. Take a few to relax, and then we open the doors," he chimes in with such certainty.

"Thank you. But I'll be fine," I respond.

Eliazar has not moved, still holding on to me. "Take a couple of bites, then let's get you up and walking a little. Or are you dizzy?"

"I'm not dizzy." I grab the sandwich and take a bite. I chew and swallow before saying, "That came out of nowhere."

I look to Natalia, and she's quiet, just watching us with a small smile.

"You got this. I told you already, but if you didn't hear me the first time let me repeat myself, I will not let you fail at this. This is the first time I have seen you so determined. So focused. So involved. Never. Never have I seen you this excited about work. You are loving this. Now let the love for it shine and stop worrying. As long as this place is well-run, we will market the shit out of it, and it will thrive."

"Really?" My eyes widen at her observation.

She nods. She's right. As much work as this has all been, I've loved every minute. Even the construction portion, with all the noise and changes.

I nod back at her; my lips pull out tightly. I want to smile, but I'm just not quite ready.

"Another bite," Eliazar directs me. He's right. I need to eat, especially if it's going to get busy.

9

ELIAZAR

MY HEART DROPPED WHEN I SAW MARISOL STRUGGLE. I DON'T KNOW IF I'VE ever been that scared in my life. My mind races with memories of my time with Angela. I don't remember a time that I was ever that worried about her. Even the time she broke her foot and she was in pain. I took it in stride, and we made our way to the emergency room. What does that say about my relationship with her?

Was I really mad at her for leaving, or was I mad because I stayed so long living in comfortableness? Maybe my anger was never directed at her. Maybe I just refused to see past it to myself. All those paintings. All that frustration. Was it my indecision about where I needed to go next in life?

My newest work flashes in my head. It had started out like all the others. Consuming darkness. But when Marisol walked into my life, it took on a new feeling. The sun shone. Life started again. I've been painting. I've been playing with new techniques and colors.

"Do you need to grab your equipment?" Natalia's voice brings me back to the present.

"Uh. Yeah." I was sitting at the table with the empty sandwich wrapper in front of me. I don't even remember finishing it once I got Marisol back to herself. I stand up, grabbing my trash and throwing it in the paper bag on the table. "I'll be right back."

As I walk out of the store to my Jeep for my things, my mind is still racing with this revelation.

Back in the shop, I walk into the storeroom to drop everything off. I take out a camera and watch the hustle and bustle. Everyone looks happy, chatting excitedly for the day. Even though the day could be brutal, everyone is in good spirits, ready to tackle it.

I start snapping a few shots. I try and stay back so I can snap them candidly. It's amazing how much better pictures turn out when people don't know they are being photographed.

"It's officially open!" Marisol says loudly to everyone with a tight smile. She's still extremely nervous.

Hoots and hollers accompany her announcement for a few seconds before everyone returns their focus to their conversations and work.

Natalia is sitting at a table with her laptop open in front of her while Marisol paces the length of the store. After a couple more snaps and one too many back-and-forths from her, I grab her arm to stop her.

"It's going to be fine. You said it yourself, it could be crazy busy, or it could be dead. All you did was send out emails to influencers and asked for quiet word of mouth. Once the stay-at-home moms make their way to the splash pad, maybe one of the baristas can go out with some latte samples to bring them in," I try to reassure her.

"That's a great idea." I see her chest fill with air. "You're right. I just need to calm the eff down." She finally greets me with a soft smile.

I bend down, kissing her lips quickly. "A good luck kiss," I whisper, winking at her.

She tip-toes to my ear, saying quietly, "If this place wasn't packed with my employees, I'd ask for a good luck fuck." She looks into my eyes, cocking her brow.

"That surely can be arranged tonight," I growl, as my cock hardens in my jeans. "And keep talking that way and your employees will know what we are talking about if they notice my woody."

A full-bellied laugh escapes her lips as she mouths to me, *I'll behave.*

Almost an hour passes, and she was about to cut some of her employees for the day when the door opens to a group of four ladies. The relief I see in her face as she greets her first customers eases my apprehension. I was watching her closely, not wanting her to experience another panic attack.

Soon after, they get busy. I snap pictures, and Natalia greets and helps in between working in her makeshift office at the corner table.

Coffee making soon turns to wine pouring. The day continues, and they have a steady flow of customers. A few drinks are sent back, but overall, the new baristas are handling the orders efficiently.

.   .   .

I LEFT for a few hours in the middle of the day to meet another client but made my way back to Sol y Luna for her evening business. She had changed sometime while I was gone. She swapped her jeans and logo shirt for a black pencil skirt with a different colored logo shirt. A few new, unknown faces of wine stewards greet me.

Marisol is still up and moving, and I wonder if she's eaten.

She comes up to me with a tired smile. "It's been a good day. I can't wait to get off my feet."

I kiss her cheek. "Have you eaten?"

"I had a taco that Nat got me," she answers.

"Do you want me to go get you something?"

"No. We are closing in an hour. I'll eat then. But what I really want is a massage." She drops her head to the side and rolls her neck out.

"You wish is my command." I bring my hand up, cupping her cheek. "Go on and finish. I'll take some pics and wait for you."

The hour passes quickly, and soon we are standing outside our cars.

"Where do you want to stop and eat?" I ask her.

"I want a hot shower and to lie down more than I want food right now."

"Here." I begin taking my house key off the key ring. "Go to my place, take a shower, and I'll pick up something for us to eat. Make yourself at home."

"Are you sure? We can go back to my place again," she offers.

While her place is nice, and I would go over in a heartbeat if she insists, I want her in my space.

I wave the key in front of her, smiling.

She takes it from my hand and gets into her car.

I KNOCK on my door with the bags of burgers and wait. I wonder if she's in the shower or maybe fallen asleep. Just as I was going to call her, I hear the lock turn and the door open to a glorious sight. Marisol in one of my T-shirts, no bra, bare faced, and hair wet— instant turn on.

Stepping in, I say, "I don't think I want a burger for dinner anymore." My voice drops a couple of octaves.

A sly smile creeps across her face. "But you promised a massage."

"I also promised a good luck fuck," I throw back at her.

"Well, before all that happens, I have a question." Her eyes dart around as she rolls on her feet from heel to ball.

"Shoot." I wonder why her demeanor changed.

She turns around and heads upstairs, so I place the bags down on the coffee table and follow her. She goes directly to my studio, where the door is open. I never leave it open.

"I didn't know which was your bedroom and walked into this." She shrugs her shoulders. "I'm sorry, I didn't mean to pry. But… uh… and that looks familiar?" She points to a finished canvas leaning against the wall. One of the dark pieces that I had brought back from the gallery.

I knew I was going to have to come clean sooner or later, I just didn't exactly know when. I take a breath, buying myself time. She turns to look at me for the first time since walking into the room.

"It looks familiar because my other pieces are hanging in a gallery. The gallery where we ran into each other."

Her eyes widen at the memory. She turns and looks around the room before facing me again.

"That was your work I…" she says dropping her face.

"It was," I confirm.

"Shit," she says under her breath.

I step up to her, wrapping her in my arms. "Art is subjective. I was nervous that night. It was my first show. I was still mad at you for the past. I…" I was about to say I was still heartbroken, but after today, I realize I wasn't.

"I'm so sorry," she mumbles against my chest.

"It's fine. We're here now, and I don't want to mess this up." I kiss the top of her head.

She pushes against my chest to pull away, gazing up at me. "Why is that one different?"

I know she's comparing my dark piece to the one still on the easel. "Which one?" I ask anyway to make sure.

She turns around and points. "That one."

MARISOL

Eliazar hugs me from behind. His arms comforting even with this new revelation—knowing I bashed his work.

"I told you about my ex."

I nod my head.

"Well, after the breakup, I was angry, and that's what came out. Piece after piece was full of frustration and anger."

"That's what Natalia said." I whisper, remembering her speech on the piece.

"Natalia said that?" he asks.

"Yes. But she also said there was hope." My voice is small; I'm scared of what's to come of this. Tears begin to collect in my eyes. What am I doing here in the workspace of an artist whose work I slammed? I had no regard for anyone's feelings. Just shooting my mouth off to make myself feel better because it's something I don't understand.

"Did she?" he sounds intrigued.

I nod my head again. "And that one?" I ask again, pointing to the unfinished work on the easel. "It looks like the outline of a woman."

"Because it is," he says plainly. "Come on downstairs so you can eat, and I'll answer any questions you have."

I turn to look at him in disbelief. How can he still want me here? "Are you sure? I don't want to pry. And I would understand if you wanted me to leave, especially after my not-so-nice comment at the gallery."

"First, I don't want you to leave. Second, I may have overreacted. Like I said, the nerves of it being my first show and all. And seeing you caught me off guard."

A single tear escapes, sliding down my cheek. He brings his hand up and swipes it with the pad of his thumb. He comes in close, brushing his lips against mine, then says, "The outline is you—mi sol."

He brings our lips back together for a short kiss and holds me tightly.

"Stay here. I'll be back," he says letting me go.

He exits the room, and I walk to the easel, looking at the painting. I stare at it, taking it in. I think of Natalia and how she looks at pieces and conjures up ideas of what they mean. Could I do that too?

It looks like it started out angry, the way the other one is. Black and dark gray around the border. It's clumped and has no rhyme or reason, like Natalia said. But then lighter colors come in. I look closer and can see the black behind some of the blues and pinks. And it all comes together in the center with the outline of a woman in yellows and soft oranges. Her hair looks like it is windblown.

"I'm back." Eliazar announces his return.

I turn around to see him carrying a blanket with bottled waters and the bag of burgers. I rush to him, taking the blanket out of his hands. I open it and spread it on the floor. He sits down and places the food in the middle.

"Come. Eat and ask."

"I don't want to pry," I say, taking my seat and grabbing one of the waters.

"You're not. I promise," he says as he grabs the burgers out of the bag and places one in front of me.

"So I guess I'll ask the same question again. Why is that one different?" I cock my head in the direction of the one with the woman.

He takes a bite of his burger, chewing and looking between the two canvases.

"The one I'm working on is different because I met you again. You have brought happiness back in my life. I told you I was shocked when Angela left. All the pieces like that," he points at the one on the floor, "were done after she left. And Natalia was right. That was anger. Frustration. Despair."

I take a bite of my burger as he explains.

"And then I you walked into my life. And I felt things again. That's what art is for me. I paint my feelings. The good, the bad, and the ugly." He shrugs his shoulders, taking another bite.

"You've called me 'mi sol' a couple of times now. Why?"

He smirks as he finishes what he has in his mouth then takes a drink of water before saying, "You caught that?" He raises a brow at me.

"It's always been out of the blue. At the motel. I guess you thought I was sleeping. Then earlier today when I freaked out. And just a bit ago."

"Because you are my light. I was living in darkness, not believing in love or happiness. I couldn't see a way out of the black hole I had destined myself to live in. Then you walked into my life, and all I see are the possibilities." There is a certainty in his voice. He looks at the painting, focusing on it for several seconds before he turns to look back at me. "The piece is called, *Mi Sol, My Sun.* You. Tú eres mi sol."

Tears I didn't expect stream down my face with his admission about the painting and of his feelings. I crawl closer, straddling and hugging him tightly, scared to let go. Is this real? Did I finally find peace in my life?

Nothing in my life has felt so right. Every guy I dated was a filler until the next. No one I wanted to give my heart to. Never mind my heart, some I didn't even want to give my time to. Every job was that. A job I did but it didn't bring me joy. Something I did to support myself.

Sol y Luna is exhilarating. I wake up wanting to get things done. And Eliazar. Since he walked into my shop, I would be lying if I said I wasn't looking forward to the next time I could see him. Even when I still thought he hated me. Even then I just…

"Hey." Eliazar rubs my back with one hand and cups the back of my head with the other. "What's going on in that beautiful head of yours?"

"I'm happy with my life right now. You. The shop. My life before was what I thought it should be, but it never felt right," I say, still holding myself tightly to him.

"It's me and you."

I pull back quickly to look into his eyes.

"I want you in my life." he says, then adds, "I don't want to be one of those guys you get tired of."

"You're not." I pause, watching him. Thinking about the feelings that I have stirring around me. How happy and settled I feel.

He kisses my nose. "Finish eating so I can give you that massage I promised."

Emboldened, I roll my hips feeling him harden a bit, then add, "You also owe me a good luck fuck." I bite my bottom lip, waiting for his response.

"That I do." He gives one of my nipples a quick pinch, and my core clenches in anticipation.

We quickly finish eating, and he walks me back to his bedroom, where he asks me to lay down on my back. I do as he says, and I watch as he sits on the foot of the bed. He grabs my right foot and begins massaging it. His strong hands kneading all the standing I did today feels amazing. He spends a couple of minutes on it before moving to the next.

He kisses my toe and places my foot down. His warm breath on my foot sends goose bumps up my leg. "Now take off your shirt, and lay on your stomach."

"You just want me naked," I tease, pulling the hem up.

"Yes. But to massage your back."

He moves from the foot of the bed to the side before I can lay back down. He cups one of my breasts in his warm hand, and I lean in wanting more.

"That's coming too." He rubs my nipple with his thumb until it hardens.

I move closer to him, wanting to feel him inside me more than the massage now.

"Patience." He stops me. "Lay down."

I grumble, but listen turning over and laying down, facing away from him. He begins rubbing my shoulders, and now I can't decide what I want more—his massage or to feel him inside me. His hands move, hitting pressure points, kneading out knots up and down my back. A few kisses sprinkled in keep my arousal steady.

His hands move to my calves, and then I feel his lips kissing their way up my leg, to my butt, then on my back. His hands are on my waist, then slide up, gliding over the side of my breasts. I push myself into the mattress needing pressure at my core.

His lips come to my ear. "Turn over."

I slowly flip over, looking into his hungry gaze. His blue eyes have darkened.

He takes his index finger and glides it around my torso lightly, sliding down to my panties. He hooks his finger on one side, and I take the other as he pulls them down my legs. He stands up, letting his eyes take me in.

"What are you waiting for?" I grab my breast and pinch my nipple.

"Not yet." He takes my hand off my breast and places it at my side. "I'll do that."

I can feel the wetness between my legs.

He strips out of his clothes painfully slow. I squirm, needing touch, friction, something.

"Please," I whimper, needing to feel him.

He sits on the side of the bed and cups my breast, bringing his mouth closer. He kisses it, then licks my hardened bead. I close my eyes, relishing the feel of him. I push into him, desiring more. His cool breath startles me after his warm mouth has been on me. His fingers are pinching and playing with my other breast.

He grabs my leg and begins trailing kisses up. He moves between my legs and continues, his lips moving closer to my wanting center. He kisses my mound, then he separates my folds, licking my nub gently. A loud moan escapes my lips.

"I need more," I groan as he continues to lick and kiss me all over except the most sensitive spot.

"Don't be greedy, mi sol, it's coming," he growls.

Before I could beg some more, a finger slides in me, and he sucks my clit in his mouth. Instant ecstasy. My body is tingling in the most beautiful way.

Kisses on my belly, then over my breasts before he reaches my mouth. I taste myself on him as our tongues dance together. He covers my body with his as he brings himself to my center. I spread my legs out farther, waiting on bated breath for him to enter me. He slides in slowly until he is up to the hilt. He rolls his hips, and I push up, wanting more.

He begins rocking into me, in and out. He lowers his body on mine, kissing me quickly before he rolls over and places me on top.

"Sit up and let me see you."

Dizzy with the rush of emotions all day long, I do as he asks. With him still in me, I sit up and ease him further in. The sensation of being in control hits, and I begin rocking my hips and feel a rumble in his chest under my hand.

He watches me with hooded eyes as I bounce up and down, controlling what feels good. Soon another orgasm is building.

"Come for me," he growls as he licks his finger and begins playing with my clit. "I'm coming with you this time."

A few more pumps and the rush of euphoria hits, and I slow down. He grabs my hips, moving them, and soon he groans and his body shudders under me. I lower down, laying on his chest, his penis still in me. I want this feeling of connection.

After a few quiet moments, he says, "Roll over. Let me get up and get you cleaned up."

I follow his request, missing the feeling of fullness as soon as he slides out. He sits up in bed and stands, going to his bathroom. The faucet sink starts running as I hear him in there. The water stops running, and he comes out with a washcloth.

"Spread 'em." He gives me a devilish smile.

"You wish is my command." I roll to my back bending my knees and spreading myself open for him.

He brings the cloth between my legs, and its warmth and his gentle swipes turn me on again. I close my eyes again, wiggling under his touch.

"You can have me every day if you desire. But now, I need a shower, and you need sleep. You have another big day ahead of you."

He takes the cloth away, and the cool air hits me. I open my eyes to look at him, and he comes down, placing a kiss and a quick lick between my folds. "My last taste until tomorrow."

My heart thumps hard against my chest. Another assumption for tomorrow. New territory for me, and it feels good. I want to be here. I want to feel him tomorrow. I want to cuddle against him. I roll to the side and watch as he closes the bathroom door behind him and the shower turns on.

ELIAZAR

I BEGIN TO STIR BEFORE THE ALARM GOES OFF. I KNOW SHE WILL HAVE A BUSY few months as she opens this new business. I remember the early days of my photography business. Always on call to pick up new clients. Juggling a part-time job to help pay the bills. Not that she will have to get a second job, but the time she'll be spending at the shop will be abundant, and she will begin to feel it.

Her body is curled up, and I'm spooning her from behind, my arm under her pillow. I don't move, not wanting to wake her before she absolutely has to be up. This right here, this is love.

I can't believe I was so blind to Angela's and my unhealthy relationship. Hindsight can be both a blessing and brutal. Things you chose not to see become glaringly obvious. Little things like this. Letting your partner sleep. Angela would get up in the morning and not care what noise she was making when getting dressed, even on the nights I worked at the bar and had a full day in front of me.

We could go days without talking when both our schedules were packed. Sometimes not even texts to check in with each other. We had become more of roommates that lovers, only going through the motions of lovemaking when one of us would bring up how long it had been. We lacked that all-consuming feeling of wanting to be with the other person. I know it doesn't last and rela-tionships evolve over time, but I can't believe the feeling of desire for the person fades.

Even in the beginning. We were friends first, but did we really move to the next level?

Before my mind can start spiraling with memories of the past, the alarm on her phone goes off. She grumbles as she begins moving around. I grab her phone off the nightstand, turning it off for her. I kiss her bare shoulder and pull her in closer to my chest.

"Another big day for you," I say softly.

"I know. I'm excited, but so tired," she croaks sleepily.

"Sleep for a few more minutes. I'll make you some breakfast to take with you. I'll check on you to make sure you got up."

"Mm-hm." She rolls out of my hold, and I quietly get up and get to the bathroom.

AFTER MY MORNING meeting with Natalia and her PR firm, I call Mateo to meet me at Sol y Luna to check on Marisol. He can see the place, and I can get my fix of her. As I walk up, I can see several customers sitting at tables—some with coffee and some with wine. I open the door, scanning for Marisol. There is a group of three ladies with strollers at the counter, and one of the wine stewards is pouring them what looks to be a sparkling rosé in the plastic travel wine glasses. She had a great idea with those.

"Hey." I feel a clap on my shoulder.

I greet Mateo, and we make our way to the counter to order.

"Eliazar, hi," the barista greets me.

"Hello." I smile at her. "Marisol?"

She tilts her head back toward the storeroom. "In there. Want me to get her?"

"No. Don't disturb her if she's busy. We'll just order and wait."

"Okay. What can I get you?"

She takes our order, and we take a seat at one of the empty tables. With the steady flow now, I wonder what traffic she'll get once it's officially open. Her grand opening is soon. This was a great idea of hers to open a couple of weeks early with no publicity so she could gauge the traffic.

Mateo and I chat for a few minutes, enjoying the coffee, when I see Marisol step out of the back room. She scans the shop before her eyes land on me. Her lips pull out into a huge smile, which makes my heart pound a little harder. How long has it been since a female smile has turned me into a giddy kid?

She walks to our table, her gaze not leaving mine.

"Hey." Her voice trembles a tad.

I wink at her in return, then add, "Marisol, meet Mateo. This is who we borrowed the Tahoe from." I nod my head in his direction.

"Hi. Nice to meet you." She extends her hand to him, and he takes it, pulling her closer and kissing the top before letting it go.

She lets out a girly giggle. "Oh, you're a dangerous one, aren't ya?" Her smile is even wider than before.

He shrugs his shoulders. "Nah. Maybe. Sometimes?"

She laughs and shakes her head. "I'll take that as a yes. Thank you for coming and checking my place out."

"It's great. I was going to try the wine that filled my car, but since I have to go back to the garage, I gotta stick with coffee."

"Okay now. You can stop flirting with my girl." I punch his shoulder playfully.

I turn to Marisol and watch as her cheeks brighten with a tinge of pink.

"Can't help it if my normal self tops your flirting skills." He laughs. "I'm getting a refill."

Mateo stands, making his way to the counter.

"Has the place been this busy all morning?" I ask.

"It's been off and on. We get a rush then it slows down. It's been nice. I'm getting a little worried about the true opening. I'm wondering if I should hire more people." The silliness subsides, and she's back into businesswoman.

"Check with who you have first. Ask them about pulling double duty for a few weeks to see if the newness busy tapers off. If it doesn't, then you can hire. That way you don't end up with too many employees." I wave my hand casually.

"I could. I thought about it but was worried about overworking them." Her brows raise and crease her forehead.

"If they are good, then it should be fine. And it wouldn't be long term. Just to see how it all plays out." I try and help her ease her mind because I think she had already thought of that but didn't want to upset her staff early on.

She smiles and nods. "You're right. It's just for a few weeks. I guess I just needed to talk it out."

"I'm always here."

Mateo comes back to the table with a to-go cup in hand.

"I gotta get back to work. Nice to meet you, Marisol. We'll definitely be back, and I think we can talk Ritza into picking us up some orders." Mateo tips his head. "See you." He looks at me, and as soon as he's behind Marisol and she can't see him, he mouths, *I approve.*

I school my face because Marisol doesn't need to know this fool's shenanigans.

"I guess I should head out too. I've got some pictures and graphics to work on." I start to stand. "I'll be home if you want to stop by again. I'll have dinner ready."

"We have spent almost every night together. Aren't you worried we are moving too fast?" She cocks her head to the side.

"I told you last night, it's me and you. So, no. I don't think we are moving too fast. But if you would like to go home, I completely understand. But I was thinking I would have another taste tonight." I give her a smirk, cocking a brow.

She licks her lips slowly, and I watch her breath hitch. I stand and whisper in her ear, "If all I do is have my favorite meal, I'll be a happy man." I kiss her neck.

A quick kiss good-bye and I walk out of her shop.

11

MARISOL

Days have turned to weeks, and I have never felt so tired, but fulfilled. The shop is doing well, steady foot traffic and lines for wine and coffee on the weekends as people enjoy the spring weather at the splash pad and outdoor areas.

More days than not, I'm at Eliazar's after work. I have started to duplicate things, so I don't have to pack a bag to go back and forth. He is the one who encouraged me to leave things. He wants to make my life easier.

The hot shower after another long day feels amazing. I've had to modify my hours because I won't be able to sustain working twelve-hour days every day. I've started to trust my managers to open and close for me so I can do one or the other. I opened this morning, so dinner, movie, and an early night is all I'm looking forward to. Maybe not so early, if I have my way. From good luck fucks to sunshining dining to good-night bites, I've made up all kinds of ways to ask for his magical skills.

I step out of the shower so I can dress and wait for Eliazar to get back from picking up our dinner. I quickly slide on comfy oversized sweatpants and a T-shirt to lounge and relax for the rest of the evening.

I head downstairs, and as soon as my foot hits the last step, my heart stops as I notice a woman sitting on the couch looking at a blank TV screen. I'm stuck not knowing whether I should run back upstairs and lock myself in my room or to the kitchen to grab a knife.

Before I can make a decision, she speaks. "I never thought I would be in the situation to kick a damn *sancha* out of my house, but there's a first time for everything." Her voice is cold and flat.

This strange woman just called *me* the sidepiece? She must be joking.

"Who the hell are you?" I yell and make my way to the kitchen for a weapon.

She slowly turns her head to look at me, her eyes narrowed.

I freeze. "Get out of my boyfriend's house!"

"I leave town for a few months for a job, and some slut thinks she can kick me out of my home." The laugh that leaves her lips is shrill. She stands and extends a hand with keys in it. "My name is Angela, and my name is on this lease. You are the one who doesn't belong, no matter what he told you. I'm home now and *you*..." she drags it out, "need to leave. Now."

It feels like a punch to the gut, the air whooshing out of my lungs. Tears instantly spring to my eyes. This can't be happening. This is a nightmare. Did I fall asleep? I pinch my arm, and I feel the dull pain.

"Seriously? Are you that dumb? I said get the *fuck* out of my house, before I call the cops."

I'm frozen in place. My feet don't move. I watch as she bends down, grabbing something from the couch. She comes up with her cell phone and begins typing on the screen.

I quickly move, grabbing my purse and keys from the entrance table, and walk out the front door. As soon as the door closes behind me, I run to my car, letting the tears fall freely. I start my car and speed away before I see *him*.

How could he lie to me? Lead me on? He said they were done. Was that all a lie? She had a key. I know Eliazar would have locked the door when he left. He knew I was going to be in the shower. He doesn't even like it when I lock up the shop at night alone. He's huge on safety.

This. This is the reason I don't settle. Because something always goes wrong. Nothing is ever right. People lie. People deceive. People do what they want to get the better of you.

What did he want from me? A piece of ass while his girlfriend was away? I need a drink. I drive to a hole-in-the-wall bar we used to frequent when we were younger. No one will bother looking for me here.

I step out of the car and realize I don't have any shoes on. I open the back door and hope I have something in here from all the back-and-forths between his place and mine. *Score!* A pair of sandals that don't match the sweats, but who cares? I slide them on and walk in. No makeup, wet hair, loungewear with dressy sandals, surely equals heartbreak.

A decent looking guy is working the bar. I hop onto a stool. Luckily, it is midweek, and the place has only a few patrons.

"What can I get ya?" Bartender asks as he wipes the counter in front of me.

I lean on the bar and answer, "Straight-up whiskey. Make it a double."

"Ice?" He offers gently.

"Nope." I shake my head. "I need it to burn."

Punishment for falling. Punishment for believing. Punishment for falling in love… Wait, I fell in love. Tears fall, and I wipe them away roughly. I will not be that girl. I was her in high school. Crushing on, falling for, and trusting the wrong guys. What gets me is that I admitted that to him. I admitted knowing I was being used and staying anyway to be popular. And he used me for…

Bartender places a glass filled with the amber liquid in front of me and holds the bottle with the other. I grab the glass and down the liquid in one large gulp. The heat makes its way from my throat to my stomach. I want and need to feel the oblivion as fast as possible. He holds up the bottle to me, and I place the glass down and tap it with my index finger. He pours another double, then places the bottle down.

I watch him move to the other side, where a man came in and took a seat several stools away from me. I place the glass to my lips and down the second drink. I grab the bottle he left for me, and I pour another. How smart is that? Not very, but right now, right now is for getting piss-ass drunk. Tomorrow, I wipe away the crushing feeling of betrayal and move on, yet again. Third glass down and the burn is nonexistent.

I open up my phone and his texts are the first thing to show up. Another tear falls, and I swipe, delete. No reason to go back and wonder what if. I open my pictures and start clicking all the pictures of us. Why did I take so many selfies of us? What am I, a teenage girl with a crush? Yes, yes I was, and look at what that got me. If I had one wish to be granted, I would want to go back to my life before Eliazar walked back into it. Trash is where those pictures go. I pour myself another.

The numbness of the shots is starting to make its way around my body. I slide off the stool and grab some money from my purse. I down the drink before walking over to the jukebox in the corner. I feed it my money then flip the pages, clicking letters and numbers for every upbeat, cheesy song I can. I may be wallowing in my misery, but I do not need to subject every other person to my shitty night.

I make my way back to the stool, and my purse and phone are gone. Fuck! I just left my stuff for anyone to take it. No keys, no wallet, no phone. Fuck, fuck, fuck! I get up on the stool and drop my head on my crossed arms.

"Looking for this?"

"What?" I answer without looking up.

"This."

I look up, and Bartender holds my purse in his lifted his hand.

I exhale loudly in relief. "Thank you." I stretch out my hand to grab it.

"How about I hold on to this," he shakes my purse, then says, "and give you this." He hands me my phone.

I take it and continue looking at him with narrowed eyes, trying to focus.

"Use that to call a friend, an Uber, or whatever ride home. As soon as you have that, I'll give you back your bag, and you can settle up."

Sounds reasonable since I'm feeling the whiskey already.

"Fine." I agree.

He pours me another then takes the bottle away.

I swipe my phone and send Natalia a quick text to come get me. No why. No reason.

She responds with a simple, *ok*. No questions. That's what I love. She knows I'll eventually tell her everything, anyway.

ELIAZAR

I unlock the door and walk in expecting to find Marisol on the couch, cuddled under blankets the way she has been every night she's stayed over. But instead, Angela's eyes are boring into me.

"What the hell are you doing here?" I exclaim in anger and frustration. "And where is Marisol?"

I scan the room, thinking I would see her.

"Mi sol!" I yell up the stairs, hoping she'll respond.

Silence greets me.

"I told her to leave my house," Angela says flatly.

I turn to look at her, rage bubbling up my chest. I clench my jaw, holding my tongue to choose my words wisely.

"Your house?"

"Yes. Mine. My name is on the lease." She crosses her arms across her chest.

"It may be, but I'm about to renew, and it sure as hell won't be again. And you didn't pay for shit, so no, not your home."

"Look. I'm sorry." Her demeanor softens, and her eyes water. "I left because I was scared. We had been us for so long. We were young and only knew each other. I just didn't want to make a mistake. What if we were just us because we were scared to leave each other? I needed to make sure it was real."

"What the fuck are you talking about it? That makes no sense. Of course, we were us. Of course, I proposed because it was us. I only wanted us. But that was past tense. Wanted. Not want. Not anymore."

"You can't mean that." She takes a couple steps closer. "I'm here now. I'm ready. The answer is yes," she pleads.

"The answer to what? Because I sure as hell didn't ask you anything. You need to leave. It's over. It's been over. I'm not in love with you."

"You already fell out of love? Really. After all our years together." Tears stream down her face, and all it's doing is making me uncomfortable. I feel bad, sure, but I'm more worried about Marisol.

"I did. I moved on, just like you said we needed to." I shrug. "Marisol walked back into my life and brought me out of the darkness you left me in."

"You can't mean that." Her voice trembles.

"Let me show you something." I walk to the stairs and look behind me. She takes a step, and I make my way to my studio.

I open the door and step in, waiting for her to enter.

"You're allowing me in your sanctuary?" The surprise in her voice is apparent.

"This one time, yes." I point to blankets and pillows in the corner of the room. "That's where Marisol naps or reads or watches me while I work."

I turn to look at her, and she is staring at the blankets with her lips pulled down.

"She's allowed in here?" Her voice shakes as she says quietly.

"Not only allowed, but welcome. She brings me peace as I'm working. Even if she's not paying attention to me, more engrossed in a book than me or sleeping, just her presence inspires me." I can't decide whether it's cruel that I'm telling Angela this or whether I'm being kinder by showing her that I really have moved on. That someone else has filled my heart.

"That's her?" She points to the canvas with Marisol's silhouette. It's hung on one of the walls. That's another hint for Angela. I have never hung up any of my works in my own home. Even if I like them. *Mi Sol, My Sun* is the first of my pieces that has found a home on my own walls. And that's where it will stay. That piece will be mine. Always.

"It is."

"I see." She wipes the tears that have fallen with both her hands. "I should go."

I only nod at her. She turns around and walks away. I stay in place, digging my phone out of my pocket and dialing Marisol's number. It rings and rings, no answer. I hang up and try again. No answer.

I run down the stairs and to my car. The drive to Marisol's apartment is long, and I call her incessantly. Still no answer. Her car isn't in the parking lot. I knock on her door like a madman, with no luck. On my way to Sol y Luna, I get a text from Natalia.

Are you with Marisol? Why does she need me to pick her up from a bar?

She's at a bar?

I hit call on Natalia's name.

"What's going on?" she answers the phone.

"My ex showed up, and I guess kicked her out of my place."

"WHAT?!" she yells.

"I know. I wasn't home. I was getting us dinner. I came home, and Marisol wasn't there, but my ex was."

"So that's why she's drunk and alone at a bar?"

"Yes," I answer, ashamed. "I'm going to get her. Don't worry. I got her."

"You promise?" Her voice trembles.

"I promise. I love her," I admit it out loud for the first time to Natalia, realizing I've never said it to Marisol.

Everything with Marisol has just come so easy, I took for granted she knew how I felt. I've never said the words. Because I never said it, she doubted and left. She ran away to preserve herself, yet again.

"Okay."

"What bar?" I ask.

"Bentley's. On McKellan. Call me if you need me."

I hang up and speed, exiting the highway to do a turnaround. The next fifteen minutes getting to the bar is going to be brutal.

I park, jump out of the vehicle, and run to the door. I swing it open, and my heart drops the instant I see her perched up on a stool at the bar, smiling brightly at the guy behind the bar. I'm simultaneously pissed at the guy for hitting on the love of my life and worried about her safety. Why would she choose to come here?

Seeing her, I can breathe a little easier, so I take a deep breath and collect myself before approaching. The guy notices me staring at her and gives me a quick nod of his head. He turns around, and I see Marisol's purse by his register. The realization dawns on me—he took her keys so she couldn't leave. Grateful there are still nice people looking out, I return the head nod when he looks back in my direction.

I slowly walk up to her, taking a seat on the stool next to her. She doesn't bother looking my way, her gaze stuck on the bartender.

"Mi sol." I place my hand on her back, and she flinches away.

"Go away! How did you find me? No one knows about this place," she spits out angrily, slurring her words. She's had one too many.

"Natalia told me where to find you," I answer her, not lying.

She grunts and says, "I need another one. Keep pouring until I pass out." She then looks to me, fire in her eyes, her features contorted in anger, and says, "Don't you have a fiancée to go home to?"

She's not thinking clearly anymore, and all I want to do is hold her.

I shake my head at the guy when he looks to me. I hope he understands I'm answering both her statements—don't pour her another, and no, there is no fiancée.

"My girlfriend is sitting in front of me. The only girl who owns me is sitting in a dive bar drunk out of her mind. The love of my life is hurting because my past came back to haunt me."

I try again, and place my hand on her back, and she drops her head on her crossed arms on the bar. The vibration on her back tells me she's crying.

"Come here." I stand trying to wrap her in my arms.

She pulls away quickly and jumps off her stool, standing but swaying, while shooting a look that could kill. "No, no, no. Go away. I trusted you. And you were still with *her*!" She yells, not caring that she's making a scene in a bar. Very unlike her.

"I am not with her. I don't know what she told you, but we broke up almost a year ago. Everything I told you was the truth. I didn't date anyone until you walked into my life again. You, you are *the one*. I love you" I try and take a small step closer to her, and she takes a step away.

She shakes her head, "Nope. It's not going to be me. It's not me. I'm fine. You can go. Natalia will come get me. Or he can take me home." She ticks her head to the bar area, insinuating she would take the bartender home.

"I'm not leaving without you. I'm not leaving the woman I love while she's hurting," I plead with her. My hands are itching to touch her, to comfort her. I rub them on my sides to have something to do.

"Well, I don't love you, so you can go." She rolls her eyes, swaying. She loses her balance a bit and grabs on to the stool to keep herself steady.

She stabs me in the chest with that statement, even though I know it's not true. She's hurt and angry and wants to make me feel the same. She has always been in self-protection mode. That's why she's never settled. If she does, and something goes wrong, she'll get hurt.

"Sol, I won't ever hurt you on purpose. And if I was home when Angela decided to walk in the door, you would have witnessed me kicking her back out. She went out searching for something more than me, and I guess she didn't find it. She thought she could come back and I would welcome her with open arms. I didn't. I told her about *you*. That I fell in love with you. That *you* are my future." I place my hand on hers, which is resting on the stool. I'm dying for any connection I can get. She pulls it away and leans back. She catches herself on the bar.

Talking to a drunk Marisol is not going well.

She's quiet for a few seconds, just staring at me, then says, "I can't." Tears fall freely, sliding down her face. "I won't be your rebound. The one that you think you love but you're still working through your past." She's trying hard to not sound as intoxicated as she is.

"You're not my rebound. You are the one I always loved but didn't have until now. The one I gazed at and dreamed about when I was a hormone-driven teen. The one that inspires me. The one that I want to come home to. The one…" I let my last statement hang. This last one I won't share until she is sober. It was something I didn't even realize until Angela made me explain why we could never go back to what she wanted.

Marisol's tears are still streaming down her face, and she sniffles. I take the step to her and wrap her in my arms. Her rigid body melts against mine. She continues crying into my chest as I grip her to me tightly, never wanting to let her go.

"Let me take you home," I whisper in her ear. "Either of our places, but I will be staying with you."

All I feel is a nod of her head against my chest.

"Let me settle up, and we're leaving."

I pull my wallet out of my back pocket and struggle to pull my card out one handed. I'm still holding Marisol with my other arm; she feels like she will topple over if I let her go.

"Need help?" the guy asks.

"Top card." I tell him as he slides my card out and runs it for her tab. He turns around, places the card back in my wallet, and hands me a pen. I close out, giving him a generous tip for watching out for her.

"Let's go." The guy drops her phone in her purse handing it to me. I grab it and escort her out. She's stumbling as we make our way to the Jeep.

12

MARISOL

My head is pounding, and I think I have to throw up. I keep my eyes closed, scared the light will make it worse. I swallow the extra saliva announcing the puke that is about to come. I rush out of bed, barely opening my eyes to make it to the toilet. I crouch down, waiting for it to come. I empty everything in my stomach, which was not much, and let the dry heaves stop before I stand back up to look at myself in the mirror. Then it dawns on me that I'm in Eliazar's bathroom. How did I get here? I left last night.

I brush my teeth and jump into the shower. The scalding hot water running over my body relaxes me. Flashes of last night come back to me. Eliazar picking me up from the dive bar. The whiskey. *I love you. The one that inspires me. The one that I want to come home to.* These words. Did I dream them?

I sluggishly make my way out of the shower, get clothes on, and pop a couple of pain relievers for my headache before going downstairs to look for him.

Just like last night, I hit the last step and see a person sitting on the couch watching a blank TV screen, but this time it's Eliazar. I would think I was in a dream if not for the pounding in my head.

"How are you feeling?" he says without turning around.

"I have a headache," I admit.

"I would think so." He huffs out a laugh. "And about me? About being here?" he continues.

"What do you mean?"

"Are you okay waking up here? That I brought you here?"

He's still refusing to look at me.

"Yes. It's fine that you brought me here. Thank you for coming to get me," I answer, wondering why he seems put out by my presence. Even after everything he said last night.

He finally turns around, and it looks like he hasn't slept. His brows are furrowed, wrinkling his forehead.

"Natalia and I picked up your car this morning before she went to work."

"Thank you." What else can I say?

"Are you ready to talk now?" he says quietly.

I nod, scared of the conversation in front of me. I'm frozen in place.

"Come have a seat."

I make my way to the side chair, pulling my legs up, hugging my thighs to my chest.

"What exactly happened last night, and what did Angela tell you?" His jaw is ticking, and his shoulders are tightly bunched up.

I take a deep breath and tell him my side of the story. He knew she was here, so I'm assuming she gave her version. I tell him everything, including all the whiskey I drank. During my story, I can't look at him, so I stare at my legs in front of me. Getting lost in his eyes is too painful if it this doesn't end the way I hope.

"I'm so sorry you had to go through that. I had no idea she kept a key. Actually, I should have known because I didn't ask for it back, but I never thought she would use it. I thought she was only in my past." He moves from the couch to the floor in front of my chair. "I told her that we could never be us again. That I had found you. That I was in love with you. That I only wanted you. Not a rebound. You are it for me."

My eyes water at his admission, and I look in his eyes, seeing a storm of emotions. "Are you sure?"

"Positive." He stands and extends his hand. "Let me show you something."

I place my hand in his, dropping my legs to follow him. He takes me upstairs to his studio. I'm confused why. The painting he was working on is still the same as it was last I saw it. Nothing new. He's looking at his unfinished canvas.

"Why are we in here?" I ask, looking at him.

He doesn't take his eyes off the piece but begins. "Because Angela was never allowed in here. I don't know why. I just never felt comfortable with her in my space. This room. My studio. I never wanted her in what I felt was *my* space. And especially when I was working. She would see my paintings once they were complete, but never in progress." He finally turns to me. "But with you, I want you in here. You inspire me to try new techniques, colors, approaches. I'm seeing things with a new set of eyes. Whether I keep this place once my lease is up or not, wherever my studio is, I want you in it."

"Really?" I hiccup, trying to hold the sniffles and tears streaming.

"Yes. For the first time last night, I brought Angela in here to show her your space in my room… Correction. Our room… When I showed her that you spend time in here, she understood I would never go back, even if she wanted to try."

"She was never in this room until last night. In all the years you dated."

"It was only this room for about a month before she left, but yes. Each place I had my 'studio,'" he air-quotes with his fingers, "she was never allowed in. In my old place, I made a corner as my work area and separated the space with a curtain. She could not look behind the curtain."

He places his hands on my cheeks, wiping the tears with his thumbs. The softness in his touch, the sincerity in his eyes and words lets me know I'm his. I got scared and ran last night. I did what I always do, try and protect myself. This time I couldn't because I had given my heart away. Luckily, I gave it to the right person who fought to protect it and me.

"If we stay here or move into a new place, you will have a comfy couch, a desk, whatever you want so you can be in here while I work if you want."

He places a kiss to my nose before placing his forehead to mine.

"I'm sorry for last night." I whisper, embarrassed by my actions, tucking myself into his strong chest.

"Don't be. That had to have been a shock. I don't blame you. But please, if you ever have doubts, come to me first. I will tell you that I'm here with you. Only you." He wraps his arms tighter around me.

I can feel the beating of his heart.

"Did you sleep last night?" I mumble.

"Not much. I was in and out checking on you."

"I'm sorry." I rub my face against him.

"Again. Don't be. That's what I'm here for. To worry about you. To protect you. I love you. Eres mi sol." He lifts his head looking at his piece by the same name and drops another bit of information. "And never have I hung my own art in my home. That one, you, is mine. It won't be for sale. It will stay in our studio, representing us. My light and my muse." He looks back down to me.

"I love you too." I raise up on tiptoes to meet his lips to mine.

ABOUT TORI ALVAREZ

Tori Alvarez is an educator by day and author by night. She spent many days and nights daydreaming different stories and scenes, so she finally took the plunge and began putting them down on paper.

Tori writes real, honest romance with a hint of steam. She is a sucker for happily ever afters, so you will always find them in her books. She is the author of the *Graffiti Hearts* series and novella *Love's Influence*.

Tori is a Texas girl, born and raised. She lives in South Central Texas with her husband, teen daughter, dog & cat.

You can follow her at:
Website & Newsletter Sign up:
http://www.torialvarez.com

    ⊙ instagram.com/mstorialvarez

    ♪ tiktok.com/@mstorialvarez

    f facebook.com/tori.alvarez.3551

    g goodreads.com/torialvarez

    BB bookbub.com/profile/tori-alvarez

    a amazon.com/author/torialvarez

    🐦 twitter.com/MsToriAlvarez

PIRATE BOOTY

RINA DAYNE

Editor: Stephenie Magister

Visit my website at
https://rinadayne.com/

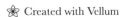 Created with Vellum

ABOUT PIRATE BOOTY

Subgenre: Contemporary Romance.
Tropes: Small-town, workplace romance.

Graphic sexual depictions, open door sex and explicit language

Blurb:

It was just supposed to be one night of anonymous sex. To give her a couple orgasms. To get her mind off the disaster of a job interview.

So imagine Phoebe Kestrel's surprise when she ends up getting the job. And her even bigger surprise when she figures out that her anonymous sex partner works for her.

Westley Jasper Herrington V is the art teacher, and favorite son of Jasper Mill. He's fantasizing about his Halloween hookup when he, too, figures out that his new boss is the woman who haunts his dreams.

Their bodies recognize each other before their minds do, and soon their relationship is burning brightly.

But can Phoebe succeed in her job—on her own merit—while dating Wes? Can Wes understand why she needs to? Or will he use his family name in an act of benevolent chauvinism that undermines her?

When it comes down to it, Wes is more than just his assets. But he does have that fine Pirate Booty.

1

PHOEBE

W<small>HAT KIND OF SMALL-TOWN, FALL-CARNIVAL,</small> H<small>ALLOWEEN-PARTY-NIRVANA HAVE</small> I fallen into? I expect a pair of ridiculously good-looking emo vampire brothers to show up any minute and tell me I'm on the set of a TV show.

Surprise, Phoebe, this isn't a Halloween party. You're a guest star on Just-Another-Teen-Vampire-Drama!

But no, this is real life in Jasper Mill.

I was only supposed to be in town for a job interview. You know, a job I told everyone at home I was sure I would get. A job, to be fair, I had all signs I *would* get.

It would have been a new life. A new home. A new step forward— this time in the right direction.

Instead of leaving town with a new job, though, I'm leaving a huge crater where an opportunity used to be.

All because I couldn't keep my mouth shut.

But Tony Capsigo had made that crack about knowing when to bend the rules and when to break them. Yes, I'd interrupted him and shared my strong views on the subject. I couldn't help myself. I believe that rules exist for a reason, and when someone suggests—like Tony had—that they're only honored in the breach, well, it pisses me off. I'm not afraid to say that. So I did. Tony got the full brunt of a righteous-Phoebe-on-her-soapbox lecture.

But he needed to know. If I were going to be the new principal of Jasper

Mill Middle-High School, I wasn't going to let them keep doing things like they'd always done. That wasn't why I'd applied for the job.

That was also, apparently, why I wouldn't be getting said job.

Now I'm wearing a Medusa costume, standing at the entrance to a Halloween carnival where I can already see a trio that can only be described as the weirdest version of the Three Musketeers in existence. A sexy (or trying to be, but *how* in that costume?) Deadpool. A T-Rex dangerously close to the... pool (*is* that a pool?). And a Pirate with the exact kind of asshole swagger that usually gets me in trouble.

As I follow my new friend Kyra inside, my feet tingle with nervous energy. I feel like the Titanic. Beautiful, but destined for tragedy. Maybe I'll meet someone dressed like Leonardo DiCaprio.

It's only as I look over at Kyra's wicked grin that I remember everyone here is on a secret mission to ditch their costumes as soon as possible.

And I hear the water's *cold* on a naked body.

Was there any point earlier in the day when I could have saved this sinking ship?

———

Earlier that day...

I start the morning trying to do something bold. To be the youngest high school principal that this town has ever seen. One trainwreck of a job interview later, I go back to the local café to drown my sorrows in a steaming cup of legally addictive stimulants.

There is no Starbucks in Jasper Mill, but there is Kyra. She owns the café, and I knew I'd like her as soon as I saw the name—It's a Grind.

Kyra catches sight of me from behind the counter and, with a familiarity that shows how she's made this place a success, she makes me a quad-shot white chocolate mocha—two extra pumps of chocolate to counter the quad shots—and gestures to the side table.

What? Why are you laughing at my white chocolate mocha? I don't actually like the taste of coffee. I just like the caffeine buzz. So my drinks of choice are the perfect balance of sugar and coffee: 90% sugar, 10% coffee.

Kyra sits, hands me the cup, and with my first sip, the tension in my body releases.

Or at least it should, but there's one part of me that's not going to get any release for a while longer. Who's got time for a date when she's about to be the next principal—

Oh. Right. I'm not going to be the principal.

"Tell me everything," Kyra says.

So I tell her. I tell her every asinine question they asked, every flippant answer I offered. She listens to it all. She doesn't judge. She just starts laughing when I finish my story.

"I bet that vein in Tony's head looked like it was going to pop out," she says, before announcing, "and we're going to a party tonight."

I freeze. Trash talking folks over a mocha is one thing—a party is another.

"I was kinda hoping to end the night with a tub of Ben & Jerry's."

Kyra raises an eyebrow and gives me the most wicked grin in existence. "You come to this party, you could end up with both of them."

"Excuse me?"

"It's a costume party. Where half the time, the costumes end up on the floor."

I push my mocha slightly to the left. Just enough to signal she's got my attention.

I can't help it. That tension in my body? It's even worse after getting my heart broken at that job interview.

"Could be fun," I say hesitantly.

"But?"

"But I don't have a costume."

"You think I didn't already think of that? I went home this morning and picked one out for you."

I raise my eyebrows at her. "You already have a costume ready for me?"

"Well…"

"Before I told you the bad news?"

"Phoebe, this is totally awkward, but I want you to stay and hang out…"

I reach out and squeeze her hand. "I'm so glad we're friends."

She squeezes back, looking relieved. "All you need to pick out for yourself is a mask."

"Why a mask?"

"Oh, everyone wears one. It's like a Halloween-masquerade combo."

"But why?"

"This is a really small town. We're all in each other's business all the time, even if we don't want to be. This is the one night a year when we can ignore all the baggage and just have fun."

"Do people really not recognize each other?"

"Sort of. Sometimes I recognize a voice, but we all try really hard to be visually unrecognizable. And even if you do guess who it is under the mask, there's like this unspoken understanding that you pretend you didn't."

"Sounds…interesting."

And an arrangement I would *never* agree to if I were actually staying here as the new principal.

Except I'm not staying here. I won't be their principal. If I go to the party, no one will recognize me because no one knows me. And after that job interview? No one ever will.

"It's totally fun," Kyra says. "After 8:00, no kids are allowed. There are a lot of shenanigans."

"What kind of shenanigans?"

"Way too much drinking and lots of sex," she says with a laugh. "We trick-or-treat for condoms after 9."

Ohmigod. Anonymous protected sex in a town I will never visit again?

It's scandalous.

It's exciting.

It's definitely what I need to forget about this day.

"Come on," Kyra says. "You know you want to."

I soften my voice, lower the pitch, all the stuff I do when talking to a crowd. I don't want to sound too eager. We might already be fast friends, but I don't need Kyra to know *exactly* how long it's been since I last got laid.

"Well, parties aren't really my thing, but I *could* use a little...male attention."

Kyra grins at me.

"But you have to promise not to tell me who anyone is. And you definitely can't use my name or tell anyone who I am. I need to be totally anonymous."

"Of course! But you know, sometimes people have enough fun to take off their masks. One couple even got married after a Halloween hookup."

"For real?"

"Totally. They wore their masks for the wedding and asked all of their guests to come in masks too."

"Was it...fun?"

"It was a lot more complicated than the couple were expecting. All the guests wanted to stay anonymous, just like on Halloween. Half the people sitting on the bride's side didn't even know her. They were just trying to disguise who they were."

"That's so weird," I say with a laugh.

Kyra shrugs and smiles at me. "So you'll come?"

Bombing the job interview for the position I was counting on is awful. I feel it down to the soles of my feet.

But Kyra is promising a night I'll never forget.

And you know what? If a night I'll always remember helps me forget the day I'll always regret, isn't that a win/win?

"Yes, I'll come." Hopefully in more ways than one.

———

EVERY WORD she said is true. We walk past a large bowl of condoms as the Catwoman-formerly-known-as-Kyra drags me to the apple-bobbing barrel. It's huge. A galvanized steel trough as large as the above-ground swimming pool I grew up with, filled with water and tons of apples, surrounded by people soaking wet and laughing hysterically.

"Watch what some of the pros do," Kyra says to me with a nudge. She tilts her head in the direction of the Three Musketeers I already spotted, who have been joined by a half-naked Waldo. Instead of a shirt, Waldo has opted to paint red and white stripes across his chest.

The Pirate catches my eye. But what does it matter that he caught it? He'll never see me again, and I'll never see him.

Except judging by the smile he's giving me, maybe I *will* see him again. He's pointing at something. Am I already so drunk that I'm fantasizing about him pointing at a private cabana where he and I can—?

Before I can finish my thought, I see what he's really pointing at.

The inflatable dinosaur launches himself into the apple-barrel-pool. Shrieks of laughter and shouts follow his lack of progress as he doggie-paddles with his comically short T. Rex arms. Laughter shakes my body.

"Bro, jump on!" the T. Rex calls to his friend to join him.

And join him he does. I watch as Waldo climbs on the back of his T. Rex bro's inflatable costume like it's a pool float. He uses his arms to paddle over to a large clump of apples.

My body can't decide whether it wants to laugh or die of shock.

Waldo lifts his mask up just enough to expose his chin and mouth and start bobbing. He manages to land about a dozen apples on his T. Rex float before running out of room and paddling back over to the edge, careful not to spill a single apple.

Though he's still in the water, he spreads his nearly-nude Waldo arms like a proud father revealing a bountiful meal.

Fun. Weird as hell, but fun.

After his friends relieve him of the apple bounty, T. Rex begins his exit from the pool. It does not go well. He's got his stubby little arms on the edge of the pool, but can't get enough leverage to hoist his huge inflatable body over the side. I feel tears forming in the corner of my eyes from all the laughing.

"Bruh, are you gonna help me, or what?" he asks Waldo. "Just pull me out." This was the wrong request to make.

"Ok, get one leg over the edge here," Waldo says. After a little rolling and cussing, T. Rex makes it happen. "And on 3," Waldo says. "1—

"On 3, what?" T. Rex asks.

"2—

"Dude, what are you going to do to me?"

"3!"

Waldo and Deadpool grab T. Rex's arms, haul him over the edge of the pool, and drop him with the same *plop* as a bundle of wet clothes.

"My nuts! Fuck!" T. Rex howls and rolls on the ground. Waldo stands over him, dripping white and red paint on his "bruh" and laughing hysterically. I'm laughing so hard I'm having trouble catching my breath.

That's when Deadpool and the Pirate walk over to me and Kyra.

"An apple for my Catwoman?" Deadpool says as he extends an offering to Kyra.

"Thanks honey," she says and then manages to grab the apple and his ass all in one coordinated move as he grabs her up in a hug and a kiss unimpeded by their costumes. I guess they know each other.

"And for you, darlin'?" Pirate says to me.

"Thank you, kind sir," I respond as I take the offered apple.

"Are you sure I'm kind?" he asks me, mischief in his voice.

"No, but it doesn't really matter to me, if you want to be my Sir."

"Medusa, I had no idea!" Kyra shrieks at me as she turns back from her man.

I'm equally shocked that I said it.

"Ok, I'm not really into the BDSM thing," I say, backtracking with a giggle.

"Too bad," Pirate responds and I can just make out a half-smirk. It adds to the whole image. He's wearing a tricorn hat proudly bearing the Jolly Roger, an obviously fake wig and beard that combine with an eye patch to obscure most of his face, a leather vest with no shirt beneath it, and these black satin pants that cling in all the right places.

"Can I escort you through this dangerous town?" he asks in a low rumble. His growly voice with a Southern twang wakes up my vagina, and I decide that this is the anonymous dick I need tonight.

"Why thank you, I would be delighted." I loop my hand through his outstretched arm, and the four of us head off to explore the rest of the carnival.

I don't know how long we spend wandering around. There are the usual midway attractions, games of chance and skill. And every time Kyra's or my red solo cup runs dry, Deadpool or Pirate are refilling them with a delicious... punch? I guess that's what you would call it. It doesn't taste like booze, but I think it's one of those college drinks that is designed to mask the flavor of the alcohol and get you drunk quickly. I wouldn't be surprised if it was Everclear and Kool-Aid.

Pirate seems to like playing games that involve hitting targets—with guns, with balls, with water. And he's good at it. He's amassing a small collection of stuffed animals that he's throwing into a satchel that I somehow didn't notice until the third stop.

Okay, I know why I didn't notice the satchel before then. I was too busy staring at his ass. Those black satin pants cling to his perfect butt. Every time he plays a game, I stand behind him and watch. I can see every muscle ripple and flex beneath the pants.

And now I've been caught.

"See something you like?" Pirate calls back to me, as he gets ready for his next shot with the air gun.

Not going to show him that I'm flustered. Not embarrassed.

I didn't get the job, but I really am a badass. I'm the youngest ever Assistant Principal in my county's history, and I know I'm ready to be a principal. Somewhere. As long as they follow the rules.

So why does this guy instantly make me feel like I want to break all of my rules?

"Yeah, I want that stuffed llama," I say as I point to the biggest stuffed toy above the game he's playing.

With another one of those half smirks, he turns back to his game and focuses on hitting the high-point targets. Five shots later, he's being handed the huge stuffed llama.

He turns around and walks—no, *struts*—towards me.

"For you, darlin'." He hands me the llama with a flourish.

"I shall call him Murray."

"Why Murray?"

"Old inside joke—it wouldn't be funny if I explained it. But thank you for sharing your spoils with me."

"Aye, it be my honor to share my booty." He winks suggestively with his unpatched eye. "Especially with such a beautiful woman."

"Even a woman with snakes on her head?"

"Yes, even with snakes that can turn me to stone. In fact, I feel myself getting harder now."

He murmured the last into my ear. If I could purr, I would. My thong is definitely damp under my barely-there toga.

I glance around, looking for Kyra, only to find that she and Deadpool appear to be involved in a serious groping session. Under the lights in the midway. Pirate's gaze follows mine.

"Get a room!" he yells.

Deadpool breaks away. "Yeah, yeah."

"Hey, can you make it back to your hotel okay?" Kyra asks me.

"Yeah, no worries."

"You're not too drunk?"

"Well, I can't exactly feel my fingers…" I hold both hands in front of me and touch each finger in turn to my thumb. Nope, not much feeling there.

"I'll get her back to the hotel safely," Pirate interjects. And bends his head down to murmur in my ear once again, "but I hope you'll want to feel *my* fingers first."

"Or something else," I respond.

"Dirty!" Kyra shriek-laughs.

"You heard that?"

"Neither of you is as quiet as you think you are."

"Whatever," Pirate says. "You and Deadpool are going to go fuck like bunnies. Maybe some of the rest of us want to have some fun too."

"On that note, we should get going, love." Deadpool finally joins the conversation. And acts like he's trying to escape it as quickly as possible.

"Hey, do I know you?" I ask him.

"Don't think so," Kyra quickly responds for Deadpool. "Plus, you made me promise not to tell you who anyone is."

"His voice just sounds so familiar." The thought is lost when Pirate begins nuzzling my neck.

Deadpool grabs Kyra by the hand and they begin walking back towards the parking lot.

"This was really fun, Medusa!" Kyra calls back over her shoulder. "Come see me in the morning! Make good choices!"

I have no intention of making good choices.

With a smile beneath my mask, I turn to face Pirate, and sing one of my favorite lines.

"I wanna do bad things to you."

2

WES

Fᴜᴄᴋ ᴍᴇ, ᴛʜɪs ɢɪʀʟ ɪs ʜᴏᴛ. I'ᴠᴇ ʙᴇᴇɴ ᴡᴀᴛᴄʜɪɴɢ ʜᴇʀ sᴡᴀʏ ᴛʜᴏsᴇ ʜɪᴘs ᴀʟʟ night. Keep catching glimpses of full lips beneath the mask every time she takes a drink. Noticing every time her laughter rings out in the cool night.

I have no idea who she is, but Kyra said she's staying at the hotel. She must be from out of town. Maybe a college friend? She seems like she could be even younger than that, and yet the certainty in her eyes tells me she's not quite that young. Most of her meekness is an act. There's a strong woman in there—the kind that's exactly my style.

I wonder what Kyra told her about the nighttime activities at the Halloween party.

"So, are you going to help me use this?" She's holding up a foil condom packet.

I guess I can stop wondering what she's thinking about. Badass.

"Hell yeah." I pick her up—she's got one of those long slender bodies and weighs less than what I lift everyday—toss her over my shoulder—she's laughing but doesn't tell me to put her down—and haul ass to my secret spot behind the mechanical building of the Jasper Mill Middle-High School.

I gently shift her body to slide down mine and set her on the ground in front of me. "Are you sure you're okay with this?" I ask.

"Okay with it? God yes. This is what I need."

"You're not too drunk? I don't want to take advantage of you."

Her mask tilts up towards me and I wish I could see her face. "No, Mr. Pirate, I'm not too drunk. I want you to fuck me."

And when she reaches down between us and begins massaging my erection, what can I say? She's convinced me.

I pull a flannel blanket out of my satchel—my purse, according to the guys —and spread it out on the ground.

"Always prepared, huh?"

"I got kicked out of Boy Scouts, but I did learn a thing or two."

Turning back to face her, I wonder why this feels so awkward. I've had plenty of anonymous sex at Halloween parties over the years. But I want to see her face, her lips. I reach out to touch her gold mask, but as it shifts a little, she grabs my forearm to stop me.

"No strings, right?" she asks.

"No strings."

"Then let's keep the masks on. We'll always wonder who the other was, and we'll never see each other again, guaranteed."

I won't lie, I'm a little disappointed. But the arrogant pirate in me takes over. "Then I better make it the best you ever had, darlin'."

As I sink to my knees before her, I hear a tiny gasp and I grin to myself. We're both going to enjoy this.

My hands circle a delicate ankle and I begin working my way up her left leg, underneath the toga. Smooth skin, soft flesh. I part her toga up to her waist where it's belted in place, and I'm rewarded with the sight of her white lace panties in sharp contrast against her tanned skin. Leaning forward, I place one light kiss on her hip bone.

"Mmmm," she responds.

"You like that, darlin'?"

"Mmm-hmmm." It ends on a sigh.

She's so beautiful under the moonlight, so responsive to every touch—I have to keep reminding myself to take it slow. But those little moans and sighs make it hard to remember. And my member is harder too.

My hands make another slow trip down and up her leg and I kiss along the line of her panties across her abdomen. She's slender, but she's not a stick. Her flesh is soft and curves inward toward her belly button. When my lips reach the apex of her thighs, I can barely restrain myself. She must feel the same because I feel her whole body shiver.

"It's been way too long," she whispers in the silence.

"Since someone ate your pussy?"

"Since someone touched me at all."

"Then let me touch you. All of you."

I reach up to grab her waist and gently guide her down to the blanket behind her. The toga is a mess—it was hardly a suitable dress in the first place

—and splays out around her. My legs are straddled over her, giving me easy access to undo her belt and unwrap her like a present. I unclasp the hook of her bra—thankfully in the front—and her skin gleams in the moonlight.

"Beautiful," I murmur, running the back of my hand lightly down one of her shoulders.

"I don't know about all that," she says softly.

"Whatever. You aren't just a priestess like Medusa was. You are a goddess. A goddess that deserves to be worshipped and treasured, like the sun and the moon and the ocean."

Why does she remind me of the ocean? Her voice, her essence, are calming. Like an afternoon stroll on the beach, hand-in-hand with an enduring love. Stopping to pick up sea glass and to share tender caresses.

When did I become a damn poet?

She shivers again.

"Are you cold, darlin'?"

"No, it just feels good. Your touch and your words. It's been a long time since…any of this. I knew I would be overly sensitive and responsive. But you…you're taking it to another level."

The best foreplay begins in the brain. I sure as hell know it, and I've done it before. The words coming out of me tonight, though, are surprising even me.

"Then let me touch some more. Let me take care of you. Give you the pleasure that you deserve." Enough words for now.

My hands move to the tops of her breasts—perfect mounds of creamy flesh, and so, so soft. I squeeze one of her nipples between my thumb and forefinger, and her soft moan fills the air.

"Harder," she murmurs. As I increase the pressure, her moan grows louder. My dick grows even harder.

"I thought you weren't into this."

She shakes her head below me. "I didn't say I didn't like it a little rough. Just not into the power exchange thing. Enough talking." Writhing beneath me, she moves my hand to the other nipple. I lean down to grab the first between my teeth and pull a little. Her back bows beneath me.

"You like that, darlin'?"

"Mmm-hmmm. You're so good at this. And it's been so long. It's gonna be over too soon."

Leaning down, I trail kisses down her abdomen until she flinches.

"The beard is scratchy."

"Fake hair will do that." I fling the beard and then my hat and wig to the side, not caring that she can now see my face. If only she would open her eyes. I continue my trek down her body. Until finally, I scoot down and nestle myself between her legs.

I place gentle kisses on the insides of both thighs.

"Wait, is your face unmasked now? I don't feel the hair."

"Mmmm," I mumble as I continue kissing up one thigh, heading for that treasure chest where her legs meet.

"I won't look, I promise," she says.

I shrug, but I don't know if she feels it because I lose all concentration in that moment. I slide her thong to the side and expose her pussy. My cock jumps at the sight. Completely bare. I can't wait a second longer, and slide my index finger up and down her slit once before gliding inside. This moan—long and deep—is the sweetest sound I've heard in a long time.

"Fuck, darlin', so wet."

She lifts her hips towards my face. "Make me come, Pirate."

"So eager. Me too, darlin'."

I slowly draw my finger out and then grasp her thighs in both hands. Spreading her wide, I go in for a taste. No preliminaries. Tongue in vagina. And fuck yeah. Her back arches, she grabs my head, and grinds into my mouth.

Using my thumb, I find her clit and make circles around it while she fucks my face. Her moans become whimpers.

"So good...almost there."

Hell yeah. It really must have been a long time for her if I can make her come this easily. I move my tongue to her clit and slide two fingers inside of her.

"Unnnngh..."

She begins to tighten around my fingers as I continue to lick and suck her sensitive nub. This *is* going to be over too soon. Like a teenage boy rushing to the finish line.

Hands grip my head again. I *could* help her slow down.

"Don't...stop..."

Maybe next time. She seems to need this right now.

She bucks her hips once...twice...three more times before they still and she screams out her orgasm.

After a moment, I feel her whole body soften. She practically melts into the blanket on the ground.

"That was so damn good," she murmurs.

"So I heard." I grin against her thigh.

"Mmmmm. I just wish it had lasted longer."

I move up towards her on the blanket, but she turns her head away from my face.

"Hey, that's okay with me. You told me it had been a long time. We can just lay here for a while, or we can go back to my place if you want. No need to be embarrassed."

"I'm not embarrassed. I just don't want to see your face."

I keep trying. She keeps refusing to let this be something more.

I mean, I knew she knew this was just supposed to be anonymous sex. But doesn't she feel what I feel? That there's some kind of connection between us?

"If that's what you want."

"It's what we agreed on, right?"

"Aye," I say, resuming my asshole pirate swagger. I spot my wig and beard on the grass about 15 feet away, and I stand up to grab them and put them back on.

When I turn back around, Medusa is sitting up on her knees in the middle of the blanket, naked except for that gold mask. Fucking beautiful.

"Come here," she orders me.

As I approach, she looks up to my disguised face with a glint in her eye. "It's your turn now."

I'm pretty sure I'll do anything she says in this moment. Why am I still dressed?

"You have too many clothes on," she says, apparently reading my mind.

I yank my shirt off and kick off my boots in the last few steps to her.

She doesn't rise. Instead, she meets me at groin level and immediately reaches for the elastic waistband of my pants. In some kind of sexy-woman-magic, she pulls my pants and boxer briefs down in one graceful maneuver, leaving my dick to not-so-gracefully spring to attention in front of her face.

I've died and gone to heaven. She lifts up her mask just enough to slide her full lips around me. But the mask…

"Ouch!" I yelp and jump back from her, struggling to keep my balance with my pants around my ankles.

She looks up at me and giggles. Giggles!

"You think that's funny, Medusa?" I say as I drop to my knees and tackle her back down to the blanket. We're both laughing now and I kick my pants the rest of the way off.

Wearing nothing but our masks, laughing beneath the stars. This night is magic in a way I've never experienced before.

"Let's see how funny you think this is," I murmur. Lowering my head, I grab one of her nipples between my teeth and tug gently.

She throws her head back with a throaty moan, and my dick swells with pride.

"I need you to fuck me, Pirate."

"With pleasure." And without any preliminaries, I slide a finger back into her delicious pussy.

"Feels so good," she murmurs.

"Good girl. Already wet for me." I slide another finger in and gently stretch her out.

I sit up and search for the condom, until I finally see the moonlight glint off the foil. When I turn back, she's rolling over onto her stomach, thrusting her ass up into the night air.

"What's that for?"

I mean, I love it doggy-style, but I have to admit that I'm a little bit disappointed. Again, I'd wanted to see more of her eyes through the mask, her body moving beneath mine.

"So I don't see your face."

Oh.

I roll the condom on, realizing once again she really does want an anonymous fuck.

What's wrong with me? Why can't I accept it for what it is?

Well, I can at least make it the best fuck she's ever had.

Straining to move slowly, I angle my dick in front of her pussy and slide just the tip in. Circle my hips to stretch her out a little more, and then slide in a little further.

"You're so tight," I grunt as I strain against the urge to slam into her all at once.

"I told you it had been a while. But you don't have to take it easy on me." She slams her hips back and impales herself on my shaft all at once.

"Fuck!" she screams out.

"You okay?" I still as I wait for her response.

"Mmmm."

I slowly move out and back in her, out and in, until I feel her juices flowing and helping me glide.

"Oh yeah." It comes out a little more guttural, a little more desperate than I wanted. But she feels…so…good.

My body begins picking up the pace, and I lose myself to the sensation. The velvety smooth gliding in and out. The sounds of her moans and grunts as I slam into the end of her time and time again. Feeling the globes of her ass fill my palms, massaging them as I move in and out of her.

Before I realize what I'm doing, I draw one hand back and deliver a resounding slap to her ass cheek. I immediately stop everything. "I'm so sor—

"Don't say it. Spank me, mark me, do whatever you want to me. Just don't stop." She punctuates her words by slamming her hips back against me again. Instinct takes over. I repeat the slap, and then grab a fistful of her hair with my other hand. I tug her head back as I resume a steady rhythm. And too soon, I feel her tightening around me.

"Oh God, yes," she says, and her hips begin moving in time with mine.

"Yes, yes—

I feel my balls tighten.

"Yes, baby—

Her words go up in pitch, her movements more desperate.

"Spank me!"

I slap her ass as hard as I dare, grab her hips, and pump in her as fast as I can.

"Don't stop!"

No. Fucking. Way.

She clenches down on me one last time. "Yes!" I explode inside of her in the same instant. Jets of cum spurting into the condom as I ride out her orgasm with my own.

And I collapse.

"Could you maybe get off me?" she asks after a moment.

I roll off to the side, and bring her with me, curling her into my arms.

"I don't think I'll ever forget this night," she murmurs.

"Happy Halloween, Medusa."

———

I WAKE myself up with a snort. Shit, was I snoring? I hope she didn't notice. I lift my head, but I don't see her. Maybe she ducked around the corner to pee.

Shifting to the side of the blanket, I realize I need to get this nasty condom off my now-limp dick. How long was I asleep? I grab a tissue from my satchel, take care of the condom, and quickly pull on my pants.

"Medusa?" I call out as I make my way along the building. "Is it okay if I come around the corner?"

No response.

"Medusa?"

I turn the corner, but there's no one there. Spinning around, my night vision detects no movement. Nothing, no one.

A familiar feeling rises up in my chest. Anger, disappointment, resignation. Usually women use me for my name. She used me for sex, but the sense of abandonment is the same.

She got what she wanted from me. And she left.

3

PHOEBE

I'm still in Jasper Mill on Monday morning when my cell phone rings. I glance down, sigh, and turn off the ringer.

"Aren't you gonna answer it?" Kyra asks from across the café table. I decided to stay in town for a few extra days during my Fall Break. It's like Kyra and I were destined to become besties, and I've had a blast just getting to know her better this weekend. It also doesn't hurt that she has supplied me with enough coffee, junk food, and alcohol to drown my sorrows about last week's disaster.

"No. It's Tony Capsigo. I don't feel like hearing the bad news from him right now. I need at least two more mochas first."

After delivering another steaming cup of coffee, Kyra stands next to me with her hands on her hips. "I'm not as patient as you are. Let's hear the message."

Sighing, I dial my voicemail and put it on speaker.

"Ms. Kestrel, this is Antonio Capsigo with the Loblolly Valley Consolidated School District. Please give me a call at your earliest convenience. There's a rather urgent matter I need to talk to you about."

"See? He wants to talk to you at your earliest convenience. He wouldn't say that if it was bad news."

It's true. People usually don't say "at your earliest convenience" unless it's good news, or a really big problem. I can't imagine that a job rejection would be "an urgent matter."

Oh, fuck.

A horrifying thought occurs to me.

"Hey Kyra? Are there any security cameras around the maintenance building at the high school?" My stomach churns.

"I don't think so. Why?"

"That's where the Pirate and I uh...met. What if Tony is calling me because they found the video footage or something? What if that's the urgent matter? Oh shit, is my sex tape going to be all over the internet? Or maybe it already is?!"

My chair screeches across the floor when I push back from the table and stand up to begin pacing. Thankfully there's only one other customer in the coffee shop right now, and he's got his AirPods in, looking out the window. I can let all my anxious energy out without anyone staring.

"Phoebs, calm down. Why don't you just call him back and find out what this is about?"

"It's not that easy!" My screech is louder than I intended.

"Sure it is. Here's your phone. I already hit call for you."

"What?!" Another screech.

He answers just as I put the phone to my ear.

"Ms. Kestrel, hello."

"Hello Mr. Capsigo. I got your message, and I'm so sor—"

"Let me stop you right there. Before you turn us down, let me tell you why you absolutely want to be the next principal of the Jasper Mill Middle-High School."

What? I thought I totally bombed that interview. What the hell is he talking about?

"Ms. Kestrel?" he asks after a moment.

"Yes. Yes, I'm here. I just didn't think—"

"Now my dear, I know I can be a bit spirited. The Italian blood and all."

It's a good thing this isn't a video call. I roll my eyes so hard it hurts.

"Perhaps you left the interview, after your verbal sparring with me, thinking it did not go well. But I love that you weren't afraid to tell me I was wrong. That was actually what made the final decision in my mind."

I thought that's what had cost me the job. But it's what made him hire me?

"And the entire school board thinks you would be an excellent fit here at Jasper. We love that you're not going to just do things the way they've always been done, and that you don't back down from a little confrontation. You have some fresh ideas that could really help the school move into the 21st century."

"I...see." I totally don't see.

"So what do you think?"

The only reason I went to that Halloween party was because I didn't get the job.

The only reason I let the Pirate fuck my brains out was because I didn't get the job.

But now this.

I had gone to the party.

He had fucked my brains out.

Could I still take the job?

"I need a little time to think it over," I say to Tony.

"That brings me to the urgent nature of my call. We'd like you to start a week from today."

"Wait—what? I thought the job started after the holiday break."

"Well, that's what we posted. But we just adore you, and we currently have no principal, so why wait?"

I glance over at Kyra, who has her eyebrows raised at me.

"I'm so flattered, Mr. Capsigo—

"Please, call me Tony."

"I'm so flattered, Tony, but I need some time. Can I let you know by Thursday?"

"Of course, my dear. I know this is sudden, and it would be a big move for you."

That's the understatement of the year.

"Thank you so much, Tony. I'll be in touch soon."

He hangs up, but I'm still staring at my phone.

How is this real life? I thought I would never see Jasper Mill again. I thought my interview with the school board went about as horribly as it could go, and that there was no way they would hire me.

I'm too young, too inexperienced, too female for this small Southern town. And oh yeah, I lose my temper if you tell me I'm wrong when I know I'm right.

But they'd seen that temper as bold leadership. What had he said? I use the options on the table.

Which, unfortunately, included having a one-night-stand with the sexiest Pirate I've ever met.

He almost certainly lives in Jasper Mill. If my typical bad luck holds true, he probably has a kid who goes to the school.

If my luck turns even worse, he works for me.

But even if he does?

A kind of confidence settles over me. Even if the worst-case scenario turns out to be true, I'd kept my head on my shoulders. And my mask on my face. I'd guaranteed that I wouldn't know who the Pirate is. He sure as hell doesn't know who I am.

As long as things remain that way, everything will work out.

I can still have the career I deserve.

Kyra tackles me to the ground with a hug, interrupting my thoughts.

"I told you so! You got the job!" She's screeching in my ear, and a huge smile breaks across my face.

"I totally got the job," I say as I return Kyra's hug. "Now get off me."

Between a lot of laughing, we manage to get off the floor and back to a table.

"So he just offered it to you? No discussion about your argument with him?"

"Yeah. He actually said the argument was what made him decide to hire me."

"Sounds like Tony," she says with a laugh.

"And then the craziest part is that they want me to start next week!"

"Next week? OMG!" She claps her hands. "We need to go find you an apartment!"

"Hold your horses there. I haven't decided if I'm accepting it yet."

Her face falls.

"Why not? Don't you want it?"

"Well, yeah. It's my dream job."

"Then what?" she asks, cocking her head to the side.

"Am I going to fit in? Will the kids and parents like me?"

"Oh, honey. Absolutely. Life in a small town is different, but I think you'll fit right in."

"Yeah?"

"Yeah. And once more folks in town get to know you, they're gonna realize what a good influence you are on the kids."

"Okay."

Kyra smiles at me. "But Phoebs, what about the Pirate?"

"What about him?"

"Well, you know he lives here, and…"

"Stop right there," I say. "I don't know who he is, I never looked at his face, and I think it's probably better that way. That was a crazy night and it's better left in the past."

She squints her eyes at me. "If you say so."

"I totally say so."

"So are you going to take the job?"

"I need to go home. Look through the offer that Tony is sending over and the benefits packet. And think about whether I can really make this work."

I already know I'm going to take the job. I'm just not ready to say it out loud yet.

"Okay. But for what it's worth, I really hope you decide to accept the offer."

"Thanks Kyra," I say with a smile. "Now I've got to drive home and decide if I'm going to upend everything."

———

THE SUN SHINES through my bedroom window too early the next morning. I shield my eyes and, with a groan, get up to hit the shower. Joseph, my ornery cat, follows me into the bathroom and grooms himself while I do the same. Our hygiene routines are remarkably similar, except I don't lick my own ass.

After feeding Joseph his breakfast and grabbing a bagel for myself, I sit down at the kitchen counter to make a list.

To Do in Jasper Mill

1. Earn the respect and trust of the teachers.
2. Connect with the students.
3. Build confidence in the parents.

You know, just all the things.

The next two days are filled with change. Telling my family I'm moving four hours away, reaching out to Jim (my asshole principal), reading my lease to see how much cancelling it is going to cost me. Then there are my friends.

"That's awesome!" Maria, my best friend since elementary school, is at my house for a girls' night. Movies, wine, and junk food.

"It is. But I'm going to miss you so much."

"I'll miss you too, Phoebs. But it's not like you're on the other side of the world. We'll just have to plan our girls' nights a little more in advance."

"You're right. I know you're right." Tears form at the corners of my eyes.

"Hey now." Arms surround me. And now it's not just Maria, but the rest of the girls too, which makes me cry even harder.

I'm soothed by a chorus of hugs and back-rubbing and shushes until I can breathe again, and collapse on my kitchen floor.

Maria drops down beside me. "Principal Phoebe, this is an awesome opportunity for you. We would be so mad at you if you didn't take it just because you have to move away from some of us."

I look to my friends one at a time, and each of them offers me a nod and a warm smile. I know these girls will always be here for me.

"Okay." I stand up. "Okay."

"Now let's drink sangria and watch Princess Bride!"

———

ON THURSDAY MORNING, I'm ready for my new life.

Ring. Tony picks up almost instantly.

"Ms. Kestrel, I hope you're having a delightful morning already."

"Yes, Mr. Capsigo. Good morning. I'm calling to accept the job offer." It all comes out in a rush. It's really real, right?

"Oh, I'm just thrilled to hear that. We'll look forward to having you with us in no time."

"Me too. Thank you, Tony. I won't let you down."

I text Kyra to tell her the good news.

Me: It's official. You're talking to the newest principal of JMMHS.

Kyra: Woohoo! I'm so excited!

Me: Can I drive back over tomorrow, and we can do some apartment-hunting? I need a place that will take my cat.

Kyra: I'll clear my schedule.

Me: Okay, talk soon!

I can hardly believe it.

The interview wasn't a disaster.

Having that one-night stand didn't tank the whole thing.

My secret identity is safe.

All of my professional dreams are coming true.

I just can't give in to the temptation to find out who the Pirate is. Even if it was the most mind-blowing sex I've ever had. And even if there did seem to be a spark of something more there.

Who needs a relationship? I've got a job.

4

WES

Another Monday. Back to the grind.

"Hey, Mr. Herrington." One of my students is early for 2-D Art this morning.

"Hey bud. How was your weekend?"

"Epic. I saw the new Avengers movie like 3 times."

"That is pretty epic."

"Yeah. Hey, what's the new principal like? I heard she's hot."

"I don't think it's appropriate for you to talk about our principal that way."

I don't have the heart to tell him the truth. I've been hearing those kinds of rumors ever since I was a kid. Most of the time, the principals end up being old white guys with bald heads and no sense of humor.

Maybe that's why I laughed as a student when my friends told me about their fantasies about teachers and principals.

Principals? They were never sexy.

And while I was clearly an exception for teachers, the only time I let that side out was under the security of a deceptively simple disguise of a pirate costume at our annual Halloween party.

The rest of the kids start filing in as I get ready for our next project.

"Welcome back everyone, take your seats."

After several minutes of jostling and shuffling, the motley crew of teenagers finally settles down.

"We have a war to wage in the next few months," I begin.

"A war?"

"Yes, a war. You see, the school board wants to cut funding for the arts, again, and we're going to war to try and prevent that."

"What do we do?"

"We make art, of course! I have this idea…"

———

AFTER SCHOOL THAT DAY, we have our first faculty meeting with the new principal. I don't know much about her, except that she moved from out of state.

One of the bigwigs from the school board is standing at the front of the room. I really hope he doesn't want to speak. And just as soon as the thought crosses my mind, he starts walking towards the podium. Dammit.

"If I could have your attention everyone." High-pitched squeaks of feedback accompany his words.

"Excuse me," he says as he adjusts the mic. "If I could have your attention."

All of the teachers find a seat, finally. It's almost as much of a production as settling down my art classes to get started.

"Good afternoon, teachers! For those who don't know me, I'm Tony Capsigo, chair of the Loblolly Valley Consolidated School Board. It is my pleasure to be here today to introduce you to your new principal, Phoebe Kestrel. Now I know most of you haven't had a chance to meet her yet, but I also know you're going to love her. She has some exciting ideas for how to bring the school together as a community."

Great, we probably have to do another bake sale. While Tony drones on, I take a look at the agenda that was passed out. Icebreaker—typical. Budget review—typical. Discipline issues—all too common.

Brainstorming? I'm shocked to see that on the agenda. Since when do we do anything interactive in our faculty meetings?

Applause interrupts my thoughts. I glance up to see a young woman approaching the podium. Did we get a new secretary too?

But wait. The way she sways her hips. Those full lips. My body reacts just like it reacted to Medusa on Halloween night.

What a bizarre coincidence.

"Who is this?" I whisper to Mrs. Sledge sitting next to me.

"The principal. Pay attention, Westley."

"Yes, ma'am."

How can this be the new principal? My eyes return to the front of the room, where she is now adjusting the microphone. Damn. She is hot. I adjust my crotch.

She tosses her hair over her shoulder, arranges her notes, and begins speaking. Her voice is mesmerizing. I'm not even aware of what she's saying as I watch her tall, slender figure move around the front of the podium. She really is an excellent public speaker. I shake my head and force myself to tune in.

"—and that's one of my priorities. To build rapport with the parents of our students, so they can trust that their children are getting the best education possible. So they don't send them to a different school."

"Uh, Phoebe," Mr. Michaels interrupts. "I think you're forgetting that this is a very small town. There is no other school."

Her cheeks turn pink. "Mr…"

"Michaels."

"Yes, Mr. Michaels. My understanding is that we've had some attrition. Families who are willing to drive their children over to Punning to attend their Middle-High School."

"Those are just isolated incidents."

"I have to disagree with you there, Mr. Michaels. A group of 'isolated incidents' becomes a pattern at a certain point." She punctuated her statement with air quotes, and didn't even stammer. Just a cute little flush across those cheeks. "And when I see a negative pattern forming, I like to address it before it becomes an even bigger problem."

"If you say so." Michaels slouches back in his chair. He's a pompous blowhard. He's been teaching social studies here since I was in high school, and I'm pretty sure he hasn't changed a word of his lectures in all that time.

"How do we build rapport, like you suggest?" This from Miss Waters, one of the new math instructors. I think she just graduated from Boroughs last year.

Principal Kestrel ignores a groan from Michaels. "Thanks for that question, Miss…"

"Waters. Angela Waters."

"Thanks, Miss Waters. I'm glad you asked. You may have seen that I have a brainstorming session planned for the end of the meeting, but I'd much rather do it now. All this routine stuff can be put in an email."

Bad. Ass. I hate having meetings for the sake of meetings.

Ms. Kestrel guides us through a 20-minute discussion of how to build relationships with the parents. No one comes up with anything too revolutionary. Just the usual stuff that we're already supposed to be doing. And I do it. But most of the older teachers don't. I get the sense that Ms. Kestrel is gearing her comments towards them, but trying not to let it show.

Color me shocked when Mrs. Sledge raises her hand. "What about a meet-and-greet over the new videoconference doohickey?"

"Yes, yes!" Phoebe responds in an excited voice.

The same voice. The voice that haunts my dreams saying, "yes, yes!"

It's just a coincidence, right? Lots of voices sound the same.

Except that I stare at her full lips. The same lips that I glimpsed under the mask.

I watch the corners of her green eyes crinkle the same way as the eyes under the mask.

And then she laughs. The same rich laughter that drew me to her on Halloween.

And oh, fuck.

Me: It's her.
Kyra: ?
Me: principal=Medusa
Kyra: I will neither confirm nor deny.
Me: Don't need to. I know. Why didn't you tell me???
Kyra: Come to the shop after school.

I don't hear another word the rest of the meeting. As soon as Mrs. Sledge and the others around me begin gathering their belongings, I hightail it out of the teachers' lounge and out of the school.

"Kyra!" I bellow as I walk into It's a Grind. Everyone turns to stare at me, but I don't give a shit.

She walks around the counter and grabs me by the arm to drag me into her office. "Keep your voice down, caveman."

When we reach the office a moment later, I close the door and launch into her.

"Why the fuck didn't you tell me that Medusa was my new principal? Do you know how much this could fuck up my life?"

"Hold on there, sport. I didn't think she was going to be your principal on Halloween."

"What do you mean?"

"She told me all about how she bombed the interview, how Tony Capsigo hated her, how she offered a lot of flippant answers to stupid questions."

"Why would she lie to you?"

"I don't think she was lying. You know how hard it is to read Tony sometimes. I was there when he called to offer her the job, and she was truly shocked."

"You guys are friends now?"

"She's my people."

"Fuck me."

"Been there, done that, got the t-shirt," she says with a smirk.

"Smartass." I run my hands through my hair. "What do I do now?"

"Nothing."

"Nothing?"

"Nothing. She has no idea who the Pirate was."

"You didn't tell her?"

"Nope. And she didn't want to know. She really just wanted anonymous sex for one night. She didn't go and catch feelings like you did."

"I didn't catch feelings."

"That's not what Liam says about it."

"Shithead doesn't know the bro code."

"Oh, he knows it. He just doesn't follow it when it comes to me." She flips her hair, adjusts her boobs, and flashes a smile at me.

"Yeah, yeah. You're a sexy minx."

"And don't you forget it."

"So I really just do nothing?" A deep sigh escapes my chest.

"Yep. Pretend like you have never encountered Phoebe Kestrel until today."

"What if I can't do that?"

She haunts my dreams. I don't know why. I've had plenty of sex. Plenty of fantastic sex, even. But something about that night, about the way she responded to me, about the way I felt when she came, lets her live rent-free in my head. Maybe it's just the challenge? Maybe because she wouldn't let me see her, and didn't want to see me?

"Maybe now that I know who she is, I'll be able to forget about her."

"Maybe," Kyra says. She doesn't sound like she believes it any more than I do.

———

When I drift off to sleep that night, I dream of being sent to detention back when I was a student at Jasper Mill Middle-High. It's weird because I never actually got sent to detention. Sure, I got in trouble lots, but the name always got me out of it.

But now I'm sitting in detention. I glance around and see a bunch of my high school buddies. We're being called to the principal's office one at a time. I'm not sure why.

"Mr. Herrington, it's your turn." Grace, the principal's secretary, leads me down the hall.

I walk into the office and am surprised to see that the principal is not, in fact, one of the old white guys I expected.

It's Medusa. Phoebe.

The woman I haven't been able to get out of my mind for months, and she's beautiful. She has this amazing auburn hair with highlights that look gold in the sunlight, and these bright green eyes. She has a couple little laugh lines around her eyes, and I know it's because she has a great sense of humor.

She's the hot principal we always dreamed of, but never got.

She doesn't say a word as she unbuttons her blouse and approaches me. Not a word as she unzips my pants and fondles my cock. Not a word until…

"Fuck me, Pirate."

How the fuck am I going to deal with her as my boss?

5

PHOEBE

THESE FIRST FEW WEEKS HAVE BEEN A WHIRLWIND. I'VE SPENT A TON OF TIME reviewing the budget, trying to figure out where we're losing money. I've been meeting all of the school board members again, trying to lay the groundwork to ask for more money. I've been schmoozing my PTA, trying to get them to help with some additional funding too. I've been holding weekly assemblies to let the kids get more comfortable with me. And, perhaps most importantly, I've been having one-on-ones with all of my teachers. I need to understand who they are and how they fit into our team.

I'm down to the last one-on-one. It's with the art teacher, Mr. Herrington. He's rescheduled on me three times already, and I'm starting to think he's avoiding me. We'll see about that.

"Knock knock." I arrive at Mr. Herrington's room right as the dismissal bell rings, so I can invade before he goes anywhere.

He looks startled to see me.

"You're a hard man to track down, Mr. Herrington. I thought I'd come to you."

"Call me Wes. And yeah, sorry I've had to reschedule."

"No bother. I'm here now. Would you like to get down to business?"

He pauses, a weird look crossing his face.

"Um, yeah. So what did you want to talk about?"

"Why don't we take a seat?" I sit at one of the student desks, and gesture towards his desk. "And I'd really just like to get to know you."

"Where'd I go to school, how long have I been teaching, that kind of thing?"

He seems really nervous.

"Sure, we can start there."

"Well, I've been teaching art here since I graduated from college. About 8 years now."

That makes him about 30, same age as me.

"And where did you go to school?"

"Over in Dallas."

"Which school?" Gah, this is like pulling teeth.

"University of Dallas."

"And what do you like to do for fun?"

"What?"

"Fun? You do know what fun is, right?"

"Uh, yeah. I, uh, play a little rec league softball. Hang out with the guys. Probably drink too much."

"Is that really something you should be telling your boss?"

"Uh…I mean…my drinking has never interfered with my job. I would never let it. I just have a beer or two every night, sitting at home alone."

Great, I've got an alcoholic on the staff.

"I see."

There's an awkward silence. It's like the guy doesn't know how to carry on a conversation.

"What are your plans for the future?"

"The future?"

"Yes, like 5 or 10 years down the road. What do you see yourself doing?"

"I guess I'd like to have a wife, a few of kids."

"I meant professionally, Mr. Herrington."

"Oh. Right. And it's Wes."

"Well Wes, I'm trying to figure out where you fit into our team."

"What team?"

Seriously? Is this guy dumb?

"You know, the team of folks who work at this school? Whose job it is to educate the next generation?"

"Right. I guess…I guess I just want to keep teaching art here."

No effort whatsoever. He didn't even try to come up with anything ambitious or interesting to say. Shouldn't he be one of my most creative thinkers? I'm going to have to do a little digging, find out what his story is.

"Well, I guess I should let you go," I say, rising from the desk.

"Wait!"

I pause and look at him.

"Yes?"

"Is there, uh…is there anything I can do to help you get settled here in Jasper?" he asks.

I cock my head and think for a moment.

Inspiration hits. Something to help me learn more about him.

"I do need something to hang on the wall in my office. If it's not too much trouble, do you think you could paint something for me?"

He just stares at me.

"Unless that's too much…?"

"Uh, no. No."

He clears his throat and stands up. He walks towards the door, obviously trying to get rid of me. I follow him to the door anyway.

I can't help but stare at his ass. Admire his swagger.

"I'll make it the best painting you've ever had, darlin'."

I stop in my tracks.

The Pirate promised me a night of sex that would be the best I ever had. Odd that Mr. Herrington used the same turn of phrase.

He stops and turns around.

"Are you coming?"

I search his face.

"Have we met before?" I ask him.

"I…don't think so."

"Maybe don't call me darlin' then?"

"Oh. Sorry."

I walk out of the room without another word.

Me: Do I know the Pirate?
Kyra: What do you mean?
Me: Like, does he work with me?
Kyra: I thought you didn't want to know who he is.
Kyra: Right?
Me: Right, right. Ok. See you later.

It couldn't be him. It would be too much of a coincidence.

But…when he said darlin'…well, that term has echoed in my head more times than I'd like to admit since Halloween. And he sure did sound like it just now.

Must be my imagination. I head back to my office for more budget studying.

———

By the middle of January, I feel like I'm hitting my stride.

I've met with all the school board members, my teachers and staff, the PTA officers. I've gotten to know some of the kids—both those who are discipline problems and those who are our top performers. It tends to be only the ends of the spectrum that make their way to the principal's office.

The folks in town, and everyone at school, seem to be taking me seriously as the principal. Thank goodness. I've always looked and sounded so much younger than I am. I can't even tell you how many times people have assumed I'm the secretary, or even the daughter.

Tonight, I tackle my first school board meeting. I haven't seen this group together since my interview back in October. I'll just observe this meeting—I don't want to be one of "those people" who comes onto a scene and, with no background or history, starts telling everyone the best way to do things. I mean, at least not until my second school board meeting.

When I review the agenda, I'm surprised to see that Mr. Herrington is listed. Why wouldn't one of my teachers come to me before going to the school board?

Maybe he has a problem with me. He's continued to avoid me as much as possible since our one meeting a couple weeks ago. My hands get clammy and my stomach begins to churn as I wait for the meeting to begin.

"It's 6:02, and I'd like to call this meeting to order," says Tony Capsigo. "We've got a few new faces in the crowd," he smiles in my direction, "so let me give a quick overview of how we run these meetings. The board goes through our routine business first, then we turn to any new business brought by either board members or members of the community, and then we reserve time at the end for open comment."

From my seat in the front row, I offer a nod and a smile to Tony, and settle in for what sounds like a boring meeting.

The board's routine business does not disappoint. Dry, boring, and predictable. When it comes to "new business," one of the board members is concerned about the state of the flagpole at our local elementary school, we need some new landscaping around Punning's middle-high school, and then it's Mr. Herrington's turn. He stands at the podium situated just in front of me.

He does have a nice butt.

"The chair recognizes Westley Jasper Herrington the Fifth."

Jasper? Like Jasper Mill?

"Thank you, Mr. Chair. I'm here today to talk about an idea I have for bringing art to the public spaces of Jasper Mill. As you know, my family has a long history with our town, and we are deeply invested in its long-term success."

Yeah, it must be Jasper-like-Jasper-Mill.

"And as the resident art teacher in town, I can't help but notice that we really don't have any public art installations. I'd like to propose that we get some."

"Mr. Herrington, let me stop you there," Tony interjects. "Why isn't this a matter for the Town Council? They would be the ones to head up art in public places, not your school board."

"While that is true, there is a piece of this project that involves the school board. I'd like to get permission to have the Jasper Mill High School kids involved. Create a special class where they can earn school credit just for working on this public art project."

What the hell?! He should have come to me with this.

It is a good idea—maybe a great idea—but there's a procedure. There are rules.

"And why isn't that a request for your principal, who I see is sitting right behind you?"

Thank you, Tony!

Wes turns around and looks at me. I see no hint of embarrassment on his face. What an ass.

"Well," he says as he turns back around, "since she's new, and I knew the board would need to approve anyway, I thought I'd just short-circuit the red tape."

That shreds any last suspicion I had that this was who I *hoped* it was. The guy I met on Halloween was smooth, attuned to my needs, and willing to follow my rules. This one has no respect for anyone's rules but his own.

"Mr. Herrington, I know that your family helped found this town. And I know that you're used to getting your way with the art program around here. But really, this is not appropriate. You need to discuss this matter with Principal Kestrel first."

That's right, Tony!

"Well actually, there's some time sensitivity here…"

Well actually. The siren song of mansplainers everywhere.

"You should have thought of that before you decided to circumvent the chain of command, Mr. Herrington. Now please, take your seat."

Murmurs spread through the crowd. Apparently no one is used to seeing Westley Jasper Herrington V not get his way.

Wes turns around, gives me a half-smirk, and heads back to his seat. We're going to have a talk about this tomorrow.

Thankfully, there are no more surprises in the Board's "new business." When it comes time for open comment, I decide I'm going to speak.

I know. I said I'd be quiet and observe for this one. But my pride, my ego won't let me. I stand in line behind the podium.

"Principal Kestrel, lovely to see you." Tony greets me with a smile.

"Thank you, Mr. Capsigo."

"What do you have to share with us today?"

"No particular item of business. I just wanted to address the room."

"Go ahead," he says as he gestures towards the microphone.

"First let me say that it's wonderful to see all of the school board members this evening. While I've met with each of you individually in the last several weeks, I don't believe I've seen the whole group of you together since October. It's a pleasure."

They all nod their heads and smile. Score points for me.

"To the rest of the folks in the room," I grab the microphone out of the stand and turn around, "I haven't had a chance to meet all of you yet, but I would certainly welcome the opportunity. Jasper Mill has really grown on me. After only two months, I feel like this is home. Like this is where I'm meant to be. And I'm dedicated to our children—to making sure they receive a balanced, world-class education right here in Jasper Mill."

All eyes are focused on me, not a sound in the room.

"And while I understand that some of you may be hesitant to place your trust in me because I'm a newcomer," a couple of uncomfortable shifts, "or want to circumvent me because I'm a relatively young woman," a pointed glare at Wes, "rest assured that I have the experience and the thick skin necessary to do this job. I will not hesitate to do what it takes to make our school, and the school district, the very best it can be."

I turn to face Wes this time. "Including firing a son of Jasper, if that's what it takes."

Turning back to face the podium and the Board, ignoring the murmurs behind me, I conclude, "Thank you for the time."

"Our pleasure, Principal Kestrel," Tony says. "And with that, I will call our meeting to a close."

I walk straight out the back of the room, ignoring the stares and the whispers. Take that, Westley Jasper Herrington V.

6

WES

Shit. I've been called to the principal's office.

Walking down the hall, a strong sense of déjà vu overwhelms me. I've been in this dream before.

Was it a premonition?

Did she call me to her office to have sex?

I mean, I wouldn't mind it.

Especially if she uses that principal-tone-of-voice to order me around.

"Mr. Herrington, she'll see you now." Grace, the long-time principal's secretary, is giving me a dirty look. And using my last name.

Walking into her office, I feel like I've just met Phoebe Kestrel for the first time. She's painted the walls this peachy-tan color—almost the color of sand—and decorated in all blues and greens. It reminds me of a walk on the beach, looking for sea glass. Like the ocean.

Just like in my dream, I can't help but marvel at her beauty. The sun streaming in through her office window highlights the gold threads in her auburn hair. Her piercing green eyes are mesmerizing. But I don't see the laugh lines today.

No, this version of Phoebe isn't laughing. She's pissed.

She's standing in front of her desk, hands on her hips, glaring at me.

"Principal Kestrel," I say in greeting.

"Mr. Herrington, take a seat." She's using the principal-tone-of-voice, and I do as I'm told.

She doesn't sit, but leans against her desk instead and crosses her arms across her abdomen.

"We need to talk about the school board meeting."

I nod.

There's a pause.

"Do you have anything to say for yourself?"

"Um...I was just trying to get the ball rolling?"

"Don't you think you should have come to me first? And don't you think you owe me an apology?"

"Uh...I'm sorry?"

"Are you asking me?"

"No, I'm sorry. I really am. I just figured it would be faster this way, with you being new to town and all."

"I see. And were you in the habit of going around your last principal?"

"Uh, no."

"Uh-huh. So perhaps you see why I'm concerned that you're treating me differently because I'm a woman."

"Oh, no, no. I'm treating you differently because you're an outsider."

Her eyes narrow.

"And somehow you think that's any better?"

"Um..."

"Right. Here's the other thing, Mr. Herrington. I've spent a lot of time going through our school budget since I took this job, and there are some puzzling numbers for your department."

Uh-oh.

"See, our total spending exceeds the amount that the school board allots us. And there's a whole lot of miscellaneous expenses for your department." She looks at me expectantly.

"About that," I say uncomfortably. "I kind of...fund the art department."

"Do what now?"

"Well, the school board keeps cutting the arts funding. So I decided I would just supplement the funding myself, and then they couldn't touch it. Grace takes a check from me once a year, and then I submit my expenses against it. I'm really just keeping track of how much we spend. So, yeah, it makes the budget numbers look funny."

"Huh."

She uncrosses her arms.

"That wasn't what I expected to hear," she says.

I shrug. I don't like talking about how I spend my money. My legacy needs to be more than just my family name and the money I inherited.

"The funding issue is also why I'm tackling this public art project. I'm thinking that if I can get more of the town to see the value in public art, the value in the arts in general, maybe we can get some more support and funding. I mean, not that I mind personally funding it. But I think this town is wrong-headed about its priorities."

"Sounds like a solid plan. But there's still the matter of you going to the school board last night without talking to me fir—"

"I said I'm sorry about that."

"Please don't interrupt me. And please don't do that again. You may have noticed that I look younger than just about every teacher in the school. I have to work twice as hard to be taken seriously, and having one of my teachers—"

"I won't do it again, I promise."

She slams her hand down on her desk, and a small picture topples onto the floor.

"Dammit, Wes! Stop interrupting me!"

I'm on my feet grabbing the picture for her before she even finishes that sentence, and I stand up to see her face flushed again.

"I'm sorry. I really am, darlin'," I say as I hand her the picture of her and a few other women about her age.

She gently takes it from my hand. When we touch, there's a warm buzz that flows between us. She takes a long look at me.

"It's been way too long," she murmurs.

"Since what?"

She shakes her head and seems to struggle to find words. "Since I…uh… snapped at someone like that."

I don't think that's what she meant.

"Oh. Well, don't worry about it. My mama always tells me I can drive anyone to drink. I guess I drove you to snap." I add a smile and a shrug.

"I'm just so focused on making a good impression here, on establishing that I can do this job, on trying to earn some respect."

Beneath her tough tone, she's just a little insecure.

"The way I see it, you've already done all those things. Everyone loves you, and you're already making major changes, teaching some of the old-timers new tricks."

"Everyone except for Michaels," she says.

"Michaels doesn't count."

Her tone turns earnest.

"People tell me I can be too aggressive. And I know that sometimes I react in the heat of a moment, instead of pausing to think through the implications of what I'm about to do."

Is she talking about the school board meeting?

About snapping at me just now?

About Halloween night?

Her eyes are searching mine. Is there a glimmer of recognition there?

"Aye, matey." It's worth a shot.

And it pays off.

Her lips are suddenly on mine. But softly, like she isn't sure if I'll be into it. She steps back.

"I…I'm sorry," she whispers.

"I'm not."

I grab her around the waist and pull her to me. My lips find hers, and the kiss is everything. Those full, plush lips parting for me. Her scent and her touch and all the feelings swallowing me whole. Like the ocean washing over me.

She lets out a low moan before she breaks the kiss.

"That was one hell of a first kiss, Pirate."

"I've been dreaming about it for months, Medusa. You wouldn't let me kiss you."

She smiles a sad smile. "I really thought I'd never visit Jasper Mill again. It seemed like a waste of an emotional investment. And now that I am here, and I figured out who you are, we still can't do anything about it."

"Why the hell not?"

"Because I'm your boss."

"So?"

"So it's not appropriate."

"Maybe not in a big city, but here in Jasper—well, the town is just too small to impose all those restrictions on who you can and can't date. You'd have no options if you couldn't date anyone you worked with, or your kid's teacher, or anyone your bro ever dated…"

"If you say so. But I'm still not comfortable with us being anything more than principal and teacher. I don't think that starting a fling with the art teacher is the best way to go, as I'm trying to establish myself in this job."

I don't know how to respond.

"How could anyone respect the outsider-girl-new-principal who immediately starts sleeping with the town's favorite son?" she asks.

"I don't think you give the folks of Jasper Mill enough credit."

"I don't think you understand what it's like to be the new girl in town trying to earn their trust."

"No, I surely don't. But I do know these people. I've known most of them my whole life, and they're good people. They know how to judge someone's work on its quality, rather than their personal life that has nothing to do with it. And you're right, I am the favorite son. That would make things even easier for us."

"Maybe. But I need to find my way on my own here."

"Is that really what you want, darlin'?"

"It doesn't matter what I want."

"If you say so."

"I do."

Her face has resumed the buttoned-up, prim mask that she wears. But I know what's underneath it. Passion. Passion for her work, passion for sex, and passion for other things she hasn't given me a chance to learn yet.

I wish I knew what she was really feeling about me. A deep, resigned sigh escapes my lips.

"You still want that painting for your office?"

"If you're still willing to do it, yes please."

Nodding, I turn to leave.

"Wes?" she stops me as my hand turns the doorknob.

I pause but don't look back.

"I wish it could be different." Her voice is pained.

Another nod, and I'm gone.

I have a painting to do.

7

PHOEBE

When Wes leaves my office, I collapse. Literally. On the floor.

Me: Wes Herrington is the Pirate
Kyra: I know

I nearly text back to her as many curse words as I can find. How could she know that and not tell me?
Because you told her not to.
And I had. I'd agreed to go to the party and wear a mask. I'd insisted she not tell me anyone's identity even if she knew. It wasn't her fault that I'd gotten the job anyway.
I even vaguely recall her trying to tell me after I got the job. And I'd shut her down.

Me: I need many drinks
Kyra: Meet me at my place in 20 minutes

By the time I get to Kyra's house, I'm a complete mess. Ugly-crying, red-faced, hot mess.
"Oh, honey," Kyra says when she opens the door. She hugs me and rubs my back for a minute. "We're going to the steam room."
Kyra's house has this epic steam room in the basement. The prior owner

put it in for their own personal fitness club down there, and it's something no sane person would spend the money to do.

But it's awesome, and it's where we have the best conversations.

Five minutes later, I'm sitting in the steam room, wearing my special spa robe, and drinking frozen daiquiris out of a huge-ass insulated tumbler. Kyra has one of those frozen drink machine things too. Like Slurpees for adults.

"I didn't think you'd be this upset," she says.

"I just…it's all too much some days, you know? Like I have my dream job here, and I feel like I'm settling into town, and people are starting to view me as an actual professional educator with good ideas."

"That all sounds good."

"It is. But it's a lot of pressure. And I have no personal life, except for you. And that's only when Liam isn't in town."

Yikes! That didn't come out right. I hurriedly add, "which is totally fine, and please don't think I'm a bitch, you're my only friend."

"Slow your roll, girl. We're good. But none of the work stuff is new. What is it about Wes that made you so upset? So what if he was your anonymous dick on Halloween? I told you everybody acts like those things never happened."

"I…I guess it's…I really did think it was just a one-night thing, and that I'd never step foot in Jasper again. And because of that, I did some things I'm not very proud of. With Wes."

"Oooh, this sounds good."

"Well, I let him go down on me, but I wouldn't let him kiss me."

"So?"

"I don't know. It just feels like I used him?"

"Wes knew what he was getting into. He isn't a stranger to the Halloween Hookup, and I happen to know that the man loves eating pussy."

"Ohmigod, Kyra! I can't believe you just said that!"

"What? I say what I mean. And I have firsthand knowledge."

"Oh shit. You've slept with Wes?"

"Yep."

"Yet another reason I can't date him."

"Don't be stupid, Phoebs. I knew who he was at the party. If I had a problem with it, I never would have let you go off with him."

"But I don't date my friends' exes."

"The rules are different here. If none of us dated our friends' exes, we'd have no one to date at all."

"That's basically what Wes said."

"He's right. Is that all that's bothering you?"

"Well, there's more about that night…"

"…Yes?…"

"As soon as he came, he passed out, and then I left without a note or a word or anything."

A pause. Kyra acts like she's waiting for more.

"Again…what's the problem?" she finally asks.

"It feels…I don't know. But I've never done that before, and it definitely feels like I used him for sex. I'm worried he got the wrong idea."

"If dude couldn't keep his eyes open after blowing his load, he deserved it. That must have been some incredible sex though!"

"It was."

"You should definitely do it again then."

"I just don't think it's that simple."

"I think it could be, if you'd let it."

My head drops into my hands and I let out a sigh I've been holding in for what seems like days.

"You don't have to decide anything right now," Kyra says. "Let's just drink and steam."

Nodding, I lie down on the bench and close my eyes.

———

A FEW DAYS LATER, I have a lunch scheduled with Tony Capsigo. We chose a spot in Punning, the neighboring town, to reduce the chances of one of my parents overhearing our conversation.

"This menu is great," I say.

"I'm glad you like it. Kind of a tapas, small-plate concept."

"I love it. I haven't seen anything like this in Jasper."

"I may be a little biased, seeing as how I live here in Punning, but I think you'll find that our culinary taste is a little higher-end. We should run over to my brother's bakery for dessert after this."

"Ooooh, a bakery."

"Save room!"

After placing our orders, Tony gets down to business.

"How are things going so far?"

"Pretty well, I think. I've done weekly assemblies with the kids, focused on fun games, and just letting them get to know me. I've been spending time with our PTA to see how they can help support the school."

"Good, good."

"And I've had one-on-one conversations with all of the teachers and staff, and think I have a real sense of who's on the team now."

"How's that going?"

"Okay. I mean, there are a few who obviously have no interest in change, and ignore most of what I suggest."

"Probably nothing to be done about that," he says, nodding.

"I think a lot of the younger teachers were immediately on-board with some of my ideas. They're similar to what they were taught as part of their education degrees."

"Sure. And what about Wes Herrington. That display at the school board meeting…"

"Was completely embarrassing and I had a talk with him the next day."

And a kiss. And a flashback to some of the best sex I've ever had.

"Are you hot, dear? You look a little flushed."

"Um, no, I'm fine."

"Do you think Mr. Herrington is going to continue giving you problems?"

"Maybe of a different kind, but I don't think he'll be going around me to come to the Board again."

"That's good at least. What other problems are you worried about?"

This is really not appropriate. I definitely should not be talking to the school board chair about my love life. And yet…

"I think he wants to date me."

Tony's eyes light up.

"That's wonderful, my dear!"

"Is it?"

"Why, yes. He's a handsome man, the town's most eligible bachelor. You're a beautiful young woman with a promising career ahead of you. You make a delightful match!"

"I'm not sure it's appropriate for me to be dating one of my teachers."

Taking my hand in his own, Tony launches into a fatherly speech. "You are going to be faced with some big problems as a school principal, Phoebe. You are going to be challenged by difficult parents, have your decisions second-guessed by a school board, be disappointed when a student you've given special attention just can't get their act together…these are all necessary burdens for you. But you don't have to do it all alone. You should have a social life, a partner, a confidante. And the fact that Wes is a teacher at your school doesn't disqualify him from that position. It may sometimes be awkward or uncomfortable. But I daresay I know you well enough to be confident that you will be able to manage it. You have the keen judgment necessary to keep yourself out of tricky conflict-of-interest situations. And you have the social acumen you'll need to make sure that none of your other teachers feel slighted."

"Thanks, Tony. I really appreciate your confidence in me."

But I'm still not convinced it's okay to date Wes.

He must read it on my face because he releases my hands and leans back. "You have to do what you're comfortable with, Phoebe. But I hope you won't worry about how other people would react to you dating Wes. As long as you keep doing your job well, and don't play favorites, it will be just fine."

Saved by the waiter. "Your lunch, my friends."

Thankfully, the rest of our meal is filled with nothing more than banal chatter. And true to his word, Tony takes me to his brother's bakery for a dessert cupcake afterwards.

"Mmmm…ohmigod," I say through a mouthful of cupcake. "This is the best red velvet I've ever tasted!"

"It's the special cocoa powder, bella," Tony's brother—Mauro Capsigo —explains.

As we leave the shop, Tony counsels me, "just don't tell anyone in Jasper that you went to The Flour Shoppe."

I wonder what that's all about. Small-town life.

Me: Hey
Wes: Hey back
Me: How are you?
Wes: Fine. And you?
Me: Fine. But I've been thinking…
Wes: ?
Me: Would it be okay—could I make you dinner this weekend?
Wes: I thought you said it wouldn't be appropriate.
Me: Can't a girl change her mind?
Wes: Of course.
Me: So will you come?
Wes: I'd love to.
Me: Good. Saturday at 7.

8

WES

I WONDER WHAT HAPPENED TO CHANGE HER MIND.

But I don't really care. I'm just glad I get to spend more time with her.

I hope she means for this to be a date.

I'm going to make it a date.

Me: Need help
Kyra: With what?
Me: Phoebe. Tell me what she likes?
Kyra: Maybe. Come fix my ice machine.

When Saturday rolls around, I'm a man with a plan. And when she opens the door, I take the opportunity to start over.

"Hi Phoebe, I'm Wes. Nice to meet you." I extend my hand to shake, and appreciate the look of complete bafflement on her face.

I'm wearing the pirate costume.

I'm not going to make it easy for her to reject me again.

"I wondered why Kyra told me to wear this," she says as she leans over to grab a Medusa-snakes wig. The moment I see it, all of my sense memories come flooding back. Halloween party, bobbing for apples, watching her sway her hips all night, her lips teasing me under that mask, her unexpected forwardness, the taste of her on my tongue, the sound of her screams, the feeling of her pussy clenching down on my dick, the best fucking orgasm I've had in…well, ever.

I clear my throat and then help her position the wig on her head. She immediately jumps into the game of starting over.

"Won't you come in, Wes? It's so nice to finally meet you. Kyra has told me all about you."

"It's all lies."

"No," she laughs—that rich, melodious laugh that I remember from Halloween, "it's all good."

"Well then, it's all true."

Stepping into her home, I'm overwhelmed by the smells. So familiar and comforting.

"Wow, you really did make me dinner."

"Of course. That's what I said I would do." She turns from the door and heads inside.

I drop my satchel to the floor of the entryway and pull out a small bouquet of white spray roses and purple alstroemeria. Follow her to the kitchen, where she finally turns back around.

"For you, darlin'."

"Oh!" She puts her hands to her face like a cartoon character might. Taking the flowers from me and bring them to her nose. "Some of my favorites."

"So I heard."

She smiles at me over the top of the flowers.

"Let me just find a vase."

"Is there something I can do to help with dinner?" I ask while she searches through cabinets. When she bends over to check the bottom cabinets in the island, I can't help but stare at her ass. I hope I get another chance to spank it. My dick strains against my zipper.

"You can just keep staring at my butt," she says.

Damn. The woman must have eyes in her butt or something. I chuckle to myself.

"Here it is!" She emerges with a beautiful deep-plum vase, obviously hand-thrown on a wheel.

I take the vase and flowers from her and set to arranging them.

"This is a beautiful piece," I say.

"Piece of ass?"

"Well, that too. But no, the vase. I'm an art teacher, remember? I know what goes into making something like this."

"Thank you. I made it in a ceramics studio class during college."

"Amazing." Flowers arranged, I'm restless. "What next?"

She's busy stirring something on the stove.

"Why don't you take the flowers to the table and pour the wine?"

As I finish filling our glasses, she carries a large platter of pot roast to the table. It smells divine, and it's surrounded by roasted potatoes and carrots, with a sprinkling of fresh parsley on top.

"Wow, *my* favorite."

"I may have heard that." She gives me the cutest little grin. I take the platter from her to set it on the table, and then turn to pull out her chair.

"What a gentleman," she says and touches me on the arm. Just that small contact sends a little thrill through my body.

Dinner is beyond any expectations I might have had. Phoebe made the best pot roast I've ever tasted. But don't you dare tell my mama I said that.

"So where are you from, Phoebe Kestrel?"

"Near Miami."

"Oooh, living the fancy beach life, huh?"

"Not exactly. My parents were kind of obsessive birders. We spent more time looking through binoculars in the Everglades than tanning on the beach."

"Perfect last name, huh?"

She lets out a small chuckle.

"If you can believe it, my parents had our last name legally changed. And did you know that Phoebe is the name of a bird too?"

I get a good laugh out of that one.

"Wait, wait. What's your middle name?"

"Wren."

"No way!" I can't stop myself from laughing. Tears leak out of my eyes. "Bird Bird Bird—Bird to the Third!"

"Yeah, laugh it up, Westley Jasper Herrington V." There's no edge in her tone. She's smiling too.

"So where do your parents live now?"

She looks down at her half-eaten dinner.

"They, uh…passed when I was in college."

Way to spoil the mood, Wes ol' boy.

"I'm so sorry," I say.

"Yeah, thanks."

She shakes her head and looks up. "What about you? Where are your parents?"

"Five generations born and bred in Jasper Mill."

"I assumed that's where your middle name came from."

"Yup. Whatever great-grandma that is was a Jasper. Her husband was one of the founders of the town, and their firstborn son was Westley Jasper Herrington. Here I am, the fifth generation Wes."

"That's kind of cool—to have such a rich family history, so bound up with the town."

"I guess." I shrug.

The family name usually feels like more of a burden than anything else.

An obligation to do things for the town.

A reason girls want to hook up with me and then get me to do something for them that no one else could get away with.

"For a kid like me, who got dragged all over the world looking for rare birds, it seems almost impossible. I would have loved a more steady upbringing."

"Do you have any siblings?"

"Nope. Birdie, the only child."

How lonely she must have been.

"I've got four. It was fun growing up, but chaotic a lot of the time."

"I can only imagine."

Maybe I can show her. Maybe I can make her part of my family.

But I'm getting ahead of myself.

We stare at each other for a moment.

"So what are we doing here, Phoebe?"

"Having dinner."

"But why did you invite me over for dinner?"

"Well, I thought you—

"Yes, Phoebe, I'm very attracted to you. But you said we couldn't date."

"I might have been wrong about that."

Huh. She can admit when she's wrong.

"But if we're going to do this, there have to be some rules." She shifts into principal mode. "When we're at school, I'm still your boss. We can't let our personal relationship affect how we do our jobs. As long as we do that, we can fuck all we want."

I just stare at her.

Who is this amazing creature?

"Unless you don't want to anymore…," she adds to fill the silence.

"No, no. Definitely no. I mean, I'm not sad to hear that you've rethought this. But what made you change your mind?"

"Enough people have said the same thing—that things are different in a small town—that I can be judged on the quality of my work, and not denigrated just because of my relationships…"

"Kyra?"

"Her, and others."

"Well, I'm glad you're listening to them."

She looks up, a shy smile on her face.

"Can I get us dessert now?" she asks.

"Darlin', can we skip the food? I've been hard since the moment you opened the door. I'd much rather have you as my dessert."

"Oh."

"Yeah, oh."

Pushing back from the table, I throw my napkin down and toss off the pirate beard and hat. In a moment, I'm by her side, then lifting her into my arms and carrying her over to the couch. I settle down into the deep cushions with her on my lap and cradle her face in my hands.

"I've waited so long for this," I murmur. As I lay gentle kisses along her jawbone, she closes her eyes. This feels different. Intimate. Right.

Almost too good to be true.

9

PHOEBE

FOR NOT THE FIRST TIME, I ASK MYSELF IF THIS IS REAL LIFE. I HAVE MY DREAM job here in Jasper Mill. The students, parents, teachers, and school board all seem to like me. This incredibly hot art teacher who was supposed to be nothing more than an anonymous hookup is now sitting on my couch, with me on his lap, nuzzling my neck. And no one in town is going to judge me for dating him. Does it get any better?

Turning my head towards Wes, I find his lips and kiss him softly. He's just as gentle in return. Like we're testing. Making sure that the other is okay.

Wes's tongue teases at my lips. And in an instant, we both dive in. Our kisses become urgent, insistent. My hands are groping at whatever parts of him I can reach. Hard muscle beneath his pirate shirt. He cups my breast beneath the lightweight dress I'm wearing, and I let out a small moan. I'm already wet and I'm practically dry humping him through all of our layers of clothes. His tongue tangles with mine and he shifts me in his lap.

Except those black satin pirate pants. You know, the ones that cling in all the right places? They're slippery. And as he tries to shift me, and I let go, and he lets go…

"Oh fuck!"

I slide off his lap and fall onto the floor with a thud. We stare at each other for a startled moment. Until I bust out laughing.

Wes stares at me for a beat longer, and then he starts laughing too.

"So much for the mood," I say as I catch my breath from laughing.

His laugh stops abruptly. He grabs his hard length through the offending black satin, and massages himself. "Darlin', nothin's gonna ruin my mood."

Oh.

"Let's head to my bedroom then. Where I won't fall off your lap."

Before I realize what's happening, Wes stands up from the couch, bends down to grab me around the waist, and hoists me over his shoulder. It's like Halloween all over again.

"Second door on the left," I say before he asks.

In my room, he lays me down gently on the bed and then looks around. The moment he spots Murray, he chuckles.

"You still have the stuffed llama from Halloween?"

"Of course I do," I say. "What about you? What did you do with all those stuffed animals you shoved into your purse?"

"Satchel. But I don't want to talk about that right now."

His gaze returns to me, stretched out in the middle of the bed.

"What am I gonna do with all this?" he asks, eyes glinting.

"Anything you want. Everything you want." I toss the Medusa wig off my head and onto the floor. I sit up, grab the hem of my dress to pull it over my head and add it to the pile on the floor.

"Mmmm. What do I want first?" He shimmies out of the black satin pants, and pulls the poet's shirt over his head. Standing next to the bed, his erection straining the fabric of his boxer briefs, he puts a finger to his lips like he's thinking.

I guess we're playing a game now.

"How about this?" I ask as I pull down one cup of my bra and pinch my nipple.

"May...be..." he says, dragging it out.

"Or how about this?" I ask as my hand covers my mound.

"I think I need a closer look before I can decide," he says and climbs on the bed next to me.

Laying on his side, Wes gives me his full attention. A gentle hand caresses my face and cheek. As he leans over and begins trailing kisses down my neck, I feel treasured. Like I'm the pirate booty he's been searching for.

His hand cups my breast and begins kneading my nipple through the thin fabric, and I moan louder.

"You like that, baby?" he murmurs as he continues kissing.

"Mmmm-hmmm," is all I can get out. But it feels like there's a direct nerve connection from my nipple to my pussy. Every time he pinches and pulls, I get wetter.

"Let me take care of this then." He gently lifts me up to unclasp the bra behind me, and throws it onto the growing pile of discarded clothing. His mouth is on a nipple before I'm lying down again.

"Ahh, Wes, so good." At least that's what I mean to say. I'm not sure how coherent I am right now. He reaches a hand down between us while he continues to give special attention to first one breast and then the other. His hand finds the small triangle of black lace—the only fabric still on my body— and pushes it to the side.

Two large, strong fingers circle my clit, and I'm writhing beneath him. I pull his head up from my chest and begin kissing him. Moving my tongue inside his mouth like I wish he would move his tongue inside my pussy. And those strong fingers move gently into me as I continue my assault on his mouth.

This is like nothing I've ever felt before. I mean, sure, the sex was phenomenal on Halloween. But this is another level. It's no longer just a physical connection between us, but a spiritual one as well.

Pulling his head back from our kissing, he manages to mutter something.

"Hmmm?" I ask, eyes still closed and enjoying the languid strokes of his fingers inside of me.

"You are so fucking wet, Phoebs," he rasps into my ear before nibbling on my earlobe. "That's right, baby," he says as I feel myself begin to contract on his fingers between us.

I can't really come like this. Can I? I've never been able to before.

But Wes keeps going. Stretching me out, then adding a third finger. Returning to kissing me, and tongue-fucking my mouth. He bends one finger inside of me, and I see stars.

"Oh, God!" I scream as I wrench my mouth away from his.

He doesn't stop.

"Yes, baby," he murmurs in my ear, continuing his relentless stroking inside of me, hitting that magical spot over and over again.

The sensation is like nothing I've ever felt before. The orgasm rising within me is so strong, I'm almost afraid of it. Like I'll literally shatter.

My legs convulse and Wes keeps going. Dropping his head to my nipple once again. As he sucks and teases my breast with his teeth, the sensations all finally overwhelm me. I throw my head back, screaming so loud I'm sure the whole block can hear it, as my pussy clenches down on Wes's fingers and I lose all control of my body.

It goes on and on and on.

But what feels like half an hour is probably only a minute in reality.

When the convulsing finally stops, I'm breathing heavily. My face is hot and my pussy is throbbing. Wes is still inside me, gently stroking with just one finger now.

I open my eyes to see him staring down at me, his trademark half-smirk on his face. He peppers my face with kisses. "So fucking beautiful." As he praises me, I feel like a goddess. Like I wield all the power of the universe. Probably all in my pussy. Because I sure as hell can't talk right now.

"Now I get to taste you," he says with a grin, and he slides down my body.

"No, Wes, I can't take any more."

But as he withdraws his finger, I feel empty. And when he replaces his finger with his tongue, I moan in contentment. It feels right. It feels comforting. His murmurs of appreciation keep me feeling like the goddess I am.

It doesn't take long before I feel that pressure again. Know that I'm going to shatter again. I reach down to hold his head in place as I move. I can feel the slight stubble on his chin on me, and it's so. Fucking. Good. I ride his tongue, his mouth. My legs begin to convulse again, and suddenly all of my muscles clench.

"Oh God, yes Wes! Fuck fuck fuck! Yes baby!" I scream.

He carries me through it, lapping at my folds, softly offering sweet nothings, and rubbing his hands up and down my legs as I come down from the high.

After my breathing returns to normal, I slowly open my eyes. He's still lying between my legs, looking like the cat that got the cream, and rubbing my body gently.

"Did you enjoy that, baby?" he asks, knowing full well that I did.

"Just a little."

He moves up the bed to cradle me in his arms as I continue to luxuriate in the post-orgasmic bliss.

As the feelings fade, I feel Wes's massive erection poking me in the ass. Reaching behind me, I begin rubbing him, feeling the moisture beaded at his tip.

"No baby, this is about you," he says in a low tone.

"Ok," I say. But I don't stop.

"You don't have to do this," he says, groaning as I continue to stroke him.

"I know."

I release him from my grip and turn to face him.

"But now, Westley Jasper Herrington V, I need you to fuck me."

A smile crosses his lips. Something soft flits through his eyes.

"Yes, ma'am," he says, guiding me back down to the bed and climbing on top to straddle me.

"Fuck me, Wes," I urge him. "Show me how bad you want me."

His cock nudges the edge of my pussy, and I open my legs wider for him.

"Show me, baby," I say.

That's all it takes. He plunges inside of me, and I let out another scream. He stops.

"Are you okay?"

"Yes. It just feels...so...good...," I say, emphasizing each word with a movement of my hips and another small gasp.

And it feels amazing. He pounds into me again and again, and I'm riding the edge of pleasure and pain. I'm so tight, but every movement he makes strokes those nerve endings that were just so thoroughly satisfied.

"How do you want to come, baby?" I ask him.

He pauses, pulls out, and flips me onto my stomach.

"Lift up that pretty ass for me," he says and smacks it as he does. The moan is involuntary.

He plunges back inside me, resuming a relentless rhythm.

"Fuck me hard," I say, gasping.

He grabs my hips and pounds as hard as I've ever felt, and then releases one hand only to smack my ass again. I feel myself beginning to tighten again.

"Yeah, baby, come for me again," he growls as his free hand grabs my throat.

I've never been so turned on. So dominated. So well and thoroughly fucked.

It seems that we've both lost all power of speech. Wes ruts into me and my pussy continues to contract. His groans become louder, my moans more high-pitched. Until finally, in a fury of wild motion and feral sound, we reach that climax together. We both scream for the other.

And we both collapse.

———

I WAKE TO A SUNLIT ROOM, and the fucking cat laying on my ass. I glance over to see Wes still sleeping.

We crashed last night in each other's arms, but I woke up about an hour later, feeling like I was on fire. He's a furnace. I had to reclaim my side of the bed and my stay-cool pillow for the rest of the night.

But in the light of day, I'm ready to snuggle up in all that heat again.

"Mmmm. Mornin' darlin'," he says as I take my place as the small spoon. "Glad to see you didn't leave me this time."

"Well, it's my house."

"Still. I was worried you'd get freaked out after last night."

"No."

I shimmy my ass up against his morning wood.

"Feels like you've been a bad boy. Should I send you to detention?"

"Only if you promise to sit on my face during detention."

"That can be arranged. I *am* the principal, you know."

"Fuck yeah," he growls as he rolls me over on top of him.

———

WHEN WE FINALLY MAKE IT out of bed, we head to the kitchen.

"I'm starving," he says.

"How about bubble waffles with fresh berry sauce?"

"Sure. Want me to call Tess's and place an order?"

"Um, no. I'm cooking for you."

I pull my batter bowl out of the refrigerator and plug in the waffle iron. I turn the heat back on the berry sauce I started last night, before glancing over at Wes. He's wearing that half-smirk and a little twinkle in his eye.

"What?" I ask him.

"You planned on me staying for breakfast?"

Oops. He noticed.

So what if I'd made the waffle batter last night?

And the berry sauce?

"The odds were good. Plus, it's not like I couldn't eat all these waffles myself if I really wanted to. Now can you make the coffee, please?"

"As you wish."

10

WES

LIFE HAS GOTTEN A LOT MORE INTERESTING THESE LAST FEW WEEKS. I SPEND MY days working with the best art students to plan the mural project. I spend every night I can with Phoebe. And when she's not around, I'm busy working on her painting.

The kids don't seem to have figured out that I'm dating Phoebe yet, but the other teachers definitely know. Sitting in a weekly faculty meeting, it comes up in the worst possible way.

"I'm sorry, Bill, but we don't have any more money to buy new band instruments this year," Phoebe says.

She's talking to Bill Dunn, the orchestra teacher who's a few years older than me.

"The art department never seems to have a problem finding money," Bill retorts. "Maybe if I were your boyfriend, we'd be getting new violins."

I launch out of my seat at the same time Phoebe tears into him.

"Bill, you know perfectly well that Wes funds most of the art department himself," Phoebe says. "If you'd like to make a donation to the school to buy new violins, go for it. Otherwise, start working on your budget request for next school year."

She is much calmer about this than I am.

"Also, don't be a dick, man," I say.

Bill turns around to face me.

"Excuse me?"

"You heard me. Don't be a dick. You know damn well that Phoebe is doing an awesome job as principal, and that we'd be in a lot worse shape without her. She's gotten additional funding from the school board, she's energized the PTA to do more fundraising for us, and she's rallied the parent volunteers to help with the day-to-day."

"How many of those is she sleeping with?"

And all hell breaks loose.

I'm in his face, yelling at him.

The football coach is holding my arms back.

Mrs. Sledge is screaming, threatening to call the police.

Phoebe has rushed over to us, her face flushed, and unable to get out a coherent sentence. While I'm looking at her, Bill tries to throw a sucker punch.

He misses, but I lunge at him and yell louder.

"Wes, stop!"

I hear her. But I don't stop.

Finally someone blows a shrill whistle.

It's Phoebe. She's standing at the front of the room, glaring at us all.

"Faculty meeting adjourned."

Kyra: Dude. What the fuck did you do?
Me: What?
Kyra: Phoebe is P-I-S-S-E-D
Me: Oh.
Me: I kind of got into a fight with Bill at the faculty meeting. He accused Phoebe of sleeping with half the town to get her job done. Asshole deserved to have his ass beat. At least I just threatened him.
Kyra: We aren't in high school anymore. You can't do shit like that.
Me: Whatever.
Kyra: Well you better apologize to her.

Apologize to her? I did her a favor. She'll see it when she calms down. Whenever that may be.

———

THE NEXT DAY AT SCHOOL, I get a visit from Sheriff Rudolph.

"Mr. Herrington," he says as he knocks on my door during my planning period.

"Sheriff. What brings you by?"

"I think you know, son."

"Was it Bill or Mrs. Sledge who called you?"

"Sledge of course."

"You know he deserved it."

"I don't even know what was said, and I know he deserved it. But that doesn't mean you can assault someone during a faculty meeting."

Assault? Well, technically. I did *threaten* physical harm.

"I guess I should apologize."

"Try not to hit him."

"Sure thing, Sheriff."

The art room is Grand-Fucking-Central-Station today. As the Sheriff walks out, Suzanne Gentry walks in. She's an English teacher, and the sometimes-girlfriend of Bill Dunn.

"Wes, that was really inappropriate yesterday."

"You're not the first to say that to me."

"I know, but I just wanted to apologize on Bill's behalf."

Wait, what?

"You...wanted to apologize?"

"Yes, what Bill said was way out of line. We all know that Phoebe is working her butt off to make improvements at the school. For Bill to suggest that she's just having sex with whoever she needs to convince, well...it sets women back a good three-quarters of a century."

"Thank you, Suzanne. I'm glad you noticed the point I was trying to make."

"Don't get me wrong—you're a brutish neanderthal for starting a fight during a faculty meeting—

"Naturally."

"But I think you taught him something"

"One can only hope," I say, laughing.

"I've said my piece. Now you better make it up to your girlfriend."

She turns to leave, but I stop her.

"Uh, Suzanne? What am I apologizing to Phoebe for, exactly?"

She lets out a deep sigh and walks back over to my desk.

"Do you think Phoebe is doing a good job?"

"Yes, of course."

"Do you think she has a problem standing up to people, or fighting her own fights?"

"No."

"And you understand she's sensitive about people thinking she's somehow less capable just because she's a woman."

I nod.

"Then why did you feel the need to defend her honor? To come at a guy she had just finished dressing down?"

"Um, because she's my girlfriend?"

"And because you think she needs protecting merely because she's a woman."

"Right."

She just stares at me.

"Oh shit," I finally say.

She stares at me some more.

"By thinking I needed to fight her fight for her, I did just what he was doing. Suggesting that she's less because she's a woman."

"Ding, ding, ding! We call it benevolent chauvinism. You think you're trying to help, but you're not."

"How big of an apology does this need to be?"

"No grand gesture required. But you do need to make clear that you understand what you did, and acknowledge that it was wrong."

At least the make-up sex will be good.

"Okay, my work here is done," Suzanne says. "I've got to go tend to the man-child's bruised ego."

"Thanks Suzanne."

She waves her hand, brushing me off, as she walks out the door.

Me: Is it my turn to make you dinner tonight?

By the end of the school day, still no response from Phoebe.

Me: Phoebs?
Phoebe: I don't know if that's a good idea.
Me: Please darlin'. I owe you an apology. Let me make it up to you.
Phoebe: Ok, I guess. But I'm not sleeping over.
Me: I understand. Come over at 7?
Phoebe: See you then.

WHEN SHE KNOCKS on the door that evening, I'm ready. I've got a kitchen towel flung over my shoulder when I open the door, and dinner will be ready in a few minutes.

"Hey darlin'."

"Hi."

She's still in a suit. Arms crossed, stern look on her face.

"You wanna come in and get comfortable? I gotta run back to the kitchen."

"I thought you'd be ready, but okay."

It's the principal tone.

I'm tossing the pasta with the sauce when I hear her call from the dining room.

"How much longer are you going to be? Can I do something to speed things along?"

"Just pour yourself some wine," I call back. Lots would probably help my cause.

I grab the huge bowl of pasta and the bread basket, and march into battle.

"It's about time. It's already 7:20."

Still the principal tone.

"Before we eat, I want to say something," I tell her.

She sighs. "How long are you going to drag this out?"

"For fuck's sake, Phoebs, I'm trying to apologize!"

She just stares at me.

Maybe cussing at her wasn't the best way to start my apology.

"Let me back up."

She nods.

"I'm really sorry for what happened yesterday. I know that I shouldn't have gotten into a fight with Bill."

"Right, because you're a 30-year-old teacher, and not a frat boy anymore."

"Well, that too. But also because I know you don't need me to fight battles for you. You're perfectly capable of dealing with dickheads like him on your own."

"And you."

"Huh?"

"I'm capable of dealing with dickheads like you too." For the first time since she got here, a small smile forms on her lips.

"Right. You can deal with all the assholes and dickheads just fine."

A full smile breaks across her face.

"Apology accepted."

I release a breath I didn't know I was holding, and walk over to her. Fold her in my arms. Kiss the top of her head.

"Do you want to get more comfortable? I can take the suit jacket for you."

"Okay." She lets me help her out of the tailored black jacket, revealing a sleeveless red silk blouse beneath.

"Oh shit. You were dressed for war today."

"Nah, I just needed the confidence to hold my ground. It's hard to stay mad at you."

She steps out of her heels, turns in my arms, and looks up into my face.

"Thank you for apologizing." She gives me a quick peck on the lips. "And thank you for wanting to be my defender, even when I don't need it."

And now it's my turn to kiss her, but I'm not settling for a peck. I taste her lips, and then make my way down her chin, her jawline, her neck, all the way to that spot just behind her ear that I know she likes.

"Mmmmm," she moans.

I nibble her ear.

"Let's sit down for dinner," I murmur in her ear.

"Tease," she says.

I just grin, and we take our seats. Our knees are touching, and I like the constant reminder of her physical presence.

"I see you were planning to win me over with bacon," she says as she digs into her pasta.

"Damn straight, darlin'. I figured with enough carbonara and red wine, you'd forgive me eventually. Even if I fucked up the apology."

"Solid bet. This is so good."

"Just wait till you see what I have planned for dessert," he says with a wink.

PHOEBE

I TOTALLY SLEPT OVER.

Wes and his magical tongue make the best desserts.

We quickly fall back into a comfortable routine. I'm the principal. He's the high school art teacher, who's also working on a public mural project for Jasper Mill. I give directions and approval. He does what I say.

And at night, the roles reverse. I let go of the burden of being in charge, and let him fuck me however he wants. Oh God, do I love being at his mercy. Those three-orgasm nights make the mornings—when I re-assume the mantle of responsibility—easier to bear.

The physical side is amazing. But I'm totally blown away when Wes invites me to his family's vacation home for spring break—it seems like a much bigger emotional step.

"Where is this place, exactly?"

"It's about a 2-hour drive, up into the hills."

"And we'll be the only ones there?"

"For the whole week."

"So it's like a small mountain cabin? Do we need to bring firewood or anything?"

He laughs. And then laughs some more.

"Oh darlin', you should know by now that the Jasper family doesn't do anything small."

"So…"

"We don't need to bring firewood. Or food. Or clothes."

"There's already clothes for me up there?!"

"No, just the food and heat. I thought I'd keep you naked most of the week though."

Good thing we're already lying naked in bed, because I'm wet again, just thinking about that plan.

"I know spring break isn't for a couple weeks, but can we get started now?"

I climb onto him, straddling his body between my legs. His cock instantly springs back to life.

"Damn straight," he says.

I lower my head to kiss him as I grind into him. Without so much as missing a breath, he lifts my hips and eases me down onto his shaft before pulling back from the kiss.

"Ride me, cowgirl."

———

A FEW DAYS LATER, I attend my first Jasper Mill Town Council meeting. Wes is going to be presenting on his public art proposal, so I want to support him. I also want to learn more about how things get done in Jasper Mill.

Glancing around, it appears that the town council meetings are quite the social event. Familiar faces everywhere—almost all of the Main Street shop owners, sheriff, fire chief, big-name families in the community, several other teachers, and even Tony Capsigo.

"Why do you think Tony is here?" I whisper to Wes. "He lives in Punning, right?"

He nods and turns his lips to my ear.

"He likes my mural project and wants to see what happens."

The Town Council chair calls the meeting to order.

"For those who don't know me, I'm Westley Jasper Herrington III."

I elbow Wes.

"You didn't tell me your grandpa was chair of the Town Council," I whisper.

He grins, but continues to face forward.

The Town Council meeting is even longer and more boring than the School Board meetings. A lot of people have a lot to say about a lot of unimportant little shit. And unlike Tony Capsigo, who runs a tight ship at the School Board meetings, Ol' Grandpa Jasper seems content to let everyone get in all their words.

Grandpa Jasper, despite the moniker I've given him, is not frail in any way. He's got to be 75, but he's like a Harrison-Ford-75. Silver hair, sparkling eyes, well-tanned, sinewy strength showing beneath his shirt sleeves. Wes has got some good genes, I'll say that.

The meeting is so long, they have an intermission. Seriously.

"Why don't y'all stretch your legs, take a comfort break, and we'll resume in 10 minutes," one of the school board members announces.

I lean over and give Wes a quick peck on the lips. "When do you think it will be your turn to speak?"

"Probably right after intermission. Gramps likes to give me dramatic effect."

"Well, I've gotta pee. I'll be back in a few."

He nods and stands, and I head off in search of the ladies' room.

The line is as bad as at a concert. When I finally make it into a stall, I take a few breaths and try to re-center myself. It's been a long day, and I want to be able to focus on what Wes has to say, and how people respond. If the public art gains a lot of attention, it could help us make a case for more arts funding at the school.

The bathroom is almost empty when I hear a group of three—or is it four?—women enter, chatting away.

I mostly ignore them, but my ears perk up when I hear one of them mention Wes.

"Did you see the new girl with Wes?"

"Kind of hard not to. She prances around on those high heels, hanging all over him."

"She sure didn't waste any time trapping one of the Jasper men."

"Well, you've got to give her credit for figuring that out so fast. With Wes at her side, her job is safe, and she can do no wrong."

"I heard she fucked him way back in October, when she was in town for the interview. She must have been a great lay."

"Good enough to get her the job, at least."

"He's probably just using her too. Get what he needs out of the art department and the high school to make his mural project work, and then he'll dump her. You know how he is."

My ears buzz, drowning them out.

What. The. Fuck.

This is exactly what I've been worried about all along. How can I make a name for myself when I'm dating one of my teachers, from one of Jasper Mill's kingmaker families?

And is Wes really just using me to push his mural project through?

And how do they know I slept with him back in October?

And *are* there security cameras on the maintenance building?

This is not good.

I wait until the gossips leave the bathroom, and when I return to the meet-

145

ing, I see that Wes is already standing at the podium. I sit at the back of the room and listen to his presentation, but I don't hear most of what he says.

At the end of his speech, he heads back to his seat, but doesn't even look around for me. I guess he doesn't care where I went. And when I see a twenty-something, blonde, groomed-to-the-hilt lady of Jasper Mill sit down next to him, and him lean over to give her a kiss on the cheek, well, that's it. I'm out.

It's another hour before my phone dings with a text alert.

Wes: Where'd you go?

Took him long enough to notice.

Me: Home.

I don't respond to any more of his messages.

———

THE NEXT DAY at school is hard. I have no interest in talking to Wes. Or even thinking about him, really.

I have a budget meeting with the school board and a curriculum study session to get through in the next week, and I have a lot of work to do to prepare for both. The last thing I need is to be distracted by…feelings.

I don't visit him during his planning period. I only go the teachers' lounge when I know he's in class. I don't meet him for lunch in our usual spot. And I head straight home after the bell rings, to continue my work in peace.

Kyra: What did Wes do now?
Me: Nothing. I'm just busy.
Kyra: I know that's bullshit.
Kyra: But I'll let it go for now.
Kyra: Girls night on Friday?
Me: Sure.

Another day successfully navigated to avoid Wes, and I'm ready for girls' night with Kyra. Tonight, rosé is our drink of choice, and we're going to re-watch Bridgerton. Season 1, of course.

"So tell me what happened," Kyra says as we settle into the couch. She even let me have the end with the recliner, so I can put my feet up.

"Nothing in particular. I just don't think this relationship is going to work."

"It seems to be working just fine."

"That's not what I mean."

"Then what do you mean?"

"It's making it harder for me to do my job. People assume that I'm dating Wes just so my job is safe, and so I can get whatever I want in terms of resources for the school. I don't see a way for me to stand on my own in my career, and still date him."

"Who are the 'people' who think this?"

"I don't know—everyone?"

"Um, no. What else is going on, Phoebs?"

"I overheard some women talking in the bathroom at the Town Council meeting—

"Who?"

"I don't know. I was in a stall, and they didn't know I was there. Anyway, they were gossiping about me and Wes, about me sleeping with him at the Halloween party, and saying that Wes is just using me to make sure his mural project gets approved."

"You know that's not true, right?"

"I know that it doesn't really matter what's true or not. Perception is reality, Kyra. If people think I'm getting special treatment around town because I'm dating Wes, then it becomes true. And how would you know what his motives are?"

"I've never specifically asked him—

"Exactly. Anyways, like I said, it doesn't matter one way or the other. I've been thinking a lot about it, and I just can't see him anymore. I've been worried about this since day one—that I shouldn't date one of my teachers, that people might think he gets preferential treatment, that they think I get preferential treatment because he's one of Jasper's golden boys. It's too messy. Being a successful woman brings a certain amount of loneliness and isolation with it, and I forgot that."

"Oh bullshit," Kyra says.

She pours me more wine.

"If you love him...do you love him?"

I shrug.

"Well if you do, none of it matters. You figure out how to make it work. I don't think you should give up just because it got hard."

"And I don't know how he feels either. Maybe he *is* just using me."

She scooches over on the couch, and gives me a hug.

"I really don't think he is, Phoebs."

I shrug again.

"But there's one way to find out."

"I don't think I want to ask him right now."

"Ok. When you're ready."

"Let's just watch Rege. He's the only man I need for the moment."

12

WES

I HAVE NO FUCKING CLUE WHY PHOEBE IS IGNORING ME. ALL I KNOW IS SHE never came back after intermission at the Town Council meeting.

Maybe I said something in my presentation that pissed her off.

I don't know because she won't even respond to a text.

So I'm spending my Saturday evening at Pig & Grapes, the best bar in Jasper Mill.

Ok, it might be one of only two bars in Jasper Mill. But it's good.

They have a ton of great beer on draft, and you can also catch a game on the televisions or play darts, or even weekly trivia nights.

Anyway, that's where I am. Four pints into the night and watching a perennially-loser baseball team out in Virginia try to pull off an upset. A bunch of my buddies and siblings are here too.

"Hey Wes, isn't that your girlfriend?" one of the guys gestures to the entrance. Phoebe's shape is framed by the doorway. Her auburn hair curls around her shoulders, her makeup is what I now know to be her game face, and she suddenly spots me. She makes her way over to our table with a look of grim determination.

"Hey darlin'," I say in greeting.

"Hey Wes. Can we talk?"

"Yeah. Whatcha wanna talk about?"

"Us."

"I might be too drunk to talk about that right now," I say.

She gives a tight-lipped smile.

"Well, do you want to come over for brunch tomorrow?" she asks.

"Ok."

Lily sidles over to me.

"Hey big guy," she says as she slings her arm over my shoulder.

Phoebe looks between us, confusion and hurt crossing her face.

"Hi, I'm Lily. You must be Phoebe." She extends her hand to shake, but all Phoebe does is the same tight-lipped smile thing and nods her head.

"Nice to meet you, Lily." Phoebe's voice sounds weird.

Lily rolls her eyes and grabs my beer.

Phoebe shakes her head and seems to recover herself. "You know what, Wes?" She puts her hands on her hips, cocks her head, and gets "the tone."

Uh-oh. This is aggressive Phoebe coming out.

"What, darlin'?"

"First of all, stop calling me darlin'. Second, forget about brunch tomorrow. We're done, Wes."

What the fuck just happened? I'm suddenly very sober.

I stand up from the table and grab Phoebe's arm so I can guide her to a quieter place to talk. We end up in the hallway by the bathrooms.

"What's going on, Phoebe?"

"What's going on is that I can't do this anymore. Do us anymore."

"Did something happen? You've been avoiding me since Thursday night's meeting."

"It's everything I was worried about coming to bear. People assuming I only got the job because I fucked you, that I'm fucking you now so I'll keep the job, and that you're fucking me just to get the mural project pushed through."

"That's a lot of people worrying about why we're fucking."

"Yes. And it isn't helping my professional reputation."

"Darlin', forget that noise. All the people who matter know you're doing a great job."

"Easy for you to say. You're the golden boy. No matter what you do, or who you do, people are still going to kiss your ass and let you have your way. You'll always have women lining up around the block for you. And it's all because of a stupid name."

Huh. That stings a little.

"Is that really all you think of me? That I've only made it because of the Jasper name?"

"It's not the same for me," she continues. "I'm working my butt off to make it work here. But you lose control in a single faculty meeting, get into an argument with another teacher, and suddenly all my work is undone."

"What?"

"I've had multiple calls from school board members and parents, concerned that I'm letting our personal relationship cloud my judgment."

"That's bullshit!"

Now I'm drunk and pissed.

"Calm down, sailor."

As I look at her, I try to see it all from her perspective. But I can't. All I know is that I care for her, and she seems to care for me. Why do we have to let other people get in our way?

"You know I'm not using you, right?"

"I don't know anymore, Wes."

"Then maybe you don't know me as well as I thought you did. And maybe I don't know you at all."

She shrugs her shoulders. Looks me in the eyes, then off to the side.

"This is for the best, Wes. We were just supposed to be an anonymous hookup. We weren't meant to be a couple."

There must be something really interesting on that wall behind me, because she won't look at me again.

"If that's what you want," I say.

"It is. Goodbye, Wes."

She turns and hurries back out of the pub.

I may as well take a piss while I'm back here.

When I get back to the table, I get a bunch of funny looks.

"What the hell did you do to her, jackass?" Lily asks me as she punches me in the arm.

"Ouch! What was that for?"

"She speed-walked outta here, red-faced and on the verge of tears."

I shrug.

"She dumped *me*."

"Smart girl."

Me: I don't understand what happened. Can't we talk about it?
Phoebe: I'm busy.

———

THE NEXT FEW weeks are a blur.

Phoebe avoids me as much as possible, and I don't try to track her down.

I do have feelings for her. A lot of feelings. But I don't get what's going on in her head.

Until I get through this mural project, though, I'm going to have to put things on pause. I got the approval I needed from the Town Council, the kids all have their mural plans finalized, Principal Phoebe gave us the latitude we need to get it done, and it's time to start painting.

I'm going to be covered in latex paint and surrounded by teenagers around-the-clock for the next two weeks.

"Hey Mr. H, where's your girl?" one of my guys asks the first day on site by the Old Mill.

"Not here."

"Duh," he says. "But where is she? My mom thought Principal Kestrel would probably be here to watch you work."

"Your mom did, huh? What other brilliant opinions does your mom have on my love life and the motivation of my girlfriend? Maybe I should call her for advice right now?"

"Whoa man, cool down."

He holds his hands up and backs away from me.

Yeah, that was probably too much to dump on one of my students.

But I'm getting sick of the small-town gossip train too.

Phoebe is doing a damn good job.

Are these people really so small-minded that they can't see past our personal relationship?

They can all go fuck themselves.

No, even better—I'll show them just how wrong they are.

Phoebe doesn't need to put up with all this bullshit in her life. And maybe once I fix it for her, she'll talk to me again.

"Hey boss," another student calls over. "You got a minute to help plot this out?"

"Yeah. Be right there."

13

PHOEBE

I'VE CRIED A LOT MORE THAN I EXPECTED THESE LAST COUPLE OF WEEKS.

Wes hasn't tried to come find me in my office, and he even stopped texting me. I guess he's moved on already. The bitches in the ladies' room were right —he just needed me to push the mural through, and now he has no use for me.

Hell, I think he moved on before I even broke up with him.

That Lily chick was hanging on him at the Town Council meeting, and then with him at Pig & Grapes. She must be his new fling.

When I'm not crying, I'm busy burying myself in work. At least the harsh phone calls from school board members and parents have stopped. And the rest of the teachers have gone back to treating me how they did when I first arrived—a little distant, but with respect.

I haven't even managed to see Kyra for drinks since Wes and I broke up. That's partially because her boyfriend Liam is in town for a month, but also because I just don't want to deal with it.

Work is good though.

I killed it at the budget meeting with the school board. After explaining how the former principal diverted arts funding to the football team, and how Wes had been funding the art department, it took the Board about 30 seconds to approve my new budget. Next school year will see us returning to balanced spending.

Yes, I plan to be here next school year.

This place feels like home, and I'm sticking around as long as the School Board will let me.

Kyra finally tracks me down.

Kyra: Hey, girls' night this weekend? We still haven't talked about Wes.
Me: Isn't Liam still in town? It can wait, no big deal.
Kyra: Liam will be fine. And I think it is a big deal to you.
Me: <shrug emoji>
Kyra: Sauna on Friday?
Me: Ok, fine.

When Friday rolls around, I show up at Kyra's house prepared. I've got my pajamas for a sleepover, the cheesecake I picked up from Tess's Treats, and my makeup already removed.

Liam answers the door.

"Hey Phoebe," he says in that gravelly sexy voice of his. "Come on in." He grabs my overnight bag from me, and ushers me in towards the kitchen.

"Good to see you, Liam. How much longer you sticking around?"

"Not sure right now," he says. "A while."

"Oh, Kyra must be thrilled."

"She is. We are." He gives me that famous smile. "But I'll let her tell you."

"Tell me what?"

"Oh, just a little something," Kyra says as she strolls into the kitchen, flashing a ring on her left hand.

"Ohmigod! You guys got engaged? Congratulations!"

I run over to give Kyra a hug, and then step back so I can admire her ring.

"And that is not a 'little something,' Kyra. That thing is huge!"

"That's what she said," they say in unison.

"Y'all are a mess," I say, laughing. "So tell me all about it."

"On that note, I'm out of here," Liam says.

"You don't have to leave on my account," I insist.

"You're not kicking me out, sweets—I have a guys' night out planned."

He gives Kyra one last kiss and heads for the door. "Have fun!" he shouts as the door closes behind him.

"Sauna time," Kyra says. "Then we dish."

Ten minutes later, we're half naked.

"Tell me all about the proposal," I say to Kyra.

"Nuh-uh. You can hear that some other time. Like at our engagement party. You tell me why you broke up with Wes."

"Well, I tried to talk to him, like you had suggested."

"That's not exactly what I heard."

"Well, I at least went to the bar where he was hanging out."

"And…?"

"And it just confirmed my suspicions. He already moved on."

"Why do you say that?"

"Some girl was hanging all over him. The same girl who I saw him with at the end of the Town Council meeting."

"Did you get this mystery woman's name?"

"Lily."

Kyra's hand flies up to cover her mouth. She must be shocked by the revelation.

I take another huge gulp of my daiquiri.

"Did you…um…ask Wes about Lily?"

"No. It didn't seem worth it. Why, do you know something?"

"This is really a conversation you need to have with Wes."

I shrug.

"I don't think I want to."

Kyra looks at me for a moment, then shakes her head.

"So, you wanna hear about the proposal?" she asks.

"Of course!"

I'm glad for the subject change.

When we finally emerge from the sauna, pruny and full of way too many daiquiris, I'm relieved I just have to make it upstairs to Kyra's guest room. I feel wrung out from all the emotions of the last few weeks.

―――

WHEN I WAKE up the next morning, I'm shocked to see that I slept for 12 hours. I can't remember the last time I did that.

I usually wake up refreshed and energized. Today, though, I just want to crawl into a cave.

I wipe the sleep from my eyes and stumble down the hall towards the kitchen, but pause when I hear voices.

"She said it was Lily," Kyra says.

"You mean…Lily, Lily?" Liam asks.

"Yep. I told her she needs to talk to Wes."

"You think she will?"

"Nope."

I've heard enough of that, and take the last few steps into the kitchen.

"Morning, sleepyhead!" Kyra says to me.

"G'morning," I mumble.

"You sleep okay?" Liam asks.

I nod.

"Good. I was worried I might have woken you when I came in last night."

I shake my head.

"Coffee?" Kyra asks, as she hands a tall mug over to me.

I nod, and take a long drink, closing my eyes as I do.

When I open them again, two sets of eyes are staring back at me.

"What?"

"You all right there?" Liam asks.

"Yes. I just don't have words before coffee."

He chuckles. "Well ladies, I have a meeting to get to. See you later."

Taking a seat at the kitchen counter, I close my eyes again and inhale the magical scent of coffee. After a few more sips, I look up and see Kyra busy washing dishes.

"What do you have going on today?" I ask her.

"Not much. Kimball has taken over weekends, so I actually have time to myself."

"That's great!" Kyra had been working herself to death, running the coffee shop all by herself, seven days a week. Kimball is an assistant store manager who has worked with Kyra for four years. It's about damn time Kyra let them help.

"What about you?"

"Nothing in particular planned. Just laundry, cleaning the bathroom, the usual."

"Why don't we for a walk, and then get brunch over at Stella's?"

"Ok, sure. I need to get a shower first though."

"Take your time."

Forty-five minutes later, I'm ready to go. Clean clothes, damp hair, and no makeup except my favorite Buxom lip gloss.

Kyra looks like she's ready for paparazzi.

"I thought we were just going for a walk?"

"We are. But I think the engagement news already hit Twitter. Never know who might be lurking around."

Maybe I should put in a little more effort.

Nah. It's the weekend.

"Ok, let's get a move on," I say.

"I'll drive us into town, and we can walk from there."

I am not amused when Kyra pulls into the parking lot of the Old Mill.

"Why are we here, Kyra?"

"I thought you'd want to see how the mural project is going."

"I don't want to talk to Wes."

"Fine, ignore him. But at least check out what some of your students have been doing."

With a deep sigh, I get out of the car.

"Hey Principal Kestrel," one of the senior boys calls out. I wave.

Jane, the senior class president, rushes over to me.

"Let me show you around, Principal Kestrel," she gushes.

After Kyra and I complete our tour around the Old Mill building—without any Wes sightings—Jane hands us a hand-drawn map of the rest of the mural walk.

The students have designed and are now painting murals all over commercial buildings in downtown Jasper.

"Thanks Jane. We'll check out the rest of the buildings," I say to her with a smile. "Keep up the great work!"

As Kyra and I continue through downtown, we see a beautiful floral mural covering a whole side wall of the florist, an abstract design with bold colors decorating the fascia above the post office, and a somewhat-predictable portrait of Ruth Bader Ginsburg on the side of a law office.

"Are you having them paint anything on the shop?" I ask Kyra.

"Yep," she says.

"Know what it is?"

"Nope. I told them to surprise me."

I nod.

I'm relieved when we finally duck into Stella's with nary a Wes sighting. If I'm being honest, I'm kind of afraid to see him. I don't know how I'll react. If I'll still be mad, or if my body will betray me.

Better to just avoid it.

"What'll y'all have?" Stella asks.

"Eggs Benedict with a side of fruit for me," Kyra says.

"I'll take…"

"Coffee, Denver omelette, and more coffee?" Stella asks.

I laugh. It's what I ordered the very first time I ate at Stella's. With Wes.

"I can't believe you remember," I say.

"Of course," she says. "When you order coffee twice, I know you're serious."

"Well, let's do it again today. Thanks Stella," I say, handing her the menu.

Thoughts of Wes and food flash through my mind. The Denver omelette, the bubble waffles, the pot roast, how I was his favorite dessert…

"Yoo-hoo, Phoebs," Kyra calls out.

"What? Oh, sorry. Just daydreaming."

"I can tell. Anything you want to share with the class?"

Just then, a familiar shape passes in front of the window, and my heart sinks.

"There's Wes and Lily again," I say to Kyra.

"Oh those two are always trouble," Stella says as she sets down my two cups of coffee in front of me. "Ever since they were kids, they've been lookin' for fun that usually turns into a mess."

Stella moves on to her next table.

"They've known each other since they were kids?" I ask Kyra. Great, they're probably part of some weird Jasper Mill arranged marriage thing.

"You need to talk to him, Phoebe. You can't avoid him the rest of your life, especially if you're going to stay in Jasper Mill. I think there's a huge misunderstanding here that can be easily resolved. But you have to talk to him."

"Why can't you just tell me?"

"Because I'm not the one you're in love with."

In love?

Am I in love with him?

"You're avoiding him to protect your heart. To avoid dealing with the consequences of your own decisions."

"What? What did I do wrong?"

"You didn't do anything wrong, Phoebs. But you made choices. You chose to have anonymous sex on Halloween. You chose to take this job. You chose to have a relationship with Wes. You chose to back off when things got hard. And now that there are a few problems, you just want to stick your head in the sand. You're sad and depressed, and it breaks my heart to see you miss out on what could be a wonderful relationship just because you want to avoid the messy parts."

"But it doesn't matter!" I say too loudly. "Wes has already moved on with that Lily chick!"

Just then, Stella returns to the table.

"Don't you know, honey? Lily is the baby of the Herrington kids. She just moved back to town last month."

No. I definitely did not know that.

"I thought his sister's name was Beth? He's told me all about her."

"Only Wes calls her Beth," Kyra says. "Her name is Lilybeth."

Oh shit.

What have I done?

14

WES

> Kyra: Phoebe just figured out that Lily is your sister.
> Me: What do you mean, she just figured it out?
> Kyra: She thought she was a new girlfriend or something.
> Me: I'm sure I told her about my sister.
> Kyra: I'm sure you didn't use the name Lily. She really had no clue.
> Me: Oh shit.

Did she break up with me over a simple misunderstanding? Because she thought I was dating Lily?

I could have sworn I told her that Beth is Lilybeth.

But why didn't she just ask me about it? And why is she still avoiding me?

I shake my head and put it out of my mind when I get back to the Old Mill to check on the kids. I'm happy to see my sister is there already.

Since Lily got back in town and doesn't have much to do until her new job starts, she's been acting as my second-in-command on this mural project. The kids love her, and I love spending time with her. I missed her while she was away at college.

And, if I'm being honest with myself, I've been lonely since Phoebe broke up with me. It's not a feeling I'm used to. I've always been happy with my life —teaching art to a bunch of kids, drinking too much on the weekends with my buds, exercising just enough to burn off the calories from the booze, and seeing my family once a month, just often enough that they don't write me out of the will.

Phoebe was something more. In such a short time, she became an important part of my day. Every day.

She was the person who I couldn't wait to tell about whatever dumb thing one of the kids said. The person who made exercising a lot more fun. The first person who made me able to envision a future where I have a family of my own. One that wouldn't be as dysfunctional as mine was growing up. She's someone motivated by achievement and compassion, not just money.

And then she left.

Because of a misunderstanding, yes. But also because she wasn't sure where she stood with me. If I was using her.

"You're thinking about her again, aren't you?" Lily asks.

I shrug. "So what if I am?"

No way I'm telling Lily what's really going through my mind.

"I really think you need to talk to her."

"She's the one who's avoiding me. She's the one who dumped me."

And I miss her like hell. I already fixed things for her with the school board. Now I need to fix this. Lily knows it.

"Suck it up, brother-o-mine. You went and caught feelings. You miss her. You need to try to make it right."

"Maybe. When the murals are done."

"Oh bullshit. I'm here to help with the murals. You're just making excuses."

"Maybe. But get back to work." I elbow her in the ribs.

———

Between finishing up the murals, and working on Phoebe's painting, another week flies by in no time.

Of course I'm still doing her painting. We may not be dating anymore, but she's still my boss, and I did promise.

Anyway, spring break has arrived, and I can finally take a breath.

"I'm really glad you could join me at the cabin, Bethy," I say to her as we head out of town.

"Me too. It's been a long time since I've been up there."

"Nothing has changed."

"We have, I think."

I laugh.

"Yeah, maybe so. Can you believe I was ready to bring Phoebe up here? I've never done that with a woman."

Lily turns her whole body to look at me.

"Westley," she says.

I pull over. She's using my whole name. It must be serious.

"Yes, Lilybeth?"

"Have you considered the possibility that you love this girl?"

Do I love her? That's a stupid question. I've only really known her for, what, four months? I mean, I "knew" her back in October, but I didn't know her.

"Westley?"

Right. None of that was out loud.

"I don't know."

"I think you do. Why would you bring her up here? Why are you avoiding talking about her, and instead pouring all of your feelings into your paintings?"

I look at my annoyingly-astute little sister for another moment.

"So what if I do? She obviously doesn't feel the same way about me. There's no point in dwelling."

And off we go, back onto the road and headed to the cabin for a week of relaxation.

But it turns out to be anything but relaxing for me. I'm restless. Can't stop pacing. Can't focus on my art. Can't sleep until I just completely exhaust myself.

———

THREE DAYS INTO OUR TRIP, I'm awoken by the sound of knocking at the door. I *just* made it to sleep an hour or so ago. Who the fuck could that be?

I stumble to the front door, adjust my boxers, and swing open the door to find…

"Phoebe?" I'm suddenly awake.

"Yeah," she says with a small smile.

"What are you doing here?"

"I…I came to see you."

"Oh."

"Do you…do you not want to see me? Should I leave? I can go. This was a stupid idea." She turns away from the door.

"Please stay," I say to her back.

She turns around with a brilliant smile. A triple-bird-worthy smile that lights up the space in my heart. That feeling of restlessness that I haven't been able to shake suddenly flies out of my body.

"Come in." I open the door wider and gesture for her to enter. "Take a seat in the living room. Let me go get some pants on."

"And maybe a shirt?" she calls as I head back to my room.

I smile to myself. She's still distracted by the sight of my bare chest.

Handing her a mug of coffee a few minutes later, I dive right in.

"So why did you drive all the way up here?"

"I, um…I wanted to talk to you. And I didn't know if you had cell service."

"I do. You could have just texted to find out."

"True. Well, the thing is, I wanted to see you. In person."

"Did something change?"

"Sort of. Yes."

"What?"

"Well, first of all, I figured out that Lily is your sister."

"Oh yeah. Kyra mentioned that."

"Well I thought she was your new girlfriend, or old girlfriend returned home, or…I don't know."

"What in the world would give you the idea that I would suddenly start cheating on you?"

"I heard a rumor."

I roll my eyes. Small-town gossip mill is about to make an appearance.

"About?"

"That you were only dating me to help push the mural project through. And once you got your approvals, and I saw you with another woman, I thought…"

"You thought it was true?"

"Yeah."

"Did I ever do anything that suggested that's how I felt about you? Because that's sure as hell not how I feel about you."

"No. But…"

"But what?"

"I guess I was just insecure. I didn't believe that you could like me for me. I was always looking for what you were getting out of the relationship."

"Darlin', I didn't want anything out of the relationship but you."

She smiles again. A smile that covers her whole face, that lights up the room, that makes me believe everything is going to be all right.

"So how's work going? We haven't talked in a while."

"Oh. Great, actually. The phone calls have stopped. It's back to business as usual."

"Glad they listened to me."

The smile drops from her face.

"Glad they…what?"

"After you told me those school board members were calling you, I went and had a talk with them. Told them that you were doing a fantastic job, and they needed to stop bugging you."

"You did what?!" she shrieks and stands up to begin pacing the floor.

"How could you do that to me, Wes? You know I want to do this on my

161

own. To earn their respect and make a real difference here in Jasper. Why would you undercut me like that?"

"I was just trying to help."

"Just trying to help? By throwing your name and weight around, so that now even more people will think I only got the job because I slept with you? How is that helping?"

"It's not a big deal, Phoebs. I was just protecting my woman."

"You were just…ohmigod, I can't believe you! Will you never learn?"

"Phoebs, just calm down."

That was the wrong thing to say.

"Calm down? Calm down?! I'm out."

She turns around, grabs her coat and bag, and stomps out the door without another word.

The second the door slams shut, Lily comes barreling down the stairs.

"You idiot!" she shrieks.

"Good mornin' to you too, Bethy."

"When are you going to learn? She doesn't want you to fight her battles for her. She just wants you to love her!" She's still shrieking.

"Isn't helping her do her job a sign of love?"

"No, Wes. It's not. It's a sign that you think she can't do it herself. Get it through your thick skull."

I shrug.

"I don't see it that way."

"Then I'm not spending the rest of the week with you either."

Lily runs out the door in her pajamas and I hear her calling to Phoebe. Fine. They both can go.

They'll figure out that I didn't do anything wrong. It looks like I'm gonna have a few days of relaxation by myself.

But I can't relax.

I'm going to wear a hole in the wood floor from all my pacing. I don't have the heart to work on Phoebe's painting. And despite having gotten only a couple hours of sleep, I can't seem to take a nap.

I replay my conversation with Phoebe over and over again.

And no matter how hard I try, I just can't shake this feeling of restlessness. If anything, it seems to be getting worse.

But I think I may have figured out just the thing to do.

15

PHOEBE

I'M SUCH AN IDIOT.

I just assumed, when I figured out Lily was his sister, that everything was going to work out with Wes.

But we've never really talked about our relationship. We've certainly never said the L-word. We have great sex, and talk about our daily lives, but never about the future.

And he still doesn't get that I don't *want* him to fix my problems for me. That I want to make it on my own terms.

Tears are stinging my eyes as I hurry back up the road to where I left my car.

"Phoebe, wait!"

I turn around to see Lily running up the hill in her pink bunny slippers.

I shake my head and keep heading for the car.

She's fast. As I open the driver-side door, she's hopping into my car on the passenger side.

"Hi Phoebe, I'm Wes's little sister Lily," she says, extending her hand to me.

"So I gathered."

"Can you drive me back to Jasper?"

Huh?

"Um, I guess?"

"Great, let's go." This strange blonde woman settles back into the seat, buckles in, and puts her bunny-slipper-feet up on the dashboard.

I have no idea what to say, so I just start the car, throw it in reverse, and drive. Away from Wes Herrington as fast as I can.

About 10 minutes down the road, my eyes finally stop tearing up. I get my breathing under control. I take a huge drink from my security water bottle. And then a deep sigh.

"You better now?"

It's the first I've heard from Lily since I started the car.

"Calmer at least, yeah."

"Nice to meet you."

"You too. Why are you in my car?"

"Wes was being a jackass. I didn't want to spend the week with him."

"What did he do to you?"

"Nothing. He was being a jackass about you."

Oh.

A few more minutes of silence.

"Do you love him?" she asks.

"I…I don't know. But it doesn't matter now."

"I think he loves you."

A snort escapes before I can stop it.

"I know you don't believe me," Lily continues, "but I've never seen Wes like this. Talking about a woman nonstop. Wanting to show her the family cabin. Thinking about something beyond his next drunken festivities with the guys."

"Hasn't he ever had a girlfriend before?" I ask.

"Sure. He's had lots of women."

"I'm not sure that makes me feel better."

"Hear me out," Lily continues. "He's had sex with people. But I'm not sure he's ever had anything deeper than that. He's always convinced that women are just out for his money. And until you, I think he's been right."

"It's a nice story to tell, Lily, but I don't think there's anything special about our relationship."

"There's something special about *you*, Phoebe."

I glance over at her.

She must see the disbelief on my face.

"You don't have to believe me," she says, "but I'm telling you, Wes is different with you. Maybe because the women in our family aren't strong like you."

"I'm not strong."

"You are, Phoebe. You knew what you wanted out of your career. You were willing to leave behind everything you knew to move to a small town in Arkansas, just to take the next step."

"Lots of people move for jobs."

She continues like she didn't hear me. "You were willing to have an anonymous hook-up with a guy you'd never see again."

"You know about that too?" I make a disgusted sound.

"You came into this town, charmed the pants off Tony Capsigo, made friends with all the other school board members, built trust in the parents, and formed a connection with the kids. You're kicking ass and taking names."

"Uh…thanks?"

"My mom never does anything except lunch at the country club and donate Dad's money to whatever her cause of the week is."

"Yeah, but you went to college," I say.

"Just to get out of Jasper for a while. But here I am, back home and ready to work as a preschool teacher. A fucking demure preschool teacher."

"I don't think demure preschool teachers use the word fuck all that often," I say with a laugh.

"Whatever. It's the least badass job there is. And I'm okay with that. Because I don't have your confidence, your strength to do big things. You're changing this town, Phoebe. You're changing my brother. And I don't want that to end."

I don't know what to say. So I focus on the road in front of me and drive us back to Jasper in silence.

———

KYRA IS in Europe with Liam.

Me: Hey. Can I use the sauna?
Kyra: Duh! Let yourself in.

I have a key to Kyra's place. I do not have a key to Wes's place.

That's the thought on my mind as I let myself into Kyra's and head down to the basement. I set up the daiquiri machine and get it running before changing into my spa robe and turning on the sauna.

Ten minutes later, I'm naked, sitting in the warmth of the sauna, and drinking a mega-size daiquiri.

What am I going to do?

I'm not sure if Wes will ever figure out how I need him to support me, but not fight my battles for me.

How am I going to keep working with him?

Because I do love my job. And this town. I'm not going to leave over a boy.

I let out a deep sigh, lay back on the bench, and close my eyes.

16

WES

I COULDN'T TAKE ANOTHER NIGHT IN THAT CABIN. I DROVE BACK TO JASPER IN the middle of the night last night, and now I'm up and out early this morning.

I know that several of the art kids are spending their spring break painting. I decide to swing by the Old Mill and see who's there.

"Hey, Mr. H!" one of the kids calls out to me. "Didn't expect to see you here."

"Just thought I'd come by and see how everything is going."

"Real good, Mr. H. We've got final outlining to do on a couple murals still, but otherwise, we're ready for the grand opening next week."

"Is everything done over at It's a Grind?"

"No, that's actually the last one we started, so it's got more work to be done still."

"Good, I want to change it."

"You want to change it? Now? How are we going to get it done before Monday?"

I clap him on the back.

"I'm gonna work around the clock to do it. If you or anyone else wants to help me, cool, but if not, that's okay too. This is a personal one for me."

"Ok, Mr. H. You know we'll do anything we can to help you. I'll see who's around."

I head over to the coffee shop and sit on the ground in the alley, staring up at the mostly-completed mural on its outside wall.

Kyra said we could paint whatever we wanted, so I had just given the kids a color palette of blues and browns, and then left the details up to them. They came up with an abstract design. Lots of chunks of color. I can work with this.

I pull out my sketchbook and get to work.

I don't know how much time passes, but when I hear the telltale sounds of teenagers approaching, I realize I'm hungry. And looking down, I decide my sketch is finished.

Standing up, I stretch and prepare myself mentally for the next couple of days. I've got to buy more supplies, direct a couple kids in how they can help, and paint my heart out.

Because this painting is my heart. For the world to see.

When I turn around a minute later, I'm shocked. It's not just a couple of high school kids here to help me. It's every art student I have this year, whether they're on the mural project or not. It's some of my former students. It's Tess and Daphne, Declan and Brandon, Pete, Carter, and of course Lily. There's Stella from the Diner. And even Tony Capsigo. Seems like half of Jasper Mill has shown up to help.

"Wow." It's all I can say.

"Yes, well, we hear you fucked up," Tony announces. I hear a few snickers and gasps from the rest of the crowd.

"Yes sir, I'd say I did."

"We're here to help you fix it. Where do we start?"

I love life in a small town.

Sure, it can be annoying when everyone knows your business.

Sometimes I get bored of the same two bars and three restaurants.

But you can't top these people.

If you need help, there they are.

No one struggles on their own.

"Thank y'all so much." I mean it down to the tips of my toes.

I turn my sketchbook around to show him.

"Here's what we're going to do."

17

PHOEBE

It's Monday, and the grand opening of the public art installation. I'm going to have to face Wes again.

But this is part of the principal life in a small town. I will show up and applaud my students. It doesn't matter what personal drama I may have going on. It's all about the kids.

When I arrive at the Old Mill promptly at 9:55, it's a madhouse. I can't find a place to park, until Sheriff Rudolph shows up and directs me to a spot up front.

"Thanks, Sheriff," I say as I get out of my car. "Did the whole town show up or something?"

"Pretty much."

"I didn't realize there was so much excitement about the murals. Wes will be so happy."

The Sheriff just nods and smiles.

I make my way to the front of the audience, and take a seat in the chair that has been reserved for me. "Principal Phoebe Wren Kestrel."

I wonder who spilled the beans on my middle name?

Wes's grandpa, Westley III, steps up to the podium and begins in his speech. In true Jasper Mill form, there's a lot of pomp and circumstance. The local Girl Scout troop leads a flag ceremony. The students who painted the murals stand to be recognized, one by one. There's even a ribbon cutting.

Through it all, my eyes keep returning to Wes.

He's sitting up there on the dais, looking so handsome. So proud of his kids, of his work. It hurts my heart to know that I won't get to know him on a personal level any longer.

He just can't be part of my life. He doesn't understand that I need to earn folks' respect for myself. That my career cannot be tied up in the machinations of a boyfriend. I don't want to succeed just because of the Jasper name.

I clap in all the appropriate places during the ceremony.

I even catch Wes looking over at me a couple of times.

And I'm relieved when it finally—*finally*—comes to an end.

I'm trying to duck back to my car when a student catches me.

"Ms. Kestrel! Over here!"

Reluctantly, I head over to the group of assembled high-school students.

"Great job, everyone," I offer in my excited-principal voice.

Wes is standing at the back of the group.

"Ms. Kestrel, will you please come with us for the walking tour?" another student asks.

"Oh, I don't know about that. I have a lot of work to get back to."

"Please," another chimes in, and soon it's a pleading chorus.

I catch Wes' eye, but he just shrugs.

I really can't say no.

"Ok, I'd love to." A little cheer erupts. Boy, they sure do seem happy to see me.

Kyra appears at my left elbow.

"Hey bestie!"

"Hi Kyra, how was Europe?"

"Fabulous. I'll tell you all about it later. Let's check out the murals."

Kyra and I follow along while the kids give the Town Council and the School Board a guided tour of the mural walk.

When we approach It's a Grind—the last stop on the tour—I see that someone has set out cake and punch. Sweet. At least I get a sugar fix out of it.

"Ms. Kestrel, why don't you come up here so you can see better?" one of the students calls to me from the front of the group.

"I'm fine, don't worry."

"Oh come on, Phoebe, let's go!" Kyra grabs my arm and drags me up to the front of the crowd.

I look up and I gasp.

Before me is the most stunning mural. A beachfront seascape in an abstract blocky kind of way. Waves are crashing onto a sandy beach. There's a seagrass-covered dune in the foreground on the left edge of the wall.

Before I realize what I'm doing, my feet are moving me closer to the mural. My fingers reach out to touch the brushstrokes. And as I look closer, I see there's a snake slithering through the grass.

My eyes trace the lines of the painting up higher on the wall, to the expanse of blue sky. I find three different birds, each magnificent in its own right, swooping through the sky. As I track down the right side of the wall, I notice a small ship in the water, the perspective making it appear tiny in a vast ocean. I move that direction and bring my nose nearly up to the wall. I can see a Jolly Roger—the pirate flag—flying on the ship's mast.

"Uh, you don't need to smell it, Phoebs." Wes's voice from right behind me causes me to jump and turn around.

"What is this?"

"It's a mural."

"But it's us. The snake, the birds, the pirate ship."

"Yes, I know. I designed it."

"Oh Wes, it's beautiful." Tears are forming in the corners of my eyes.

"I'm glad you like it," he says softly. "Our first meeting may not have been the stuff that romance books are made of, but it was special to me."

"And me." I look up into his eyes and he leans his head down towards mine.

The kiss is gentle, but deliberate. Tender and passionate. Taking up more time than we have, but not long enough.

Tony Capsigo clears his throat next to me.

Oops. I forgot we were standing in a crowd of people.

"If I may interrupt, Ms. Kestrel."

"Yes, of course," I say, smoothing down my hair and shirt.

"Would you kindly take a look at the signatures on the mural as well?"

I turn back to the wall.

What I originally thought were swirls of sand at the bottom are signatures. Hundreds of them. Maybe a thousand.

Oh no.

I quickly swing around to face Wes. "You didn't make them—

"No, no, my dear," Tony interrupts.

"We heard what a dumbass Wes had been," Kyra says as Lily waves at me from across the crowd.

"And we wanted you to know," Tony continues, "that we all love you. Not because of Wes. Maybe in spite of Wes. But you have made it. You've established yourself in our community and in our hearts. And now we just want to see you happy."

Wes circles his arms around my waist and I turn to face him.

"Can we try again? Will you forgive me?"

"Yes, Westley, of course I will." He kisses me on the nose.

"Good. Because I've been doing some thinking these last few days, and I…"

Another kiss on the nose.

"…I think I love you."

He looks into my eyes, searching.

A small smile breaks across my face and I stand on my tiptoes to place a soft kiss on his lips this time.

"Oh Wes, I love you too."

And the crowd goes wild.

We rush through the cake and punch. I think the whole crowd has figured out that Wes and I are desperate to be alone together.

But for just a few minutes longer, we're surrounded by the love and support of a whole town.

Me and my love. Together.

ABOUT RINA DAYNE

RINA DAYNE

Rina Dayne is a storyteller. Whether she's working as a romance author, as a lawyer, or as a teacher, she shares stories of the human experience.

As a romance author, Rina writes steamy contemporary romances. There will be profanity and open-door sex scenes, and her content is recommended for an over-18 audience not easily offended.

Rina lives in Colorado with her husband, two kids, dog, and three cats. The humans and dog love to camp, often spending 30+ nights per year in their camper. It's a busy, challenging, rewarding, amazing life.

You can follow her at:
Website & Newsletter Sign up:
https://rinadayne.com/newsletter

facebook.com/rinadaynebooks

instagram.com/rinadayne

ONCE UPON THAT TIME I STARTED A MAJOR SH*T SHOW

MARIA ANN GERMAIN

Maria Ann Green
ONCE UPON THAT TIME I STARTED A MAJOR SH*T SHOW
Copyright © 2022 Maria Ann Germain

Editing by Carly Green & Jackie Hritz

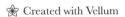 Created with Vellum

Romance Subgenre: Contemporary Romance
Trope: Enemies to Lovers

Graphic sexual depictions, open door sex and explicit language

Blurb:

Charli had a terrible relationship that nearly damaged her
beyond trying again. But then walks in Quinn. He's confident, hot as hell, but
the problem is he's a heartbreaker. Or that's what she's heard from most people
who know him. They're maid of honor and best man in their friends' wedding,
though. So they're stuck together a lot. And sparks start to fly, even as Charli
continues to put her foot into her mouth over and over. And over.

The Wait Really Is Over

So, we finally invite you to the wedding of **Thomas Michael Stone** and **Claire Elizabeth Shaw** on Friday the Thirty-first of October at Three in the afternoon at Salem Woods Park, 152406 Willow Street. There will be cocktails to follow from Four until Five at Salem Library, 333 Berry Lane. Dinner and Dancing will then begin at Five in the evening and continue until the last ghost returns to the grave – or at Midnight, whichever comes first.

Costumes aren't mandatory, but they are absolutely welcome and will be judged, with prizes.

Are You In?

M_____
(write your name(s) above, preferably somewhat legibly)

{ } GLADLY ATTENDING
    { } regretfully declining
    { } resentfully attending
    { } enthusiastically declining
    { } declining to respond, but will show up at the last minute anyway

---

ClaireBear is getting married girls!
That's right, MARRIED.

So we're celebrating the end of her life...the single life, that is. And Since she and Tom are having a Halloween Wedding, we figured the carnival was a good choice for her last hoorah. Prepare to get your drink on, and leave your inhibitions at home! There will be embarrassing adornments added to whatever dress you don.

RSVP to Charli at 651-555-5309 by the 10th if you plan to join in the celebration. Then meet us at the entrance to the fairgrounds in St. Paul, MN at 7pm on Friday, October 17th.

"Hi, you've reached Emma. If your number isn't already saved in my phone, you better leave me a message after the obnoxious beep, or I'll never call you back. And if this is you, Mom, I still won't call you back... Kidding!"
Beep
"Hello Emma, this is your *mother*. JUST KIDDING. I miiiiiiiiiss you. And I wish you were here partying with us, Em! Not that I don't wish you were so pregnant you're ready to pop. Because believe me, I cannot wait to smooch that little munchkin's face after you push her out. Smooch, and pinch, and smell. Oh my god she's going to have that sweet newborn smell! Wait...why did I call? OH! I wish you were here having margaritas with us. They're so good, and they have all these Halloween-themed flavors. Like Claire's is called Werewolf Wildberry. Mine's something about zombies...or is it cannibals? It's not the same here without you. Shut up, Clementine, I'm not saying it isn't still fun. Anyway, tell Colton to give that tummy extra kisses for me. See you next week, babes."

"Hi, you've reached Emma. If your number isn't already saved in my phone, you better leave me a message after the obnoxious beep, or I'll never call you back. And if this is you, Mom, I still won't call you back... Kidding!"
Beep
"Oh God. You're probably sleeping. Shit. Just delete these voicemails tomorrow morning before listening. Love you. Swear I do. Don't' hate me."

Journal of Charli Ann Tartt

HOLY FUCKING SHIT, I'm hung so over.

I haven't felt this bad in a long, long time. I'm too old to feel this awful. Though, to be fair, if I wanted to prevent the vom-fest in my bathroom this morning, I probably shouldn't have drank like I was still in college.

Probably.

Since it's been A WHILE since college. Thirty is balls sometimes. I mean when I was twenty I could drink all night, then rally by eight to get to class, and not puke once. I'd even manage to eat greasy food for lunch and keep my skin looking glorious and my waist the same.

Now…

Now I feel like my bones are mad at me, and my joints are on fire, and my eyes won't un-puff for a week. Plus the rat's nest that is my hair may never be the same again. We're talking permanent damage. I look like a raccoon who slept on the wrong side of the dumpster last night.

Well, anyway. Almost all the girls were there last night to celebrate Claire, our sweet bride-to-be. The carnival-fair, whatever you want to call it, was such a perfect idea (thanks Clementine) and Claire's already texted me saying it was better than she even imagined.

And that's all that matters, really. Right?

RIGHT?

That's what I keep telling myself.

I know Claire had the night of her life. Though, that may have a little something to do with the fact that we were celebrating her and the upcoming nuptials to her soulmate. But who knows. Clementine was woo-hoo-ing all night long, Hailey, Mackenzie, and Sadie all have boyfriends they were sexting the entire time. And Beatrix is just Beatrix. She made out with some guy on the merry-go-round and he's already pledged his undying love to her.

Not shocked.

But my night. Ugh.

Emma wasn't there for one. And she would have stopped me from making such a fool of myself, I just know it. But instead, nope. I want to crawl into a hole for a while. Maybe disappear for a bit. Or rewind a few hours and un-do my stupidity last night.

Sigh.

The night started out fantastic.

Everyone was sporting their penis themed accessories and jewelry – which was absolutely mandatory. Claire had her sash and blinking tiara. There was so much delicious fair food to choose from, which was my favorite part. The drinks were delicious and people kept buying them for us since we were such an obvious party. And there were so many fun costumes, even though Halloween is still two weeks away.

It all started out so great.

We had shots. Too many shots.

And Cheering on Claire to make toasts and order the weirdest sounding drinks. It was just the perfect girls night.

For a while.

No one cared when they spilled on their white dresses – another must of the night – or when strangers bumped into us. The nigh was cool, but not too cold which you never know into October here. We even got Sadie to go on some rides. The tamer ones, and nothing that spins, but still.

After I called Emma – which I'm still embarrassed about by the way even though I don't remember what I said exactly, I just know I went on and on – we finished those drinks and walked toward the Ferris Wheel. Not that we went quickly. We stopped for mini donuts and for the bathroom three separate times, plus we took at least two wrong turns. The fair grounds are way bigger than I ever remember. And of course we were talking the whole time.

Claire asked, "Has anyone heard if Emma and Colton have second guessed their decision to come yet? I felt like a jerk even inviting them after I found out we'd picked her due date, but she's insistent on coming."

"Fiesty mama," Mackenzie shouted then, and we all chimed in. Because she is.

"Why Salem?" Hailey asked next.

"Why not?" Claire answered in the least helpful answer ever.

But I've heard the real reason. She and Tom went there on their first vacation. They'd been arguing about where to go on a road trip and neither would give in. So they made it a game, they are just the cutest jerks ever making it seem like perfect love is out there. They put up a map and played darts. Salem won, and she'd loved it ever since. They've gone several times, and I swear if he let her they'd pick up and move there.

So, in a sense, her answer still fits.

Why the hell not?

"When is everyone leaving?" Sadie asked, always the one to worry about doing things right.

"I'll be there for eight days I think," I chimed in.

"Me too," said Clementine, since we're flying together and picked rooms with an adjoining door, right next to each other.

"Just a week for me," Hailey said, and Mackenzie nodded along.

Beatrix was in her own little world, staring at her phone as we walked, so who knows when she'll show up in Massachusetts. Maybe in time for the wedding, maybe not. And just when I thought she wasn't listening she opened her pouty lips and contributed. "Who has dibs on which groomsman?" she changed the subject so fast I swear I missed a step and almost fell, dizzy.

Or maybe that was the shots kicking in. Either way.

"So I assume you'll be making out with the best man, Charli, since you're the M.O.H." And I swear when Claire said that I choked on the two mini doughnuts I'd just shoved into my mouth. Yes, two. I get hungry when I drink, okay.

"Excuse me?" I choked out, truly almost choking.

"I mean, that just makes sense," Clementine added. Such a traitor.

"It's practically tradition," Beatrix said, like it was just fact.

"Rude. You are just rude," I said, pointing at each of them, one after the other. "From the little I've heard, not much of it is any good," I added.

"I haven't heard anything," Hailey piped up.

And then I got to hear more than I had yet.

Claire started, and almost couldn't stop once she was on a roll. "Tom's known him since they were little. I swear Quinn would have proposed if I hadn't met Tom when I did," Claire joked, slapping her own leg as she laughed so loud. IT was sort of adorable, because it wasn't funny at all. Which is what made me laugh.

"I heard he's a huge player," someone suggested, but I didn't see who. She said exactly what I was thinking anyway.

"I wouldn't say that exactly…" Claire tried. But it wasn't very convincing.

"So he is," Clementine interrupted. Love her.

"I mean. He's hot, that's not in question," Claire says. "Not that any of you will ever tell Tom that I admitted that. Swear on your lives." At this point we all crossed our hearts because Claire may be sweet and adorable, but she can be scary too. And she had that crazy look in her eyes at that particular moment. We all swore. "It's never been a new girl every night or anything, but I wouldn't say he's had the best luck with love." Claire added.

But then there was little else she would say on the subject of his dating history, which obviously only means bad news. She was being kind, I'm sure of it. Quinn probably shouldn't be trusted by any woman, if I'm reading the signs.

"He is hot, though," Beatrix offered up once we finally could see the Ferris Wheel.

"How do you know?" I asked, with too much high-pitched squeak in my voice.

"I've met him, duh. He was at that bowling night. And even pictures don't do him justice," she said.

My mouth may have hung open for a moment longer than I'd like to admit, but I made no response. Hailey and Mackenzie did, but I honestly don't remember what they said after that. It was something about the other grooms-men, and who was walking down the aisle with who.

My focus was on the couple we passed in line for a twisty, upside down ride.

They were arguing in the line, making everyone around them incredibly uncomfortable. That was obvious to me and Clementine who I made eyes at as we passed, but the screaming two seemed oblivious to it. She was calling him selfish, and he reiterated several times how unkind she is. It was embarrassing me just to listen to it. The names they called each other. It seemed like they were so wrong for each other, and everyone but them could see it.

It gave me a sinking feeling in my chest, that fell all the way down to my stomach.

I remember that feeling. Like I was trying to mold myself into the right shape, that if I could just do what I should, if I could turn myself into the puzzle piece that fit, then everything would just work out. Ray was such a mistake. And even if we never argued like that in public, the look on the woman's face reflected how I used to feel all the time.

"I'm so fucking glad I'm single," I mumbled. Only Clementine and Claire heard me, but they both nodded. Claire put her arm around me and Clementine blew me a kiss. Because they wanted him gone too. They knew I'm a better version of myself now, more real.

Then we were in the Ferris Wheel line suddenly.

And that's where the night took a turn for the worse for me. That's the part I'd erase if I could.

If only.

2

Girl Gang Group Thread

Me: OMG this group of bros behind me is the worst.

Clementine: Are you really texting us from feet away?

Me: Well, I don't want them to hear me, do I? No. No, I do not.

Claire: What are they talking about?

Beatrix: Any hot?

Me: I have no idea what they look like. I see backs of heads at the moment.
But they have the maturity of a bunch of five-year-olds. They're actually telling
poop jokes.

Sadie: That's disgusting.

Me: Don't worry. I've got this

Mackenzie: Got what? What are you going to…hahahahah omg

Claire: What? I couldn't hear! What did she say to them?

Me: It's possible that I told them to use their time in a more productive
venture, and find some holes in bathroom stalls.

Sadie: omg, you did not. Tell me you didn't.

Me: It didn't even phase them. Unfortunately. Only one turned around and
blew a kiss at me while winking.

Claire: I heard their cackling laughter after. I'd offer to switch with you, but it
is my night. So…sorry.

Me: Gee, thanks.

Clementine: We're getting on. I just counted. Girl, you're not going to like it.

Me: What do you mean??
Me: CLEMENTINE?
Me: OMG

Hailey: Is riding by yourself really that bad? I mean we can go again, and I'll ride with you.
Me: That is so not the problem.
Claire: ???
Me: The first one. He jumped into my bucket with me.
Clementine: WHAT

Me: Turn around and see for yourself.
Me: I'm dead serious.
Me: And he keeps talking to me.

Hailey: How did that even happen?

Me: I have no idea. I sat down and then all of a sudden there was the strong smell of cologne, mixed with tequila, and a big, warm arm around my shoulders.
Me: I think maybe he paid the ride attendant.

Beatrix: Conspiracy theory much?
Me: He's already told me I'm rude for texting so much while he's trying to get to know me.
Mackenzie: Classic
Me: Like I asked him in here with me. I so did not. He practically pushed me into the bucket and then jumped in after me.
Clementine: Exaggerator
Claire: What is he saying to you? I can hear you both, but I can't get a good angle to see you.
Hailey: Me Either.
Claire: HELLO?
Beatrix: Did he murder you already?
Claire: OMG don't even say that Bea.
Beatrix: We would have heard the scream.
Clementine: Or seen her body fall.
Claire: CHARLI ANN TEXT US BACK IF YOU ARE OKAY RIGHT NOW!
Me: He didn't murder me. God. What is this a True Crime podcast? He's just talking my ear the fuck off.
Mackenzie: Good thing we're still going.

Claire: Was that you Charli? Why are you laughing so loud? You sound like…
Me: Don't you dare.
Sadie: Like who?
Me: No one.
Clementine: Her mother
Me: Bitches
Beatrix: Good think you dyed your hair after you dumped that asshole. Otherwise…
Me: CUT. OFF. Every one of you.
Claire: Nooooo I didn't say it. You can't ice me out. It is my bachelorette party. I demand that you tell me what the hot guy who beat away all the competition and paid to sit with you.

Me: Now who's exaggerating?
Me: This guy is so annoying.
Me: I swear he thinks he's God's gift to women

Hailey: What's he saying?

Me: He's bragging about his job.
Me: And flirting uncontrollably.
Me: Even after I told him I'm not interested.
Me: At all.
Me: Even if he is hot, which I did not share. But still not interested.

Mackenzie: Ouch
Sadie: Harsh

Me: What? It's the truth.
Me: But he did say the same thing.

Claire: Maybe because he really likes you?

Me: He just met me. He's can't even know enough about me to like me.
ME: He did also tell me I need to get a filter. That mine might be missing. And I might have just gone off on him.

Clementine: Oh shit.
Hailey: ? Why did you go off on him for that?
Beatrix: Forgive her, Char, for she is but blissful.
Hailey: Forgive me because I'm happy?

Me: That's it, Hail.
Me: And I went off because…
Me: because…

Clementine: Because she lost her filter after Ray. Rightfully so.
Hailey: Ray?
Me: My ex.
Claire: He tried to suppress everything that made Charli, Charli. Until she was nothing but filter.
Clementine: She was this quiet little thing. So not like the amazing Charli we have with us tonight.
Beatrix: It was shitty.

Me: Awwww you guys.
Me: Also I think I may have told that story before, because I pretty much told him the exact same thing. Almost word-for-word.

Claire: AND WHAT DID HE SAY?
Clementine: Yeah, stop burying the lead.
Me: He tried to change the subject real quick. Asked me why I'm here tonight
Claire: And you said to celebrate your very bestest friend and how perfectly amazing she is, right?
Me: Not exactly…
Clementine: Hahahahahahahahahaha
Claire: shut up
Me: I told the truth.

Beatrix: Wait, Char, I think…
Beatrix: I'm not sure. But just wait.

Me: Wait what?
Mackenzie: drama, drama, drama
Hailey: Oh, like you don't want to know
Mackenzie: Oh hell yes, of course I do. I didn't talk shit about drama, just pointed it out.
Hailey: You would
Me: uhhhh
Beatrix: Tell me you waited to spout off, like I said to.
Me: I definitely did not.
Beatrix: omg lolololol
Clementine: Serves you right.

Me: This is
Me: Embarrassing

Claire: If you three don't explain to me exactly what is going on I am going to explode, I swear

Me: You don't want to know.
Me: I promise.

Claire: YES I do.

Me: No, you really do not.
Me: Of all people, you really don't want to know what I just did. Swear.

Claire: OMG
Claire: Tell me now.

Me: Bea?
Clementine: You're on your own babe.
Me: Fuck.
Claire: Spill
Me: Okay, well just remember how much you love me, okay?

Claire: I will not.
Claire: Spill

Me: Well I started with what we're here for, like you said.
Clementine: To celebrate the great and powerful, Claire.

Me: Exactly.
Me: But of course, since it's me, I didn't stop there.

Beatrix: I'm going to pee my pants, I cannot stop laughing.
Claire: STOP INTERRUPTING HER
Me: So, I kept going about how I'm the M.O.H. and how I'm dreading meeting Tom's best man because all I've heard about him is bad, like narcist, avoid-at-all-costs bad...except for how lickable he is. Like all over. Face. Body. LICK-ABLE.
Sadie: OMG
Hailey: You did not!
Me: I did. I said lickable. Several times. And I even licked my lips. I also said exactly how shitty said best man is, as in why – that he's such a player, and so

189

not someone I want to spend ANY of my time with. Even if it was solely to lick him since he's supposedly hot af.

Claire: Okay. while that's a lot of information for a stranger…

Me: Shut up. I know.

I blame the booze

Claire: I don't get why that's so embarrassing.

Mackenzie: Claire, watch them get off the ride.

Me: Yeah…

Claire: OHMYGOD

Beatrix: peeing

Clementine: Can't breathe

Me: I hate you all.

Sadie: Ummm your mouth is still hanging open.

Claire: You are my hero, Charli. I cannot CANNOT believe you said all of that to Quinn's face without recognizing him. Complaining about him TO HIM.

Beatrix: I'm dead. From laughter.

Hailey: Whoops

Me: h a t e

Mackenzie: What a cute way to meet someone LOL

Me: Or a disaster

Me: I'm the disaster

Claire: An adorable one

Me: the loveable shit show. The clueless, but kind of cute disaster. No meet cutes for me. Just straight up disasters. Just great. That's how I want to be known. Fuuuuuuck

3

Victoria Rose Shaw requests the honor of your presence for the wedding shower of Claire Ann Shaw and Thomas Michael Stone on Thursday the Twenty-Third of October. Cocktails and hors-d'œuvres will begin promptly at seven in the evening, at Chez Fig. This is a black-tie event.

Please RSVP to Victoria by Monday, as those who do not will not be on the list and thus not allowed entrance.

———

FROM: "CLAIRE" CLAIREBEARBABE@XMAIL.COM
  To: "Charli" misscharles@xmail.com, "Clementine" GinAndJ@email.-com, "Hailey" HaileysCommet@mymail.com, "Mackenzie" QuarterPound-Zie@mymail.com, "Sadie" SadieSaid@mymail.com, "Beatrix" TrixForTat@xmail.com, "Emma" AlmostSpelledTheSameWayBackwards@email.com
  Subject: Let's Shower Together

OKAY LADIES,

I have the run down for tonight. Victoria is…prim is probably the nicest way to say it. Charli may use another adjective. But in the end, she's family, and she's throwing this shower especially for those who can't make the trip to

Salem. So please, please don't piss her off. If you do I'll have to hear about it for years from my aunt Rose. And that's just not gonna happen. Alright?!

Okay, with that out of the way – she wanted me to let the wedding party know about the itinerary. I can hear your eye rolls, so shush. Whatever you do, DO NOT show up late. I will never hear the end of it. So Beatrix that means you need to leave AN HOUR earlier than you originally planned, okay? Seriously. She plans drinks and food to start right on time, and for toasts to start half an hour later. Then she wants me to open gifts at nine. She even has a few games planned before that, at eight. I hope they aren't too embarrassing. But you all have to participate no matter how cringey they are. She means well.

And lastly, when I say this I mean it. No drama. That will send Victoria into a full-on spiral. Don't call her Vicky – that means you Clementine. Don't leave early (that's almost as bad as showing up late). And get along with each other. That means the whole wedding party...Charli. I'm sorry but I have to reiterate it. Play nice or you will regret it.

Okay? Okay!

Xoxo

Claire

FROM: "CHARLI" misscharles@xmail.com

To: "Claire" ClaireBearBabe@xmail.com, "Clementine" GinAndJ@email.com, "Hailey" HaileysCommet@mymail.com, "Mackenzie" QuarterPoundZie@mymail.com, "Sadie" SadieSaid@mymail.com, "Beatrix" TrixForTat@xmail.com, "Emma" AlmostSpelledTheSameWayBackwards@email.com

Subject: RE: Let's Shower Together

I FEEL ATTACKED.

FROM: "CLEMENTINE" GinAndJ@email.com,

To: "Charli" misscharles@xmail.com, "Claire" ClaireBearBabe@xmail.com, "Hailey" HaileysCommet@mymail.com, "Mackenzie" QuarterPoundZie@mymail.com, "Sadie" SadieSaid@mymail.com, "Beatrix" TrixForTat@xmail.com, "Emma" AlmostSpelledTheSameWayBackwards@email.com

Subject: RE:RE: Let's Shower Together

ME TOO.

. . .

From: "Beatrix" TrixForTat@xmail.com

To: "Clementine" GinAndJ@email.com, "Charli" misscharles@xmail.com, "Claire" ClaireBearBabe@xmail.com, "Hailey" HaileysCommet@mymail.com, "Mackenzie" QuarterPoundZie@mymail.com, "Sadie" SadieSaid@mymail.com, "Emma" AlmostSpelledTheSameWayBackwards@email.com

Subject: RE:RE:RE: Let's Shower Together

Rude. But fair.

———

Journal of Charli Ann Tartt

I'm a coward. I can admit that.

Because I'm currently hiding in the back of the coat closet at the fanciest restaurant in Minneapolis avoiding a boy. That's right. I'm avoiding Quinn behind a bunch of autumn and winter coats, with my pretty dress on the dirty carpet, and my face full of appetizers.

I snatched an entire tray from a poor wait staff as I power walked in here. I swear he looked like he was about to faint when I grabbed it. He stuttered after me as I rushed toward a dead end.

And now here I am, on the floor, regressed to elementary school. Writing in what is essentially my diary – food in one hand pen in the other – not even worried about anyone seeing me because obviously if I can't see them, they can't see me.

Wow. I'm pathetic.

But still, knowing that even, I can't make myself stand up and walk out of here.

First, that's embarrassing. So I'll be living her for the rest of my life. That's a given.

But second, because I'm an idiot who deserves the time out I'm in.

I guess that needs context. So here goes. I'm hiding, of all places, in the closet at Chez Fig, where reservations go weeks out, for Claire and Tom's wedding shower. The fancy one her cousin planned. Which I did not dress fancy enough for. I swear Vicky – oh, sorry, *Queen Victoria* – is out of her damn mind wearing a straight up cocktail dress fit for the Met Gala. She bought Claire this dress that guaranteed was more than her wedding dress, which is the most gorgeous wedding dress I've ever seen. Anyway, it's super fancy and my online lace keyhole dress seemed really great until I got here, and now I feel like a toddler wearing my mom's clothes while trying to fit in.

So, I was already negative points when I walked in. At least I was on time, otherwise I might have been turned away I swear.

But as soon as I walked in Quinn smirked at me with those lips. Those gorgeous pouty lips that no man should be in charge of let alone wearing. And his lashes. God, they're so dark and thick. Why does the universe only give those kinds of lashes to cocky men? It isn't fair. And in his tightly tailored suit – black on black on black is far too alluring on him – his muscles are highlighted without being obnoxious. I think I'd have liked it better if he was more obnoxious tonight.

He smirked and I went running. That's right. Went, not came. I ran the opposite direction. I'm still mortified about our meeting. Just because I'm a more blunt me these days doesn't mean that I feel good about absolutely hating on the man to his face. Especially before meeting him once.

I was doing my best to follow the rules, though. I was avoiding him so that there wasn't another run in. I didn't want to upset The Queen by arguing at her fancy-pants party, which I was explicitly reminded not to do. Twice.

I swear I tried. I really did.

But Quinn just…he just pushes my buttons like no one else ever has. Not even Ray. Not even Claire or Emma or Clementine and collectively those three have known me longer than I've been alive. He knows how to get under my skin with just a glance, a lifting of his eyebrows and a twitch to his lips like he knows what I'm thinking and is already over it.

Just writing this has my blood boiling, because it's the truth.

He's such a jerk.

Only the problem is that so am I apparently.

When I thought I was avoiding him pretty damn well I lost sight of the jackass, and then next thing I knew I could hear him talking. Talking about *me*. I heard him say something about the Ferris wheel and I immediately knew. Beatrix and Clementine were trying to distract me, but they ended up giving up and listening in with me instead, I think. I'm not completely positive. I think I've blacked some of it out already out of sheer mortification.

I heard words like, "Rude," and "regret," and "impossible." And I just saw red. I mean, how dare he? I was giving him space so that we didn't have to be anywhere near each other and he goes out of his way to talk shit about me?

I wasn't about to lie down and let him walk all over me. I'm done with allowing that.

Only…ugh these bacon wrapped whatevers are delicious. And the kabobs too.

They're almost helping me to forget how I turned around and started raising my voice. Calling him out on his bullshit.

His bullshit that I had so wrong.

Because it wasn't about me at all.

He was telling Emma and Colton, I mean of all people, about our meeting. How dare he? She already knew what happened. Though, I guess I'd missed her ask for his side. If I'd known she had started the conversation maybe my voice wouldn't have gotten so loud, and so shrill, as I confronted him. Ugh.

I went on and on about how he should really stop talking about people behind their backs. And how that night he could have interrupted me at any point – which he tried to do right then and I stopped him with a single finger and a look filled with poison – to tell me who he was instead of letting me go on and on and on. And on.

His smile grew as I let my cheeks flush and my head weave back and forth with my sure attitude.

Then Emma finally told me to shut up. That's when I knew I'd put my foot in my mouth again. Red bottomed stiletto and all. Because Emma doesn't yell at me, ever. And she made sure to shut me up real quick.

Colton tried to cover up his giggles while Emma calmly explained to me how Quinn had been telling her just how rude *HE* had been to me. How he'd thought it was hilarious that I told him just how I felt, and how he had respected me for it. That my brazen honesty was refreshing, and he thought it might have been impossible to be more impressed by our meeting. How when he told the other groomsmen about our meeting he defended me, saying I wasn't wrong about most of my assessment of him anyway.

The more she said the lower my eyes focused until my toes peeking through the front of my heels were all I could see. I don't think I've ever been so warm with embarrassment. Not even when my skirt was tucked into my thong in the tenth grade for fifteen minutes of walking through the packed hallway.

As someone who's been underestimated a lot in the last few years, I never meant to do that to another.

But then he went and made it worse.

He said my name with the sweetest smile on his face. I could hear it before I looked up, and then sure enough it was even more gorgeous than I'd thought. He winked at me and added, "Don't worry, I don't change my mind easily."

And that's when I ran.

He made me realize just how shitty I've been to him, and I couldn't face it in the next breath. I mean that filter that used to be too much could have come back for like just a second, just a fraction of it.

So I'm stuffing my face, eating my feelings like I've never done before. I mean I've done it plenty before, I'm just doing it better right now with fancier food and more of it.

Shit I see some shoes coming my way that I wish I didn't recognize.

Crap.

———

Charli and Clem's message thread

Clementine: Where the hell are you?
Me: Moved from the closet to the bathroom. I live here now.
Clementine: WAIT
Me: I don't wanna talk about it.
Clementine: Too damn bad.
Me: Quinn
Clementine: I need more than that
Me: I yelled at him.
Clementine: Yes, I heard that part. Everyone heard, actually.
Me: great
Clementine: But then you just disappeared. Claire asked about you. I think she thinks you left. You better get out here.
Me: I don't want to.
Clementine: omg stop
Me: shut up.
Clementine: hiding in the bathroom where everyone will assume you have diarrhea sure as hell isn't going to make you feel any less embarrassed, I hope you know that.
Me: I reiterate.
Me: shut
Me: and up.
Clementine: Fiiiiiiine
Me: no, don't
Clementine: Make up your damn mind.
Me: He tried to come apologize to me.
Clementine: in the bathroom?!
Me: No, when I was still in the closet.
Clementine: Wait…you were in the closet?!
Me: Ugh
Me: yeah.
Me: You're going to have to keep up if you want to hear the whole story before I die from shame.
Clementine: Fine. You were in the closet and he apologized. So is everything better then?
Me: Turns out, not really
Clementine: Okay…well
Me: I started talking at the same time. I didn't KNOW that he was coming to

apologize. I thought he was coming to rub it in that I made an ass of myself again.

Clementine: did he give you any reason to believe that's why he was coming over.

Me: Stop using your logic on me. Okay? It's not helpful.

Clementine: lol

Clementine: continue

Me: Anyway, if you must know

Clementine: I must

Me: I figured.

Me: Anyway, we both started talking at the same time, and as he said he was sorry I opened my full mouth and spit out crumbs all over myself to try and say something at the same time.

Clementine: Feeling less and less sorry for you by the second

Me: I know. I don't know why I'm acting this way. What is wrong with me?

Clementine: A lot.

Clementine: But we can get into that later.

Clementine: What did you say as you also sprayed it?

Me: fuck my life

Clementine: I know that's not what you said.

Me: I felt so stupid sitting there on the floor, with a mouth full of appetizers that should have been circling the party, and two empty champagne glasses next to me. And you know how I get when I'm embarrassed.

Clementine: Super defensive.

Me: YUP

Clementine: You're painting a beautiful picture – without actually telling me what you said.

Me: Yeah, I thought maybe you'd drop it.

Clementine: Really?

Me: No. But I hoped anyway.

Me: He held out his hand as he said he was sorry, and asked if we could start over. But it was at the exact same time that I said I was sad for Tom that he had to have Quinn for a best friend.

Clementine: You didn't.

Me: I wish I hadn't.

———

Girl Gang Group Thread

Clementine: Soooooooorry

Me: why?

Claire: Get your ass out here now.

Me: oh
Me: I can't.

Claire: WHY?

Me: Didn't Cleme tell you? I have horrible diarrhea. It's basically deadly. So I might die. From diarrhea. So you can't actually be mad at me. Then it would be the last feelings you had about me before my horrible death. And you'd feel so guilty afterward. I'm trying to save you from that remorse.
Me: That work?

Claire: What do you think?
Me: Not even close

Claire: Bingo
Claire: You know what? Nevermind

Me: Wait. I don't like the sound of that.
Claire: too bad
Clementine: What are you doing?
Me: She sent Emma in after me.
Claire: Can't say no to the pregnant woman.
Me: rude.
Emma: But true!
Me: Can't I just go home now PLEASE?
Claire: Honestly? Can't you just suck it up.
Clementine: This night is about Claire.

Me: Okay.
Me: Okay, you're right. I'm sorry ClaireBear. I really am.

Claire: Thank you.

———

Charli and Clem's message thread

Me: I feel like an ass.
Clementine: Well, that's because you kind of have been.
Me: You should have seen the way his face fell when I was such a bitch. He

tried to hide it, but I think I really hurt his feelings. I wasn't even sure he *had* feelings until I hurt them. I'm worse than an ass. I'm the hairs on a large, flappy butthole. That's how bad I am. If one could die of shame, I'm pretty sure I'd be dead. Died. Dead, dead, dead.

Clementine: Well, now that you've recovered from your deadly diarrhea, which *unfortunately* didn't kill you anymore than your embarrassment and disgusting imagery...maybe you can apologize to him?

Me: Yeah. Maybe I can.

Clementine: Shots first.

Me: Deal

———

Claire and Tom's Bridal Shower
Private Event Group
Discussion Page

POSTED BY **VICTORIA ROSE SHAW**: 10/23 6:55PM

"Hiiiiiii everyone! Victoria here. Feel free to post and share all of your photos in this private space from what will surely be an amazing party tonight. I've invited everyone who RSVPed, of course. This way Claire and Tom can save the memories forever. See you in a few. Kisses!"

POSTED BY **JOSHUA JAMES**: 10/23 8:16PM

"SHOTS FOR THE BRIDAL PARTY!! WOOOOOO!!"

Posted by **Bea Trix**: 10/23 8:17PM

"You're buying next round, **Josh**y ;)"

POSTED BY **EMMA ELIZABETH**: 10/23 8:20PM

"**Quinn Page**, always the life of the party"

POSTED BY **CLEMENTINE CROSS**: 10/23 8:25PM

"**Charli Ann** Really?!

POSTED BY **VICTORIA ROSE SHAW**: 10/23 8:26PM

"I really hoped this would just be a place to hold memories and photos from tonight..."

. . .

POSTED BY **THOMAS STONE**: 10/23 8:35PM
"Anyone know where **Quinn Page** went? He's not answering my texts."
Posted by **Charli Ann:** 10/23 8:36PM
"He left."
Posted by **Thomas Stone**: 10/23 8:38PM
"**Charli Ann** Really?!"
Posted by **Charli Ann:** 10/23 8:38PM
"really"
Posted by **Quinn Page**: 10/23 8:45PM
"Sorry **Thomas Stone** but something came up…"
Posted by **Charli Ann**: 10/23 8:46PM
"gross. However, not shocking."

POSTED BY **THOMAS STONE**: 10/23 8:47PM
"**Quinn Page** is dead to me. Who wants to be my best man instead?"
Posted by **Emma Elizabeth**: 10/23 8:46PM
"I volunteer as tribute."
Posted by **Thomas Stone**: 10/23 8:47PM
"done and done. You'll look a hell of a lot better anyway!"

POSTED BY **TRENT QUARTZ**: 10/23 8:56PM
"Actually, I accidentally got a video of **Quinn Page** leaving with **Theresa
Lyn** when I was trying to take that group picture with the fancy drinks."
Posted by **Thomas Stone**: 10/23 8:57PM
"**Charli Ann** omg is that really what I think he said to you as he left?!"
Posted by **Charli Ann**: 10/23 8:58PM
"Yup"
Posted by **Quinn Page**: 10/23 9:01PM
"I mean, was I wrong? Did you leave with anyone **Charli Ann**?
Or did your attitude get in the way, like I thought?"
Posted by **Charli Ann:** 10/23 9:02PM
"Actually, you said my attitude would stop me from
getting laid tonight, not from leaving with anyone.
At least be accurate if you're going to insist on being
a dick.
Posted by **Quinn Page**: 10/23 11:18PM
"fair enough"

4

Saturday October 25th

Saturday October 25th

Book (Raptured in Rome by KT Rattner)	$12.99
Journal (pink glitter cover, spiral bound)	$19.99
Pen	$2.99 X3
	$8.97
Bottle water	3.99 X4
	$15.96
Beef Jerky	$8.99
Gum	$4.99
Mints	$5.99
Sub Total:	$77.88
Tax	$5.84
Total	$83.72

Charlie Ann Tartt

Signature...

```
BestAirs Airlines                              Name
Name: Tart/Charlotte              800B5S
          Tart/Charlotte


From: Minneapolis/St. Paul, MN         To: Salem, MS Date
25 OCT


Date         Departs              Flight  Class  Seat   Gate
25 OCT       11:30 AM             BA 013 V      26F    H5

                    ZONE 5
                                   Boarding 10:40 AM
                                   Time
```

CHARLI'S TUNE OUT THE TURBULENCE PLAYLIST:

If You Wanna Be My Lover by Spice Girls
Hit Me Baby One More Time by Britney Spears
The Show Must Go On by Queen
I Write Sins Not Tragedies by Panic! At the Disco
Don't Stop Believing by Journey
Geek Gets the Girl by All American Hi-FI
Hey There Delilah by Plain White T's
Let It Go by Idina Menzel
Dirty Pop by N'Sync
I Want It That Way by Backstreet Boys
Faith by George Michael
Lips Of An Angel by Hinder
River Lea by Adel
Million Reasons by Lady Gaga
All the Single Ladies by Beyoncé
Over by Tove Lo
Sober by Demi Levato
Wrecking Ball by Miley Cyrus
Take Me To Church by Hozier

```
BestAirs Airlines                          Name
Name: Page/Quinn              8OOB5S        Page/Quinn

From: Minneapolis/St. Paul, MN    To: Salem, MS Date 25 OCT

Date          Departs          Flight  Class  Seat  Gate
25 OCT        11:30 AM         BA 013 V       26E   H5

                    ZONE 5

                         Boarding 10:40 AM
                         Time
```

Journal of Charli Ann Tartt

IN CASE YOU EVER WONDERED, I panic far more places than just at the disco. I wish I could just take advice from the band. But no. I panic everywhere. Like now for instance, right the heck now.

Because of the however many flights there are from Minneapolis to Salem half of the wedding party ended on the exact same one on the exact same day. And guess who lucky old Charli is seated directly next to.

That's right.

Quinn.

Who by the way keeps trying to peek over to see what I'm writing in my journal. Doesn't matter that I've told him about ten times already how rude that is. Ten times and we aren't even in the air yet.

Ugh, hold on.

Okay I told him what I'd do if he tried to look one more time, and it's the first time I've seen genuine fright cross his beautiful eyes. Wait, I didn't mean beautiful. Why did I write beautiful? Why do I *keep* writing it?

His plain eyes. Boring, depthless eyes. Ones that you definitely can't get lost into. Just regular old Quinn eyeballs. The eyeballs I threatened to puck from his skull with a melon baller if he keeps snooping on what I'm writing. Granted I don't have that particular utensil with me, but I have several to choose from back at home. And I'm sure they have plenty in Salem.

He asked why I was so nervous if I wasn't writing about him. That's when he got the death glare. It wasn't as effective as my threat to take away his sight – in fact he might have laughed and tried to cover it up with a cough – but he tore those ~~gorgeous~~ eyes away from me anyway.

Anyway…what the hell was I talking about before this derailment?

Oh. Yeah.

Quinn. Both my main point and my derailment are both about him. It feels like everything is about him lately. And it's making me crazy. Or a little crazier than I already was.

I'm panicking like I'm at the disco.

But instead I'm panicking on a plane. On a plane with Quinn, near me. Actually he's so close I can smell whatever his cologne is that's spicy and sweet and making my mouth water. No wait. I didn't write that. Damn it.

I don't mean to panic like this. I don't want to be so awkward around him.

But I am. I just am, and it might be time to admit that to myself finally.

Quinn makes me panic.

I'm not even sure I can pinpoint why.

I mean of course he's hot. But I knew that even before I met him.

He thinks he's way funnier than he is. But he is smooth as hell, a charmer. Maybe that's part of what has me squirming and saying the exact wrong thing every time I'm around him. Maybe.

Or maybe it's my lady bits, namely the vagina because the heart and the head are nowhere to be seen anymore, short-circuiting every time I encounter Quinn and his perfect facial features and his muscles and…

Oh god.

I wish I'd have known he was on this damn flight, that he was going to be sitting right next to me. Because if I'm really honest with myself there are two parts to the equation that has the sum of my freaking the fuck out. One: I still feel like a complete asshole about how I've treated him. Unintentionally once, and then unfairly the next. I'm embarrassed of myself and my shitty behavior. I'm really a nice person.

I swear.

Or I used to be.

And it bothers me that he hasn't had the chance to see me at my best. Only my worst and somehow below what I thought was my worst. I've always cared more about how others feel, and how to be kind and supportive. But Quinn has seen NONE of that. In fact he's seen the exact opposite and it's really getting to me.

So back to the math. One is my embarrassment.

And two…two I think I'd rather like him than hate him.

And that scares the shit out of me.

Oh

My

God.

I tried to apologize just now. I started with "I'm so…" and then my mouth just stop working. Actually my brain did too. Nothing came out. I wanted to say I'm annoyed with myself, not him. And that I'm sorry to being rude, for jumping to conclusions, but nothing came out. I didn't know how to put any of that.

And he's still staring at me as I write this. After I said nothing. And he said nothing, letting me just sit there in my big pile of uncomfortableness. I was the rude one, the one who needed to apologize, but now with his freaking smirky grin, the smug look in his eye, maybe it's easier to just stay mad. Keep being rude and continue hating him like I'd been doing before. It worked better than whatever this weird silence is.

It feels weird. Like there's something bit between us, even though his arm is only a centimeter away from mine. I could just push my elbow over and touch him. I could…

He just signed.

It may have been the most annoying sound in the world. But also the most adorable. I don't know. Maybe I have a brain tumor that's making me such a lunatic.

Well if he's annoyed, then I can keep being annoyed too.

We can both just stick to hating each other.

I'm going to follow his lead and put my headphones back on to listen to the playlist I made for the plane. He's probably listening to some smarty-pants podcase about how to stay charming and handsome and…yikes. *Charli, get a grip*.

Music it is.

––––

Quinn's passing the time up in the air playlist

Fat bottom girls by Queen
True by Spandau Ballet
Every Rose Has It's Thorn by Poison
Pour Some Sugar On Me by artist
Faith by George Michael
Don't Stop Believin' by Journey
Man In the Mirror by Michael Jackson
Bohemian Rhapsody by Queen
Rocket Man by Elton John
Dance With Somebody by Whitney Huston
Butterfly by Mariah Carey
Toxic by Britney Spears
Here I Go Again by White Snake
Danger Zone by Kenny Loggins

Bed Of Roses by Bon Jovi
We're Not Gonna Take It by Twisted Sister
Carry On Wayward Son by Kansas

—————

Journal of Charli Ann Tartt

OKAY, I have about a three minutes, maybe five if there's a line for the bathroom – I haven't dared to turn around and check.

Because then he'd know I'm thinking about him.

Which at this point how can I not be?

His arms keep bumping into mine, and his smell is all over this damn plane. He keeps making obnoxious laughing noises that he tries to cover as coughs. I can't tell if he's been looking at my phone screen to see what songs I'm listening to, or if he's listening to some tragic comedy album.

Or, who knows, maybe he's the actual devil and he's listening to the stock market crash or scenes of couples braking up. What the hell do I know.

Okay.

That was harsh.

But I swear I can just feel that he has it out for me somehow. I can sense it coming of him in waves that keep bumping into me along with his pointy elbows. And his devious plotting smells a lot like aftershave and cinnamon toothpaste.

Oh, there he is, coming back from the bathroom.

That was a quick minute.

I swear to god, every flight attendant on this aircraft has been obsessed with him since he sauntered onto the plane. And the one with the giant tits and legs that go on forever just abandoned her drink cart to intercept him. I shit you not. There's a poor grandma looking around like she imagined the pretzels she was supposed to be handed. All because of Quinn.

Granted, the flight attendant is gorgeous. There's no questioning that. But I still want to punch her in the throat. It's not my fault. I bet half of the women on this plane feel the same way about her sweet smile and perfect fucking hair. Seriously, how doesn't she have a single fly away. And no dark circles – isn't flying exhausting for her? It is for me.

Right about now I'm wishing I wasn't wearing my sweatpants that are ten years old – okay maybe a lot older than that – with my high school logo down the sides, and the tshirt I inherited when my dad died with the bleach stains and a hole in the armpit. My hair in a messy bun, and now that I think about it I never did wash my face before bed last night so I probably have racoon rings from my day and a half old mascara.

No wonder she's so appealing to Quinn. She actually looks human, a gorgeous one at that, compared to the sack of potatoes he's been sitting to all flight. OH MY GOD. I brushed my teeth this morning right?! I mean, it was a 6am flight, so I've basically been awake since the middle of the night.

Breath test into my hand isn't promising.

The goddess with flight-wings pinned to her bouncing chest (it really is perfect, and as much as I want to hate her, I kind of love her a little bit too, just light the entire male population in this air craft) just put her hand on Quinn's arm like she's marking him. She might as well lift a leg and pee on his shoes.

That's not the worst part through. He turned toward her, showing off those perfectly white teeth, only one a little crooked to prove he's indeed human, and his dimples. Those dark brown eyes are probably mesmerizing her as much as they were for me...scratch that. They're just mesmerizing her. Now he's running his hand through that black hair of his and mussing it up just enough to show her what he looks like after sex. Probably. Oh, and she definitely didn't miss the flex in his arm as he did it either. I'd put all the money I don't have on that bet. His tattoos look extra sexy when his muscles bulge like that.

Okay.

My mind has run away.

I know it now.

The proof is in all the scratched-out words above here. I'm going to claim temporary insanity right now. Quinn makes me absolutely crazy, and it's his fault if I do anything else stupid from this point forward.

He's SOMEHOW torn himself away from the literal goddess of Midwest Magic Air, stupid name I know, and is sitting next to me again. I think he must have put more of his cologne on too because it's fogging up my brain, like toxins. It's making me even more annoyed.

I will not say something stupid.

I will not do something stupid.

I will be a normal person, civil. I'll just ignore him.

...

WELP, that didn't work.

My annoyance, however irrational, just couldn't be contained any longer. And I picked a fight, like I knew I shouldn't. Like he doesn't really even deserve. Probably. But, of course, because I just poked the bear. Antagonism is apparently one of my superpowers.

I actually asked him if he was chatting with the flight attendant to schedule a time they'd meet in the bathroom.

What is wrong with me?!

He's currently staring at me.

Probably thinking that I've been the one to screw up every time we've managed to be near each other. That I've been the queen bitch, and he's just tried to survive being anywhere in my vicinity.

Oh god. He's opening his mouth to say something back.

I don't want to know.

I cant take it.

5

Saturday October 25th

Saturday October 25th		
Bloody Mary mixed drink	$12.99 X2	
	$25.98	
Margarita mixed drink	$12.99 X2	
	$25.98	
Vodka mini bottle	$8.99 X2	
	$17.98	
Rum mini bottle	$8.99 X2	
	$17.98	
Sub Total:	$87.92	
Tax	$6.59	
Total	$94.51	

Quinn Page
Signature..

Journal of Charli Ann Tartt

SO I OPENED MY MOUTH AT THE SAME TIME, TRYING TO CUT QUINN OFF. I WAS way too afraid of whatever he'd been planning to say. Surely something I deserved. Something cutting, but true.

But we were both interrupted.

Thank hell.

Because the busty, beautiful flight attendant came over in the nick of time. She brought with her a Bloody Marry and a Margarita. The Margarita for me, with a splash of grenadine. I have no idea how he knows one of my favorite drinks, but suddenly there it was being handed to me as Quinn's grin widened and softened at the same time, his eyes actually hopeful instead of watchful or guarded.

It shut me the hell up, other than to sputter out a few thank yous.

He wasn't flirting with her.

AGAIN I assumed wrong. Making an ass out of myself. Which turns out is a fantastic talent of mine. Maybe a superpower you could say. That plus picking fights, which we already established meer minutes ago. Neither of which paint me in the best light.

I swear I used to be a kinder person. I used to care more about others than myself, at all times. And true, I'm glad I found my voice; it's better that I'm able to stand up for myself. But I'm thinking I need a bit more of a balance. The old Charli meets the new one.

Charli 3.0. That's my goal on this vacation.

So, again Quinn has proven me wrong. He paid attention to my likes and bought something to help me calm the fuck down. It's a stretch, but at this second he may be my hero. Because the tequila in this margarita is really helping.

"I needed this," I said to him after taking a break from scribbling in here. She just smiled, knowing better than to agree.

"Cheers to the beginning of a beautiful friendship," Quinn said. I sucked in a breath. So silly. Maybe it's the altitude or the pressure or something making me emotional but I almost cried. A line from one of my favorite movies.

Then something in my gut sank – it's still sinking just a little bit – and I'm not exactly sure why. He's being sweet, and saying all the right things. Doing the right things. But I somehow I'm still left wanting a little more.

Just a little. But even that feels selfish.

"Cheers," I was able to squeak out before coming back to write more. I want to remember this, and after not eating anything today – no breakfast other than a Venti latte, and my muscle relaxer before the flight so I don't clench the whole time and flare my TMJ – it's making for quite the effective drinks.

Oh, yeah. I forgot to mention. We're on our seconds, both of us. And the flight attendant, who's actually incredibly nice it turns out and I feel back for thinking rude names and attributed for her, brought over some free snacks – the good ones that you normally pay for – after Quinn ordered two little shooter bottles for each of us.

It's getting a tiny bit hard to write.

But Quinn's really getting a lot more charming the more he drinks.

Or maybe it's the more I drink.

Both?

I don't know, but this flight seems a lot less stressful right now.

I'm going to be brave.

Hold on…

————

THE FLIGHT IS HALF OVER, but I've had the best hour with Quinn after I put my journal away.

I sucked it up and asked him if we could just start over.

He laughed at me, thinking I was joking. So I have him the glare, and he sucked in his giggles, trying to look serious. "Why, yes madam, I would love to make your acquaintance," he said in his most dashing voice.

Then he had me laughing right back. The loud and embarrassing kind, but real.

"I'm Charli Tartt, friend of the bride. And you are?" I asked in some weird imitation of of an English accent. I went for posh, but I'm pretty sure it was far more cockney than anything else. Maybe a bit Irish too. I'm not totally sure.

As dorky as it was, it felt exactly what we needed.

"A fresh start," Quinn echoed the thoughts I'd had rushing through my head at the time. Like he was reading it.

We've been amicably talking since.

And drinking.

And talking.

And drinking.

I now know that he has FIVE, that's right f I v e brothers. He's heard all about my relationship with Ray and why I've been so obnoxious as of late. He actually high fived me after that, approving of my sass even toward him.

And now, I'm about to sneak off to the bathroom. Because of course I spilled all over myself while gesturing during a stupid story. It wasn't even a funny story. Thought Quinn did laugh. But now my nipples are quite obvious in this ratty t-shirt and bralette only, So I'll be right back…and probably write more later!

————

Midwest Magic Air wifi
Payment received from Charlotte Tartt $15.99
Thank you for your continued patronage with us!

―――

SEARCHING FOR...QUINN PAGE
   818 found

Quinn Page (Minneapolis)
   FaceBook profile set to private
   Request friend? **[NO]**

SEARCHING FOR...QUINN PAGE
   @QuinnForTheWin (Quinn Quinn)
   Instagram profile set to private
   Request friend? **[NO]**

SEARCHING FOR...QUINN PAGE
   222 found
   Quinn Page (@QuinnForTheWin)
   SnapChat profile set to private
   Request friend? **[NO]**

―――

Girl Gang Group Thread

Me: What's the deal with Quinn and his social media lock down?
Claire: Why are you asing?
Me: Can't a girl be curious
Beatrix: you know what that leads to
Sadie: Really good sex?!
Beatrix: I mean the cat and all that
Sadie: Exactly. Pussy.
Me: OH MY GOD
Claire: how long have you been cyber stalking him?

Me: Just the last few minutes. He's totally private.
Me: do you think that's because he's such a player?
Me: because he has so many girlfriends that he want's to make sure they never accidentally find each other on there?

Hailey: Or MAYBE, just maybe, he's a normal guy who doesn't want creepy strangers all up in his business.
Hailey: Like you. I mean you.

Me: I want to argue.
Clementine: But you have no legs to stand on

Me: Possibly
Me: So dish. What's his deal?

Emma: maybe you request to add him and find out!
Me: whoa, whoa, whoa. That escalated quickly.
Mackenzie: Chicken
Me: Why do you all insist on picking on me so much lately?
Claire: That's just how you're taking it. Because you're being a baby. We're not doing anything different than you have or would for us.
Me: shut up.
Beatrix: I mean what could it hurt now? You've already made a total fool of yourself, just request him and see.
Me: Tell me more about him ClaireBear. Pleeeeeeease!
Claire: Well his middle name is Payton.
Me: is that supposed to be helpful?
Claire: He loves soccer and musicals.
Me: I feel like you're making this up to get me to embarrass myself again.
Claire: Tom's known him for ever and ever
Me: I give up. You all can suck it.
Sadie: Or you can invite him to the bathroom to join you and *YOU* can suck it…
Beatrix: I second.
Emma: Votes?
Claire: Yay
Hailey: Yay
Clementine: Yay
Mackenzie: oh hell yes
Emma: And it's unanimous. Sorry kid, no RBG to dissent this time.
Me: Worst friends ever
Claire: You're lucky to be stuck with us
Me: I know

———

QUINN PAGE (MINNEAPOLIS)

FaceBook profile set to private
Request friend? **[Yes]**
Status: **Accepted**

@**QuinnForTheWin** (Quinn Quinn)
Request friend? **[Yes]**
Status: **Accepted**

Quinn Page (@**QuinnForTheWin**)
SnapChat profile set to private
Request friend? **[Yes]**
Status: **Accepted**

———

Journal of Charli Ann Tartt

I just got back from the bathroom.

He probably thinks I have IBS or something with how often I've found myself hiding in there around him.

The general feeling is even better than when I got up and hid to stalk him and gather intel from the girls. If that's possible. Maybe it's the fourth drink kicking in for each of us. Or maybe it's something else.

But after he accepted my requests within seconds I haven't been able to get the smile off my face. He noticed when I sat down, even.

"You know, your eyes really light up when you're hiding something behind that beautiful smile," Quinn said. And now I'm going to hold onto that feeling and go back to chatting. Putting this thing away. The girls said we were laughing too loud, but I don't even care. It's nice not to feel like an ass around him for once.

6

Me: Worst friends ever…
Status: unsent

─────

"THIS IS YOUR CAPTAIN SPEAKING. Sorry about that turbulence folks. It's going to be quite a bumpy ride for the next half hour or so. Keep your seatbelts fastened, tightly, then have another drink, and we'll be out of it before you know it."

CLICK AS RADIO TURNS OFF

─────

Girl Gang Group Thread

Clementine: You okay?
Me: fuck
Claire: how you doing Charli?

Me: I'm about to die in a metal tube that's full of flammable people. That's how I'm doing. I'm okay. It's okay. Everything's okay.
Beatrix: sounds about right
Me: I don't even have the energy to yell at you Bea. That's how scare I am.
Emma: sounds about right

Me: My fingers are going numb from holding onto my phone too tight. May need new cell after this.
Me: IF WE DON'T DIE THAT IS

Hailey: Take a deep breath
Mackenzie: In…
Sadie: and out…
Me: I think I forgot how to breathe.
Beatrix: they literally just spelled it out
Clementine: Her brain has short-circuited

Me: I think you're right.
Me: I've broken.

Claire: I texted Quinn, so he knows what's going on.
Me: Oh great, so he can know what a fucking freak I am.
Clementine: I'm pretty sure he already knows based on how much you're sweating. I can see it from here.
Me: You're half the plane away.
Claire: Precisely

––––––––

Journal of Charli Ann Tartt

WELP.

The plane didn't crash.

Despite my absolute certainty that it would.

I've never been tossed around so much midflight before. It was truly terrifying. After the girls text Quinn he promptly slid my phone out of my sweaty hand and shoved it into his pocket before slipping his hand into mine. He let me squeeze as hard as I wanted. I swear I saw him wince at least three times. I used to play softball, basketball, and have three brothers, so my grip is no joke.

But he smiled the while time, and talked to me nonstop. To keep me distracted.

At first I didn't realize what he was doing when he started asking me questions. First it was get to know you stuff. Have I always lived in Minneapolis, or at least Minnesota? How many siblings do I have? Are my parents still together?

Yes.

Four.

No.

But then, eventually, he moved into more fun stuff, and he started sharing too, when the ride got really bumpy and I started to feel a little light headed. Only after we landed safely did he tell me that I'd first lost all color in my face, and then began to turn green. He thought for sure he's end up having to throw his shirt away after the flight.

I learned that his last relationship, serious one, was two years ago. And that contrary to what I've been lead to believe that she broke up with him. After he found her in bed with his cousin. He'd tried to make it work for all of a day before he came home from work to a half empty apartment. She didn't even have the decency to face him. She just scurried away like the cockroach she is.

He also shared that despite what everyone thinks, he hasn't been on a date in months, and the only one night stands he's ever had were in college.

His favorite color is green.

He likes, barf, football and hockey.

And despite my disbelief his actually does like musicals. Well, not musicals plural, but one musical. Rocky Horror Picture Show. And he's been to a midnight showing in costume at least three times.

He prefers a stiff drink over a beer.

And he'd rather stay in and watch a movie than go out dancing.

Wow…

I didn't really realize until sitting here to write it all down how much he shared, how well he distracted from my sheer terror, from the immovable fact of my pending death that I'd been sure of.

But he did.

He got me to talk, and then when that wasn't enough *he* started talking. He asked me all kinds of questions about myself, and my life. My favorite color, song, app to scroll while on the toilet. And then when he ran out of questions he started telling me all about himself.

It was surprisingly perfect.

Actually, he made me feel safe. Protected. And even if something went wrong, I knew at least I wouldn't be in it alone. I can't think of a single man who's taken the time to do that for me. Certainly not Ray.

My girlfriends, of course.

But a man…other than my dad before he died?

Never.

When we landed a tingle started to come back in my hands. But it wasn't

217

from like the pins and needles I normally feel after it goes numb. It was something more, something electric. More like a spark.

And when he pulled his hand out of mine, somewhat reluctantly I'm pretty sure, it's almost as if that spark arced across the air between our fingers for just a moment. Like electricity.

I know I sound crazy, okay.

I know.

And it may be partially due to the couple Xanax Claire let me have when the seatbelt sign turned back off and she could come over. *Maybe.*

But still.

I felt something.

I just wish I knew if he did too.

And that wish…yeah, it might be wishful thinking. Because even after the turbulence landed he didn't stop holding my hand until it was time to stand up and grab our bags. And he got my bag down for me, then carried it through the airport, in the cab ride, and all the way until we parted ways in the hall of the hotel. We're on the same floor, but opposite sides of the hall and at least teen sets of doors between us.

I'll admit it here, and to NO ONE out loud. Ever.

But I think…I might…nope, not yet.

I will share that I turned around in the hallway to see if he did too. I so wish he had. I felt stupid as the only one. But I'm also pretty sure it won't be my only smitten, longing glance of this trip.

I wish I could say I was that strong. Be stoic and keep my feelings out of my mind and off my face.

But let's face it. I'm so not subtle, or stoic.

Clumsy? For sure. Emotional? Without a doubt.

But I'm so not that graceful chick who men run after because they aren't sure if they have a chance. The one everyone wants, but no one knows who she wants back. I'll never be Holly standing in front of the big glass window.

Though, to be honest her life wasn't all that glamorous, like she wanted it to be. So maybe I do fit that archetype better than I originally thought when I started the comparison.

ANYWAY, that's beside the point.

He didn't turn to look at me longingly, or at all.

So, maybe he'll go back to being an ass now that our lives aren't in danger, and he's sure I'll be able to care for myself like a grown ass adult, not on emergency anxiety medications.

Not ideal, but I think I'll understand if he doesn't.

Or I'll try anyway.

And I'll pay one of the girls to hold me accountable to being civil and as normal as I can be either way.

7

Claire and Tom's Wedding Rehearsal and After Party
Private Event Group
Invitation and Discussion Page

POSTED BY **CHARLI ANN**: 10/30 2:00PM
If you forget to come to the rehearsal you will straight up be denied access into the afterparty. And you don't want to miss the afterparty. Because the number one rule will be NO talking about the afterparty. So, show up, practice the walk, and then you can get your booze on after, I promise.

P.S. WOOHOO **Clair**Bear and **Thomas** are fiiiiiiiiiiiiinally doing this damn thing!

POSTED BY **BEA TRIX**: 10/30 3:00pm
"I'm pretty sure we all know how to walk."
Posted by **Emma Elizabeth**: 10/30 3:01pm
"Keep telling yourself that **Bea**."
Posted by **Bea Trix** 10/30 3:05pm
"You should talk, Mrs. Waddle."
Posted by **Emma Elizabeth** on 10/30 3:06pm
"I may waddle, but I can still kick your ass."
Posted by **Bea Trix** 10/30 a 3:15pm

"that was ONE TIME."
Posted by **Charli Ann** 10/30 3:15 pm
"One glorious, unforgettable time."

POSTED BY **THOMAS STONE**: 10/30 6:00 pm
"And with that over, it's FINALLY time for toasts all about me."

POSTED BY **JOSHUA JAMES**: 10/30 6:01 pm
"I swear to god, if that officiant is drunk again tomorrow I'm gonna punch him in the throat and
lead the ceremony myself
Posted by **Quin Page:** 10/30 6:05 pm
"How do you know those hiccups weren't from something else. Maybe he has a medical
condition that gives him red cheeks, hiccups, and a little balance trouble. You don't
know his life."
Posted by **Thomas Stone** 10/30 6:10 pm
"Besides, **Josh**. You'd make the next worst choice. I'd prefer his hiccups
over whatever the hell you'd end up saying.
Posted by **Colton Ryan**: 10/30 6:11 pm
"Good call Tommy Boy."

POSTED BY **EMMA ELIZABETH**: 10/30 6:12 pm
"If you boys don't shut up and start drinking I'll never get to live vicariously through you all."

———

Day before the wedding

AKA the one where we rehearse and then get rewarded for rehearsing

SHOW UP to the park for ceremony practice 4:00pm
Girls tell Beatrix she's supposed to be there at 3:00pm
Head to the library for receiving line practice 5:00pm
Move the party to dinner at Sweet Bee's 6:00pm
Drinks, drinks, and more drinks after dinner

. . .

ANYONE WHO SHOWS up to the wedding hungover tomorrow better watch out for Claire's pissed off side. Only a select few of you have seen it. And, I promise, you do not want to see her when she's pissed.

Just kidding, as long as you don't puke during the ceremony or on her dress it's fine. Probably.

———

MENU for Claire and Tom's Rehearsal Dinner at Sweet Bee's

DINNER OPTIONS
    *pick one…duh
    Prime Rib with garlic mashed potatoes and grilled asparagus
    Shrimp scampi linguini with roasted peppers and capers (Dairy Free option)
    Vegetable pasta *(Vegan option)*
    Chicken nuggets and tots *(option for the grown ass men who still eat like toddlers)*

SIDE OPTIONS
    *pick up to two
    Raspberry vinaigrette and feta salad
    Seasonal fruit plate
    Grilled vegetable plate *(with dressing on the side)*
    Waffle Fries with seasoned sour cream

DESSERT OPTIONS
    Chocolate lava brownie *(with caramel and fudge layers under a dark chocolate ganache sprinkled with cookie crumbles)*
    Nothing else, that's the only dessert anyone should ever need in their life, and everyone gets one. If you don't finish yours fast enough, it will be made available for the bride.

DRINK OPTIONS
    Mimosas *(bottomless and covered)*
    Sangria *(bottomless and covered)*
    Keg *(first come first serve)*
    *Any other drink will be cash bar

———

Girl Gang Group Thread

Claire: You guys
Me: I knoooooow
Claire: YOU GUYS
Beatrix: This is better than the last time I had sex. Than the last ten times.
Me: And that's really saying something

Beatrix: shut up
Beatrix: But also, true

Emma: best dessert ever
Me: I want to bathe in it
Clementine: count me in
Me: it's a date
Claire: who wants to start bets on the first guy to tap out?
Me: eh
Clair: EXCUSE ME?!
Me: I mean, forgive me, oh glorious bride. We are here to serve you.
Claire: damn straight
Hailey: I vote for Josh, he's a lightweight
Mackenzie: I say anyone but Quinn. He'll stay as long as Charli does
Me: ignoring you
Sadie: I put $100 in that they leave together by the end of the night

Me: OMG
Me: stop
ME: I hate you guys

Claire: except me

Me: obvi.
Me: But only because I'm not allowed to.

Emma: and also, me
Me: who can hate the golden one about to bring new life into the world
Emma: exactly
Me: so, it's decided then?
Emma: ??
Me: I'll be godmother
Beatrix: WRONG

Emma: We will be doing contests for that.
Emma: feats of strength
Emma: riddles

Me: you're ridiculous
Claire: also, Sadie, I'll take you on that bet. But I say it'll happen within the hour
Me: oh, stuff it, bridezilla

––––––

Drink tab

Claire: Champagne x4, Water x5
Tom: Water x3
Charli: Bottomless Mimosas x2
Quinn: Bottomless Sangrias x4
Emma: Shirley Temple, Water x5
Colton: Water with lemon x3
Sadie: Bottomless Sangrias x 3
Josh: Keg beer x8
Beatrix: Bottomless Sangrias x6
Paul: Keg beer x5
Hailey: Bottomless Mimosas x4
Travis: Keg beer x9
Mackenzie: Bottomless Mimosas x3, Bottomless Sangrias x3
Daniel: Keg beer x7

––––––

Girl Gang Group Thread

Sadie: so, turns out I win
Me: that's bullshit
Claire: is not
Me: YES IT IS

Beatrix: techjlkjk
Beatrix: technically
Beatrix: she was still right

Me: but we ALL left together.

Me: I didn't leave WITH Quinn, the entire bridal party walked out of the restaurant TOGETHER and over to a bar down the street to karaoke

Claire: Yeah, but still
Beatrix: technically
Me: shut it with that technically Bea
Beatrix: never
Me: I DID NOT LEAVE WITH QUINN
Emma: get me up to date

Me: no, prego.
Me: You lost out on knowing anything when you went home with your husband to get a good night's sleep.
Me: like an adult
Me: Unless you are on my side, in which case yes I will be the godmother to your sweet unborn baby

Claire: We all got drunk, someone shouted karaoke, and now that's what we're doing
Emma: Well then clearly Sadie won
Me: traitor
Mackenzie: Seconded
Beatrix: I vote yes too. If she buys me a drink.
Sadie: Fine
Hailey: Yay!
Me: I hate you all
Claire: And yet you're stuck with us forever

Emma: Amen sista'
Emma: Also, goodnight

Hailey: P.S. it defeats the point of trying to argue with us when you start singing a love song WITH HIM
Me: It's not a love song

———

Karaoke Playlist

WRITE your name(s)the song you want to belt out

Claire and Tom: Power of Love

Claire and the bridesmaids: Spice Up Your Life
Tom and Quinn: Danger Zone
Just the bridesmaids: All the Single Ladies
The groomsmen: Who Let the Dogs Out
Josh: Ice Ice Baby
Beatrix and Clementine: Barbie Girl
Sadie and Mackenzie and Hailey: I Will Always Love You
Claire: Another One Bites the Dust
The groomsmen: Smooth Criminal
The groomsmen: 1999
Quinn: Lips Of an Angel
Quinn and Charli: Time of My Life

———

Journal of Charli Ann Tartt

It's possible I'm writing this while still at the bar.

While the groomsmen are jamming out to Michael Jackson.

Wow Paul really cannot dance. And Dan somehow did the splits – and so did his pants unfortunately. Well, fortunately for us because his boxers have little cacti holding rubber duckies on them. He blushed for all of a moment and then moved into the next lyric. True Rockstar.

Wait.

None of that is the point of why I broke out my notebook to jot down a quick note to myself about what's going on. Because yes, I'm still documenting this whole trip. Maybe someday Claire will want to read some of this.

Or maybe not, I don't know lol.

ANYWAY.

Oh shit… Quinn is getting up to sing alone. Hold on

———

Journal of Charli Ann Tartt

Okay.

Wow.

Just *wow*.

I'm back in my room and trying to collect my thoughts.

It's not the easiest thing I've ever done. My heart is going all kinds of crazy. It's fluttering I think, like a moth stuck in a cage. Which makes me think of the evil death-face month from Silence of the Lambs and that's really NOT what I want to be thinking about at the moment. I mean, it is a fantastic movie. But so not relevant this second.

Omg.

What is wrong with me?

Scratch that, there are too many things to list.

Anyway, Quinn sang my favorite song.

Right after the entire set of groomsmen finished their first song – the own I was writing during – they did a second number, which was just as embarrassingly amazing. But then the rest of them left the stage and Quinn stayed up there.

He stared directly at me, and the girls started whistling and cheering.

I may have temporarily died before reentering my body, which was then about a hundred degrees hotter than before. But the smile just would not leave my face. I tried to rub it away, literally, but it kept peeking through my fingers.

He sang my angsty-college-self's favorite song, which to be totally honest really is a terrible song for anything romantic. Unless one knows it's my favorite. And he does. He remembered.

Quinn sang with bravado too. Like all hooded eyes and gravelly voice. I felt like the only other person in the room for most of the time. Except when Claire was elbowing me in my side and Beatrix and Cleme were whooping. But still. Even they couldn't ruin it.

It felt like lightning, or an electrical current, was bouncing on top of my skin. I had goosebumps all over, and I felt lightheaded. The booze was wearing off already, it had been for a while, but there was a flash of...I don't even know. It was like my head was two sizes bigger than normal and floating a bit above my neck. I forgot how to speak.

It was so sexy watching him sing to me. Sing something he knew would make me happy. And DAMN did it.

He strutted across the stage and did silly emo hair flips making me laugh so loud, truly obnoxious. But I wasn't even embarrassed. Normally I SO would be. But somehow, right then, I wasn't.

Also, he knew every single word. Like, he didn't have to look at the screen at all which somehow made it even hotter. I was basically on fire in my seat. Which I almost slipped out of, if you catch my drift.

And well of course you do because you are me. This is my journal. Omg.

After the song ended I swear someone else took over my body. I jumped up on stage before he could leave and held onto him like he might try to run away.

He didn't.

And I picked the first lovey-dovey song I could find, barely even reading the titles. Of course, it was from Dirty Dancing. Of course.

We sang it together. My awful voice and his surprisingly amazing one kind of balanced out. It didn't faze him anyway.

Though, he did have to read the words on the screen this time. I guess he wasn't as aware of Baby's status regarding corners as I am. But he looked at me every time it was my turn to sing. And he really *looked* at me. In a way, he didn't even on the plane. He looked at me like he wanted me.

No, that's not quite right.

He looked at me like there was nothing else in the entire world he wanted but me, and the rest of his face reflected the fact - he already had what he wanted, and it was a forever kind of have.

Maybe I read too much into that.

But I'm gonna go with it anyway.

His eyes practically glittered, I swear.

We danced while we sang, and made idiotic smoochy faces, being dorks. It was the most fun I've had in I don't even know how long. And that's saying something because after getting rid of Ray I've been a lot happier. Having more fun.

But this was just the let-your-hair-down, not-give-a-single-fuck, kind of fun. Inhibitions abound. Smiles so wide my cheeks hurt. And I loved every single second.

And then at the end of the song, he leaned in. It wasn't a big lean. I could have pretended I didn't notice it. But there wasn't even a moment's hesitation in me. I leaned right back.

AND WE KISSED.

I kissed Quinn.

Or he kissed me. I don't know. I don't even care that I don't know.

We kissed.

And it was amaze-balls.

8

Please
DO NOT
Disturb

S<small>EARCH</small>...<small>HOS TOO HAV</small> 1 <small>NIGHT STAND</small>

S<small>EARCHING</small> "hos too hav 1 night stand"
  *Did you mean "**how to have a one-night stand**"*

Journal of Charli Ann Tartt

I'M IN A NEW DIMENSION.

Or maybe just a new world.

Where nothing makes sense, but everything feels right.

Which, of course, that doesn't make sense on the surface. And yet somehow it does to me.

Okay, I know I have to rewind and record it all. Or in a week I won't believe it actually happened. And if I'm honest, I don't want to forget. This whole night is one memory I want stored for viewing again later.

Last I was writing about our shenanigans at the bar.

THAT KISS.

Sorry, my time is limited, and I need to get this all down, but I just couldn't resist.

It was epic.

Anyway, I stopped writing because there was a knock at my door. And I swear my heard did a flip-flip like a gymnast on a floor routine, or a fish dying out of water. Those are two very different examples, and yet they both fit perfectly to what was going on inside my body.

I sort of just sat there in my pajama shorts and crop top – fancy af when I sleep, I know – trying to get a bit unwound so that I could get some actual sleep before the wedding of one of my very best friends tomorrow. *Whoops. Still not sleeping.*

And I sat there, staring at the door. Not even sure anymore if I'd actually heard the sound or if it was in my imagination. Then the knocking came again and I had the exact opposite reaction. I threw this poor innocent journal practically across the room as I flinched and jumped up, all at the same time. I think a squeak popped out of my mouth too.

What can I say, I'm a classy bitch.

But I went to the door, and I tried not to think any thoughts. Clear mind without expectations or hopes. But...yeah right. When I looked through the peephole, because no matter how much I've had to drink or how giddy and dizzy I'm feeling, my mama did not raise a fool. I check the backseat before getting into my car. *Always.* And I check the peephole before opening a door.

I will never be the first to die in a scary movie.

Second?

Sure.

But never first.

Omg. ANYWAY.

It was Quinn. He looked sheepish and so fucking handsome somehow in his gray sweatpants, tight white tee, and mussed-up hair like he'd been running his hands through it since we all got back to the hotel.

Cutest I've ever seen him. Legit.

And I opened the door so fast after seeing it was him knocking that I think I scared him. Which was even better because he let out a little squeak that was very comparable to the one I'd let out as I'd jumped out of bed just a minute before.

If that's not a sign I don't know what is.

He cleared his throat, completely glossing over his reaction, as his eyes went straight up to the popcorn texture of the hallway ceiling, collecting himself. It was *SO* hard waiting for him to say something first. I wanted to interrupt so freaking bad. But I held out, fidgeting the entire time cracking my knuckles and trying to keep my poor nails out of my mouth.

"Hey…you're up too." Quinn finally said.

And I shouldn't admit that I started laughing. Not the cute sort of girly giggle either. No. Nothing elegant or charming. I went into a hysterical fit of laughter with snorts and tears leaking from the corners of my eyes.

It was horrendously embarrassing. Worse than most things I'd done in front of him yet.

But I waved him inside while I was still making a fool of myself, literally trying to wipe the grin off my face with my sweaty palms. Instead of helping, it made me even more anxious and then a final burst of laughter fell from my mouth. Real loud. Real obnoxious.

"Sorry. Sorry," I did finally get out when he was finally on the other side of my door…in my room. I looked around and almost lost it again when my eyes fell on the bed. The one bed. "What's up?" I asked to distract myself from the dirty thoughts that flashed into my head uninvited but very present.

"I can't sleep, and I thought…well…" he trailed off as he looked at the same spot I just had, no longer able to form sentences either apparently. ~~The Bermuda triangle of words.~~

Okay, scratch that, it sounds dumb.

Anyway!

I wonder how many times I'll write that before I actually get to the point.

"The truth?" Quinn asked suddenly, pulling my eye back to his.

We were standing almost a foot apart, but I swear I could feel the heat pulsing off of him. The fear in his tone hit me right in the feels too. I hadn't expected it. This confident man had talked me out of a panic attack on a plane that very well could have killed us. He stood tall against all of my harassment and unfair judgments, smiling – or maybe sneering, but still. He was nervous right then. As much as I was.

I nodded. "If you think I can take it," I added as an afterthought.

I meant to laugh, a pathetic and strangled sound, sure. But nothing else came out.

I couldn't look away from his eyes, and after I finished somehow, hand to god, something changed in the room. All of the nervous energy changed. It turned inside out and was a whole lot more peaceful. I wasn't afraid of what he'd say anymore. I was…excited.

"I thought I was ready to say goodnight to you earlier. But I just wasn't." Quinn smiled after he finished, clearly feeling the same relief as I had.

"Want to watch some terrible late-night TV?" That's how I responded. Not like a normal person who might say something as simple as 'me too' or, I don't know, validate his feelings. No. I asked him to watch trash television.

"Sound fantastic," Quinn answered, totally shocking me with a nod and that award-winning smile. Seriously, if he hasn't gotten some prize money or at least one of those little ribbons for first place grin, I don't know what's wrong with this world.

"Here," I picked up the remote as I said it, and then I shoved it into his chest. "I'll be right back," I very eloquently followed it up with. I then ran into the bathroom with my phone. And I'm a tiny bit ashamed to say I googled how to have a one-night stand while pacing the tile floor of the teeny space.

There was nothing helpful, and I felt like more of an idiot afterward.

I then proceeded to look into the mirror, and I told myself to grow some ovaries and get out there. It's possible I had to tell myself a few times. But eventually I went back out.

I have no idea how long I hid in the bathroom collecting myself, so it's possible I furthered the illusion of my irritable bowel problem. So that's great.

OH MY GOD. I just realized I never ran the sink water after doing a fake flush. So, he officially thinks I don't wash my hands. I wish I hadn't just realized that, because it will never leave my brain again. That little nugget is officially burned into me forever.

"Look what I found!" Quinn said, super proud of himself, as he pointed to the tv across from the bed. My bed. My bed, where he was lounging in his sweatpants and t-shirt and looking *lickable*.

That's right. I said it again. *SO* Lickable.

Because when I said it to his face it was just speculation, based on what I'd heard. But turns out he really is. My mouth watered imagining treating him like a lollypop. Then I shook my head and actually tore my eyes away from him to look at what he was talking about.

"I love this movie," I cried out. Then I cringed because it was way too loud, and the clapping I'd done while shouting was even worse.

But still it's the truth.

"Schwing!" Quinn announced just as loud, patting the spot next to him on the bed.

"Who said you get that side?" I asked as I shoved him over.

"Everyone knows the left side is the best. So yeah, clearly the left side is mine." My panties caught on fire then, I swear. Spontaneous combustion.

But I also realized, thinking of my panties, what I was actually wearing. Total cheek covering, cotton, underwear with a random day patterned across them. Like a toddler. It would only be worse if it was my name.

I didn't let the though distract me too much, though, as I finished pushing him over to the right side of the bed. Right as in correct. But also, right as in right.

"I don't care about left or right," I corrected him once I was snuggled up against the headboard, the covers pulled practically to my chin despite being sitting instead of laying, and as close as I could get to him without actually pressing myself into his side.

"What the hell? You just wanted me to be wrong?" he joked.

"No. No! Not at all," I sputtered out, trying to think of a less embarrassing way to explain what I meant, but coming up with nothing. The truth it had to be. "I don't care about which side of the bed, because it depends on where the bed is in the room."

Quinn looked at me, pure pleasure written across his face, and I almost leaned in to kiss him again.

"Because...?" he prodded me. He actually poked my shoulder as he said, emphasizing his interest in the stupid answer.

I regretted it already.

"Because I like to be on the side farthest from the door. You know, in case a murderer breaks in. Gives me a few more seconds. Or if someone is there with me...I die second at least." I looked away, stopping just short of slapping my forehead.

"Okay. That's legit," Quinn said, totally shocking me yet again.

I'm not sure when I'll stop making incorrect assumptions about him. But it's gotta stop soon.

"I know it is. If someone breaks in here while we're watching, and I'm quoting the lines, sorry-not-sorry, this way you can get stabbed first. I'll have more time to scream and freak out before it's my turn."

He laughed, and even though we were both facing the TV finally, I saw his eyes flick over to me, because obviously mine were trying to watch him from the corner of my vision instead of the movie I've seen a thousand times.

"So..." Quinn started to say, and something just hit me.

I could be brave. I could go for what I wanted. And it turns out, very expectedly, I wanted him.

Before he could say anything else. I climbed on top of him and pressed my lips against his. It was a rush. My head felt a bit too light, while my blood was pumping through me so fast. I've never felt so much adrenaline all at once, not even that time I tried to train for a 5k race, which I never did show up for.

It's safe to say I shocked him.

Straddling his lap, my hands around his neck, and my mouth pressed against his, he froze. And I started to panic. Like immediately. I started to pull back, apologies already on my tongue ready to start spitting out as I began to die of shame.

But it only lasted for a moment.

Less than a second.

Because as soon as he realized what was happening Quinn kissed me back.

He opened his mouth and took over mine possessively. It wasn't rough exactly, but it wasn't gentle at all. There was a charge, a need, that had us pushing harder into the moment, into the kiss.

I can very confidently say that those ugly undies were soaked, just from kissing.

His tongue took over, and his hands rested on my hips. I could feel his fingers drumming a rhythm on my heated skin as he itched to move them higher. He was holding himself back, and that excited me more than anything else.

Because if THAT was holding back, I wasn't sure I cared if I lived past him going full-force. I'd die happily in bed with Quinn.

After who knows how long of my sitting in his lap, holding onto him as tight as I could, I pulled away. It was so hard to do. Even for the breath I knew we both needed to take. I was actually painful to separate, and I was instantly shier.

"So…" I said, having to bite my lower lip so I didn't smile too big. My eyes still closed as I pressed my forehead to his. Not willing to pull back any further than I had to.

"Holy fuck," Quinn whispered.

And I started laughing again. I don't know what my problem is, but hearing him so out of breath but still yearning, a catch in his throat. It was so perfect, so unexpected from how I'd started the day. Just…I couldn't help myself.

"What do you say we throw all rules out the window?" I asked.

"The windows don't open in this hotel," Quinn answered. Such a shit.

"You know what I mean." I gripped him tighter, wanting to shove him, but also not willing for him to be any farther than pressed up against me. "No strings. Just this once. Let's just go for it tonight." My eyes were open finally, no longer hiding, and I saw the reaction he tried to hide the moment it crossed his face.

That wasn't what he'd wanted to hear. Not his first choice anyway.

The disappointment was clear in his eyes, like there was a neon sign in each blinking at me and buzzing with electricity in two words. *Not. Enough.*

Before I could second guess, though, he covered it up. And even now, afterward as I write all of this down while he snores next to my ear, I'm still not sure if I really saw that. Or if it was my brain filling in the space of where my hopes and my expectations didn't quite meet.

His slack expression snapped like a rubber band into one of hunger, of ravenousness. He licked his lips before speaking, and I watched the motion, rapt.

"Well, if that's all I get. I guess it better be unforgettable," he said it low, but it felt like he growled, like the words weren't really in my ears but etched into my skin.

"I dare you," I started to say, but he cut me off with another kiss.

This time he pushed me backward, no longer satisfied having me on his lap. With his weight on top of me, everything seemed to click into place. I got out of my head for once in my life, I didn't worry about what to do with my hands, and I just melted into the experience.

Quinn's hands pushed up my top and when he grazed my nipple I swear to god I stopped breathing for a second; it was pure bliss. Then I have no idea how he did it so fast, but my shirt was off and his hands were having a hard time deciding if they wanted to be on my tits or down my shorts. It only took a moment for them to split the difference.

His lips wouldn't leave mine, though.

It felt like I was breathing in air he was giving me. And no matter how I arched my back or where I dug my nails, he didn't feel close enough. I needed more.

"Please," I begged.

That's right. I begged. And I'm not ashamed.

I had a hot man on top of me and I wanted him inside of me ASAP. Nothing wrong with that.

"Shit," he hissed.

Which, to be honest, is not what I expected to hear in response. Not exactly.

"I mean, please don't," I said. Because I'm hilarious.

He pressed his forehead against mine, like I'd done to him before. "I just mean, I didn't plan this out. I hadn't expected to…"

"Hold on," I interrupted and slipped out from beneath him. Topless and my hair in who-the-hell-knows how bad of a rat's nest, I rushed over to my purse. "I think it glows in the dark or blacklight or something, but Beatrix thought these were funny for the bachelorette, and I've been too lazy to clean out my purse since then." I held the condom out like it was a priceless gem.

And, in that moment, to both of us, it kind of was.

"You're amazing," Quinn said, catching me off guard. The honesty in his voice slammed into me like a wall of confusion and admiration and I don't know how to describe what else. One hand on a hip, my shorts askew, and my prize held out between us I was anything BUT amazing. And still, there was no doubt he was serious. That's how he felt.

I ran back to the bed.

"Tit for tat," I said as I handed him the condom and proceeded to rip his shirt off.

"Mmmm, I'd say so," he answered as he dropped his lips to my nipple.

The words that came out of my mouth were very dirty, and I can't even remember the confused string of them I'd put together. Let's just say I told Quinn exactly how good what he was doing felt.

Surprising me, again, he lifted me up until I was on his lap again, like we'd started. I wanted more, though. Greedy, or not, I don't care.

Getting on my hands and knees, I smiled and then pulled his sweatpants down.

And I may have blacked out.

Obviously, I'd felt his dick before that moment. I felt it pressed against my thigh just minutes earlier. But I guess I just hadn't comprehended the impressiveness of it. When I came to, I was sitting back up on my knees and he was already slipping the condom onto himself.

He surprised me as he grabbed my chin then, making sure I was paying attention.

"Ma'am. My eyes are up here." If I had had time to laugh I would have. Or, really, I would have yelled at him for calling me ma'am. I'm no ma'am yet. Instead he moved himself with some kind of superhero speed, and in the time I blinked he pulled me up to him. His lips consumed me as his hands directed my hips until we were lined up perfectly. The heat of him, right against my pussy, had me feeling like we might light up like fireworks.

It was delicious, and I couldn't help myself from rubbing against his head for a few moments. I was so wet, as I used his body like a toy, rubbing him against my clit, I actually worried there wouldn't be enough friction for me to come.

I shouldn't have worried.

"Please," he groaned against my mouth, never breaking from me even for the one syllable.

"Since you asked so politely," I said as I slowly moved down and he filled me up. It was stupid, silly, and somehow the perfect thing to say. I don't even regret it. I could have started speaking in tongues, and I'm not sure I'd feel any regret right now. Because, damn did he fill me up.

It's been several months since I've had sex. So that's probably part of it too.

But it was just on the brink of pleasure and pain, in the best way possible.

I know how cheesy this sounds, okay, so I'm fine with it. But in that moment before either of us started moving again, it felt like we were made to fit together. It was about as close as I could get to coming without actually tipping over the edge.

And then he breathed out my name and everything went into fast forward. I rocked against him and he matched my movements. His hands were everywhere at once, and if it hadn't felt so amazing I might have worried about extra limbs in the mix.

But the best part wasn't what I'd have guessed.

Normally, I'd say it was the expert way he moved his thumb between us as his other hand held onto my hip with possession, and he rubbed my clit as I bounced and grinded on top of him.

Or I'd try to claim it was the breathless speed we both moved, and the intensity of his kissing that he continued – in a way that kept us connected by as many points as possible for as long as possible, like even buried deep inside me he couldn't get close enough.

But in reality, what made it beyond anything I've had in…I want to say years, but definitely ever…was the way he kept holding onto my gaze. He'd turn my head, or tip my chin, anything to get me to look into his eyes. And I don't think anyone has ever wanted that from me, to watch my face and hold my gaze as he touches me.

It was…idk, just something more.

I didn't overanalyze it in the moment. Then after he begged me to come so he could too and I sped up my movements to a frenzied, frantic, pace, I couldn't think about anything at all for several minutes. No words came. I was fucked that good. Or I fucked him that good. Whatever.

He kissed me all over after I'd basically collapsed on top of him. And he didn't pull out or away for a long time.

"Tell me the truth," I mumbled against his shoulder. Or maybe more his clavicle.

"Always," he said into my hair.

"How crazy is it?" I asked.

He pulled back, his eyes searching mine for what I meant, and I realized the mistake I made. I was trying to be funny. But when I finally said, "How bad is my hair right now," it fell flat. I swear it was like I shit the words in the middle of the floor. He pretended to laugh, his smile was almost believable, but something in the air changed.

"I think you should wear it like that for the wedding today," he said.

And then I panicked.

"Today, oh god." I jumped up and apologized profusely as I tried to sort of back into the bathroom because I didn't know what was worse giving him a huge glimpse of the stretch marks on my booty or seeing the true terror on my face. It was basically a tie. "Clair is going to kill me if her cousin has to brush this mess out of my hair in the morning. I'm just going to shower really quick," I practically spit out.

And yes, I'm not ashamed to say that I locked the door.

I needed to get my head on straight.

The hot water didn't help as much as I hoped. But after I got out and slipped into new jammies, his shirt because I was trying to make up for all my mistakes earlier, he kissed me just as passionately as before and then jumped into the shower himself. That's when I started writing all of this.

I took a break when he came out and naked as hell got under the covers with me and pulled me against him. He's holding onto me, still sleeping, as I finished the novel of what happened tonight.

And I am trying so hard not to overthink all of this.

It's just been so unexpected. So fast.

So, ugh, wonderful.

Why does he have to keep pleasantly surprising me? Why can't he just be the jerk I expected, the kind of jerk I'm used to.

I don't know if I'll ever fall asleep tonight.

I feel too wired to ever…

9

"THAT'S RIGHT, YOU'VE REACHED CHARLI. BUT IF YOU'RE LEAVING ME A voicemail instead of texting me, you probably don't know me well enough for a call back. And if you do, text me to call you back, because I probably won't listen to your message anyway."

Beep

"Charli Ann Tartt. You know this is serious because I *am* leaving a message. Where the fuck are you? You were supposed to be here in Claire's room ten minutes ago. And considering Bea has been here for five whole minutes already, you're seriously pushing your luck. Get over here NOW!"

———

"THAT'S RIGHT, you've reached Charli. But if you're leaving me a voicemail instead of texting me, you probably don't know me well enough for a call back. And if you do, text me to call you back, because I probably won't listen to your message anyway."

Beep

"Giiiiiiirl. How the hell am I here before you? You in trooooooouble."

———

Charli and Clem's message thread

Clementine: Where the hell are you?

Clementine: I just left you a voice mail. A. Voicemail.
Clementine: Are you dead?
Clementine: You better be dead. Or Claire is gonna kill you. Or I will.
Clementine: Seriously. Omg!

Charli and Beatrix's message thread

Beatrix: I repeat.
Beatrix: Girl, you in trouble.
Beatrix: Claire is sweatier than normal. She's laughing too loud, and drinking faster that she did last night. You better get her ASAP before she loses her shit.

Charli and Clem's message thread

Me: oh fuck
Clementine: SHE LIVES
Me: fuck shit fuck fuck fuck
Me: FUCK!
Clementine: drama queen, calm down.
Clementine: But calm down quick and get your pretty ass here.
Me: ON IT

Charli and Beatrix's message thread

Me: Stall for me
Beatrix: hell no
Me: What?! Why?

Beatrix: this is making my year
Beatrix: My life

Me: do you hate me that much?
Beatrix: I love you so much that I'm helping you be a better person but not making excuses for you
Me: oh, fuck you
Beatrix: love you too

Girl Gang Group Thread

Me: Oh, hey girls, my last minute errand ran long, I'm almost there.
Me: So sorry!

Claire: Surprises? Yay!

Me: of course.
Me: only for you.

Mackenzie: She's only nervous-pooped three times. Proud of you ClairBear

Me: You're a riot.
Me: Love you Claire

———

The Wedding Day

AKA the one where we get hitched...FINALLY, I know, I know

GUYS GET ready and get Tom to the PLACE for pictures any time till 1:00pm

Girls head to Claire's room 8:00 am
Hair and makeup 9:00 am
Quick lunch 12:00 pm
SEPARATE bridal party shots 1:00 pm

Wedding guest arrive and are seated 3:00 pm
Doing the damn thing! 3:30 pm
Full bridal party, and family, pictures 4:00 pm
Drinks between pictures
Contest winner awarded for best costume 5:15 pm
Dinner, dancing, and all the rest 5:30 pm

Charli and Quinn are responsible that the entire bridal party lives through the night. Tomorrow all bets are off. But no alcohol poisoning on the damn day.

———

Girl Gang Group Thread

Me: don't
Claire: Oh, but we must
Me: well. Shit.
Clementine: If Claire wants it today, then it shall be.
Emma: Wait. What am did I miss?

Me: nothing.
Me: Nothing at all.

Emma: filthy liar
Emma: Spill

Me: I'm genuinely worried your water may break.
Emma: I'm fine with that
Claire: She got it on with Quinn last night!!!!!!

Me: First of all, you don't know that for sure.
Me: Second, you have no proof.

Claire: We literally watched him leave your room after you rushed over here
Claire: without any gifts, I might add

Me: Umm, hello. Breakfast delivered. By that very cute delivery boy, I MIGHT ADD

Claire: Fine. Fine.
Claire: But you still screwed Quinn

Me: OH MY GOD
Emma: Hallcluiah sweet baby jebus
Me: not you too
Mackenzie: the smile on his face
Me: lah lah lah, I can't hear you
Clementine: Em, her face is sooooo red. It's the cutest thing I've ever seen
Me: I'm going to look like a tomato in the pictures if you all don't stop already
Beatrix: never
Me: you still have no proof
Sadie: the grin on his face, and that impressive chest as you shoved his t-shirt into it, and the way he looked back at you after you rushed down here – it's all the proof we need
Emma: daaaaaaaaamn
Me: I plead the 5th
Claire: I want every single detail tomorrow at breakfast

Me: ugh
Me: fine

———

Journal of Charli Ann Tartt

So.

Yep. That's about what I have left today. And dinner hasn't even started yet.

My brain is mush.

It's happy, confused af, mush.

I fell asleep all tangled up with Quinn. And neither of us remembered to set an alarm before. So of course, we both slept in. Why wouldn't we? After a second round of mind-blowing sex – that's right, just as I put my journal away I had this urge wash over me. And I woke Quinn up in a very creative way.

With my mouth.

That's right. I'm a sexy bitch now who does stuff like that.

But it really meant we barely slept. So, I got yelled at for being late. And allllllll day long Claire and all the girls have been making eyes at Quinn. And making very dirty references. Which is embarrassing.

But also, he's totally unconcerned. And he might even like it. Or he's really good at faking that he likes all the attention. After a whistle sounded in the hallway he shook his butt as he walked back to his room.

And a huge smile has been plastered to his face all day. Literally every time I look over at him he's looking back at me with this goofy grin. Plus, he keeps making excuses to touch me.

His hand finds the small of my back as he walks by. He brings me drinks between photos and his fingers touch mine.

And he smiles. Every time.

It's possible the happiest I've ever seen him.

Tom keeps looking back and forth between us like he's trying to figure something out. I don't think Claire has told him yet, and she's enjoying seeing how long it takes him to piece it together.

The day has been wonderful though. The ceremony was. Oh god. It just was perfect. Everyone came in costumes, but classy ones. And I bawled at the wedding. Obviously. Their vows were beautiful and funny, and I swear it was hard to stay standing up there as I held my breath to try and keep the tears from falling.

It did not work.

Also, I almost passed out.

But when we walked back down the aisle, after the MARRIED couple, Quinn gave me his pocket square so I could try and fix my face. And he didn't even blink when I handed it back with one of my fake eyelashes attached to it.

Oops.

I honestly don't know how I'm going to make it through my speech.

I'm dreading it.

At least I get to go before Quinn.

Everything I heard about Quinn before this…it wasn't flattering. It made him out to be this guy who couldn't be bothered to look twice at someone after getting into bed with him. But he's looking. At me. Still. And a lot.

And I like it.

I really do.

Maybe the girls were wrong about him. Maybe whoever said the crappy stuff was upset, or jealous. Or maybe I've lost my damn mind. Who knows. Could be any of those possibilities.

Oh crap. It's my turn to be in more pictures.

More.

Pictures.

I swear they'll have a billion after today.

But then, soon – it HAS to be soon – is dinner.

Ugh, I hope he doesn't watch me while I eat, though. It's not exactly graceful.

———

Dinner will be buffet style

Dinner options

Stuffed chicken breast, wrapped in bacon *(nothing healthy here)*
Pulled pork
Vegetable pasta with vodka sauce *(Vegan option)*

Side options

Greek salad with vinaigrette dressing and blue cheese crumbles
Seasoned potatoes and vegetables
Cheesy shredded potato dish
*can you tell Claire like potatoes?!

Dessert options

The hot chocolate bar
The chocolate fondue station
The chocolate wedding cake
*YES, you can have some of everything!

Drink options

Red, white, and rosé options *(free)*
Keg *(first come first serve)*
*Any other drink will be cash bar
The bride and groom suggest trying from the many Halloween Themed drinks
available

––––––

#HalloStonedWedding

POSTED BY **CLAIRE STONE**: 10/31 5:35PM
"That's the kind of hashtag you get when you let your HUSBAND pick it
out. That's right. Notice the name change bitches!"
#HalloStonedWedding

POSTED BY **THOMAS STONE**: 10/31 5:36PM
"That's my wife everyone."
#HalloStonedWedding

POSTED BY **VICKI SHAW**: 10/31 5:35PM
"You two have never looked so beautiful. My eyes will be puffy for days!"
#HalloStonedWedding
    Posted by **Claire Stone**: 10.31 6:01PM
    "Love you, mama!"
    #HalloStonedWedding
    Posted by **Vicki Shaw**: 10/31 6:05PM
    "And the rosé."
    #HalloStonedWedding
    Posted by **Claire Stone**: 10.31 6:17PM
    "To be fair, I get that from you."
    #HalloStonedWedding

POSTED BY **CHARLI ANN**: 10/31 6:39PM
    "BEST DAY EVER!"
    #HalloStonedWedding
    Posted by **Quinn Page**: 10/31 6:39PM
    "agreed!"
    #HalloStonedWedding

. . .

MORE POSTS
   …loading…

———

My speech

~~I HAVE KNOWN…~~
   ~~Claire and I~~
   Let's face it, we all saw what a mess I was during the ceremony. So, I'm going to keep this short and sweet.
   Claire, I adore you. And you'll always be one of my best friends. Whether you like it or not. I'm never going away. Tom, I apologize. Kind of.
   I'm so happy to be here tonight.
   FINALLY.
   Claire, you make Tom better. And he makes you better.
   And that's all you really need in life, isn't it? Someone to make you better. Someone you want to be around all the time, even when they're annoying. Someone that you can see yourself growing old with. And I've never seen two people more perfect for each other than you two.
   Raise your glass to Claire and Tom. May they be together long enough to trim each other's ear hairs, yell loud enough when their hearing aid batteries are on the fritz, and count the years before they met as less than the ones they've been together.
   CHEERS!

———

Journal of Charli Ann Tartt

IT WAS TOO perfect not to write down.
   His toast was perfect.

"Tom, I've never seen you as happy as when you're with Claire. I see it in both your faces, that spark. You light up the room for each other. There's nothing else you need in the world than that.
Sure, a house and some money are great. I guess you need to eat too.
But really, all of that comes along easier with love in your life.
Two the best couple I know. Everyone raise your glasses.
To Claire and Tom. May we all be as lucky as these two, and find out person."

   And then he looked at me and winked.

I'm dead.

———

Girl Gang Group Thread

Me: Did I imagine that?!
Me: Tell me I didn't make it up.

Emma: YOU DID NOT. RED ALERT. YOU DID NOT IMAGINE THAT.
I SAW IT TOO
Me: My eyes hurt from the shouting
Emma: sorry. Sorry. Pregnant lady got too excited. It was like I was reading a romance novel and it was THAT MOMENT. Ya know?
Claire: OMG. That's what it was. That was THE MOMENT.
Me: You two are nuts

Beatrix: I agree with Charli. That mushy crap is too much.
Beatrix: But he winked. 100% he did.

Me: I think my brain short circuited.
Clementine: Well, that should actually help then. Now you won't overthink it all. Just go with how you feeeeeeel.
Me: But should we trust my feelings?
Beatrix: iffy
Claire: I mean your feelings go you into Ray

Emma: strike one.
Emma: Though, they also got you out

Sadie: ALWAYS go with feelings. Logic is shit for relationships.
Mackenzie: I'm with Sadie. I say yay.

Me: Hurry up and make my decision for me
Me: This is like torture

Hailey: Do we trust him though?
Emma: I'll kick his ass of we can't.
Claire: I say yes
Me: And you're the one in charge tonight. So yes it is…

10

Music Playlist for #HaloStonedWedding

All of Me *First Dance*
I Gotta Feeling
I Wanna Dance with Somebody
Marry You *Dollar Dance*
The Macarena
I Will Always Love You
Dancing Queen
Single Ladies *Bouquet Toss*
Raise Your Glass *Garter Toss*
It's Gonna Be Me*Bouquet and Garter Couple dance*

REQUEST LIST:
~~Who Let the Dogs Out~~ *Banned List*
Cupid Shuffle Okay
Chicken Dance Okay

Girl Gang Group Thread

Me: get outta town

Emma: world's cutest first dance
Emma: EVER

Me: dorkiest song
Claire: hush you
Me: I mean considering you guys have been together for a million years, you're luckier it's not worse
Claire: Truth
Me: I wish it was a boy band though
Clementine: sameeeee
Me: life goals
NAME: Okay, it's almost time for the dollar dance. Make me some money honeys
Me: Well, that's really up to you.
Beatrix: Work it girl.
Sadie: Damn.
Hailey: Make it rain
Claire: I mean did you expect anything less?
Me: never!
Claire: good
Me: okay you hooligans, get off your phones for a while
Emma: what's the angle?
Beatrix: She wants to make eyes at her new BOY instead of texting with us
Me: I'm literally standing next to half of you…
Beatrix: I said what I said.
Claire: If anyone says I threw that to her on purpose I'm going to smack you.
Clementine: I was honestly about to text to ask you that.
Claire: I mean Mackenzie and Sadie literally shoving her forward as I threw it probably helped.

Me: this is horrendously embarrassing
Me: Why did you have to do such a cliché song choice?

Beatrix: You shut your filthy mouth. She's the queen.
Me: Correction, a queen. Gaga is one as well.
Clementine: Seconded
Beatrix: Losers

Me: oh
Me: my
Me: god
Me: who set this up?

Hailey: I can't stop laughing
Claire: I swear, no one!
Me: don't make me do this
Mackenzie: You have to
Emma: It is TRADITION
Me: like you get any say in tradition! You didn't even let us come to the court-house wedding you snuck to.

Emma: GET ON THE DANCE FLOOR IWHT YOUR HOT MAN.
Emma: Or so help me I will deliver this baby right now, and make you help hold my legs the whole time

Me: deal
Claire: No!

Me: oh my god. Did you have to pick THIS song?! It's going to haunt my dreams.
Me: also shut up with all your yelling.

Claire: Then stop making everything so sexually charged
Me: never

———

Bridal Party's Specialty Drinks:

1. Bridesmaids' Bloody Mary, Bloody Mary, Bloody Mary *(Obvi)*
2. Groomsmen's Graveyard Bash *(Whisky on the rocks with a tombstone straw)*
3. Bridal Suite Slayer *(Manhattan but with vodka)*
4. Haunted Honeymoon *(tequila, orange juice, champagne, crushed pineapple, grenadine, plus a toothache)*
5. Panic! On the Disco-Floor *(basically a fruity long island)*

———

Clom-Taire Drinking Game Rules:

1. Basically, it's a mix of poker and bullshit, both of our favorite card games
2. Every time anyone swears we all drink
3. Every time a king or queen is face-up the bride and groom drink

4. Nose goes
5. The winner of each hand gets to pick someone to drink

———

Journal of Charli Ann Tartt

I'M WATCHING these dorks play a drinking game.

And it makes literally no sense.

Claire got tired of dancing, but she didn't want to leave. She said if she was going to sit down then she was going to make us all sit down too. I have absolutely NO idea where she pulled the deck of cards from but suddenly it was on the table.

I played two rounds, but I got way too lost and they kept making me drink.

So now I'm sitting behind Quinn and just watching.

Also, obviously I brought my journal to the wedding. Why wouldn't I?

Don't judge.

My feet are in Quinn's lap as he plays, since we're sharing a chair, and he keeps rubbing them. It feels so freaking good I start to zone out and just feel his strong fingers constantly touching me, reminding me we're touching.

After I was set up to catch the bouquet, and he kind of tackled Paul to get the garter, we danced. It was so silly because it was a boyband song, and even with that awful detail I couldn't hate the moment. I wanted to. I really tried.

But he kept smiling as he lip-synced the lyrics – knowing as many words as me, if not more. And then he kissed me. Right there in front of everyone on the dance floor. It wasn't as earth-shattering as the kiss at karaoke.

Oh my god.

I just realized we kiss with background music most of the time so far, and it's setting a dangerous precedent.

It wasn't as shocking, the kiss tonight.

But it was special.

It was deeper, even though it wasn't especially long or even whistle-worthy.

What I mean is, I felt it deeper. In my heart.

Deeper than that even.

I don't know if I'm making sense. But it was a new feeling.

And it scares me.

A lot.

Quinn keeps trying to sneakily read what I'm writing, but it's getting more and more obvious the more he plays. It's cracking me up. And still…I don't know. I have this feeling in my chest. It's kind of good, but kind of not. More terrifying than anything.

Maybe I need to go to bed soon. It's been a long day already.

11

Girl Gang Group Thread

Me: What the fuck happened while I was putting my notebook away in the bridal dressing room?!
Me: I was gone for a minute!

Claire: I've been asking Emma when I can scratch her eyes out. She just appeared out of nowhere. And that costume is atrocious. I got stiletto shape for a reason. I'm gonna use 'em.
Beatrix: Settle down there sparky, you look rabid
Claire: might be
Me: BUT WHO IS SHE
Emma: Give me a sec
Me: do not

Emma: too late
Emma: brb

Me: can shame kill you?
Me: Like can you die of embarrassment?
Me: Because it feels like you can

Claire: Dish
Me: wait

Emma: yeah
Clementine: now she's got a real problem

Me: don't Cleme.
Me: everyone take a breath

Sadie: okay I'm lost

Me: it's nothing
Me: no big deal, seriously
Me: can we all stop staring please

Claire: HEY! I have an idea
Claire: and it's MY wedding, so you all have to say yes
Me: yes
Claire: let's go trick-or-treating
Me: hell yes
Claire: done

Charli and Quinn's message thread

Me: I see you
Quinn: huh?

———

#HalloStonedWedding

POSTED BY **EMMA ELIZABETH**: 10/31 9:22PM
   "If they thought they were being sneaky, they were sorely mistaken. See the dozen photos I took of their *sneaking*."
   #HalloStonedWedding

POSTED BY **EMMA ELIZABETH**: 10/31 9:25pm
   "They stole the centerpiece vases for their buckets!"
   #HalloStonedWedding

POSTED BY **EMMA ELIZABETH**: 10/31 9:22pm
   "Bride wins for best costume, though. For sure. Perfect sendoff for this preggo tonight! Love you **Claire** and **Tom**!"

#HalloStonedWedding

———

Girl Gang Group Thread

Emma: I might be in bed, but I still want to know what you said to him before leaving for trick-or-treating
Me: nothing
Emma: bullshit
Me: Seriously. She walked away before I got to him, and then he turned around and I panicked and walked away.
Claire: more like ran
Me: it was this super awkward half run, half dance
Beatrix: I'll never forgive myself I missed it.
Emma: So…
Me: So, nothing. I haven't talked to him about it.
Mackenzie: Yeah, but
Sadie: You're going to, right?

Me: Honestly?
Me: Idk

Claire: EXCUSE ME, WHAT
Me: omg stop
Claire: never
Me: I think Emma fell asleep
Hailey: go talk to him now
Me: noooooooooo
Clementine: girl
Me: what?
Clementine: grow up
Me: never
Claire: Seriously. Go talk to him.
Me: You, Mrs., do not get a say in the matter.
Claire: What? Why?!

Me: You brought him along for our outing. He said yes so fast and then you dragged me along too. I thought you were going for a fun distraction.
Me: Not a sabotage.

Claire: Can't it be both?

12

Girl Gang Group Thread

Claire: Muahahahaha
Me: omg
Clementine: you are SO competitive.
Beatrix: I love it
Claire: only because I was born to win

Me: I repeat
Me: but I'm glad you're having fun lol

Claire: because I'm the winner.
Claire: and also, CANDY

———

Last Minute Candy Score Card

NAME TOTAL PIECES PLACE

Claire 273 1st (YEAH baby!)
Tom 99 10th
Quinn 0 worst
Charli 10 69th

Paul 269 2nd
Beatrix 201 6th
Josh 177 7th
Clementine0 2nd worst
Trent 42 blah
Mackenzie 204 5th
Derek 88 11th
Sadie 136 8th
Joe 222 4th
Hailey 223 3rd

p.s. holy shit, we have a huge wedding party!

———

Girl Gang Group Thread

Me: where the fuck did Quinn go?
Me: also, it's FREEZING

Claire: isn't he…
Claire: wth

Me: I'd have gone back already if he wasn't out here. I wanted to talk to him
Beatrix: Hold up
Me: recon?
Clementine: everyone, get your aisle buddy

Me: dorkiest name ever
Me: but I love you babes

Claire: Tom has no clue
Beatrix: mine either
Me: ugh
Hailey: nope
Sadie: sorry

Me: I mean did he die?
Me: maybe of hypothermia

Mackenzie: possibly, because I got nothing either

Me: omg
Me: If he did I will feel so bad about being this pissed

Claire: he didn't die
Me: then I can stay mad
Claire: Always
Beatrix: 2nded
Me: ugh

Friday October 31st

Large Sweatshirt	$29.99
Medium Sweatshirt	$29.99
Sub Total:	$59.98
Tax	$3.75
Total	$63.73

Quinn Page

Signature...

Journal of Charli Ann Tartt

WELL.

It's been a night.

Which, of course it was. Claire and Tom finally got married. And it was beautiful, and wonderful, and perfect.

But also, not at all for me.

After pictures we had dinner and drinks and dancing. Then we played drinking games. And Claire got drunk and decided we needed to competitive trick-or-treat. After I saw Quinn at the bar with that Theresa girl from the wedding shower I needed to get him alone. But just when I got up the courage he straight up disappeared.

I was so frustrated.

And shivering.

So, I bailed a few minutes early to get back to the wedding.

And when I saw Quinn standing in the hallway looking around my heart fluttered. The damn skull moths were back, and it stopped me in my tracks. I didn't want to feel that way after seeing him standing with someone else. I mean, nothing happened. But still. I was all frustrated and flustered, and I didn't like it at all.

And then he saw me and his face lit up.

I swear it made my feet start moving, on their own.

And then. UGH. And then she walked up to him again. I swear I have no idea why Claire invited her to the wedding, but I wish she hadn't. I don't even know how Tom knows her, but she ruined my night.

Though, to be fair, it wasn't her fault. How could she know?

Anyway, I'm not making a whole lot of sense without the context. She came out of nowhere, walking way faster than anyone should be able to on a pair of tall stiletto heels. I mean, who is she, a top model?

And she grabbed Quinn's face and started playing tonsil hockey with him. I swear it looked like she was trying to swallow his face. It was…a lot.

His eyes bugged out, and he froze. He FROZE. Eventually he pushed her off, but it took too long. Way too long. And he did it so gently, not wanting to hurt her feelings I'm sure. But damn, did it hurt mine.

My stomach sank as I stopped walking. His eyes stayed flickered back and forth between her face and mine, but I knew. I knew immediately as my insides hit the floor between my feet and crashed through it making a sinkhole, that I wished nothing more than to sink down into; I knew. I'd been waiting for it. Because it didn't feel surprising this time.

It felt inevitable.

And that's what hurt the most.

I felt so stupid. My gut, my heart, everything except my brain expected this. Almost every part of me was just waiting for it to happen, other than you know my consciousness. That fucking stung.

It stung so bad my eyes started to betray me and I started running.

Well, first I took off my heels, then I started running. I ran right past him without stopping, and I wanted to get away so bad. I thought maybe, just maybe, I could go fast enough that he'd leave me to my misery without adding to it.

Nope.

He started yelling my name. Even with the music playing so loud I know a few other people heard him too as a couple heads turned and watched me rushing toward the exit. So, slowed down, which I so did not want to do, but it worked in getting the few dancers who'd glanced over to look away. I think.

The room got a little wobbly then, bending like I was underwater instead of fleeing a beautiful library all dressed up for a wedding I should have been enjoying the fuck out of. Ugh. Why can't I just do anything normally? Do it right…

Since I'd slowed down he caught up to me pretty damn quickly. His shoulder touched mine and it felt like my skin was on fire. Confused but still drawn to him. Pissed and hurt and a million other things, and my body still betrayed me and longed for his skin against mine.

Stupid hormones.

He left her, the woman kissing him without his needing to ask, to talk to me. Knowing I was livid. But it wasn't enough.

I stopped. But I didn't turn. He said my name again, and still I was a statue, doing everything I could just to focus on my stupid tear ducts and not let a single droplet fall down my cheeks.

I didn't let him say anything more than my name. My stupid name on his lips that sounded way too good.

I practically growled at him when I told him, "Go back to her."

He was in front of me then, a blurry blob of handsome, even through the layers of my anger. And I could see the shock change his face. I couldn't quite look into his eyes, but I felt his confusion rolling off of him in waves. Angry waves. And that spurred on my frustration again. Which helped.

"Since you're incapable of sticking with one woman, according to every single person here, I think she's a better fit," I added. And then I started walking past him. I wanted to shove him, to bump into his shoulder as hard as I could. But I also was terrified of touching him.

I blinked a few times, wanting to see the realization sink into him.

But as I did all I saw was his features hardening. He wasn't shocked for long before it turned to disappointed anger. He lowered his voice so that I could barely hear him over the thump of whatever song was playing. I have no idea what it was, something fast and making my heart speed up along with it. Or maybe that was from Quinn. I don't know.

But his voice was a rumble as he narrowed his eyes at me and said, "That's fine. Just fine. Because while I was getting you a sweatshirt," he paused then as I pulled my head back in question. "Yeah, I heard you complaining about being cold. Whatever. The hotel gift shop only had ugly things. So, I bought one, but was second guessing it. I checked in the dressing room quick to see if anyone brought something you might like better and…"

"And what?" I practically screamed it. Or whispered. I'm not actually sure, both seem equally possible.

"And I saw your journal," he said as he pulled it out from under the armful of fabric he had. A sweatshirt he got for me.

And my private thoughts. My journal.

I couldn't see straight anymore and the edges of my vision went white; I was so angry. I still am as I write this. Because I could read it all over his face.

He'd looked at it. He'd opened it to see what was inside and he read some of my secrets.

"Don't look at me like that," he said, embarrassed as hell. "It was knocked over, I'm guessing. On the floor and opened to a page. A page that said some pretty fucking shitty things about me."

When he finished I felt hollowed out.

"So, it's just as well. Because you clearly never intended to take the time to get to know the real me. Like I was trying to do with you. You had zero plans to be real with me. To even try. All of which I was all in for with you. But at least I know the truth now."

He sounded so flat then. Like all of the air, and hope, and been let out of him.

I didn't think there was something more than hollow, but if there is I felt it then. I was so empty it was like I was a black hole in the middle of the room. I was where happiness went to die.

He shoved my journal and a lump of bulky, warm fabric into my arms. Then he stormed off, leaving the library altogether. He rushed off, and the longer I stood in place the worse I felt.

I didn't even say goodbye to Claire before coming back here to my room.

And now, several little bottles of booze later, I just want to sleep. Possibly for a week. And forget, if I can.

Forgetting would be ideal.

13

Saturday November 1st

Saturday November 1st		
Room	$159.99 X2	
		$319.98
Rented movie (Terms of Endearment)	$9.99	
Mini bar (tequila)	$9.99	
Mini bar (vodka)	$9.99 X2	
		$19.98
Mini bar (gin)	$9.99	
Mini bar (candy bar)	3.99 X2	
		$7.98
Robe	$59.99	
	Sub Total:	$437.90
	Tax	$27.37
	Total	$465.27

Charlie Ann Tartt

Signature...

Journal of Charli Ann Tartt

UGH. I CAN'T SLEEP.

I may be crying my eyes out right now, in the middle of the night, watching a movie by myself instead of spending the night with all the other girls (minus Claire and Emma). Might as in that's absolutely what I'm doing.

I already know my eyes will be totally puffy tomorrow and uncomfortable to blink. But I can't turn the movie off. I just want to be sad. And sit in my sad, all uncomfortable and whiny. Seems fitting.

Plus, I'm drinking. A lot. Possibly too much from the expensive as hell minibar. Do I regret it? Not yet. But would I do it again? Absolutely.

I don't want to go to sleep either. I mean I know for sure I'll regret that tomorrow. But it seems worse to let go and dream about worse things. Plus, I never sleep well when I drink. I know I'll toss and turn until the sun breaks through the dark and I'll be cranky as fuck tomorrow.

Sitting here, crying I've made several realizations.

One: I developed actual feelings for Quinn.

And, two: that's so stupid.

I told him one time. I said it out loud, and he agreed. But I saw the disappointment in his face, and I knew he wanted more. And deep down I knew I did too. I didn't want to feel that way, and I knew I'd get hurt. It was just dumb to let myself fall for him.

But fall I did.

And then I went and wrecked it before he could.

Good one, Charli.

_____

Girl Gang Group Thread

Beatrix: come to our sleepover
Beatrix: COME ON

Clementine: pleaseeeeeee
Emma: What?! Why wasn't I invited!
Beatrix: You were already snoring, I could hear it through your door
Emma: I will be again in about two minutes after I pee.
Sadie: Charli come over! We're eating popcorn and watching 90s movies.

Hailey: Forget him!
Hailey: Seriously, come on.

Beatrix: Your loss…
Mackenzie: She's probably sleeping

_____

Claire, Tom, and Charli's Group Thread

Tom: Claire is worried about you. Answer the girls.
Me: I can't. I'm sleeping.
Claire: What happened?
Me: I told him off. It wasn't great.
Claire: Why though?
Me: He kissed her.
Claire: I'll kill him
Tom: Welp, it was nice having a best friend for a while.
Me: Don't kill him. Let him live his sad little life.
Tom: Hey now
Me: HE KISSED HER.
Claire: That's not what he says.
Me: Traitor
Tom: She kissed him. That's what I saw. And then I saw him push her away and run after you.
Me: lips were touching
Claire: He didn't ask her to do it. And he'd rather be kissing you. That's what I got from that.
Me: IT IS YOUR WEDDING NIGHT WHY ARE YOU TWO WORRIED ABOUT ME?
Tom: Because we love you. And I love Quinn. And I think
Me: don't say it
Tom: I'm pretty sure he's ass over head in love with you
Me: What a nice way to say such a mean thing.
Claire: Hear him out babe.

Me: Ugh.
Me: Fine.

Tom: get ready for a novel
Tom: So. Thing is. None of the rumors about Quinn are true. I don't know why they're so prevalent, but he's a really good guy.
And the thing is he loves hard, and he doesn't sleep around. He's good-looking (yes, it's obvious, shut up) and he makes everyone laugh and he gets a lot of phone numbers. But he doesn't do one-night stands, and he's all in or not in anything.
The stupid rumors started in college because he had this cocky attitude and charm and he never denied it. But that's it. It's how OTHERS perceive him. Quinn has actually only had two long-term relationships. One was before I met him in high school. And his second was the second half of college. He had a ring and was going to propose, when he walked into their apartment and caught her in the middle of cheating on him. He tried to make it work, forgave

her, and then she moved out and ghosted him while he was at work after class a few days later.

It hurt him, and he hasn't been with anyone since. He's been on a few dates, but hasn't connected with anyone in a while. Not until you. Because Quinn has been talking about you ever since you met. He's been my best friend for forever, and I know him. I can tell when he has real feelings. And he has them for you.

Theresa has been all over him because she's liked him since they had a class together freshman year. He's never been interested. Even when he "left with her" from the shower they didn't go anywhere together. They shared a cab and he took her home first, then went home alone. He doesn't like her, and he never slept with her.

But he likes you. A lot. And he's upset. He's my friend, and he's hurting. So, I had to tell you because you're Claire's best friend and we both love you too. But honestly, you screwed up.

I know that's harsh. But it's true too. And I only say it because we love you. Quinn is the real deal. And I think you two could be great together. If you give him a real chance.

Tom: It could be great.

Me: Thank you for the information. And I love you both too. Really.

Me: Now go back to YOUR WEDDING NIGHT and stop worrying about me.

Journal of Charli Ann Tartt

UGH.

Ughhhhhhhhhhhhhhh.

In the wise words of Tom, I screwed up.

I screwed up big time. In fact, I fucked up.

Turns out he actually liked me. And I liked him. Then I fucked it all up making assumptions and not giving him the benefit of the doubt. After the jerk I was with before I think I lost trust in anyone I didn't already know, anyone who hadn't already proved I could trust them.

And in that I ended up losing out.

I lost out on Quinn.

I think Tom is right, and we could have been good together.

I don't blame Quinn AT ALL for just walking away after what I wrote, and what I said. I gave him zero chance, expecting the worst the whole time. Even when I when he was kind to me, when he encouraged me to be myself, to open up and share even when it was the weird stuff or the embarrassing. The entire time he's known me he's shown me nothing but his real self and expected the same from me.

And I blew it all up.

He's basically the opposite of stupidass Ray who nearly broke me down into a blank slate he could rewrite. He turned me into a non-person. An almost person. Someone who didn't trust herself to talk or to think without checking in first. I was quiet. I wasn't me.

And Quinn kept asking about me. Laughing at my jokes. And wanting me for real. More than just once.

I am so stupid.

I really fucked up.

———

MESSAGE TO **QUINN Page**

I fucked up. I'm sorry. I don't like apologizing, but you're worth it. And I really am. Sorry I mean. Can we try again? Start over like on the plane?

If not, I understand.

But I hope you can look past my flaws and give me another chance.

We could be great together. Even Tom thinks so…

STATUS: draft

14

The Next Day
AKA the one where we have brunch, hungover, and watch Claire and Tom open gifts

Get your butts out of bed by 10:00 am
Get to brunch at Sweet Bee's10:30 am
Eat, drink, and be merry10:30am-11:30 am
Watch gift opening11:30 am
You're free after gifts

EVERYONE IN THE WEDDING PARTY HAS TO COME, NO MATTER HOW HUNGOVER... them's the rules

———

MENU for Claire and Tom's Gift Brunch

Brunch buffet options

Blue cheese and berry salad
Omelet station
Waffle bar
Cheesy hash browns
Bacon

Sausage
Spicy sausage pasta
Scrambled eggs

Drink options

Mimosas *(bottomless with choice of juice: pineapple, orange, guava, mango, cherry)*
Bloody Mary Bar *(bottomless with lots of fixing choices)*
Water *(for those of us barely keeping our brunch down)*

———

Girl Gang Group Thread

Me: Can I please just skip?
Me: It's the only thing I've wanted to!

Claire: hells no
Me: PLEASE
Emma: You told us to make you come in
Beatrix: Sure did
Me: I take it back
Claire: too late
Clementine: and she's still the bride
Claire: True. Today still counts. After today you can skip things that aren't mine.
Me: I'm very much regretting this
Hailey: but you haven't even done it yet
Emma: Get out of your car and get your ass in here NOW.
Me: geeze, remind me to tell Colton to give you some loving.
Claire: she's having contractions dummy
Me: WHAT
Emma: they're over ten minutes apart and sporadic. There's plenty of time.
Me: omg
Mackenzie: stop stalling
Emma: I can talk through them still. They may even go away. Besides, this baby wants you to come in here and go through with your plan.
Me: I might throw up
Claire: That's fine. Throw up, then get in here!
Me: …
Claire: I'm not above making a scene at my own brunch. I will go all Bridezilla on you and everyone here.

Me: fuck
Claire: yeah, stop stalling!

––––––

Clementine's Notes
Saturday November 1st 10:10AM

CLEARLY Charli is busy.

And someone had to write this shit down word for word.

It's too perfect, and magical, and romantic NOT to!

Claire is not-so-secretly videotaping it too, so I can make sure I don't miss anything. Charli just walked into the front doors for brunch at Sweet Bee's in a big ass elephant costume with humongous ears. It's a knock off, but the hat and frilly neck thing (no clue what that's called and I don't have time to look it up) are perfect, so we all know who she's dressed as.

She's taking her sweet time to get over to our private room, but it's French doors and huge windows all around, so I don't know why because we can all see her very clearly. Her face is so red; it's the cutest thing ever.

"Hi," she's saying.

Literally everyone I can see is staring at her. It may be Salem, but it's still the day AFTER Halloween. She's the only one in a full-on costume at this swanky place. It's very hard not to laugh.

Beatrix isn't even trying not to.

"Can I talk to you?" she asks after finally walking up to Quinn.

His face is so torn. He's trying his damndest to hold back a smile, but it's making his eyes water with the effort, and both corners of his mouth are still turned up.

Oh shit, he's shaking his head no!

"That's right. Make her work for it!" Emma shouts. Harsh, babe.

But I love it.

"I'm all ears," Quinn says. And now he's got a goofy grin across his face as Charli starts to twist the fabric of the left ear on her costume.

"Say it already!" Tom shouts.

"And so we all can hear," Claire adds.

This may be the best day of my life.

"Fine," Charli mumbles.

OH MY GOD. She's standing up on the table. He's still shocked and frozen in the buffet line, and she's standing on the table where his plate would be if he had gone through the line any faster. She's really going for it.

"I was so dumb." Charli barely said a few words before a fit of giggles took her over. She's only looking at Quinn, and his hand is on her ankle, rubbing his thumb in circles. I don't know if I want to gag or cry or shout for them to make out. "I know I was," she finally starts up again. "I took first impressions, based on gossip and other people's opinions, as gospel. When all along I should have listened to my heart. I knew I was falling for you, but I didn't want to see it, to admit it. I really thought all men were awful – not you, Tom, but everyone else. And when I met you I was so rooted in that belief I kept making dumb mistakes and then doubling down on each. I wanted to prove that I know I messed up. But I'd like a second chance if you'll give me one. I hope you will. And I figured after all this maybe you'd take pity on me…"

She trails off, leaving her statement to hang in the practically silent room.

Everyone's waiting.

What the…

A server just came over to help Charli down, and he's got a trash can with him too. He's setting it down at the end of the buffet line where Quinn's waiting. And Charli just threw a pink, sparkly notebook into it.

I'm a little confused, but Quinn doesn't seem to be at all.

"What do you think?" Charli's asking him!

———

#HalloStonedWedding

Posted by **Emma Elizabeth**: 11/1 10:35am

"Tom…how does **Charli**'s proposal to **Quinn** compare to when you asked **Claire**?"

#HalloStonedWedding

Posted by **Thomas Stone**: 11/1 10:39am

"Absolutely incomparable. Hers was way better."

#HalloStonedWedding

Posted by **Claire Stone**: 11/1 10:41am

"It's could be the hangover, but I can't stop crying."

#HalloStonedWedding

More posts

…loading…

———

Girl Gang Group Thread

Beatrix: you two are so cute I'm gonna puke
Clementine: AH-MAZE-BALLS
Emma: That show stopped my contractions, even the baby was enthralled!
Hailey: that may be the new video I watch any time I need to cheer up

Mackenzie: oh my god
Mackenzie: that kiss is doing things to me. I think I need a date

Claire: And to think, this all came together because of me
Sadie: GET IT GIRL!

15

BRAND NEW Journal of Charli Ann Tartt

QUINN SAID AFTER I THREW MY OLD JOURNAL INTO THE TRASH, "WELL AS LONG as you can admit when you're wrong." He grinned and then he pulled me in for a kiss.

It took my breath away.

Seriously, as he dipped me in my ridiculous costume, I sucked in air because I suddenly couldn't breathe. I'm was so happy.

I AM so happy.

Everyone laughed and clapped as we kissed, and it was this strange feeling of perfection. One I've never felt before.

"I'm sorry," I said to him again after pulling back to look into his eyes. Because I am. I have zero issues apologizing when I'm in the wrong. And I was so in the wrong here. But he shook his head then, his eyebrows pulling in together.

"I should have told you how I really felt," he said.

And I swear I started on fire and melted right on the spot.

"Me too," I admitted.

"I should have gone after you last night instead of walking away mad. But you'd already said just once, and I figured you were reminding me. I can make all the excuses in the world, but that's all they are. It's an excuse. I should have talked to you," he said.

"I guess we're both okay with admitting when we're wrong," I said as I took the hat off my elephant head and placed it onto his. "We were both a little dumb."

Then I yanked him back to kiss me again to the sound of raucous clapping and some dirty shouts from the bridesmaids.

And after brunch, he bought me this new journal so I could write it all down, even though I'll remember today for forever.

———

<u>Saturday November 1st</u>

Brut champagne bottle	$25.99

	Sub Total:	$25.99
	Tax	$1.62
	Total	$27.61

Quinn Page

Signature.......................................

———

BestAirs Airlines		Name	
Name: Tart/Charlotte		551B1M	
Tart/Charlotte			

From: Salem, MS   **To**: Minneapolis/St. Paul, MN
Date 1 NOV

Date	Departs	Flight	Class	Seat	Gate
1 NOV	11:30 AM	BA 013	V	2F	A13

ZONE 2

Boarding 11:00 AM
Time

BestAirs Airlines		Name	
Name: Page/Quinn		551B1M	
Page/Quinn			

From: Salem, MS   **To**: Minneapolis/St. Paul, MN
Date 1 NOV

Date	Departs	Flight	Class	Seat	Gate
1 NOV	11:30 AM	BA 013	V	2F	A13

UPGRADE: changed seat

ZONE 2

Boarding 11:00 AM

STATUS UPDATE: POSTED BY **CHARLI ANN**: 11/2 10:05PM

    Charli Ann is in a relationship with **Quinn Page**

    Posted by **Emma Elizabeth**: 11/2 10:06PM

    "Ummmmm excuse me. First you steal the show at brunch, and now you're

    making it official on Penny's BIRTHday? Love it."

    Posted by **Clementine Cross**: 11/2 10:06PM

    "**Charli Ann**, **Quinn Page** yassssssssssssssss!"

    Posted by **Bea Trix**: 11/2 10:07PM

    "I mean…finally."

    Posted by **Quinn Page**: 11/2 10:08PM

    "damn straight."

BRAND NEW Journal of Charli Ann Tartt

YES, we're official dating.

He asked me tonight, on his drive over after work. He said he couldn't wait until he got here. He wanted to be all in.

Damn straight I'm swooning.

It's amazing how every time I see him it's better and better. He makes me happy.

Ahh he's here, and my phone is buzzing like crazy.

Will write more later <3

―――

Girl Gang Group Thread

Emma: P.S. I used your post to announce the baby.
Emma: She's huge.
Emma: And squishy, and wrinkly, and the cutest thing ever.

Claire: CAN I COME TO THE HOSPITAL ALREADY?
Claire: I'm still mad you didn't let me be in there for the delivery

Emma: what is wrong with you?
Claire: Oh, also YAY Charli too!
Me: I want to come too! Can I come to the hospital tonight too?
Emma: You both can come in the morning, during visiting hours, like normal people.
Me: lame

Beatrix: Look at all of you being so normal with your cute babies, your beautiful weddings, and your sweet relationship statuses
Beatrix: makes me sick

Me: called that second message
Me: Love you too Trixie

Clementine: Took you two long enough
Claire: Yeah
Me: Are you serious?
Sadie: So, when's the wedding?
Me: blah
Mackenzie: How amazing is the sex?
Hailey: BOW CHICK-A WOW WOW

Me: buzz off
Me: Love you girls

―――

Charli and Clem's message thread

Clementine: Happy for you babe
Me: guess what?

Clementine: ummm
Clementine: This feels like a trap

Me: you're next
Clementine: don't bet on it
Me: love you
Clementine: love you more

———

Charli and Quinn's message thread

Quinn: Can you come in here?

Me: where are you?
Me: And why are you texting me from inside my own apartment?

Quinn: your bedroom
Quinn: I have something very interesting to show you

Me: COMING!

Quinn: Not yet, but very soon

ABOUT MARIA ANN GERMAIN

Maria, a badass USA Today and international bestselling indie author, lives in Minnesota despite the frozen winters. She's a creative, mouthy, introverted, proud bisexual, miscarriage warrior, highly-sensitive INFJ, chronic-pain spoonie champion, battler of anxiety, Slytherpuff, dork with a sweet-tooth. She will always believe that though not every story is for her, and her stories aren't for everyone, every story has a reader.

You can follow her at:
Website & Newsletter Sign up:
https://linktr.ee/mariainmadness

facebook.com/MariaAnnGreenAuthor

twitter.com/missmariaann

instagram.com/mariainmadness

bookbub.com/profile/maria-ann-green

goodreads.com/mariaanngreen

pinterest.com/mariaannwriter

ON THE ROCKS

G.G. GLEASON

ABOUT ON THE ROCKS

Subgenre: Contemporary Romance
Trope: Enemies to Lovers, Forced Proximity

Graphic sexual depictions, open door sex and explicit language

Trigger Warning: Discusses past drug addiction and loss of family members.

Blurb:

All Skyler wants to do is get away from her life as it crumbles around her. She catches a flight to Sedona, her safe haven in this crazy world. Unfortunately for her, an annoying Mr. Grumpy Pants is seated next to her on the plane. And when he invites himself into her life and home under the guise of "help", her safe haven is shot to hell.

Seth might be a lot of things – arrogant, pushy, and grumpy beyond measure, but his muscles and tattoos quickly worm their way under her skin, not to mention that mountain man beard of his. It might be fun for Seth to watch Skyler get worked up, but unfortunately for Seth, turnaround is fair play.

1

THIS AIRPLANE STINKS.

I'm all the way in the back, which of course means I'm sitting right by the goddamn toilet, and it already stinks. I barely made this connector flight, hit several people with my bag as I hurried to my seat, and got just as many mean looks as I went.

It's not my fault there wasn't a gate open for my flight from Charlottesville. It's not my fault that I had to run across the *entirety* of the Charlotte airport in order to catch this stupid connector. At least it's only a few more hours until I reach Sedona, Arizona. That is my mecca. I'm almost there.

As I sit down, middle seat of course, I apologize to the very nice woman in the aisle seat, and glance over at what looks and smells like a drunk asshole on the other side of me. Perfect. He appears to already be passed out, which is good news for me.

That is, until I accidently smack him with my backpack as I hurriedly try to shove it under the seat in front of me.

"Sorry," I say quickly, my voice all high and pitchy. The drunk guy opens on eye, just enough to glare at me, then goes right back to sleep.

"Relax, honey," the woman next to me says. "You made it. Take a deep breath."

I look over at her, her dark eyes smiling at me. She has "grandma" written all over her. Mid-sixties, curly black hair, and a bright pink sweater that compliments her dark skin perfectly. It's her kindness and her smile that finally have me taking a deep breath for the first time in weeks.

"Thank you," I say to her. "I really wasn't sure for a minute there."

She pats me on the arm and I can already feel tears prickling at my eyes. Kindness. It's been a while since I've felt kindness.

I sit back and stare forward, trying not to cry, trying not to touch angry drunk dude, and feeling thankful for the stranger sitting next to me that's showing me kindness for no other reason other than she, herself, is kind.

As the plane takes off, I gently reach over sleepy drunk guy to lift the visor on the window. I can get claustrophobic, and it helps to be able to look out the window. I make sure not to touch him, and begin to lift the blind. I get it about halfway up before Mr. Grumpy jolts up in his seat, scaring the shit out of me, and slams the visor back down.

Now both his eyes are open and glaring at me. Holy shit, if looks could kill.

"Could you not see that I was fucking sleeping?" he spits at me, rage hanging on every word.

"I …" I stutter, my eyes wide. He continues to glare, his nostrils flared, and my heartbeat continues to climb. "I just, uh, wanted to see as we took off," I tell him, trying my best to not look like a deer stuck in headlights.

Mr. Grumpy stares at me a little longer, and I stare right back. I can hear the nice woman beside me humming, and a part of me wants to jump in her lap like the scared kid I feel like.

"Do you ever think about anyone other than yourself?" His words are soft but lethal. Lethal in the way he grinds them out, and lethal since they cut me to my core.

"That's uncalled for," I tell him, now angry myself.

"Whatever," he mumbles, trying to get comfortable again in his seat. "Just leave me alone."

His eyes close again, his arms fold across his chest, and I sit there, eyes wide, jaw hanging low, just staring at him. Never in all my years of flying has someone been such a complete and total asshole.

Leaning back, I do my best to not overreact and keep control of my emotions, which is no easy feat. I've been a walking, talking emotional nightmare going on one week now. It's why I'm getting out of town. It's why I *had* to get the hell out of Charlottesville for a while.

"You okay, sweetie?" the nice woman asks as we fly along.

"Just a bit overwhelmed," I tell her honestly.

She smiles knowingly at me. "Boy trouble?"

I'd like to tell her that not all problems women have are boy troubles. I want to tell her that I'm a career woman, a boss ass bitch, a real player at my job. All of that is true, and she is still absolutely right.

"Unfortunately," I tell her, looking as guilty and depressed as I feel.

"Want to tell me about it?" she offers. "I've been around the block a few times," she adds with a laugh.

The polite thing to do when on an airplane with a total stranger is to decline, thank them for their interest, and mind your own damn business. But am I going to do that? Nope.

"Can I ask your name? I'm Skyler."

She sticks out her hand to shake mine. "It's nice to meet you Skyler. My name is Dorine. My babies all call me Momma D, though."

"Ms. Dorine, it's a pleasure to meet you."

We shake hands, and she says, "come on. We've got two hours to kill. Tell me all about the bastard."

And so I do.

I tell her how I'd been with Vince for almost two years. I tell her how magical it was being with him, and how much he spoiled me. I mention the breakfasts in bed he used to bring me every Sunday morning. I tell her about the gifts he'd leave on the dining room table, "just because." I tell her how he used to hold my hand and remind me just how special I was on a daily basis.

"Sounds like a fairy tale," Dorine says skeptically. "And that shit never lasts forever."

I give her a knowing nod and sigh. "Last Sunday he brought me breakfast in bed, as usual," I continue. "Orange juice, bacon, eggs. But instead of sitting on the edge of the bed and kissing me good morning, he stood there, and waited for me to wake up on my own." I shake my head as it replays in my brain. "Out of the blue, and I swear it was out of the blue," I insist to Dorine, "he tells me we need to break up."

My eyes are wide, bewildered, because it still doesn't make any sense to me whatsoever.

"Honey, I'm so sorry. It sounds like there might have been more going on behind the scenes than you realized. At the very least, he wasn't being honest with you."

Grumpy dude on the other side of me grunts and changes positions. I send a glare his way then turn back to Dorine. "But I don't know what changed," I nearly cry. "We were so great together. My family loves him. His family loves me. Hell, we moved in together six months ago! How ..." I stop and let my thoughts wander a moment. "How can you tell someone they're your every-thing, and then not twenty-four hours later end it?"

Dorine watches me with sad eyes. She takes a moment before she speaks, and I can tell she's doing her best to be careful with her words. "Sometimes people do the wrong things for the right reasons." I can feel my eyebrows move together as I frown at her. "What he did was wrong, honey. But in a guy's mind, maybe he was just trying not to hurt you until he knew for a fact that he was no longer invested in the relationship."

"But," I begin, my voice suddenly small, "the lies hurt so much more than the truth would've."

"I know, sweetie." Dorine puts a comforting hand on my arm. "But, well, men are idiots. They're always just looking for the easy way out."

A loud huff leaves my throat. "You can say that again." I swear I hear Mr. Grumpy huff as well, but I'm sure he's still asleep, so I let it go. "I just wish Vince would've been upfront with me. If he was having second thoughts, or if moving in together wasn't going as smoothly as I thought it was, I just wish he would've told me. We could have worked on it. We could have fixed whatever needed to be fixed."

"You know what, though, if this is how he handles things, consider yourself lucky, honey." Dorine shakes her head then adds, "if he wasn't mature enough to come to you with the small stuff, then he was never going to be mature enough to come to you with the big stuff. And a man like that isn't worth keeping around."

"But I love him," I protest.

"I'm sure you do, baby. I hate to break it to you, but The Beatles were wrong. You need a whole hell of a lot more than love to make a relationship work."

At that I laugh, and Dorine smiles. "You're not wrong," I tell her, narrowing my eyes, letting her know that I don't like just how right she is.

"Let this Vinny guy go," she says with a wave. "You left him behind for a reason, right?" I nod my head. "He's old news now. Never deserved you. A hot young thing like you? Honey." She grins at me, and for the first time in days, my lips break out into a genuine smile.

"It's Vince," I say coyly, still smiling. "He's letting me keep our place, at least. That's one of the reasons I'm going to Sedona; so he can be all moved out by the time I get back." My voice gathers a bit of anger as I add, "I never want to see him again."

"And I hope you don't," Dorine laughs. "But if you do, just remember that no one deserves to be treated the way he treated you. You don't need him, right?"

I nod over at her. I absolutely do not need him. I make my own money. I have my own job. Shit, I'm more successful than he is. Maybe that was one of the small problems in our relationship he never bothered to tell me about. Maybe my success made him insecure. Prick.

"Dorine, you should be a therapist or something."

She just laughs and shakes her head. "I have four children and three grand-kids to keep me busy." She nudges me with her shoulder. "Not to mention gorgeous young women I meet on planes."

The two of us continue to talk until the plane lands. Mr. Grumpy never speaks a word, which is fine by me. Even after the plane lands, he doesn't budge. We're all in the way back, so there's no reason for him to move for a while. But as more and more rows exit the plane, he still hasn't budged.

Two more rows left before ours. This guy was a dick, but I'm not. I don't want him to miss a connecting flight, or whatever is waiting for him here in Phoenix. As gently as I can, I lean over and tap him on his shoulder. No movement.

"Sir?" I ask, my voice all high and pitchy. I inwardly cringe at how ridiculous I sound. Still, "uh, sir," I say again, poking him a little harder. Finally, he moves and his eyes meet mine. "Sorry," I say, my cheeks going a bit flush because his big dark eyes are focused on me. "We're about to get off." I point towards the line of people walking off the plane, and then turn away.

I don't dare look back at him, but I can hear him rustling around and getting ready to walk off. When it's our turn, Dorine goes first, then me, and I notice Mr. Grumpy is still fumbling in his seat. Several other people file out behind me, and I'm sure he's going to wind up being the last person off the plane.

As we walk into the terminal, I turn to Dorine and give her a hug. "Thanks for being the best plane buddy ever," I tell her. She laughs and hugs me back.

"Enjoy yourself, honey. You're far too talented and lovely to waste your energy on a jackass who doesn't deserve you."

I rub her back before saying, "thank you. Your family is beyond lucky to have you."

She lets out a little chuckle and waves as she walks away. I take a moment to breathe, finally relaxing because I'm in Arizona. It's still a two-hour drive to Sedona, but it's an easy one. Just as I'm finding my calm, an elbow meets the middle of my back.

"Ow!" I turn and glare at whoever just fucking touched me, and I am in no way surprised to find Mr. Drunk and Grumpy himself. "What the fuck!" My zen is gone. My cool that I'd just found has died. This guy has been a little prick to me for absolutely no reason, and now that I'm not trapped next to him, I get to give him a piece of my mind.

Mr. Grumpy continues to glare at me as he walks on, and I'm not having it. I grab him by the elbow and force him to turn around and look at me. My eyes are wide as I shake my head. "Really," I say, "what the fuck?"

"You were in the way," he growls back at me, like I should be me apologizing to him.

"Are you a twelve-thousand-pound man that needs ten feet to pass?" I ask. A quick glance at his body tells me that, no, he is not. While I'm still on the verge of slapping this dude's face, I'm disturbed to see that his body, while not twelve-thousand-pounds, is actually quite fit. When my eyes meet back at his, I'm once again taken aback by his large brown eyes, as well as the full beard I hadn't noticed on the flight.

Shit. Mr. Drunk and Grumpy also happens to be Mr. Fit as Fuck.

The guy just glares at me. If glaring were an Olympic sport, I'd award him gold right here and now. I shake my head at him, just waiting for him to say something, literally anything.

"Jesus Christ," I mutter, finally letting go of his elbow. "I don't know what the hell your problem is, but I know it isn't me. So maybe stop being an asshole to people who don't deserve it."

In an effort to get the upper hand, I walk past him and purposely, aggressively, brush my shoulder up against him, knocking him out of my way. A small little grin spreads across my face. Then, not two seconds later, it drops off the fucking planet never to be seen again.

I am frozen. Fucking. Frozen. Because standing right in front of me is none other than my ex-boyfriend. And he is not alone.

2

I AM FACE TO FACE WITH THE PERSON WHO JUST BLEW UP MY LIFE; THE PERSON who I just got on not one, but two airplanes to get away from. What the hell is Vince doing here? He's supposed to be back home. He's supposed to be packing up all his shit and getting it the fuck out of our – wait, *my* – apartment.

And who in the goddam hell is he with?!

I must've been staring for longer than I realize, because Vince's eyes look up, and directly into mine.

"Shit," I hear him mutter. I watch as his jaw drops, and his cheeks begin to flush. He quickly lets go of the woman he's with as a look of guilt washes over his face. An incredibly awkward chuckle leaves his mouth, and then he bites down on his lower lip.

The lower lip I used to kiss every single night before I fell asleep next to him.

Vince walks up to me, as slow as he can, like he thinks he can somehow avoid this moment of pure hell. I'm frozen to the spot, unable to wrap my brain around what is truly happening.

"Hey, Skye," he says to me, like I'm not about to murder him right here in this airport. "What, um, what are you doing here?"

I gasp. I gasp because he has some goddamn nerve.

"What am *I* doing here?" I growl. "What *am I* doing here?!" Oh shit. I'm about to make a scene.

Vince's arms are already moving, trying to tell me to calm down, but it's not going to work. "Skye, please," he mutters desperately, sending an apologetic smile back to the unnamed woman his hands were just on.

"*I* have property here!" I bark at him. "This is *my* favorite place! This is where *I've* been trying to get *you* to come to FOR OVER A YEAR!"

Okay, now people are looking. Yup, everyone is staring. I need to cool down before I get arrested and never make it to Sedona.

"Baby, please. There's no need for that." An arm goes around my shoulders and the cool words flow from my left side. I look over, stunned, as Mr. Grumpy comes up next to me, speaking to me like we are, what, friends? "This man is clearly lost and looking for meaning in his life." Mr. Grumpy turns and looks at Vince. "Not that I blame him after losing out on the holy grail of women." Mr. Grumpy turns, looks me dead in the eye, smiles, and says, "which you very much are." Then – *and then* – this total fucking stranger leans in and kisses me on the damn cheek.

The only part of my body that I can move are my eyes. I'm staring at Mr. Grumpy, who looks really freaking sure of himself. Then my eyes flutter back to Vince, my ex, who is so red in the face you'd think he'd been in the Phoenix sun for the past twelve hours.

The two men look at each other, feeling each other out, and all I can do is stare.

Mr. Grumpy breaks the silence and asks, "who's the woman?"

It takes Vince a second to register, and snaps his head like he doesn't know who he's being asked about. Mr. Grumpy, with his arm still around me, nods his head towards the blond woman who has been watching this entire shit show go down.

"Uh," Vince stutters, "she's, um, she's a friend."

"Sweetheart," Mr. Grumpy shouts, motioning for the blond woman to join us. The way he smiles at her, all confident and sexy as hell, I don't blame her for returning his smile and joining our dysfunctional pow-wow. When she gets close enough, his arm leaves my shoulders, and reaches out to shake her hand. "Hey there, I'm Seth. And you are?"

God damn, he's smooth. The woman doesn't even flinch.

"Becky," she says sunnily. "How do you know Vince?" Oh man, this woman. I want to fuck her shit up.

"Old friends," Mr. Grumpy says with a wave of his hand. "What are you in Phoenix for?"

"Oh nothing," she smiles. "We're heading up to Sedona."

I ... am ... going ... to ... kill ... him.

"Oh, what a coincidence, so are we." My eyes move over to him, wondering if he overheard me talking about Sedona on the plane. I wonder if he really is going to Sedona as well.

"How long have you two been together?" Mr. Grumpy asks her then.

I see Vince flinch. I see him physically move to stop her, to cut her off, but she's not paying attention. Her eyes are fixed on Mr. Grumpy, and she answers so easily and freely, that it tells me she has no idea who I am, or that I ever existed.

"Two months. It's so good to finally meet some of Vince's friends." She giggles and nudges him with her hip. "Back home he's always so busy!"

"I'm sure," Seth, aka Mr. Grumpy says. "What, with him having another girlfriend most of that time, I can only imagine how busy he was."

Becky's face falls. Right next to her, Vince's face goes slack as well. Seth's hand slowly reaches around my waist and pulls me into him. "Well, it was great meeting both of you. Now, if you'd excuse us, we have places to be. Enjoy your visit!"

I let him lead me away towards baggage claim. I say nothing, carrying my backpack over one shoulder as he pulls his carryon luggage behind him.

I have no words. Vince. He was cheating. Not only was he lying to my face but he was cheating on me, too. Two months. Fucking *two months*.

By the time we reach baggage claim, I don't know if want to cry or just give up and go walk into traffic. But there's one question I have to know the answer to.

I turn and look at Mr. Grumpy. Seth, as he introduced himself. His eyes meet mine, and I can see that he's not okay. There's so much going on behind those brown eyes of his that I find myself studying them before I speak. Hurt, anger, pain, resentment.

"What?" he finally asks as he looks away.

"Why did you do that?"

His arm falls from my waist, and although it never should have been there in the first place, I find I miss its warmth.

Seth shrugs. "That guy was a dick."

"Uh, that's it?"

He turns and glares at me. There's the plane guy again: Mr. Grumpy is back. "What else do you want?" His tone is not gentle.

"Look, pal. I didn't ask shit from you, and you just inserted yourself, I don't know, into my life." Still, there is little to no reaction from him. "What the hell? Why would you do that?"

"Jesus," he growls. "Some thanks I get for saving your emotionally damaged ass."

The loud, dramatic gasp I let out grabs the attention of no less than ten people that are standing around us. "What the actual fuck did you just say to me?"

Then, this mother fucker grins. I have my hand on my chest, my body angled away from him, ready to smack that gorgeous beard off his face, and he has the audacity to grin at me. "It's nice to see you're not as much of a pushover as you seemed to be from the heartbreaking tale you told to that poor woman on the plane."

"Excuse me?"

"You wouldn't shut up," he groans, bending his knees slightly as he says it. "Talk, talk, talk, cry, feel sorry for yourself." He stops and stares directly at me. "At least Dorine gave good advice. Fuck that guy. Move on."

I don't even know what to say. I don't have one clue what the hell to say to this guy. He listened to our entire conversation. Why the hell is he acting like he cares?

"Stop staring at me like that."

I clear my throat and finally lower my eyes. "I'm sorry, I just," and then I pause. "Actually, no, I won't apologize. You listened in on a conversation that was none of your business. You made snap judgments about me, and were rude as all hell. Then you insert yourself into my life, into my relationship, and you're still the one who is angry with *me*?"

I'm expecting him to shrug, or walk away from me, which he very easily could do. This whole thing should be over right now, if he would just walk away. Instead, I watch as his eyes wander around the baggage claim, and then land back on mine.

"You're welcome."

Alright, I really am going to hit him. I move my bag off my shoulder to free up my arm to clock this dude, when he takes me by surprise yet again, and leans his head over me, pressing his lips right up against my ear.

"I wouldn't make too much of a scene, sweetheart," he grumbles into my ear.

The rage burning inside of me could start a nuclear war. Unfortunately, feeling his beard against my skin has also started lighting another part of me on fire. My vagina snaps to life like it's dying of thirst, and this bearded man can bring me back to life.

Simmer down you thirsty little bitch, I tell my lady parts. This mother fucker is just that; bad news and off limits.

"And why shouldn't I make a scene?" I finally growl back at him, my eyes closing from feeling his hot breath on my neck.

His hand reaches up and runs through my reddish brown hair, and I can feel goose bumps rise across my arms and down my chest.

Mr. Grumpy hums into my ear and I nearly die. "Because your ex and his very disgruntled-looking lover have just joined us." I can feel him move even closer to my face, letting his bearded cheek brush seductively against mine. "Wouldn't want them to think there was trouble in *our* paradise, would we?"

I can barely speak. Gone is the smell of alcohol. This close to him, he smells of ocean and musk. Manly, rough, yet there's something gentle and mysterious about him. I wonder if he tastes as good as he smells.

I clear my throat as he moves his face away, smiling down at me as he does.

"There is no *our paradise*," I remind him, doing my best to hide just how flustered he's made me.

I don't get flustered. Ever. What the hell was happening to me?

An evil grin spreads across his face. "There is now, sweetheart."

I huff out a quick laugh, my cheeks burning red, and say, "sure, I guess we'll just head to my place in Sedona together and live happily ever after."

Mr. Grumpy shrugs. "Not forever, but the rest sounds just perfect."

"Uh," I start, narrowing my eyes at him. "You're joking right?"

He looks across the baggage claim and I follow his eyes. Vince and his new girlfriend, Becky, are both watching our every move. When Seth knows I've seen them, he turns his gaze back on me. "Gotta keep the façade going, don't we?"

"You … you can't stay with me," I tell him, doing my best to be firm, but the only firm thing happening between us are the muscles on his arms that I've just caught a glimpse of and would now like to sink my teeth into.

He chuckles, and it's so deep and dangerous that my nipples immediately form into peaks. He leans in towards me again, kisses me on the cheek, and says, "think of it as thank you." I feel his hands run over my shoulder and down my arm. I should hate him. This absolutely cannot and should not happen. And I should definitely, without a doubt, not be panting like a cat in heat.

I look over and see the anger radiating out of Vince. Never in the entire time that we were together did he get jealous. I've never seem him so much as upset, let alone filled with anger, fuming, and ready to punch someone's lights out.

I wasn't sure if it was my lights he wanted to punch out or Seth's, but either way, he deserved to be messed with for a little while longer.

My eyes land back on Seth, and I smile up at him. Now it's my turn to grin dangerously at him. I run my fingers through his very dark and, god dammit, very soft hair, and as gently and sweetly as I can, I say, "okay, mystery man. But if you even so much as think about putting a hand on me," I pause and run my fingers over his beard before they land on his lips. "I will stab you to death and dump your body in an alligator infested pond." I wink at him. "No one will ever find your remains."

Mr. Grumpy grins down at me, wider than ever. He places both his hands on my shoulders and gives me a quick nod. "Sure thing, sweetheart. I wouldn't dream of touching you without your permission."

I tap his cheek with my hand, a fake smile still plastered on my face. "Good boy."

"Seal it with a kiss?"

Before I'm given a chance to respond, the beastly man pulls my body towards his, grabs my face with both hands, and presses his lips against mine for the whole world to see.

My first instinct is to push him away. Run. How dare he? I just said not to touch me.

What my *actual* reaction is, is *good god*. Those lips. Those plump, full, gorgeous lips, trapped amongst the best beard I've ever seen. His warm hands on my face, and the small little hum that leaves his lips as they're pressed against mine.

I do not push him away. What I do instead, is open my mouth to him, and let my tongue dance against his.

On the second swipe, I regain my clarity, and quickly pull away. My fingers immediately go to my lips as my eyes search his.

Hunger. That's what I see in him. Followed closely by torment, confusion, and maybe even a bit of surprise.

"That ..." I stutter airily, "was not part of the agreement."

"No, it wasn't," he responds, his words full of air, like he's still trying to catch his breath. "But it sure as shit was fun."

3

Mr. Grumpy Pants Seth follows me through the airport with his bags. He gets in line with me at the car rental kiosk, and stays by my side as we wait for my rental to be pulled around. We do not speak. I do not dare to even look at him, even if I think he's looking at me.

Once our luggage is in the trunk of the car, and I slide into the driver's seat, my nerves can hardly take it. I put the car in drive, move about four feet, then slam on the breaks. The car jolts and a startled Seth turns and looks at me.

"Really, why are you doing this?" I ask hurriedly. "Are you really coming with me? Why? What's in it for you? Are you going to murder me? Rob me blind? I don't have a lot, just so you know. It's a small place; my grandmother's place actually. I inherited it from her."

I'm rambling and scrambling and the words just keep pouring out of my mouth, because what the hell is this hunky stranger doing in my goddamn car?

As I finish asking my multitude of questions, I stare back at him, waiting for him to give me a response. I have to wait a long ten seconds before he sighs and finally responds.

"I just happen to be going to Sedona, too," he says gently, in a way that assures me that he does not plan to kill me and keep my bones as trophies. Another sigh and he adds, "I saw that guy, and that girl, and your face..." He stops and shrugs. "I wanted to give that asshole a taste of his own medicine."

Just as I'm about to say something, he turns his body fully towards me, and I do not miss the way he eyes travel across my body. "I also happen to not have a place to stay lined up." His eyes take their time on my lips. "And I think you and I could have an … adventure together."

Oh Jesus, just shoot me now. He's pretty much eye fucking me with those big brown eyes of his, and it is turning me *on*.

"I don't," I start to say, then stop. I want to tell him I'm not that type of girl. I want to tell him he's reading me all wrong. But I can feel the flush on my face, and I can feel my hardened nipples pressing against the fabric of my bra as this rugged mountain man stares me down. When I don't say anything else, he tilts his head and looks at me curiously.

"Don't worry, sweetheart," he says, as he moves his giant hand onto my thigh and squeezes me lightly. "I promise I will not kill you. There is nothing in it for me other than shelter, and perhaps, the company of a lovely woman."

I gulp down my nerves while my mind tries not to freak out from his touch. "W-What kind of company?" I stutter. I'm torn on what I want his answer to be.

The bastard grins. Oh, does he grin. "Whatever type you'd like it to be."

I have no response to that. I give a curt nod, put the car back in drive, and take off towards Sedona, towards my grandmother's house that is now my own. Once we're on the highway, my mind still very much on his last comment, I decide to pick the conversation back up where we left it.

"I don't do that," I say, eyes forward on the road. "*That* type of company," I clarify. "I've never, um," I stutter.

"Are you saying you're a virgin?" he cuts in, surprise registering on every word.

"What?!" I squeal, my face beet red. "No! Oh my god, no." I can see him visibly relax next to me. "I meant messing around. I don't do that type of thing." Then, just to further clarify, "I mean with strangers."

"Are we still strangers?" he asks, his deep voice, I swear, reverberating in *my* chest, and maybe between my legs as well.

"Yes," I tell him angrily. "You never actually introduced yourself to me. You're sitting in my car, piggy-backing on my solitary trip, and you never even had the common courtesy to tell me your name."

Mr. Grumpy turns towards me, an amused expression on his face, and says, "hi there. I'm Seth Parson. It's nice to officially meet you." I huff and roll my eyes. I already knew his name, but at least this time he said it to me. "And you are?"

My gaze leaves the road for just a second so I can glare at him. "You know my name.

"And you already knew mine, but you said we needed to do this properly," he insists, crossing his arms and letting me know just how annoyed he currently is.

"Fine," I grit out. "I'm Skyler Netrio." I send another glare his way and add, "most people just call me Skye."

"Well it's a pleasure to meet you Skye." His words are drowning in sarcasm, and for half a second I want him to drown in them, too.

"Why are you being like this? I'm doing you a favor. Can't you just be nice?"

"I'm sitting here playing your game by your rules, sweetheart."

"Stop fucking calling me sweetheart! Don't you know you shouldn't call women that? It's sexist."

Seth lets out a quiet laugh and I can see him shaking his head. "Alright," he says eventually. "I will stop calling you sweetheart."

"Thank you." My tone has not changed. I'm still angry as hell.

Nothing about this scenario is me. I do not lie. I do not pick up random men in airports and bring them to my house. I do not have shouting matches with ex-boyfriends in the same airport. And I do not, I repeat, *do not* get turned on by angry assholes that take liberties with me and make me feel out of control.

I'm pissed, but I'm pissed at myself. I'm pissed that my mind and body are so fucking confused right now that they think this hot as hell guy next to me is the answer to my woes. Every time I catch a glimpse of his hands, or his arms; every time one of his muscular legs repositions itself in the seat next to me, I squirm.

"So can I ask a follow up question, *Skye?*" He emphasizes my name, making it clear that he's let the whole sweetheart thing go. I sigh and nod my head. It's a long drive. Talking might help, if he can behave. "You're saying you've never had a fling?"

Kill me. Sweet Lord, just take me now. His tone is light, but I can hear the interest in that deep voice of his, and it takes all I have to keep my eyes forward and not swerve off the side of the road and scream, "Take me now!"

Seth waits patiently for me to answer, and it takes me a hot second to do so. "I don't know," I finally say, and feel like a teenage idiot. I shake my head and try again. "No, okay? I haven't. I've always been a relationship person." I can see him nodding his head. "I just, I have to like someone, a lot, before I'm interested in, um, you know; the other stuff."

His soft chuckle pulls my eyes to him. "And by other stuff you mean sex?" A single eyebrow raises on his perfect face and I'm almost willing to risk a crash just to keep staring at him.

"Yes," I say, fully embarrassed. I'm also fully confused because I hate this guy, but my body sure as shit hasn't gotten the message.

"Have you ever tried it?"

His question surprises me, and I'm forced to think about it. "Not really," I admit. "There was this one guy years ago in high school. Gorgeous. Also a total asshole." I shrug. "After I saw his personality, the sex appeal quickly died."

"How old are you now?"

I consider giving him a lecture about asking a woman her age, but refrain. "Twenty-seven," I tell him honestly. "What about you?"

"Thirty-two."

I wait a second, then decide to keep on this path, and ask basic information questions. "What do you do for a living?"

"Photographer."

Okay, that's impressive. "Is that why you're going to Sedona? For work."

Seth's demeanor changes slightly, and his voice drops as he says, "no."

"For pleasure then?" I follow up. He doesn't answer. I might not know this guy, but I know a dead end in a conversation when I see one. "Where do you live?"

His sigh sounds sad, but he answer me. "Here and there, honestly. But I call Washington D.C. home."

I nod and wait for him to ask me the same question, but he doesn't. "I'm in Charlottesville, Virginia," I volunteer. "Been there since I was a kid. It's a nice place."

"I've been there," he says with a nod. "Not a bad place to call home."

I'm impressed with the easy back and forth, and I'm thankful that the topics have gone G-rated. I wasn't sure I could handle the whole drive talking about why I don't hook up with strangers. Mostly because any answer I'd give him would be met with a ton more questions.

As we near my grandmother's house, I decide to divulge a bit more information. "So, we're going to my Grandma's place. She lived here the last fifteen years of her life, so I spent a lot of summer vacations and winter breaks out here. My parents weren't the most stable people on the planet, but Granny made sure I always felt like I had a home to go to."

"That's sweet," Seth says sadly. "How long since she, um, passed on?"

"About a year." I pause as I think of her beautiful face, and the way her smile always lit up a room. "I still miss her, but at least I can come here, and it really helps me feel connected to her again."

"And your ex never came?" The question throws me for a second but I shake my head. "Not even for the funeral?"

This was a huge point of contention between Vince and me. I was devastated when she died, and I was also in charge of planning the funeral. I had to take a week off work to come out and handle everything by myself, because lord knows my dad wasn't going to lift a finger. Vince promised me he'd be at the funeral. He promised me he'd find a way to take off work and that he'd show up for me. He never did. Instead, the morning of the funeral, I woke up to a text that simply said, "so sorry I won't be able to make it. I'll make it up to you when you get home."

There is no making up for something like that. In my darkest hour he was MIA. Still, when I got home, I told him it was okay. I told him that I understood. He had to work. I handled it on my own. I survived. I told him, and even myself, that I could get over it. I could forgive his mistake. But, as I sit here in this car, next to a stranger, I realize that I never really did forgive him. Mostly because letting me handle the death of the most important person in my life completely alone is the definition of unforgivable.

To answer Seth's question, I simply shake my head. He doesn't need to know the specifics; he wouldn't care.

"Fucking bastard," he grumbles. His backhanded sympathy actually makes me smile. It feels good to know that someone else out there believes that Vince was in the wrong as well.

"You know," I say to him, "I think you're right."

For a moment, we look at each other, smiles on our face, and my heartbeat calms. I relax. Things are going to be okay. Maybe he's not the giant asshole I took him for. Maybe there is some hidden softness in there somewhere. Maybe behind that gorgeous face, that perfectly trimmed beard, and those mammoth hands of his there is a sweet man who hides behind a dick-ish exterior.

"So clearly you have shit taste in men."

Aaaaaand maybe not.

"Why's it always on the woman? *She* has shit taste in men. Never, wow, that guy is total shit."

At that, Seth laughs, and it's the first time I've heard him really belt it out. It's beautiful. His laughter is deep, sensual, and, well, fucking dangerous.

"Okay," he says in between laughs, "you got me there."

"I'm glad we are back in agreement," I mutter, but a smile is creeping over my face. His laughter is contagious. He smiles at me as his laughter dies down, and I nearly forget how to breathe.

I turn my head forward and turn off the highway. We're almost there.

I should be excited to be back in Sedona. I should be relieved to once again be in the place that was my sanctuary as a child. Instead, as I turn right, then left, then go through two green lights, the only thing on my mind is whether it would be the *worst* or *best* idea ever to bend the rules for this guy.

So I've never had a one-night stand. I've never been attracted to a guy that I wasn't emotionally invested in. And how has that worked out for me? Not great, if I'm honest.

As I turn onto my street, my stomach fills with butterflies.

Maybe?

Maybe Mr. Grumpy can be the one to put a smile back on my face.

I click open the garage door and shake my head as I pull in.

I need to get a grip. Sex is dangerous, and it's always a letdown.

Sex will not solve any of my problems. It'll probably just make them worse. That's all it did with Vince. Why would it be any different with Seth? Seth doesn't even like me. I couldn't make it work with Vince and we loved each other.

I'm pretty sure I'm just a lost cause.

Still, watching Mr. Grumpy get out of the car, walk back and open the trunk and pull out both our suitcases, I nearly have to wipe the drool off my chin. He's so calm, so casual. Yet here I am, just watching him, losing my shit.

I need a glass of wine. That'll help me get clarity, right? Calm my nerves … Right??

4

SETH

W𝐇𝐀𝐓 𝐓𝐇𝐄 𝐅𝐔𝐂𝐊 𝐀𝐌 I 𝐃𝐎𝐈𝐍𝐆

I'm standing in the middle of a stranger's living room in Sedona, Arizona, wondering what the fuck happened to land me in this spot. I'm fully aware that it's about ninety-nine percent my fault, but still.

All I wanted to do on the plane was pass the fuck out. I'm exhausted. This trip is happening for one reason, and one reason only, and nothing about that reason is fun. All I wanted to do was get in, do what I have to do, and get the fuck out again.

Instead, I stayed awake and listened to some pouty woman gush about her broken heart for the entire flight. When I finally fell asleep, it was her sweet voice and soft touch that woke me, letting me know the plane hand landed.

She was not part of this plan. But when I opened my eyes and started back at her, something in my gut shifted. Shoulder length brownish red hair, and green eyes like I'd never seen before. She was startling. I don't like to be startled.

So what did I do? Shoved past her the first chance I could; not because I'm a giant fucking asshole, which I definitely was, but because I knew I'd never see her again, and just needed to touch her. *Needed* to, even if the only way I could was by being an asshole.

Then I heard her say the name of the guy who fucked her up. Vince. The freaked out look on the guy's face, the other woman standing next to him, it was obvious what was going on. And for whatever reason, man, I felt for this girl. She was all broken hearts and emotions and here her ex was, completely rubbing it in her face.

I couldn't *not* step in. Even as I did, even as I swung my arm around her, the voice inside my head was screaming, "Don't! She's not yours to save! Get on with your life." But I couldn't. No one should be treated the way she was.

Do I think she's beyond naïve? Hell yes. Two hours of how perfect this Vince guy was, how perfect their relationship was, I lost count of how many times I rolled my eyes as I pretended to sleep. No guy's that perfect. If they are, there's so much going on behind the scenes that you do not want to know about.

The asshole had it coming. I have no regrets about that. But I know I took it way too far. The second my arm was around her and I was speaking for her, I knew I'd crossed a serious line. Not only because she's a stranger, but also because I quickly realized that there was something about her pouty lips that made my dick twitch.

And this is not a dick twitching type of trip. Not at all.

Still, I led her to baggage claim. I stayed with her. My heart was beating out of my chest, but every time I caught a glimpse of her ex, I moved in closer to her. Closer to her felt good; it felt really good. The way she puckered her lips in distain at me only made me want her more. The way she glared up at me made me feel like a king amongst men. Having her eyes on me lit me up in a way I wasn't prepared for.

And then ... well then I crossed way over the fucking line and invited myself into her goddamn home. *And then I kissed her.*

That fucking kiss. That glorious, unexpected, all consuming kiss, that she returned immediately.

"That was not part of the agreement," she said to me, and she was right. I had agreed to keep my hands off her, and to not touch her without her permission. I guess I decided to bend the rules, put on a show for her ex, but also, I needed to know if she tasted as good as she looked.

Now here I am, after an excruciating drive from Phoenix, standing alone in her house while she goes to the store to grab groceries. I'm shocked that she left me here. That's quite trusting of her. I assured her I meant her no harm, which is true, but I might mean her a little bit of devious fun.

The woman needs it, god damn. Never had a one-night stand? Never messed around outside of a relationship? Who can say that? I sure as shit can't. Almost all my experiences have been just that; meaningless, detached, just sex. For me, that's the best way to do it. I move around way too much, and no place is really home.

That's the way I like it. Just me.

I stop at that thought and let out a deep breath. It really is just me now. It's official. I'm the last of my family. My parents died a long time ago, and I my sister was lost to me not long after. But now she's truly gone, and it's hit me much harder than I thought it would. I'd given up on her. I had to give up on her. Still, she haunts my dreams every single night.

I'm only here for her. I'm here because this was her final wish. As fucked up as she got, I will do this for her. She may have lied through her teeth, robbed me blind, stolen my car, and ripped my fucking heart out of my chest, but she was my sister. My baby sister.

Walking around the living room, I see very few photos. There's one by the fireplace of an older woman and a young girl. I pick it up and examine it. The little girl is missing her two front teeth, her wild red hair covering half her face, but that smile ... that smile is the purity and happiness that only a child can know.

I think back to the Skyler I just met today. It's hard to see what this little girl and that grown woman still have in common. Her hair is still somewhat red, but there's no smiles to be had.

I bet I could make her smile ... shit, I bet I could make her cry happy tears of joy as I rail her from behind, wiping away both our hurt.

I shake my head and put the photo back. I can't be thinking about Skyler like that. I'm lucky she hasn't killed me yet, or called the police and had me arrested. I barreled my way into her life, into her house, and she's honestly taken it a whole lot better than I would.

When we were driving, I caught her looking over at me more than once. Her eyes wandered over my body, and a little sliver of hope bloomed in my chest. Maybe she's looking for a little stress relief as well. I don't think I'm alone in whatever this fucked up attraction is between us.

And there is definitely something here. She sat in her car and watched me carry the bags into the house, but not like angry watched me; more like hungrily watched me. I knew she was looking, so I took my time.

She wants a show? Baby girl, I will give you a show.

Assuming the cops don't surround the house and haul my ass off to jail in the next half hour, I have a new mission for this trip.

Get under Skyler's skin and find out what makes her tick. Loosen her up. Relax her. Get her to tell me why she's got a massive stick up her ass. Then maybe – maybe – offer to fuck it loose for her.

The woman is a goddamn stunner. That Vince guy is a fucking fool.

Hopefully his loss can be my gain.

5

SKYLER

"Dumbest fucking thing I've ever done," I mutter to myself as I peruse the aisles of the local grocery store. It's a small store, but I can make do. Most importantly, they have wine, so I'm just fine here.

I cannot believe that guy is at my house right now. Mr. Grumpy Seth is at my house, alone, doing god knows what. Shit, I hope he's not robbing me. I hope he's not poisoning food to serve me later. Then I realize I'm at the grocery store because there is no food, and therefore no way for him to poison me. At least that's one less thing to worry about.

I have to go down each aisle twice because of how distracted I am. Fucking Vince. That lying, cheating, no good bastard. Why couldn't he have just told me something was wrong? I had no idea. Shit, I still have no idea what the problem was. Now I'm just blatantly aware that there was one.

And then there's Seth. Mr. Grumpy. What the hell am I doing with this guy? Honestly, what the hell am I going to do with him? So far, I've let him pretend we know each other, pretend he's my new boy toy, let him *kiss me* in the middle of an airport, and then I drove his ass all the way to Sedona and invited him into my home.

An anxious groan leaves my lips, and I notice several people looking at me, wondering if I'm off my rocker. I smile back politely, apologetically, but in truth, they might be right.

It must be the breakup. It's just made me loopy. Because why else would I make a scene in an airport, then let a total stranger kiss me? Oh, and then let my lady bits get way too excited and worked up just sitting next to said stranger in a car for two hours.

The thought of his lips on mine, his big, rough hands on my body pulls me back out of reality. Shit, he's a really good kisser. Like, a really, *really* good kisser. No one has ever kissed me like that.

It felt like … lust. There was an urgency, almost like he was claiming me as his own. I hate that shit. I absolutely hate all that macho bullshit. Still, when he grabbed me, it was all I wanted in that moment.

"Excuse me, but are you going to move anytime soon?"

I snap back to reality and notice three people impatiently waiting while my distracted ass and my cart are taking up the entire aisle.

"Sorry," I mutter, my face beginning to flush. I quickly move my cart, grab three boxes of rice, and move on. I need to get my head back in the game. Thankfully, the wine aisle is just ahead. That's my real goal. I need to get enough wine to make this entire thing feel not as fucked up as it truly is.

I came out here to get a break, relax, and get my mind off things. Wine happens to be an integral part of my plan. I don't know if Seth drinks wine. I really shouldn't care, but I still want to be a good host; even for a guy who bullied his way into my house and into my life.

I'm here for two weeks. I have no idea how long he'll be squatting at my house, but I need to be prepared. I grab an empty wine case box that's sitting next to the wine, and fill the whole thing up. Twelve bottles should get us through.

The amount sounds extreme, but I remember his drunk ass on the plane, and my hunch is that he'll be helping quite a bit. Better to over buy than be under prepared.

After grabbing sandwich meats, ground beef, veggies, some chicken breasts, cheeses, bread, and a bunch of other things, including four bags of Doritos just because I freaking want to, I head to the checkout.

My foot is anxiously tapping against the floor as I pay for my order and load everything back into my cart. I have no idea what's waiting for me back home, in my own house.

All I know is that this relaxing little getaway just got a whole lot more complicated; and fuckload hotter.

I cannot stop thinking about his hands. They're just all man.

Vince had good hands, too. They were soft and regularly manicured, and he always kept his nails short. He was meticulous. They just happen to be the exact opposite of Seth's.

Seth's a photographer. He works outside. He works with his hands. I bet he's good with his hands.

I look up and am stunned to see that I've driven all the way back to my house, and am sitting in my driveway. I gulp back the anxiety that's eating me alive, refusing to call it by it's proper name, sexual tension, open up the garage door and pull in.

6

SKYE

BECAUSE I'M A STUBBORN ASSHOLE, I DO MY BEST TO CARRY EVERYTHING I purchased inside in one run. Except for the box of wine bottles, of course. It's not easy to do when you've got two week's worth of food to get inside the house.

Still, my arms are loaded to the brim with grocery bags, and I'm kicking, yes kicking, the door handle in the garage, hoping I'll suddenly turn into a ninja and it'll open magically for me. Six kicks in, no such luck, but I'm no quitter. I bend my knees a moment, letting a few of the heavy bags sit on the garage floor as I catch my breath. Then I raise them all up again, take a deep breath, and kick once more, because it's working well for me so far.

Just as I'm about to kick again, the door flies open, and I am met with an angry, glaring … holy fucking shit half naked, dripping wet man with nothing but a teeny tiny towel around his waist.

I freeze, unable to take my eyes off of the gloriousness in front of me. Seth on the other hand, looks about ready to murder me and eat me for lunch.

"What the actual fuck?" he barks, one hand on the door, the other holding that delicate little towel in place. "What the fuck are you doing?"

Jesus. Angry Seth is somehow even hotter than cranky Seth. Maybe it's the nakedness. Perhaps it's the … oh my … the tattoo that wraps around his shoulder and flows over the right side of his chest then down his arm.

"I-I-I," I stutter, my jaw on the floor, my arms officially losing all feeling.

I hear him scoff loudly, then swing the door fully open and reach for my arms. He takes several of the bags from me, and, still with one hand on that towel, he marches them over towards the kitchen, places them on the counter, and saunters back over to me, where I have yet to move a muscle.

"I'm going to put on clothes," he growls. "Then I'll help you."

I watch as he marches into my guest room, slams the door, and leaves me standing like a god damn marble statue in the heat of my garage.

Once he's out of sight, I finally start breathing again.

Wow. Wow wow wow.

I knew he was a handsome, manly dude, but sweet Mary, mother of God.

The abs. The pecs. The tattoo. The dark brown chest hair that pointed my eyes down, down to the area the small towel hid from me. His angry, brown eyes focused on me. His calf muscles, shit. The man had thighs that could choke me out, and an ass that, I'm sure, could crack a fucking walnut.

I could eat breakfast off that ass.

I clear my throat even though I'm alone, then do my best to get my shit together, and carry the remaining bags into the kitchen and set them down next to the other.

Back in the garage, I go to reach for the case of wine, when suddenly there are two very manly hands grabbing at mine.

"Let me do it," Seth barks, and I equal parts want to tell him to go fuck himself, and also beg him to immediately do me.

"I can get it," I huff out, my cheeks on fire, unable to look at him because I might just die, or lose all control and kiss his beautiful face while running my fingers over his perfectly chiseled body.

He doesn't respond before he picks up the box like it's nothing and heads back into the house. I slam the trunk closed and pout as I follow him inside, closing the garage door and the door to the house behind me.

I do allow myself to hang back and watch his ass as he carries my wine for me. Yeah, there are worse views than a hot as hell man and a full case of wine. They go quite well together, actually.

Once he sets the wine down, he starts peeking in the bags. The scowl leaves for just a second as he eyes up my massive Dorito purchase.

"Like Doritos much?" he asks.

"I'm on vacation," I say defensively as I head his way. "And this is *my* house. I can eat whatever the hell I want here."

That damn grin is pointed at me. "Never said you couldn't, sweet- I mean, Skyler."

I grin right back, silently thanking him for correcting himself. "I never get to each chips back home, so when I'm here, I indulge."

"Good for you." His words sound so sincere I take a moment to study him. "Stop staring at me," he says, catching me. Then he turns, and an evil grin has spread across his gorgeous, bearded face. "Surprised you're still interested. You know, now that I have clothes on."

I'm dead. Died. Deceased. The way this man is calling me out, I have no defense. None at all. His nakedness slayed me, and there's no pretending it didn't.

"I didn't," I begin with a huff. "I wasn't," I try again, but there's no hope for me. Instead I scowl, hang my head to the floor, and sigh.

Seth comes up behind me, letting his chest brush gently against my back as he pretends to put stuff away, in a kitchen that is not his. "Didn't say I minded," he practically purrs in my ear. "Did I?"

My head leans back all on its own. I no longer control it. It leans back and finds his hardened chest and another, more desperate sigh escapes my lips. His hands land on my hips, steadying me.

"Hey, Skyler," he says, his beard brushing up against my cheek, lighting my lady bits on fire. I hum in response, unable to form words. "Where should I put the bread?"

My eyes open back up, and his hands leave my hips. That stupid fucking grin is no longer my friend. Now it taunts me, and I'm not having it.

"Give it to me," I snap, grabbing the loaf from his hand and turning away from him. "Just leave it. You don't know where anything goes anyway. Just go away."

He lifts his hands in surrender, but I know he thinks he's won. This round, he has. I was ready to let him bend me over my grandmother's kitchen counters and fuck me raw, and no one is more ashamed of that than I am.

"Truce?" he asks, and all I can do is glare. "I'll just put a few of these bottles of wine in the fridge, okay? Let them chill a bit."

"Fine," I groan, but I get to the box before he does. I yank out a Merlot and step back. "This doesn't need to be chilled. This I can drink right fucking now."

"Stressed, are we?" he coos, and I hate him. I hate him for toying with me, and I hate myself for the effect his every word and movement has on me.

I pull open a drawer with way more force than is necessary, and grab my bottle opener. Ten seconds later the cork is out, and I'm ready for my first drink of the day.

"Not for long," I say, a warning glare being sent his way across the kitchen.

"Want a glass for that?" he asks, condescending to the last drop.

I'm so angry I almost start drinking straight from the bottle just to prove a point. But that would only hurt me.

For my grandparents' twentieth anniversary, my Granddad gifted his wife with really beautiful, hand blown wine glasses. She'd always wanted a fancy wine glass that made her feel posh. That year he made that wish come true. Every time I come here, after turning twenty-one of course, I've considered it a privilege to use those glasses. I would not let his man-candy jackass take that privilege and that pleasure from me.

I turn from him and reach into the cabinet above me, carefully pulling down one of the delicate glasses. I can feel his eyes on me as I pour a generous amount, not giving a fuck what he might think about it.

I pick up the glass, turn and face him, and let him watch as I raise the glass to my lips and take my first sip. My eyes close as the first drop enters my mouth. Yes, this is what I need. This will take the edge off.

Except that when I open my eyes, the angry man-candy is standing directly in front of me. I flinch, surprised to find him there. He leans towards me, and for a second I'm sure he's going to kiss me again. Instead, he presses his chest against mine, making my nipples stand at attention, and reaches over me, grabbing a glass for himself.

The game ends the second I see his hands on that glass.

"Be careful," I say quickly. "Those glasses are expensive and really, really important to me, and irreplaceable."

Seth pauses for a moment, then continues to pull down a glass for himself. I notice that he's slowed his pace, and is actually taking care not to break the glass.

I watch as he sets the wine glass down, grabs the bottle, and pours himself a glass just as big as the one I just poured for myself. He picks it up, raising it to mine, and I do the same.

"What are we toasting to?" I ask, agitation back in my voice.

"How about, to not killing each other while I'm in town?"

I snort out a laugh, but clink my glass to his. "Here's hoping." We both take a sip, then I add, "jail would put an unfortunate wrinkle in my life plan."

"Or if we do wind up killing each other," he smiles, as I go to take another sip, "let's at least agree to do it naked and fully fucked."

Wine comes out of my damn nose as I gasp, and then I'm choking. I'm choking on my relaxing wine as Seth slaps me on the back while I gasp for air.

"Shit, I'm sorry," he says, seeming to genuinely mean it. When I finally stop coughing, my face redder than it's been yet, I take another cautious sip, and thankfully this time it goes all the way down. "It was a joke," he says.

I look up at him, my hand over my nose that was just leaking wine, and search his perfect brown eyes for the truth. He lets me, standing still as I study him, our eyes staying locked for way too long for two people who claim to hate each other. "No," I finally say, "it wasn't."

An awkward silence falls between us as we sip our wine. When he clears his throat I look up at him. Seth sighs, shrugs his shoulders and says, "fuck it. You wanna just get drunk or what?"

That leads to my first genuine smile since getting to Sedona.

"Fuck yes."

7

SETH

Two hours, and two bottles of wine later, things are going well. We're sitting in her living room, shooting the shit, talking about nothing and everything all at once. The wine was a great idea. Thank god she got so much. It might be the only thing that can cut the tension between us, and that shit is thick.

Her body is leaning up against mine in the kitchen, and I'm about to lose my mind. All I want to do is slam her up against Granny's counters and take her, right here and now. The desire to pull her hair, open her neck to me and sink my teeth into it is almost overwhelming.

At least she enjoyed the view I gave her after my shower. It wasn't planned. There I was, taking a shower, trying to wash the plane off of me, and suddenly it sounded like someone was trying to break down the damn door. And it would … not … stop.

Pissed to hell, I grabbed the first towel I saw and anger walked to the door just to make it stop. If someone was trying to break in, one look at me would tell them they had another thing coming.

Instead, I was met with Skye, her arms piled with groceries, and the most shocked look I've ever seen on another person.

Maybe I'm an asshole, but I loved it. Hey eyes were glued to me, and as pissed off as I was about the noise, damn, her gaze set me on fire. That's the real reason I had to go get dressed. I couldn't be standing there in nothing but a towel while my boner grew to attention. I needed to put my jeans back on so I could hide that shit.

Now things seem more at ease. Skyler is on the couch, I'm sitting in a recliner, and we're just chatting as we drink, like we're old friends.

"More wine?" she asks, finishing off her own. She stumbles a bit as she stands up, and out of instinct, I'm on my feet to steady her. "I'm fine," she says quickly, brushing me off, but my hands don't leave her body. I'm trying, really trying, to tell my hands to let go, but they don't. They do not want to leave her sides.

Her eyes wander up towards mine, fear, anxiety, anticipation fueling her gaze.

Thinking on my feet, I reach for her empty glass and say, "allow me." My hands finally cooperate, and I walk into the kitchen, her empty wine glass in hand. I pull open the fridge door and let out a deep breath. We're both drunk. That's really a bad time to lose my shit and decide that bad things are suddenly a good idea.

"What do you want to drink next?" I shout over to her in the living room.

"Not sure," she says, and my body stills, because she is right behind me. "Do you have a preference?"

Oh no.

I turn around quickly, slamming the refrigerator door as I do. She's not there by mistake. I know this, she knows this.

I stare at her, watching and waiting to see if she moves away, but she doesn't.

"I do," I tell her, my voice low. I let my eyes wander to her wine stained lips, and then lick my own.

"I-I meant for the wine," she stutters unconvincingly. And then she bites that plush bottom lip, and that does it.

My hands go to the sides of her face and pull her lips to mine. There's nothing gentle about this kiss, nothing at all. I am in control, and right now she is the air I need to breathe.

Skyler reacts instantly, her hands wrapping around my waist and pulling herself flush with me. I can feel her tits on my chest and a low growl leaves my lips. Our tongues meet quickly, desperately searching each other.

Her hands fall to my ass, and this time the growl is coming from her. "I wanna eat breakfast off that ass," she sighs, and my dick stands at attention.

"Fuck me," I mutter, going right back to kissing her. I press my hands to her perky ass and lift her off the ground. Her legs go around me and I carry her back into the living room.

Our bodies fall onto the couch together, and we are a total mess; a sloppy, sexy, horny as all hell mess.

"Wait, wait, wait, wait," I say, gaining some control as I back away from her. "We're drunk. We're both drunk. We can't be doing this."

"Seth," she says, an air of annoyance in my name, "I have never been so turned on as I am by your mean, grumpy ass." My eyes light up with surprise. "So can you do me a favor and just kiss me?"

Yeah, she doesn't have to ask twice. My tongue is back against hers, my hands exploring her body, and hers are doing the same.

"Just kissing," I mutter against her lips.

"Obviously," she growls. "I don't do one night stands, remember?"

I grin into our kiss. She may not do one night stands, but I'm going to be staying here more than one night. Fuck, the way she feels wrapped around me, I could stay here forever.

"I remember," I growl back. I press my erection against her and watch as her head tilts and her eyes close. "And why is that?"

The sweetest moan escapes her lips as my hand travels down to caresses her breasts.

"Because," she mutters, her body arching into my hand, wanting more from me. "I don't like sex."

That stops me cold.

My hand stops, my lips stop, and I move to look down at her.

"I'm sorry, what?"

8

SKYLER

GREAT, HERE WE GO. ANOTHER GUY GETS TO TELL ME THERE'S SOMETHING wrong with me. Another guy gets to tell me that with him, it'll be different. Just trust him. He knows better than me. Barf. I've heard it all so many times. After the fourth time, however, I just stopped listening. I have no idea why men think they know more about a woman's body than a woman does, but they all do.

"I'm sorry, what?" Seth asks me, his glorious hands no longer on my tits, and that tongue of his now in his mouth only.

I let out a loud frustrated sigh and run my fingers through my disheveled hair.

"I don' like sex," I say again, giving him an unapologetic shrug.

He stares at me a long while, so long I'm a little worried I've broken him. "But," he finally says, his confusion apparent, "you like this, yes?"

"The thing we were just doing, oh yes."

Another quizzical stare. "And you wanted more?"

I sigh again. "I'm not the one who stopped," I remind him heavily.

"So," he says, leaning back on the couch, away from me, trying to figure me out like a damn puzzle. "Can I ask since when?"

"Uh," I have to think about that one. "I don't know. I guess since I started having sex in high school."

"How many guys have you been with?" My eyes go a bit wide and he follow quickly with, "sorry, that's personal. You don't have to tell me that."

"I'm not ashamed of my number," I tell him, because I'm not. "I've been with twelve men." It's not that many, and it's also not too few. I'm fine with my number. No shame in this game.

"So," he says again, and I let out a deep, loud, frustrated breath.

"Yes," I say, answering his silent and annoying question. "Yes, I've had sex with twelve guys, and each time it's just," I shrug, "okay."

"Okay?"

"Yes," I glare back at him, "okay." When he doesn't say anything else, I roll my eyes and continue. "It's not bad, exactly. Well, two of them were downright awful. I walked away in the middle of sex with one." I shake my head and shiver. "Ugh. Worst experience ever."

I glance at him, and he's sitting there, bottom lip hanging down, hanging on my every word. "Each guy claimed they'd be able to pleasure me." Another eye roll. "Each guy was *so sure* they had the magic cock that was going to blow my mind and make me fall in love with them." Another eye roll. "For some reason men internalize my lack of interest and make it a personal goal to make me come, and it's so goddamn annoying."

"But they never bothered to ask you what you want." Seth is shaking head head, his voice solemn, like he actually gets what I'm saying. I can hardly believe it, so I don't.

"Pretty much, yeah," I sigh. "I stop being a person and immediately become some type of challenge for their manhood. After that I'm out."

He lets out a long breath of air as his fingers dance across his beard. "Yeah, no, I can't blame you there." He pauses and looks at me. "I'm sorry guys can be such assholes."

I nod at him, thankful for his apology on behalf of all men.

"Can I ask," he begins.

"Ask whatever you want," I say, resigned. "I'm not ashamed anymore. I'm so over all of it. My body is the way it is, and that's that."

"How did your ex feel about all this?"

I shoot him a warning glance, but decide to answer the question. "The same as the others at first," I admit. "He wanted to 'be the first' to make me come. He kept telling me that he loved me, so that was going to be the ticket." I stop to take a sip of my wine, only to realize that my empty glass is still sitting in the kitchen.

Seth sees me, and hands me his still half full glass. "Thanks," I mutter. "After I a while though, he gave up, but he was nice about it. We had sex if he wanted to, and he stopped worrying about me and what I got out of it."

"Uh," Seth says, sounding slightly annoyed, "I don't know how I feel about that."

"Why?" I ask, helping myself to his wine.

"He knew you didn't enjoy having sex with him, still asked you to have sex with him, then totally gave up on making it pleasurable for you at all?"

"Uhhhmmm," I stutter. Then the talking points I'd rehearsed over the years flood back to me. "He still wanted sex, so I wanted him to be happy. I mean, I wasn't getting orgasms, so what was the point of him trying to do anything other than get his, you know? In and out, quick, and then we went back to other stuff. It wasn't a big deal."

The grimace on Seth's face slowly turns to full on distain, hatred, anger, and honestly it's a bit scary.

Scary hot.

"That is, with all due respect," he adds, "the biggest load of bullshit I've ever heard in my life."

The two of us just stare at each other, my Bambi eyes wide, his narrowed together in rage.

He shakes his head, letting go of some of the anger. "I'm sorry he treated you like that," he finally says, his voice a bit softer. "Honestly, you deserve way better than that."

"How?" I mean it. I genuinely do not know the answer to this question. How do I keep a man, keep him happy, give him what he wants, if the thing he wants gives me no pleasure? How else do I keep him with me other than to suck it up and take one for the team? I have to put myself aside. I have to put him first, or he'll leave me.

I watch as Seth sighs, shakes his head, and reaches for my wine glass. He places it on the coffee table in front of me and takes my hand.

"Like this," he says softly. He holds my hand gently, letting his thumb run over my knuckles. I have no idea what he's talking about, but it feels nice. A flutter of butterflies goes off in my stomach, and I bite my lip.

"I don't get it," I admit.

"Kindness, sweet- shit, sorry. Skye. Kindness."

I gnaw on my lip, contemplating what I want to say next. It's a risk, but dammit, it's how I really feel. "Then how come you've been nothing but an asshole to me and I can't keep my hands off you?"

Seth grins, and his eyes fall to the couch. "Alright," he admits, a shy smile on his face. He lifts his head and looks at me again. "You got me there, gotta admit." I smile at him while those butterflies keep doing circles in my gut.

"So maybe I like mean guys?" I ask. I really hope this isn't the case. That would really suck.

"No," he laughs, squeezing my hand. "You don't like mean guys, I promise."

"But," I begin, my stomach fluttering away, "I like you."

Seth's smile fades as his eyes undress me and bare my soul.

"Skyler," my name a near whisper on his lips, "you are free to think what-ever you like about me, but I'm not a mean guy. A mean guy wouldn't have stopped what we started in the kitchen. A mean guy wouldn't … a mean guy wouldn't care if sex made you uncomfortable or hurt you. They'd only care about getting what they wanted from you and then they'd move on."

"Well, what you want from me?"

It's the wine. I completely, totally, one hundred percent blame the wine.

This time his hand reaches up and brushes across my cheek.

"Maybe I did want something from you," he admits, his brown eyes fixed on me. "Maybe I still do. But you know what I want *for* you?" I shake my head, unable to breathe. "I want you to feel happy in your own skin." His hand moves as his fingers brush into my hair. "I don't want you to feel like you have to compromise your body or your boundaries to keep a man." When his hand lands on my bottom lip he adds, "no one is worth losing part of yourself for."

His words hit me like a freight train. No one has ever said anything like this to me. Never in my life did I feel like I was compromising parts of myself to please someone else, but I know in this moment that he's right. That's what I've been doing. That's what I've done my whole life.

He's also right, that, I need to stop. It has to stop. And it will stop.

"Thank you," I say slowly, reaching out and placing my hand on his while his thumb dances on my bottom lip. I kiss it then, and let my teeth gently press against his flesh. His eyes close, and I know what he still wants from me.

I move his thumb into my mouth and let my tongue feel him as my lips wrap around it.

"Skye," he sighs, biting his lip which is making me hungry for so many things. "I didn't tell you that as some ploy." I swipe my tongue against his thumb again. "You don't have to do that," he tries to say. "I don't want you doing anything you don't want to do."

I let my teeth sink into his thumb and he lets out a short gasp.

When I release his thumb, I say, "I know. And I appreciate you saying that, really I do."

Then I move my body off the couch, straddle his lap, and press my center against him. The hiss that leaves his lips drives me a bit mad, and it just makes me want him more.

"Skye," he whispers, his hands on my hips. "What are you ... what are you doing?"

"Exactly what I want."

With that I take his head in my hands and press my lips to his. This is what I want. From the moment he kissed me in the airport to this moment now, this is what I've needed. I need to kiss him. I need him to kiss me back.

"Are you sure?" Seth whispers against my lips. I rock my hips against him, surprised by how good it actually feels.

"Yes," I answer, nibbling at his lip. "Is this okay?"

His growl is all the answer I need, but he still says, "yes, fuck yes."

"Even if it never leads to sex?" I ask.

He kisses me hard, letting his tongue find mine. "Anything you want, sweetheart," he mutters into my mouth, "and nothing you don't."

His words release me. I relax, knowing that boundaries have been set, knowing that we are on the same page. I don't want to ruin this moment, what we have, with sex. I do want to kiss him for hours and run my hands over his gorgeous body, hair everywhere, all man, and never stop.

He won't make me, or ask me to do anything I don't want to do.

I'm free to be me. I'm free to just have fun, enjoy the moment, and get lost in his perfect, dangerously delicious kisses.

9

SETH

I KISS SKYE UNTIL I PHYSICALLY CAN'T ANYMORE; UNTIL MY BALLS ARE WRAPPED so tight that I'm afraid they might just fall off. All our clothes stay on, my hands only explore areas she's already deemed as safe: her face, her arms, hips, ass, and breasts.

Not once do I try and move my hand between her legs. Not once do I try to strip her naked, fuck her on the couch, and have my way with her.

I won't make her a challenge.

She set limits, and I'm in her damn house. I am going to respect them.

It's nearly 1A.M. by the time our lips finally detach, and I gather up the resolve to say goodnight. Her lips are so swollen from mine that it feels impossible to actually physically walk away. I hold her hand as we walk back towards her bedroom. I know I'm not going in with her, and that's okay.

I kiss her goodnight, and go into the guest room, closing the door and locking it behind me. Fuck. What a night. What a day.

How long has it been since I just kissed a woman? The second I started having sex as a teenager, that was the end goal. All the other stuff became foreplay. Less and less attention was put on really good kissing, touching, holding someone as your lips brushed against theirs.

I'm shocked by how full I feel inside. That was ... really nice. Kissing her and knowing it wouldn't lead anywhere, it felt freeing somehow.

So I kissed her. I kissed her until my dick was about to fall off, and I had no other choice but to duck into her guest room and pump myself until I spilled out all the desire she'd spent the last several hours pumping into me.

I whispered her name as I groaned out my release, stunned by how hard I came, and immediately wanting more from her.

After a second go with myself, I finally crawled into bed and fell asleep.

This has been the strangest, most unpredictable day of my life, and I'm a photographer. I've been in the jungles of Africa, the mountains of Europe in winter, and the dessert in Dubai. This fucking day with her still takes the cake.

I cannot wait to see what tomorrow brings.

10

SKYLER

I wake up the next morning with a smile on my face and a light headache. It takes me a second to remember where I am, then another to remember that there's a stranger in my house; a stranger that kisses like the devil and looks just about as tempting.

I wondered if I'd wake up this morning and regret what I did last night. There was wine involved, and I had to admit that I was in a bit of a delicate place emotionally. But as I stretch and look out my bedroom window, I have no regrets. In fact, the biggest feeling I have is gratefulness. I told Seth my big bad secret, the one that horrifies all men, and he'd taken it with stride. Not just with stride, but he continued to let me kiss his face off for another several hours.

As I get out of bed, I wonder if he's up yet. I wonder if I can also pick right back up where we left off last night. Those lips are mesmerizing, and I want more.

I quickly put on a pair of yoga pants, a sports bra, and a loose fitted workout shirt and throw my hair up into a ponytail. I'm in Sedona, after all. Some of the best views in the world are just outside my windows. Whenever I'm here I always try to take full advantage and get out and see the red rocks as much as possible.

When I walk into the kitchen, I'm greeted by the sight of Seth brewing coffee, shirtless. His back is turned towards me, and I notice the disheveled bed hair, as well as a few lines on his back left from the bed he slept in.

I tentatively walk up to him, clearing my throat gently to announce my presence. He turns around, and hot damn. He's even more gorgeous than I remember. That tattoo of his, thick lines and shapes dancing over his shoulder and chest draws my eyes, but then they quickly fall to his full, muscular physique.

"Morning, sweetheart," he says with a grin, fully aware that I'm ogling him and not giving two shits.

"Morning," I answer back shyly, reaching to tuck my hair behind my ear before remembering it's all up in a ponytail. "Did you sleep okay?"

He's eying me up, taking in my yoga pants and lose shirt. I wore a little makeup yesterday, mascara and a bit of pink lip balm. This morning my face is bare, and I wonder if he notices the difference.

"Eventually."

There is *so* much meaning hidden in that tiny little word, and his tone tells me all of it. I got him hot and bothered. He had to take care of himself. He came last night while thinking of me.

My face begins to flush, and I self consciously touch the back of my hands to my cheeks to try and cool myself down.

"So," I say, breaking away from his intense stare and reaching for two coffee mugs, "what are your plans for the day?" I stop at that, and turn to look at him. "Actually, why are you even in Sedona in the first place?"

Seth lets out a low chuckle, and that noise has me panting for him in an instant. Could he be anymore more manly? Tall, dark and handsome, glorious chest hair that's trimmed close to his chest but still plenty for me to run my fingers through. And I do want to run my fingers through it.

"I guess I never did tell you that," he admits, pulling my thoughts from his chest that I want to lick for the next hour, at least. Instead of answering, he continues to smile at me, like he's trying to decide what he wants to tell me. "Come on a hike with me this morning."

It's not a question, but he asks it so nicely that I think it is. "Well," I start, "I was planning to go walk around the red rocks anyway, so I guess we could, um, go together."

He reaches for the coffee mugs and fills both of them with fresh brewed coffee.

"There's a specific trail I'd like to go to. Is that okay?"

"Sure," I say, reaching for one of the mugs. "Which one?"

"I looked it up last night before I fell asleep. It's about twenty minutes from here. It has a vortex on it."

"Ooooh," I say slowly. "Those places are something else."

"So you've been?"

I narrow my eyes as I think. "I doubt I've been to whichever one you want to go to, but I've been to one, a long time ago. They say it's a portal to another world. It sounds crazy, I know, some real *Outlander* type of shit, but I'm telling you." I shake my head. "When you're there, you understand why people say it is what it is."

"So you believe in portals to another world? Or another time?" Seth asks, very interested in my answer.

"I don't know to be fully honest," I tell him. "But I can completely understand why someone would. They're special places, at the very least."

He nods his head and takes a sip of his coffee.

"What makes you want to go there?" I ask, moving to the fridge to grab the carton of eggs I bought yesterday.

When he doesn't answer, I turn and look at him. He looks so pensive, and lost in thought. "Can I tell you when we get there?" he offers, and there's just enough pain in his voice that I know to drop it. I nod at him, and then go back to making us some breakfast.

"How do you like your eggs?"

"I don't," he laughs. Just as I'm about to roll my eyes and tell him he's annoying, Seth comes behind me and wraps his arms around my waist, taking me by surprise. My body eases back against his, like it's done it a million times before. "I had fun last night." His chin is resting on my shoulder, and I can feel his breath on my neck.

"Me too," I say softly, moving my hands on top of his. "Thanks for, um, you know," I stumble, "not pushing me or giving me a hard time."

The beast of a man kisses my neck and I melt, *melt* against him.

"Of course, Skye. I'd never want you doing anything you weren't fully into." I feel him shrug. "What's the fun in that?" He says it like it's common sense, like all men think the exact same way, but they most certainly do not.

"I was into you last night," I mutter, surprising myself by how bold I'm being, and before I've even had a full cup of coffee.

He hums against my neck and I let out a raggedy breath. "I was very into you as well."

His arms fall from around me, as one travels down to my ass, then gives me a soft pat before walking away.

My hands are shaking as I try to crack two eggs into my skillet on the stove. Thankfully Seth isn't watching me, or I'd be mortified.

I eat quickly while we both sip our coffee, then agree to head out to the vortex that he wants to see.

11

SETH

A HALF HOUR LATER, WITH SKYLER DRIVING THE RENTAL CAR, WE PARK AND get ready to hike the trail that gets us to where I need to go. My backpack is with me, with precious cargo inside. I do want to tell Skye what we're doing, but it's hard. It's complicated, and I hate being in a position of vulnerability, especially with a woman I barely know.

Knew her well enough to let her ride my dick over my pants till I almost came, but that's a different story.

We each get out of the car, double check that we have our phones and water bottles, and take off. I offer to put her water in my backpack so she doesn't haven't to carry it and she accepts with a shy smile.

We walk in silence as we head towards the vortex. I really don't know what to expect, but this isn't my show. I didn't pick this place, so whatever we find, it's how she wanted it to be.

It's a brisk twenty-five-minute walk until we reach our final destination. Even though it's still somewhat early, before 11AM, the heat is strong, and we're both sweating; me more than her, since my body is covered with thick, black hair everywhere.

"Here we are," Skye says, and I can hear the struggle in her breath. It was a trek, no doubt. "So," she says, turning back towards me, a smile on her face, "what do you think?"

It's gorgeous. Stunning. Nothing but red rocks, nature, silence, and I feel so immediately at peace I nearly cry. Now I see why she wanted me to come here. I get it. This place feels … spiritual. It feels other worldly.

Skyler is watching me, waiting for me to respond. "It's breathtaking," I finally say. "I had no idea." I wipe my arm across my forehead, getting rid of some of the sweat. "I can't believe I've never been here before."

"Better get your camera out and take some pictures then," she says, a teasing smile on her face. I give her a quizzical look, and she laughs. "That's what's in the backpack, right? Your camera? There's no way you could come here and not want to capture the beauty of this place."

She isn't wrong. But I know no camera will ever do this place justice. I have to capture this place, and this moment, in my heart.

As Skye puts her hands on her hips and looks around, something tugs deep at my heart. It feels like it's all happening for a reason; like she is supposed to be here with me. Almost like this is part of my sister's plan. It sounds so crazy, even to me, but in my gut, I feel that this is exactly where I am supposed to be, and Skye is absolutely supposed to be here by my side.

"I didn't come here for me," I say, gently placing my bag on the red, sandy ground. Skyler turns and looks at me. "I came here for my sister."

"You have a sister?" she asks, her eyebrows slightly narrowed.

I unzip my backpack and slowly pull out a small cardboard box. I hold it in my hands, all that is left of Lena. "Had," I say solemnly.

Skyler's expression changes quickly. She goes from happy and carefree to full on nurturer in a spilt second. "Seth," she says heavily, coming to me and placing her hands on my wrists as I hold the box containing my sister's ashes. "I'm so sorry. I'm so sorry." She looks down at the box, and then back into my eyes. She watches me a moment, then asks, "would you like to tell me about her?"

I nod my head. Yes, I really would.

I place the box on the ground between us and take her hand. "Can we sit?" We find a flat place, and I pull out a towel that I brought along, and we both sit on it, close together. The box of ashes sits between us, and I still feel like I need to be gentle with it; like I still need to take care of her.

"Lena was a wild child," I begin, a small smile spreading against my lips. "We had a difficult childhood. Both our parents died young, and pretty close together. She got really mixed up, and started to depend on the wrong people." I feel Skye's hand reach out and squeeze mine. I squeeze it back and continue.

"She had a boyfriend at the time, and I thought he was helping her through." I shake my head. "Turns out he was a piece of shit. He was cheating on her, lying to her. He was nice to her face because he didn't want to upset her, but in reality, he was checked out. When she found out, she lost it. She got drunk for a month. Then she fell in with this scuzzy guy who wound up getting her hooked on cocaine."

"Jesus," she mutters, shaking her head.

"It just went downhill from there. I tried to intervene. I sent her away to rehab, several times. I had her move in with me. But I wasn't around enough. Instead of helping her, I came home to find my place trashed, emptied out, and my car stolen."

"Oh my god."

"After that I had to cut my losses for a while. It was killing me seeing her like that, and it killed me not being able to save her." I turn and look at Skye. "I was all she had left. I should have been the one to save her, but I couldn't."

Her hand starts caressing my arm. "I believe you did everything in your power to help her. I truly believe that. Not ... not everyone can be saved," she says reluctantly.

"I lost track of her for a while. Over a year. Then one day she showed up on my doorstep, telling me she was in deep shit and needed my help. She swore she'd get sober and clean and do whatever it took to salvage our relationship." I stop and look down at the box. "I sent her here," I tell Skye. "There's a rehab place not far from Sedona, and I checked her in for six months."

"How'd that go?"

I give a sad smile. "She did really well. Lena loved it here. She sent me emails, cards, and called me at least once a week to tell me how this place made her feel whole."

"That's really great."

"It was," I say, knowing how things turned out. "She must have updated her will, or hell, written her will, when she was here. Not six months after leaving this place she was found dead of a heroine overdose."

"Oh my god," she says, her hand over her mouth. "That's horrible."

I shrug, doing my best to find peace with what happened to her. "She never did conquer her demons. They found her, and in the end, they won." I take a moment to let her hold my hand and comfort me. It feels really nice not to have to go through this alone. "I lost my sister a long time ago," I say with a deep breath. "I know losing her this time is the final time, and in a fucked up way, that almost feels easier to deal with."

I shake my head, hating myself for admitting the truth. But watching her suffer for all those years, not being able to save her, always feeling that I had to while knowing I couldn't, it killed me. Her struggles killed me a little bit every single day, because I loved her too much to never not care.

Beside me, Skyler nods her head. "I know what you mean." She takes a deep breath and looks at the ground. "I know it sounds fucked up, but I get it. When my grandmother got sick, we all knew it would get her in the end. She was old, she'd lived a great life, but there was nothing anyone could do for her this time. Every call terrified me. I kept waiting for it to be *that* call, the final call. And watching her suffer..." She takes in a deep breath and I can see the emotion bubbling over in her. "It killed me," she admits. "Every single day, it killed me a little bit more inside."

My stomach drops, realizing that she's used my exact same words.

"When I finally did get that *final* call, I was devastated. Absolutely devastated. And yet, I also felt relieved. She was no longer in pain. She was at peace. The battle was over. I didn't have to lie awake anymore, terrified that she was going to die alone. It was over. For both of us, it was over."

I pull Skyler to her feet along with me as she wipes tears from her eyes. The second we're both standing, I pull her body against mine, and we stand there, embracing each other, letting our tears fall for the ones we loved and lost.

There's no judgment, there's no anger, and being here for each other, I can feel the pain begin to slip away.

When we finally pull apart, I look into her eyes, then lean in and kiss her. It's a soft, sweet kiss; a thank you for being here with me in this moment in life. She smiles, and kisses me back, just the same.

"Are you ready to do this?" she asks, taking a deep breath and looking at the box.

I nod my head. I am. It's time.

Together we remove the tape, check the direction of the wind, and stand looking out over the beautiful landscape that surrounds us.

I close my eyes, picturing my sister as I choose to remember her: a little girl, so full of life and happiness. I say one final farewell to that sweet, innocent girl, and I feel the wind on my back. I raise the box above me and tilt it, letting the wind carry her away.

12

SKYLER

IT WAS BEAUTIFUL. BEING WITH HIM, SETH SHARING HIS STORY ABOUT HIS sister, sending her off into another world. A final farewell. A part of me felt like I was saying goodbye to my grandmother, too. I'd done that at her funeral, yes, but I still carry so much loss inside me because of her. Being out there with Seth today, the way we held each other as we cried, I felt a shift in me.

It's crazy, but I felt like I was supposed to be there, right there, with him. Not just for him, but for me as well.

As we walk back towards the car, we do so in comfortable silence. We shared a moment that neither of us will ever forget. Something powerful just happened, and I feel in my bones that I will be forever changed because of it.

I sneak a peak over at Seth as we walk. His dark hair is sleek with sweat, and I can see trickles dripping down his neck. I want to kiss him. I want to hold him again and have him hold me.

Just as I think about reaching for his hand, movement to my right catches my eye. When I look over, I jump about six feet in the air and squeal out a barely coherent, "*snnnaaaaaaakkkeeee!!*"

I am running so fast in the opposite direction that it takes me a second to hear Seth shouting at me to slow the fuck down, and get the fuck back here. When I finally stop running, my heart beating out of my chest, Seth is right behind me.

"What the actual fuck!" he shouts, both out of breath and annoyed to all hell with me.

"There was a snake!"

"Yeah, I fucking gathered that," he says sarcastically. I watch as he rolls his eyes, breathing heavily. "Did you see what *kind* of snake?"

"No," I say defensively, crossing my arms over my chest. "Either way it's one that could kill me and I'm not having it."

The man looks at me like I've gone insane, but I refuse to budge. I don't do snakes. I hate snakes. Like, hate hate snakes.

"So, what's your plan then?" he asks angrily. "Hmm? You just going to stay out here forever?"

I pout and frown at him. "I hadn't gotten that far," I reluctantly admit.

"Jesus Christ," he mutters, as he moves his hands through his sweat soaked locks. "How about we go back to the car," he says, but I'm shaking my head like a crazy person already. "Stop," he groans. "I'm tired, and covered in sweat, and I want to cool the fuck down. For all those things to happen, we need to get back to the car, and that requires you coming with me."

"But the snake!" I cry.

"I will deal with the snake," he says, so calmly that for whatever reason, and with no logic at all, I believe him.

"You promise?"

Another deep sigh. "Yes," he says, "I promise. Now can we please go?"

I let him lead me back down the path, my eyes fully alert for any and all movements. I'm sure we're back where I saw the snake, but it's nowhere in sight.

"Must've slithered off," he says, grinning over at me. I shiver, not ever wanting to run into another snake for as long as I live.

We make it back to the car, and the second I turn the key he's blasting the AC. "Sweet fucking relief," he groans, making me laugh.

Once back at the house, we both agree to take showers and change, then grab some lunch. I resist the temptation to wait for him to come out in a teeny tiny towel again. God, do I want to see more of that.

Instead I remain a good little girl, and when we're both dressed and ready, we head back into my car.

"Just," he says, stopping me before we get in, "one quick thing." I look at him, confused, and then he pulls me into him, and kisses me hard. My purse drops to the garage floor as my arms wrap around his neck. I open my mouth to his, desperate to have his tongue against mine.

When he backs away, I let out a very audible whimper of disapproval. His smirk makes me bite my bottom lip. "Plenty more where that came from," he teases me, "but first, I need food."

13

SKYLER

THE LOOKS THIS GUY IS GIVING ME OVER THE TABLE - BE STILL MY BEATING heart.

We've already ordered and are waiting for our food, but Seth cannot stop looking at me. He's not just looking at me in a nice, casual, isn't this a lovely day, type of way. No. He's looking at me like he knows my body is on fire and the only thing that'll put that fire out is him.

"Stop," I finally say, hiding my flushed face behind my hand. I can hear him chuckle, and I shake my head, doing my best not to smile my corny, *I'm way too happy right now* smile.

Thankfully our food arrives, but before I can dig into my salad with salmon, he takes big forkful of his lasagna and moves it across the table to me. "You've gotta try this."

I mean, there are so many things I do want to try that belong to him, but I guess I'll settle for the lasagna. I'm also in no way upset that he's feeding me from his own fork. I purposely lean over the table, letting my shirt hang, giving him a good peak at my tits. I watch his eyes dart to them, and I feel pretty proud of myself. Turns out I can affect him just the same as he affects me.

"Hey," Seth says, his voice light and gentle. I look up at him, all ears. "Thank you for this morning. It, uh, it meant a lot that you were there and supportive."

I reach over and grab his free hand. "Thank you for letting me be part of it."

He takes my hand, raises it to his lips, and kisses the back of it, filling my already full belly with butterflies. I feel him tug at my hand, as he nods his head. "C'm here." His voice is so soft, but deep in a way that I know there's nothing innocent about this man.

I lean over the table as does he, our lips meeting in the middle. Kissing him has quickly become my favorite thing to do. Kissing him in public, at a gorgeous restaurant, surrounded by gorgeous scenery – it doesn't get much better than that.

"Ahem." I hear someone clearing their throat and I back away with a giggle. Busted. I gaze up at our waiter, and am shocked to find Vince there instead.

"What the hell," I say, without even thinking about it. "I mean, uh, hi Vince. What are you doing here?"

He's wearing the world's deepest scowl, and it makes me shrink back in my chair. I let him glare at me and over at Seth for another moment before I say again, "what are you doing here?"

"Can we talk?" He's refusing to look at Seth. His body is turned away from him, almost like he's hoping that beefy hunk of man will just disappear.

I glance over at Seth. He does not look thrilled, but at the same time, I can tell he doesn't feel threatened. Good. There's only one man I want in my bed tonight.

Oh shit… I want Seth *in my bed*? Where did that-

"Skye," Vince say hastily, breaking me out of my thoughts. "Can we? Please?" He motions towards the side yard of the restaurant, away from all the tables.

While I don't feel I owe this jackass anything, I agree. I wait for Seth to give a quick nod of approval, and then excuse myself and follow Vince to a quieter spot.

"What?" I say, crossing my arms over my chest.

"Who *is* that guy?" Vince is not happy, which makes me feel pretty happy. I take a moment to soak him in. Tall, thin frame, blond hair that's styled impeccably, well dressed as always, and a disapproving scowl on his face that I'd learned to live with every single day we were together.

I glace at Seth, sitting at our table, over Vince's shoulder. Tall, dark, handsome, built up with muscle, that tattoo, the beard. The two could not look more different.

"That's not your concern," I say sharply, cutting off the line of questions I know are coming my way. "I could ask the same of your other girlfriend," I shrug my shoulders, "but I won't."

"Skye," he says, in the way he did when I was still his. It makes my stomach churn. He reaches for my arm and I quickly pull away. He no longer has the right to touch me whenever he pleases.

Vince sighs, but retracts his hand. "I'm sorry," he says. "I didn't know how to tell you that I wasn't happy. The whole sex thing was just too much for me," he admits. "I thought I could handle it, and then I met Becky. Getting to know her, the way I feel about her, that's how I knew what we had wasn't enough. I'm sorry it went down the way it did, though."

"Okay," I say, rolling my eyes. "A little advice for the future; don't tell one woman you love her while you're fucking someone else."

He physically cringes and moves away from me. He's not used to hearing language like that from me, I get it. He doesn't recognize the woman standing in front of him. In fairness, neither do I, but I think I like her.

"I-I-I said I was sorry," he tells me again, like I've insulted him.

"I heard you. I appreciate that. Is that all?"

There's that pursed lip look I despise on him. He wants to lecture me. Vince wants me to know that he's right, once again, and that I am wrong. That was always so important to him.

"I'm concerned about you," he adds. I scoff, then let out a loud, unconvinced laugh. "I'm serious!" I just look at him, wondering if he hears the bullshit that's coming from his mouth. "You don't know that guy, Skye. He could be bad news." Vince turns and sneaks a glance at Seth, whose eyes have not left us. "He has a tattoo, Skye. A big one. He could be dangerous."

There are so many things I want to scream at this man-child, but it would do me no good. We're over. He is out of my life, just like he wanted. I will win nothing and potentially lose my shit if I engage like Vince wants me to.

Instead, I stand tall, smile at him, and say, "you're right. He could be dangerous. But that's for me to find out, not you. Go back to your new life, Vince. And stay the fuck out of mine."

I leave him standing there, his perfectly shaved jaw on the floor, and walk back to Seth. His brown eyes are glued to me, and mine to him. His chest his heaving, and I can see him gripping the arms of the chair harder than usual. He's worried. He doesn't need to be worried.

I walk up to him, place my hands on both sides of his luxurious beard, and slam my lips against his. I need him to know this is for him, and not for Vince. I crawl into his lap and let him wrap his arms around me. When I break the kiss my eyes are only on his, telling him as best I can that this is where I want to be. Nothing else matters to me; not anymore.

"Take me home?"

Seth nods his head as his tongue darts out to lick his bottom lip. I kiss him one more time then go back to my seat. I do not look to see if Vince is still there, watching. It doesn't matter. He made his choice, and it wasn't me.

Now I've made mine.

14

SETH

GOOD LORD. THIS WOMAN, THIS STRANGER I JUST MET, IS ALL I CAN THINK about. I cannot stop looking at her. I don't ever want to stop kissing her. I refuse to even think about what'll happen when I leave in a few days. It doesn't feel real. Leaving this place and this moment with her doesn't feel real.

I hated watching her go off and talk to that loser ex-boyfriend of hers. He just showed up and expected her to give him what he wanted. I don't know what they said. All I do know, is that when Skyler was finished, she came for me. *Me.*

It wasn't for show. She didn't kiss me to prove a point. She didn't crawl into my lap to make another man jealous. No. She did it because that was what she truly wanted to do.

"Take me home?"

Baby girl, I'll take you anywhere you want to go.

I quickly pay the check, and grab her hand, walking us both back to her car. It's a short drive to her place, but I don't let go of her hand as she drives.

Once we're back at her place, we walk into the living room, hand in hand, and I pull her body towards mine. Her arms wrap around my neck, and her green eyes gaze into mine.

"Are you okay?" I ask her, unable to hide the desire in my voice. She nods, then leans up and kisses me. "Do you want to talk about it?" My breath is already heavy, but I want to be there for her.

She watches me a moment, letting her fingers run across my jaw line.

"Okay," she says softly. "I can tell you about how I can't stop thinking of you." Jesus. "Or how all I want to do is kiss you, get you naked, and explore every single inch of your body."

"I-I-I," I stutter, letting her press her breasts up against my pounding chest, "I meant about lunch," I manage to get out, my hands having already found their way to her hips, pressing her further against me.

Skyler leans in and kisses me again. "The only thing I want to talk about," she says, stopping to kiss me again, "is that tattoo." I feel her hands move to the bottom of my shirt and hesitate. "May I?"

I nod quickly. Yes, yes she can take off my shirt. I'm thankful I lost my appetite when her ex showed up. Instead of being full, I'm starving for her. Skye lifts my shirt over my head, and the little gasp that leaves her lips makes me body shudder.

"Can I ... touch you?"

"Sweetheart, you can touch me anywhere you want."

I'm about to apologize for calling her that, but a grin spreads across her face. I stand there as she takes her time, her fingertips grazing over my chest and chest hair, up to my shoulder, and down my arm.

"What does it mean?" she asks of my tattoo.

"My granddad was Polynesian," I tell her, my eyes shuttering closed from her touch. "He grew up in Maui. Came to the U.S. mainland when he met my grandmother and married her. She was Italian and wanted to go back to be closer to family." I can barely talk as her hands explore my body. "The tattoo is part of his and my culture. I wanted to honor him after he passed. He was a good man."

"Mmmm," she hums as her hands slowly bring me to my death. She looks up at me, like she's studying my face. "I can see that," she says. "It looks good on you."

"Do you have any tattoos?" I ask, just to keep my heart beating.

Skye giggles as her hands continue to move down my body. "No," she tells me plainly.

"Why not?" I tease.

Her hands stop at the buckle of my jeans, and her eyes dart up to mine. "I never felt the need to get one," she says. "But I do have a large scar on the back of my left thigh. I figure that makes me unique enough."

It's only then that I realize I've never seen her legs; and how much I desperately want to see her legs.

"Want to show me?"

I watch as she bites her pretty little lower lip in contemplation. Skye looks my body over one last time, then nods her head. "Okay."

15

SKYLER

I'm fully aware that his interest in seeing my scar is a ploy to get me naked. Maybe he doesn't realize my bringing it up was a ploy to make him *think* about getting me naked.

God, what is wrong with me?

Never in my life have a felt like this. I've been with men; enough men to know better. I always have high hopes that things in the bedroom will be better, and they never are. I go in open minded, and leave annoyingly frustrated yet again.

With that said, I have never, ever, crawled into a man's lap in public and kissed him while an entire restaurant watched. I've also never invited a stranger into my home, then kissed and dry humped him for *hours*, then woken up desperate to do it again the next morning.

The last time I felt this … needy, I was sixteen years old, and dying for my boyfriend to shove his hands in my pants and make me feel good. He finally did, but it did not feel good.

As I watch Seth follow me into my bedroom, my entire body is on edge. Tingles and jingles everywhere. I feel like a goddamn teenager again; all hopeful and ecstatic to see this man naked as the day he was born.

Once he's inside my bedroom, my cheeks go red. I don't want to play games. I just need him naked.

I start to unbutton his jeans, and his hands go to my button as well. I freeze for just a second, but that's all it takes for Seth to stop.

"I'm sorry," he says quickly, removing his hands.

"No," I say, shaking my head. "No I want this, I swear."

"Are you sure?" His words are so soft, but I can still hear the fire in his voice. "I don't want you to do anything you don't want to do. Ever."

A devious growl leaves the back of my throat as I push his body onto my bed. His eyes shoot wide open as his back hits my mattress. I climb on top of him, and go right back to unbuttoning his pants.

"You have to stop saying stuff like that to me," I growl.

"Jesus," he mutters, his eyes fluttering, letting me undress him. "What stuff?"

"Being all understanding," I tell him hastily. "It's such a fucking turn on."

Seth laughs deliciously underneath me. "I really am just being honest, Skye. You don't owe me shit, and I want to make that plain as day."

He stops talking when I pull down his zipper, move to the side, and shove his pants and boxers off his body in one fell swoop.

Oh, my.

I take a moment to just drink him in. Glorious tanned skin, muscles that are so defined I think he could hold water between his abs. His tattoo that suits him so well and draws the eye, but right now my eyes are fixated on the eight inches standing at attention right in front of me.

My mind is swarming with so many thoughts it's hard to pick just one.

Beautiful. Gorgeous. Sexy. Juicy. Thick. Throbbing. Delicious.

I want to taste it.

I snap my head up, shocking myself with my final thought, but yes, yes I really do. I move my hand onto him, and wrap my fingers around his thickness, loving the groan that leaves his body as I do.

"Skye," he whispers, reaching for my hand on him. "You don't …" His words fade out as I begin to move my hand against him. "Shit," he mutters, his hands moving above his head as he takes several deep breaths.

"Hey, Seth," I say timidly. He raises his head and looks at me. "You're kind of beautiful."

I can visibly see his react. His chest settles, like he's let out a deep breath he didn't know he was holding. The tension in his shoulder disappears, then he sits up, both hands reaching for my face, and he kisses me like I'm the only woman in the world.

"You're the beautiful one," he whispers against my lips. "So fucking beautiful."

His tongue dances across mine as his hands move down to finally remove my jeans from my body. I grin, with my hands moving south helping as well.

Once they're off, I let him look me over. I'm still wearing my shirt, bra, and panties, but I doubt they'll last much longer.

"Damn," he mutters, letting his fingers brush against my hip. "Fucking gorgeous."

"Want to see the scar?" Seth nods his head, his eyes not leaving my legs.

I roll over onto my stomach and let him see the faded scar on my left leg. It's just below my ass, and has thankfully healed nicely over the years. His fingers trace over it, and my eyes close from his touch.

"How'd you get it?"

I smile back at him. "Amusement park." He quickly looks at me, and I grin. "Seriously. It was a water ride, one of those where you sit in the big cart and go down a ramp and get splashed and soaked." His fingers trace the scar again. "It was a new ride, and when I went down, a piece of the seat broke off and slashed my leg open."

"Holy shit. How old were you?"

I shrug. "Twelve. My Gran had taken me, and boy was she pissed. I mean, there was blood everywhere, and she was screaming like I'd never heard before." I'm laughing as I tell the story. Remembering Gran be super woman for me will always make me smile.

"I had to be taken to the hospital and get stiches, then had to stay overnight because I couldn't move my leg. It was miserable, honestly."

His fingers continue to move across my leg. "Did you sue the place?"

I move my body onto the side and grin up at him. "Guess how she was able to pay for this house – in cash."

"No."

I laugh. "Yup. Turns out one slashed kiddo leg buys you a pretty nice place in Sedona."

"Wow."

I sit up and wrap my arms around his neck, and kiss him gently. "It's fine now," I smile. "It's a fun story I get to tell guys when I'm trying to seduce them."

I can feel him smile against my lips. "Are you in the habit of seducing men you meet on airplanes?" he asks coyly.

I kiss him again as his hands move to my hips, and I move to straddle him. "You're my first," I sigh.

"Mmm," he hums, "let's keep it that way."

Our kiss intensifies, my hands moving across his gorgeous chest, his hands moving to the bottom of my shirt, waiting for me to say yes, then tugging it above my head.

I want to be here with him. My body feels alert and turned on, and I want more. I reach behind me as our tongues intertwine and remove my bra, my panties the only article of clothing left between the two of us.

My hips are rocking against him, having a mind of their own. He feels so good against me that I can hardly believe it. Seth's hands on the small of my back steady me, and keep me rocking against him at a steady, numbingly delicious speed.

His kisses are a drug I cannot get enough of. His hands on my body have me losing my mind. Every time I touch his shoulders, chest, run my fingers through his hair, I can feel my body tighten further. The feeling's so intense I'm afraid I might explode.

I'm panting, loving how much of him is touching me. I moan into his kiss as a delirious feeling grows inside me. "Seth," I whisper, my eyes shut, my brain firing at ten thousand miles a minute to keep up with this overwhelming sensation of pleasure.

Each one of his kisses has it building further. I can feel my legs begin to tremble beneath me, but I don't feel tired. I don't want to stop.

I gasp against his mouth as he rocks my hips against his hardened length.

My fingers clench around his shoulders as the tension in my body threatens to destroy me. Just when I think I can't stand it any longer, I scream, digging my nails into his flesh as my entire body spasms, explodes, and comes undone under his touch.

I cannot stop crying out. I cannot let go of him. His hands steady my hips, keeping me in place as I'm overcome with pleasure like I have never known before.

I'm gasping for air, saying his name like a prayer, and when I finally come back down to earth, I open my eyes and stare directly at him.

"Did you just-" he begins, his eyes wide and just as shocked as I am.

"Holy shit."

16

SETH

DID SHE JUST …

Skyler is still on top of me, her breath jagged, her hands digging into my shoulders.

"Holy shit."

I wait for her to say more. I don't know what to do. Has she ever orgasmed before? Or was it just with sex she doesn't orgasm? Did she say? Fuck, I can't remember.

"Are you okay?" I finally ask, my hands running up and down her spine as her breathing steadies.

"Yeah," she says breathlessly. "Wow. I think I, um." She looks at me again. "I think I just …"

"I think you did, too." I watch her, as she looks surprised and sated. "Have you ever, um, any other time?"

A small chuckle leaves her flushed lips. "Not like that."

My dick is still hard as a rock under her, but I don't dare move it. I don't know if he's in trouble or about to be praised, but either way, I'm letting Skyler make that call.

Suddenly a look of embarrassment spreads across her face. "Did I do it wrong?"

My eyes go wide. "No!" I nearly scream. "Jesus, fuck no." My hands run down her arms and up again. "That was," I have to stop and gulp down my lust, "very, very, uh, right. Really fucking hot, and, uh, very good."

This would not be the ideal time to blow my load. I need to keep it together, even though the image of her coming on top of me will *never* not be on my mind ever again.

Skyler smiles and I can see her visibly relax. She moves her body and lies down next to me, her hands going to my chest.

"That was something," she laughs, making me smile, even though my dick is screaming for release.

"Yes it was," I agree whole heartedly. "Are you okay, though?" I ask quickly, turning to look at her. "Was that too much? I hope I didn't cross any lines."

"Oh no," Skyler says, her words sounding sexier than they did just a moment ago. "You were just right." She gives me a little grin, then buries her head in my chest. "I'm okay," she says gently against my skin. "I think I'm way more than okay."

I let my hand graze across her naked back, begging my manhood to let it go, promising I'll service him later. I just want to be here for Skye in this moment. It's a big one for her.

When I finally calm myself down, I ask her if she wants to go for a walk. It's still a gorgeous day, and the middle of the afternoon. There's still so much for us to do.

Do I rub one out super quick before I put on a pair of shorts and shirt and meet her in the living room? You're goddamn right I do.

The woman is quiet but all smiles. I don't think I've ever seen a woman smile so fully as Skyler currently is. If I didn't know why, I'd probably be genuinely freaked out. However, I know that she just came for the first time with someone else, so that smile is well deserved.

We lock up the house and take a walk around the neighborhood. I bring my camera, and she's more than happy to take me to her favorite spots that provide great views of the red rocks. When she's not looking, I take several pictures of her as well. She's dressed in a tight workout shirt and three-quarters-length yoga pants that hug her body and make her look like the stunner that she is. Put her in front of a breathtaking background like these red rocks, and that's one gorgeous, timeless photo.

She asks me about my work, and I tell her all the places I've been. I ask what she does, and she tells me she's an accountant, but she doesn't sound too enthused. "I'm good with numbers, and it pays the bills," she explains, still smiling away.

She asks me about my family, and I tell her more about how shitty growing up was. In return, she tells me more about how her parents weren't the greatest, and how the only place that ever felt like home was right here in Sedona. As we walk on, we both sneak looks at each other, realizing we have a lot more in common than we ever could've known back on that plane.

We take our time, talking, laughing, and admiring the view as I stop and take photos. I set up the camera and get both of us to smile, my arm around her as my camera snaps our photo. Eventually, I get her to pose for me. I promise her it'll be a silhouette photo; just the outline of her body against the rocks. That's mostly what I take, but a few times I adjust the lens, and focus the light on her face. She's too beautiful not to photograph.

I would be a shitty photographer if I didn't capture the beauty that was right in front of me.

And god damn, is this woman beautiful.

Once back at her place, we agree to shower and change, then make dinner. During my shower, my mind wanders, and I find that now *I'm* the one who can't stop smiling. Skyler is gorgeous, yes. But getting to know her, somehow she's even more beautiful on the inside.

After I shower, I change into sweatpants, since I doubt we're going back out. My thick, dark hair is still damp, but I leave it. I trim up my beard and shave my neck, then head back out, ready to hug and kiss and worship the woman I had the good fortune of being an asshole to on the plane ride here. I'm not a religious man, but damn, maybe I should be. Skyler feels like an answered prayer right now.

I walk into the kitchen and find her elbows deep in an opened bag of Doritos and I can't help but laugh. She turns and grins at me, her fingertips already orange from the chips.

"No judgment," she laughs. "I was starving."

"No judgment here," I confirm before going over and planting a sweet kiss on her Dorito flavored lips. "Mmm," I say before kissing her again. "You taste good."

"Taste me as much as you want," she grins, and then her eyes go wide, like she just figured out how incredibly sexual her comment is. Instead of apologizing or explaining what she actually meant, the woman shrugs, and says, "hmm, maybe," and then *walks away*.

I'm left there, standing in the kitchen with my jaw on the damn floor. Did she just say what I think she said?

"Hold on," I call after her, raising my hand to steady my thoughts. She giggles and continues to head towards the living room, then plops down on the couch. I walk over and stand directly in front of her as she nibbles away on her precious chips. "Did you mean what I think you just meant?"

Another giggle escapes her orange covered lips. "Maybe."

My eyes go wide and my dick is instantly at attention. I try to move my hips to get it in a better position, but I'm not smooth. Her eyes go directly to it, and then, sweet Jesus, she licks her lips.

I stand there, waiting for her to say something, and I'm also thinking of what the hell I can say right now that isn't *take your clothes off so I can do every single thing to your body*.

"I mean," she begins, and man does she have my full attention. "That," she points to the bedroom, "was pretty unexpected." She bites her lip a second. "But it was kind of awesome."

I smile, because I'm still genuinely glad it was a good experience for her and she didn't kick me out of the house afterwards.

"Maybe," she shrugs, "I don't know. If *that* was good, maybe other stuff could be good, too." Her voice is small, but hopeful. Like she's reading my mind, she quickly adds, "I don't want to get my hopes up too much, and I don't expect you to be a miracle worker or anything like that." She's nervous. I get it. She doesn't want to put pressure on us, and I feel the same exact way. "But," she shrugs again, "maybe."

After I start breathing again, I go and sit next to her on the couch. "Skyler, I am open to anything you want to do. But I just want to say again that I don't have any expectations of you, and you do not in any way have to do anything you don't want to do." She goes to speak but I cut her off. "With that said, if you want to try something, again," I huff out a deep laugh, "I'm all for it. But if it's not working for you, you tell me and we'll either stop all together, or we can try something else. Whatever you want."

Her cheeks flush, but she nods her head. "I do want to try stuff," she tells me nervously. "I feel like it might … be different with you." Her cheeks are crimson, but she's so damn sweet that I take her chin in my hand and move her lips against mine.

I sigh, and kiss her again. "I don't think it's me, sweetheart." She studies me a moment. "As much as guys love to take credit for this shit, they shouldn't. The credit goes to you. You figured out you're worth a lot more than what those assholes were giving you. You stood up for yourself and made your own decision as to what was best for you." I brush my fingers against her bottom lip. "The difference is you."

17

SKYLER

THIS MAN IS *KILLING ME* WITH HIS WORDS.

"The difference is you."

I nod silently as I put my bag of Doritos down, and reach for a napkin to clean off my face and fingers. His hand goes to my elbow in a reassuring way, but all it really does is further light my body on fire.

Since I orgasmed, my panties have been soaked; continuously. It's like my body got a taste of the good stuff and wants more. And I want it from him.

He's still talking, saying reassuring things that I'm sure are sweet as hell, but I'm not paying attention. I take a long sip of water, nod along to whatever it is he's so passionate about, and pop a stick of gum in my mouth. I smile at him, nod again, just waiting for the peppermint flavor to overpower the Doritos so I can suck this dude's face off.

"So," I hear him say, "I'm open, sweetheart, but I have no expectations. I just want to enjoy this time with you, because so far, it's kind of been the best two days of my life."

Fuuuuuuck me.

No, literally. I desperately want him to fuck me like I've never wanted to be fucked before.

I clear my throat. "Seth?" I ask gently.

"Yeah?"

"Would you do me a favor?"

"Sure, sweetheart. Anything."

"Would you please take off all your clothes, then my clothes, and experiment sexually with me until the sun comes up?"

I think I broke him. Seth sits there, eyes wide, jaw on the floor, staring at me like he's just seen a ghost. In a way, maybe he has. I haven't felt this sexually liberated since before I started being sexually active. I should know better by now. I really should; my expectations are way too high. But my body wants him, and dammit, I want to give my body what it wants.

Just to let him know that I heard him, and was listening to what he said, I add, "I promise I will tell you if I'm not enjoying something. Okay?" I rest my hand on top of his. "Let's just have fun, okay? No expectations."

Every single part of me wants to mean that. Most of me does. I just want to have fun. I want to feel good. I want to make him feel good. We need to just leave it at that.

"Okay," he finally says, his voice cracking on the word, making me laugh. He clears his throat and laughs as well. "Sorry," he chuckles. "You really caught me off-guard there."

"But you're up for it?" I'm being flirty, but I'm worried it's coming off more vicious temptress.

Seth leans towards me. I think he's going to kiss me, but before I know it, I'm being lifted off the couch and carried back to my bedroom. I laugh as I lie there, hauled over his shoulder. He plops me down on the bed and I laugh again.

"Okay," he says, slapping his hands together. "First things first. Right." He rips his shirt over his head, followed quickly by his sweatpants, and holy crap is he amazing. Yes, I've seen him before, but honestly, I'm pretty sure his naked body is going to take my breath away ever single time I see it. "You're next," he grins at me, and I sit up, hands over my head, eager to have him undress me.

Once we're both naked, my hands refusing to leave his flesh, he asks me what I'd like to do first. "I want to go down on you." I spit the words out so quickly that he looks at me like he must have misunderstood me. I nod at him, that, yeah, that's really what I want to do.

"I don't know how that goes into exploration for you, but I said you were calling the shots."

"That's right," I say firmly.

"And that's what you want to do?"

"That's exactly what I want to do." I stop and smile at him, and remind him again: "I'll tell you what I want. I promise."

Seth lets out a loud sigh, and as he does, I swear his dick grows another full inch and raises to meet my lips. I take his hand and position him on the bed before I wrap my lips around him, taking in as much of him as I can. He tastes as good as I knew he would. His thick, throbbing dick in my mouth gets me even wetter between my legs, and the grunts and gasps that leave his lips are not helping. I'm so wet I can feel it running down my leg.

God damn.

When he gets close, his legs start to shake, and he calls out my name, letting me know he's close. I move him further in my mouth, telling him it's okay to let go. I want to taste him. I want to make him feel as good as he made me.

He shouts my name as he comes, his hand on the back of my head, holding it in place as he does. I let it rest there as he comes down, catches his breath, and then moans my name one final time.

"Do you, uh," he pants, "like doing that?"

His breathy voice makes me grin. "Yeah," I say, coming up and kissing him. "It's fun," I giggle. He kisses me hard, letting his tongue brush up against my tongue that just tasted him. "Thanks for not being a dick about it and letting me set the pace."

"Oh, sweetheart," he growls, kissing me passionately again, "you needed no help to drive me absolutely fucking insane." We kiss, our bodies pressed up against each other, and then he rolls me onto my back. "Do you mind if I try and return the favor?"

I know what he means. I've never liked men going down on me. Somehow it always seems to be for them and never for me. But this was my idea. I want to try. I am going to be open minded, and I'm going to communicate. I nod that yes, he can go down on me. Seth can tell I'm nervous. Instead of throwing my legs over his shoulder and eating me like I'm a free buffet, he kisses me gently several times, then moves to my neck, then my shoulder, and down my body.

He takes his time, warming me up, making me feel safe. It's exactly what I need. By the time I feel his breath in between my legs, that same tension is already building in my body again. He's just so gorgeous, and patient, and fuck me if that's not the biggest turn on ever.

"Let me know what you like and don't like," he reminds me, and I nod enthusiastically. When his tongue touches my slit for the first time I gasp. He's warm, and soft, and he moves in slow circles around me. I'm not ready to explode, but it feels good; nice. He moves to the right, and the feeling fades.

"It was better before," I tell him, my eyes closed. Seth moves right back to where he was, and I moan. He tries going to the left, up a little, then down, and it all feels good, but none of it is wow. I tell him just that. He tells me he's going to put two fingers inside of me, and I agree. The first goes in, and wow, okay, yeah that's feeling pretty good. He moves the one several times before he inserts the second. "Okay," I mumble. "Yeah, okay, that feels pretty good." His fingers move gently inside of me as his tongue starts back up again, and my back arches instinctively. "Fuck, Seth," I groan, reaching for his head. I grasp his hair, and before I know it, I'm riding his face, chasing the high that my body is building towards once again.

"Don't … stop…" His fingers are pressed into me, his tongue dancing around my clit and my hips move against his face. It's so much. It's too much. And then it's not enough. My body is wound so fucking tight that I feel like I'm going to explode.

And then I do. All over his gorgeous bearded face.

18

SETH

HOLY. FUCKING. SHIT.

First off, that blowjob – is she fucking serious with that thing? No wonder so many idiots stuck around after she told them she didn't like sex. If she was still doing that, who the fuck needed penetrative sex? It was that good.

Still, her riding my face, my fingers inside of her, tasting her on my tongue and lips – that takes the fucking cake.

She came. She came again, against me, with me, and then I nearly followed her over the edge. Everything about Skyler is intoxicating. The way she smiles, feels, smells, and tastes. I want it all. I cannot get enough.

"What would you like to do next?" I ask her after I run to the bathroom and clean up my face. It didn't bother me any, but when she saw her juices all over my face and in my beard she laughed. I love her laughter, but the way this night is going, I'd rather that not be the main focus.

"What's left?" she asks with a satisfied giggle.

I send a devious grin her way. "Whatever you want."

"Can we take a food break?" she asks, sitting up and letting her perfect breasts jiggle against my arm. "I'm starving."

I wrap my arms around her and kiss her shoulder. "Sex is hard work," I tease, then gently bite her.

"Mmm," she hums, "I kind of like that."

My dick immediately responds, and since I'm naked, there's no way to hide it. Skye grins down at it then looks back at me. "Maybe I help finish you off, *then* we go eat."

"Whatever you want," I say for at least the tenth time. Man, do I mean it. Whatever she wants. I'd give this woman anything she asks for.

Her hands wrap around me and my eyes close. "It might not take too long," I groan as she begins to pump me. "Watching you come nearly made me do the same."

She hums again, then moves so she's straddling me, still pumping away. With her free hand, she moves my hair out of my eyes and watches me as she works me. It feels so sensual, so intense, and so intimate that I'm both scared and so turned on I can hardly stand it.

My eyes close again as I feel myself nearing the edge, ready to dive over. "Hey," she whispers, and my eyes fly open again. "Kiss me."

And I do. So deeply, so passionately that they need to create a new word for what we are doing. Her tongue finds mine and I can feel my legs shaking below me, my breath so jagged I can hardly breathe. Another swipe of her tongue against mine and the moan that leaves her lips sends me toppling over the edge.

I groan, crying out, and I open my eyes to see myself explode onto her perfect skin. Skye just kisses me again, letting me whimper against her lips as she pumps me a few more times, letting me ride out my orgasm as long as possible.

When I catch my breath, I take another look at the mess I've made. "I'm sorry," I say, reaching for the box of tissues next to the bed. I hand her a few, nervous that it'll all be too much, but she's wearing a sweet smile as she wipes me off her body.

"You're fine," she assures me. "I like making you lose control. It's a real turn on, if I'm honest." She bites her lower lip, like she's embarrassed by her admission.

"Everything about you is a turn on," I tell her breathlessly, and fuck do I mean it.

Her green eyes go dark, hungry even. I know what she's thinking, but I have to be the bigger person here. "Food," I remind her. "Food break. Then," I pause, "we'll see where the night takes us."

19

SKYLER

SETH MAKES ME TAKE A SEAT IN THE LIVING ROOM AS HE INSISTS ON COOKING
for me. I can't recall the last time a man made me a meal, but I don't want to
be so far away from him. I compromise by sitting on a stool by the kitchen
counter, so I can watch him and drool at his gorgeous body as he moves
around my kitchen wearing nothing but a pair of grey sweatpants.

"Hungry, sweetheart?" he teases as he cuts up peppers.

"For so many things," I practically purr.

I have no idea who this version of me is, but she is one hell of a good time.
I'd say it's Seth's influence, but I already know he'd counter back, and remind
me once again that it's all me. I've had this part of me all along; I'm only now
letting it out to play.

And boy oh boy, do I want to play with him.

Seth chuckles as he continues to chop the peppers, sliced steak already
sautéing in a pan. He throws the peppers in, and the sizzle makes me smile.
Fajitas are what's for dinner, and I'm starving.

I go into the kitchen just to pour us both a glass of wine, and Seth reluctantly allows me to do that one thing. I grin and purposely bump booties with
him more than once as I make my way around the kitchen.

This is fun. I could get used to do this. I could get used to doing this
with him.

I bite my lip and quickly take a sip of my wine, pushing down the butterflies in my stomach that tell me that this is special, and I need to hold onto this

somehow. No clue how I'll manage to do that. He's a world traveling photographer, and I'm just an accountant. We don't even live in the same city. Yes, I could technically work from anywhere, but would I really like seeing the world and always being on the move?

Yes.

The answer sneaks up on me so fast that I feel like I've smacked myself across the face. Still, I need to lock this up. This is just a few days. This is just some fun. He hasn't asked me for anything past the now, and as much as I want to, I can't ask anything of him, either.

I look back at Seth and a laugh escapes my lips. Mr. Too Sexy to Wear a Shirt is jumping back from the stove to avoid the sizzling oil as it jumps off the pan.

When he's satisfied, he pulls the pan from the stove, grabs the soft tortillas, and walks both over to the counter where I'm sitting. He offers to make one up for me, and I smile and give him a nod. I don't mind this mountain man taking care of me one bit. It's nice having someone do nice things for me. I wish it had happened more in my life, but I was always the giver. The giver never seems to receive.

"This is so good," I groan after my first bite. "Oh my god. Seth. You are amazing."

He smiles shyly at me and takes his first bite. "Glad you think so."

The second bite is just as good. "Man, you can cook for me anytime."

"I'd love to," he says as he shoots me wink. "Name the time and place, sweetheart."

That stupid term has gone from annoying the shit out of me to filling my stomach with butterflies and my head with wild dreams of a happily ever after where I get to stare at this man shirtless for the next fifty years. It's dangerous.

"How about here … for the next two weeks." My heart nearly stops as I say the words, completely unsure what he will say or how he'll react. But I know it's what I want. I hold my breath as he watches me, trying to figure out if I truly mean it or not.

"Okay," he says tentatively, his eyes never leaving mine.

"It's okay," I say quickly, tucking my hair behind my ear nervously and staring down at my plate. "I'm sure you have a million other places to be. It's fine. Don't feel like you have to, um, you know, stay longer than you were going to."

I shake my head lightly, feeling like an idiot. It's way too soon to be saying shit like that. The hopeless romantic inside of me needs to chill the fuck out.

I feel Seth's thumb on my chin as he slowly raises my head up to look at him. His brown eyes bore into mine, and it feels like he's reading the emotions that are plastered on my soul.

"Do you want me to stay?" he asks softly, giving nothing away.

I take a deep breath and answer honestly. "Yes."

He studies me another minute then leans over and kisses me softly on my lips. "I want to stay, too."

I nearly melt in relief at his words. I let out a heavy breath I didn't know I was holding, and it makes Seth smile.

"You really don't have anywhere else to be?" I ask cautiously.

Seth kisses me again. "That's the beauty of working for myself, sweetheart." Another soft kiss. "I can make my own schedule."

"Do you want to stay?"

It's like I can't believe that a man like him, or any man, would choose to be here with me. Seth is gorgeous, talented, successful, and a damn good cook. Too many years have gone by where I never thought I was worthy of a man like this, or a man treating me like this. Even though Seth is right in front of me, in my home, kissing my lips, there's still a part of me that questions if it's real.

"Skyler," he says gently, and my name on his beautiful lips melts my heart. "Do you really doubt how crazy I am about you?" A quirky smile plays at his lips, and it makes me smile, too. "I've known you just a few days, and I'm already," he stops and chuckles, "kind of obsessed with you."

I can feel my cheeks blush, but my stomach fills with relief.

"Oh thank god," I laugh. "It's not just me."

Now Seth, in all his glorious naked stomach and chest and manly hair and his perfect beard, blushes. My goodness, it's the cutest thing I've ever seen in my life. Who knew you could see rosy cheeks under such a thick beard? Well, you can.

"Definitely not just you."

We grin at each other, both feeling nervous admitting there's something real going on between us. I don't dare ask what happens at the end of the two weeks. We'll cross that bridge when we get there, if we get there.

Gosh, I really hope we get there.

We eat in anticipated silence, sipping our wine and sending each other sweet little mischievous looks.

It's going to be a very interesting few weeks in Sedona.

20

SETH

A week later, I'm still in Sedona, but no longer in the guest bedroom. The night of the fajitas, I moved into the main bedroom with Skye. We kissed all night long, shared some seriously hot naked snuggles, and fell asleep in each other's arms.

Our days were spent seeing the sights, and me taking so many photographs I might as well have been on assignment. It's been a blast. The woman has me smiling nonstop.

After our morning hikes and sight seeing, we come back to her place to get cleaned up. We either eat here, or I take her out for lunch and do my best to spoil her. Skyler is a woman you have to spoil, because with every look she sends my way, she makes me feel like the luckiest guy in the world.

We have not had sex, and I couldn't care less. We've done practically everything else, and watching her explore her sexuality and truly enjoy it has been beyond amazing. She's stunning, and when she comes, when she digs her fingernails into my skin and shouts my name, I'm in heaven. She's also given me more orgasms in the past week than I've had in the past year. I have zero complaints.

Tonight I'm pulling out all the stops. I bought two beef tenderloin steaks at the store, along with asparagus and red peppers. I'm grilling my favorite meal for her tonight. While that grills, my beautiful girl is inside preparing a salad for us. I told her I'd do it all, but she smiled at me in her irresistible way, and said she wanted to help. I couldn't say no.

I flip the steaks and sneak another peak inside the house at her. Skyler's wearing a floral knee length dress that cinches at her waist and makes her looks both strong and beautiful. When my eyes go down to her legs, I lick my lips. I'd love to lift her up on the counter and kiss between her legs. Again. I already did that today. Doesn't mean I don't want to do it again.

"I see you," she laughs between the screen door that separates us. "If you burn my steak I'll never forgive you."

I grin down at the steaks, loving that she caught me looking, and loving even more the way it's making her grin over at me.

When the steaks, peppers, and asparagus are all cooked to perfection, I turn off the grill and head inside. She's made the table for us, and poured us both a glass of wine in her grandmother's special glasses.

I give her a knowing look, and quickly move my place setting onto the same side as hers. It makes her laugh, but I insist. I'm not sitting across from her. I'm sitting right next to her, so I can touch her the entire time we eat.

Skyler shakes her head, pretending like she doesn't love just how crazy I am about her. I tell her every day. Every day she blushes, which tells me she still doesn't fully believe it yet. That's fine. I'll tell her every single day until she does.

We chat about light topics as we eat. The weather, what we want to do tomorrow, where we want to go hiking, how the east coast is doing without us. Neither of us is in any hurry to get back to real life. This place is so much better.

After we finish eating, I take the dishes and begin to clean up. As I'm washing the last dish, Skye comes behind me and wraps her arms arms my waist, letting her hands dip down to the front of my thighs.

"Want dessert?" I tease, placing the clean dish on the drying rack.

"Only if it's you."

Yup, freaking obsessed with her.

I turn around and immediately kiss her, both my hands on her face, pulling her to me.

"Bedroom," she coos, and I'm at her mercy.

She lets me undo the zipper on her dress, and I love the way it floats down as it hits the floor. She makes quick work removing my pants from my body, and I'm already hard for her. Fuck, I'm always hard for her.

"What'll be tonight, baby?" She always gets to decide. I always leave it up to her, and trust me, I have never been disappointed.

Skyler bites her lip, and I'm surprised to see her nervous. We've been doing this for a week. Whatever she wants, I say yes. She's been so amazing about being honest with me and telling me what she wants, likes, and doesn't like. Every time we mess around isn't always a home run for her, and that's fine. We try again the next day and it is.

She's learning to trust her body and trust her mind, and embrace every sexual thought and fantasy she has. I have loved being along for the ride.

"I was thinking," she says slowly, letting her eyes wander down my naked body and back up to my face. "Um," she stutters, "what if we, um, tried having sex?"

21

SKYLER

"What if we, um," I stammer nervously, "tried having sex?"

Seth takes a moment before he responds, and I do not breathe while I wait.

"Is that what you want to do?" His voice is calm and assuring, the way it's been this entire week.

"I know it hasn't really been my thing," I admit, "but I think I want to try it again. With you."

"Okay," he says, and while I can tell he's nervous, he's also trusting me to make my own decisions, and that's huge. He doesn't try to talk me out of it, or remind me that it hasn't been great for me, like I could ever forget. "Do you have condoms here?"

I nod my head. "I, uh, picked some up yesterday when I went to get gas."

The cheeky little grin that spreads across Seth's face eases my nerves.

"So you've been thinking about this for a bit then?" he smirks.

"Only since I saw you almost entirely naked when you opened the door to the garage the first day you were here."

That gets him. Seth's eyebrows shoot up, and the shocked look on his face makes me laugh out loud.

"Wow," he mutters, grinning uncontrollably at me. "Well, well, well. Okay then."

Before I can stop laughing, the beast of a man picks me up under my naked ass and tosses me onto the bed. I'm still laughing, but when I get another glimpse of how hard he already is for me, I stop.

Instead I grab for him, settling Seth in between my legs as I pull his face towards mine, eager to kiss him endlessly.

We take our time warming up. Lots of kisses, his hands explore my body, as mine do to his. I love the feel of him. I love the way he smells, tastes, and teases me.

I love so many things about him that I need to be careful the way I throw that word around.

I reach into the night stand and pull out the box of condoms I bought yesterday, just so they'd be there when we're ready. I see Seth stare at the box, knowing I want to use them tonight. I can feel his hesitation. He doesn't want to hurt me. All this man ever wants to do is make me feel good.

"It's okay," I whisper into our kiss. He hesitates, and I know he needs to hear the words again. "It's okay. I want this." I kiss him again. "Seth, I want you."

He nods his head, and his nerves are so apparent that they almost calm mine. Of course I'm nervous, but I'm more excited. Even if it's not great for me, I know it will be okay. Seth won't be mad. He won't yell at me. He won't ask me to keep going if I don't want to.

I trust him.

I trust him completely.

I reach inside the box, grab a condom, and hand it to him. He takes it, and slowly rolls it down his length, and my insides tighten at the sight.

Yes, I want to like sex. That would be great. Right now, though, I just need to feel him. I'm so fucking crazy about him, and I need all of him; to be as close as I can be to him. I stare at his thick manhood, standing at attention, wanting me. I want it, too.

Seth moves on top of me, his face close to mine and positions himself at my opening. I can feel him, and it makes me close my eyes in anticipation. He kisses me, staying right there, not pushing inside of me, and I'm grateful for it. We're taking it slow. That's more than okay.

As our kiss deepens, I feel him pulse next to me, and my hips move to him instinctually. His dick pulses again, and my hips react, this time pushing the tip of him just inside my opening. A small gasp leaves Seth's lips, and the sweet sound makes me want more.

Slowly, I move my hips back, bringing him into me bit by bit. He's thick and swollen, and it takes my body time to adjust to him, but he feels good. As I stare into his eyes, it feels even better.

This is not just sex. This is not even just sex with Seth. This is … love. I really think it is. This feeling I feel right now is only happening because I'm with him.

I move my hands to his ass and slowly push him the rest of the way inside of me. I want all of him, and I'm done waiting.

Seth stays inside of me, letting me feel how full he makes me. We kiss each other zealously, and when his erection pulses again, this time it makes me pulse with him. I let out a quick moan, and then Seth begins to move.

Slow at first, short movements, warming me up. In truth, I feel plenty warm.

"You feel good," I whisper, and I can see his shoulder relax.

"Do you want me to pick up the pace?" I nod my head, then kiss him again.

I don't know what I was expecting, but it wasn't this. This is so fucking sensual I could die. He looks into my eyes, kisses me endlessly, and moves so slowly in and out of me that it feels like a deadly combination of torture and pleasure.

I'm enjoying myself. He does not rush me, and the slow and steady pace he keeps is hitting a spot inside of me that I didn't know existed.

"That," I breath, "feels ... good." I'm so stunned by the sensation that words are hard to use.

My hands drift down to his ass and feeling the muscles move tightens the muscles in my body even further. My head tilts back, and Seth begins to kiss my neck, forcing out another moan from my lips.

"Seth," I whisper, my breath becoming fast and jagged. "You feel," I mutter, my mind slowly becoming undone, "so good."

Inside of me, I feel my body tightening. It's a new feeling, but one I'm slowing recognizing as sexual arousal heading towards the heavens. Seth never stops, he never slows, and he never goes too fast. My fingers begin to dig into the muscles of his back as I start moaning uncontrollably.

I can't form words. I can't tell him I want more, but I do, I do.

My head lifts up then slams back down, my legs begin to shake, I can feel my chest beginning to perspire, and still all I feel is Seth on top of me; hear his breath, my moans, smell is manly body that drives me absolutely mad.

Then my body takes over, and I give up control.

I cry out as I orgasm around Seth, loving the way he feels inside of me, and loving the way he makes me feel.

As I cry out, my body quaking underneath his, I feel his whole body tighten, just as mine did, before he cries out my name, biting my neck as he comes, then collapses on top of me, breathing heavily.

Neither of us move; neither of us can move, as his body rests on top of mine, each of us dusted in sweat, still unable to form words.

I move to wipe sweat from my brow but wind up smacking myself in the head instead. It makes me laugh, which makes Seth whimper, since apparently my laugher just squeezed his dick that still inside of me.

When he pulls out he kisses me three times, then jumps off the bed to dispose on the condom. Five seconds later he's back, and his lips are back on mine. I kiss him lazily, happy to let him kiss me while I don't move.

"Are you okay?" he asks gently. "How was that for you?"

I scoff and wrap my arms around his neck. "How do you think it was for me?" I tease. I kiss him again, this time letting my tongue run against is. "Thank you."

"There's no need to thank me."

"Of course there is," I say, nearly cutting him off. "I've had sex with a dozen other dudes and none of them were as kind and patient and under-standing as you've been."

"They're just assholes," he grins.

"True," I laugh. "Still, thank you for listening to me, and just being amazing overall."

He doesn't say a word. Instead he stares into my eyes, then kisses me in a way that says more than words ever could. He thinks I'm amazing. He's happy with me. He doesn't want this to be over in another week. He never wants this to be over.

We hold each other, no words needed.

We've become something special, not just to each other, but together.

Seth sees parts of me that I thought were there, but no one else ever saw. He sees them all. Even more, he loves them as much as all the other parts of me. He gets me.

When I look at him, I see his Polynesian roots, his difficult childhood, and the sister he lost way before she took her last breath. I see his struggles, his fight, and the love he carries inside of himself. And I get him, too.

We will have to go back to the real world. We've always known this. But right here, in this moment, this feels more real than anything else I've ever known.

This is my real. This is my world.

Seth is my guy. I know it. I know it in my bones.

He's my lucky number thirteen.

ONE YEAR LATER

SETH

"Sweetheart, can you grab the long distance lens?"

Skye saunters over to me, a wicked grin on her face, and hands me what I've asked for. "Anything for you, darling."

We're off the coast of South Africa, one of the most beautiful places in all the world, and she's helping me set up for a sunset photo session.

Every time I come here, I'm stunned by the beauty of this place. The coastline, the waves, everything.

I have my camera set on a tripod. I'm going to get it mounted, and have it set to take interval pictures while my love and I can enjoy the view for ourselves.

Ten minutes left to get everything in place.

"Sucked having to get up at four this morning for a conference call," Skyler says, "but this view is definitely worth it." She turns and smiles at me and my heart lights up. "Being here with you is definitely worth it."

I stand up and kiss her. Fuck the sunset. It can wait.

She laughs, and lightly smack my ass, then moves her hands into my beard, giving in a quick scratch.

"I love you, you know," I tell her playfully.

"I love you too, Mr. Grumpy Pants."

I shake my head and grin. Her little pet name for me from when we first met rears its head from time to time. Always changing time zones can be rough, but the work is always worth it. This morning I might have, indeed, been a bit of a grumpy pants. It'll all be worth it tonight, though.

These photos will be worth all of it.

"Alright," I announce, slowly backing away from the camera to set up on the tripod. "I think we're good to go."

I go to my bag and pull out two travel cups and a bottle of champagne I snuck along with us today. Skyler sees them and laughs.

"Are we celebrating?" she asks, happily taking one of the travel cups from me.

"Sweetheart, every day I get to spend with you is a reason to celebrate."

We clink the metal together and take a sip. "Still spoiling me rotten, Seth," she says with a shake of her head. Skye smiles deviously at me and adds, "don't ever change."

I laugh, then tug at her shirt and pull her lips to mine.

"Come on," I say, putting both our cups down. "Let's go watch the sunset."

I pull her near the edge of the cliff we're standing on, and take her hand in mine, both of us looking out at the spectacular view that surrounds us.

These rocks are so different from the ones we stood on together in Sedona. Yet they are of the earth, of life, and hold us together.

"It's so beautiful." He words are dreamy, just like she is, just like this moment is.

I reach into my pocket and click a button that starts my camera taking pictures. I'm going to remember this moment for the rest of my life.

"Skye." When I say her name she turns and smiles at me, once again making me feel whole, as she always does. "Thank you." I stop and run my thumb across her cheek, her hair whipping around in the wind. "Thank you for believing in me, and in us, and coming with me as I travel the world. I'm so fucking lucky to have found you, and I'm thankful every single day that you're right here next to me, where I always want you to be."

I let out a deep breath, and drop to one knee.

This is how it needed to be. I needed to be in the most beautiful place in all the world to ask the most beautiful person in the world the question I've been wanting to ask since the moment she held my hand in that red rock dessert. I knew then that I was better with her, and that I'd never again be whole without her.

Skyler's hand flies to her mouth as she gasps, but I hold her left hand in mine, tears threatening, and look up into her gorgeous green eyes.

"Sweetheart, Skyler, love of my fucking life, will marry me?" I try to choke down my tears but they come up anyway. I don't bother to hide them. I hide nothing from her, and she loves me all the same. "You're my everything, baby. I never want to know life without you smiling by my side."

Hands shaking, I reach into my pocket and pull out the diamond ring I've been carrying since we left Virginia over a week ago. I had it made just for her. The main diamond is from her grandmother's ring. Two smaller diamonds surround it, which came from the ring my grandfather gave my grandmother. The band is sparkled with small diamonds. It needed to shine. The ring needed to shine as brightly as she does.

I hold the ring up, taking her left hand again, and move it onto her finger, her hands shaking just as much as mine.

"What do you say, sweetheart? Marry me?"

Skyler lets out a loud cry as she falls to her knees, her arms wrapping around my neck, holding me tighter than ever before. We cry into each others arms.

I look at the ring as it shimmers on her finger. It's a perfect fit, just like us.

"Yes," Skye cries, not even bothering to wipe the tears from her eyes. A soft laugh leaves her as she looks into my own tear soaked eyes. "Of course I'll marry you. You're my everything."

We hug and hold each other as the sun goes down.

As we watch the last of the pinks and oranges sink below the waves, she turns and looks at me. I take her hand and kiss her fingers, knowing my camera behind us has captured the whole thing. I am in no hurry for this moment to end.

"Where should we get married?" Skye asks me with a laugh.

"I was thinking Sedona," I say with a knowing smile. I move her hair back behind her ears. "Back where it all started."

Skyler hums as her eyes close, loving my fingers on her body. "Back to where you kissed a stranger in an airport then invited yourself into her home."

"Damn straight," I smile. "Best decision I ever made."

The End

ABOUT G.G. GLEASON

G.G. Gleason is a contemporary romance author who lives in Pennsylvania with her two crazy cats. She has a Masters Degree in History, and writing has always been her passion. She wrote her first full length book in 2012, but didn't begin to self publish until 2018. This anthology will be her tenth published book.

G.G. suffers from chronic heart disease. She was born ill, and has had multiple surgeries to keep her ticker going. Her most recent procedure was a nine-hour surgery in January of 2021 to correct several arrhythmia issues. More arrhythmia issues have popped up since, but she's doing her best to stay busy and positive, and enjoy life.

After five wonderful years living in Charlotte, North Carolina, she has recently relocated to central Pennsylvania to be closer to family and the doctors that keep her as healthy as possible.

You can follow her at:
Website & Newsletter Sign up:
https://gggleason.wixsite.com/website

FOLLOW ME

KELLY KAY

A ChiTown Stories/5 Families Vineyards Series crossover

Editor: Aimee Walker https://aimeewalkerproofreader.com

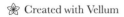 Created with Vellum

ABOUT FOLLOW ME

Subgenre: Contemporary Romance
Tropes: Rockstar Romance, Instant Connection, Forced Proximity

Graphic sexual depictions, open door sex and explicit language

Blurb:

Ever dream of getting stuck in a closet with a dreamy rockstar? Sounds romantic unless you're Ingrid Schroeder and prone to panic in small spaces. As charming as he is, the timing is all wrong. Being on the arm of Ian Reilly won't help her case for independence.

What happens in the supply closet stays in the supply closet.

But fate won't be ignored that easily. Ingrid might have to listen when chance comes knocking. If she doesn't get out of her own way, she could miss out on her "one perfect thing" and the life and love she was meant to have.

Ian Reilly has made A LOT of mistakes in love. But letting Ingrid slip away might be the biggest one yet. Of course, he'd tell her that if only he could find her.

A ChiTown Stories/5 Families Vineyards Series crossover coming to a supply closet near you.

INGRID

"Ingrid. Ingrid!"

Flashes pop, but it's daylight, so it doesn't bother me. However, the dude walking backward recording me is annoying.

"Mademoiselle Schroeder! Ingrid Schroeder. Rumor has it Dior fired you."

Fuck. I can't even quit a job without judgment. Do they think I can't speak French after three years in this country? Why yell at me in English?

"Représentez-vous Dior?" A pointed man says. I ignore him.

No, asshole, I don't rep Dior. I fucking work there.

I shield my mouth and talk into my phone. They have literally lip-read conversations before. People feel like I abandoned my 322k Instagram followers. But what were they following anyway? I hate this.

"Daddy, there's paps. I haven't been an influencer for three years. Why can't they leave me alone?"

"The more you don't want attention, the more they want you, Little Bell."

I turn to my stalkers. "Translate this: Your family must be so proud. Taking a picture of a girl walking to lunch. You're the bee's knees." I scowl and push through.

"They asked if Dior was a glamour job. I worked my ass off for that job. I quit on my own terms but they think I was fired." I glare at the man who asked if I repped Dior. No. I fucking bought this dress.

"Little Bell. Focus on my voice and your speech. Walk away." Always my father's advice.

"There's no second act for an influencer and party celebs. Kim, the

Grande dame, can't even have legitimate businesses without everyone thinking someone's doing the work for her."

"Have your farewell lunch so you can hurry home to Sonoma. I'll have pancakes waiting."

I smile, and the cameras go nuts as I yank open the door. I'm early. I don't love talking to groups. I'm freaking out about it because, inevitably, someone will film it and post it. I know it makes no sense for someone who's been photographed as often as I have to be nervous. But that's all a machine that feeds itself. I'm famous for nothing.

I fell in with Gigi and Bella because we loved fashion. They're great friends, but everyone posted about me, and then the Coachella incident happened. Then people gave me clothes and bags to carry. I saw the world on someone else's dime, as long as I posted about it. Not a bad first job after college. There's lots of money to be made in appearances. It was so dumb, but my dad, a winemaker, taught me you make wine or hay when the sun shines. You live and die by the harvest and never know what it may bring. Grab all you can while there's something to grab. You also put it all away for a rainy day. After three years of being a brand and three years working my ass off in Dior's merchandising department, I have enough money to do the thing I really want to do.

Every product I brandished was for my end goal. To carve out the career I want. My father and his friends have all worked their asses off for their dreams. I paid attention. I learned you plan, put your head down, and go after what you want. Wine's not my thing despite it being in my blood. It's always been music. Not performing but creating and shaping it.

"You can't tell anyone what I'm doing. I need a fresh start outside this media-created spotlight. And away from being a part of the 5." The five vineyard families are my extended family. Love them, but they're a bit overwhelming.

I look at the hostess, "Dior lunch?"

"You're the first." She leads me to the room. I stand there for a moment.

"Merci." She winks at me. "Dad, did you tell people about my plan?"

"Just your sister and well, I'm sorry, he asked about you, so I told Sam."

"DAD! Sam is the worst secret keeper. Everyone knows now." Sam's best friends with my brother and his crew and is like a cousin to me. Since birth, the five of them have been inseparable. All from different winemaking families in Sonoma. Now they own a winery together. I'm the youngest of all the siblings, and they're all overprotective.

He laughs. "Goldie is very excited. She's planning a party." She was my mom's best friend and the proudest of my aunties. I look at the ceiling. Dammit. I scoff. "You know they love you."

"Too much. I want to be something other than Little Bell."

"My darling girl. You'll always be Little Bell, but it's ok to be someone else too."

"I love you, Dad. Stop telling people things."

"You know there are no secrets between the 5."

"That's like thirty people."

"Ok, feisty. Relax."

"Talk later, Dad." I hang up.

I sit down on the velvet bench and try to get my shit together. I came to Paris to find out who I was out of the shadow of my insanely sizeable extended family and my charming overprotective father. My mom died before I could figure out if I hated or loved her. I look like her, so everyone calls me Little Bell for Bellamy. The mother, who by all accounts was spectacular. Only her best friend ever tells me her flaws. Hearing her faults makes her human to me. Goldie tells me she used to get angry at the littlest things and let the larger ones slide. It means she wasn't perfect, and I don't have to be a miniature version of her.

My sister, Tommi, always talks about how she glided into a room. That shit can't be real. And my brother, Bax, who was ten when I was born and thirteen when she died, tells me how wise and funny she was. And my dad never talks about her.

My work frenemy sneaks into the room. She doesn't see me as she checks the place cards. She's constantly trying to take credit for my work. Looks like she snagged a sample from the newest collection. I'm wearing vintage. That's the difference between us. She sees me and pretends she didn't move her place card closer to our boss. I exit the room, and she follows me into the hallway.

"Chérie, tu es divine." We air-kiss.

"Tu es si magnifique dans cette vieille chose. Vous devez être nerveux." Bitch. I look magnificent in this old thing. Vintage does not mean old.

I answer her in English, which I know she hates. "So nervous. I'm going to pop over in here and practice." I squeeze the mean girl's arm and turn towards a random door as if I know exactly where I'm going. I want away from her— from everyone for a second.

It's dark and smells like industrial cleaners. I find the lights and realize I'm in a large cleaning supply/storage room. This will do. It's bigger than a closet but not massive. I won't be in here long. I'm not a fan of enclosed spaces. My brother once locked me in my dad's wine room when I was nine. Never really recovered. I set my bag down and pull up my speech on my phone. I pace and practice. Ok, it's not small at all. There's a lot of room to roam around. My mind wanders.

After a quick visit home, I go to the Chicago doorstep of a woman who has never treated me like a kid or cared who my family was. In high school, I interned at Meg's film festival. I wasn't the little sister or the sad girl who lost her mom too early. Instead, I got to be Ingrid. Her rockstar husband is letting me learn to produce music at his studio. I want to help shape and form something beautiful for the world.

I came to Paris to get out of LA. To distance myself from what I was becoming and be an independent woman. Didn't quite work. No one lets me forget my three years on the influencer circuit. Time to get lost and pivot completely toward what I want instead of someone else's idea of what I should be.

Being the youngest member of my tribe takes a toll. They've all achieved miraculous things and then patted me on the head. Music has always been my savior, and I want to give that to someone else.

I flip through my note cards and pace a little as I say the speech quietly. I loved the Dior perks. My shoes are exquisite. But the job wasn't for me. I do another lap through the shelves.

My back is to the door when it startles me, and I feel all of my curated positive air sucked out of the room. Please don't be a janitor. I peek around the large shelves and instantly recognize the man with dark shaggy hair. He slams his palm on the door and then shoves something in his pocket.

I'm not alarmed but oddly curious why someone as famous as musician Ian Reilly would be in the supply room in a French restaurant in Paris.

I've done a lot of research for my new job, and his name came up a time or two. Given my mentor, how could it not? If I'm going to produce and mix music, even something as poppy as his, I wanted to know it all. I made myself a student of every genre and era of music.

Ian does have one perfect album. It's deep, rough, and riddled with loss. It's more profound and lyrical than his others, and I know exactly where it came from. And oddly, it's his most successful. Nothing has compared to the album "First Heartbreak" since then.

He's moving from side to side, staring at the door. It's as if he's commanding the space around him with the sway of his hips. There's a vibe, almost like an electric current, drawing me to him and into his aura. I feel a little lighter just watching him, despite his evident agitation. He's humming, and it's filling my nervous heart. I don't know the tune—it's calming me down but seems to be agitating him.

This is a beautiful man. He's sexier in person. His Irish complexion is creamy and perfect, with a glimpse of red in his cheeks. He's incredibly tall but not as gangly as I thought. His linen shirt hangs off his broad shoulders. He turns, and his broad back tapers right down to a fabulous ass. Damn. Maybe his music is better than I thought. His figure cuts elegantly through the space like a dancer.

He's running his hand through his famous dark brown hair. He glances at his phone, then puts it to the side. I'm watching like a voyeur but not a fan, fascinated as I stare at a man who seems to be entirely at home in his body and mind. Then he picks up a glass off of a serving tray and hurls it against the opposite wall screaming, "Bitch!" As it smashes, I shriek.

IAN

Oh fuck. I didn't know anyone was in here. "Are you hurt? I'm so sorry." I turn towards the stacks of industrial metal shelves. There's a tall stunning brunette woman with a severe chic low bun. Shit. By the time I reach her, I'm already lost in her dark brown sparkling eyes, and the slight upturn curl to her painted wet coral lips. She's fucking gorgeous.

"No. Just startled. Are you ok?" Her voice has a slight trill to it. I don't know if that's fear or if she's naturally a musical sound, but I like it. She's a melody yet discovered, and fuck is she hot. The tight beige dress accents her hourglass shape and was designed by someone who knew how to make my heart flip. And here, I thought it was dead. Turns out it was waiting to find a woman in a supply closet.

"I'm not ok, clearly. I just smashed a glass in a closet instead of eating my lunch. So nope. I'm hungry and insane and now trapped with a stranger. You're not a serial killer, are you?"

She steps towards me. "Worse. I'm a super fan. I keep all your pictures on my phone, Mr. Reilly." My face drops as she giggles at her joke. I don't want a fan. I'm so sick of being Ian. I keep fucking up my life in such spectacular ways. "I have a tattoo of your face on my back. Will you sign it? Then I can tattoo your name across my ass."

I laugh at her as she crosses her arms over her spectacular chest. She's funny. That body, that face, and that voice belong to someone funny. It's too much for me.

"At least you have good taste." I smile and extend my hand so she can step over the glass. I'm loving the feel of her hand in mine. Damn. Then I grab a case of paper towels and gesture for her to sit. She's so damn regal sitting on the case of paper towels she makes it look like a throne.

"Thank you." As I'm sweeping the broken glass away, she gets a curious look on her face. "Did you say trapped?" I pull the snapped off door handle from my pocket.

"Oh. No. No. No. I have to get back out there." She pulls up her phone and shrieks. "No bars. Oh my god. What is this, a bomb shelter? Stone Age Wi-Fi? Shit." She stands up, and her black patent leather pumps, with a strap and like a death-metal heel, clack as she scurries to the door. Then she click clacks all around the room to see if there's better reception. "Ian. Mr. Reilly. I mean, you, call someone." I stare at her and realize I know who she is as well.

I follow her on social media, and I assume she follows me. "For someone who posts as often as you do, that's odd, Ms. Schroeder, that you don't have a backup WiFi router in your purse." Her face snaps to mine, and there's simmering anger that started long before I made a comment, but now I'm trapped in taking the blame.

"I don't do that anymore. And please don't assume you know who I am because of some stupid pictures." She sits back down.

"Same."

She nods sharply. "Fair enough. And it's Ingrid."

"Ian."

She grins and shakes my hand. Her delicate touch is more than I can take in my current situation. I grab my own case of paper towels and settle in across from her.

She hops up and reaches for me. "I'm rather handy. Please give me that."

She takes the broken handle, and I lean back against the shelves and watch her futile attempt. Good view of her ass, though.

"All we have to do is turn this pin, and it will unlock."

"You go, safecracker." She turns to me and rolls her eyes. Then flips me off. I like feisty. She grabs a fork and starts to scrape metal on metal. As much as I'd like to get out of here, a larger part wants to get to know her. I hear a loud metal snap and "Oh, fuck." I run to her. The fork is bent in half and stuck inside the small handle hole. She rubs her finger, and I inspect it.

She peers up at me through her long eyelashes, and I swear I can hear her heart stop. I rub the part that looks the angriest. "You ok there, MacGyver?"

Her voice is breathy and sweet. "I guess." She pulls her shoulders back, snapping out of our moment. She abruptly turns away and begins pounding on the door.

"Help! There are people in here. PEOPLE! I'm in here and a famous singer/songwriter pop star is in here!!"

I laugh and yell, "And a very attractive woman who no longer fancies herself an influencer, but you would totally know who she is!" I keep banging.

She looks up at me and sneers. "Not funny."

"Little funny."

"AHHH! NO!" She goes back to screaming at the door instead of me. "Help! Anybody!" She turns to me. "Help! I'm trapped with an ego!" I stand over her, caging her to the door, and I don't hate being this close to her. We both beat on the door, screaming for a couple of minutes. Nothing. I grin. Things could be worse for me.

She clicks and clacks in a tight circle in front of me. Then she begins to expand the circle muttering to herself. It's freaking adorable.

"Why are you in here?" I ask.

"I have a little speech thing and needed practice. And to escape a bitch I work with. Oh. Jesus. I'm having a hard time breathing. Is there enough oxygen in here?" She bends in half. It's adorable.

"You're fine. Breathe in and out slowly." I rub her back.

She snaps up. "You touched me."

"My apologies."

"No, it was familiar and nice."

Familiar. I agree. Even though the thought is wild. She flops back on her paper towel chair. I grab a couple more cases and fashion an actual throne for her. She scoots back towards the wall of cardboard, and only her feet dangle over the edge. She looks like a little girl in a giant chair. She's spectacular.

I roll my hands in the air towards me. "Let me hear it."

"Shouldn't we be trying to get out of here?" She's clutching her phone but seems to be breathing ok.

"We'll have to wait until someone needs more dishrags." She smiles, and even that's too much for me. I'm about to be humiliated and disgraced. She'll run from me once she gets service and sees my viral shitstorm. But for right now, she has no idea that my ex-wife just published a tell-all chronicling how she cheated me out of money and the staggering volume of dicks she cheated on me with. I'm a joke outside of these walls, but in here, she doesn't know yet. I have one last chance to get to know someone before they know what an idiot I am.

"Come on. You worked hard on it. Someone should hear it."

She raises an eyebrow. "Someone?"

I raise my hand. "I'm someone."

She sits up a little straighter, pulls her legs onto her makeshift chair, and bends them to the side. There's some blockade of cool I'll break down.

I know about hiding behind the persona and blaming behavior on circumstances. I tried to be different with Abbey. Hell, I married her to prove it was destiny, not a lack of moral character, ego, and youth when I cheated on Meg. But in the three years, I've been with Abbey, I did nothing, despite all I could have done. I didn't even flirt with other women as if that would right the wrong I did to Meg. The cheating isn't why we broke up, but it didn't help. I never want to be that shit heel again. My exie-bestie, Meg, has forgiven me, and she's incredibly happy in her marriage. And I got karma'd.

The Abbey book scandal broke, so I came to Paris to get lost. Hoping the hashtags wouldn't follow me. But they don't know international boundaries. #ianreillygetsplayed #playergetsplayed #tellall #ianreillywellhung.

That one, I don't mind so much. But my ex-wife ranked my dick against my roadies and crew. I'm glad I'm bigger, but she shouldn't have a working knowledge of my band's cocks.

Ingrid purses her lips and traces a tiny imaginary circle on top of the cardboard. "My speech? We're trapped in a room. And I'm supposed to be having bubbles and foie gras. They're going to think I blew them off."

"Yup."

She stands and gets in my face. "Yup?"

"Yup. All that's true. But who cares what their reaction is? They're not here. I am.

Give me the speech." I gesture for her to get on with it.

She blows out a forceful exhale. "Do you speak French?"

"Sure."

She stands in front of me. I spark up my phone's translator app. I push my sleeves up, and she stares for a second. Even though there are billions of pictures everywhere, there's always a look the first time I expose the ink. And it's always telling. Her look says she's intrigued.

"Je pense que tu es plein de merde et que tu ne parles pas français mais que tu essaies de me faire sentir mieux. Alors merci."

She does a little bow. It's the sexiest thing I've ever seen. This woman speaks French, which is also sexy as fuck. I nod as if I approve of what she's said. Then I reach for my phone, but she grabs it first. She's laughing as she sees what I've done. She holds it up.

"Read it to me then, smarty French pants," I say.

She does. "I think you're full of shit and don't speak French, but you're trying to make me feel better. Which is oddly sweet from a stranger who trapped me in a supply closet. So thanks." Now I'm laughing. She seems lightened by it all, not as severe and worried as when I came in.

I stand and pull my phone from her. We're close enough that I can now get a full whiff of the insane lilac and peony coming off this formidable flower. She's stronger than those scents. There's something to the steel versus velvet thing she's got going on. Like she could grow where planted. She could bloom under pressure.

Her breath catches when she looks into my eyes. Then she's off. She's racing in a circle, putting her phone in the air again, searching for bars.

"I can't breathe. There's not enough oxygen in here. Is there a window?" She flips from steel to vulnerable velvet. I dig her dichotomy.

I go over and place my hand on her back. "You're going to make yourself hyperventilate."

"I need a bag. A bag, I tell you." She grabs her purse and begins to breathe into her purse.

"You're fine. We're not in a sealed chamber. It's a room."

She peeks up from her purse. "You don't know. This could be our tomb. This is our tomb, Ian! At least I'm wearing Dior." She breathes heavily in and out, then buries her face back in her purse.

"Don't panic."

She stands straight up, and my hand flies off her back. "I haven't begun to panic. But, needs are starting to come up, and I don't know what to do about them!" Her eyes are crazy, but she's breathing regularly.

"Needs?" I lift an eyebrow hoping to distract her. I spin around the room.

"Stop moving so much. You're using up all the oxygen. We have to conserve our energy for the long haul. It could be weeks before they discover our bodies."

New tactic I move in front of her and take her purse from her. She reluctantly lets go as I place it down on a stack of tablecloths. "I'll find you some air. First thing they teach you in adventure school..."

"Adventure school?"

I put my palms up. "Look, I don't know what to tell you. That's what it's called. When trapped in a cave or a storage room, make a list of your assets first. What can we use in the cave for survival?"

Her eyes are perking up, and she seems more involved in my jackassery than her panic. That's a good thing.

She nods at me and hangs on my every word.

"Get your pencil and notecards out." I say. She does as she's told but gives me a look. "You know if we end up somewhere dangerous someday, we're doomed. So far, your adventure skills suck."

She says, "You're a jackass."

I'm over by the shelves, and I jerk my head back to hers, "Hold up there Wildflower."

She pops a hip and says, "Is that a pet name?"

"It is now. Beautiful, snappish, and out of control."

She stalks over. "Ok, pop star, I'll start a list."

I head into the metal shelving. "Oyster crackers! Score."

"You're way too excited about them."

"Bottles of water. That's lunch and dinner, baby!"

I move around the shelving and find a door cracked open in the back of the room. "Holy shit. There's a tiny room back here."

"Shut up!" Her heels quickly clack upon the cement floor.

I open the door all the way and search for light. There are lockers and a slop sink. There's a mini-fridge and... "There's a bathroom!"

She pushes past me and, as she closes the door, says, "Thank god. Don't listen!"

I step away and survey our provisions. Lu Petit Beurre biscuits. I crack one open, and they taste like butter cookies. I slide a sizeable unopened box of Comet cleanser to be a makeshift table—between our two paper towel chairs. I drape stark white linen over the chest and arrange our lunch. Water, two packages of biscuits, oyster crackers, I hear her emerge.

"I found crème de citron, some sort of tinned rillette, a pre-packaged jambon sandwich, and a bunch of what appears to be saucisson." She's holding up food, then sees the set table. She continues, "Those are baby teething crackers but will be perfect with the lemon curd!"

"Did you find some oxygen in there?"

"I simply stopped panicking."

I place her items on our dining table and hug her. She's stiff at first but yields to me. "Congratulations on passing adventure school."

"Is there a badge or something?" She smiles as she sits.

I nod, "And there's arts and crafts later."

"Can we make a WiFi tower?"

"Sure, just after we finish weaving potholders."

INGRID

We put the potted meat and the sandwich back in the fridge for a possible dinner. I bite the end of the salami and peel the outer coating off. When I'm done, I look at Ian, and his eyes are wide. I realize I chomped into a long tubular thing, and there's a heat to his eyes. I take a demure bite off the top and pass it to him.

He puts his hands behind his head. "Nah. Just gonna watch you eat that. It's all yours."

My face flushes, and I hop up to grab cutlery and plates for us. I cut a slice of salami, and he sighs. Then he says, "How about I watch you eat a banana sometime?"

"I prefer strawberries," I say, curbing the phallic talk. He makes me itchy in a forbidden kind of way. I've settled into being trapped in a room, but my body now realizes it's trapped in a room *with him*.

He smells like resin and sex. Nine months ago was my last one-night stand. He said the right things, and I was taken in. After the inevitable silent phone, I swore off men. It was time to get the hell out of France and get on with life. Ian's messing with my head and my equilibrium.

We dine on our crackers, biscuits, and salami. "What would you have ordered?" I ask.

"Something with beef. And you?"

"Niçoise salad. I always have that, but I should probably switch it up."

He shifts, and his box sags a bit. He trades it for a different paper towel box.

"You're so damn beautiful."

My body freezes and burns simultaneously. "Thank you, but you don't have to say that."

"It's a date, and I wanted to compliment you. I don't ever do anything because I have to." He waggles his eyebrows.

What is actually happening here? Damn. "It's not a date." I continue, "It's adventure school."

He leans towards me. "I had my first kiss at adventure school."

I raise an eyebrow. "Counselor or camper?"

He smirks at me, and his lips curl up like he'll swallow me whole. "Counselor. Chocolate or caramel?"

Rapid-fire game. I'll play. "Chocolate. Beach or lake?"

"Beach. Coke or Pepsi?"

"Really? That's a question? Try again."

"Fate or destiny?"

I ask, "What's the difference?"

"Destiny, you can change, fate you can't." He tents his fingers.

I answer, "Destiny."

"You'd rather choose your path?"

I say, "Hell, yes. So you'd rather leave it up to a mythical force to decide your path?"

"Fate put a guitar in my hand. I certainly didn't put myself on the path I've been on in the last couple of years." A slow smile creeps up at the corners of his mouth and then fills his whole face. "Fate broke that handle, not me."

Oh damn, that's smooth.

I look down. "I'm scared of my next step, but leaving Paris is the right. Doesn't make me more comfortable, but I'm choosing destiny."

"That's how you know you're making the right choices. They come with nerves and exhilaration."

"I've never told anyone I'm scared before. Did you drug me?"

He shifts and crosses his long legs off to the side of our 'table.' "Nah. We're trapped. Why not chat about stuff we'd never tell anyone else?"

"Tell me something vulnerable."

"You're stunning. I'm not worthy of this moment. But I'm going to inhale every fucking second of it."

I gasp. He's so odd. And beautiful. I'm having a hard time concentrating. I'm trapped with a scorching rock star. I need my purse again so I don't hyperventilate. His kind and alive eyes are fixed on me. I fold the napkin in front of me. Then I rearrange the pieces of salami on the plate. And put the top on the curd. Then I look up at him. I'm back in control.

I kind of want him. The way he moves through space is effortless. Mine is calculated, so I don't make a misstep, but here's a man who's made many yet doesn't seem to lack confidence in any step he takes.

IAN

We're going on hour seven in this room. I know all about her childhood nemesis, and she knows about where I buried treasure when I was seven. Every second I spend with her, she is lovelier and more attractive. "Are you nervous?" I'm captivated by her little fidgets. "I mean about the speech?"

"Oh, um, yes."

"Then we should dance."

I need to touch her. I want to hold and protect her. I've never felt this immediately possessive. She doesn't resist as I capture her delicate hands with my calloused ones. I know her from pictures and a little about her family in Northern California. But I never expected this, certainly not after the year I've had. She's a whisper of a future that doesn't involve pain. I need to know if she feels this too.

Her eyelashes are fluttering. "But there's no music. If only there were someone around who might be able to make some."

"Any requests?" I move a little closer to her. And the air is smacked with fucking voltage. It's like right before a summer storm—you feel it in the air, the ground, and on your fingertips. I gently align her hips with mine.

She whispers, "Stevie Wonder."

Ironic. After I shamelessly discounted the man years ago, I did some work on myself musically and emotionally. I know every word, piano lick, and baseline. He's been my soundtrack for the last couple of years. Fate.

I pile boxes on top of each other. I'm a tall guy, 6'3", and I need a tall congo drum. I begin a slow, steady salsa beat, and she begins to sway a bit. I'm humming the beginning of Stevie Wonder's *Don't You Worry 'Bout a Thing.* Her smile widens. Then she hums.

I keep the beat going. "You sing?"

"Not to anyone who will listen."

"I'll listen."

I grab a set of spoons and slap them in rhythm to my hand. She sways to the beat and hums a descant over my percussion. She picks up a closed can of Comet cleanser and does the shaker backbeat. It's sexy as hell that she knows the song that well. I sing the opening verse to my very best audience. And she joins me in the chorus. She loves this song. Damn, did I pick correctly.

I sing the line about how life's not working the way it should, and she finishes it with the next. The one about starting over in a new place.

I pull her closer. We let our "instruments' go and keep singing. Our hips are in rhythm, and fuck, if my cock isn't getting into this mess. There is zero way she doesn't feel me. I don't care. She's going to ruin me. I can feel it. But it's going to be the path that fate put me on. I pull at the back of her tight bun, and nothing happens. We both laugh. She reaches up and pulls a long pin out of it, and it cascades down onto her shoulders.

I need to step away from her, or I'll attack her right here. I dance back to my drum and pound on it in rhythm to the chorus, and she sings full out, and it's gorgeous.

INGRID

I'm all starts and stops right now. I curl my finger as he looks up from his drum and comes when called. I dance in front of him, swaying my hips to the beat. He slides one of his palms onto my hips, and I put mine on his biceps. I pick at his loose-fitting white linen shirt. His biceps are bigger and harder than I imagined. Damn, he's cut for someone so tall, verging on lanky. He keeps the fake maraca beat, and we fall into a salsa step. His voice is raspy but pure. He's raw and real, and it's magic when he sings like this. When he's overproduced and poppy, it loses all that magic.

Even though his world is falling apart on the other side of that door, he's so confident. His ex-wife is trying to destroy him.

He pulls me closer, then his lips are near my ear as he sings and slowly moves my hips in a swivel pattern. I make a figure eight, and he keeps singing low and sexy.

"Don't you worry 'bout a thing, Mama." He sings the title of the song. Shit, he's hot. I slide my hands up his arms and brace them around his neck. I let my thumbs trace a pattern on his back to the timing of the music. Then, as the lyrics swell, I swirl around in a circle, never missing a beat. Our feet are in perfect rhythm as he sings, and I let go. I pick out harmony and join him. He dips me and pulls me back up. We're nearing the song's end, and now he's let go of me. I'm freestyling and clapping along to us singing.

He wraps me in his arms with a flourish and spins me one last time. He lights me up—I can't explain it. I feel safe with him, right here in the confines of our adventure school.

"Ingrid."

I whisper, "Yes."

He traces my cheek with his hand, and I close my eyes and relax into his touch. He's pushed some button deep inside me and freed me from all my bullshit.

"We should probably get going." He gestures his head towards the door.

I laugh, and his lips are on mine faster than I can process time. They're hard and fast and impetuous and perfect. Fucking perfect. I don't think of judgment or pleasing anyone except me. The room vibrates around us as I let my hands roam and his go to my ass. He gasps as he breaks away from me.

"Fuck. I'm not sure they have a name for what we just did. But it might be my new favorite hobby."

I flex my eyebrows at him. "Foreplay."

He doesn't hesitate to take me back in his arms, and I wiggle my Dior dress up over my hips.

"Christ, woman. You're in my head. I want all of you. You cool with that? I can't stop touching you now that I've started."

"You have all my yeses."

IAN

I'm crazed to get her under me. I need to feel her from the inside. My tongue is sliding against hers, and it's real and raw. I grab the back of her head. I can't be close enough to this woman. I've enjoyed our banter, but there's this simmering thing neither of us can overlook. She moans, and I'm freaking gone.

"Jesus, you're—"

"Amazing," she says with this little lilt, and it's driving me nuts.

I dive back into her, kissing her neck and muttering, "Wildflower, this is too powerful. What I feel and want to do to you." She throws her head back and gasps. I tear myself away from her and throw all of our silverware and picnic remnants aside, then push all the boxes together.

She giggles. "I thought we'd do it against the wall."

"No, I need to see you come undone."

She sucks her breath through her teeth. I look over, and her hand is on her heart. I brace the boxes with a wall. When I'm done constructing our fuck pad, I realize my shirt buttons have come undone. She's staring at my chest. Not sure if it's the ink or me.

She walks over and finishes the job. Her lips are on my chest, licking and lighting nipping.

She looks up at me. "I need you. And I'm seriously terrified at how much."

"Then we should dance." I attack her lips and unzip her dress while our tongues wildly chase each other. Her dress falls to the floor. She reaches for my zipper, and I see her lacy bra and nipples pulling hard against it.

Digging into my back pocket, I grab my only condom from my wallet. My crew gave it to me last year at the tour's end as a joke. They told me I was going to need it. I laughed, but they knew my future ex-wife was fucking around. I don't know if they meant I should use a condom with her or if I was going to be single soon. Fortunately, she stopped having sex with me when she fucked all of them.

Ingrid stops groping me and pulls my chin down to her face. "Where did you go?"

"Doesn't matter. This does. Can you read the expiration date?"

She takes it, and suddenly it's no longer a symbol of pain but of rebirth and closure.

"We're good. We have a year and a half. I think we can get to it before then." I kiss her hard and long, then lift her and lay her down on our boxes. I grab a stack of tablecloths and stick it under her head.

"Aren't you the gentleman?"

I growl at her. "That fucking ends right here." I lie on top of her, and the paper towels groan but hold. My goal is to flatten them. I let my hand drift to her thong and reach inside. "Hmm, someone seems rather wet for me." She moans and lifts her hips as I make contact with her clit. "Good thing because my dick is weeping and hard as that metal door we can't open."

"Let's do this until they find us." She hisses out, and I cover her mouth with mine while I explore.

"Good idea."

———

She's draped in a tablecloth and nestled into me. I gulp the moment down. We flattened the boxes, so we're sitting on the floor. I'm stroking her hair and kissing the top of her head. She periodically kisses my chest or arms. This is fucking perfect.

I say something that might shatter me, "Can I see you again?"

She doesn't hesitate to answer but also doesn't leave my arms. "I'm trying to become my own person, and being on Ian Reilly's arm won't help. You have a lot of collateral damage to fix of your own."

I raise one eyebrow at her. "Explain, my beautiful Wildflower." Her voice is so beautiful. She has an innate musicality. I don't know if she knows that.

"The book. You can't be seen with a woman right now."

Holy shit, she knew this whole time about my messy life. I pull her closer, taking in the fresh and intoxicating scent of her shiny hair.

I smile and say, "What do you know about the book?"

"All of it. I turned down an advanced reader copy. Not a fan of take-downs, but I know the details." She turns to me, and I caress her cheek. I gently remove my arms from her, run to the bathroom, and grab my clothes. I need a moment without her. I can't believe she likes me knowing the ex-wife drama. Abbey didn't rob me of this. This was all mine, and I get to savor it repeatedly.

I yell from the back room, "We don't know when we'll get rescued, so as much as this pains me, I think you should get dressed."

"On it."

"WAIT!" I run out without my shirt buttoned, and she's standing there in her bra and panties. I pull a breast out of the cup and let my tongue show her how much I'll miss her perfect tits. She holds my head, and I want to make her come again. I nip, and she squeals. Then I dry off her nipple and tuck it back into her bra. I address her boobs, "You girls be good. I'll see you again, and we'll have more fun, ok?" She laughs, and I zip her up, then she turns and buttons my shirt. It's all very domestic for a moment. I tuck my shirt and kiss her softly.

We sit, and I'm running my hand up and down her arm, and she's cuddled into me. She belongs in my arms in a way beyond comprehension by a mere mortal. This fucking goddess. Both afraid of the world and controlling every-thing around her. She's so strong and soft. Even Meg didn't feel like this, and I thought she was it. Until I realized I wasn't ready for someone of true substance. And it certainly wasn't Meg. This space in my life and heart seems to have been reserved for Ingrid.

———

We wake abruptly as the door swings open with a clang. We've fallen asleep entwined. She grabs her heels. The cleaning crew is holding a crowbar and staring blankly at us. My favorite watch says it's close to three a.m. We've spent twelve hours in here. I nod at our rescuers, who are all muttering in French.

Ingrid nods and says, "Merci, ça devenait terriblement étouffant ici. Et merci pour ton sandwich au citron caillé et au jamon. Ils étaient délicieux. Bonsoir." I guide her out of the closet by placing my hand on her back. I growl in her ear as we glide past a slack-jawed cleaning crew.

"I thanked them for the sandwich and told them it was stuffy in there."

We both laugh very hard as we push our way out to the street.

"Walk you home?" Our fingers interweave as we wander into the unseason-ably warm spring night. She doesn't put her shoes back on and walks across every grass patch she can. We don't let go of each other's hands. After six blocks or so, she stops in front of a gorgeous home and nods. "This is me. Well, three rooms of it are me."

"I get it, but I don't like it. I haven't slept that well in years. How will I do that again without you, lovely Wildflower?"

Ingrid presses her lips to mine. It's gentle and light, and as much as she means this to be goodbye, it feels like a new day. "Take care of yourself. Good luck with the book thing." She's soft and quiet.

"Good luck with your new path and wherever it leads you." I'm still holding her. I desperately want to keep her, but she was only mine in anonymity.

"You'd be surprised where my first stop is." She smirks.

"Shock me." I move her hair behind her ear. "But first, I'm not sure if you've heard this enough. You're tremendous. Not just other orbits gorgeous, but strong and so fucking smart. And funny. You're more than you give yourself credit for."

"Same to you. You're more than the sum of your parts."

"Shock me another time then," I say because I want more. Because I don't think I could handle it if this is it.

"Ian—"

"Shh. I know. Let me have the fantasy." I pull her closer. It's been a transformative night in a closet. But now we're out, I get it. I'm a lot of baggage right now, and she's hell-bent on forging some new trail out of the spotlight.

I add, "Or we can go back and live in the closet."

Ingrid's laugh peals out of her, and she fills the night. I kiss her again. She squeezes me and quickly heads to her door, and we're done. I wait, and I'm rewarded with her beautiful face framed by moonlight and the moment. She presses her palm to the window, and I return the gesture.

I turn down the street, determined to finally get my shit together. I want this moment to be permanent. There's only one way I can figure out how to do that right now. After that, I'm guessing it's time to disappear and write a whole bunch of shit lyrics about the perfect night and perfect girl that might be my someday.

INGRID

I've changed clothes several times. I left Chanel on the bed and opted for jeans and a simple flowered peasant blouse from Anthropologie. I'll feel better in something that's simply Ingrid.

I'm terrified to meet Morgan, the sound engineer, and the rest of the band. I don't want to walk in there and have them think they're doing Jake a favor. Jake is my friend Meg's rock star husband. He and his band, Grade Repeated, built a studio here in Chicago to stay home to record and be with their families. It works for them, and today, I get to be a small part of the process.

I've studied for this. But no one knows yet. I spent every spare moment in college at USC's radio station, KXSC, pouring over the music and dissecting tracks with every music geek I could. Then I danced at Coachella next to Justin Timberlake. The photo changed the course of my life. It was all circumstantial. I dressed for whimsy, which is my favorite. It was thrift shop couture, but people made a big deal of it. And Jessica was dancing with us the whole time, but the solo angle of Justin and me alone went viral. Jess, even DM'd me to apologize for the mess.

Then it snowballed. I did appearances at clubs, parties, and shows. I was front row at global fashion weeks. But the entire time, I listened and cataloged. I studied and stood by DJs learning from them. I spent time with engineers or different bands backstage. The pictures portrayed me as a party girl, but I was learning. I've taken all the teasing from my brother's crew over the years for being the so-called "it girl."

But I was studying the way sound can bend and stretch. Or how it can fill the background or affect a mood. Understanding how music communicates and bonds became my religion. Figuring out what messages in a bottle song-writers slip into lyrics. I'm far from musical, but I think my brand of analytical supports that kind of genius.

Just a touch of Tom Ford's deep coral lipstick, *Twist of Fate*, sent by a family friend who has a freaky gift of picking the perfect shade for people. It came in a box for my first day. So much for keeping secrets from my tribe. I lift my boobs back into my bra and throw my shoulders back. I'm the queen of fake it until I make it. I can assess any situation, see what it needs from me, and morph into that. But this time, I want to be just Ingrid, not what someone else thinks Ingrid is.

———

It's hour four of the same song. I'm fascinated as this green-haired pixie floats around the board and lays the vocals into the music. The entire band is recording today before they lay down solo tracks. It sounds like a silly song about a bar fight, but it's about heartbreak and giving up. Remarkably, this message is wrapped inside the ridiculous, and it's beautifully deceptive. But it's off.

They've tried different approaches, currently working with a ska feel. Morgan groans. She's petite and gruff, dressed in jeans and a ripped shirt as if she doesn't want anyone to know she's beautiful. She's five feet and scares the shit out of me.

She presses the studio button. "STOP. This is shit. Fuck. Let me try something."

They're frustrated. I'm fascinated. Jake scrubs his face with his hands. The buff and tattooed Rob Westerbrook, the other lead singer of Grade Repeated, is jumping up and down and groaning. The other members walk away from their instruments. They let the front men moan and bitch, as if they've seen this before.

Jake says, "Fuck it. Beverage break."

I meekly say, "Morgan. Sorry. Morgan." She doesn't turn around.

Eventually, she pulls her headphones off and turns to me. "Yes?"

"You heard me?"

"I hear everything." She climbs on her chair, squats down, and spins it around in a circle like a child. "What?"

"Penny's Noodles and beer will be here in a second."

"Maybe it will help this shit song we've wasted three fucking days on. We're going to have to scrap it." I crack the door to the studio, and Jake tries to greet me warmly.

"This Ingrid. She fancies a career behind the music. Be nice. Sorry, it's a crap-fest today."

I meekly wave my hand at them. It's odd. The room smells like the rubber backing of the rugs and men. The rest is woodsy and a bit like the glue that holds instruments together. Almost a pine resin. I love it. It's intoxicating. He smelled a little like this. The man I shouldn't still be thinking of who I did in a closet. That was more like my sister-in-law than me. She's wild and uninhibited. It works for Tabi, but it doesn't work for me. I'd feel guilty if it weren't for that connection I'd never felt before. I keep picking up my phone to text him, but I don't have his number. He's a phantom pain, but I keep thinking he's there somehow. I have to tell Meg. It's strange, but it's not like Meg, and I are related.

My mind wanders to him as it does too often. What's he doing? And the world, including me, wants to know where he is. He disappeared, but I guess I did too. One last searing kiss as he dropped me off at my house. Jake's voice breaks me out of my Ian fog. I have my fingers on my lips as if I'm trying to feel him again. "Ingrid, yo."

"Sorry. Lunch is in the conference room."

"We call it the hub since we got couches and shit in there," Tyler, the drummer, says with a silly voice. He's a squatty man with a rubber face and a killer sense of rhythm.

Rob slaps me on my back, then curls his arm around my shoulder. "Welcome meek one."

I turn to him. "I'm not meek." Everyone files past us.

Jake smiles as he passes. "Prove it."

Rob puts his hands on my shoulders and pushes me to the hub.

———

They're done eating. I tried to clean up, but no one would let me. They kept saying I'm not an intern. I can't stop thinking about their song. I'm putting the leftovers into Tupperware, and they're bitching.

Rob is up and springing around the room on the balls of his feet. He's super fit and cut. Short dark hair peppered with a bit of grey. "Morgan, fix it," he whines.

She's blunt, "I'd trash it."

Jake says, "What if we push the bridge towards the end, write another verse and fill in the space with a better riff."

Thad, the bassist, says, "Lipstick on a pig."

I mutter as I snap a lid shut, "The guitars need to be crunchy and move to a 136 bpm." The song keeps running through my head like older songs my dad loves, not the ballad or ska they keep trying to force.

Rob's voice is booming behind me, "WHAT DID YOU JUST SAY?"

I whip around, and my face is red. "Nothing really." I didn't realize I said it aloud.

Jake nods and sits forward on his chair. He rests his forearms on the table as if he's about to leap. Morgan stands, and her smile curls like a cartoon character with a plan. "Come, little rabbit, let's hear it."

I catch my breath. I smooth my blouse to my body and hold my stomach for support. "Ska doesn't work...." Everyone nods. "But when you were messing around before the last couple of takes, I heard it differently."

Jake stands. "Continue," he says in a pleading voice.

I say it quickly, as if my dumb idea will sound better faster. "If you pull the rhythm up and pan to the drums, smooth out the bass and crunch up the guitars, you could pull off a '70s vibe."

Rob is jumping up and down and looking up at the ceiling. "Describe."

I get excited and nervous. They're listening to me. Maybe all that observing has paid off-I know this is what this particular song should sound like. Tyler begins a slow drum beat on the table. Jake flails his hands as if he wants me to speak faster.

"Put in the pocket of The Little River Band's 'Reminiscing' or the Eagles, 'Take it Easy.' Twist it a little modern like Amy Winehouse's Rehab.' Something sunny and dusty with all sixteen tracks weaving into some old-school magic to highlight the song's irony. Give them nostalgia that isn't. Because that's what heartbreak is really, nostalgia." I slap my hand over my mouth. There's silence in the room. Rob is in my face and removes my hand from my mouth. He kisses my forehead.

His eyes are earnest as he points to my chest. "Don't ever stand in the background again."

Jake's beaming with pride. He yells above the drumbeat, "When will you assholes remember, despite her klutziness and apparent disorganization, my wife is a fucking genius who can always find the right place for people. Fuck, I'm buying Meg something shiny."

Thad says, "No, I am."

Tyler says, "Let's get her a GameStop gift card." He's such a dork. Then Morgan speaks, and I hold my breath—her opinion carries serious weight.

"Back to the studio. We have a ton of work to do." They all run out of the room, and Morgan looks at me. "Text Meg, you two won't be home for dinner."

My heart is so full it's going to leap out of my chest. Hasn't felt this way since the storage room months ago.

IAN

It's been almost four months living among the Swanton, Vermont locals. And they don't give a shit about me. It's hot, and I wish this fucking cabin had air. I've managed to live through the chaos of the book dropping and the constant speculation of where I disappeared. Eventually, I got more press for my absence than her stupid fucking book. Take that, bitch. Now the media speculates I've gone crazy. People keep reporting sightings of me like a yeti.

I am really fucking sick of myself. I'm not sure what the next step is. I don't know where to go. I know I don't want to go home—or the building where most of my stuff is—not sure it's home anymore. I want to record, but I don't know if I have anything to say. I released a random song before hiding. It did ok. But it didn't do what I wanted it to.

I have all these thoughts and rhythms itching to come out and make sense of my head. I'm a bit adrift and paralyzed. That's why I'm still here. Inertia. A body at rest stays at rest, and a body in motion stays in motion unless knocked by a great force. There's nothing to knock me, so I stay. They have a Dunkin', so it's all good. I walk and sing. I play and think. The other day I lay on the grass out front and listened to music. I simply listened like I used to do in my bedroom as a kid.

I've written many songs about water and rocks. None of them are good, but it fills my day. I do that and think of a supply closet 6000 miles away. It was only twelve hours of my life, but it was different. I pined for Meg once, but not like this. I don't want to be anywhere but beside Ingrid. I want to learn everything she's ever thought and then weave it into my own narrative.

On the back deck, I'm lying on a chaise overlooking the Missisquoi River.

Perhaps this is who I'll become, the grizzled bitter guy who never bounced back after his wife slaked her thirst with dozens of roadies and other musicians. I can never look my road manager in the eye again, and he's been with me since I was seventeen. Ingrid seems to be the only true thing besides music. And I don't even really know her outside the confines of our cleaning supply kingdom. She's disappeared too. I can't find her anywhere, and I don't have her number. No one does. I asked around.

I don't use my cellphone except for demos. I don't want to talk to anyone. My parents have the landline number in case they need me. Everyone else can fuck off. I don't know who to trust in my life. I don't know who knew about Abbey and when.

There's a loud crash. I pause and sit up. A bear? Then the distinct thumping of someone knocking. No one comes here. It's not easy to come here. That's the fucking point.

I ignore it. Whatever they need will take care of itself. The thumping continues, then a loud, jarring voice pierces my self-pity utopia. Of course, she's here.

"IAN! Open the fucking door. I fell on your stupid-ass steps, and I'm bleeding." I groan, make my way to the front door and swing it open—it's like she's been stranded in the woods for a month. Her hair is wild, with branches and leaves stuck in it. Her eyes are crazed, her face has actual dirt on it, and sure enough, her shin is bleeding. And I didn't know how much I missed my friend. I pull her into a hug, and she wraps her arms around me. After a minute or two, she speaks, buried in my chest.

"Do you think I need stitches?"

I laugh and release her from my arms. "You did this on the front porch?"

"No. I did fall on the porch, but I didn't think the Prius would make it up the drive. So I hiked up your *driveway*, full of treacherous rocks and evil little holes. And I'm not an outdoorsy girl, so I got spooked by some noise in the woods. I may or may not have tried to run." She pulls air quotes, and my mouth curves into a broad smile.

"Sit." I dampen a cloth with warm water and soap. "How and why the hell are you here, Meg?" My exie-bestie is standing there, blood dripping down her leg.

I pull off my ratty t-shirt and grab a clean shirt. She turns away but then turns back.

"I'm here to fucking kick you in the ass. And your mom told me... Um, that's a lot more ink than when you know, we, um...."

"Did it?"

She smirks. "Yes."

It turns out Meg and I are soul mates in a different way. She's Jake's everything, and all my hard feeling about that are completely gone. As well as any flicker of a torch for who's turned out to be my closest friend. Thank God she forgave me for my karmic jackassery. I cheated on her with my now ex-wife.

"You still talk to my mom?"

"If I have to, and this sitch has gone on long enough. So, I had to."

She stands, and before I can pull my shirt down, she traces the small watch face by my grandmother's lily, now joined by a tangled bunch of wildflowers. My breath catches because I never intended for her to see the watch. I don't want her to misinterpret.

"Is that me?" She whispers.

"No, Bae. The watch is all things about that time, not you." I evoke the name even though its meaning has shifted. I trust her before anyone else. "It's the idea of you. That there might be someone out there somewhere who devastates me the way Jake devastates you."

She smiles and places her hand on my cheek. Her eyes fill a little. "Your real woman is out there. I'm sorry I wasn't her."

"Oh. No. NO. Meggy, you were never that girl. I just thought you might be at one point. You never need to feel guilty. Not after what I did." She pinches my arm, nods sharply, and then limps back to the kitchen chair.

"You can never tell Jake I saw your chest again."

"Clearly." I grin. Even though it's splashed all over the internet.

"Who's the bunch of wildflowers?"

She might know Ingrid from Sonoma, and I want her all to myself. "No one. Sometimes a tattoo is just a tattoo."

"Fine. You'll tell me later. Grab your shit. You're done here." She stands and starts collecting my clothes. She grabs sheets of scribbled lyrics and notes and stacks them on the table.

"Where are we going?" I cross my arms over my chest.

"My house." As she limps at high velocity, it looks like she's in the eye of a tornado, not an off metaphor for her. Turning and kicking up dust like a memory. I stand in awe of her, putting the pieces of my life back together as if it were her job. The force to knock me out of my state of rest. Inertia.

I didn't go to bed after I dropped Ingrid off. Immortalizing the moment in time when, possibly, my molecules changed seemed more important.

"Look, Jake is being pretty cool with this crazy plan of mine. Start shoving things in a bag. Have you ever been with a kid who's cutting molars? It sucks ass. Wailing and drool everywhere. Multiple outfit changes. And we're in the midst of it with Pearl."

I laugh very hard at the idea of this international rocker, Jake, trying to calm a baby. I stand and cross the room to look out at the river. She curls into my side. I throw an arm around her. It's intimate but very different, and the realization that I don't want to fuck Meg is crazy to me. I just want her to listen to me whine. She's right. She's not it, and Abbey's not it. I'm not ready to tell her about Wildflower, mostly because I don't trust myself. What I feel can't be honest, and it can't be trusted.

"How long have you been up here?" She squeezes around my waist once more, then picks up the remains of my breakfast dishes out here on the back porch.

"Sixty-two iPhone demos worth of time. Mostly songs about trees and my inability to move towards hope. And—"

"Terrible heartbreak songs? I'm sure the songs inspired by our breakup were much better."

"Multi-platinum, Grammy for song of the year and album of the year, and number one download of the year. So, yeah, yours was better. Now what?"

She puts her hands on her hips, and I see the mom Meg has morphed into. "Home. You go back to work and figure out things in our carriage house. Jake will hate every second of it, but he loves me and knows what he married."

"You collect lost men." She has a trail of men on her speed dial who confide in her. I adore our relationship but know I'm not unique.

"I guess I do."

I kiss the top of her head. "Thank fucking god."

She says, "Rent for a couple of nights in the carriage house. I need a favor."

"Anything."

"Can you mentor a quick ChiKid thing for me? The film kids shot footage, but they want to know how to score it. Can you play different genres of music behind a couple of clips, so they see the difference music can make?" ChiKid is the youth program she runs for the City of Chicago.

"That's why you came all the way up here, isn't it?"

"Yes." She stands, and I pull her into an embrace.

"Liar." I squeeze my friend closer.

She kisses my cheek sweetly. "Ok. Maybe your pathetic ass needed a kick. I'm not flying to the middle of fucking nowhere again. If you'll excuse me, I have to hurry back to Chicago, so my husband can take a shower and jump onto Lollapalooza's stage tonight."

"Ok. Let's go."

She beams and raises her eyebrows. She always gets what she wants.

IAN

I did her seminar yesterday, and it felt good to play for an appreciative audience. They are nine-to-fourteen-year-olds, so it worked out well. There were four clips the kids put together, and I played different moods behind them. They saw how the piece changed with the music. I forget the power music has. I won't do it again.

It's ass-crack early, and I was up all night playing. Just playing and fucking around with sound and words. This place has excellent acoustics. I'm on to something here. I'm open, and I don't want to mess with it.

My flight's today, but I don't want to go to LA. I want to write and figure out what the next phase of my life sounds like. I think I could do some seriously fucking great stuff here. I even had a fantastic conversation with Jake. He told me if I needed to use the studio to call Morgan for some time. That's a solid man. I want to be a solid man. Instead of a man-child struggling to figure it all the fuck out.

Whatever someone is cooking smells divine.

IAN: Hey, you up?

MEG: I'm married, don't start. What?

IAN: What are you doing?

MEG: Pouring milk for the princess. She rejected six of eight sippy cups. Weaning sucks.

IAN: What made the cut?

MEG: Spiderman and Olaf. Nothing makes sense anymore. What do you need?

IAN: Can I stay?

MEG: In my backyard?

IAN: Yes. For like a week or two. There's something here that I want to explore.

MEG: Sure. Oh shit. Olaf is down. Fucker has been rejected. I'll run it by Jake. Some-one's staying upstairs. Don't be alarmed if you hear them.

IAN: Check.

MEG: Fuck me. She just "poured" herself more milk. Talk later. Headed to the office this morning.

IAN: Thank you, BAE.

The carriage house is set up for two occupants. Usually friends or nomad musicians stay here. It's an excellent setup. Everything has been painted white, so it's clean and bright. The ceilings have to be at least fifteen to twenty feet. The large doors where the coaches used to go through to be housed for the night are still there. They've been sealed, and the windows expanded, but the outline remains. The vibe is casual, rock star comfort. The kitchen's small, but it's not like I cook. Maybe learning to cook will make me a man.

There's a sunroom and a little patio overlooking the backyard. It's got a stackable washer and dryer in a closet. But the best part of this place is the enormous dining table. It looks like reclaimed wood. And smells of history. It faces the big picture garden window. I grab a notebook and start scratching out something a neighbor in Vermont said that stuck in my head. 'Flowers don't continuously bloom, but they're still there, waiting.' She was bitching at me to dig up the tulips and split them or some shit. I ignored her, but her phrase stayed.

I'm writing away when I hear the other occupant come down the stairs. I have zero desire to be friendly. Gonna stay here until Jake takes the session musician to work with him, then sneak in the house and grab something to eat. I'm starving. A slip of paper slides under the door. I ignore it. Instead, I'm feverishly writing notes and tapping out beats.

When I look up from the song, which is really fucking good, it's been almost two hours. Shit, now I'm ravenous.

I grab the note.

Your music gave me the best night's sleep. You're very talented. I made these this morning.
Thought you might like some. Thanks for the guitar.

I

Shit. Someone knows I'm here. Why the "I"? I fling open the door, and there's a covered tray. I take it to the kitchen and discover it's an icy but plentiful plate of pancakes. I toss them in the microwave. Upstairs has also provided juice, cut fruit, and syrup. No butter, though.

I bite into the most unique pancake flavor. I smell it. It's like a Christmas cake, and the pancake itself is whole wheat. Holy shit. It's carrot cake. So fucking good. I move the flapjacks and syrup to the table and scroll my phone while I devour them. I read my version of the morning paper, then dunk the last bits into the syrup.

I've read the Schroeder Vineyard blog, creatively titled 'Grapevine,' every day for four months. I relish any tiny piece of information like I'm a reporter on a beat. Mr. Schroeder is my only connection to Ingrid. I know she went from Paris to home but then set out again. He includes snippets of memories about her, and I love it. But nothing today, just something about leaves.

My belly is warm and wonderful, and I flop down on the couch with my guitar, picking out the new song and writing down riffs that work.

———

Last night I raided Meg's kitchen and took half a case of wine. I'll munch on her leftover Kung Pao in a bit.

I make coffee and settle in at the magic table. I had another idea last night. One, unfortunately, about her again. Ingrid doesn't show up on Google news or her social. There are a billion pictures of her if you google, but the ones with her family look most like my Ingrid.

I sit down and pull up the blog. Today's was about these five wineries and the friends he's close to. He also gave me this gift, 'Ingrid always loved the lush vines.' That's all he said, and I'm going to fucking dine on it. He misses her too. I hear you, brother. My Ingrid fantasy is interrupted by another note. I don't run to it, but I walk over, hoping to catch a glimpse of mystery pancake person.

I like the third version of whatever you're working on. It has more soul. Enjoy the breakfast. I made too much as always.
I

Holy fuck. There's a smidge of pink lipstick smeared on the corner. This is a woman and definitely not Meg. She hates makeup. And this woman is listening intently. I pick up the tray and lift the lid. They're red today with a tiny pot of something white. Red velvet and cream cheese dip with a side of bacon and fruit. Jack-fucking-pot. Whatever is with this woman, she knows her way around breakfast. I finish them while trying to remember the third version.

———

Last night's song was yummy comfort food. Move the refrain up and double the chorus, in my humble opinion. I made sourdough pancakes. (Yes, I have a tiny bit of starter with me. I'm a geek like that.) Enjoy.
I

This woman is a fucking savant. Musically and with batter. I can't help but be obsessed with her. What does she looks and sounds like? I might stake out the door tomorrow. I want to talk to her. She's dead-on about the song. Perhaps she's European or Australian because she addresses the notes in reverse.

I tape a note for her to my door.

Thank you for the batter and suggestions. You're kind of spot on with both. You keep strange hours, and I find the mystery of it all enticing. Why the pancakes?
Yours in syrup,
I

———

Ever had a Japanese pancake? Here you go. Last night's song felt undone as if you're waiting for something. What are you waiting for?
Pancakes are a thing I do with my father. I make them to comfort me or when I miss him.
I

Jesus, these are strange, like mini soufflés. I sit and think about what I'm waiting for while reading Adrian Schroeder's latest winery post. His son and daughter-in-law are launching a new wine using some of his grapes for their own winery. I've had Prohibition wine. It's good.

Perhaps I'm waiting for news of a girl who's more fantasy than reality these days. Or maybe I'm waiting to see who I'm going to become.
I

———

Well, those could be lovely lyrics. Perhaps some piano and light percussion to add to the melody you kept trying to finish. I hope you hear about your girl. I, too, am searching for a lost connection that feels like something, but there's no time.
I

I fuse her words and mine into the chorus. Melding the two yearning for something or someone more. This woman is twisting my brain. She's wise. She must be older.

And she's made me an apple Dutch baby pancake. That's fucking commitment. I can't take this anymore.

Piano will be critical. I can hear it when I play. I hope you find your connection today. I'm striving for it again.

I

———

Rushed. Here are my signature regulars. Floated on that countermelody last night. Why don't you ever sing when you play? Or are you a songwriter?
I

That's it. Four days. Four songs. Four sets of pancakes. I need to meet this woman. I don't care what she looks or sounds like. I want her to sit and analyze what I'm writing. She's so damn insightful in these little snippets. The mystery is killing me.

I sing but haven't felt like it lately. I'm starting to want to lay down tracks of these songs. I haven't believed in my music in a little bit, but suddenly, I have something to say. Thank you, pancake girl. Please knock in the morning. I'd like to have breakfast with you.
I

———

There were no pancakes this morning for the second day in a row. Is she that skittish?

I'm sorry if I overstepped. I just wanted to thank you in person.
I

———

No pancakes. My note is still taped to the door, unread. No movement upstairs. I think I've lost another woman. On the upshot, Ingrid visited her father over the weekend. Knowing where she was for even a brief moment sets my heart right. She poured wine into the tasting room. There was a wedding celebration for her winemaker sister with all the winery families. Sounds like Adrian and his kids had a good time. She's gone again, but I know where she was for the first time in almost five months.

Oddly, I'm now invested in this man's life. Ingrid is a bonus these days. I'm captivated by learning how he and his best friend, a guy named Will, spent the day trying to fix something called a gondola. I don't know what it does in wine-making, but they needed it. His life has a purpose. He's an adult. I'm a thirty-five-year-old struggling with how to be relevant, pining over a woman I'll never see again. And that seems to be my only plan. I need to be more like Jake, and Ingrid's father, Adrian.

That's it. No note. No pancakes. Step one to getting a new life plan- asking Meg about pancake girl. I want her opinion on some riffs I'm playing with. It's early, but the chaos in that house rises at dawn.

She'll kick my ass because she will think I'm trying to bed pancake girl instead of using her musically. We may be legit friends now, but she's always had a thing for the long hair. I keep it shaggy and head over to her kitchen.

"Hey," I say as I enter.

"HOLD UP!" She twirls around, wholly stunned to see me. She knocks over a stack of folded cloth napkins. "You startled me!"

"I live in your backyard. How startled can you be?"

I bend over and pick up the napkins, and she pours me a cup of coffee. She shakes some sugar in it. She pours herself some more and takes a sip. It dribbles from the bottom of the cup down her shirt.

She gestures at it, "None of this should be a surprise. Where have you been? Are you writing? I hear things at night. You good?"

She jumps up onto the counter, a patented Meg move. Jake actually removed an upper cabinet in his kitchen to give her a perch where she wouldn't bang her head.

Canyon, her flatulent French Bulldog, trots over to my legs. I sit on the ground behind the island and take her into my lap. We used to be pals. She's licking and wiggling as if she remembers our time together.

"She still snore?"

Meg nods. "Do you?" She tosses a wadded-up paper towel at me, and it easily misses. Canyon runs towards it, sniffs, licks, and begins to eat it. She's always hungry and not very bright. I take it from her mouth.

Meg says, "I'm not going to like this. I see you. Floppy hair doesn't work on married women who have no interest in your way-too-sincere pop star stare." She takes two fingers and points from her eyes to mine.

I sit at the nook in the corner by the back door. I stretch my legs out and in runs both of her stepsons. Ben, the older one, is like thirteen. The other one is maybe nine.

"Sup, gentlemen." I salute them.

"Meg! You took in another stray? How charming." She throws one of the newly retrieved cloth napkins at Ben. The floor is becoming littered with her chosen shrapnel.

The younger one sits next to me. "Who are you, and why are you in our kitchen? Usually, the dudes stick to the carriage house. I mean, the girl can come inside because hubba-hubba." I laugh at him while he elbows my arm. Maybe the kid knows more about pancake girl.

"I agree, little man, some girls are definitely hubba-hubba indeed. What's she like?"

"Meg, make it stop," Ben pleads.

Meg's voice cuts through my nonsense. "Ben, are you headed to Ethan's this weekend? You can fly out Friday midday. You don't have camp, right?"

"Yes. I already booked my ticket, and Liam and Jillien have my times."

"I enjoy a system that takes care of my flaws. Are you guys here tonight, or is your mom picking you up?"

Jonah answers, "Dad said while he has to be away tonight, you'd need men to watch out for you."

I grin. He's safeguarding his woman from me. As if he needs to.

Meg rolls her eyes. "Fine. I'll see you later. Go, or you'll be late." They both hug her, and she kisses the tops of both their heads even though Ben almost has her eye to eye. They exit, and she watches them go with a dreamy look in her eye. I smirk until she turns back to me, narrowing her eyes. She leans forward on the kitchen island and rests on her elbows. I stand to come over to her.

The backdoor opens, and we're interrupted. Meg smiles and nods to the person coming in, and I turn my head. The girl's eyes bug out of her head, and my heart drops to the floor. It's her. The air crackles like just before a summer storm, same fucking feeling. Hell, my DNA crackles. It's her. It's fucking her. It's the woman, other than the pancake girl. I dream of every god damned night and beat off to every morning. The woman I scan the "news" for every day in the shape of her father's blog. The only woman my dick and heart want to be with at all, Ingrid Schroeder.

Her stunning face is pale, but the rest of her is perfect in tight dark-wash jeans that hug all the angles and curves of my chestnut-haired goddess. Her eyes are popping light fireworks on a distant horizon, and I'm drawn to her. Meg doesn't even notice the two of us suspended in the moment.

I'm a whisper from her face. "How?" I want to touch her and kiss her immediately. My hands twitching.

"Ian." Her voice is breathy and laced with tomorrows.

"Yes, Ingrid. How?" Her hand goes to my chest, and I'm overwhelmed at how at harmony I am in an instant. There's a calm Meg brings to my life, but Ingrid is all-encompassing peace. She smiles, and all of my senses wake up, but my dick, unfortunately, responds as well. He's so damn happy to see her.

Her words are delicate and soft but sure of themselves, "I don't know how or why, but I'm so happy to see you. To know you're ok." My heart flips that she cares. She might have thought about me as much as I fucking obsessed over her. Worst mistake ever, not getting her number. Fucking ex-wife took away my swagger for a moment. But she's here in front of me.

Meg interrupts us by standing just on the other side of Ingrid's arm with her face between us. She sips her coffee.

"What's happening here? Ingrid. What do you need?" She shakes her head and steps back from me. Ingrid's hand slowly leaves my body until our soul point of contact our her eyes. And our sole point of contact is her fingertip. Finally, she turns towards Meg, breaking the spell.

She stutters as if embarrassed by them, "I need pancake eggs...." My eyebrows shoot up into my hairline. And my fucking world flips again.

"YOU'RE pancake girl!? You were signing your notes, not addressing them to me. I." I facepalm, then look directly at her.

"Oh. Shit. You're the music." She shakes her head. The two women who rule the thoughts of my day are the same woman. "I didn't know."

"I assumed, or you'd possibly have said hello." I grin at her, and Meg smacks my arm. I turn to her. "What?"

She hands Ingrid some eggs and says, "There you go. Jake said they're starting in an hour. You can see how the master is woven together."

My head spins to her. "You're mixing?" That's her path. My path. Music.

"Learning. Producing hopefully." And another piece snaps into place. She knew exactly what she was doing when she commented about my music.

Her lips curl at the corners, and she turns to leave. I want to run away, buy a giant Winnebago where all we do is fuck and eat pancakes. She can mix all my music if she agrees to the camper plan. She turns back, her cherry-red lips still in a hopelessly large smile. "See you around, neighbor." And she leaves, and I stare at the door.

Meg hits me again. Her voice is sharp. "Do not fuck Ingrid."

I pretend to pledge her an impossible task, "I promise not to fuck Ingrid...." But I can't lie to her. I close my eyes tight as I say the next word, "...again."

"WHAT ARE YOU TALKING ABOUT, Ian Reilly?"

I put my hands up to try and calm her as she rounds the kitchen island and punches my arm.

"Not here. Four months ago! It was Paris. She was everything. I didn't know you knew her."

"She's my ward!" Meg screams.

I back away from her. "Ok, settle down there, Bridgerton. Your ward?"

"I'm watching out for her. I always have." And then it dawns on her how odd this is. Her eyes slowly close as she puts her hand over her mouth. She talks from behind it.

"Ew. You slept with Ingrid and me."

I talk to her calmly as if I were a hostage negotiator or a flight attendant during turbulence.

"Meg, I didn't know your connection. She knew it was me, so maybe hammer her a little bit and stop smacking me. We got locked in a storage room in Paris for twelve hours. It just happened. It was the day the book dropped. We don't think of each other like that anymore."

She looks at me sideways as she heads back to the coffee pot. "You're right. You're like a big dumbass brother to me."

"Exactly, nutjob."

"Watch it."

I grin. She holds her mug close to her chest, and there's a comfortable silence. I've missed just existing with other people. Despite our past, Meg gets my head to settle down faster than any dope I can get my hands on. She's just a different drug to me now.

She says, "Do you think of Ingrid that way?"

I blow my hair out of my face and admit something I thought was simply loneliness after my shitshow of a divorce. "All the fucking time. I can't stop since that day. We were in that closet for twelve hours. And sex was only for like an hour."

"How many?" I smirk, knowing precisely what she means. I flop back down on the kitchen chair.

"Fourteen or so."

"You already wrote more songs about her than me?!"

I say, "Yes, but I've only released one."

"Hold up! *Glitter Girl?*"

"Aww, you listened." I randomly released it, hoping she'd reach out. It was a desperate move after Paris.

"And you have a problem. Do not pursue this if you're going to be all Ian about it. No flaky. No cheating. No denying her feelings or your own. And you have to tell her about sleeping with me."

She's always been daffy and occasionally clueless. "The world knows we slept together. I have six Grammys to prove it." She flicks her thumb against her teeth, then turns and pulls the coffee pot. Facing me, she pours a new coffee, for I assume Jake. She doesn't look and leans back to place it on the counter. It's happening, and I can't stop it. The cup is a couple of inches short of the back counter and crashes to the floor. Just as this happens, her husband walks into the kitchen.

"Ah, the sounds of Meg in the morning." I laugh and nod. He's a good man. "Don't move, my love. I'm guessing you're barefoot." She nods. He leans over and kisses her very romantically.

Then he turns to me. "Mine," he growls. I don't know if he truly hates me, or it's simply fun to pretend I'm a rival. I never really had a chance. They're fated.

"All yours." I put my hands up.

"He banged Ingrid." My eyes shoot to Meg. "What? You know I'm not good holding stuff from Jake."

"Cool, we have like a fucking Noel Coward play around here. Perhaps we get my ex-wife to take up space in the attic?" He reaches for the broom and hands it to me. Then he walks behind the island and lifts her up onto his shoulder. She's losing it, and her colossal laugh fills this room and the one next to it. He glides past me.

He smacks her ass. "Mine." I grin and begin to sweep the broken ceramic.

"And we have a toddler, so sweep it up real good there, Pretty boy Popstar douchebag."

As they leave the room, Meg lifts her head and yells, "Does she devastate you?" Jake doesn't wait for an answer. But for the first time in my life, the answer is yes.

INGRID

The stairs creak under every footfall. I'm panting as I enter the house and slam the door. As if that will stop him from being here. I've got a lot of excess adrenaline, and I don't know what to do with it.

I've never been happier or more terrified of anything in my life. I made the man pancakes and critiqued his playing. I thought it was some journeyman session, dude. I thought he was older because the guitar sounded so seasoned. I didn't know it was him. Why the hell didn't Meg or Jake tell me? Oh god. Now I have to tell Meg about the super awkward thing we have in common.

I can't see him again. I can't want him. I have to wear a hood whenever I go downstairs. I'll sleep at the studio. My head is clouded. I'd finally shoved down all the thoughts and hopes of him that dominated both my REM and my awake cycles for months.

Now all of those thoughts are running amok in my head. He's not living rent-free but certainly subletting my brain. Jesus. How can he be here? How can I have cooked for him? That smell. My un-dry-cleaned Dior dress lives in a large Ziplock in my suitcase. I might have slept with it a time or two, then realized I was a freak. I had a handle on it until now.

The sunlight is streaming in the window, and I sit cross-legged below it. I'll hide. Seems logical. Eventually, he'll leave, right?

There's a banging at the door and that voice teen girls dream of. "Open the door, Ingrid."

I clear my throat. "Cleaning service. She's not home."

He guffaws. I wasn't trying to be funny. He turns the knob. I didn't lock the door, and I'm hiding. That's like hiding 101. Lock the door of the place you're hiding. Dammit.

He steps through the door with the sun at his back, and I can't make out his face. But he clearly sees me sitting in the middle of the room, ducking just under the windows. He folds his arms across his chest.

Then the sun recedes, and I can't mistake the smirk on his face. It's mischief and mayhem in a perfectly symmetrical set of lips. I exhale. He found me.

"Awful jumpy, Wildflower." My shoulders make their way back to their normal position. I cross my legs and sit up completely.

He sits in front of me. That smirk. It's my undoing.

We stare at each other, and I crack a smile that gets wider as he licks his lips. Oh man, do I want those lips back on me. Everything I've guided my life on in the last sixteen months goes out the window as I stare at him. He moves slowly as if I'm a chipmunk that can be scared off. His hand reaches for me, and my breath catches. He tugs, and I look down at my hands.

"Hand me the carton of eggs, and no one gets hurt." I snicker at him. The eggs are placed to the side, and he pulls me to standing. I submit to my desire and him.

There's no doubt or hesitation as he takes me in his arms. His mouth is on mine, aggressive and hot. His kiss is urgent and desperate but not as desperate as mine. Our tongues crash into each other's mouths. That's not enough for me. I jump up and hitch my legs around his hips, and he groans. He's so hard already. I know how big that thing can get, and I want it now. I flex my hips.

"Christ, it's crazy how much I fucking missed you." He gasps against my lips.

"Me too. And…" I pull back from the kiss as he forces my head back and starts kissing and sucking on my neck.

"Fucking now, talking later." He walks towards my little bedroom but misses the door, and I'm thrust up against the wall. We both groan as I frantically search for friction between my legs. I'm aching for him. He thrusts into me, and I might come with our clothes on. I grind down on his cock and try to find relief.

"Ingrid, I've never wanted anyone how I want you."

"Same. Now shut up and kiss me again."

His mouth is on mine with such force I'm shocked my head doesn't dent the wall. He doesn't stop, but he does finally finds the doorway. We make it to the bed and stop abruptly when his knees hit the mattress. He tosses me on the bed. His hair and eyes are wild. They're dark and hooded, and I want to capture every second of this in my memory. There's no rational thought, only lust. Everything is lost except those eyes and this ache in between my legs. He flips his shirt off and stares at me, licking his lips.

"Why aren't you naked? I want to see all of you." I grin and unbutton my shirt. I'm supposed to be headed to work in an hour. I don't want to go. I go up on my knees and toss my shirt to the side. He hisses at the sight of my orange bra. I love orange.

I think he'll like what's on the bottom more. I stand on my bed, and he stares up while he steps out of his jeans and boxer briefs. He strokes himself, and I'm lost in the rhythm of watching him tug on his tremendous cock. I walk to the edge of the bed and wiggle my jeans off my hips.

"Fucking commando. Jesus, you're hot." I forgot to do laundry. He moves to me, then his hands are on my ass as he rakes me towards his mouth, which is at the perfect height. I grab the bed posts on either side of me. He kisses my inner thigh, then angles my ass so I'm presenting myself to him. I look a bit like the sacrifice in *King Kong*. There was no worshipping of each other's bodies in the supply closet, just hard stranger fucking. Albeit on pallets of paper towels. Now, I feel like a goddess.

He moans as his tongue makes contact with my clit. "You're so wet for me, Wildflower." I moan as he sucks me into his mouth and his teeth graze my clit. One hand leaves my ass and makes its way to join his mouth.

He looks up at me. "You're seriously all the fucking gorgeous in the world."

He chuffs, and I look down.

"What?"

"You're like an Amazonian goddess waiting to be worshipped." I laugh too. He might as well be kneeling at my altar.

"So, what are you waiting for?" I giggle. I really need to come. He's driven me out of my mind.

"Yes, your highness." He dives between my legs and spreads them wide. He's licking and sucking the most intimate parts of me. Then he spears me with his tongue, and I cry out as his fingers strum my clit. My knees buckle as I let go of the posts and fall literally and figuratively.

I can only scream, "Ian," as I do. He grabs my thighs and pulls me to him. I slide down his body, shuddering and tossing my head back. Our faces meet, and my eyes focus again as he kisses me softly.

We're standing naked, bodies pressed against each other. His erection digging into my stomach. He licks his lips. "You're the only thing that will ever taste better than your pancakes."

IAN

I've never made a woman come so hard she lost all sense of balance, but I've never made a woman come while standing above me. She's blisteringly hot. I haven't spent nearly enough time on her perfect tits, but there's no time now. I place her on the bed, and her smile slowly curls up, lighting up the fucking room and every piece of me.

I'm standing at the end of the bed as she opens her legs to me. "I can't believe I get to have you."

I crawl up her body. I kiss the hell out of her. Our tongues and hands are relentless. I settle between her legs, and she pushes on my chest, pulling out of the kiss.

"Condoms."

"Shit. I've been celibate since you."

Her eyes widen. "Really?"

"I'm not sure what you do not understand about how fucking bad I want you. You've invaded all of me. Every other woman is dull. Boring. Unattractive. It's a sad world out there for me when the only thing I find beautiful or sexy is the one thing I couldn't fucking locate. So yes, no one since you. Except an ember spark for pancake girl. Now you talk." I raise my eyebrow and point at her. Her chin lifts, then she grins and looks off to the side.

She bites her lip. "Me neither."

I kiss her again and moan into her mouth as I peel myself off her. She looks alarmed.

"Where are you going?"

I shrug. "Walgreens with the most painful fucking blue balls and hard dick I can imagine. Gee, I hope there's paparazzi." I jump into my jeans, getting ready to smash my dick into them. I turn to her with my fly open and my cock still out and bouncing a little to make her giggle.

She crooks her finger. "Shot. And totally STI-free, I promise. No one since you."

I pump my arms in the air, and my dick bobs up and down again. She actually guffaws. "FUCK YEAH, I knew you were my girl. I'm clean but pretty sure I'm packing sperm. So can't help out there." My jeans are gone, and I'm back on top of the perfect woman in seconds.

Her breath catches when we make contact. I kiss her again, but the lust has shifted. We savor each other. Her gentle lips meet mine in a sexy steady series of small kisses. I capture her lips and take over. I slide my tongue back where it belongs, and it's met with the perfect amount of resistance. I groan as she arches her back.

Her voice is raspy. "Ian."

"Ingrid?" I answer.

"Can we be past this part? I promise we can be gentle and sweet later."

"The fact that you promised me later means you get whatever you want now." I notch my cock between her legs, and she reaches down between us and helps me slide in.

I back up to get more control over this situation. My head flies back as my eyes almost roll back into my head.

"Christ, that's so good. You're so tight and fucking perfect."

She moans, "It's been too long. Harder. I need you deeper, closer. Be closer to me."

I look at her face. I'm stunned she went from fantasy to what I want my future to look like in seconds. I pull back and slam into her, and she gasps and moans in the most beautiful way. My dick won't last, so I need to get her there faster than I'd like. I want to take my time and pull like six torturous orgasms out of her, but instead, I push back into her.

I pick up the pace. The slapping of our skin fills the room, and I need her closer. I can't be close enough to her. I'm mad for her. It's fucking insane. I sit down on the bed and pull her onto my lap. She eases down on my cock, and we both groan as she begins to move. My hands are on her face and her breasts. They're everywhere at once, but our eyes never leave each other. Then my fingers grip her hips, and I help her speed up by slamming her down on my cock.

"Fuck me. Fuck me, my beautiful fairy pancake princess."

"I'm coming. Ian. I'm coming. Oh god. It's so much."

"I've got you. Fall apart for me, Wildflower." My balls are tight to my body. I'm so ready to release into her. Shit. I reach down and put pressure on her clit, and she seizes up and clamps my cock in the very best way. I groan.

"Ian. Oh, God. Yes." She shatters around me, and I clutch her as she rides the waves of orgasm. Her head is back, her rich brown hair hanging behind her. She snaps it all forward and stares at me.

She exclaims, "This is what sex should be!" I grin. I'm still inside her, aching to come. "Now you." She grinds down on my cock, and I lay her down. I lift her leg and piston in and out of the perfect place. "FUCK." I'm coming in a way that's unique to her. It has to be the bareback and not the soul connection. I'm a fool for her already. I need to maintain some dignity. Shit. I jerk and make a noise that no human or dolphin should utter. But there it is.

I flop down next to her as we attempt to catch our breath. All I can say is, "Good."

She laughs. Her arm collapses onto my chest. "Good."

We stay entwined for another minute, then I extricate myself.

"Got what you need, and you out?"

I laugh. I run a washcloth under warm water and drape a hand towel over my forearm like a waiter. I bow to her at the edge of the bed. "Shall I clean the lady up?"

She cracks up and says, "That would be delightful, sir. Thank you." She spreads her legs and is so fucking gorgeous. I wipe her down, then pat her dry as I say made-up French words.

She sits up on her elbows. "Ce sera assez homme sexy chaud. Tenez-moi."

I jerk my face to hers and kiss her. "You know I can't resist when you speak French."

"Hold me. Tenez-moi."

I whisper the words back to her, skating over her lips with mine.

I toss the towels to the side and slide into bed. She places her head on my shoulder, and I lean towards her soft and stunning face. People accused her of using a filter, but she's that luminous in person. The gentle and perfect blush to her cheekbones as it contrasts with her peach skin tone and dark eyes and hair. She's the basis for all filters. Life through the Ingrid lens is more beautiful than anything I can write or play.

I move my fingertips through her hair, and she smiles.

She says, "Where did you go?" Her hands are cozily curled into my chest.

"Middle of nowhere, and even there, I was lost. I should have followed you."

"Perhaps."

"I kind of stalked you," I say.

"How? I paid people to post bullshit."

"I know that. But you underestimate how connected to you I felt." I roll her on top of me so we're face to face.

Her eyes brighten. "Right? I can't explain you."

"Me neither, but I was desperate for any information about you."

She shrugs. "There isn't any."

I sit up, and she sits on my lap with her legs wrapped around me. I clear my throat. "And I quote, 'My girl's favorite pinot blocks aren't flourishing. She sang to those vines as a little girl because they were her mother's favorites. Maybe I should force Little Bell to come back here and sing to them, and they'll fruit.'"

She gasps. "Are you kidding me? You read my dad's blog?"

"Every morning like it's the news. I'm a huge fan of Adrian Schroeder. And his best friend. Can't remember his name, but he's fucking funny."

"Will Whitter. He is. He's family to me."

"They all seem to be family to each other. I mean, there's what like seven wineries all connected. He randomly talks about them all. I can't keep people straight, but I like it."

"Five. Well, six if you count Prohibition, which my brother, his wife, and their friends own. We all grew up together. I'm the baby by ten years, but they're as close as anyone's blood relations. I don't have a single memory in my entire life that doesn't involve one of them. Will and his wife, Sarah, are like second parents to me. Their son, Josh, is my brother's age and rather protective of the women in his life. I'd be careful."

"Is there a flow chart or a class I can take to keep them all straight?"

She rolls on her back and laughs. "I'll make you a family tree. I have to go."

"No." I hold her in place.

She giggles. "I can't take the day off. They're doing the final mix of my song."

I sit straight up and pull her to me. I'm blown away. "Your opinions on the songs about you were actually valid and professional. Hmm."

She rolls back on top of me, her hair a curtain shielding us from the world. "About me?"

I kiss her and hold her cheek. "They've all been for you since Paris."

Her eyes fill with emotion. "Too much. Back off, Mr. Temptation. That's way too fucking much to take in."

I push her off me, one of the hardest things I've ever done. "Go. Get out of here. Jesus, I'm sick to death of ya." I roll over as she jumps to the ground. She scoops up her clothes, and I watch her pert little ass scoot into the bathroom. She emerges, and I quickly shut my eyes.

She laughs, then kisses me. "Have a good day."

"Have dinner with me."

"Takeout, or are you cooking? Because I'm not blowing my cover over you just yet." She's tying her hair into a knot in the back of her head. Even that's fucking sexy.

I pull the covers up and say, "Fair. I'll think of something." I close my eyes, so I can let her walk away.

"Good." I hear the front door slam behind her, and her delicate footsteps head down the old wooden staircase.

I've always fallen hard and fast. A sucker for the idea of a forever. Meg and Abbey were both a wrong fit. I only hope I'm not mistaken. This feels different, not the same road I've been on. As if this road has been repaved recently and new streetlights were hung. It all seems straightforward and smooth. Hopefully, it's not fool's gold.

INGRID

I don't even notice where I am until I'm sitting on the bus. My phone is in my hand, and I feel it buzzing. The world is floaty and bright. Jake's wondering where I am.

I heard the lyrics last night about his girl's crooked smile, and I didn't recognize him. Ian Reilly thought about me as much as I thought about him. Whether it's sex or more, this morning was perfect.

I want to tell someone. My brother's assistant is the closest in my massive brood to my age. She used to hit clubs and have dinner with me when I'd visit Bax. Now she's part of the tribe, married to one of my older "brothers." She's good with secrets, unlike my dad.

INGRID: He's at Meg's! He was the musician I was making pancakes for.

NAT: I'm knee-deep in an argument with a very sassy little girl. She's flimflamming feisty. Hold, please.

My lips curl up, thinking of her redheaded stepdaughter. The second feistiest of the next-gen winery set.

NAT: Sadie's settled. She'll be out of sorts until David gives in to her demands. But for now, there's no cookie. And OMG. No one could find him, and he's been in Chicago?

INGRID: Was in the woods, now here. And most recently, he was under me. DO NOT TELL BAX.

NAT: Because we talk about your sex life. Duh. Was it everything?

INGRID: It was tectonic plate shifting. It was a tsunami, an earthquake, and all the lousy weather things that can describe really otherworldly sex.

INGRID: But I can't date him.

NAT: Oh yes, you can, girl. Look, my heart is totally David's, but that man is delicious.

INGRID: You'll be happy to know he is actually delicious.

NAT: Blush.

INGRID: My stomach is fizzy. My blood is buzzing and snapping under my skin. I'm a bowl of Rice Krispies of lust and emotion.

NAT: Ride the wave. But still do the engineering thing. Don't stop learning or striving for that because he's good in bed.

INGRID: I won't. I promise. But here's a secret. He's good out of bed too.

NAT: You're in trouble. Jesus. Sadie's climbing the kitchen counter now.

INGRID: Love to David and the kids. Kiss the Irish hellion for me.

————

Morgan looks up. "Where the fuck you been?"

She doesn't scare me anymore. I say, "Fucking," then clamp my hand over my mouth because I can't believe I said it.

There's a pause. I stare at her. Her green-black pixie cut looks fresh. I concentrate on her hair so I don't have to look at her piercing crystal eyes of judgment. She tosses one hand in a fist in the air and offers me the palm of her other.

I return her high five.

"Cool. Next time text so I can plan. Listen." She pushes the studio button, and the sound fills the room. It's haunting and so beautiful. These two men harmonize about the agony of knowing things could be different, but no one bothers to change it. The lyrics are tricky. It could be interpreted that someone's in love, but it's actually about giving up on love. I have an idea. I want Rob's voice, which is only on the chorus, to be dreamier. Truly haunting but leave Jake's where it is. Morgan nods and grins.

"Girl, you're fucking made for this. That's an awesome idea. Sometimes these men kill me." She interrupts them. "We're switching it up."

She puts a different mike on the shock mount and removes the foam. I'm holding up the door frame when she elegantly gestures to me.

Jake smirks. "Well. Well. Well. You know our houseguest?"

Rob nods. Oh god. They know. Rob's in my face. "No precious little angel, baby engineering savant. You don't know anything but our music. You live here now. No more going back to the multiplatinum pretty boy. Do not make his music. Do ours. Only ours. Enjoy your life here chained to our studio while you finish our album." Everyone laughs as Rob pretends to tie me to the door. "There. That should hold. Now. Why the nakey mike. Wanna hear my mouth breathing?"

Morgan shrugs. "It's the savant's idea to make you sound spooky."

He coos at me, "Baby angel savant. Let's try it." I smile and look at the floor. Maybe it's a dumb idea. "Baby angel savant, lift that chin. Take credit for the good and the bad. Apologize when something doesn't work, but always try. Failing is part of this business."

Jake says, "Your wackadoo take on our sound is genius. It won't be for everyone, but we're lucky you stumbled into my carriage house."

They all clap, and I bow. I set the levels for the new mike.

"Hey, Rob, sing the first line of the chorus?" I clip it and throw the playback into the studio. They all cheer, and Rob does a split in the air. He's got like four or five children and a tattooed rock god body. Jake pushes his glasses back up his nose and signals to me as Morgan slips back out of the studio.

The take is perfect. Morgan lays it over the guitar and piano tracks and sends it back into the studio. They pace and listen, and when it finishes, Jake runs into the booth. He lifts me out of my seat and twirls me around. "Do you just hear it or see it?"

Morgan pipes up, "She's got problems technically, but Jesus, that ear is hep." I laugh.

Jake puts me down. "How does it feel?"

"What?"

"To get your first liner note producer credit?"

Moran rolls her eyes, but I scream. "REALLY?"

Jake nods and heads back into the studio. "Ok, idiots, what's next?"

I sit back in my chair. I'm not sure there's ever been a better day in the history of fucking days. My phone buzzes. He demanded my number.

IAN: Am I supposed to lie here naked, waiting? You've been gone for days. Hurry home, Wildflower.

Nope. Never been a better day in my entire life. I have a nickname that isn't about my family or my dead mother. I have a man who doesn't care I'm actively throwing away an influencer's empire. And I spoke up. I did the thing I've always dreamed of doing. I'm pretty sure someone is going to get hit by a brick. But not right at this moment. I'm so making pancakes for dinner.

INGRID

The music curls around the back gate before I can see him. There's a blues slant to it all, and I can't help but listen. He's singing nonsense lyrics along with the melody.

"Buddy mayonnaise makes sense to the world because
All I want is you and some dijonaise."

I cover my hand to stop myself from laughing. I accidentally kick a garbage can. He stops playing.

"Rat or perfect woman? Either way, show yourself."

"I'm far from perfect." I peek around the corner, and he's sitting in the garden, paper scattered all around him.

"Thank fucking god you're back." He's in front of me, kissing me quickly. There's sunlight all around us, and I feel his heat and light.

He puts his forehead to mine. "That's too long. I thought you took off again."

I cock my head. "I'm not the only one who disappeared."

"True. But see, I knew where I was. I didn't know where you were." He holds my waist. "That's where you belong with me. It's not hard to figure out. You're a smart girl."

I laugh at him. "Wine?"

"No."

Panic fills me for a second. "No, you don't like wine? Might be a dealbreaker." His tongue tells me his intentions, and the hard length on my hip reinforces the point. I say on his lips, "Oh. You want to do that first?"

"First, next, now, later, last. I only want to stop if we have a muscle spasm or to replenish fluids. Tell me you don't have to work tomorrow."

It's seven at night. I don't actually have to work. They said it was a gestation day. See if everything gels.

I untuck my Josie Natori lilac silk, ribbed tank from my cigarette-cropped jeans and head for the steps. He follows me.

"I don't think I've discussed your ass enough."

I don't look at him but bite my lip. "Perhaps we can do that all day tomorrow."

He growls, then pushes me forward. "Faster. I need to fuck you faster."

He cages me at the front door, and I fumble with the key. He moves my low pony and kisses the back of my neck.

"Concentrate on opening the door, or I'm going to explode, and Meg's kids will see something beyond their years."

I laugh and finally get the door open. He closes it with his foot, his lips on mine. His touch skates up my skin, removing my shirt. I grin when we have to stop kissing to get it to pass over my head. I reach for him at that moment and whip off his shirt. I stoke his colorful mosaic skin. His broad shoulders and cut chest are almost too much to handle while trying to catch my breath.

I kiss an intricate Japanese design—words woven into waves with koi fish edging the tattoo out to his arm. It's stunning. As is he. "I'm lost in you."

He says, "I'm happy to find you." His fingers are tracing my jawline. I close my eyes and relish the feeling. "And now we're done with the worshiping portion of our evening." He lifts me up by my ass, and I wrap my legs around his waist and kiss his chest and neck.

He sets me down and raises his left eyebrow in the sexiest way. "You're wearing too many clothes." He pulls down his shorts, and his deliciously long dick bobs out. I stroke it, and he moans. His voice is gruff and low, his eyes dark and demanding. I've never been this turned on in my life. "Naked now."

I quickly remove my pants and lingerie. His kiss is rough and demanding.

He notches right at the beginning of me and then takes my breath away as he finds his way inside me. We both gasp.

———

"I'm ravenous, I say."

His hands are diving between my legs as I stretch. "Is she up? I'd like to snack on her, then we'll find something to satisfy your cravings."

I flip over and look at him. We've been up and down all night. Three times I found myself entirely fulfilled by this man. It's about nine in the morning, and I really want an egg slider from Stray Hen. I lie on top of him.

"If I have sex with you right now...."

"I'm listening." He moves my hair behind me and smiles.

"Would you walk with me somewhere?" I trace his eyebrows, then his cheekbones.

"Is this a perilous walk?"

I laugh and straddle him. He's thickening under me, and it feels divine to have that kind of power. "Maybe. But I would think the reward is worth the risk." I grind down, and he groans.

"Ok, sign me up." I lift up and grasp his full length, then slowly sink down on top of him. Divine.

———

"Meet me here in thirty minutes." I pull on some shorts and a peach t-shirt. It's my favorite. It's all faded, but it says, "Never Go Against the Five Families." It's from a gathering the five winery families had after a whole thing we went through.

"We can't go together?" he pleads.

"No. I can't risk being spotted with you. No one knows where we are."

He sits up in bed, and the sheet falls just low enough to see the V and the beginning of the only thing that might pull me back to bed.

He strokes himself, "You look too sexy in that. Do you have a kaftan or possibly a burlap dress of some sort?"

I laugh and pick up one of the pillows from the floor. I threaten to throw it at him. "That seems extreme." I hit him right in the face.

"If I could make my legs work right now, I'd chase you. But it seems all the blood in my body has relocated to one particular area."

I kiss him goodbye, and he talks on my lips. "Ingrid. You have to help me redistribute the blood to the rest of my body."

I stand. "You're insatiable."

His hand finds the back of my head, and he pulls me back to his lips. "Only with you."

"Good answer. I'll see you in thirty. And bring your guitar."

IAN

I find her in the booth of Jake's studio. We kiss, and her lips are new to me each time, like a never-ending puzzle of pleasure and fascination. I quickly grab a piece of paper and pencil and write that down. It's perfect.

I flop in the chair next to her and see a white bag. "Best egg sandwich. It's so freaking good. I got you two. I figured you needed some protein."

"Aww. You care about my sperm."

She turns to me. "I do. And in return, will you help me practice running the board?"

"Ah, the guitar." I lean back, unwrap the sandwich, and then shove the food into my mouth.

"Yes. I thought we could demo that bluesy song you were playing the second night you were in town."

"You remember which night I played what? Do you catalog everything or just music?"

Working the board, she glances over and rolls her eyes. "Just music and sexual positions. Now, did you record anything?"

I slide my phone to her. She holds it up, and I smile for the face recognition. Then she finds the files and downloads them. She plays them for us to hear. It's not bad. She stops the recording.

"Here. It needs this hook. Repeat this at the beginning and then before you hit the chorus."

I'm watching as she becomes alive and even more vibrant. She talked about her family and fashion and Paris, but nothing has lit her up like this. It's intoxicating to be around. She makes me want to play. She's good.

"Does that make sense, or am I totally crazy?"

I lean over and pull her chair to mine so we're face to face. "You have some sort of instinct. Don't doubt whatever comes into your head. I won't. The moment I start to see a flaw or second guess is the moment I get plunged into writer's block. I decided a while ago to never doubt. Forge ahead. If it's shit, it's shit. If no one likes it, then so be it. You can fix it all in post. But it's what was true in the moment."

She smiles and cocks her head to the side. I rub her arms. I can't stop freaking touching her. I want to record this song with her on my lap and my arms around her. I put my arms around her while she's still working the board. I brace them on the edge of the cabinet.

"True in the moment. I like that." She shivers as I kiss the back of her neck.

"Good. Because it's just became a lyric."

"It's the title." She stands and turns in my arms. "Go."

I abandon the coffee and sandwich. I race with my guitar into the studio. I put on some headphones, and now I'm connected to her entirely differently. Recording music takes trust. In the process, in the music, in myself, and in those who handle it. I trust her with this, and that's a hell of a lot different than wanting to sleep with her.

I tune for a moment or two and then break into my first hit. I can see her laughing. Then she pushes the button to connect her voice with only my ears.

"Sounds like a winner. But a little young for who you are now."

I grin. "Let's see what you got, Schroeder." I prop up the lyrics I scribbled in the middle of the night. I was going to call it The Best First Date, but I like *True in the Moment.*

The red light flashes, and I play like she suggested. It doesn't feel right.

"I'm going to start again." I do what I hear in my brain. It's hard to explain to people that it sometimes comes out like this. I've written a song in half an hour. And I've written some that take weeks. This feels like it's almost done in my brain, so I play it.

My mind goes only to the music. Nothing else matters when my fingers connect to the strings. I close my eyes and sing the lyrics I wrote and things that pop into my mind.

I open my eyes and see her standing when I'm done. She leans down and messes with the board. Then gives me the cutest thumbs-up. I come into the booth, and she starts the playback. I grab her hand as I sit next to her.

"It's good but could be better. It's terrific. But what if you tweaked the words?"

———

And that's how I wrote a song with this infectious creature. Four hours later, not only do we have a demo, but she's mixed the track. I played some piano, which I haven't done in years, then she laid some drum over it from a session musician, a discarded track from Grade Repeated. It's genius. I text the drummer, I've seen him around, and ask if we can use the beat. He's all in.

She sits back and stretches. She hasn't stopped moving or leaning over the board. I was abuzz with her energy. I'm watching every tiny move she makes. She's collecting materials and rendering the track. She really is fucking good at this. Not just lust clouding my judgment. I don't fuck around with my music. I thought we'd come here and mess around, then I'd trash the track, and she'd get some practice. But she's got this. I'm not worthy, but I'm going to try and be. I see beyond my infatuation with her, which scares me, but I'm ready. I didn't think I would ever be again after the last two disastrous forays into romance. Perhaps I'm ready, or maybe we were always meant to be right here in the pocket of this groove together.

She turns to me. "You ready? I'll meet you there. I can take a different route."

I pull her to me and kiss her. "What does it matter? Come on. Let's go together. Let's be together. I mean, we're basically anonymous. No one ever recognizes me. And you look like shit. Cut-offs and a t-shirt. That's not your brand. If you're not posing with billion-dollar sunglasses or on the arm of Christian Siriano, no one cares."

She lightly pats my chest with a huge smile. "I care. I'm not done learning and being out of the spotlight. And you, my sexy, insanely gorgeous, and funny man, are indeed a spotlight. Although, I don't see you like that. I never really have. Perhaps, I've simply been waiting for you all this time."

I slide my tongue into her mouth, and it's insistent. My hands pull her ponytail out to get into her hair. I need to be inside of her now.

I pepper her jawline with kisses while I wrap her hair around my fist. She sighs and gasps. Then says, "Here. I want you here." I quickly remove her shirt and kiss the top of her breasts before removing her bra.

I pull off my shirt, and her fingers drift to my bicep. She hasn't asked, but I know it's crossed her mind. I lay her on the couch, and she's still tracing the tangled grasses and bright flowers surrounding the watch and Grandma's lily. I answer her question.

"Yes. I got it in Paris, twenty-five minutes after leaving your side." She kisses me with tears in her eyes. "Wildflower."

I look up at her, and she reaches for my belt. "Let's not record this session."

She laughs and pulls down my zipper.

INGRID

A slight chill signals my summer of sex is almost done. My eyes search the sea of diners. Bored faces of couples and business meetings fade to the back as I search for a face from home. There's a handsome man my eyes skim over until he begins waving.

I get close and shake my head to get a clearer picture. Chiseled beard-free jaw, brown hair held back with swagger hair product, built and cut body where there was once was a squishy belly and a huggable "brother." But it's his dark eyes that are the same. The sad sack, sweet face of Sam Langerford stares at me, smirking. It's been three years since I've seen him. He wasn't at my sister's wedding. He and I texted occasionally, but no one told me about his transition.

I'm in his strong arms and exhaling a bit since he's such a piece of home. He kisses the top of my head and mutters, "Little Bell." I squeeze him harder, shocked his Winnie the Pooh-like status is gone. He was always the scruffy love-able man in our crowd. He owns Prohibition Winery with my brother and sister-in-law. The other owners are two overprotective sweethearts who are my brother's age and have always felt the need to watch out for me.

I sip my water and stare.

"It's still me, Little Bell."

I sit back. "Well, shit, Sam. Look at this. You're like a thirst trap."

"I know. I'm gorgeous now." He throws his hands up and laughs.

I grin. "You've always been gorgeous. You're just so different."

He takes my hand and squeezes it. "Enough me. Tell me about this life here, and are you ever coming home?"

"Did she do this to you?" The sentence thuds in the middle of the table. "Sorry. Never mind." His girlfriend ghosted him about the time I went to Paris.

"It's ok, LB. Sammy's still a little raw, but I decided to take care of myself instead of being a sad sack full of shit. She's gone. Not even Mel can find her." This is shocking since Mel, my sister's wife, can hack anything and locate anyone.

He continues, "I'm in a tricky bit of a grieving stage. No one's heard from her. I fear for the worst, and I think that's how I have to handle this. Taking care of myself started with Josh forcing me to go running. Then basketball with David and tennis with Bax. Anything to fill my non-winemaking time. Then it evolved into CrossFit and Krav Maga."

"No shit."

He grins and says, "No shit. What the fuck are you doing here? Radio or some shit? Do you have a card I can pass on to the high school? Maybe you could spin the senior prom."

I throw a small piece of bread at him, and he bats it away, squealing a made-up Chinese word. "Cat-like reflexes now. Baby, I'm the whole fucking package now."

I laugh loudly. He's the funniest of us, shit secret keeper but funny.

"I'm helping produce Grade Repeated's new album."

His eyes almost bug out of his head. "Like a real job. You're all grown up, Little Bell. I don't care for it. That means I'm old. I'm going to end up that old bachelor in a velour tracksuit unzipped a bit too far. I might be a new me, but the forest on my chest will gray up and stick out of the front of that suit."

I wipe the tears of laughter from my eyes, but he won't stop.

"I'll be the one at the pool pinching waitresses and regaling them with tales of how I keep my skin so leathery." He lifts his biceps like he's showing off. I'm dying.

"Ok, I won't grow up anymore."

He shoves a big bite of salmon into his mouth and says, "You do that. My fate's in your hands." He chews, and I sip some wine he's brought along. It's a little funky but good. It's a Grenache/Cinsault blend from Prohibition called *"Are You Happy Now?"* I know it's a reference to my sister-in-law's favorite grape, and they weren't growing it for a long time. He catches my eye. "You, ok? Happy?"

"Very."

"One of us should be."

My heart is breaking for him. His girlfriend was really cool, and they were perfect together. A raspy voice interrupts us.

"Interesting. You won't go to dinner with me, but this guy?" My head whips to Ian's face and his pursed lips. I'm not sure if he's jealous, pissed, or kidding.

Sam's up, and his face is raw and angry. He gets in Ian's face, and I'm terrified of my overprotective new Krav Maga edition of Sam.

"Why don't you move along?" Sam is huge when he stands. I mean fucking thick and ripped. Jesus. I try and stand, and Sam, without looking, guides me back to my seat with his hand on my shoulder.

"Sam. It's—" Ian's face is now screwed up too.

"I've got this, Ingrid," Sam says.

Ian steps back a bit. "You do, dude? You got this?"

Oh shit. "Ian. Don't."

Sam's head whips to mine. "You know this lanky muthafucker?" Is Sam on roids? He's never angry like this.

I nod, and Sam backs down for a second. "Talk, Little Bell." Sam doesn't move but stares at Ian.

Ian says, "You don't tell her what to do. What the fuck is your problem? And who the fuck…." Ian's face relaxes then he steps behind me and addresses Sam. "You said Little Bell. Hulking overprotective brother vibe. My guess is Josh."

I say, "Sam."

"Really?" I've told him about all the guys.

I turn. "He's lost weight and is cut like an MMA fighter now."

He extends a hand. "Sam Langerford, and who are you, and why are you touching Little Bell?"

Ian shakes his hand. "Do you mind if I sit, so we can have less attention?" Sam slightly nods. "I'm Little Bell's boyfriend."

We've never said the words. There's no reason to define things in the privacy of our carriage house, but I guess it's true.

Sam sits back. "You ready for the gauntlet for defiling my little sister?"

I roll my eyes and put my hand on Sam's enormous forearm. "Sam, he is. And I'm happy."

"What do you do, boyfriend?"

Ian looks confused. He's been famous since he was seventeen years old. I shrug.

"Hey, man, I'm not trying to be an ass, but I'm Ian Reilly."

"Doesn't mean shit to me."

"I'm a musician."

"Bum, or have you done something?"

I google Ian and slide the phone to Sam. "Oh, shit. Well, that's a few more hits than I get. I'm not good with names. I'm sure I've heard something." Sam has to be bluffing. He plays guitar in a bunch of local bands.

Ian kisses my cheek. "This is the first time we've been out in public. She won't risk being recognized. And I got ruffled she was with another man."

Sam says, "Oh shit. That's why we're eating at like four in the afternoon."

Ian sips my wine. Sam toasts him. "Understandable. She's sitting here with an Adonis of a wine god and you with your measly kabillion google hits. I'd be intimidated too."

Ian cracks a smile. "You get it. I mean, seeing her in here with a male model of your stature, I couldn't help but drown in my own inadequacies."

Sam chuckles.

"What are you doing here?" I ask Ian.

"I heard the mac and cheese was dreamy. I had to sign some papers at a lawyer's office down here, so I wandered in to pick up some mac for someone I know." I shovel a massive bite of it into my mouth. And he wipes my mouth with a napkin and settles back into the chair. He stands up and refrains from kissing me. I appreciate it.

Sam stands and shakes his hand. "It was a pleasure. Now, never touch Little Bell again."

Ian replies, "To meet a piece of this woman's home is truly an honor. And even though I'm pretty sure you could crush me flat, I'm probably going to get lucky in like...." He looks at me, and I grin.

"Like an hour or so," I say.

"I speak for like thirty people when I say, don't hurt her. Don't fuck this up."

He clasps Sam's elbow and hand. "I don't intend to. Take care." He squeezes my shoulder and exits, carrying two huge bags of carryout.

I squirm in my seat and stare at Sam, cutting his salmon. He shakes his head.

"How long?"

"Six weeks officially, but, Sam, I'm pretty sure it's been going on for longer than either of us can fathom. Only Nat knows." He pretends to button his lip with elaborate locks and zippers.

"He's your Sammy. I see it. Let him take you out." I wince. Sam still thinks of her as his soul mate.

I squeeze his arm before he can take a bite. "I love you. Thanks for having my back."

"Love ya, LB." He winks.

———

Meg asks as I hustle around her kitchen, making grilled cheese for everyone, "Does he do that thing with his feet?"

"The rubbing back and forth as if he's trying to get closer to your feet?"

"Ok, women. That's quite enough compare and contrast. This is strange."

Meg turns to him and says, "Only for you. I was secretly in love with Jake at the time. I don't remember a lot." She winks at him.

He groans. Pearl is on his lap, and he looks domestic and perfect. Jake's boys run through the house.

"Grab your stuff. You're going to be late for school. And, Jonah, grab Pearl and take her up to her crib for me. I'll be up in a second."

"Why am I the baby Sherpa?" I adore Jonah's vocabulary. But I guess that comes when your dad is a songwriting genius.

The kids exit and Meg looks at him. "Seriously, I'm not feeling a thing." She gestures to her whole body and almost knocks over a cup. She wanders out of the room, and I straddle Ian.

"Let's get some oxygen. I miss getting dressed up. Take my pretty clothes to dinner."

"You know the only purpose of a date is to get those pretty clothes off. Let's just do that."

I slap his arm. "No one knows we're in Chicago or even know each other. There was no fallout from Sam's meal. I don't want a Meg tattoo situation. I simply want to do something with you out of the house."

He kisses me slowly, and I nip his lip. "What's that about?"

"You do that to me. You make me want to do really naughty things."

"Stop fucking in my kitchen. Oh my god. Ian, as hard as it is for me to squash another man's game…."

"Is it? Is it really? Considering our history?" He shakes his head. "You know I like to bust your balls there, Jakey. All those years of calling me PBDB." I look to Ingrid, "Pretty Boy Douchebag." She nods and laughs.

"Just stop fucking in my kitchen. My kids could walk in. And shouldn't you people be moving out of my backyard?"

"Soon."

IAN

We scoot down the alley behind Gentry. A piano bar in the heart of Boystown. She's stunning in a yellow-flowered dress that flutters around her knees. She made sure I knew it was Nanette Lepore. You can take the influencer's phone away, but... you can't take the influencer out of the girl. I put on a pink linen shirt and shorts. And the shirt is ironed. Of all the places we could go to, I know for sure we'll be judged here.

"Ready for our first date?" I ask.

"You promise no one will know us."

"I never said that." She tries to pull away. "I said no one will take it public."

"You're delusional."

I open the back door, and it lets us behind a curtain. The room is filled with people and waitstaff scurrying around with cocktails and eggs bennie. The MC for brunch and my contact in this scheme is off to the side of us, and we can't quite see them.

We hear in a loud, gravely cheeky voice, "All right, bitches. Everybody here signed, right? Gals, no holdouts, or you're out! The waitstaff is collecting your agreements now. Yo! I'm talking up here. All eyes are on me, as they should be. Who did not sign their life away to sing Sondheim and sip some damn bloodys?"

One hand goes up. We're still well hidden.

Ingrid is giddy. "I love karaoke. But do we need to sign?"

I shake my head no at her, and my lips curl into a small smile as I wink at her.

"Ok, now we're all damn legal. No one leaves, and no one comes... or enters… until we're done. It's like deathmatch karaoke today." There's a massive roar of laughter, and we giggle too. "Do not think that Gaga is here for a command performance. It's just two straight, cis white people who wanted to have a first date without a goddamn hassle. So shut it, bitches."

The crowd collectively says, "Aww."

Ingrid gasps, "They signed NDAs?"

"Yup," I whisper back.

The host says, "So if the urge to take pictures arises, remember to point your peepers and cameras at me, dahlings. I'm always ready for my close-up!"

I take Ingrid's hand and step out from behind the curtain. The host, Ms. Mac A Damia, rushes to us. "Aren't you more gorgeous than I thought?" We air-kiss, then Ms. Damia squeezes Ingrid carefully, not getting their makeup on us. The crowd is murmuring.

I turn to the crowd. "Hi! Yes. Yes, and yes. We're dating, and you're the only people on earth who know that. You can take your NDA copies home and show people once we've gone public. Thanks so much for this. We can't wait to hear you all sing."

The crowd answers me, "Honey, we don't give a shit." There's a roar of laughter, and Ingrid lifts her head with a smile. "As long as you sing a show tune, you're welcome here."

We sit, and the men next to us swoon a bit at my girl. She is stunning and almost otherworldly. One of the men leans over. "Your pictures are trash. Sweetheart, you're flawless."

A platinum blond man leans toward her, and I can see her starting to relax. "I was YOU for Halloween!"

She laughs. "Then I should go as you this year."

He pulls out his phone, and she covers it and frowns. Dammit. No fucking selfies today. He looks at her and then realizes.

"Oh shit. No. I was just going to show you the picture."

She smiles and says, "Just send it to my DMs, and I'll see it there. I'm a bit camera shy these days." He nods and winks at her.

"OK! Enough oohing and ahhing. Get the vodka flowing, and up first is Gehart with…."

The room answers in a groan, "'The Impossible Dream.'"

He takes the stage as a waitress arrives. "Catalog and menu." She tosses it down, and we order drinks and settle in for Broadway Brunch.

There have been lots of straining voices, but some are really good. Ingrid is clapping and chatting with everyone around us.

I sang a stirring rendition of "Let the Sunshine In" and was asked to take my clothes off. Respect. We've inhaled mimosas, bagels, and lox. Every time she takes a sip, I can't help but watch her lips. I squeeze her arm and make my way over to Ms. Mac A Damia.

"Thank you. For everything."

"No problemo. Such a unique request. I love young love."

I hand over my Amex. "Run it for everyone. Tip the staff well."

They squeal in delight. "You don't need to do this."

"But I can. And look how happy my girl is."

They nod to the stage. "Yeah, but can she sing?"

"Hi. I'm Ingrid." Everyone laughs. "I'm insanely nervous, but you've all sung, so why the hell not? There are chorus parts I need help with. I'm sure you know every word like I do." The crowd cheers. "This is 'Satisfied' from Hamilton."

The music starts, and a man stands and addresses the crowd. "All right, all right…."

I move to stop him, but Ms. Damia stops me and whispers, "It's the first line of the song." I squeeze their hand and head back to my seat. The man fills in the Alexander Hamilton parts to the song. And the crowd sings everything else.

Her voice bursts forward, and she's entirely on beat with the rap section. I'm not that familiar with the show. I saw it. Who didn't? But something is haunting about Ingrid singing she will never be satisfied. She's so close to something that's only hers. She's brilliant and amazing. Fuck, I'm underwater, and she's my oxygen.

The room goes nuts as she finishes the last note, holding it beyond the music. Perfect pitch and tone. She could have been a singer. She could have been anything. I'm just glad she's mine.

INGRID

Ian's been in LA for two days. I've been so spoiled. He's been all mine for three months. Lately, his music has been super bluesy, so I snuck him into Kingston Mines last week. I watched from afar as he played with some of the best blues musicians. He was magnificent. They're all brilliant musicians doing what they love for the sake of loving it. No press or IG stories are being captured. They just play because it's in their soul. That's my favorite part of music. When the artist can't help but do anything else.

I'm heading to the studio to grab my phone. I left there yesterday. We Facetimed last night on my iPad. I'm ok, but I'm not alright. I miss him. I'm in too deep to get out, I think. I told my dad I met someone. He pressed for information, but I knew Sam had already filled him in.

There's a crowd in front of the studio. I'll go around back. I hope I don't disturb anyone recording. It must be someone super popular. I head in the back door, and Morgan's there, but no one's recording.

"Shit. How the hell did you get by those assholes?"

"Alley. Who's coming in? What's this about?"

Morgan pops up, starts arranging carts and files, and then looks at me as if I've got food in my teeth. "Girl, you're clueless. You, it's your shitstorm. They're looking for Ian and Ingrid. You're trending."

My body is numb, and I'm hoping not to throw up. This can't be happening. "No. No one knows." I shake my head, and Morgan hands me her phone.

I slide through a series of pictures. It's the two of us at the blues club on opposite sides of the room. There's one of us on the street, the distance between us, but clearly in front of Meg's house. Shit. Oh god. One of us kissing at the karaoke club kills me. Assholes. I hope they use the money wisely. Shit. Everything is crumbling. I plug in my phone, and it doesn't stop notifying me for a full minute. I scan for only one name.

Morgan's eating a giant sandwich, and it's all over her face. "Hey, girly, you're also trending on Spotify. It's a fucking good song. I'm proud of you, baby savant."

"What are you talking about?"

I pull up my Spotify, and *True in the Moment* is the number one played song today. He gave me credit for the song. Holy shit. Why didn't he tell me? I scroll Twitter, something I avoid like the plague. And find our hashtag: #ingridian. Not very original, but I start to read the thread. Most of it is what I expected. Gold digger or pretty boy snags a party girl. Hateful but useless. And then there's a thread about the song—him giving the party girl a job—how I fucked him for a song credit. Tears flood my eyes. My phone rings, and it's him.

I pick it up but don't know what to say.

"Wildflower, speak to me. Ingrid." My breath hitches. "Oh, sweet, beautiful Ingrid. Ignore all of that. Focus on your song being a hit and me. Don't."

"It's ruined. I'll never be taken seriously. I've exposed Jake and Meg's house. It's all destroyed. They think you gave me the job. I'm a joke. I'm once again in someone else's shadow. I can't, Ian. I can't go back to being a brand, a nothing. I can't be with you." My words are punctuated with sobs. Morgan rubs my back. I hang up on him as my phone drops to the ground.

"Oh god. What do I do?"

Morgan pulls me to her, and I unleash the melodramatic beast. I sob until I can't anymore. My brain repeating, "Your career is gone." I don't see a way out. I have to break my heart. I can't be his arm candy. And I'm not sure I can be without him. I can't be in his shadow and never accomplish my goals. Everything I ever do will always be because I'm with him. Or my father's daughter. Or vapid Instagram girl. Or Bax's little sister or in the shadow of the 5 and their hip winery, Prohibition. It's hopeless.

I sit up finally. Morgan says, "Let me take you back to Jakes's."

"Why are you being so nice to me?"

"There are very few women in this career who seek out this kind of work, and fewer have your fucking ear. So regroup. Go build that studio you were talking about. Fuck em. And if no one wants to record with you, I'll threaten some people." I throw my arms around her.

———

IAN: Do not panic. Focus on how I feel about you and how utterly good-looking I am.

IAN: Your first produced song hit number one in the course of a day. And it's one of the best songs I've ever recorded. I should have told you it was being released. Sorry. I was just so excited.

IAN: Talk to me, Wildflower. Talk to me, my perfect girl. Don't go dark. I'm jumping a jet to get to you. I'm coming for you, and I don't care who takes my picture. Talk to me.

INGRID: I'm ok.

IAN: Then I worried about nothing. See. Things are rosy and bright.

INGRID: Talk later.

IAN: Well, that was reassuring. Call me.

IAN

Not the first time I've raced across the country for love, but it's the most important. I do mean love. I should have told her. It's right there in front of our damn faces. I released the single, thinking I needed a sweepingly romantic moment to be worthy of telling her. But it backfired a touch. Fuck. Ingrid is all the music I could ever want to write. I have to fix this.

I didn't like being away from her when she worked but being in LA for two days was sheer torture. What if she made pancakes and no one ate them? I want to eat all of her pancakes. Twitter is a cruel bitch right now.

I summon the flight attendant, whose blouse mysteriously keeps getting unbuttoned. Ingrid is so strong, but I want to protect her. I can't believe releasing the song turned out to be the dumbest move of my life. I thought it was better than candy and flowers. Shit.

"Can I get a Stella, and is it possible for me to use Facetime?"

"Sure, just log on to the cabin wifi. The password for this flight is 'Dreamy.'" She scampers for the beer, then lingers too long. I head back to the bedroom. I'll keep calling until she picks up.

I'm on call seven when she finally answers. Her eyes are red, and my heart sinks. Her forced smile fills the screen. Her hair is on her head in a messy bun, wisps framing her delicate cheekbones.

"You're so gorgeous. I miss you so much, Wildflower."

She smiles but doesn't mean it. "Hi. Where are you?"

"Bedroom on the plane."

Her eyebrows raise. "That's a thing?"

"Oh, it's so much of a thing I'm going to need to show you someday. I'm going to—"

She puts her hands up. I stop talking.

"Please stop. This is hard. I can't do this." Tears stream down her face, and I'm in physical pain that I can't hold her.

"Ingrid. Whatever you think you're doing, you need to stop. This is not the time to decide destiny for both of us. I'm sorry I didn't tell you about the single." And then I realize there's a fate worse than her crying. She's becoming the Wildflower. She's steel and pain. I don't want any part of this.

"Listen. You're not quite understanding. My life, the one I thought I could have—career, partner, and respect. All gone. All fucking gone. I know you didn't mean it, but it ruined me."

This is like sitting on hot glass. That makes no sense, but I'm pretty sure it would be as fucking painful as this. What is even happening?

"Hey, are you sure you're not exaggerating? We can figure out how to be together. This is a blip that will blow over the next time Kanye starts his own religion. Calm down."

Like a car accident, I saw it coming. I knew I shouldn't say it, yet my dumbass mouth let it fly. If someone told me to calm down, I'd launch on them. Turns out it's a universal thing.

She stands, and I can see boxes. What the fuck does she think she's doing?

"Are you running? Are you leaving?" She moves to a different part of the room, and her face fills the frame. Shit. I fucked up.

"You can date me, and your integrity is restored. That whore cheated on, wrote a book, but look how he bounces back with hot influencer Ingrid Schroeder."

"What are you saying?"

"I'm paraphrasing everyone from the Twitterverse to memes to Jimmy Fallon."

"Don't listen to Fallon. It only matters what we say." I stand and walk around a little. This can't be happening. She's not the villain or the twit.

Her voice is strong and true, and it scares the shit out of me. "Ian, I end up taking the hit. I'm the vapid girl who gets a career handed to her. Troubled influencer finds a sugar daddy. Paris was a bust. On to the next career, she might try on. You win, and I lose. And I can't have that. I'm rapidly falling in love with you, but I can't sacrifice my entire being to be with you."

She's stopped pacing and is steely. I'm holding onto that she's falling in love with me. I caress the edges of my phone, wishing I was there.

"I'm always the little sister, daddy's girl, the dilettante, the wine princess. I'm Lohan or a Kardashian. Who, by the way, have worked their asses off to be treated fairly, and it's still not happening for them. I know Kylie the best. I'll use my sweet friend as an example. She started her own line, modeled her ass off, and all anyone asks is, "Who's her baby daddy."

"You're not them." My voice vibrates. I'm so angry at all of this. All that's slipping through my fingers while I'm on a fucking plane.

She says, "Which sucks because they're probably going to find their way out the other side. I won't have that chance. Women are always their worst day in the press. And men, well, they get redemption and another chance. And famous men, shit, Ian, you could probably get away with anything. And me, I can't even get away with being really fucking good at my job and having a talented boyfriend."

"I'm sorry it's like this. I hear you. I see you. I'll even shut my mouth because I can't imagine what this is like. I'll pick up takeout on my way to the carriage house, and we can come up with a plan. I'll get my PR on it, or I don't know, but I do know I need to see you. We can fix this."

"You can't fix this." Her face is back to the vulnerable one. Tears fill her eyes. "Goodbye, Ian."

Before she can hang up, the only word I can get out is, "No."

INGRID

I throw my phone across the room. It rings, but it's not him. It's my brother's ringtone, some random Barry Manilow song he put on there. If I don't answer, my father will freak out. Dammit. This hurts. I'm building that fucking studio and hope he's still there after I figure this out. I deserve both. I can make this happen. "Daybreak" squeals from my phone again.

"I'm fine." I throw stuff into a box.

"Oh, such the slinger of bullshit. You're not fine. Who do I get to kill?"

"Tab? Hey."

"This all sucks. I'm not done..."

My brother clearly ripped the phone away from my insane sister-in-law. I'm headed to a hotel. I can't stay at Meg's with the press outside on her sidewalk.

"Ingrid. This isn't like you."

I sit down and play with some leftover crepes. I fold and stretch them. I take a small piece and put it on my tongue while my brother talks at me. Still tastes good cold. My heart has a hole in it. I might want him more than I want things for myself. Maybe we reinvent ourselves. Change our names and head to the Oregon coast. Tabi always says Oregon can fix things. We could open a small club and have local acts perform.

"LB, you're not listening. Don't make me put Tabi back on." I rip the crepe by accident. And then I rip them all.

"Bax, this is all hopeless. I appreciate you, but there's nothing to be done."

"Are you in love with this pop star?"

"Dad or Sam?"

"Nat and then Sam. Sam had a lot of good to say."

"Dearest brother, I'll never be seen as anything but someone's accessory. It doesn't matter that I fucking produced the shit out of that song. That I'm really good at this. I love it so much. I'm a punchline."

He pauses and clears his throat. "I know a bit about being thrown under the bus and being a punchline. You're the one who told me to get my shit together. So I'm returning the favor, but first—drive."

"What?" I throw the crepe pieces in the sink and pull my favorite travel mug out of the cabinet. I toss it across the room into a box.

"Drive. Be with yourself, and you'll figure it out. Don't hide. Don't give them the satisfaction of taking things away from you. But don't go to the airport or a train. Don't go where they're looking. Come home. Regroup and attack your life from here."

Ok, I don't always hate being a little sister.

I say, "That's the first solid piece of advice you've given me, ever."

He laughs. "You told me to relax and figure it out. I'm just spitting it back at you. Stop fighting against it but find strength from it. Come spend time with all of the kids running around here. Let them remind you, you're no longer the baby."

I smile. "Can you tell Dad?"

"Nope. You know that's not how Adrian works. You're his girl. You call him. Give him a heads-up you're coming home."

"Can I stay at your place?"

"Our rental?"

"What happened to the house this time?" I giggle at Tabi's insistence to renovate that piece of shit farmhouse. It's been like four years of nightmares. Each one is funnier than the last.

"Flooded. All of it. Like every inch somehow. We're all jammed into a three-bedroom house on the west side."

I squeeze my lips tight. "I love you, Bax."

"Love you too, Bell."

"Not Little Bell?"

"You're too old to be Little. Drive."

He hangs up, and my eyes fill. Maybe I can do this. I need a plan. I need a whole new plan.

———

I'm taking my money and building a studio on the fallow land in the vineyard. I asked my dad if I could buy it with my influencer blood money, but he said no. Instead, he's going to parcel it off and put it in my name, and I'll pay taxes on it.

I'm getting another entrance dug out, and I was thinking of maybe building a series of one-bedroom cottages. Bands could take up residence while recording.

I don't tell anyone, but I made millions going to parties. I never spent it. I'm Daddy's girl. You always pay your bills and put half of what's left in savings. It wasn't easy, but I did it. And now I have the money to do what I want. The more I drive, the more it makes sense. I finally want to be from somewhere. I want to be home. I'm proud of who I am. Fuck the press.

Now, if I could stop crying about Ian, I'd be fine. I can build a studio on the DL, but if that man's in my life, there won't be a moment where I'm my own person. I'll always be Ian's girlfriend.

I can't believe something as stupid as his fame is going to take him from me. I'm aware I'll never love anyone like I love him. That's melodramatic. I might as well wear black and throw myself on a picture of him and sob. It's time to go. I need distance.

IAN

MEG: She's packing and somehow has a car now. Like out of nowhere. Boom. She owns a car. I'm panicking. I can't stall her. I don't have the talent. I'll end up telling her I texted you.

IAN: Where's she going? I'm about an hour away. Fuck. I landed, but your fucking city has the worst traffic. And I'm from LA. At least our shit's predictable. STOP her.

MEG: It's a big car. She's going somewhere

IAN: I don't care about the car size. Throw my shit in a duffle and grab my ax.

IAN: I'm heading back to you. Fucking stall her. You owe me.

MEG: I'll try.

Even I know that's a reach. That woman owes me nothing. I'm drumming my hands on the back of the car, and we're not fucking moving.

"Jesus, man. Is there no other route?"

He turns back to me. "You do see, we're basically parked. No one's moving. I'm not a genie."

I text her again. She's not answering me. So I go back to Meg's texts.

MEG: I most certainly do not owe you.

IAN: You kissed Jake before you broke up with me.

MEG: And you fucked your ex-wife before I broke up with you.

IAN: Yeah. There's that. And sorry about that again. But um, OH! How about you're pretty.

MEG: Cram it, Pretty Boy Douchebag.

It's an eternity, but we start moving again. Fuck.

MEG: I'm so sorry. I'm so so sorry. I, um. She hugged me and left. She won't listen. She said she had to think.

IAN: FUCK.

"Hey, man. Take your time. Nothing matters now. Pull into Mcdonald's. Fries on me."

"Fries are always a good idea. But I'm sure it does matter. There's always an alternative route."

———

Follow me, and you'll see what you want to see.
Follow me, and you can pretend all that you want to be,
But if you follow me, you'll never really know me.
My heart isn't in the pixels. It lies beating for your skin. You're the only one who can't see that
all I want to do is follow you.
Lead me wherever you want. My heart is yours. Lead me towards the open water, and I'll
swim to your shore.
Lead me beyond all of this so we can get to the other side, my love.
I'll follow you to the end.

This is my only idea. I spent the night trying to figure out where she would go. But why go by car? I ache to talk to her. I offered iHeartRadio an exclusive acoustic mini-set. I played *Wildflower* and then our song *True in the Moment*. And followed it up with my newest song, *Follow Me*. I wrote it on the plane home. I figured it all out last night. I want to record it with her when I find her. The host comes back into the booth with her blue index cards.

"That's a gorgeous song. Was it written for anyone in particular?" Her voice goes way up at the end of her sentence. Sly. I shove some McDonald's fries into my mouth. Music and fries. That's all the joy I'm ever going to get. I should probably write them a jingle and be done with it.

I smirk at her and say, "Are you fishing or asking?"

"Both."

Fuck it. I have no filter. "They're all for her. Every note and rhythm. And every song I write can only be improved by her ear, care, and talent."

"Talent? No offense." She scoffs.

I made this mess, but this woman is the problem. My girl isn't taking one more second of this shit.

"Damn, you aiming to offend? Yes, talent. She's a music-producing genius with more skill and music knowledge than almost anyone I've ever met. Grade Repeated just cut an album. And Pearl Jam sat down with her to hash out a couple of new singles. And she's been asked to consult on Mavis' new album. I'll be lucky if she has time for mine. No offense, but perhaps you do a little more research than TMZ."

"How was I supposed to know?"

I draw my first word out slowly to belittle her more. "R-esearch. Isn't it part of your job? You're like the kid who copies Wiki for a paper. Twitter's not a source."

"I said I was sorry." She stares at me with pursed lips.

"No, you didn't, but I could care less for your hollow words."

I shrug and settle my guitar back on my lap. "No matter. I'm contractually obligated to play four songs in your tiresome company. I'll wrap up with a hit. I'm aware none of this will make it to air, but it all needed to be said."

The petty woman shifts in her chair. As if my story could be distilled down to blue note cards.

I could play my first hit, the nostalgia money song, or I play something from the soul. All I want now is to write music on my own terms and her. But, this, I play for her, whether she hears it or not.

I finish my song, and everyone is stunned. Now I'm going to say all the promo shit in one sentence, and they can cut it together. I move around the room, summon a car and toss my gear in the case.

"Hey, Jack. Start the cart recording." He's a good guy. I've known him for years. He bounces from station to station. I didn't know he was here in Chicago. The dude has my back. Maybe my rant will make it to air.

I clear my throat over the woman asking a notecard question. I've gotta go.

"Wow, that was so fun. Thanks for having me. Thanks so much for listening to iHeartRadio. Acoustic Sessions. I'm Ian Reilly. I'm Ian Reilly, and this is Acoustic Sessions on iHeartRadio. iHeartRadio, stream it today. Acoustic Sessions has been brought to you by T-Mobile. This is Ian Reilly, and you're listening to iHeartRadio. Hey, it's Ian Reilly. I've got four fresh new acoustic songs for you coming up next on iHeartRadio Acoustic Sessions."

I bow to the woman and reach for the exit. I glance over at the engineer, and he gives me a thumbs-up as I whip the body mic off.

"You can't just leave."

"You came to this 'music' session with takedown in your eyes, darling. That's not a game I consented to play. Take your invasive cards and shove them up your ass. Ingrid Schroeder has more integrity and grit than you'll ever know. She's worked her ass off to become an expert in a male-dominated field, and she's only beginning. God forbid anyone wants to step out of the box they've been put in."

I glance back at Jack, the engineer, and he smiles. Then he says over the intercom, "And that's a wrap. Good stuff, Ian. Tell your girl if she ever wants to get into radio to look me up. If she really does have board skills."

I grin. "She does, but I think she's a producer." I bolt out the door and scramble into the car.

MEG: I'm sorry. No word from her.

My heart falls. My fingers go numb. Fuck. Ok. Pivot. Plan B. I'm good at insanity. I'm done waiting for my love life to work out. I may be an idiot chasing the wind, but I have to try. I love her, and I forgot to let her in on that little secret. I won't let her choose something other than us.

"Pull over right here, man. Keep the full fare. I gotta run. Thanks, man." I unfold my legs from the tiny-ass Nissan Uber. I take off down Michigan Avenue towards the Hancock while I google a number. He'd freak if he didn't know where she was going. It's time to meet the parent.

I blurt out my pre-rehearsed statement. "Hello, I'm trying to reach Adrian Schroeder. Is this a good number for him?"

"It's a terrible number for him. This is Prohibition Winery, and he has his own winery. But I could take your number for his son."

"Bax." It pops out of my mouth. "Yeah. Um. I don't even know where to start with this. Who am I talking to, and do you know Ingrid Schroeder?"

"We have no comment at this time." She hangs up the phone. Shit. I call back, and she doesn't answer. I look up Schroeder Estate Vineyards and Winery.

"Schroeder Estate Winery, how may I help you?"

"Adrian Schroeder, please."

"I'm sorry, sir, your number is part of a blocked list. Have a good day." She hangs up. Shit. I was blackballed pretty fucking quick. I bust into a coffee shop, and I want to be recognized for the first time in my life. I walk over to a couple of women. Both of their phones are on the table.

"Hi. My name is Ian. I need a favor. I need a phone."

"Ian Reilly?" Eyes wide but smiling.

I nod. The woman slides her phone across the table, and I seize it. I take a quick selfie with the ladies, then give them the cheeseball wink. The one I used to actually use to pick up women. I was a clueless fuck.

I redial Prohibition.

"Prohibition Winery, this is Natalie." She sounds nicer.

"Natalie. Do not hang up...." And she clicks. I put down the phone and scoop up the other one. Now I've gained the attention of the rest of the coffee shop. I wave to them.

"I'm trying to find her, ok. She left because of you people." Three people who were filming me put their phones down. "Hell yeah, you're a part of the problem, strangers in this coffee shop." There's a silence, and I need them on my side. I'm cranky as fuck, and I need to curb it.

"Now, I might need all your phones. So nobody goes anywhere." I nod to the barista, who is taking my picture. "Anything you people want to eat or drink is on me, ok?"

A girl in the back walks up to me and offers me her phone. "You look good together. And I'm sorry I clicked on the pictures. I just wanted you to be happy after what that woman did." I guess not all fans are jackals. I grin. I take her phone and take a selfie with her. Then I turn back to my mission.

"Prohibition Winery, this is Natalie."

"Baxter Schroeder, please. It's life or death."

"If I used crass language, this would be a good place for it. I don't know what press organization you work for but stop harassing us." Click.

I look around. "They think I'm People fucking magazine. Who's next? Give me a phone."

Another voice, a deeper feminine voice, answers, "Prohibition Winery, this is Tabi."

"May I please speak to Baxter Schroeder?"

"The fuck you will. I don't know who the hell you are, but it's in your dick's best interest to back off this line of questioning. I can do this all-fucking day long."

"Please let me explain."

"Oh my god, the balls on you. Well, sorry to tell you, mine are bigger."

"Tabi! You're married to Baxter. You're the...." Click.

I move on to the next phone. She answers right away, "Not today, asshole."

"What if I was a customer?"

"Don't care." Click.

I scream. "They think I'm the freaking press! Help, anyone. I'm open to all ideas. What do you have?"

There's a girl about sixteen years old. "I have an idea."

She dials and puts it on speaker.

"Prohibition Winery, this is Tabi."

"Hello, my name is Chelsea, and I have an Ian Reilly on the line for you."

"Ian Reilly? Chelsea, for real?"

"Yes, ma'am."

"Fine. I'll talk to him."

"Don't hang up," I say.

Her voice explodes in laughter. "Shit, why didn't you tell us it was you?"

INGRID

"Dad." I burst into tears.

"Little Bell. Are you hurt?"

"Everywhere. It hurts everywhere without him." I cry for a bit, and he's silent. I regulate my breath. "Dad."

"Oh, honey. Trust me, of anyone on the planet, I know that feeling. Every day, it still hurts that your mother died and left my cranky ass alone. Are you on your way?" He lets me stew in it for a moment. Then, I wipe my face, so I can see the road.

"I'm on I-80 now." I sniffle.

"You know I won't sleep until you're here safely. So let me ping your phone from time to time."

"Fine."

He says, "Tabi and Natalie had an exciting day." He pauses for dramatic effect. He likes to do that. "He called Prohibition."

"Who?"

"Him." My breath is gone. I pull into the right-hand lane and slow down a little.

"What?! What did he say?" My heart is racing and aching. Is that a sign of love or a heart attack? Maybe they're the same thing.

"He wanted to know where you were and talk to me. Unfortunately, I was out in the blocks with your sister and missed the call."

I blurt out, "He reads your blog."

I run my hands over the steering wheel. There's no way he's ever going to get over that I ran at the first sign of trouble. Jesus. I'm not vibrant, beautiful, strong wildflowers. I'm a plain ole ratty-ass stepped-on crocus.

"You there? He reads my blog? At least that's one." My dad laughs at his dad joke.

"He read it when we were apart. He said it was the only way to get any information about me. He reads it every morning like the paper."

"He's got good taste." I smile. "Where are you, Bell?"

"Not far. I couldn't really motivate. I'm going to take my time. I slept downtown last night. I'm a couple of hours outside of Chicago." I look at the next exit. "I'm in Iowa City."

"Pull off. Pull yourself together and get a hotel. Order in room service."

"That sounds like a great idea, Dad. I'm so sad. I miss him so desperately, but the situation is hopeless."

I pull off at the exit and search for a hotel that will have room service instead of a breakfast buffet.

"Bell, I say this for your own good. Nothing is hopeless. He's not dead. Pull your head out of your ass."

I laugh at my dad. We've always said everything to each other. My brother and sister were out of the house by the time I was nine. It's always been the two of us. Because I didn't know her, I missed the idea of my mom, but not her. I had my dad and the aunties and the winery families.

My dad starts again, "He's a mess. And Tabi, well, Tabi hung up on him a dozen times because she's——"

"Tell me no one told him I'm coming home."

"Would that be such a bad thing? Having someone who loves you know where you are?"

"But I don't know if he loves me."

"Then unravel your drama. Who gives a shit what people say? In the face of being alone, do you really care if they think he gave you a job?"

I smirk. "Careful. I made a lot of money off of those people."

"Perhaps this is all payback for such an easy huckster job."

"EASY? Do you know what it's like to smile non-stop or wear shoes six inches tall for hours on end?"

He chuckles. "Easy. I'm going to go drop some fruit and check brix on the back Syrah block. So don't mind me as I head off to my easy work."

"But you love it." I grin and ease back into the seat.

"And you love him."

"Completely." I let the phone be silent for a moment as I pull into a hotel called The Graduate. I put the car in park and sit there listening to my dad listen to me.

"Bell. I love you."

"At least someone does." He laughs, and I hang up. He's right. And my father didn't call me Little Bell. Just Bell. Did they have a meeting and decide to drop the 'Little?' Perhaps the world is shifting.

IAN

I haven't slept. I hate everything and everyone. The trio at her brother's winery told me they'd get her to listen to the iHeartRadio thing. They said they'd make sure, but it's not like they can force her. I want her to hear the music. They'll cut the other stuff, I'm sure. I'm headed to LA tomorrow. I can't stay in exile, in my exie-bestie's carriage house, licking my wounds forever. Until she resurfaces, I'll have to wait it out.

I miss the small things. Sex is the best there will ever be, but it's the way she holds a spoon or wipes down the sink after she brushes her teeth. I don't want anyone else in the fucking world to know that when she's about to fall asleep, she flips her pillow over. That's all mine from now on. She's delusional if she thinks I'm not going to chase her. Hold her and remind her that fate put us in the damn Paris closet. I'm a sappy boy now.

Here's what I'll do. I'll find her, woo her back and then stay. I'll just make music for locals in the park. I don't have a choice about making music, it's who I am, but I do have a choice about the fucking fame. If I'm gone long enough, my name will only surface in those "Whatever happened to that poor schlub" segments on weekend editions of ET.

I'll be Mr. Mom to our kids. I don't want anything to take me from her side, and I don't want anything to take away from her work.

Fuck. I scrub my hands through my wet hair and pull-on clothes. I don't care about anything. My shit's all packed up but not very well. Meg shoved it all into random places, but I don't care enough to sort it out.

I make a cup of coffee and check the door in case there's a pancake delivery. Dumbass wishful thinking. Where the fuck did she drive?

The cream swirls as I open my iPad to the "morning paper." I expect nothing, but I do want to know how the Chardonnay pressing went. I'm invested at this point.

The vines always have a way of coming back. Finding their way home. No matter what Little Bells and whistles you try and figure out to coax them home, they find it on their own. So if you've lost something, you might be able to catch it on 80 before it finds its way back home. Perhaps if you hurry, you can catch them outside of Iowa City, where we're welcoming some new distributors. The Zinfandel blend is unique and very special and has been called "One Perfect Thing," a phrase coined by my best friend about his wife. If this Zin is your One Perfect Thing, then you can't be without it.
I'm honored you're reading and look forward to meeting you here at Schroeder Estate Winery and Vineyards. And while you're here, perhaps you can chat with the folks at Prohibition Winery. I know my daughter-in-law is itching to make everything hospitable for you.

Holy shit. What did I just read? Is he talking to me? Is this a message on how to fucking find her? Ok. Shit.

The back door slams behind me. Pearl runs up, and I settle her on my hip.

"Pearly girly. Where's your mama?"

Jake enters. "Work. What's up?"

I quickly explain the blog and hope he can help me. He smirks at me and pushes his big black glasses up his nose. "That's amazing. Ok, let's see."

"Little Bells is a reference to her. Her family calls her Little Bell."

Jake points to the article. "I'm from Iowa. Interstate 80 goes right through Iowa City, and if you stay on it, you end up on the other coast."

I put Pearl on the counter, and her dad puts a hand on her while I pull up maps. "Holy shit. She's driving home. 80 ends right near Sonoma."

He picks up Pearl, who reaches for his glasses. He smiles. "And the rest of it sounds like you got her father's permission to pursue his daughter. Literally across the country."

Jake grabs a sippy cup and begins to fill it with water. He hands it to Pearl, and I'm staring at him. My heart bursts open and warms. I want that. I want a tiny Ingrid in my arms while I prepare to write music for the day. I'm staring at them and smiling. Jake interrupts my thought process.

"Shouldn't you be getting on the road?"

"Man. I can't thank you enough for all of this. For being cool with Meg and I being friends and the studio and…."

"Hey, if she makes you even a sliver of how happy Meg makes me, you're wasting time talking to me. You're welcome. You're still a douchebag, but you're a douchebag with a good heart. And some killer blues riffs. I heard the demos. Go in that direction. Ditch the pop shit. You've got some pain in there that needs to come out. And if you don't record with her, come on back. Morgan will take care of you." I kiss his cheek and Pearl's nose.

"Tell Meg I'll call her."

I shake his hand, and the door slams in my wake as I focus on trying to rent a car.

INGRID

The world is brighter and clearer now. Full of life and sunshine at noon. I had an excellent breakfast and grabbed a chicken salad sandwich for the road. I'm going to get to Sonoma and ask him to visit, and we'll see how it goes. No one gawked at me here. Perhaps there's life outside the spotlight. I've been in hiding for too long.

The machine is still churning, though. His single is being lauded, but not because I had anything to do with it. They keep asking, "Who really did the work?" Morgan went apeshit for me and posted all she could to her small cult. I adore her, but the machine is too big to be the ghost for me.

Ian keeps texting. I'm saving them up to read all together like a novella of sadness. I swing onto the highway just after one. I'm listening to NPR and podcasts. I need to be without music for a minute.

I'm an hour in when my phone pings a reminder that I didn't set. It echoes through the car that I did not pair it with. My sister's wife must have hacked my phone. She does that for a living. She's what they call a white-hat hacker, hacking for good, not evil. We've all gotten used to knowing Mel is watching. She mostly sends me funny little messages through all kinds of electronics.

My phone speaks, "Turn Your Radio On." I didn't opt for satellite radio, but it pops on, and iHeartRadio comes blaring into my new SUV. My phone goes silent when the radio tunes in. Mel is scary good.

His voice throws me. Apparently, my tribe is trying to send a message. I pull into the right-hand lane.

"Hey, I'm Ian Reilly, and coming up next on iHeartRadio are three new acoustic songs and a classic." Three? He only had two completed. I'm hungry, and if I'm going to listen, I might as well make it an event. Dust kicks up as I ease to the side. The sun and cool breeze flow through the roof and windows. I leave all the windows and the sunroof open and blast the radio. I spread a blanket over the car's hood and gather my picnic. The first song is *True in the Moment*. And although it hurts, the song is really fucking good.

I sip my soda when song number two comes on. The one that's super bluesy, and I love it. I love him. I really do. I love the way he loves me. The song is fun and dark and funky and perfect. And it's called Wildflower. The patter in between is annoying, and this woman is clearly trying to get some kind of scoop.

I don't know the third song. But it's beautiful. Its soul oozes into mine, and I realize it's about us, not just me. *Follow Me.* I love it.

Oh god. I shouldn't have run from him. I should have trusted we could figure it out. But I was so ruined by what everyone was thinking about my work. I forgot to let it stand on its own. The song ends, and tears are streaming down my face. I need to talk to him. I scramble off the car and collect my things as well as myself. Maybe someone can teach me how to tune out everyone but him.

My hand is almost on the handle when I hear him yelling at this woman. Defending me. Telling them how talented I am. I bend in half as I really cry. I threw away my one perfect thing. I hope to god I can get it back. I pull my t-shirt down and straighten up. I wipe my tears and begin to twist my hair into a bun. A car pulls over in front of me. Shit. Some asshole who thinks I'm a damsel in distress. I ignore him and pull the handle.

"STEP AWAY FROM THE CAR!" I look inside my car and then back at the voice bellowing on the side of I-80. It's him. Both of them are him. He's jogging and gets to my car pretty damn fast. I turn and hit his body with too much force. While an acoustic version of *Don't You Worry 'Bout A Thing* plays.

His dark eyes are glittering in the sun. His cream skin blushes as I stroke his cheeks. His hands find their way around my waist. "May I have this dance?" He pulls me close, and good tears stream down my face. His version is wonderful. I can make it better.

"How? Yes. Yes. You can have all my dances."

"I'm so sorry I'm late. And I forgot to tell you something."

I smile at him. "What?"

"I love you."

He kisses me instantly, and his lips are soft and perfect. My body hums with a rhythm that's all ours. He loves me. I'll never hear or create anything as beautiful as those words. Then his tongue sneaks into my mouth, and I moan around it. I hold his neck as he pulls me closer. And he sways, turning us in a circle. We're dancing and chasing each other's tongues around for a solid five minutes, and when he pulls back, he has a big dopey grin on his face. "You're the jelly, the soundtrack, and the syrup."

"What the hell are you talking about?" I laugh.

"To my peanut butter, to my life, and to my pancakes. Wildflower, I love you so fucking fiercely even your family already knows we're written in the stars."

I shift my hands tighter around his neck. We're close. "They made me listen."

He kisses me softly. "They told me where to find you. You really should read my 'morning paper.' It's quite illuminating." My eyes are wide as I stare at him.

"My dad?"

He kisses me softly, and I let it languish. He whispers, "Your dad. Among others."

My tribe. They're a fierce bunch. "Sam. This plan has Sam written all over it. I'm sure Bax wouldn't listen to Natalie, but Sam can get anyone to bend. And he's the most romantic of all of us. Or used to be."

"And you're here. You came after me."

"I'm not sure what you're not getting. I'd follow you anywhere."

"You'd follow me?"

"Anywhere. Nothing else seems to matter at all except that. You call the shots. And I think you're going to be pretty busy. I got a text today from someone who wants to know if you have openings in your recording schedule."

My eyes go wide. "I'm sorry, what?"

"I told Ed you were booked up with my new album, but maybe you could fit him in later in the fall."

I walk away from him and kick all the dirt around me. My car's radio is still a descant over the horizon as I stare at it.

"And he wants me?"

"Yes. He wants Moment's sound, and Morgan slipped him a couple of demo tracks for Jake's new stuff. He wants you. Not your followers." I grin uncontrollably and turn to him.

My words burst out with pure raw emotion as if they were a shotgun. "Then we better get busy building a studio. Tell your friend, Ed, yes."

He takes me in his arms, and all the pieces of me come together to be more than I could have ever imagined. "Ok then. I'll let Mr. Sheeran know."

"Oh, My Fucking God." His mouth silences me as my body zings. This is all too much. Good thing I have a couple of days' drive.

He pauses. "I love you so very much. Like forever love you." I slide my fingers into his floppy brown hair. He grins.

"Then you should probably follow me home because I love you more."

"Hotel first, then home."

"You know this trip is thirty-one hours, and I've only managed five hours in two days."

"Cool. Let's take our time. Like a month or so?" He squeezes me to him. A month. I could do that. It will take that long to pour the foundation and get some walls in my studio.

I kiss him. "Deal."

"Now, about that hotel?" He grinds his pelvis into me, and I laugh.

"Next exit?" He smiles, then kisses me quickly, turns me around in his arms, and pushes me towards my car. I'm still standing, stunned and laughing. I strain to hear him over the zoom of cars.

"Chop chop, woman. We've got forever to get to. And I really need to meet your dad. He's going to need help with that tricky Merlot lot."

I grin, turn around, and race towards my car and future.

The End

EPILOGUE

INGRID

OUCH. FUCK. THAT HURTS. I'M ON MY STOMACH, PROPPED UP ON MY ELBOWS. The buzzing sound is actually soothing. The outline was done a month ago, and today I'm here for color and shadow. David Gelbert, one of my brother's friends, drew the perfect tattoo for me. Wildflowers entwined around a guitar. The studio is thriving, and we're adding two more one-bedroom bungalows next month. Turns out some of the bands like to come here and write before they record. It's quite the little village vibe I've created.

Ian's not toured or left my side as I produce music. Well, he follows my father around, learning all he can. He's obsessed with becoming a vintner. He's calling it his second and third act. He stands at my sister's side when she starts making her magic with our wine. He's also started poking around the other vineyards in the '5' to learn it all. Glad one of us likes the winery business.

The bell over the door dings, and then he's in front of me and down on one knee. His brown eyes sexy, dancing, and earnest. His hair is cropped a little closer to his head now, but I fucking love him so very much. He shoves something toward my face and everyone around the shop gasps. He flips the top, and there's an enormous sapphire ring. It's stunning. The buzzing on my lower leg stops.

"Ingrid Sarah Schroeder, you're my entire world. I love you. Will you marry me?" There's heightened tension in the air as I roll my eyes at him.

"Nope. And you have got to stop asking." He snaps it shut and pulls a chair over. He sits backward on it and kisses me. The buzzing continues, and I wince.

He says, "You can take the slight pain there, dream-killer. Are you ever going to say yes?" His lips curl into a smile that sets my toes on edge. Sets all of me on edge. So damn hot.

I say, "Eventually. But not yet. The rings are getting prettier, though."

He grins widely. "What should we do with this one?"

"How about you return it?" He shoves the ring back into his tight jeans pocket.

"Is it the ring or the proposal you have a problem with?" He grins at me, and I want this tattoo business to be done so we can retreat to our own little home on the back half of Schroeder Estate Winery. It's a three-bedroom California bungalow, and it's perfect for us.

The studio has a room off the back that's all windows exposed to the vineyards and hills that my family's winery sits at the base of. That's the room Ian wanted for himself. I never let other musicians use it. It's his sacred space. We've produced and released an album and five songs together, and when he won record of the year last year, he asked me to accept for the two of us. A spotlight I made myself and was thrilled to step into.

He started asking me to marry him the very first month we got to Sonoma. We have time. But it doesn't stop him from asking me frequently. Sometimes the proposals are elaborate, and some seem spur of the moment, like today. It's getting harder and harder to say no—I think that's his plan.

He kisses me again, and his lips still breathe life into every cell of my body.

"Maybe I'll ask you," I say on his lips.

"It's more fun asking you repeatedly. Wait until you see the next ring."

"Everything's more fun with you." I wince again. "Except getting a tattoo."

"I love you, Wildflower."

"I love you too. You're my favorite person. How could I not?"

"Come on, marry me." He pleads.

I shake my head, and he sits back down.

"Why do you want to marry me so badly?"

He puts his hands behind his head and says, "I want to be in Adrian's will. Duh. That's a pretty sweet piece of property you're set to inherit. I'd be a fool to let you slip away on a technicality."

I laugh hard, just like I do every day with him. I wince again as laughing shakes my body. Much to the chagrin of my tattoo guy, who forces my leg back into position. I rest my head on my forearms and stare at my forever.

In a dreamier voice than I intended, I say, "You can have it all as long as I get you."

"Is that a yes?"

"Not yet. But soon."

"I'll take it." He leans the chair towards me, kisses me one more time, then hops up.

"Where are you going?"

"I've got a ring to return and buy. And the aunties want a word with me about a ritual or some shit. Be back later."

I grin as he waves to me through the window. And now I know exactly when I'll say yes. Once the five families get involved, everyone is helpless against them and their tide of love. He'll see.

The end.

ABOUT KELLY KAY

She's a steamy, funny romance writer that attempts to give you all the feels. She's married to a writer, mother of a creative dynamo of an eleven-year-old boy, and currently, she's a little sleepy. She's a klutz and goofball and loves lipstick as much as her Chuck Taylors. And most likely, she has a glass of wine or a cup of coffee in her hand right now. She's the author of eleven Contemporary Romance/RomCom books. She cleverly figured out a way to drink wine and write at the same time by creating her Five Families Vineyard Series. It's available, along with all her books, on Amazon and free in Kindle Unlimited.

Website:
www.kellykayromance.com

Spotify:
http://bit.ly/KellyKayPlaylists

instagram.com/kelly_kay_books
bookbub.com/profile/kelly-kay

DAYLIGHT: A WITCH OF KITCHEN LAKE NOVELLA

MARISA MOHI

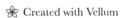 Created with Vellum

ABOUT DAYLIGHT: A WITCH OF KITCHEN LAKE NOVELLA

Subgenre: Paranormal Romance
Tropes: Magical heroine, forbidden love

Graphic sexual depictions, open door sex and explicit language

TW/CW: This story includes mentions of blood.

Blurb:

Jo Bonneville is the witch of Kitchen Lake, one in a long line of witches who have practiced the craft and sold their services on the shores of that little body of water. But the trailer her granny left her needs a new roof, and her bartending shifts at the Lakeshore Inn aren't really paying off like she needs them to.

That's when a vampire walks into the bar on dollar beer night offering big money for a complicated spell. Jo can heed the warnings her granny gave her and say no, or she can take a chance with a dangerous man and hope it pays off.

Jo Bonneville reached into the cooler under the bar top and prayed the inventory was suddenly replenished. There hadn't been this many customers at the Lakeshore in she didn't know how long, and it was only a Tuesday.

The bar was packed. All the regulars were there, but so many other people were there too. That was the problem with the summertime. There was no telling how business was going to be. Either no one was at Kitchen Lake that week, or everyone and their brother hitched their pontoon boats up to their truck and decided to party. This was clearly one of the party weeks. The bar top was full, with people standing behind the seated customers. All the tables were full, and customers milled around on the dance floor as a few people danced. St. Caroline and the Cookie Dusters was what the band was calling themselves on that particular evening, though Jo knew that by her next shift, they'd have a new name.

Luke scrambled around customers, carrying a few cases of Miller High Life bottles to the reach-in cooler before darting back into the walk-in to change the Coors Light keg for the second time that night. Jo could've sworn his hair was somehow turning grayer by the minute, but he smiled the whole time because big money nights for his little business were few and far between.

Matt held fast by the door, arms crossed against his broad chest, trying to keep a count of how many people had entered the Lakeshore, and calculating how many more could enter before he'd have to turn people away. He was six and half feet tall and ridiculously good-looking with a new close-cropped haircut for his upcoming MMA fight. Jo wasn't ashamed to admit she'd had a few impure thoughts about him, even if he was ten years younger than her. But they all faded away as soon as he opened his mouth to reveal that he barely had a thought between his ears.

"Two more and tab us out, Jo!" Leon called from the end of the bar where he sat with his wife, Melinda, of fifty years.

Jo nodded to him as she poured two more Jack and Cokes, adding a maraschino cherry to Melinda's. She tapped a few buttons on the bar's register and printed out their tab, then dropped the drinks and bill in front of them.

"Some night, eh?" Leon said.

Jo shrugged. "Dollar beer nights are always a little crazy in the summer."

Melinda smiled, reaching across the bar to hold Jo's hand for a second. "You make sure you get plenty of sleep after this shift, all right?"

Jo smiled. She loved her regulars, and Leon and Melinda Collins were extra special to her. They'd been coming to the bar for years, and they had been around the lake since Jo's grandma lived in the trailer that Jo lived in now. They got married the day after they graduated from high school, and they'd been together ever since. Jo thought it was sweet, even if the idea of marrying someone from her high school made her want to puke a little. She loved how the two of them always seemed to be looking out for her, and if Jo ever needed help finding a handyman to do work around her trailer, she knew she could ask Leon and he'd find her someone who wasn't going to rob her blind.

Which was good, because Jo needed some help.

She'd been working herself harder than normal trying to earn enough in tips to cover the cost of a new roof for the trailer before the fall rains hit. She loved the trailer her granny had left her, but by the time Jo had inherited it, so many repairs that her granny had been putting off were coming due.

"Watch Nattie Rae tonight," Luke whispered in Jo's ear as he walked past to grab empty pint glasses off tables.

Nattie Rae was enjoying the band from her usual seat at the bar. That was always a bad sign, at least for the staff. Nattie was another regular, with a haircut that Jo didn't know you could get after 1985. She had a million stories about which bands she'd partied with back in the day, and even though Nattie was in her sixties, she wasn't opposed to taking her top off and dancing on the bar. It didn't matter how much Luke or Jo told her that the Lakeshore wasn't that kind of place. Nattie was who she was, and if she was there, well . . . It tended to become that kind of place.

Jo moved down toward Nattie to keep an eye on her, but regretted it immediately when Dave, who was sitting next to Nattie, winked at her.

Jo knew that men like Dave were part of the whole bartending gig, and even though he drove her crazy, he still wasn't a bad guy, per se. He wasn't good by any means, but he just wasn't someone that Jo wanted to speak to except to get his order. Dave, however, always wanted to strike up a conversation.

He was a few years older than Jo, though Jo didn't know how many, and he had been recently divorced. He spent his evenings flirting with Jo, or at least trying to, and then eventually going home with one of the bar patrons. He had a 1965 black Chevelle with white racing stripes, which Jo had to admit was pretty cool. But what wasn't cool was how often he tried to remind her how roomy the backseat was.

"How about another beer," Dave said, leaning over the bar to get closer to Jo, "and a smile, while you're at it."

Before Jo could respond, Dez Spellman, the leader of the Belle Starr Outlaws, Oklahoma City's finest lesbian biker gang, sidled up to Dave and prodded him in the ribs with her thumb. Dez smiled, crinkling the bright blue eyeliner wings she'd expertly painted on. Jo always loved how Dez managed to match her eyeliner to whatever color her mohawk happened to be that week.

"How about you act like your mama raised you right, Dave," Dez said. "Jo, when you get a second, we'll take one more round of tequila shots."

"I gotcha. One for you, Frankie, and Tina, right?" Jo leaned in to be heard over the music.

Dez nodded, then looked back to Dave. "You know our girl here is working her ass off, and you come in here acting like a pretty woman like her has the time for a man like you? You know you're just gonna go home with a lake party girl anyhow. So why don't you drag your happy ass up to the dance floor and hit on that chick in the tube top?" Dez pointed to a woman who was dancing in a much more suggestive manner than the music called for.

Jo poured Dave another beer and handed it to him. He grabbed his drink and elbowed his way to the dance floor with a gleam in his eye, Jo all but forgotten.

"Thanks, Dez," Jo said, salting the rims of three shot glasses. "He's mostly harmless, but annoying as hell."

"I think we could say that of all men," Dez said. "When you decide to quit barking up that tree, let me know. I know some women who would love to date you."

Jo smiled and shook her head. She poured tequila into the shot glasses, placing a lime on the rim of each one.

The song ended and Nattie Rae let loose a "woo" that surprised those around her. But Jo said nothing because at least Nattie still had her top on.

Jo went up and down the bar top, filling orders and tabbing people out. Customers came and went as she washed glasses and tried to restock the coolers as fast as she could. A small fight looked like it wanted to break out in the corner of the bar, but Matt was there in a flash, and both parties were thrown out by the collars of their shirts.

The band took a half-hour break to go smoke on the wood deck out back that overlooked the lake, and a handful of patrons left for the night. The bar was finally slowing down. There were a few tables she could run and bus really quick, and she wanted to make sure no one had been over-served. It was always hard to monitor on busy nights, but she could do a quick sweep of the room and make sure all was going according to plan.

She grabbed a tray and set out, picking up all the empties around the room while checking on customers, asking them how they were doing, if they needed anything else, or if they liked the band. It was hard to monitor on busy nights, but it was easy to see how far gone someone was if you could make them talk with you.

As the tray filled up, she stacked some pint glasses and carried them in her hand back to the bar. But before she got to the swinging doors that separated the bar from the rest of the room, she could feel the hair on the back of her neck stand up.

It couldn't be.

There hadn't been a vampire in Oklahoma in over a generation. In fact, her grandmother had been the one to banish the last one. This vampire had a lot of nerve to show up in her bar. And the vampire had to know it was her bar, because if she could sense him, he could sense her.

Setting the pint glasses and tray down, she absentmindedly reached for the quartz necklace she always wore. Her grandmother had given it to her right before she died, when it was clear that Jo would take over as the witch of Kitchen Lake. Jo scanned the room, trying to find him. The crowds were thinning, and Matt held the door open to let out a gaggle of sorority girls who were staying in the cabins across the lake for a bachelorette party. Even though Jo thought they were annoying and ordered stupid drinks, she hoped they would get back to their cabin safely and didn't invite anyone in that night.

As Dave left with the woman in the tube top, Jo spotted the vampire. He was sitting against the wall, nothing but two rows of tables and a bar top separating them. He hadn't ordered anything yet, and he watched Jo from where he sat.

A kernel of fear started to wake up in Jo's gut, like a piece of popcorn in a hot pot. She stared back at him, hoping to get a sense of his business, but it was no use. She couldn't always sense what a person was feeling, at least not before having a conversation with them. She needed to get to know him a little before she could feel it.

They made eye contact, and the vampire smiled. Jo didn't like it. She moved to the other side of the bar and signaled to Matt. He came up to the bar, sidling in between two patrons.

"Watch him," Jo said, trying to nonchalantly motion to the vampire.

"Why? Did he say something to you?" Matt asked, his neck stiffening as his chest puffed out.

"No, not at all. He's just someone I've never seen before and he's not drinking anything. Looks suspicious." Jo appreciated that Matt's sense of chivalry was what drove him to be the best bouncer the Lakeshore Inn had employed in the ten years she'd been working there. She didn't need saving, though. But that didn't mean she couldn't use Matt's desire to be a knight in shining armor to her advantage. "Just make sure he's not trying to take anyone home or slipping things into drinks. You know how some people are. And since I've never seen him before, it's weird that he's here, and dressed so nicely. This is a lake bar, not a city club."

Matt smirked and walked back to his post by the door.

Jo kept pouring drinks and cleaning glasses, hoping she did the right thing. It didn't matter that Matt was a semi-pro fighter with his heart set on becoming a heavyweight champ. When it came down to it, he wouldn't last one second against a vampire, and Jo worried she may have just sentenced him to death.

2

John Laurent sensed her even before he walked in. She was a strong witch, and he was more afraid than he cared to admit. But this was important. He needed to talk to her. She was really his last hope.

And after that week wasted in New Orleans, he didn't have any more options.

He parked his rental Mercedes toward the back of the gravel lot. He'd thought it was a low-key sort of car that no one would notice, but that was before he realized he was going to a dive bar near a lake. The rest of the lot was filled with trucks and SUVs, and a few motorcycles near the front.

John knew he was out of his element. But he didn't have another choice. He needed her help, and from what he'd heard, she was descended from a long line of witches—all of them strong like her.

He hit the lock button on the key fob and made his way to the bar, momentarily angry about how dusty his Italian leather shoes would be from this place. The young man at the door gave him the once over and let him in.

Once across the threshold, John could feel her power even more. She had an aura, almost pure golden light, like a fine outline around her. He couldn't stop staring. Someone behind him brushed past him to get to the bar, and John realized he was standing still. He shuffled over to the wall where he could stare at her across the bar.

He could tell when she noticed him. She had been picking up glasses around the bar, and her back stiffened. Her head shifted around the room, searching. Back behind the bar, she finally spotted him.

God. She was pretty. That was something John never thought he'd say about another woman. Not after . . . It had been so long ago. Before he was turned. But there she was. Her hair was black and her skin an even bronze that really stood out against the white V-neck T-shirt that hugged her body.

She had a French last name too. Bonneville. Maybe they'd have something in common. Of course, it's possible she'd never been to France. But he tried not to think of what would happen if they didn't hit it off, or if she couldn't help him.

Or if she flat out refused.

Though he thought he looked good before leaving the hotel, he now realized he stood out like a sore thumb. A button-down long-sleeve shirt in August in Oklahoma? Probably not his smartest move, though the heat didn't really affect him. Everyone else was in cutoff shorts and sleeveless shirts. This was not his scene.

He kept staring at the witch until she finally looked up at him. There was something about her gaze that reassured him. She was powerful enough to handle what he needed. But at the same time, he was frightened. She didn't look very happy to see him.

There weren't that many vampires in Oklahoma in the first place, so maybe it was just shock. He knew this would be an uphill battle—and he was running out of time. It didn't matter how sharp her glare was. He needed to ask.

"Ladies and gentlemen, we're St. Caroline and the Cookie Dusters!" On the stage, a funny-looking man in a tie-dye T-shirt arranged a guitar strap on his shoulder as the two other members of the band took their spots, one behind a drum kit and the other next to the keyboard.

The band went into a rousing version of Metallica's "Enter Sandman" that left much to be desired, but they did it with the sort of gusto that John had to give them credit for. As they eased into the first chorus, several patrons shuffled out to leave, and John saw his chance.

He grabbed an empty seat at the bar right in front of where Jo was standing.

Jo's head shot up from the reach-in cooler. She glared at him. "Can I help you?" The question was the sort of thing a bartender would ask a patron. But the tone was all wrong.

John cleared his throat. "Just a beer, please." He smiled, hoping it would defuse the situation, showing that he meant no harm.

"Which one?" Jo asked, hands on hips.

John hadn't noticed her hips yet. But there she was, drawing attention to them. He pulled his eyes away and pointed at the dollar beer sign. "One of those." He kept his eyes on the stack of coasters on the bar.

Jo grabbed him a bottle of Miller High Life, expertly pulling a church key out of the back pocket of her cutoffs and popping the cap off. She reached across the bar and placed it on a coaster, then paused before taking her hand away. "You cool?" Her eyebrows were raised.

He cleared his throat. "Yeah. Cool. I swear."

"Because if you're not cool, we're going to have a problem."

"No, no. Just here to have a beer and listen to the music." He knew she could tell he was lying, but he wasn't ready to lay it all out on the table just yet. He lowered his voice. "I'm not here to feed, if that's what you mean."

"Good. Because if you so much as look at one of my customers the wrong way, I will ruin your night." She moved away and kept her eyes on him.

"Fair enough." He took a sip, gagging on the beer.

"Not a beer fan?" Jo asked, wiping down the bar top.

He shook his head. "More of a wine drinker, really."

She pointed to a box of wine next to the two beer taps. "We have that, if that's your thing."

Franzia in a box. John really was out of his element.

"No, this beer is fine. Just here to enjoy the music."

John could feel someone getting close to him. Before he could turn around, he heard the deep voice of the bouncer behind him.

"There a problem here, Jo?"

"Not at all. Our new guest here is just enjoying a beer and he was getting ready to go tip the band." She smiled at John. "Right?"

"Absolutely," John said, trying to be as agreeable as he needed to be. "Love a good Metallica cover." He walked over to the tip jar on the edge of the little stage and dropped in a twenty. She was going to make this hard.

He had known it wasn't going to be easy, but he had so precious little time left. All the witches in New Orleans turned out to be fakes, so she was his only hope. He needed to do whatever it would take so she wouldn't turn him away.

John hated feeling so desperate. It wasn't like he had any other choice.

3

AFTER "ENTER SANDMAN," THE BAND WENT ON TO PLAY SOME CLASSIC ROCK covers of Creedence Clearwater Revival, Kansas, Queen, Blue Oyster Cult, and the Steve Miller Band. Nattie left her spot at the bar and made her way to the dance floor. Luke covered his face with his hands, and after checking with Jo to make sure she could handle the bar for a bit, he stood watch near the dance floor, just to make sure Nattie's top stayed on.

Business stayed steady, and at 12:45 a.m. the band did their last song. Most of the customers had left by then, and only a few stragglers remained. Nattie continued to dance, even though the band was sipping High Lifes on the back deck, and the only music was the local soft rock station playing through the speaker system. The Belle Starr Outlaws sat in their regular booth but were getting ready to head home. A few remaining customers weighed down tables, finishing up their drinks. The bar top was completely empty.

That's when he came back to take a seat. Jo had almost forgotten about the vampire in the rush to get the bar ready for closing while still serving the remaining customers.

Almost forgotten.

He'd been like a dull ache on her senses since he walked in. Like a pebble in her shoe. But if she was being honest, it wasn't painful. Just a subtle awareness of something that was there that she didn't normally sense.

Jo couldn't get over how he looked. There was some sort of magic that happened when vampires turned. It gave them the jawlines of movie stars and the posture of a flamenco dancer. And Jo secretly believed that the best skin care routine was just being a vampire—because they never seemed to age.

"Can I get you another?" she asked, looking at the bottle of High Life he still held in his hand. It looked like he had only taken that one sip.

The vampire looked down at the bottle, his face betraying how disgusted he was by the prospect of having to purchase and consume a second beer. "I know you know what I am. And I know what you are. I know it's not normal for you to see men like me at this bar, but I need a spell."

Jo paused. That was a new one. It wasn't unheard of for vampires to come to witches for help. But vampires generally tended to fear Kitchen Lake, especially after what her grandmother had done to clear the place. These days most of her witching was done on the down-low. It wasn't that she wasn't proud of who she was. But she wasn't exactly established as a business yet, and she didn't have any word-of-mouth sales coming her way. It had been a whole year since she did any spellwork for a customer.

Of course, there was always a witch at Kitchen Lake. And even though her granny had been the one that really created the legend, Jo was glad that she got to carry on the legacy.

John continued. "I thought I could get what I needed from some witches in New Orleans, but it turns out they're mostly there to scam tourists."

Jo laughed loudly, a throaty sort of laugh she didn't get to release on the world nearly enough. "You're not wrong. Of course, there are great witches there, but most of them are fakes. You gotta know who to look for. The vampires and witches in New Orleans run that city like the Mafia, in case you didn't know, and there's no way you're getting help from a real witch there without paying at least triple what it's worth. Even then, they'll extract so much more from you afterward. As interest."

"Well, I did not know that. I tend to stay away from that place."

"I thought your kind loved that city."

He shrugged. "It's fine. But that's where all the new vampires like to hang out. It's like running around with a bunch of high schoolers, and that is absolutely not for me."

Jo smiled and reached her hand out across the bar. "My name's Jo."

He took her hand. "John. John Laurent."

"I'm sorry I didn't give you the benefit of the doubt earlier. It's just we're not used to vampires around here."

John nodded. "I'd heard that this wasn't a great place for vampires. At least, before you became the witch of Kitchen Lake."

Jo nodded slowly. "Yeah. My granny had a thing against y'all. There were a few really bad vampires here in the 1970s. They actually came up this way from New Orleans after a hurricane destroyed the place they were staying, and she'd had it with folks getting drained at the lake. So, she banished them."

Jo left it at that. They both knew that when a witch banished vampires, it meant the vampires died.

"Understandable," John said, slowly peeling the label off the beer in his hand. "There are bad elements everywhere, and not all vampires behave ethically. That's another reason I typically stay away from New Orleans."

Was she actually having a civilized conversation with a vampire seated at her bar? She couldn't believe it. It went against everything she'd been taught, but she also knew that inherited prejudice didn't serve anyone. This vampire hadn't burst in here searching for his next victim. He sat at the bar like any regular would, making a concerted effort to fit in, peering around every so often, more nervous than anything. Still, she kept her guard up. She'd always heard that vampires were good at lulling people into a false sense of security, so he could just be buttering her up before an attack.

She didn't want to have to use any magic in front of her customers, but she would if she had to.

"Well, what do we have here," Dez said, sidling up to John. "This one's real clean. Not from around here, are ya, sweetheart?" She patted John on the hand. "We'll take our tab when you get a chance, Jo."

"All together or separate?"

Dez sighed, her blue mohawk seeming to slump with the exhale. "Together. I lost a bet on the last run, and now I'm here paying for all the damn tequila in the place."

Jo printed the tab and put it in front of Dez.

"Not as bad as I was expecting," Dez said, taking a card out of her back pocket. "Give us one round of dollar beers too." She passed the card over to Jo.

Jo added the beers to the tab in the register and ran the card. As it was printing, she popped the caps off three beers and passed them to Dez. "You know, our friend, John, here, loves these." Jo tilted her head toward him.

John blushed a little. She didn't know vampires could do that. Maybe she was imagining it.

"I don't think he's here for the beer, Jo," Dez said, signing the receipt. "He's been holding that bottle for the past hour and a half, staring at you the whole time." She winked at John.

His blush seemed to deepen. "Are you watching me?"

Dez shrugged as she picked up the three bottles. "Not on purpose. Frankly, you're not my type. A little too clean cut. A little too male. But you do stand out, so it's hard not to watch." She waved goodbye and went back to her table.

"In my defense," John said, "I thought I was doing a very good job of blending in."

Jo laughed, not meaning for it to be so loud. Where did this man think he was? A small lunch café in Greenwich, Connecticut?

"It's not that some folks in Oklahoma don't dress this way," she said. "They do. We have a lot of oil and gas money in this state, and a few billionaires and debutantes too. But the thing is that you're at the Lakeshore Inn. It's a dive bar among dive bars, and it's at Kitchen Lake, the most affordable lake getaway in the Oklahoma City metro area, so even the brokest of folks can come enjoy a weekend. Hell, we have a dollar beer night, John. We don't do that because our clientele is flush with cash."

"Yeah. I realized when I pulled in that a rental Mercedes maybe wasn't the best option."

She laughed again. "I sure do hope it's still there when you leave."

"Oh god," he said, turning toward the door.

"I'm kidding. No one is gonna steal a car, and I'm sure you set the alarm on it before you came in. Besides, no one here thinks a Mercedes is worth the money. They all have their eyes on trucks with leather interiors and the like."

"Makes sense."

After a while, Jo forgot she was speaking with a vampire. He seemed nice. There was something about him that just seemed normal, like talking to a regular person. That wasn't what she had expected at all. Gran's bias hadn't prepared her for that.

And if she were being completely honest, there was something about him that she really liked. Sure, he was polite. But he was also ridiculously good-looking: his jawline should've belonged to a movie star, and his blue eyes were like a clear sky in the middle of the day. His black hair, graying at the temples, gave him a dignified look. She couldn't have manufactured a better-looking man if she tried.

As customers paid their tabs and left, Jo and John continued to make small talk. Finally, at 1:15, Luke stood up on the stage and turned on the microphone.

"Last call! And we'll see ya tomorrow for trivia night!" As Luke stepped off the stage, Nattie tried to pull him into a two-step, but he dodged expertly and went to turn off the music and call a cab for Nattie. The usual closing routine.

"Well, I guess I should ask you what I came here to ask you," John said.

"Yeah. I'd love to know the spell you need." Jo continued wiping down the bar top and putting things away.

He glanced around. Almost everyone was gone, except the bouncer and Nattie. "I know that you may not be the type to do spellwork for vampires. But I do hope I've proven the stereotype wrong."

She stopped cleaning and leaned in closer. "I help people who need it. I don't discriminate, unless you're an ass. And so far, you've been a perfect gentleman, even if you insult the finest beverages the Lakeshore Inn has to offer." She grinned.

He laughed. Her mood was contagious. "I promise it's not that bad. It's just. Well. I'm not used to it."

Jo shrugged. "I'll be honest. It's probably not worth getting used to."

He pulled what was left of the rest of the label off his beer, like pulling off a band-aid, then looked up at her.

Jo smiled at him. Not her bartender smile. The friendlier version she reserved for people she had an actual relationship with. She didn't realize she was doing it until she'd been doing it too long. *Get it together, Jo,* she thought. *You're too damn old to be falling in love at first sight, and with a vampire at that.*

———

JOHN KNEW his time was limited, and he had to hurry. But something wasn't right.

This witch was smiling at him, and he could've sworn it was a spell in and of itself. It made him feel weird—light and giddy. Like he wanted nothing more than to sit at that bar for the rest of his existence and stare into her eyes.

He knew that as a three-hundred-year-old vampire, he shouldn't be going weak in the knees over some woman he just met. But there it was. He couldn't deny it.

So, against his better judgment, he took out his wallet and put a ten-dollar bill down on the bar to pay for his dollar beer. "I do need a spell, but . . ." He stood up and put his wallet back in his pocket. "I'll come back tomorrow. I want you to have the night to decide whether you want to work with a vampire. I know your family history, so I want to make sure we're on the same page. I mean no harm to anyone here, but I want you to feel comfortable before I ask."

And with that, he turned and left before Jo could even say goodbye.

4

AFTER CLOSING TIME, JO COUNTED THE CASH IN THE REGISTER AND GAVE THE cash drawer to Luke. She stacked the chairs on the tabletops and swept and mopped the floors, just like she did at the end of every shift. She did a quick inventory to let Luke know what he needed to order more of.

Then, as always, she nodded to Matt and led him to her Jeep.

Jo had been giving Matt a ride home ever since his girlfriend got pregnant. They had a car the two of them shared, but Matt wanted his girlfriend to have it during his shift in case she needed to make a quick run to the doctor or wanted to run an errand. So, his girlfriend dropped him off, and Jo didn't mind taking him home. Matt was a good kid, though Jo worried about his career choices.

Working as a bouncer at a crappy lake bar and trying to become a professional MMA fighter didn't seem like the sort of career path that would make fatherhood easy on him. But he was only 23, and Jo figured there wasn't much she could say to him that would shift how he thought about things.

Plus, she didn't really have a leg to stand on in that conversation. She may be ten years older than him, but she was also still a bartender at the same crappy lake bar, trying to build up her witch business. She wasn't exactly a career counselor.

They drove with the top down and Matt's smile continued to get bigger and bigger as they got closer to his apartment on the other side of town.

"How's Meg?" Jo asked, sensing that Matt wanted to chat.

"Good! We went to the doctor the other day." A grin spread across his face that Jo caught out of the corner of her eye. "It's a girl."

"Oh, that's so wonderful, Matt! Have you thought of a name?"

Matt shook his head. "We have a list of about five hundred names. And every time Meg hears a pretty word or a flower, she adds it to the list. I told her we should name our girl after one of our grandmas or something, but she nixed that idea when she realized they all had names like Maude and Agnes and Myrtle."

Jo laughed. "Can't say I blame her there. But you'll hear a name, and you'll know when you hear it that it'll be perfect for your baby."

"Is that some witch knowledge?" Matt asked. He always seemed to revere any sort of witchcraft that Jo did, like he wouldn't heed the information unless he could determine that Jo gleaned it using her powers.

"A little," Jo said, shifting the Jeep down a gear and putting on her blinker to turn into the parking lot. "But it's also just because I know you, and I know you do the right thing when you've figured out the right thing to do in a situation."

"You already know the name, don't you?" Matt crossed his arms over his chest.

Jo tilted her head, with a hint of a smile.

"Are you going to tell me?"

"I can't, because that will change how you feel about it, and you won't use the name. You need to hear it on your own time, and fall in love with it that way, or else you won't fall in love with it at all. But it's a good name."

Matt smiled. "Good. It's not Agnes, right?"

Jo laughed as she pulled up to Matt's front door. "I will tell you it's definitely not Agnes."

"Thanks, Jo." Matt unbuckled his seatbelt and unfolded all six-and-a-half feet of himself and stepped outside the Jeep. "See you later."

"Bye, Matt!" Jo waved and watched as Matt made his way through the door. She could feel that Meg was inside sleeping quietly in their bed, and Jo could even sense the baby girl that they would choose to name Magnolia.

Jo was happy for Matt. He was ridiculously in love, and young enough to think he could do all the things he wanted to do. That was something Jo envied of him.

She pulled out of the parking lot and headed back toward Kitchen Lake.

There was a time when she thought she could have a relationship and do the work she wanted to do. But the last man she'd dated had always kept her at arm's length, until finally he couldn't handle it anymore. Maybe it was all the herbs she always had drying in her home, or maybe it was how she'd say she knew something that was going to happen. But eventually it wore him down and he left. Jo saw on Facebook a few days ago that he'd married someone, a very normal-looking woman who worked at a bank.

Jo's granny had warned her that was how it would be. "Men won't like what you can do, baby girl," she'd always say. "So if you fall in love, know that it will probably lead to heartbreak. There's a reason men used to burn witches. They don't like your power."

Jo always felt that wasn't right. Being a different generation of woman, she didn't believe that men still acted that way.

But she'd been mostly wrong. In the end, it wasn't her power that made men leave. It was her sureness—she knew what she wanted, and she was going to have it. She was going to become a powerful witch, just like her grand-mother, and she was going to do it whether the men she dated liked it or not.

Her thoughts shifted to John. What a night. The first vampire to visit Kitchen Lake in forty years came in on the busiest night of the year. On her shift.

She wasn't stupid enough to think it was a coincidence. She knew he prob-ably needed something from her—that much she could sense.

But she couldn't sense any bad intentions. Only a pure soul, which was odd considering he probably punched holes in people's throats and drained them, like the plastic bag inside a box of wine.

He was different, for sure. But she couldn't say why yet. She needed a bit more information.

And honestly, she wanted to see him again. She wanted to spend time with him.

That realization hit Jo in the gut, and she took her foot off the gas pedal a little as the shock of it set in.

She wanted to spend time with a vampire.

What would her granny think?

John seemed different, though. Then again, Jo had never met a vampire before. At least, he seemed different from what her granny told her vampires were like.

John was well-spoken, and he didn't murder anyone. At least, not in the time he was in the bar. And he was good-looking. Very well-dressed. He abso-lutely didn't belong in the Lakeshore, but there he was.

Jo felt butterflies her stomach, thinking about him standing against the back wall and smiling at her as she stocked the beer coolers. What an odd thing to happen.

As she pulled back into the drive that led to her trailer on the other side of the lake, she resolved to keep her guard up for now. If she saw him again, who knows how he'd behave. And who knew what he was hanging around the lake for.

It could be completely harmless. And it could be nothing but trouble.

And at the end of the day, nothing could come of it. Even if he was ridicu-lously good-looking, she couldn't be with a vampire. Her granny would roll over in her grave.

———

JOHN PULLED his rental Mercedes into the parking garage near his hotel. Why had that gone so well? he wondered.

He'd heard horror stories about Kitchen Lake. Wasn't it the site of the biggest vampire massacre in the United States? And hadn't Jo's grandmother been the one who orchestrated it?

Despite this, he couldn't completely blame her. It wasn't like vampires were heroes, and in many cases, they were quite terrible. Vampires were much like humans in that not everyone adhered to ethical standards, or even thought they were necessary.

And, well. At the end of the day, so many vampires were turned by vampires who just wanted to party forever. It was all about the blood and the lust and the rock 'n' roll lifestyle. And sure, that was out there.

But when John had been turned, it had been because he was dying. The bubonic plague had claimed so much of the community he had once belonged to, his wife and daughter included. It was pure chance that a vampire traveling through had found him and took pity on him.

Pity, or a curse. John wasn't always sure. He had taken this second chance at life, or whatever it was he was up to these days—he didn't really know if being a vampire was being alive—and tried to make sure he was worthy of it. That meant doing right.

He'd started foundations and organizations all over the world. From the outside, he looked like the descendant of some rich man who had inherited these companies. But really, they had always belonged to him, and when there was more than one lifetime to earn money, it was easy to accumulate wealth.

Recently, he'd sold off some East Coast property he'd purchased in the 1850s, using the proceeds to start an afterschool program in the area. It was the least he could do. He didn't need the money, and he always felt guilty that for him to live, it meant that some human had to give up their blood.

But he'd never killed anyone. He was proud of that. A time or two, he'd almost lost control, but to him blood was like alcohol. When he was younger, it held more of an appeal. He could understand why younger vampires liked the idea of it, and why they saw the opportunity to feed as a party.

But he was quite old now, even for a vampire. And it was much simpler to get some blood bags from a trusted source than to have to court his next meal. And honestly, he didn't mind the occasional rabbit or deer either.

He knew that made him an outlier. But he also knew that living any other way wasn't for him.

The humid Oklahoma air clung to his skin as John walked from the parking garage to the lobby of the hotel. He was surprised to find himself thinking about the bartender. Jo. She was absolutely nothing like anything he expected.

For starters, she was nice. He was expecting someone a little rougher around the edges, perhaps the sort of woman who opened beer bottles with her teeth. But Jo seemed nice and capable, and if he was being honest, pretty.

It had been so long since he thought any woman was pretty.

Not that he hadn't been attracted to other women. Hormones and brain chemicals still created sexual attraction, even in vampires. But pretty was different.

It wasn't a biological urge. It was aesthetic appreciation.

It was something he assumed he'd only feel for his late wife for the rest of his existence.

And that Jo was a witch only complicated matters.

It wasn't unheard of for vampires and witches to work together, or even to have relationships. But it was absolutely unheard of for a vampire to come to Kitchen Lake, and for the witch of Kitchen Lake to be open to seeing them come around again.

John didn't know what Jo's motives were, but he didn't sense anything that made him ill at ease. She seemed genuine. Like she wanted him to come back to the bar.

John stepped into the elevator and punched the tenth-floor button.

Of course, he did need something from her. But it wasn't like he was keeping it from her. He knew he was going to be asking a lot, and the spell he needed was likely more than she was used to doing for a client.

He was ready to pay, naturally.

He just hoped Jo was as sweet and welcoming when he asked her for the spell. He was running out of time, and he needed to move the bodies as soon as possible.

5

Jo hated how she could never predict how busy the bar would be. Sure, she could see some things, like what Matt would name his baby or if there'd be tornadoes next spring. She knew when Luke would be in a bad mood, and if she should do a protection spell before her shift because a fight was going to break out on the dance floor.

But try as she might, she could never tell how busy it would be at the bar, and by extension, how much she'd make in tips.

So, as she stood behind her bar, wiping the counter and watching Nattie Rae slowly sway as the Last Chance Teapots (what the band had decided to call themselves that night) played Journey covers, she was a little sad that she probably wouldn't be able to get the roof on her trailer fixed for another month or so.

A few customers came and went, having a beer or two before heading out, and Jo found herself wondering if it was time to find a new job. There were tons of places to work in Oklahoma City, especially if she didn't mind the commute away from the lake. She could make decent money and get health insurance if she applied at a call center or even at a chain restaurant.

Every time she started down this path, she remembered what she was really meant to do. Sure, the money at the Lakeshore Inn was sporadic and not as much as she'd earn anywhere else. But it gave her time and freedom that she wouldn't have with any other job. Plus, the commute meant just driving around the lake.

You're either time rich or money rich, Jo, and time is the one thing you can never get more of. Another gem from her granny that never got old, but she hated feeling the squeeze of not being able to get the money she needed when she needed it.

She put the bar towel down on the bar top and took a deep breath. It was just a sign that it was time to build up her witching business, as her grandmother would call it, and the best way to get started with that was by letting the universe know that was what she wanted.

The bar was slow enough, Matt almost asleep leaning against the wall, just waiting for some patrons to trickle in, and Luke busy in the office. No one was paying any attention to Jo.

Jo took a book of matches from the bowl on the bar top. They were free to patrons and had the bar's terrible logo on the cover. She pulled out one match, lit it, and reached for a highball glass from the shelf behind her. She swirled the match inside, cleansing the vessel. The match wasn't exactly incense, but it was good enough.

Any spell worked in the Lakeshore Inn was more of a Hail Mary than a sure thing, and Jo assumed that Spirit understood that.

She grabbed an orange wedge from the container they kept the garnish in and squeezed it into the highball glass. "For abundance," she whispered. Then, from the tray she used to salt the rims of margarita glasses, she grabbed a pinch of salt. "For clarity," she said, sprinkling it into the orange juice. She double-checked to make sure Luke couldn't see her, then poured a splash of Fireball cinnamon whiskey into the glass. "For success."

She took a quick look all around and knocked it back.

The concoction wasn't great, but most spells weren't. And at the end of the day, she probably should've used real cinnamon and not a cinnamon-flavored whiskey. But Jo believed magic was intentional, and if the intention was there, the universe could meet her halfway.

She put the highball glass into the dishwasher under the bar to hide the evidence, and then tried to concentrate on the intention of the spell.

Ball's in your court, universe, she thought.

Rather than sit around and wait, Jo decided it would be best to clean up behind the bar and maybe do some of the organization she'd been meaning to get to for ages. It wasn't that Jo herself was disorganized. But it wasn't like the Lakeshore Inn was a well-oiled machine either. And it always felt that all the hard work and cleaning Jo did was always undone on her nights off when Hailey or Jason worked the bar. Both of them were good bartenders, but they didn't really take care of the bar itself, and that drove Jo mad.

As her granny had always told her, *If something brings you something good, you have to take care of it*. Even though the bar was nothing special, it was bringing her something good in the form of income. So, using this shift to take care of it a little would be a good way to help nourish her spellwork and keep her occupied until she was done for the night.

She wiped down all the shelves and cleared away all the sticky residue left by spilled beer and mixers. She organized the glass storage and was about to step into the walk-in to wipe it down when she felt a little twinge in her belly. It was like butterflies, but she couldn't tell if it was good or bad. Her senses were strong, but it was always so hard to tell the difference between excitement and anxiety.

She looked toward the door as John walked through.

He smiled at Matt and shook his hand. "Good to see you again," John said.

Jo bit her lip to keep from laughing. She had never seen a patron shake hands with the bouncer before, and she didn't know if she'd ever see it again. If John looked out of his element the day before, his attempts to act natural now didn't really fix it.

As he made his way to the bar, the neon lights from the beer signs on the wall reflected on John's pristine skin. It was odd to see anyone so pale in Oklahoma in the summertime. Even the fairest skin turned a bright shade of sunburnt by this time in the season.

But that wouldn't be possible for John. His skin never saw the sun.

The feeling in her stomach edged toward anxiety. Even though he was charming and a fun fish out of water to watch, Jo needed to remember he was a vampire. And even though he didn't seem to act the way her granny had told her vampires would act, that didn't mean he wasn't capable of doing all those terrible things.

Jo had heard stories about how seductive vampires could be. How they lulled their prey into a false sense of security and took advantage of them. Even though she didn't sense any evil intentions from John, it was best to be on her guard.

As a bartender, the best way to be on her guard with a potentially bad customer was to make them feel at ease and happy.

She took a deep breath, letting the air fill her lungs and then feeling the air go into every part of her body. A quick calming spell for her nerves. Then, she shook her dark hair a little, a quick glamour spell to combat the humidity's effects on her ponytail.

"Hey there, stranger," she said. "Haven't seen you in a while." She smiled and gestured to a seat.

John smiled and approached the bar, taking a seat right in the center. "Good to see you too."

"What'll you have tonight? Another beer?" Jo laughed.

John shook his head and grimaced as he remembered the previous night. "No. I think I'll have a cocktail tonight, if you don't mind."

"Not at all. You look like you may be a bourbon man."

"When the occasion calls for it. And I suppose today is as good an occasion as any. What kind of bourbons do you have?"

"Jack Daniel's and Weller."

"I'll take a Jack and Coke then."

Jo grabbed a highball glass and filled it with ice. She pulled the bottle of Jack from the shelf and turned it upside down, counting out an ounce-and-a-half pour. Then she put the bottle back on the shelf and grabbed the soda gun to top it off with Coke.

She could feel him watching her, but not in a malicious way. It felt more like he was intrigued. She wasn't prey to him. It was more of a curiosity. Maybe a desire to get to know her. There were tinges of other things there, like he intended to return often because he felt she was important somehow. But she also didn't quite feel like he trusted her yet.

She took a beverage napkin from the holder, placing it on the bar in front of him, and then put the drink on the napkin.

He tilted his head. "You know, it occurs to me that you could do a lot of spellwork on patrons here. If someone didn't know you were a witch and wasn't well-versed in cocktail recipes, it wouldn't be too hard for you to slip something in."

"Are you accusing me of something, John?" Jo put her hands on her hips and smiled playfully. But her guard was up.

John laughed. "Not at all. But I wouldn't put it past you if you needed to calm a patron or protect one from a leering admirer."

Jo relaxed a little. "Well, I may have done that a time or two. But to tell the truth, we don't necessarily have the best ingredients for spellwork here. The salt and citrus are fine, but any of the herbs I need are mixed in with liquor, and that can always make a spell a little wonky. I do envy those fancy mixologists at the hipster bars who have dried lavender and rosemary to use in their drinks. But no one wants a fancy cocktail at the lake."

"Cheers," John said, picking up his drink and taking a sip. "And fancy or not, this is delightful."

"Well, it's hard to screw up a bourbon and Coke."

John laughed. "I suppose you're right."

The band finished a song, and Nattie Rae howled in delight from the dance floor.

"Is she here every night?" John asked.

Jo nodded. "Most of the time. She's been coming here since before I was old enough to drink, back when Luke's dad owned the bar."

"Interesting," John said, taking another sip.

Jo couldn't decide if what she wanted to ask was rude or not, but she couldn't hold the question back any longer. "Can I ask why you've decided to come here?"

"What, you don't think I fit in?"

Jo laughed. "You absolutely do not, and that's a compliment."

John looked down at the bar top and swirled the ice in his glass. "Well, I need a spell. It's a complicated one, and I'm willing to pay as much as you charge for it."

Jo could feel the butterflies in her stomach transforming into a warmth, like a fire. Less than an hour since her abundance spell, and here he was, coming to give her money. She wanted to squeal with happiness, but she also didn't want to seem like she was desperate for work. She'd be able to fix her roof before the fall rains hit after all.

"As long as you aren't looking for curses or hexes, I'm your witch."

"Well, forgive me for seeming a little forward," John said. Jo could've sworn he was blushing, but maybe it was just the glow of the lights on his skin. She couldn't imagine a vampire blushing. "I have to ask this after knowing you for such a short time. And I'm well aware that you're a professional, and so you're probably used to requests like this. So, forgive me if I seem a little timid."

Jo leaned in. "No worries, John. No one here is listening, and I assure you that you can't be asking for the most embarrassing spell I've ever done. I did all manner of terribly cringe-inducing spells when I was a teenager. I assure you, I've seen and done it all."

John cleared his throat. "Sure, and again, you're the professional and this is all so new to me. You see, I need a daylight spell."

Jo stared at him, stock still. She felt as if the floor had dropped out from under her. The silence hung heavy between them for a long moment, and she realized John was beginning to panic.

"Daylight spell, eh? Well. I've never done one before, but I do know how to do it. Umm, you do know that, well, you know we'll have to . . ."

"Sleep together? Yes. That's why I felt so odd asking after just meeting you yesterday. In any other situation, I would think a formal courtship would be in order."

Jo laughed at that, finally feeling like she was coming back to herself as the shock of the request wore off. "Well, that's kind and very generous of you to assume that I'm the sort of girl who deserves a formal courtship. But I think we can make this all happen."

John nodded, visibly relieved. "Please don't think less of me for being so forward."

"Not at all."

"Also, please don't think I'm trying to be insulting when I say that if there's any other way to generate the necessary energy for the spell, I'd be fine with it. Which isn't to say that you aren't a very nice woman. And quite lovely. Any man would be honored to have the pleasure. Which isn't to say that it's about the pleasure." John looked around the bar, flustered, then picked up his drink and took a long gulp. "I'm sorry. I'm saying that if you don't want to do the spell the way that I've understood it to be written, I won't be offended if you can do it another way."

Jo wasn't sure what to think. How had the one prude vampire in existence found her, and asked for the one spell that actually required sex? And was she finding his flustered embarrassment to be cute?

She smiled warmly, placing her hand on his. "I can definitely do this spell, John. But you should know there is no other way. The daylight spell exists to allow vampires to walk in the daylight. It's like giving you human life. So, you have to engage in the symbolic act of giving human life to make it work. There's no way around it."

John exhaled and his jaw unclenched.

Jo went on. "And like I said, I've never done it before, but I know what's involved. The good thing is that it's not one of those spells where anyone can get hurt in the process, and there won't be any backfire. But if it doesn't work, we'll just have to try it again. And I'm not saying that to scare you off. I just want you to know that it may not be as simple and straightforward as one try. There's always a learning curve with a higher-power spell."

Was he blushing again?

"I'm not saying this to trick you into sleeping with me multiple times." She took a deep breath and tilted her head to the side. She was trying to be reassuring and realistic. Why was the idea of having sex so distressing to this vampire? "I just want to be upfront with you. I feel confident that I can figure it out, and we'll probably be done after the first time. But just in case." She paused, trying to find the right words. "Basically, I don't want you to pay money for something if you don't know what you're getting into. And you're the first vampire I've ever met, so know that there's a learning curve there too."

John finally relaxed, and with a smile he looked up at Jo. "Thank you for being honest."

She smiled back. "It's always best to be. Lies are like bad spells. You speak them into existence, and crooked words create crooked results. The more honest we are upfront, the easier it will be."

This seemed to put John at ease. "That's the most direct thing a witch has ever told me."

"You know a lot of witches?"

"No. But before I came to you, I went to New Orleans to see if I could get this spell. And so many of the witches I talked to didn't seem to know what they were talking about. They said it required ingredients like lemons and yellow crayons and a light bulb."

Jo laughed so loudly that Matt turned toward the bar to make sure everything was okay.

"There are a lot of fakes in New Orleans for the tourists. And so, when you mentioned the daylight spell, they probably didn't know you were a vampire or what the spell did. They just told you they would need a lot of things that reminded them of daylight. It's a pretty common practice. I respect their hustle, but it's not a real spell."

"Yes. Well, when I asked one of the witches about the other component," he said, raising his eyebrows, as if he couldn't mention sex again or he might explode, "she almost slapped me and told me I should at least buy her dinner first."

Jo laughed again. "No wonder you were so worried about asking tonight." John nodded.

"Well, I have the day off tomorrow, and I have a friend who owns a metaphysical shop. We should be able to get a few things from him after dark, if you'd like to come with me to get the ingredients."

"I'd love to," John said, his eyes lighting up.

Jo couldn't figure out why he was so excited to spend more time with her. Or why, for that matter, she was so excited to get to see him again on her day off.

"Awesome. Here's my number," she said, scrawling it on a bar napkin with a pen she kept by the register. "Just text me or call me when you're ready to leave your hotel. And I'll arrange it with my friend. He's pretty chill and he'll be really excited to meet a vampire."

"Perfect," John said. "And as a matter of payment," he began.

Jo's stomach dropped out. She'd forgotten about payment. And for whatever reason, she always felt so much stress when it came to talking about prices and why she charged what she charged. And if she were being honest, she had no idea what this spell was worth. She didn't have time to research, and she didn't want to shortchange herself. She needed a new roof, and that wasn't going to be cheap.

"Even the most fake New Orleans witch wanted to charge me a thousand dollars. So, if a fake spell is worth that, the real thing is worth so much more. Is fifteen thousand dollars okay?"

Jo's jaw dropped. She had never asked for so much money.

"If that's not enough, please tell me," John went on. "I'd hate to insult you."

"I don't think there's a single Oklahoma witch who has ever made that much for a spell."

"Well, it seems like you may not be charging for the actual market value here. We'll say fifteen thousand, but if there are any complications, just let me know and we can adjust it." John watched Jo expectantly. "Is it a deal?"

It took a minute for Jo's ears to stop ringing. She would be able to fix her roof and maybe take fewer shifts at the bar to actually build up her business.

"It's a deal," she said, reaching across the bar to shake John's hand.

6

JOHN SAT IN A WINGBACK CHAIR IN THE CORNER OF HIS HOTEL ROOM. THE curtains were drawn, and even though there was a flatscreen TV mounted on the wall across from the bed, he didn't turn it on to pass the time.

John knew he didn't need a girlfriend. Or a woman of any kind, really. He'd known love once, the pure kind of love that really mattered. His wife had been beautiful, smart, and capable. She'd been everything he thought he ever needed, until she gave him his perfect daughter.

He thought about them every day, and it didn't matter that he hadn't seen them in over three hundred years. They still meant the world to him. That's what this whole daylight spell was for, wasn't it? So he could get back to France quickly and move their remains before a developer dug up their graves and sifted them into whatever dirt pile they created while building a new tourist attraction.

He knew that their souls weren't with the bodies anymore, but still. It mattered to him. It was the least he could do to honor them.

And even though he hadn't quite been celibate since then, he had never started a relationship. He couldn't do that to them. Nor did he need one. He was quite fine on his own, making real estate deals and setting up nonprofits. He felt good about the work he did, and he didn't need anything else.

Except there was an odd feeling in his stomach since he met Jo, and it wouldn't go away. Maybe there was more out there.

She was so young.

Well, not so young. She was obviously in her thirties. And it wasn't exactly her fault that he'd been turned immortal. He never understood the appropriate age for propriety when it came to vampire-human relationships. But he also never felt the need to understand it, since he wasn't going to be joining any of those relationships.

Well, not in the traditional sense.

He supposed the nature of the spell required that he'd have a bit of a relationship with Jo.

She was so unlike other women who knew what he was.

It wasn't like he flaunted it. And it wasn't exactly like most humans actually believed vampires existed. But every once in a while, a young woman would seek him out, looking for the sort of relationship promised in salacious novels where some roguish vampire lustily turns a young woman into a vampire, and then they have hours of unbridled, passionate sex.

One such young woman had found him in New Orleans. John had politely tried to listen as she explained the plot of her favorite TV show, but he felt bad for making her cry when he declined.

Jo was different. She didn't seem to care that he was a vampire. At least, not in that way. He could tell that she was still not completely sure of him, and didn't always trust him. Which was smart. He wished more humans were wary of vampires.

She worked hard, and from what he'd heard, she was descended from a line of very powerful witches. He had no idea why she was bartending, though, if that was the case.

But he also supposed it was none of his business.

He didn't want to get more involved than he had to. And even though he loved the way her legs looked in her cutoff shorts, he told himself he absolutely wouldn't be thinking of her after the spell was over and he had moved his family's remains.

It was a business deal. Nothing more. Even if she was pretty and kind.

He reached for his phone and sent Jo a message.

―――

THE NEXT DAY, Jo went through her herb stores, checking what she had hanging to dry and what was already stored in jars. She had converted the trailer's extra bedroom into her office. As much of an office as it could be.

The closet was full of herbs, candles, incense, and crystals. There was an old kitchen table from a thrift store in the center of the room, with a few mismatched chairs tucked in around it, and in the corner was a bookshelf loaded with almanacs and her granny's old diaries and spell books.

In the opposite corner of the room was an altar made from an old secretary desk, where Jo left offerings and did her daily tarot readings.

Sure, she wanted to make it a bit nicer, but there wasn't money for that at the moment. After her granny died, Jo found out just how bad she had been at bookkeeping. The trailer was paid off, free and clear, but a few debts and property taxes hadn't been paid in years. Jo couldn't handle the thought of losing the place. There had always been a Bonneville witch at Kitchen Lake, and she wasn't going to be the one to stop that tradition.

So, she'd used all her savings to get the property taxes up to date. And once that was done, it seemed like all the repairs started rolling in. A busted pipe. Mold growing under the trailer. A busted window—and, of course, the roof.

Jo had friends who worked in construction, and they'd helped her do what they could. But the roof needed to be entirely replaced, and that would cost money Jo didn't have.

That's why she found herself taking inventory for a daylight spell that would change everything for her.

She put down the shopping list for the metaphysical shop, suddenly unsure about the whole thing. Was she doing the right thing helping a vampire like this? She had no choice though—she couldn't bear to lose the trailer. John seemed like a good guy, nothing like the vicious murdering vampires her granny had dealt with before she was born. John would never do anything like that. Would he?

Jo couldn't imagine what she would do if she were in the same situation her granny had been in. It was the summer of 1978, and three little girls had been murdered at a family campout at the lake. The news reported the slayings as the work of a serial killer, but anyone who knew vampires could tell what had really happened.

That was when Gran had banished them, using a powerful type of magic that destroyed one of them on impact, made another go so crazy he walked out into the sun in the middle of the day, and caused the other to walk to the bottom of the lake, where he probably still sits, immortal and decomposing, to this day.

No vampires came back to Kitchen Lake, or Oklahoma City, after that.

But John had. He was different. Jo didn't know why he needed that spell, and she felt guilty for not asking. Shouldn't she do some kind of due diligence? Gran had always told her to watch out for vampires, and here she was, just offering up a spell to one.

"You know," Jo continued, "I don't feel anything bad with this one. He has good intentions. And you always taught me to follow my gut instinct. My intuition is stronger than ever, and I think this is the right thing to do."

She pulled a few candles from the closet and set them up on the table. "I know vampires once almost ruined Kitchen Lake. But I think this one may help us fix up our home."

What was she so worried about anyway? In the end, she'd do the spell because everything in her told her it would be fine. It wasn't like she was starting a relationship with the man.

Sure, she had to sleep with him. But it wasn't like he was her first one-night stand. It was all part of the work she did. That was the thing with being a witch. You had to find energy and work with it. And in some cases, you had to create the energy. Though usually that was by lighting a fire or through breathing practices.

This was going to be just like a basic breathing practice, she told herself.

It had to be. She didn't have time for a relationship, especially not with a vampire. She had work, and a business to build. At the end of the day, her granny had instilled in her just enough prejudice against vampires to keep her from ever falling in love with one.

Jo took down a spell book from the bookshelf in the corner and laid it on the table by the candles. All they needed were the ingredients and a full moon.

Maybe after the roof was fixed, she could finally take down the fake wood paneling on the walls too. And trade out the old avocado green laminate countertops for some butcher block too…

Jo felt her phone vibrate in the back pocket of her shorts. She reached for it and read the message.

Good evening, Jo. The sun officially sets at 8:03 p.m. this evening, and I'll be ready to leave the hotel around 8:20. Can I come pick you up?

Jo grinned. "Looks like I'm finally going to get to see the inside of a Mercedes, Gran!"

———

Jo HAD FUSSED with her hair more than she cared to admit before John showed up. He'd only ever seen her at work, when her hair was pulled back into a messy bun. But she told herself she wasn't doing it for him. She was doing it for herself, so she could feel confident in doing this spell. Like someone buying a brand-new suit for a job interview, Jo wanted to feel like she could do this, and she wanted John to sense she believed in herself. So, she was going to do whatever it took to radiate confidence.

She riffled through her wardrobe, pretty slim to begin with since she never went anywhere with a dress code, and finally decided on a blue floral sundress with spaghetti straps. It always made her feel pretty, one of the few things she owned that didn't always smell like stale beer from the bar.

She slid on a pair of sandals and slapped on some lip gloss.

Jo didn't know if this was the sort of professional image she wanted to project, but it would have to do for now. Someday, when she was rolling in money from her hard work, she'd go out and buy a wardrobe that made her look like Stevie Nicks. Until then, she'd wear the best clothes she owned, even if they were sales rack dresses from two years ago.

John pulled up to the trailer at quarter to nine, and Jo suddenly felt out of place in her own home. The second-hand bits and pieces she normally loved now made her feel inadequate. She had always been very proud of her trailer. It was hers. Her grandmother had bought it with the money she earned from her craft. But she had never invited anyone with real money to the place. Hell, she'd never met anyone with real money. Even though her home was clean and cozy, and just the way she liked it, she felt nothing but shame. Before John could walk up to the door, she grabbed her bag and stepped out onto the front porch.

John was making his way up the walkway, and he smiled at Jo as she locked the front door and turned to him.

"Thanks for coming to pick me up," Jo said, trying to regain the sense of confidence she had before the shame took over.

"My pleasure," John said. "It's the least I could do. I know it's your night off, so I'm sorry to be taking it away for more work purposes."

He led Jo to his car and opened the passenger door for her.

Jo's cheeks flushed. It felt like a date. Though, if she were being honest, she'd never been on a date where a man opened the door for her, nor did she think she'd ever like that. It seemed so old fashioned and silly when some men did it. But when John did it, it seemed right.

As John helped her into the car and gently closed the door, it occurred to her that maybe John was old fashioned because he was insanely old. She tried not to giggle at that.

John got in and started the engine. The dashboard lit up with various screens and displays, and the radio started playing. Even though Jo had seen this particular car model in a recent car commercial, she still couldn't believe how sleek and futuristic the whole thing looked.

"Is the store far?" John asked, turning the radio down.

"Not at all," Jo said, giving him directions to the shop.

They made small talk for the fifteen-minute drive, and Jo felt herself at ease in his presence. That wasn't something she was expecting. It never seemed like she needed to have her guard up. Try as she might, she searched her intuition for any sort of deeper feelings she may be missing, but there were none. John appeared to be exactly who he said he was.

The lights in the shop were off when they pulled into the parking lot, but Jo had told Brian that they'd be there around nine. He was very excited to meet John.

John insisted on opening Jo's door again, and as he helped her out of the car, Jo thought it was probably important to mention that Brian was going to be weird.

"John, I just want to warn you about something."

"Oh?" he said, offering his arm to Jo as if they were a couple promenading around the castle gardens in a regency romance.

"Brian's a really good guy. But he's going to be weird, and probably ask you all sorts of questions about being a vampire. I warned him that he needs to be civil, but he's also the sort of person that doesn't understand how to act under normal circumstances. So, if he says anything that offends you, please know that he doesn't mean it. He's just, well, weird."

John laughed. "Noted. How weird?"

"Well, when he introduces himself, he's going to say his name is 'Brian the Warlock.'"

Jo led John to the back of the building, an old stand-alone structure that looked more like it should be a small gas station instead of a metaphysical shop. When they reached the steel back door, Jo knocked a very specific pattern.

"Secret knock?"

"Yes, but I assure you it isn't necessary. Brian just prefers this."

The door opened, and the two of them stepped inside.

A buzzing fluorescent light hummed above them, bathing the stockroom in a sickly glow. In front of them stood a man about five and a half feet tall with a blond hairstyle suited more to a 1980s hair metal band. He wore a black button-down shirt starched crisp, and a pair of Wrangler jeans with red cowboy boots.

"Sister!" he said, wrapping Jo in a hug that she didn't immediately reciprocate. "It's good to see you."

"Good to see you too, Brian. This is John." Jo stepped back and gestured to John.

John bowed his head slightly. "A pleasure to meet you."

Brian smiled and wrapped his arms around John. "Good to meet you, brother. My name is Brian the Warlock, and I'm happy to help you in any way that I can."

John, for his part, accepted the hug even though Jo could tell he wasn't happy about it.

Brian led them from the stockroom into the store, making idle conversation about the position of the stars and occasionally asking if they felt a presence.

Jo hated how Brian tended to put on a show, but that was his style. And even though he was very knowledgeable about herbs, crystals, and rituals, Jo knew he couldn't sense anything. His shop was as spiritless as they came, but he wanted so badly to feel the things that Jo could. And for that, Jo felt pity for him and put up with his behavior.

"What can I get for you?" Brian asked, stepping behind the counter.

John stood close to Jo as he glanced around the shop.

Jo procured a list from her bag. "Okay. Do you have dried mistletoe? I have some, but it's not dry enough yet and I need to be able to burn it."

"We do!" Brian turned to a shelf behind the register. It was covered in various jars filled with herbs and greens. "How much?"

"A half-ounce should do. But I also need some mountain ash bark. Do you have any of that, or do you know where to get it?" Jo gave as much detail as she needed, and nothing more.

"Hmmm." Brian mumbled to himself, deep in thought, as he measured out the mistletoe. "That only grows on the East Coast, right?"

"Mostly."

"Not a very common spell component." He flipped his mullet as he put the jar back on the shelf behind him.

Jo didn't say anything. It was only a matter of time before he figured out what spell they were doing, and then he would make it weird.

Brian turned to John, his eyes wide. "You need a daylight spell."

Before John could speak, Jo said, "Yes, but that's really none of your business."

Brian put his hands up in mock defense. "You're right. You're right. It's interesting, though. Vampires haven't been around here in years, and then this one comes out of nowhere to ask the witch of Kitchen Lake for help. Is this a trap?"

"A trap?" John asked, more confused than ever.

"Yes. A trap. Are you seeking vengeance against Jo and her grandmother for the banishment?"

"No, I would—"

"Because I'm quite skilled. Jo is a trusting soul, bless her heart," Brian said, trying to pull himself up to be a little taller. "But I won't tolerate anyone coming to my city to do harm. I'm a very powerful warlock. And while you seem like a good vampire, I can't risk anything happening. We have a reputation to uphold."

"You do?" Jo asked, too confused by the last statement to be offended by what he'd insinuated.

"Yes, Jo. We're very powerful, and if you were taken advantage of in any way, it would reflect poorly on the craft-practicing community here."

"Taken advantage of?" Jo put her hands on her hips.

"Jo, sweetie. This man is trying to sleep with you."

Again, Jo could've sworn she saw John blush.

"Brian, you need to stop. I know what kind of spell I'm doing. I know what it requires. And I'm well aware of what I'll be doing. I've already vetted John, and you don't have anything to worry about." Jo wanted nothing more than to be out of that shop. She would definitely think twice about shopping there in the future, especially when she could just get everything online these days.

Brian reached across the counter and put his hand on Jo's shoulder. "I'm just looking out for you."

"A noble gesture," John said, regaining his composure. "But I assure you my motives are pure. There's no impropriety here. I simply need to be able to travel to France, and quickly, which would mean hopping on a plane, and that would expose me to some sunlight."

Brian sighed, and shook his head at Jo like he knew something she didn't. He grabbed a stepstool and put it in front of his herb shelf. He climbed to the top and carefully retrieved a jar. "How much?" he asked Jo.

"A few strips of bark is all I really need."

He pulled out the bark with some tweezers and put it in a plastic bag. "Anything else?"

"That'll do." Jo felt her skin crawl, her discomfort growing by the second. She wanted to be out of there fast. It wasn't her intuition going off. Just plain awkwardness.

Brian rang up the items and before Jo could pay, John handed over his credit card. "Allow me."

After all was said and done, Brian escorted them through the stockroom and out the back door.

Once they were both in the car and safely on the road, Jo exhaled.

"I'm sorry. But all in all, that was way less weird than I was expecting."

John just laughed. "He seems nice enough. You're right though, very weird. He just has a crush on you."

Jo laughed. "Yeah. He thinks I should date him so we can create some kind of magical empire. But he's absolutely not my type."

"What is your type?" John asked. "Not that it's my business. I just can't seem to figure you out. You're a smart and capable witch, but you work in a . . . very interesting bar. And you're good at dealing with odd people—I've seen that tonight and at the bar. It makes me wonder what you're looking for."

Jo shrugged. "I don't think I have a type. All the women in my family who practiced magic were always single. Or if they were married, it didn't last. I don't think you can practice magic and have the happily ever after."

"And so you just wish to practice?"

"Mostly," Jo said. "I'm working on building the business side of things. And making my granny's trailer work for me. Redo a few things here and there to work better with how I practice."

John nodded. "I see."

"I've done a lot, though I guess you can't really tell if you didn't see it before. I wish I would've taken photos. There's a lot more I want to do. But one step at a time, I guess."

"I'd love to see," John said. "I've never been in a witch's workshop, you know."

The feelings of shame Jo felt earlier bubbled up again, but she pushed them aside. It was a witch's workshop. It was hers. And it had been Gran's too. So why shouldn't she be proud of it? It wasn't fancy, but real witches never were. And what did she care about expensive stuff anyhow? Her work spoke for itself.

"Let's go."

7

"So, what exactly is it about the lake?" John asked. They were standing at the front deck of the trailer.

"What do you mean?" Jo dug her keys out of her purse. Most of her embarrassment and shame were gone, but still. She wasn't sure about showing her house to this man. She was proud of it, but anyone who could casually suggest fifteen thousand dollars for a spell wasn't the type to think her trailer was cute.

"Well, why did your family choose it?" he said.

"I don't know if it was a choice, really. Our ancestors were relocated to Oklahoma by the government back in the 1800s, and this is the same land allotment from back then."

"Oh, I didn't know. I just assumed you were French."

"We are. Some of the tribes in the midwestern part of the country traded with French fur trappers, and some of the French fur trappers married into the tribes," Jo said, unlocking the door.

She set her purse on a small table by the door. "Would you like something to drink?" she called over her shoulder as she walked toward the kitchen.

John stood in the doorway, smiling politely.

"Oh, I'm so sorry," Jo said, coming back toward the front door. "Please, come in."

John laughed. "I know it's silly. But it's part of the curse of being a vampire."

"I didn't even think about it," Jo said. "You were able to enter the bar and the store, so I assumed it wasn't real."

John shook his head as he crossed the threshold and entered the trailer. "Both are public places where it's implied that all are welcome. Unless there's a specific spell done on the building to prevent me from entering, I can always go to a public place."

"Noted," Jo said. "How about a drink?"

"You aren't going to give me a beer, are you?"

"No. In fact, I can make you a really good drink here."

Jo led him through the living area and into the small kitchen, motioning for him to take a seat at one of the bar stools next to the laminate counter. She turned to the small pantry cabinet next to the refrigerator and got out a bottle of bourbon and put it on the counter. She plucked a few sprigs of mint growing in pots over the kitchen sink. Then, from a fruit bowl on the little dining table, she grabbed a few limes.

She set to work, with John watching her intently.

Jo got two glasses from a cabinet and dropped in some mint. She cut the limes, squeezing the juice of half a lime over the mint, then sprinkled a bit of sugar from the uncovered sugar bowl over the mix. She then reached into a drawer and pulled out what looked like a thick dowel rod and used it to smash the mint leaves.

"What's that?" John asked.

"A muddler. It gets all the good stuff out of the leaves."

John was taking it all in. "Is this some kind of mojito, but with bourbon?"

Jo shrugged as she continued fixing the drinks. "And a few other things. This is something my granny used to make, even for me, when I was a teenager."

"Even with the alcohol?"

"Always. It was part of a ritual. She said all good spiritual practices needed some kind of holy alcohol. The church has wine, and she always preferred bourbon. So, that's what we used. She mixed these drinks on special occasions, like New Moon ceremonies or holidays like the Summer Solstice. It was always nice to have, and there's a lot of good stuff in it. I think if we have a couple, it will make it easier to get to work. You know, it's the whole symbolic gesture of breaking bread or sharing drinks together."

"Makes sense," John said, fascinated as he watched her work.

Jo reached into the fridge, retrieving a knob of ginger. She cut off a small piece and used a spoon to peel off the skin. "The daylight spell is kind of a lot. I know I can do it, but it will require a lot of you too. You have to basically lay your soul bare and tell the truth about why it's needed. It's like a symbolic rebirth, and you have to absolve yourself of sins."

"Sins?" John asked, his brow furrowing.

"Not like in the churchy sense of it. But in the sense of all the stuff that weighs on you. You can't carry that with you into the light. You have to give up those things to the darkness, and only then will you be able to move into the sun."

"Oh." John was quiet.

Jo kept working, grabbing a zester from another drawer and zesting the ginger into the glasses with the lime and mint. "I want you to know that I don't have to hear it, you know. When you confess and get rid of your sins. I can leave you to get it off your chest. But it'll have to be done before we, well. You know."

Finally, she filled each glass with ice on top of the mint-and-ginger mixture and poured about three fingers of bourbon for each of them. She put a glass on the countertop in front of John, then took a sip of her own.

"The best part of mixing drinks at home is that I can have one too."

John smiled, picking up the glass. He took a moment to smell the drink. It was fresh and fragrant, the alcohol of the bourbon subtle but still there. It fit the moment perfectly. He took a sip, relishing the taste as each of the flavors came forth. Heady and refreshing. It was the best drink he'd had in a while.

Jo smiled. "You like it?"

"I do."

John insisted on a full tour of the trailer. He wanted to know where Jo did her work, and he was pleased by how important family was to her. Though she had been slowly changing up her grandmother's trailer, it was clear that she did it in a way that still honored the family tradition.

They toured the kitchen and the living area that Jo had worked hard to brighten, the refinished furniture and vintage finds transforming it into more of an artist's loft in a big city than a trailer at a lake. Jo showed him the workshop and explained all the plans she had for it. How she desperately wanted to get rid of the fake wood paneling.

Her priority right now was the roof, she explained. Even though it was livable, she didn't want to spend another rainy fall placing buckets and pots in various corners of the house as the roof sprung new leaks.

She even gave him a glance of her bedroom.

That flush crept across his pale cheeks again. Though she felt wicked for doing it, she thought it was also quite fun.

From there, she led him out the front door and onto the deck and down to the yard on the side of the trailer, where she kept her garden. From there, she showed him the rows of tomato plants, jalapeños, cucumbers, and strawberries. She pointed to places where she'd plant garlic later in the year, and where she'd probably try to grow some potatoes in the next season.

Beyond the garden she pointed to the woods near the lake, where she often foraged from different ivies and barks that she used in spells.

"This is all incredible," John said, holding his almost empty glass and admiring the view.

"It's not much, but it's mine. And it's home."

"No, really. I can't believe you've done all this."

"Well, my granny started it, really. I'm just carrying on the legacy."

"That's important," John said. "Can I see the lake?"

Jo smiled, wondering if it would live up to his expectations. But he was there, and it didn't make sense to say no, even if the small body of water wasn't much to write home about. "Sure. It's not much, and it's manmade, but it's pretty at night."

Together they walked along a worn stone pathway that one of Jo's uncles had laid down for her grandmother years ago, through a grove of trees and tall grass, until they were at the shore. The water level was low from the summer drought, but by the time fall rolled in, the rains would have the lake full again. They settled into a pair of cheap lawn chairs, Jo sitting across from him.

"I'm glad I met you," John said, taking the last sip of his drink. "I can tell you do this for the love of the work. And because it's your birthright. It must make your grandmother proud."

Jo smiled, taking another sip. "I hope so. It's something I always knew I wanted to do, and it's an honor to do it. It was always so important to my family."

"I had a family once," John said quietly. "Before I was turned." He paused, staring at the melting ice in his glass. "It was a long time ago. Three hundred years. I had a wife and a daughter."

"What were their names?"

"My wife's name was Thérèse and my daughter was Giselle."

"Oh, are they still in France?"

"Yes. But not in the way you're thinking. We were in our home, dying of the bubonic plague in 1721. We all went to sleep one night, thinking it was our last. I woke up to find that I'd been turned. They were not."

"I'm so sorry."

"Don't be. I've made peace with it, and death is normal. I used to think about how I wished I had died with them. But it wasn't meant to be."

"How did it happen, if you don't mind me asking?"

"My turning? Well, it was quite boring in comparison to what you see in the movies. As I lay there dying with my wife and daughter, a group of vampires, who were roving the plague-ridden city looking for people to save, found me. They wanted to turn as many as they could, believing they were saving humanity. The man who turned me truly believed he was giving me a second chance at life. I suppose he was. But it's been lifetimes."

"What happened to your wife and daughter?" Jo asked.

"They were both dead when he found us, so he could only turn me. I buried them under the shade of a tree, where I'd kissed my wife for the first time and where my daughter liked to play. It reminded me of them."

Jo was quiet for a moment. "So, the daylight spell. It's for them, isn't it?"

John nodded slowly. "Yes. There's a developer who plans to build some sort of spa hotel retreat in that location. The tree will be dug up, so I wanted to move their bodies to make sure their remains don't wind up in the foundations of some hotel. I know they're no longer there, not in the spiritual sense, but I need to do this. To honor them."

"I understand."

JOHN FELT LIGHTER. He hadn't spoken the concern out loud. To anyone. He'd carried the weight of it all for so long. His guilt for being turned while his wife and daughter died. The stress of knowing he had to do something to save what was left of them.

And all the while, Jo just listened. She heard what he had to say, and she understood. That was something he never thought he'd experience again. A person he could confide in who would understand.

A woman who valued family and legacy and worked hard to preserve it.

He watched as Jo stood from her lawn chair and held out her hand to him. He took it and stood, looking into her eyes the whole time.

"Let's go in," Jo said. She started to pull away, but John drew her back toward him. He slipped his hand around the side of her neck, gently cradling her head as he tilted it up toward him.

"Thank you," he said, bringing his mouth to Jo's, slow at first, a simple kiss. He brought both his hands to her waist, pulling her in closer. "What did you put in this drink?" he whispered against her lips.

"Nothing you didn't see," Jo said. "But it's a spell on its own, for clarity of mind and finding joy." She unceremoniously dropped her glass on the ground, the vessel shattering on the dry earth. Jo put both her hands on the sides of his neck. "My granny made it to help celebrate and bring people together."

"Did she now?"

Jo chose not to mention that the spell could be augmented or intensified by how the recipients felt about each other. At the moment, other things seemed more pressing. She kissed him slowly, deeply. John pulled her in closer, pressing his body against hers.

"I haven't felt like this in literal centuries," John said, moving his mouth from her lips to her ear, softly kissing the lobe.

"I think you've just unburdened yourself. You don't have the shame and guilt anymore. You let it go." She smiled. "You've already started the spell."

John pulled back suddenly, as if he'd done something wrong. "Is that a problem?"

Jo laughed. "No. It's not like a recipe. Time isn't a factor other than what needs to be done on the full moon. We're just ahead of the game now."

John leaned in again, his hands wandering from her waist to the small of her back, dropping lower. "Then there's no harm in practicing a little, is there?"

Jo took his hand and began to walk. "Follow me."

8

Jo PULLED HIM INTO THE HOUSE IN A BLUR. ONCE THEY HAD CROSSED THE threshold, she unbuttoned his shirt and stripped it off him, dropping it in the middle of the living room as they made their way toward her bed.

As they crossed the threshold of her room, John pulled her close, both his arms wrapping around her body and grabbing for the zipper of her dress, his body pressed against hers.

Jo's breath caught in her throat.

"Is this okay?" John asked, his mouth trailing from her earlobe down the side of her neck.

Jo's skin tingled all over. Goosebumps raised on her skin. "Yes," she said, her breath a ragged whisper.

He pulled the zipper down slowly with his right hand, and with the left, he slid the strap of her dress down off her shoulder, placing a kiss at the spot where her shoulder and neck met. When the zipper was completely undone, he pulled her dress off, taking a moment to look at her. He reached around her back and undid her strapless bra, letting it fall to the floor. Pressing his body against hers, he pushed her into the wall.

"Can I . . ." he began, relishing the exposed flesh of her neck as he tilted her head to the side. He gently caressed her skin, trailing his fingertips in circles.

"What?" Jo asked breathlessly. She was so turned on that there wasn't anything she wouldn't agree to.

"Can I bite you?"

She shivered, her desire mixing with fear. He was a vampire after all. Was this how she was going to die, in the home of the woman who had raised her to hate vampires, after a vampire drained her blood?

Before she could say anything, John went on. "I won't drink your blood, just taste. I promise. It's just . . . I . . ." he leaned in closer to whisper in her ear. "I usually drink blood from blood banks or animals. Feeding off humans is more of an erotic experience."

She searched her mind, and his, and found that he was telling the truth. The way he asked made it seem so harmless. And she knew that if he didn't completely drain her, and then make her drink his blood, she wouldn't be turned.

"Yes," she whispered.

He playfully nibbled her earlobe, then let his mouth trail down the side of her neck.

She felt a small stab, then his tongue against her skin where a small drop of blood slowly trickled down.

"Jesus," he cursed, pulling her away from the wall and throwing her down on the bed. He pulled off his pants and lay down next to her, bringing his mouth back over the same spot on her neck as his hand made its way down her torso and into the waistband of her panties.

His fingers searched before entering her, and she gasped. John sat up slightly, using his other hand to grab hers and pin them over her head. He brought his mouth to hers, kissing her greedily.

Jo felt out of breath, and out of her mind. She could only feel what John was doing to her, and she couldn't think straight. As her arousal grew, she moaned through a kiss, causing John to pull back.

He stared down at her, his eyes dark. Then he smiled.

With vampire speed, he let her hands go and gently pulled off her panties, and before Jo could realize what was going on he was between her legs. John held her wrists above her head, pinning her in place before entering her.

She moaned again, wrapping her legs around his waist as he brought his mouth down on her breast, taking a nipple in his mouth.

John thrust into her, over and over again, his eyes looking feral as he gazed into hers.

"John, I—" she said, gasping. "Oh God, I'm—" but before she could finish her sentence, he sent her over the edge, following directly behind her.

———

JOHN DIDN'T QUITE SLEEP, even though he could've. He lay next to Jo, her breathing quiet and calm. He had been in control of himself through it all last night. But then why had he slept with her?

He'd laid out his guilt and put it into the world, and that had felt like a release. He'd been grateful for it, even. Especially if it was part of the spell. But what had gotten into him?

Jo was a nice woman. That he couldn't deny. And he loved everything about the life she was building for herself. But how had he forgotten Thérèse and Giselle?

It was like he'd let them die all over again while he got another chance to live his life.

No, that wasn't quite it. Even though there were feelings of guilt and shame, this still felt right. Like a step he was meant to be taking. But feeling like it was meant to be only made it worse in his mind.

He had betrayed them again.

John couldn't just up and leave. He still needed the spell. And knowing that he needed Jo, even though she was the reason he had betrayed his family, made him angry. It was a slow, simmering sort of anger, the kind he could put in the back of his mind and still do what he needed to do.

He needed to get out of Oklahoma and as far away from Kitchen Lake as possible, as soon as possible. He couldn't be tempted like this again. He owed that to his family.

He sat up and reached for his pants next to the bed, grabbing his phone from the pocket. It was a quarter till six. He had enough time to gather his things and get back to the hotel. He couldn't stay at Jo's place, even if he wanted to. She had far too many windows, and all her curtains were sheer.

The thought crossed his mind that he should just get up and leave. He wanted to. But a part of him wanted to stay and cuddle up with Jo until the last possible minute.

What had she done to him? It had to be a spell. It likely wasn't, and the blame for forgetting his family was squarely on him.

He got up and threw his clothes on quickly, deciding to make a quick pot of coffee and wake up Jo and let her know he was going. She'd understand that he needed to go, and the friendly gesture would keep their working relationship sound.

———

Jo HEARD her coffee maker brewing in the kitchen. She slowly opened her eyes, remembering the night before.

What had she done?

She'd slept with a vampire, invited him into her trailer—her grandmother's trailer, really—and she'd slept with him. Not for a spell. Just for fun.

She lay naked under the covers, trying to figure out how it had happened. She hadn't done anything. Sure, she made the drink, but it wasn't anything special. It was just for celebrating, not for making anything happen.

Had John seduced her? Did he have some kind of sexy vampire powers that could make her do whatever he wanted?

That didn't seem right. And honestly, if he did, there's no way her grandmother wouldn't have taught her about it.

Jo had slept with a vampire, plain and simple. It was on her. She hadn't been forced. She hadn't been mind-tricked. She wanted to do it, so she did.

And maybe he had too? After all, why was there a vampire in her kitchen making coffee? Jo glanced over at the alarm clock on her nightstand. It was barely six in the morning. As a bartender, she wasn't the sort to wake up that early, especially since she'd normally be crawling into bed just a few hours before.

Jo stretched and got up. She went to the dresser on the other side of the room and pulled out a pair of cotton gym shorts and a T-shirt and threw them on. She went to the bathroom, making sure to fix her hair and splash water on her face so she didn't look terrible, and then made her way to the kitchen.

John was leaning against the counter, his shirt wrinkled and untucked. He was sipping a cup of coffee and staring out the window toward her garden.

"Good morning," Jo said.

John turned toward her. There was a flash in his eye, a strong emotion. Not dangerous. Desire.

Jo shivered. Maybe what happened had been more mutual than she realized.

John seemed to blush again, which made Jo smile.

"Good morning," he said, pouring her a cup of coffee. "I hate to wake you, but I need to leave soon, and I didn't want to leave without saying goodbye. So, I made an offering of coffee."

There was something about his manner, his body language. The way he was fighting with himself, Jo could sense that there was something wrong. But she didn't know what.

She chalked it up to awkward small talk after a one-night stand. Or, well, one night of sex before the sex required for a spell. There wasn't a phrase for that, at least not that Jo knew of.

"Thanks for the coffee," Jo said, trying to put John as much at ease as possible. "And thanks for last night."

John choked a little on the coffee he was sipping. He was incredibly uptight. But also, this was probably far beyond the sort of propriety he was used to, so Jo decided to be as friendly as she could.

"I don't mean that in a weird way. I just wanted to be honest. I had a good time." She took a sip, watching John. It was like a storm cloud in his head, and she couldn't get it all.

"I did too," he said, but there was a shadow over his words. Like he felt guilty for having fun.

Jo tried to shift the conversation back to business. "So. Three days. That's how long we have until it's time to cast the spell. We'll need the full moon, so I guess we should make sure we've got everything we need. And, um, I guess if there's anything you need in the meantime, you can always drop by. I'll be at the bar tonight, but I have the next couple of days off."

"Good. Yes. Perfect," John said, putting his empty mug in the sink, reverting back to his business tone. "I'll be reaching out."

"Okay. Yeah. So, I guess we're all set."

John nodded and then awkwardly walked around her toward the door. "I suppose I should get going, before the sun rises." He patted the pockets of his pants, looking for his keys.

Jo spotted them on the table by the door. She walked toward them, picked them up, and turned to hand them to John. She took one of his hands in hers, turning it palm up, and placed the keys in it, curling his fingers over them.

His skin was cool to the touch, and she sent calming intentions toward him, hoping it would help him relax around her. She didn't want him to feel that way about her—the storm cloud in his mind. And worse, she couldn't have that around when they were working the spell. It would ruin everything.

John's muscles relaxed, and he looked down at her. They held each other's gaze for a moment.

John bent down and kissed her hard.

And then it was broken. They each pulled away, realizing they wanted more.

John cleared his throat.

"You can come to the bar later, if you want," Jo said, feeling the heat rising off her skin.

"Sure," John said. "I'll see you then."

He was out the door and in his car fast. His tires spun in the gravel for a second before gaining traction and he drove away.

Jo went back to the kitchen and topped off her coffee mug.

This was all new territory for her. Because she could sense that he wanted her. But in that last kiss, she could sense in the storm of his mind that maybe John hated her too.

9

Jo SPRINTED AROUND THE BAR, TRYING TO KEEP UP WITH THE NEVER-ENDING orders and trying to make sense of who was on what check. She was officially getting her ass handed to her, and Luke was having a full-blown panic attack.

Four generations of some family had decided Kitchen Lake was the perfect site for their family reunion. After their scheduled day's activities, every adult of legal drinking age descended on the bar, all wearing matching bright green "Hutchins-Murray Family Hoe Down" shirts, and not a one of them could hold their liquor.

Two had puked in the parking lot already, and a whole pack of them were heckling the band (called Poolside Manner that evening) and begging for them to play "Freebird." And then the rest just seemed like they wanted a fight.

Jo had said as much to Luke and Matt, but Luke said they needed the business and Matt agreed that he couldn't bounce anyone if they weren't actually causing trouble.

So Jo did a small protection spell by creating a barrier of salt on the floor behind the bar, so no one could get to her, and she put some in the pockets of her shorts too.

From there, it was a mess trying to keep up with orders, and there was a whole contingency of Hutchins-Murray cousins that kept ordering shots that Jo had never heard of. It wasn't like the Lakeshore Inn had the most well-stocked bar, and it definitely wasn't like they had mixers beyond what their average campers and bikers ordered. So when Jo tried to explain why she couldn't make gummy limbos, Frankenstein bloopers, or grizzly tricycles, she could feel the cousins getting a little wound up. She even asked Luke if he knew how to make those shots, but he just looked at her like she was crazy.

Granny had always told Jo that she would know if she had ever been cursed because she would be able to feel it. And to Jo, this night felt like a curse.

Leon and Melinda, her favorite regulars, left without even ordering a drink. They waved and said they'd be back when this reunion was over. And the night only got worse from there.

The Belle Starr Outlaws showed up just before the sun set, and as soon as someone hit on Dez, just as she was getting off her bike in the parking lot, the biker gang threw down. Jo didn't see it happen, but the three bikers took out seven of the cousins, and left before even going in. They waved to Matt, who nodded approvingly at their work, and said they'd come back another night.

Inside, Nattie Rae was attempting to dance to the band, but the calls for "Freebird" were drowning out the music. As the band shifted into a rendition of Van Halen's "Jump," one of the Hutchins-Murray cousins threw a beer at the stage. They didn't hit anyone, but Nattie did.

She turned, wishing she could drop them with a look. She easily spotted the cousin who had done the throwing because he was laughing and pointing at his handiwork. She made her way toward him and tipped her amaretto sour over his head. Before he could react, Nattie was already on her way to settle her bill. She plopped a twenty on the bar top in front of Jo, visibly annoyed, and mentioned she'd come back another time, kissing Matt on the cheek as she left.

Dave, for his part, was happier than a hog in slop. There were so many female Hutchins-Murray cousins between the ages of 21 and 50 that Dave didn't know what to do with himself. Unfortunately, Dave was a little too drunk that night, which meant he was on even worse behavior than normal.

He put his arm around a woman in a Hutchins-Murray shirt and leaned in to whisper something in her ear. She pushed him away, but Dave grabbed her hand to pull her back in. Dave didn't ever hear a "no" that he took at face value, which was why Jo usually spelled most of his drinks. But she'd been too busy that night to protect Dave from himself, and one of the male Hutchins-Murray cousins noticed.

Drinks flew across the tables, and fists followed suit. Matt dove in headfirst, trying to create a semblance of order out of the chaos, but there were just too many people. Luke jumped in, and together they tried to push as many people out of the bar as they could.

Just then, the cousins calling for "Freebird" jumped onto the stage, taking over the band's instruments and causing a full-on disruption. Band members tried to fight back, but before all was said and done, someone's foot had gone through the bass drum.

527

Jo stood behind the bar in shock. Never had she seen a bar fight quite like this one, and she didn't know what to do. The chaos surrounded her but couldn't get to her behind the bar due to her protection spell. She needed a spell to stop the fight, and she needed it quick.

Unfortunately, her granny's grimoires said nothing about spells to stop bar fights.

Maybe she could cleanse the place. She'd need a lot of smoke to do it, though. She could roll up some napkins and drink menus, hold them like a torch, and light them on fire. Maybe that would help calm things down. But it wasn't enough. Cleansing would need to be done when the cousins left, just to get their energy out. But it wouldn't physically get them out of the bar.

She could douse them with water, and with the proper words, she may be able to cool down some tempers. But she didn't have enough water, and the bar's soda gun only shot so far. Best case scenario, she'd just irritate some patrons.

As she racked her brain for potential ways to stop the madness, John walked into the bar.

She hadn't expected him to actually show up, not after how awkward the morning was, and that he seemed mad at her for something. But there he was, in black pants and a white button-down shirt. He surveyed the chaos, and saw Jo trapped behind the bar.

John set his jaw and got to work.

He pulled cousins out of the fray two at a time, dragging them to the door and throwing them out. Jo had heard that vampires were strong, but John had never been anything but gentle with her. She'd never seen anyone pick up two grown adults and literally throw them.

He was diligent, seeming to pick up speed as he went. Jo watched in awe—but also a little terror.

Gran had been right. Vampires were dangerous. Even though she was glad John was clearing out the bar, it made her worry. She knew he was strong. She knew humans didn't stand a chance against him. And though she was thankful John was a danger to these particular humans, what if he could do the same to Matt or Luke or someone she cared about?

What if he could do the same to her?

Jo couldn't tell who it was in the crush of bodies, but a fist flew up and hit John square in the jaw. Jo could've sworn his eyes turned red, and she said a quick prayer to all the spirits that no one be killed that night.

John seemed more determined than ever, pulling three or four grown men out at a time. As the bar started to clear, some of the Hutchins-Murray clan realized that it was better to leave willingly than be thrown out by a freakishly strong man.

Matt and Luke continued to push others out, and in a few minutes the bar was nearly empty, aside from the band who sat on the edge of the stage, nursing their wounds and lamenting their broken instruments.

As Luke locked the door and turned off the neon "open" sign, Matt started picking up overturned tables and chairs. There was broken glass everywhere.

Jo stood behind the bar, her breath coming in short gasps. What had she done? She'd brought this man into her life, into her workplace, into her own home. He was a literal monster, and she had slept with him.

John's chest rose and fell with quick, ragged breaths as he came toward Jo. "Are you okay?" he asked, his voice gruff and angry.

Jo didn't say anything. She just stared at him, her eyes wide open, as if for the very first time.

"Well?" he asked, putting his hands on the bar top and leaning in.

Finally, the trance was broken. "Yes," she said. "Yeah. I'm fine. I made a salt barrier in the bar to keep myself safe. I just didn't know what to do to get the fight to stop. I didn't have a spell for it."

John took a deep breath, his calm demeanor returning. "Good." He looked around the bar. "Good."

Matt came up to him and clapped him on the back. "Good work, man. You're strong. What do you do, CrossFit? Or like, just bodybuilding? Because, damn. I need to get on that workout."

John relaxed even more, his eyes back to their clear blue, as if the conversation was helping to take him out of that space. "I do like to lift weights," he replied casually, though it was clear to Jo that John had never set foot in a gym in his whole vampire life.

Luke reached in the cooler and got some beers for the band, then gave a beer to Jo, Matt, and John. "Thanks, man. What's your name?"

"It's John," he said, looking at the beer and trying to seem grateful for a drink he despised.

"Well, John. You really saved our asses tonight." Luke turned to Jo. "Jo, just clean up as much as you can. I'll get a crew in tomorrow morning to deal with the broken glass and smashed tables. You were right about that family reunion." He took a long swig of his beer. "They were ready for a fight. Is that your witchy sixth sense or something?"

Jo rolled her eyes. "More like common sense," she muttered.

"Never had too much of that," Luke said, smiling at Matt and John.

John sat down at the bar while Jo cleaned up as much as she could, stealing glances at John as she moved, but not quite sure what to say.

John didn't seem to have much to say either. He stared at the wall, letting Jo finish her work.

She stocked everything and made the bar ready for the next shift, but it wasn't much work since she'd protected the space earlier. She chugged her beer, and when Luke wasn't looking, she took John's and did the same.

"I'm going to head out," Jo called to Luke. "Matt, do you need a ride?"

Matt was on his fifth beer, chatting with Luke and the band's drummer. They were sharing fight stories, and Jo could tell they weren't in any mood to leave.

"I'll give him a ride," Luke said.

"Okay then. See you tomorrow." She knew Matt wouldn't make it home until after sunrise, and she also knew his girlfriend would be so mad at him that she'd lock him out of the apartment for most of the day.

Jo walked out from behind the bar, and John followed. He didn't offer his arm to her this time, and even though it was the sort of over-the-top gesture that Jo didn't think she liked or needed, it suddenly felt wrong not to have it.

They walked out of the bar and into the parking lot. John had parked his Mercedes next to her Jeep.

"Is it always like that at your job?"

"No. Are you always so ready for a fight?"

John's face fell like her words hurt him. "No. I saw you behind the bar in the middle of all that chaos, and I knew I had to do something."

Jo relaxed a little, realizing her shoulders were up around her ears. She was tense, and even though they had just gotten out of one fight, part of her wanted to start another. "I'm sorry. I appreciate what you did. I'm just a little freaked out right now."

John seemed to relax too. "I understand."

Jo looked at the man she'd known for so little, trying to find out what she could about the storm in his mind. She wished she could've sensed it before she let him get so close.

———

THE AIR WAS HUMID, and John, though naturally cool, needed to cool down more. He was grateful for the fight, for the chance to expend some energy and anger. But now, standing in front of the woman who was the source of his anger, he couldn't help but feel worked up all over again.

And like he wanted to throw her in the back seat of his car and reenact the previous night.

How was she able to do that to him? Her hair was a mess and she was sweaty from work, and there was a beer stain on her tank top. What sort of magic was she doing to bring him in?

He knew it wasn't her. He knew it was him—his desire.

"I think we need to talk," Jo said.

She looked tense. And John wanted to talk to her. He really did. He'd love to sit up all night and chat with her about anything. Mostly, he wanted the talk to turn into something more. But that made him feel so guilty.

Why was he so capable of forgetting his family when he was around her?

"So talk," he said, a little more brusquely than he intended.

Jo looked at her feet. "Is everything okay? I mean, since this morning. It's been weird, right? It doesn't have to be weird. I'm sorry if I did anything to offend you."

That was like a knife to his heart. John knew he was being an asshole. He knew he wasn't being the best version of himself, and he knew Jo didn't deserve it.

But he also knew he had to do it to keep her at bay. He couldn't handle how she made him feel.

"It's nothing." He stepped back from her and leaned his back against his car. "Don't worry about it."

"Okay. I won't. But you seem different than you were last night."

He shrugged.

"I just don't want you to think that what happened last night has to change anything."

"Does it change anything with your other clients?"

"What?" Her face shifted from confusion to hurt.

"I'm just curious."

"I don't sleep with my clients."

"Oh. Am I just a special case?"

She crossed her arms. "Look. I thought we were both into it yesterday, so I went with it. I know that the work I do sometimes includes sleeping with someone. I can't change the nature of spellwork. I really can't. I didn't create the spells. I just use them. And if we're being honest, you're the one who came to me for work. What happened last night was just two people hanging out."

"Well, I imagine if a client is going to pay fifteen thousand dollars, you'd want to give him his money's worth." It was out of his mouth before he could take it back. And as soon as he'd said it, he felt like he'd been punched in the gut.

Her face fluctuated between hurt, disappointment, and a slowly simmering rage. John had never been afraid of a human, not during his life as a vampire. But he was now.

"Fuck you." Without another word, she got in her Jeep and sped out of the parking lot.

John sat leaning against his car for a long time, trying to figure out why he said what he said.

10

Jo drove home faster than she should've, her Jeep going up on two wheels as she took one of the sharp turns. She needed to calm down, and fast.

Once parked, she stomped her way up the deck stairs and unlocked the door of her trailer, slamming the door behind her as she headed straight for the kitchen. She needed another beer.

She pulled one out of the fridge, standing in front of the open door to cool off as she chugged a can of Coors Light. When she was done, she grabbed a second one, and pulled herself up onto the counter where as a kid she used to sit and watch her granny make potato salad for picnics, where she'd mixed the bourbon drink for John the night before.

Everything had gone so horribly wrong. And she had no idea how it all happened. And what was worse—she had let a vampire into her life. Her granny had warned her enough. But she'd done it anyway.

She sipped the beer slowly. She needed to come up with a plan. She didn't think John was going to hurt her, at least not in the way that vampires normally did. He could hurt her plenty just by being an ass.

So she decided that she'd take as much time as she needed to cool off and relax, then spend the next day reading her granny's journals and spell books. She'd do what she needed to do to keep herself and her livelihood safe. And she'd forget all about John.

The trailer settled as the wind shifted, and Jo thought about the roof. Sure, that money would've been good, but it was too good to be true. If she needed to, she'd pick up some extra shifts at the bar. She could put out some feelers and see if any local stores wanted her to read tarot cards for big shopping days or art walks or any local events. She'd make the money she needed, and she'd do it without that asshole.

She would figure it out.

She should've known all along that vampires were trouble. And having learned the hard way, she'd never forget it.

———

AFTER WHAT FELT LIKE AN HOUR, John finally got up off the cold ground and into his car. He exhaled. What the hell had he done?

He'd never been particularly good at expressing himself or holding his emotions, or even knowing what his emotions were. And now that little short-coming had really screwed him over.

He couldn't believe what he'd just said to Jo. And what was worse, he'd said it because he felt guilty. It wasn't Jo's fault. He knew that. But how could he just forget his family like that? He felt torn.

Sure, he'd slept with other women in the three hundred years since his wife died. But none of them meant anything, and it wasn't like he sought them out. It just happened after a few drinks, and nothing was expected afterward.

But now, with Jo, he'd slept with her because he wanted to. And he'd done it knowing full well that he couldn't just leave the next day since he needed that spell. He didn't want to leave, and that somehow felt worse. He hated that shitty little bar and he hated that Jo worked there, but he'd gladly go there every night for the rest of his life if it meant he'd get to see her more . . .

No. No, I can't. He slammed his fist against the dashboard, perhaps a little too hard for a rental.

He was done with Jo. He'd lost his head a bit, and now it was time to clean everything up. He couldn't be running around like some lovesick boy, just following around a bartender because he thought she was pretty.

And smart. And capable. And her head was in the right place. With a sense of duty and a desire to preserve her family's legacy. And she had asked nothing of him that he wasn't willing to give.

He sighed. He had to stop thinking that way. She was a distraction. Nothing more. He'd get the hell out of Oklahoma tomorrow night. He'd be done with her. She'd never hear from him again. And he'd never spend another moment thinking about her. Or her legs. Or the way she smiled. Or how she wanted to build her own business on her own, and how attractive he'd never realized that was.

He headed back toward downtown, driving much faster than the speed limit and making record time. Which was good because he needed to make a phone call.

Once in his hotel room, he'd call a lawyer friend of his in France, and they'd figure this all out. His friend knew what he was and was capable of discretion, John was sure of it. Surely a lawyer could find a crew to exhume the remains of his family and put them somewhere until he could make the long trip to France by boat—the only way to avoid the sunlight.

He'd figure it all out. He always did.

He didn't need a woman like Jo in his life. He had a family that he loved desperately, and he'd never do anything to dishonor their memory again.

Jo didn't sleep at all that night. How could she? She had work to do.

After her second beer, she made herself some tea. Chamomile for calming. Lavender to soothe. Honey to soften. Mint for luck. Stirred three times clockwise with a cinnamon stick.

She sipped the drink slowly, thinking about her intentions.

First, she was going to get John out of her life for good. She'd cleanse her home of him, and then reseal the door against him. She'd make a plan to get the money she needed for the roof, and she'd make a list of people to call. If that meant picking up some shifts for the next few weeks and smoothing things out with Brian so she could sell some tinctures or spell jars at his store, she would do it.

She felt good. For the first time in a while, she felt like she could do this all on her own. She was Jo Bonneville, the witch of Kitchen Lake, and she didn't need anyone.

That feeling was invigorating. So, around 3:30 a.m., when she should've long been asleep, she decided it was time to deep-clean her home. She set about opening the windows and lit some sage. She cleansed the whole space, making sure to pay special attention to the areas John had spent the most time. She got out all the cleaning sprays and sponges and went over every surface, disinfecting everything, even things that probably didn't need to be disinfected. She topped that off by rearranging her furniture. Then she did two loads of laundry, swept and mopped the floors, and organized her closet, collecting a bag of old clothes she didn't want any more to donate—the blue floral sundress chief among them.

At 8:30 a.m., she realized the sun had been up for some time, so she chugged a glass of water, and then made a pot of coffee, being certain to push every memory of the coffee John had made her out of her mind.

She made breakfast, a piece of toast with two fried eggs on top and two slices of bacon. It was something her granny made her often, and it was something she felt would give her the strength she needed for the day.

After breakfast, she took a shower and got dressed in a simple black tank top and cutoffs. She didn't have to go to the bar that evening, so she'd spend some time doing the work she was meant to do.

As she walked into her office, the air felt a little lighter than it had last night. The cleaning and cleansing rituals had done wonders.

She went straight to the shelf with the journals and spell books, grabbed what she thought she needed, and brought them to the table, flipping to the pages she felt were most pertinent.

"You were right all along, Granny," she said. "And I'm an idiot. But don't worry. I'll reseal the trailer today and figure out what I need to do to keep that vampire away. I don't know if I need a full-on banishing spell, but I think it might be time to prepare for it, if it comes to that."

Jo didn't think it would, but then again she'd been wrong about John once before.

She flipped through a few spell books until she found the spell for resealing the house. She'd have some use of that mountain ash bark after all.

JOHN LAY in bed in his hotel room all day, doing nothing. He snapped at the maid when she knocked on the door, and he could hear her scurry away down the hall.

He couldn't figure out if he was doing the right thing. It seemed like the right thing. But if that was the case, why did it feel so bad?

Surely this was the right thing. He was doing right by his family, and there was nothing that was going to stop him. He'd made the necessary calls, and it seemed like everything was in order.

But something was off. He couldn't figure out what.

He decided to stop by Jo's trailer that evening. He just wanted to formally end it—a clean break. He'd tell her he no longer required her services. That was it. He wasn't going to see her, and he absolutely wasn't going because he thought there might be a chance she wasn't still mad at him.

No, he'd go to end the business deal, and then he'd head out of town. That would be that. He didn't need to stay in Oklahoma any longer. There was just this last formality.

And maybe he'd apologize for what he said.

Not because he wanted to spend more time with her or because he needed her forgiveness. But because he wasn't an asshole. He wasn't the type of person who said things like that.

And honestly, had his wife heard him say that to Jo, she would've been angry at him. In the end, he needed to do what he could to make things right.

12

Jo felt like a brand-new woman.

Her trailer was clean and resealed, so no more vampires could enter ever again, and she'd done so much to her home that it felt like a new place. Sure, there was magic in spellwork. But to Jo, there was always a little bit of magic in cleaning up.

Jo had nothing left to do. She was completely exhausted, having spent the whole day cleaning and working and not sleeping at all the night before. She'd earned an early night's sleep, and she was going to take it.

She went into the kitchen and washed up the dishes in the sink while a cup of plain chamomile steeped on the counter. Her shoulders were tight, and she needed to relax. She'd done so much that day, but now it was time to mentally clear her head so she could sleep.

John's gone and he doesn't matter, she reminded herself. *You don't need him.* With the plans she'd made, she'd be able to earn enough to fix her trailer without him.

As she put the last plate on the drying rack, there was a knock at her door.

That wasn't common since she lived in the middle of nowhere.

But it was also uncommon for her not to notice someone approaching her home. Usually, she could feel the energy shift, or at the very least, sense someone's intentions. But this time, she felt nothing.

She chalked it up to exhaustion and lack of sleep. That was one thing Jo's granny had always told her. *Witches need to take care of themselves, Jo. They need their energy for the work they do, and if they don't have enough energy, it could be dangerous.*

Not that Jo thought there was danger at her door. In fact, it could be anything. A census taker, or maybe someone who got lost on the lake trails looking for a phone to use.

She picked up her cup of tea and headed to the door, quickly checking in with her intuition to see if she could feel anything, but she couldn't. Her senses felt like the frayed ends of a thread. She would just have to open the door.

As she did so, her stomach dropped.

John stood there, in freshly pressed clothes, looking as good as ever.

She hated that even when she was mad at him, he still looked good.

Jo glared at him.

He cleared his throat. "Good evening."

"Is it?"

"Well, I guess it could be."

"Sure," she said, leaning against the doorframe.

"Look," he said, running his fingers through his hair. "I came to apologize."

"Well, better get to it, then."

Jo knew she was being difficult. But she didn't care.

"I apologize for what I said." He looked to her, as if that fixed everything.

Jo glared harder.

"I also wanted to let you know that I'll be leaving tonight, and I won't require your spellwork."

"Good. Glad you wasted my time."

"I'm trying to be civil," he said, frustrated that this apology wasn't going in the straightforward way he thought it would.

"I'm not."

"Clearly."

Jo rolled her eyes. "Well, if that's all, I guess you can go."

————

JOHN COULDN'T FIGURE out why, but that hurt. He thought an apology would fix everything. He thought it would take away what he said. He thought it would fix it, and then he'd go about his life and never think of her again. He'd continue to honor his family, and all would be fine.

But that wasn't how it was going. He couldn't figure out why, but somehow, he felt worse now. Like the idea of leaving was a bad idea.

He reached for Jo's hand, but his fingertips couldn't make it across the threshold.

"What?" He looked down, confused, and tried to push his hand past the invisible line between the open door and the deck.

Jo smiled. "I honestly didn't think you would come back, but if you did, I wanted to be ready."

"You resealed it?"

Jo just raised an eyebrow and took a sip of her tea.

She was infuriating. And knowing that she'd spent her time that day ensuring that he wouldn't have access to her again made him feel like a bigger villain than he already did.

Everything was wrong. This wasn't going how it was supposed to. John wanted to apologize and leave and feel good and never think about any of this again. He wanted to pretend like he'd never met Jo, that they'd never slept together, and like he'd never forgotten his family in the first place.

John took a deep breath. "I deserve that. And for what it's worth, I'm truly sorry. I never wanted any of this to happen, and I'm sorry for any pain I've caused you. You didn't deserve what I said, and I didn't mean it. I took my emotions out on you, and those are things I'll have to deal with myself."

Jo tilted her head, confused. John could tell she hadn't expected that. But it didn't matter. He'd already ruined everything. He needed to go.

"I'll be leaving tonight, and I'll never bother you again."

Before Jo could say anything, John turned to leave. Jo just stood there as he pulled out of the driveway in record time.

———

Jo CLOSED the door behind her. What had just happened? Did John really come over to apologize to her? And had he been hurt that she resealed the door?

It didn't make any sense.

Hadn't he been the one that started all of this?

She threw her hands up in exasperation.

Though she'd been tired just minutes before, now she felt wide awake. The air in her trailer felt stuffy, and she needed to breathe if she was going to wrap her head around what the hell was going on in her life.

She stepped outside, mug of tea in hand, and decided to go for a walk. She wouldn't go far, and she'd just stay on her property. But she had to get this weird energy out of her body.

Putting one flip-flop in front of the other, she eventually found herself at the edge of the lake, in the spot where she and John had kissed for the first time. It had been mere days ago. And yet, there she was, all alone and John was gone.

She sat down in one of the chairs, looking at the shards of the glass she'd dropped when he'd first wrapped his arms around her. Everything reminded her of him.

Such a funny thing. One minute he was sharing about his wife and daughter from lifetimes ago, and then he was kissing her. The weight of that admission had been lifted from him, and even though it was such an important story for him to carry, he had shouldered it too long on his own.

Jo wondered what John would do now.

How would he get to their remains?

Even if he was an asshole, maybe she could still help. She knew she didn't owe him anything, but there was something she didn't know. There had to be some little piece of information she was missing. The real reason he'd lost his temper. And if his apology was true, then he hadn't meant to say what he'd said.

But it was too late, wasn't it? He was already on the road, and if his speed leaving her trailer were any indication, he was probably to Tennessee by now.

She took a sip of tea. She could still help him. Maybe. But for now, she needed some sleep. She stood and made her way back to the trailer, locking the door behind her.

13

Jo was not an early riser by nature. That was why bartending was easy for her. She could stay up and work one of the few jobs that welcomed people who slept in.

So when someone began knocking on her door at 7:00 a.m., Jo was not pleased.

She pulled herself out of bed and dragged her feet from the bedroom through the hall to the living room and opened the door to a construction crew on her porch.

"Morning, ma'am," said the one who appeared to be in charge. "You Jo Bonneville?"

She nodded, confused.

"We just need you to sign this, and then we can get to work."

"To work?"

"Yes, ma'am. We'll be fixing your roof today. We heard you had a leak or two."

"How did you hear that?"

The man pushed the clipboard with papers at her. "It's here in these papers we need you to sign."

Jo took the clipboard and skimmed the form. "John hired you?"

The man shrugged. "I don't take the calls at the office. I just go where they send me."

Jo looked back down at the clipboard. It seemed that John had been paying attention when she told him about all the things around the trailer she wanted to fix. In a little section for notes, whoever took the call had recorded exactly what she had told John as they walked through her home and garden.

"Can I have just a second?" Jo asked the worker.

He shrugged. "Absolutely. But we do get paid hourly, and even though we aren't working yet, we're still on the clock."

"Noted," she said, closing the door behind her.

She sprinted back to her bedroom and grabbed her phone off her bedside table. There were no messages or notifications. She decided to call him.

"Good morning." He sounded like he had been expecting her call.

"Just what in the hell do you think you're doing?"

"I'm sitting in my hotel room. Why?"

"I thought you left."

"I was going to. But I realized I had some unfinished business."

"How in the hell is my roof your business?"

He paused for a moment. "I don't mean to overstep my bounds. But I made a business deal with you and went back on it. In any dealings I have with others, I wouldn't be giving them a refund if they backed out at the last minute. But you didn't ask for a deposit, or have me sign a contract. So, I thought I'd pay you anyway, but I didn't have an account to wire the money to."

"What the actual fuck, John? You're just going to fix my roof?"

"Is that a bad thing?"

"I can handle my own home. I don't need your charity." Jo was fuming.

"It's not charity. It's business," he said matter-of-factly. "I know that witches often operate with handshake agreements, but that's not how I work. And I honor the agreements I make. So, even though I won't be taking your spell, I'll still be paying you."

"John," her voice cracked. "It's too much." Tears ran down her face but she didn't care.

"Please don't cry," he said, his professional tone suddenly gone. "I was awful to you. And you didn't deserve it. I've been wrestling with the idea that I have to let my family go. And it's hard." He paused for a long moment. "When I realized I spent an afternoon idly thinking about how your skin feels but couldn't tell you the shape of my wife's face anymore, I felt like I'd betrayed her memory."

Jo's legs gave out at the revelation and she found herself sitting on the floor of her bedroom. "Oh, John. I didn't know."

"I know. I didn't say anything. I didn't know what to say. And if I'm being honest, I only just realized it. That I need to let it go. My wife and daughter have been dead so much longer than they were ever alive, and I can't keep pretending like isolating myself is being loyal to them."

Jo was silent. "I'm so sorry, John."

"Don't be. I'm sorry."

"But you're still here?"

"Yes. For a few more days."

"Good. I'll be stopping by tonight."

They said their goodbyes and Jo signed the work order. The crew made quick work of her roof, finishing by four o'clock, and Jo was glad. She knew that whatever crew she could afford to hire would probably take at least five times as long—and wouldn't be quite so professional.

While they hammered away above her, Jo got to work.

First, she added a handful of dried blackberries to her food processor and ground them until they were a fine dust. Then, she ground a teaspoon of fennel seeds in her spice grinder. All the while trying not to think about what her granny would say about her not using a mortar and pestle, but Jo had a lot to do in one day.

She mixed the blackberry and fennel together and put them in a jar. Then, it was time to make the burning bundle. She took what was left of the mountain ash bark and tied it with some dried mistletoe and the dried leaves of a garlic bulb from her own garden. She bound them together with a white cotton string, keeping the intention of the spell in her mind as she worked.

The final step was to prepare a candle for that night's ritual. Jo retrieved one of the shorter candles and a brass candlestick holder from her office closet, and using a thick embroidery needle from Gran's sewing kit, she meticulously scratched the word "daylight" into one side of the candle and "John Laurent" into the other.

When all the preparations were done, she hopped in the shower and worried more about her hair than she had for any other spell she'd ever done. It wasn't that the spell required it. It was more that she was excited to see John.

———

JOHN TRIED TO RELAX, but he just couldn't. Jo was coming over. And even though he was older than the average man, the idea made him feel like a teenager. He didn't really care if she could do the spell or not at this point. But he was excited to see her. He spent most of the day pacing his hotel room, the blackout curtains tightly drawn.

He had struggled with the idea of hiring a crew for Jo, but in the end, he knew he had to do it. It wasn't fair that he'd taken so much of her time, only to back out for no good reason. And even though she seemed mad about it at first, he knew she was happy in the end.

John didn't really know how to prepare a hotel room for a visit from Jo, but he thought it might be nice to lay out some food and drinks. He ordered room service, and realized he'd perhaps gone a little crazy when the trays were delivered.

Since he didn't know what Jo liked, he ordered a few bottles of red and white wine, as well as a fruit tray. The dessert menu looked promising, so he got one of everything. And because he felt he'd erred too far on the side of sweets, he ordered the cheese tray too.

It was the sort of thing he'd never really done, simply because as a vampire he didn't need to. But it all looked so nice as the hotel staff wheeled it into his room and set it up on the table.

As he waited for Jo to arrive, he spent his time fussing with the plates, moving them half an inch this way or that way, trying to make sure everything was perfect.

When she did text him to let him know she was on her way, his nerves fully took over. He'd never felt this way. At least, never as a vampire. To take his mind off it, he turned on the TV and flicked through to the best music channel that the hotel's extensive cable package offered. He wasn't sure what Jo liked best, but he assumed it would probably be nice for her to have a night where she wasn't forced to listen to classic rock songs.

He settled on an instrumental piano channel. Though, he thought that might make him seem old and boring to Jo, but before he could change it, there came a knock on the door. It was her.

He crossed the room in two fast strides. Before he opened the door, he looked back at the room to make sure everything was as perfect as he could make it. Then, he looked at his clothes and smoothed out his shirt.

He took a deep breath and opened the door.

14

Jo carried the spell components in an over-the-shoulder brown leather purse she'd got at some thrift store a long time ago. She had her hair pulled back in a ponytail since it was always easier to do spellwork if she wasn't being bothered by her hair, and she wore a green wrap dress—another thrift store find—along with her quartz necklace and a pair of Birkenstocks she'd had since her early twenties.

She knocked on the door of John's hotel room and was shocked at how quickly it opened. Like he'd been waiting by the door for her.

"Hi," she said, feeling the heat rise from her chest up her neck and into her cheeks as she looked at John.

He smiled. "I'm glad you came." He motioned for her to come in.

"Jesus, John. Are you hosting a party?" Jo asked, looking at the spread he'd set up.

He laughed. "I guess. I mean, I didn't know what you'd like, and I thought it might be nice to have some options."

She smiled. "It's nice. But you didn't have to buy out the entire hotel kitchen."

John shrugged. "Well, would you like to start with a glass of wine?"

"Sure." Jo laid her bag down on a wingback chair. John poured them each a glass of red wine, then motioned for Jo to join him on the couch. They both took a seat.

Jo sipped her wine. "This is pretty nice."

"Oh, you're a wine drinker?"

"No, but it tastes nothing like what we serve at the Lakeshore, so I assume it's expensive."

John laughed. "To be fair, you serve the worst boxed wine at that bar."

"It gets even worse when you find out how long it's been sitting on that shelf. I'm sure it's vinegar by now."

As they made easy conversation, talking about little things that didn't matter, as if they needed to ease into the real conversation they should've been having, Jo sipped her wine slowly, knowing she couldn't have too much. Meanwhile, John sipped faster than he should've, knowing as a vampire he wouldn't get drunk, but he needed something for his hands to do.

When there was a break in their small talk, John put his glass down on the coffee table. "Look. I need to apologize again. I can't believe I said what I said."

"Stop right there," Jo said, putting her glass down next to his. "I think we need to be more intentional about this conversation." She stood up and got her leather bag from the wingback chair where she'd left it. "I have all the stuff we need for a daylight spell, if you still want it. I know you said you hired those contractors because you honor your deals, but I do too. So, we can still make this happen, if you want to. But if we do it, you need to really unburden yourself. You've gotta confess your sins, John. And it's all that shame and guilt. I now know that's why you lost your temper, only I couldn't see it then. I could only feel the storm in your mind, but not what was causing it."

John leaned back. "You can see inside my head?" he said, the shock evident on his face.

"Well, not really. Kind of. A little," Jo said, trying to think of a good way to explain it. "I can sense feelings more than anything. And it has to be a big feeling. You know, the overwhelming kind. I can also tell what people are dreaming if they're sleeping near me, since their guards are down."

"So you've been able to sense that this whole time?" John looked a little hurt, a little angry, and a little fascinated.

"Yeah. But don't worry too much. You're not much of an open book. You're a little too put together for me to know too much about you."

He relaxed a little.

"But that just means it may be harder for you to get it all out. The guilt and all that. I mean, we don't have to do the spell if you don't want to. But I want you to be able to go back to France. I want to help you. I can't imagine carrying what you've carried for that long, and I want to help you in any way that I can." She put her hand on John's where it rested on his knee. She continued. "All you have to do is express everything you've bottled up for so long. Just get it off your chest and you'll be free and clear."

He looked away, shifting in his seat. Jo's reassuring presence held the silence until he was ready to speak.

"Okay," John said. "I'll try."

———

HE GOT up and brought the bottle of wine back to the table and topped off his glass. He would need it. The idea of sharing the deepest feelings he'd been harboring for centuries seemed impossible. Jo shook her head when he offered her more. He sat back on the couch and told her everything.

He started with how he met his wife. She was beautiful and perfect, and they'd grown up in the same town together. They fell in love young and were married soon after. They'd had a daughter, Giselle, and John explained how there was a moment so long ago when he felt the happiest he'd ever been. It wasn't a remarkable day—just a sunny afternoon with the three of them together, as they sat outside under a tree eating grapes and enjoying the nice weather.

That was his favorite memory.

He shared how he didn't think he should have been spared from death. His daughter deserved it the most. After all, she was only twelve years old when she died, and she was still innocent and perfect. His wife had always been a better person than him, and she deserved a second chance as well.

But somehow he'd been spared instead of them. And though he tried to make his existence as a vampire worth it, he didn't know if it was.

He told Jo about the businesses he'd started and the charity organizations he'd donated to. He shared all of it, and how he felt it was never enough. He felt he'd never done enough to honor them.

He felt like he'd betrayed them by leaving France. He felt like he betrayed them every time he slept with someone else. And most of all, he felt like he betrayed them by being so miserable and sad and lonely all the time. Because if he had this second chance, shouldn't he be happy? Wouldn't his wife want that for him?

Jo listened, saying nothing. It wasn't her time to speak. She needed him to say it all before she did anything, and as he finally sat back and sighed deeply, she knew he was done.

"John," she said, reaching for his hand again. "Thank you for sharing all that with me. It's a lot."

"I guess so. I've never said it out loud before."

"I know. You started that night at the lake, and I thought you were done. But it was so much more than feelings of guilt or shame. It was also the feelings you had about your feelings."

"I suppose."

"How do you feel?"

548

John looked around the hotel room. "Lighter, but not completely. It's like I know I'll have to do this over and over just to feel right."

"Yes, but I'm always here."

He smiled and pulled Jo in for a hug. "Thank you."

Jo rested her head on his chest. "Don't thank me yet. There's still plenty of time for this spell to backfire."

They sat on the couch in the hotel room for a while, enjoying each other's company. And when Jo checked the clock on the wall, she let John know it was time.

He opened the curtains to reveal the full moon in the sky. They were on the tenth floor, and the view was mostly unobstructed, though there were a few other taller buildings that flanked the sky.

"Tell me what to do," John said.

Jo instructed him to get some hot water, so he called the front desk to have a carafe of it delivered along with two coffee mugs. While he did that, Jo opened a window, though it only slid open a crack. She lit her bundle and began the process of cleansing the room.

After the hot water was delivered, Jo took the jar of ground blackberry and fennel, and divided it among the two mugs. She topped the mixtures with hot water and let them steep. It was a sweet smell, though Jo knew it would be a little bitter to the taste.

Finally, she took the candle and placed it on the bedside table.

"Umm. So. It's time."

John nodded.

Jo brought the cups of tea to the bed and motioned for John to sit beside her. "Ready?"

He nodded again.

Jo lit the candle. "This is a spell of rebirth, so keep that intention in your mind. You've let go of the things you've carried for so long, and now it's time to become a new person."

Jo lifted the mug to her lips and motioned for John to do the same. They knocked back the liquid, and when both mugs were empty, Jo placed them on the bedside table next to the candle.

"Now what?" John's voice was almost a whisper.

Jo leaned in, taking his cheek in her left hand. "This."

She kissed him, softly at first, then slowly opened her mouth to his. John put his arm around her waist and pulled her closer to him, then they both stood, facing each other at the foot of the bed.

Jo reached for the buttons of his shirt and slowly undid them, from top to bottom. Her hands were shaking, and she realized that this was probably more than a spell for her. She didn't know if she'd get to spend much more time with

John after tonight, but it didn't matter. She had this night, and she had to make it count.

Once his shirt was unbuttoned, she pulled it off him. She reached for his belt, but he grabbed her hands.

He put his mouth on hers again, his kiss forceful, taking what he wanted. With one hand on her waist, he used the other to pull the tie of her wrap dress, sliding the fabric off her shoulders and letting the dress fall to the floor. He then put his hands on her waist again and pulled her in closer to him.

"Do we have a time limit?"

"A what?" she said, breathlessly.

"Do we have to complete this particular portion of the spell in a particular amount of time?" he said, his mouth moving to the place just behind her ear.

"Just as long as the moon's up." She gasped as his hand squeezed her ass..

"Good." John put a playful bite on her neck before pushing her onto the bed.

He pulled her bra and panties off faster than Jo thought possible, and when she was naked, he stood over her, admiring. Jo felt self-conscious, but only for a minute.

John moved over her, kissing her mouth first, and then trailing tiny kisses down her throat, chest, and stomach. Jo's skin tingled, goosebumps popping up in his wake. He continued moving his mouth down her body until he reached her inner thigh, playfully biting her soft skin before moving to her pussy. He slowly licked between her folds, causing her breath to catch in her throat.

She entwined her fingers in his hair and moaned as he slowly brought her to the edge. Her breath came in ragged gasps, but before she had gone too far, John pulled away, standing to take off his pants.

Jo squirmed on the bed as she watched, thinking he couldn't move fast enough.

He came back down on the bed, positioning himself between her legs, bringing his body over hers, and his mouth down on her neck. She felt a small jab, the tip of a fang, in her flesh as he took a small taste of her blood before entering her.

His strong hands held her as he thrust into her, his face over hers, staring into her eyes. She wrapped her legs around his waist, pulling him closer.

John gasped, slowing down momentarily.

Jo seized her opportunity. She unwrapped her legs and shifted her weight to push John onto his back, straddling him.

He looked surprised at first, then pleased. He held her firmly in place as they both rode out the wave of passion to its peak.

EPILOGUE

Jo had never been out of Oklahoma, much less all the way to Europe. She sat comfortably in her first-class aisle seat next to John and held his hand as he stared out the window at the bright blue sky. Jo had let him have the window seat so he could enjoy all the daylight spell had to offer.

I could get used to this, she thought.

She didn't have a passport, but John knew people who knew people, and it didn't take much for that expedited request, but it did occur to Jo that there was probably a significant exchange of cash.

Jo didn't know what this relationship meant, not really. It was hard to say. But for now, they were enjoying each other's company, and they would roll with the punches as they came.

"What are you going to do when we get back?" John asked. He'd been very interested in Jo's business plans, especially after experiencing the true power of her magic.

Jo shrugged. "I think I'm going to set up a website. It would be easier to advertise that way."

"I know a web designer," he said. "Very efficient."

"Well, I'm sure I can figure it out. I used to be really good at modifying a MySpace page, back in the day."

"You could, but you didn't get into business to do that."

Jo agreed, sighing in relief. One less thing to do.

"I also asked a lawyer friend to draw up some basic contract templates that you can use for client work."

"You don't have to do all this, you know," she said.

"I know, but look what you've done for me." He gestured to the window. "Do you know how long it's been since I've felt the sun on my skin? Do you understand how much easier you've made my life?"

Jo didn't say anything. Maybe it was time she received help when it was offered to her, just to let the universe know she was open to it.

She sipped her glass of wine. "Maybe I'll start a coven," she said, thinking out loud.

"A coven?"

"Yeah. A whole group of witches. I love working alone and always have, but I'm sure there's work out there that will require more than just me."

"Why not? It's always good to have partners, right? Do you have any witches in mind?"

Jo shrugged. "No. But I'm sure I'll find some. Witches are all over the place. And there are some who don't even know they're witches because they didn't have family to teach them."

"And what about Brian the Warlock?" John asked, raising an eyebrow.

"Why? Would you be jealous if he joined the coven?" Jo playfully poked him in the ribs.

"No."

Jo could tell he was.

"Well, you have a whole flight to think it through, and then a whole flight back."

John smiled, holding her hand a little tighter. "Thank you for coming with me, by the way."

She leaned her head on his shoulder. "Well, it wasn't like you had to twist my arm."

He laughed. "I know. But it's good to have you here. You did the spell, and you've helped process some things from the past three hundred years or so." He looked out the window. "I'm not the same as I was when I met you."

She smiled and sighed. "Me neither."

ABOUT MARISA MOHI

Marisa Mohi is a recovering forever student, blogger, and tarot reader. She has worked as a ghostwriter, technical writer, and writing instructor.

Marisa lives in Oklahoma City with her husband, Chris, and their unruly mutt, Rosie.

You can follow her at:
https://marisamohi.com

facebook.com/MarisaMohi

twitter.com/theMarisaMohi

instagram.com/themarisamohi

pinterest.com/themarisamohi

bookbub.com/profile/marisa-mohi

goodreads.com/marisamohi

youtube.com/marisamohi

CAUTION IN LOVE

K. RODRIGUEZ

Editors: Alyse Bailey & Sarah Jones

❈ Created with Vellum

ABOUT CAUTION IN LOVE

Subgenre: Contemporary Romance
Tropes: Interracial, Miscommunication

Graphic sexual depictions, open door sex and explicit language

Blurb:

The best way to get over a man is to get under a new one...

At least that's what my mother has been reminding me of since I moved back home. Thanks to the cara de culo *(shitface)* of my ex I'm practically homeless, broke and still heartbroken. A new man in my life is the last thing I need..until *him*.

Chase is just my personal trainer, but the heat in his eyes, the burn from his touch and the sweet words that fall from his lips are proving to be a real threat to the dick hiatus I put myself on.

PROLOGUE

IZZY

<small>Proverbs 4:23 - Guard your heart above all else.</small>

My mother's favorite bible verse. The fact that she even has a favorite though is absolutely laughable. My mother, Lourdes Maribel Peña, a God-fearing Christian who never misses a Sunday or Wednesday mass and dutifully gives up carbs for lent. The same unmarried woman who has five different baby fathers for each of her children, cusses worse than anyone I know, and who, even at forty-four years old, never misses a *Ladies Night* at the club.

She must thank God every day for Sunday confession.

My mother is so many things. Resilient, badass, over the top, and slightly hypocritical but damn it if she wasn't telling the truth about Proverbs 4:23.

I should have listened to her words.

———

"Stop the car and back the fuck up. He broke up with you in a text?"

My best friend Mya's voice blares through my car's speakers. I tighten the grip on my steering wheel and clench my teeth. I fight the urge to turn my car around and speed back towards Esteban's apartment to really give him a piece of my mind and maybe slam my fist down his throat.

"Ese cara de culo!" *That shitface.* Mya shouts through the phone as if he could hear her from our Philly apartment. Correction *his* Philly apartment.

"I know." I respond.

"And on your anniversary! Ooooh, he is lucky I'm carrying this baby right now, or I swear to God he'd be catching these hands!"

"I know." The image of her rolling her sleeves up and removing her hoops flashes through my mind. It should make me laugh or at least chuckle at the thought of her wobbling around to defend me.

"Fuck him. He isn't shit without you. Never was and never will be."

"I know." I say again. My throat squeezes into a tight knot. The emotions I've been trying to hold back for at least another five minutes until I can end this call or get to Mom's house, threaten to break free.

"You okay?" She asks, her voice growing soft.

"No." My voice wavers. Big fat tears fall down my cheeks as the dam holding them back finally gives out.

I'm so stupid!

"I thought he was going to propose!" I cry out, slamming my hand against the steering wheel. "I got my stupid fucking nails done. Did my makeup. I spent my entire last pay check on fucking lingerie and a dress I could barely breathe in. And then..and then," I hiccup and take a lungful of air. " I waited for two mother-fucking hours, calling and texting, worried something had happened to him. I was two seconds away from calling the hospital when I tried calling him one more time and he finally answers. Except it isn't him but some woman who claims she has been seeing him for a little over a year.

"Izzy-boo," She starts. "Come home; we can have a girls night like we used to. Kev can make us snacks and bring us the remote." The image of Mya's sweet husband catering to us all night long does put a smile on my face, and I do miss my best friend more than words can explain but thinking of her I picture her ripe pregnant belly.

She's entering her ninth and final month of pregnancy and though I should be happy for her.. I am happy for her, I can't help but envy her. Mya was the wild child, miss independent. She never even wanted kids or marriage, constantly teasing me for my own Disney like dreams of a happily ever after with my one and only and our very own brood of children made with nothing but love. But here she is absolutely glowing, the happiest I have ever seen her, married and starting a family she swore she would never want. I can't help but feel she's living my life. The life I'd always wanted. Visions of the children I had pictured having with Esteban flash through my mind.

"I just got to mom's but raincheck?" I tell her as I pull into a parking spot.

"Of course. And now that I don't have to commute all the way into the city to see you anymore, we get to make up for lost time before this baby gets here." She says excitedly. The pit in my stomach squeezes tight as I remember how horrible of a best friend I have been to her lately. Since I started dating Esteban, I threw myself into our relationship, into him, and neglected so many other things, Mya being one of them. But like the amazing friend she has always been to me, she is still here. I don't deserve her.

"Tell Kev I said hi and give extra belly rubs to my niece or nephew."

"Yes Aunty Izzy. We love you."

"Love you, back."

I end the call and stare up at the red brick row house I grew up in. I haven't lived here since college and thank God that was just for holidays and the few weeks in summers I wasn't spending with Esteban and his family. Constant trips to the Dominican Republic where his parents still lived, the farm he grew up in, and a life I could only ever dream of.

I'd never left the country, let alone flown in an airplane before I met him. So many firsts I'd given him, thinking it meant something.

Thinking I meant something.

If I had known what I know right now I wouldn't have given in so quickly, so easily, so goddamn naively to the first pretty boy who smiled my way. Who am I kidding… One look into those soulful brown eyes of his and I was done. Basically reached into my chest, tore my heart out, and put it in his hands to do with what he wanted. *Never again.*

If only I had listened to Mom, that precious proverbs verse, and guarded my heart, been more cautious with my love, I wouldn't be where I am today.

Twenty six years old, brokenhearted. Betty, my old Toyota Prius, filled with my entire life in garbage bags.

My life is basically trash and the cherry on top of it is having to move back home. Back to the chaos it has always been. And to sharing one bathroom with at least eight other people.

Fun.

It's okay. I'll be okay. I can survive a few months here. I did it once before. This is temporary, just until I can save up and get my own place.

I take one more deep breath before shutting the car off, and grab a bag, trudging slowly up the steps. The TV on the other side of the door is playing so loud I can feel its vibrations through the porch floor, along with screaming I know for a fact is coming from my sister's badass kids.

There's no place like home, right?

1

IZZY

Four Months Later

"Isadora Leticia, get your ass up." My mother's voice tears me from my slumber.

"Five more minutes, please." I beg, even though I know it is only going to get the sheets pulled right off of me. I clamp my fingers around the thin fabric, squeezing my eyes shut and holding on for dear life as I listen to the steady drum of her feet stomping towards me. And just like I expected, in one quick motion the blanket is torn from my body. My legs curl up into the fetal position in an attempt to keep warm.

Why is this house always so damn cold! We are four weeks deep into freaking Spring and still in the damn forties.

I tuck my arms out of the sleeves of my sweatshirt and wrap them around my chest.

It's been seven months since my return back to the hell I grew up in.

Okay, okay, I'm being dramatic, not quite hell, but sure not peace.

And privacy. God, I miss having my own space–four walls and a door I could call my own. I would gladly take a cupboard under the stairs to my mother's stiff as a board mid century vintage sofa complete with plastic and vinyl covering.

"Por favor nena! *Please, little girl.* Mamá is rolling around in her grave watching you live on her sofa like this."

I groan and search my body for at least a semblance of energy to crawl out of this cocoon so I can get away from my mother and her nagging right now.

"It's my day off, ma. Why do I have to wake up so early?" I ask, sitting up and cringing at the bright light that seeps through the windows and into Mom's narrow living/dining room—my current bedroom.

A blend of new and old school Dominican thanks to Mamá Ingrid. She passed away a few years ago and left it all to mom, who of course kept all of it. The furniture, the clothes, even the vintage Pyrex collection.

"Early? It is well past noon. Now, come on, my living room looks like a pig sty. Get up, get up." She says folding my blanket and rushing me up off of the couch.

"I'm going." I groan.

Before I'm even up the stairs I hear Aiden and Alfonso, my nephews, charging down the hallway.

"Finally! We've been waiting all day to play. " Aiden says as he brushes past me down the stairs and straight to the Xbox in the living room.

"Old people sleep so much." His little brother, Alfonso adds.

Little shits. The level of disrespect in kids these days is ridiculous. I would never even think about talking to an adult that way at his age. Hell, even at my age I still wouldn't. I see it all day, everyday as a teacher and you know what? I blame youtube.

When I reach the bathroom the sight in the mirror makes me jump back though I mean by now I really should be used to what I'm seeing by now. My red rimmed eyes are puffy from another restless night, which only makes my deep set eyes more prominent. My dark wavy hair tied up in a knot hangs crooked on one side of my head. And then there's the glob of pizza sauce glued to my chin.

One look at me like this, you wouldn't think I spent the week prior as a fully functioning human, molding young minds in a classroom, and changing the world one student at a time would you?

No.

I look homeless.

Shit, I am homeless.

"Izzy! Hurry up! I've gotta go!"

My head falls back at the sound of my older sister, Leslie, pounding her fist on the other side of the bathroom door. I swear her bladder is connected to the door swinging shut because every damn day, as soon as I shut the door behind me, not a second passes that she isn't on the other side rushing me out.

Deciding to ignore her, I carry on with the rest of my morning routine, taking my sweet ass time. I brush my teeth, cleanse and moisturize my face, comb my hair, and then let the water run for another few minutes just because. Her banging on the door nearly knocks the towels off of their hooks.

Fuck you Leslie. I don't know what I ever did to her, but we have been like oil and water for as long as I can remember.

I finally decide to unlock the door, but as soon as I press the button on the knob to unlock it, Leslie barges in, leaving the door wide open and not wasting any time rolling her pants down before plopping onto the toilet.

"You're such a bitch! Go get some dick to get that stick lodged out from your ass, Izzy." She hollers. I slam the door shut, smiling and feeling very pleased with myself.

Whatever. I spent my whole life being the dutiful daughter, sister, and girl-friend, and you know where that has gotten me? Nowhere but right back where I started.

DOWN THE STAIRS, I pass my nephews already heavily engrossed in some combat game I'm pretty sure they are way too young for. The tv screen slows down on a character getting their throat sliced. The graphics make it look so damn real I have to look away.

No, I will not think of my nephews as little psychopaths. It's not their fault their parents let them do whatever they want.

I turn away and head straight for the Keurig.

"So, what are your plans for the day?" Mom asks in that tone that tells me she knows damn well what my plans are. They have been the same every weekend since I moved back in.

I pop a Café Bustelo into the k-cup holder.

Sleep in, coffee up, and cyber stalk Esteban and his girlfriend's social media accounts until Monday morning. *If I wasn't at an all time low, I would be disgusted with myself—or maybe I'm too numb to realize it.*

"Same as usual, Ma." I say breathing in the mouth watering richness as it fills my mug.

"Well, Liam is with his father today and the twins have volleyball practice."

"Okay." I say, unconcerned by my other siblings. I will miss my little Liam; he's my favorite little brother, and not just because he is my only brother.

"Leslie and I are headed to the gym. You haven't used the membership I got you for your birthday. You should come."

I must not do a good job at hiding the grimace that comes across my face because she immediately purses her lips and cocks her brow in a stern look.

"Don't look at me like that. I got you a six month members pass."

"Yes, Mom. Thank you for letting me know the fat slob you think of me as."

"That is not why I got you the membership, Izzy, and you are not fat, honey, you are thick in all the right places." She says, wrapping her arms around me and leaning her chin down on the top of my head. "It's just that spending your weekends holed up in the living room clinging to this raggedy old sweatshirt isn't doing you any good, mi reina."

"For. Real." Leslie chimes in, walking into the kitchen. "Do us all a favor and put that thing in the trash." She busies herself with making a protein shake.

I glare at her and give her my middle finger. She reciprocates without even looking up, sticking a manicured finger in my direction.

"Don't you two start. Grown ass women still bickering like children. Izzy, come with us. It will be fun just us three, like back in the day before the twins and Liam," Mom says, standing beside Leslie. I notice their coordinated gym wear: Leslie's dark, leopard print leggings and matching sports bra and mom's white leopard print leggings and sports bra.

The outfits highlight every one of their shared assets: petite hourglass figure and wide hips; a family trait that, of course, skipped me.

Compared to them, I stand out and not in a good way. I'll never have a body like theirs, hell, I'm already jealous of the curves on my little sisters who are barely even sixteen. And mom, even on her worst day, though those are few and far between, can easily pass as one of our sisters, whereas I look like a distant relative.

Her afro-latina roots shine through her and every one of my mixed siblings. Where they are varying shades of tawny and hazelnut, almond shaped eyes, curls and curves I would kill for, I am the latina equivalent of plane fucking Jane. My skin is pale and instead of getting tan it very easily burns under the sun. My curves are more subtle and any excess weight goes straight to my hips or thighs but not my ass because a girl can't have it all, right. But I've got a good rack.

That's what Esteban always told me at least.

"You know you're never going to move on like this. What have I been telling you?" And because she has been saying it practically everyday since I've been back, Leslie and I repeat what we know word for word she will say.

"The best way to get over a man is to get under a new one."

"Ahora si. *Now, that's it.* Good to know my girls are listening."

Ladies and gentlemen, my mother.

"So, you're saying this new man I'm getting under will be waiting for me at this gym?"

"I don't know. Maybe, but you will never find out by moping on that couch."

"But if you're not coming, can you babysit the boys since Jimmy is a no show?"

Fucking Jimmy! Leslie's deadbeat ex and poor excuse for a father. Sucks he bailed on the boys again, but it will be a cold day in hell when I babysit those heathens.

"Oh, no. You couldn't pay me to watch those monsters. The bruising on my ass has still not healed from the last time you left me with them."

"Tsk, so dramatic. There is no way you are bruised, it was just nerf guns."

"When you get blasted in the ass by a fully automatic nerf gun for one hundred rounds, then you can tell me that shit doesn't hurt."

"See, this is why you should come with us. Get some muscles on those glutes, like your momma." Mom says turning around and smacking her ass.

Lord, you really outdid yourself when you created her didn't you.

"Mira, mira." She says flexing her ass cheeks.

"Okay, okay! I'll go just please stop.

"Also, where the fuck is Jimmy with my car, Leslie?"

My archaic 2003 Toyota Prius in her prime was the safest most reliable car in the market. Even after nearly nineteen years, any problems I had were minor things that needed replacing but of course when it rains it fucking pours. I should be saving up for my own place, but instead I've been dumping all of my savings into repairs.

"Do I look like a mechanic? I don't know shit about your car. Call the garage if you need an update."

"You're the one that pressed me into taking the car to his shop!"

"Shh, I'll text Jimmy, just go get dressed, and you be nice."

I turn around and walk out to the hallway closet where I have been storing some of my things and pull out a pair of relaxed black sweatpants and v neck t-shirt.

In the mirror hanging on the back of the closet door, I try to give myself a quick once over but my eyes catch on the frayed sweatshirt I've been clinging to for months and turn away.

I hate the person on the other side of the mirror. I hate that I let myself become this pathetic, this level of pitiful for a man I know never deserved me, never valued me, never loved me, and who honestly I never loved back.

"Not anymore." I mutter to myself as I rip the sweatshirt off over my head.

The best way to get over a man is to get the fuck over it.

———

DAMN, I wish I was hoe.

Getting under a new man would at least involve a more enjoyable type of cardio.

You know what, fuck getting over my ex. I'd gladly take an elbow deep carton of my favorite ice cream right now instead of this. Shit, I would even take my chances babysitting my nephews.

This sucks, and the gym female-to-male ratio here is pretty high. Nothing but women in Lululemons, and barely there outfits, like this is a strip club and not a fitness center.

"I'm…" I wheeze. "…dying!" My hands grip my knees as my body tries to recover from the abuse it is currently enduring.

That earns me a chuckle from Mom and Lindsey.

Leslie apparently has been teaching herself all about nutrition and fitness. She even put together a little HIIT workout for us—whatever the fuck that means—because the only thing getting hit right now is my confidence.

I am not about this life and neither are my lungs.

"Just five more minutes. Stop being a baby." Leslie calls out, dropping down into a pushup.

"You got this!" Mom cheers, popping up and off of the floor effortlessly.

I shake my head feeling the nausea roll in as sweat trickles down my neck.

"I can't." I say.

I place my hands on my sides and walk around in small circles, appreciating the slight breeze I'm getting from the large overhead fans.

"I'm going to walk." I wheeze, pointing behind in the direction of the treadmills we had passed earlier. I turn around, feeling dizzy and stumble, crashing right into a set of dumbbells. The heavy set crashes to the floor just nearly missing my feet and the sound echoes through the wide space. My ears burn as I feel every other person's eyes piercing into me, and of course Leslie bursts into laughter as Mom rushes to my side to help me replace the dumbbells.

"I was thinking we should get you set up with a personal trainer. They'll be able to guide you into these workouts better than your sister and-"

"No, mom. It's fine." It's not that I don't appreciate her concern, because I do. Honestly, this is the first time in a long time she's worried about me. Even though I was second born, I was always the one taking care of everyone and everything while Leslie was busy practicing baby making, the youngest two were still in diapers, and Mom was working full-time and going back to school for her nursing degree.

"I'm just worried about you." She says and the look in her eyes makes my stomach curl. I look away as I drop the last weight in place.

"I'm okay." I say and head as far away from her and Leslie as possible.

Way on the other side of the gym, it is surprisingly less crowded and thank God for that. I need a break from my family, if for only a few minutes and while doing some cardio.

It's quiet here, nothing but the steady sound of machines.

God, I miss peace and mother fucking quietness. It's like my family is allergic to it.

Growing up with so many different personalities in too small of a home, it always felt like the different noises were battling with each other while the noise in my own head screamed and shouted for my attention but I couldn't hear it. The quiet became something I craved because it was the only way to silence it all.

I take in the endless rows of treadmills, stair climbers, and ellipticals facing an endless wall of mirrors as large TV's above play the news, Family Feud, and an episode of Friends.

I decide to take my chances on a treadmill in the perfect position of the tv playing Friends. I can get lost in Friends any time, even while busting a sweat. I pop T-Swift into my ears and randomly press buttons on the treadmill until the machine finally starts moving. I stare up at the TV screen and can't help laughing to myself. I've watched these episodes so many times I don't even need to hear them to know what's going on. Leslie's big head walks in front of me, and I narrow my eyes at her as she hops onto the treadmill two rows down from me.

And there goes my peace and quiet.

She sticks her tongue out at me before turning her machine on and going straight into a run.

I narrow my eyes at her before raising the speed on my own machine, my ankles moving in a wobbly jog because seriously when was the last time I fucking ran anywhere?

Jesus, maybe it is about time I got into shape.

I can hear the beeps from her treadmill as she raises her speed again, picking up her pace and going into a full run. She glances back at me with a mischievous smile painted across her lips.

Fuck her and her ridiculous abs. Why couldn't she get fat after having kids?

I move my fingers up the screen to increase my speed again to catch up with her, even though my lungs have been completely against this from the moment I started pressing buttons when I notice a man stopped in front of my treadmill. No, not man. A god. Mother fucking Thor incarnate.

The white t-shirt he wears clings to his muscles in ways that make my mouth water as I imagine the contours of tight muscle that lay underneath that broad chest. He's tall, so tall I have to arch my head back just to meet his eyes, but I make a pitstop at his mouth, surrounded by a short trimmed beard that makes his plump pink lips stand out. He opens them to say something but the words don't reach through the pounding in my ears and the T-Swift and Ed Sheeran harmony going on in my earbuds.

All of a sudden, my feet snag on something and I trip, falling down fast and hard. I squeeze my eyes shut, bracing for impact, and for some reason I picture real life Thor's eyes. The way those warm hazel green eyes burned into my soul. They set fire to something unknown, yet familiar. Shifting the broken pieces inside of me.

My face connects with the moving belt of the treadmill and everything goes black.

2

CHASE

ONE MINUTE I'M STARING INTO A PAIR OF DARK SULTRY EYES AND THE NEXT she's on the ground. I witness pure fear distort her pretty face before she crashes down in front of me.

"Shit." My body reacts on instinct and I leap forward, kneeling down over the girl I'd been too busy eye fucking instead of, at least, trying to warn her again about her untied shoelaces.

I pull the red safety key hanging on the treadmill to shut the belt off before I give the unconscious woman on the ground my attention. My heart hammers in my chest as I follow the steady rise and fall of her back as she breathes in and out. A woman a few treadmills down rushes over.

"Izzy! Izzy! Oh my God, is she breathing?" The frantic woman asks.

"She's breathing. Just knocked herself out."

"Should we move her? Call an ambulance? You know what, let me go get mom, she'll know what to do."

She runs off before I can say anything, because I mean...I really don't know what to do in this situation. Maybe if she were a small animal- cat, dog, or gerbil–all situations I can handle. This..not so much.

She–Izzy, the frantic woman had said–lets out a soft moan and the sound shoots straight my dick. *Fuck, get it together! Ogling still unconscious, moaning women is definitely not okay.*

"Hey, are you okay?" I ask, placing my hand on her shoulder and give her a shake.

She moans again and mutters something under her breath that I can't make out.

"You tripped on your shoelaces. Are you okay?" I say, leaning closer. She does smell sweet. Like a juicy tropical fruit in the summer. Suddenly, she jerks her head up, crashing into my face.

Pain erupts across my face as we both groan in pain. She slowly sits up, caressing the side of her face.

"Is your head made out of Uru, too, Thor?"

"Uru?" I ask standing up and rubbing the sting from the force of her head.

She drops her hand and the angry red skin on her left cheek makes my stomach sink.

"You need to get ice on that." I say dropping back down into a squat in front of her.

"Is the ice magical?"

"What?" Shit, the girl is delusional, that can't be a good sign.

Without even thinking about what I'm doing, I reach out and touch the side of her face with the palm of my hand, lightly brushing the inflamed skin with the pad of my thumb. She sucks in a breath at my touch.

"Does it hurt?"

She shakes her head. Those eyes hold me still as she watches me and bites down on her bottom lip. Curiosity and a bit of something else shine in her dark eyes.

"Are you sure?" I ask, unconvinced that she isn't at least in some sort of pain.

She simply nods her head again.

"Can you walk? There's a first aid kit up front." I say as I stand.

She attempts to sit up but quickly shuts her eyes again, groaning in pain.

"Take your time. You fell pretty hard." I say, putting my hands out to help her.

"I'm fine, really." She says in a voice that's low, a little bit raspy, and sexy as fuck.

"Just take your time." I tell her, reaching my hand out to help her up. She slides her small hand into mine, and I pull her up as electricity courses up and down my arm, burning through our point of contact.

I'm pretty sure she felt it too, because her breath hitches in her throat. She stands on shaky legs and I have to fight myself from reaching down and lifting her up in my arms.

"Just a headache." She continues. Suddenly, her eyes roll back and I step forward as her legs give out next. I bend down and catch her small frame in my arms.

"I'd be saving you a whole twenty steps if you let me help you." I try to convince her.

"Okay," She sighs. "You win. Carry me away, Thor." She says and I chuckle to myself, quickly lifting her up as her arms wrap around my neck. Her sweet scent engulfs every one of my senses.

These twenty steps are going to be a lot harder than I thought.

"How tall are you?" She asks, squeezing my neck tight.

"Six two. Are you scared of heights?" I tease.

"Not usually but you should probably come with a height requirement."

"You're in good hands, trust me."

"Says every serial killer to his victim."

"But I mean if I were a serial killer don't you think I would have had my chance when you were laying there unconscious."

"I suppose."

I laugh. "You're safe, besides this gym has got cameras in every nook and cranny."

We reach the front desk where the receptionist is greeting members as they enter the gym. She turns, cocking an eyebrow at us in concern.

"Hey Chase, is everything alright here?" She asks.

"Yea, we're good, just need some ice and the first aid kit."

"Should I get Damon?"

"No, we're okay." I say walking past her into the trainer offices.

"Okay, let me know if you need anything else." She says handing me a bright red first aid kit and bottled water.

"Thanks, Britt."

I place Izzy on the desk and kneel down, opening the bright red container and tear open a packet of ibuprofen, handing it to Izzy along with the bottle of water Britt brought over. Izzy doesn't ask any questions as she takes the anti-inflammatories, and I get to work squeezing the cold pack to life, rupturing and shaking the contents inside until it finally gets cold. I grab a folded gym towel from the shelf beside me, and I wrap the cold pack before handing it to her.

"Thank you." She says as our fingers graze against each others and that electricity zaps up my arm again. Her breath hitches in her throat. Reluctantly, I pull away and tuck them into the pockets of my sweats.

"I'm Chase, by the way."

She cocks her head to the side and screws her face tight, pursing those plump lips of hers. "I think Thor suits you better."

"I don't mind being your Thor." I say, cringing and regretting my words instantly.

Who the fuck even says that?

I clear my throat, scratching my jaw as she stares up at me. Raised voices outside gain my attention, reminding me of the girl who ran up beside her earlier.

"Your friend who was with you, I think she said she was getting your mom?." I ask as I take a step back towards the door.

"Ew, no. Leslie is not my friend, more like the bane of my existence and unfortunately my older sister. I came with her and our mom. They thought the gym would be a good distraction for me, but I'm starting to think I was safer at home." She rambles before wincing in pain.

"What did you need a distraction from?" I ask, curious.

"A breakup." She mutters, looking away. She places the ice pack down and reaches up and releases her hair from its hair tie. The long thick locks fall down past her breast as she busies herself with the ends, still avoiding my eyes.

Fuck me, she is gorgeous.

"I'm sorry I distracted you." I say, hoping that gets her to look up. "I just wanted to let you know your shoes were untied before you tripped on them but sure enough."

"I fucking fell anyways." She says, laughing softly as I shake my head, replaying the image of her falling all over again followed by the hollow sound of her face hitting the hard surface of the treadmill.

"You're laughing but I was pretty sure I killed you there for a few seconds."

That of course makes her laugh even harder. The sight of which tug on the corners of my own lips, pulling a genuine smile out of me. The sound of her laughter, a sweet sound I could listen to and replay for the rest of my life. I sound crazy.

I have no business thinking these thoughts especially of a woman I just met.

"Oh God, that is exactly how I would die! My headstone would read 'And here lies Isadora Leticia Peña Yotun De La Vega, death by a fucking tread-mill.'" She continues laughing, but I pause wanting to hear her name again, slower this time so I can burn it into memory.

"Can you say that again?" I ask.

"What? Death by treadmill?"

"Your name."

"Isadora?" She says in a Spanish accent.

"It's beautiful."

"Izzy is way easier for everyone else to say."

"Is-a-dora." I try to mimic her accent but I'm pretty sure I butcher the hell out of it and should be embarrassed.

"No, not Dora like the explorer! You gotta roll your r's, Thor. "

"Yea, wouldn't guess I took Spanish all four years of high school, huh."

"If it makes you feel better I'm only fluent in Spanglish and can barely hold an entire conversation."

"Where are you from?"

"I'm from here. Born and raised. My parents, too. Mom is Dominican and Puerto Rican and Dad was mixed Chilean and Peruvian."

"So that makes you?"

"A mut, basically, but most likely the only Domini-rican, Chile-ruvian, you will ever meet."

I chuckle. She's right.

"I did go to school with a kid that was Dominican and Peruvian."

"Me, too. Mya, my best friend, is Domini-ruvian."

"I'm sorry about your Dad."

She sucks in a breath before releasing it. "He passed a long time ago. I barely remember him."

"So, you train here?" She asks and I nod my head, mesmerized again by how fucking beautiful she is. How easily I could lose myself and everything else around me by just looking into her eyes.

Dude, what are you saying?

I place my hand over hers and move the cold pack back onto her face.

"You want to keep that on there for at least another fifteen minutes."

"Maybe you could train me." She says, tearing her gaze from mine and looking down at her sneakers. "I mean, I clearly don't know what I'm doing and, as funny as death by treadmill sounds, that's not how I want to go out."

"I can do that."

Do what exactly I have no idea.

"Oh, okay." She smiles, pulling her full lips across her cheeks.

"But maybe we should wait until you have been cleared by a medical professional."

"Psh, I'm fine."

"That's what you said before and almost passed out again, remember."

"Izzy? Isadora? Where is she? Did the ambulance come and take her? *Ay Dios.*" A loud woman's voice comes from the front desk.

"I should get out there and let her know I'm still alive." Izzy groans.

"I could give you my number and you can shoot me a text when you're ready to start." I say, not ready to let her go just yet.

"Sure." She says, handing me her phone.

I type in my number, smirking as I save it under Thor.

"Can I at least walk you out there? I don't think I'll be able to unsee you almost dying a third time today." She takes my arm, wrapping her small hands around my bicep and hops down from the desk. I wait patiently for her shaky legs to slowly gain their balance before walking her out front to the two women causing a scene as they look for her. They look more like sisters than mother and daughter, and nothing at all like Izzy, who seems to be more on edge than relieved to see them.

She squeezes my arm tight once more and I look down, realizing just how small she is compared to me and how much I like it–how much I like her. That's crazy.

I just met her and apparently now I'll be training her? It's fine. This is fine.

I offer tips and help whenever I can when I'm here and someone is struggling. It's nothing new.

But I've never been this attracted to any of them.

I'm fucked.

3

IZZY

FIRST TIME I STEP FOOT IN A GYM IN YEARS AND WHAT DO I GO AND GIVE myself?

No, not sore muscles or burned calories but a damn near concussion. The entire left side of my face, from my temple down to my jaw, is still radiating in pain from the impact it made against that godforsaken treadmill belt. Oh, and let's not forget Thor's doppelgänger coming to my aid.

Ah, I can't believe I called him Thor outloud and I asked for his *help* at the gym.

I don't do that!

Clearly, I've suffered some sort of brain damage, though Mom's quick medical assessments determined I was fine. I mean, she is the nurse here, but I think I need a full exam. CT scan, full neurological workup, MRI.

IN MY FAVORITE pair of pajamas and raggedy sweatshirt, I cradle the phone in my hand and fight sleep as I fill Mya in on the latest humiliating events that is my life.

"I am never ever contacting him. Ever. I'll just avoid the gym which should be easy enough because I am never going back there after this!"

"That gym is right around the corner from your house, Iz. What if you bump into him? Just call him and tell him you changed your mind."

"I can't call Thor and tell him no!"

"You do understand this man is not actually the God of Thunder himself, right. I mean damn girl, how hard did you say you hit your head?"

"Hard. So hard I passed out for a good minute. I'm so fucking humiliated, Mya. One second I'm racing Leslie on the treadmill and the next he's there, standing in front of me looking all perfect and other worldly. Then BAM, lights out."

"Well, at least this bump to your head finally has you moving on from he-who-shall-not-be-named. Now, tell me more about tall, blonde, and godly."

"Moving on? What? No." I stutter. My heart, palpitating in my chest as denial runs rampant through me, "He was just a nice looking guy at the gym who happened to not be a total tool for a few minutes. He's probably a brainless meathead."

"You don't even know him, and a brainless meathead wouldn't have taken the time to make sure you weren't severely hurt."

"Okay, fine. He must have a big old heart made of pure fucking gold for falling to his knees and helping my clumsy ass. "

"I bet you Thor most definitely does have something big and meaty, though." She says, chuckling.

"Mya!"

Her laughter erupts on the other side of the phone.

"He was just doing his job."

"All I'm saying is you aren't doing yourself any favors locking up your heart like you've been doing. You are young, beautiful, and smart as fuck. Just because *cara de culo* was too much of a selfish, overgrown man child to see the amazing badass woman he had the fortune of sharing four years with, doesn't mean someone else won't see it. A real man will appreciate your selfless heart and love you the way you deserve, Izzy boo."

But why couldn't Esteban be the one to see it?

That one thought alone drives the knife lodged in my heart forward. Pain, still so fresh, tears through me. I close my eyes and take a steadying breath as my heart continues to bleed. Pictures of Esteban and his new girlfriend's face fill my mind. Their smiles and the stupid endearing look in his eyes as he gazed down at her in their last post.

"I'm done with love and done with men." I say, shaking my head and trying to force them out of my mind and my thoughts on anything else but him, her, and all the things we will never be.

And, for some reason, I'm taken back to a forest of green and golden brown.

My skin still burned from where Chase's hands had been on mine, wrapped around my hips as he carried me across the gym like Prince Charming and me the damsel in distress.

"Well, your new personal trainer is a God, so he doesn't count, right?" Mya chortles.

"Are you even listening to me? He is not my personal trainer."

"Ah, but you agree God of Thunder doesn't count as a regular man and could definitely get it. You know what, I think I'm ready to start working on my post baby body and join the gym.

"Mya."

"Get me a big, blonde God of a trainer to work me out."

"The fuck?" Kev's voice comes from her side of the line.

"Oh shit." She laughs.

"Who's going to work you out?" His deep voice is closer now, and I try to stifle my own laugh.

"I'll call you back."

"Mhm," I chime, as she laughs into the phone before hanging up.

I toss my phone down onto the marble coffee table and stare up at the popcorn ceiling. Mom's boujee crystal light shudders under the weight of the boys jumping from their bunk beds upstairs.

Mom is out on a date and Leslie is clocked into the call center downstairs. She said she would put the boys to bed before she logged in but clearly they think, *bed* is a trampoline park. My head throbs painfully as a loud thud shakes the entire house, making me jump up.

What in the hell?

I rush up the stairs, taking them two at a time. Passing Lydia and Layla's room as their door swings open.

"What was that?" Layla asks in concern.

"You were supposed to be making sure they stayed in bed!"

"Sorry." She says.

I push the door open, hoping to catch these little monsters in the act. My eyes widen at the sight of the top bunk bed dangling dangerously on one post as the bottom bunk looks like it has caved in on itself.

"What the-"

"We weren't doing anything." Alfonso and Aiden say in unison as their mother walks into the room, her headset still on her head.

She gasps as she walks.

"What did you do!" She shrieks. Their shoulders jump high up their necks as she lists off all of the privileges they will be losing and the butt whooping they will be getting.

My eyes land on Liam, the only one who looks apologetic. "I'm sorry." He says unlike the other two who jumped straight into denial."

"You two, downstairs, now!" Leslie looks at Liam. "And you, Mom, can deal with tomorrow." She says before stomping off.

"I know." He says dropping his shoulders and turning into his bed.

"At least you still have a bed to sleep in tonight." I say.

He doesn't respond but turns around and faces the wall, covering his head with his dinosaur comforter.

Liam is the youngest of us at just seven years old. He came in way under the radar when Mom had just completed her nursing degree. I still remember all of our shock, hers included, when the stomach bug she was so sure of turned out to be a five month old fetus.

I sit down next to him, brushing his soft curls back.

"You okay, sweet boy?"

"Mhm."

"Do you want me to tuck you in?"

"No, you can go, Izzy."

"Are you sure?" I ask, letting my fingers dance up his neck.

"Mhm." He sniffles and my heart cracks.

"Baby boy." I wrap my arms around him and pull him into me as bursts into a sob.

"It isn't fair! They always get me into trouble and I wasn't even jumping. I told them not to jump but they never listen. How am I supposed to be the man of the house when no one ever listens."

I rub the palm of my hand over his back reassuringly.

"Those are some big shoes to fill. You have your entire adult life to be a man, why don't you focus on being the kid of the house, huh?"

"But Dad says I'm the man of this house and need to watch out for you girls."

"You tell your Dad us girls don't need a man to take care of us. We have been doing just fine without one. And you promised me you would never ever grow up to be a stinky old man!" I say tickling his ribs until he's begging me to stop.

"Izzy, please!"

"Promise you'll stay little forever!"

"I promise!" He wails.

"Good." I pepper kisses across his face and tuck him in.

"Is mom going to be home soon?" He asks.

"I don't know, bud. It's ladies night, so-"

"Okay." I don't miss the quick twitch of his bottom lip. My heart can't help but ache for my little brother, knowing myself what it feels like to be in a house full to the brim of people of your own yet feeling so fucking alone it hurts. All while waiting for the one person who loves you to just show up.

"Move over." I say pushing his bedding back and sliding into his twin bed.

"What are you doing?"

"Going to sleep, obviously. That couch is killing my back." I say, closing my eyes.

His little arms stretch across my chest squeezing me as tight as he possibly can.

"I love you, Izzy."

"I love you more, sweet boy."

"I love you most."

"Impossible. I loved you longer."

"Fine." He says yawning and not another minute later he is fast asleep.

I close my eyes as my body gives into the soft mattress. Even with him already sticking to me with sweat, I might just be able to get a decent night's sleep.

4

CHASE

Something is wrong with me. I've completely lost my shit and have finally gone off the deep end. I'm not even the one who possibly suffered a brain injury, but I have most definitely gone mad and need medical attention, stat!

It's been days and I can't get her out of my head.

Those dark eyes and full lips of hers have been flashing through my mind on repeat from the moment she walked away from me. Since then, I've been perched at every corner of this gym watching and waiting for her to walk through those tinted glass doors like some deranged stalker. Just hoping to catch at least a glimpse of her long dark ponytail. My mind picturing all the ways I'd love to have it wrapped around my hand as my other gripped her full-

"You competing for the next bodybuilding competition, bro? You've been here everyday this week." Damon asks, smacking my shoulder as I release the two hundred pound weight I'd been pulling on and distracting me from where my thoughts were about to go.

Get it together, Chase!

My dick and dirty mind have been acting like a horny teenager that's never seen a beautiful girl before, at least none as beautiful as her, but even then it doesn't matter. I gave her my number and she hasn't called or texted. Unless she really did suffer a concussion and is in the hospital.

"What's going on with you? Is it Nora? Is she on another bender?" Damon asks, wrapping his tattooed biceps around the frame of the Reverse Delt Fly machine I'd been sitting at.

"When isn't Nora on a fucking bender?" I grunt as if he should know better than to ask that. Nora, my mother, hasn't been sober since..shit, probably since she was pregnant with me. I hope.

I reach for my bottled water on the floor beside the machine and take a swig, trying to cool my muddled thoughts.

"It's nothing." I tell him, hoping he'll let it go.

"Bullshit." Of course he can't let it go. Like he always has, Damon can smell my bullshit a mile away. Best friends since, fuck I don't know a time in my life where Damon wasn't there. Neighbors to best friends to the closest thing to a brother I could ever have.

I sigh, dropping my towel. Knowing he won't leave me alone until I tell him. "I was hoping to bump into someone I met last week." I say, wrapping my hands around the handle bars and pulling the weights back. Every one of the muscles in my shoulders and upper back were burning in pain at the torture I've been putting them through. I tear through, not stopping until my hands reach my sides before pushing forward.

"Cause that's not what stalkers do."

"Fuck you." I breathe out.

"She must be hot if you're forgoing a rest day." He says looking up. His brown eyes searching the room as if he'd be able to pinpoint her. "Is it the girl you helped off the treadmill?"

"She asked for help with her workouts. I just wanted to make sure I was here if she showed up."

"Oh, we're playing that game, huh." He says, rubbing the palms of his hands together in excitement. "I like it. You need me to grab you a trainer t-shirt from the back?"

"I'm not playing any games. Maybe I'll just set her up with Ant." Though, the thought of Ant touching Izzy as he *"helped"* her stretch sends a surge of jealousy through me as I reach forward moving the pin to add another twenty pounds to the weight and push the handles back, ignoring the fire spreading across my shoulder blades.

"Man, fuck Ant."

My thoughts exactly.

"What is she looking to do? Trim down? Muscle up?"

"I didn't ask." I grunt. My mind picturing the kind of body she only hinted at underneath the oversized t-shirt she was wearing and thick baggy sweats.

"Well, if you're going to be playing personal trainer you need to know what you're doing. Luckily you have me in your pocket to help guide you."

"I told you already I'm not playing a game. I'm not even entertaining this thing with her."

"Oh, so there's a thing."

"No. It's just me. It's been a while I guess. I don't know, maybe I just need to get fucking laid."

Yeah, that must be it.

"Don't tell me it's been since Jenna."

I complete my set and let the weights slam down against each other. Grabbing my water and towel off of the ground, I walk away from Damon towards the locker room while trying to shake that goddamn name from my thoughts. It's been well over a year since that woman and time has done little to numb the ache her memory brings. The good times, which thanks to Nora were few and far between, and the bad ones which again were usually brought on by Nora. I should have seen Jenna's ultimatum coming, but still, the fact that she put me in that spot still rubs me the wrong way. Her or Nora, it wasn't even a choice. What kind of son would I be to turn my back on my mother?

"Damn, man. That's not right. No wonder you're here everyday trying to burn up all that pent up frustration." He says, following me to my locker.

"You're a jackass, you know that right." I say, grabbing my gym bag and slamming the locker shut.

"Hee-haw, motherfucker." He jokes. "But for real, tell me about this girl. You know I respect bro code to the end man, and if you don't tell me I could end up talking to her without knowing it's your girl."

My girl? I think to myself walking out of the locker room with Damon hot on my tail as I try to dodge his badgering. My sneakers suddenly skid to a stop and my hand juts out in front of Damon, stopping him as well.

It's her.

My eyes take their time trailing over her body as she walks over to the elliptical machines. The outfit she's wearing this time seems more fit for a workout than what she wore last time. Her dark hair is tied up again in a ponytail and the faded black t-shirt she wears clings to her chest, begging for air through the deep split collar while her black, skin tight leggings let me see the thick thighs I'd imagined wrapped around me.

I watch her as she laughs. Her wide lips stretching across her face and the thick sultry sound that escapes carries through the gym and fills my entire body.

What the fuck is this?

"Earth to Chase?" Damon says, waving his hand in my face. "And I'm the jackass." He mumbles before turning around and following my gaze.

He whistles low. "Go, talk to her." He says while nudging my shoulder.

"I can't." I turn around, not wanting her to catch me staring at her like the creep I'm apparently becoming.

"What is this middle school all over again, O'Rourke?"

"I gave her my number and she hasn't used it. It's been a week."

"So? Stop being a little bitch and get your ass over there or I will."

I turn around and can only assume she had been watching me since her eyes lock on mine immediately. Those deep hooded eyes of hers, a pool of infinite darkness I want to dive into.

And now I'm a goddamn poet?

She raises her arm up in an awkward wave as Damon murmurs beside me to go.

I move my feet towards her while my mind figures out what the hell I'm going to say.

Sorry for being a creep but can I take you out sometime?

Take her out and then what?

Between my twelve hour shifts at the veterinary office and chasing my mother's drunk ass around town and then cleaning up after her, I can't offer much else outside of these walls. This is the one break I get and what do I do with it? Abuse my body until it's numb.

The ghosts of relationships past whisper in my mind and the one choice I could never make.

Before I know it I'm in front of her, my six foot two frame nearly swallowing her whole. I can feel the woman beside her eyeing me but all I see is Izzy and I can't look away. Her eyes trail up as she cranes her neck back and meets my eyes. Her lips pull up in a soft smile that triggers a dimple in both of her cheeks.

"Chase, right?" She asks, squinting her eyes. The fact that she remembered my name makes my stomach do flips.

"And here I was pretty sure you had amnesia and forgot all about me." I smile.

"I did hit my head hard," she says pointing to the faded yellow bruise on the side of her face, and I wince at the sight of it marring her skin.

"But you are harder to forget." She adds, looking away and biting her lip.

I swallow hard, searching my brain for something else to say to that but I can't think of anything else other than the fact that she's been thinking about me, too. Maybe as much as I have.

"Excuse me, Thunder God?" I perk my eyebrows at the woman beside her. Just a few inches taller than Izzy with tan skin, and large probing eyes. Izzy mutters under her breath. "Izzy mentioned the free training included with her membership. I just signed up but the receptionist up there says the gym doesn't offer personal training."

My throat goes dry as they both eye me suspiciously.

They think I'm a personal trainer? What?

"Actually-" I start before Damon cuts me off and smacks my shoulder.

"Bethany up there is new. Still training and yet to know all the things we offer here." I turn my head slowly, glaring at the side of his smug face as he speaks.

Where the fuck is he going with this?

"I'm pretty sure her name tag said Brittney." Izzy says, raising an eyebrow at Damon.

Damon shoots his hand out with his card in between his fingers like a magician.

"Damon Chambers, personal trainer and owner of this fine establishment lucky enough to be graced by you beautiful ladies tonight." He says eying Izzy's friend seductively.

"Mya. Happily married, new mom, and best friend to Izzy here. So, -" She pauses.

"I'm sorry, do you prefer Thor, Thunder God, or is there something else you go by?"

Izzy bumps her shoulder and widens her eyes at her while I try to hide my burning cheeks as my brain recalls the memory of her calling me Thor last week.

"Chase is fine." I say stretching my hand out to shake hers. My large hand engulfs hers but she doesn't let that intimidate her and squeezes tight. I apply just the slightest pressure in return to hopefully reassure her and maybe gain me some brownie points.

"So then you can train us both together?"

Damon cuts in. "Ah, Chase here is one of our most sought out trainers. Unfortunately with adding Izzy here to his schedule, he's booked up." He turns to me and winks while I stare back in horror at his words. What the fuck? I'm not a personal trainer. Sought out? By who? The starving cougars who throw themselves at me like it's part of their cardio? "And I think taking anyone else on would just be a disservice. We offer a complete personalized workout and nutrition education to each individual client we work with. You know, quality over quantity. Unless you'd rather try one of our weekly classes, I, however, do have availability in my schedule for one more."

Damon has lost his mind. *Personalized training and nutrition education?* I don't know anything about any of this shit.

"Best part is you get a two week trial before committing to anything long term. What do you say?"

"That doesn't sound bad at all. Sign me up."

"Great, shall we get started then? Or are you ladies done for the day?"

"We just got here." Izzy says.

Damon bumps his shoulder into mine, clearly pleased with himself.

"Mya, why don't we record some numbers and work on a plan."

"Okay. I'll catch you later, Izzy-boo. Thor, it was nice meeting you." She says before following Damon to the back towards his office.

Fuck! Fuck me and fuck you, Damon Chambers and your constant meddling in my life.

5

IZZY

GODDAMN YOU, MYA.

She shows up at my mother's house unannounced, dressed for the gym, and suckers me here with the excuse of getting her body back to a semblance of what it once was. Even though I have to disagree with her because she definitely doesn't look like she was the size of a planet before birthing a whole tiny human just a few months ago. And now she leaves me alone with *him*. Even worse though is the measurements and scale I will have to face in front of him.

My stomach clenches tight at the thought before the mountain of muscle beside me distracts me.

"Mt. Joy?" His deep velvety voice snaking all around me as he nods at my chest. "Never been before."

"It's a band."

"What kind of music do they play?"

"Alternative indie."

"Really?" He says surprised.

"Yes, really."

"Hm."

My eyebrows raise. "What?" I can't help feeling defensive over my music choices. Esteban was always ragging on my *gringa* ears and forcing his Dominican as fuck playlists down my throat. I could go the rest of my life never listening to another, but the last few months I have enjoyed drowning my ears in whatever the fuck I want.

"It's nothing." He says, smirking and as cute as that smirk looks across his lips, I react. My hips jut out and my hand is in a balled fist on my side.

"What, cause I'm hispanic, I'm only allowed to listen to reggaeton and salsa music?"

"No, no. That's not what I meant." His eyebrows pull together as he takes a step forward. I turn around and try to push down this uneasiness in the pit of my stomach.

"Let's just get these numbers over with."

"Hold on." He stops me, wrapping his large hand around my wrist, completely engulfing it. The contact on my skin burns.

"I'm sorry. I didn't mean to offend you, Izzy. Indie, country, rap, you listen to whatever you want. I still play Eminem's 8 Mile track like it's 2002."

"Of course you listen to Eminem." I say rolling my eyes.

"Why don't we forget the numbers for today and do something easy." He smiles down at me as my knotted stomach explodes into a swarm of butterflies.

His soft hazel eyes bear into mine, begging me to forgive him. I'm being dramatic, and I know it. It was not that serious at all. I might just be searching for something to be wrong with him at this point so I can finally get him out of my head, but dammit everything about him is fucking perfect. From the curves of his lips to the sharp angles of his cheekbones, to those perfectly placed specks of gold in his eyes.

Like a kid staring up at the sun, knowing all too well it will hurt, I can't look away from him and my heart revels in the burn sure to come.

"We can steer clear of the treadmills if that makes you feel better."

You can make me feel better.

What! No! Get it together, heart! We are not falling for another pretty face that is most definitely going to make us throw caution straight out of the window.

Been there, done that and it's not worth it.

Guard your heart. Stay strong, even though Chase's contradicting softness makes it so damn hard and for some reason all I can do is picture him petting a small bunny in his mammoth sized hands.

A laugh escapes me at the imagery.

"What's so funny?" He asks, a small smile stretching across his lips.

"Nothing." I say. Suddenly noticing the gym bag hanging from his shoulder and sweat staining the collar of his shirt.

"Were you just leaving?" I ask.

"I was but I don't mind staying for you."

"For me?"

No, not for you. He's just being nice and doing his job.

"I-" He stutters and his cheeks grow pink. Holy hell is Thor blushing? My own face flashes with heat as he pushes the words out. "You never messaged me about a time, and I sort of hoped I'd bump into you the next time you came in. You know in case you needed help."

Of course. Falling on my face again wouldn't be good for his place of business, I'm sure.

"Right. I would rather avoid any further brain injury. "

"Agreed, so how about your choice, Isadora. What will it be?"

"Not Dora, *Dorra*. Roll those r's, Thor." I chuckle, enjoying teasing him and his sad attempt at saying my name correctly a little too much before scanning my eyes over every piece of metal machinery. All of it makes my stomach twist and turn as I imagine the pain I'll be in. Hell even biking and my ass swallowing that tiny seat will be a bitch I'll feel for the rest of the week.

Looking up, my sight hangs on the open second floor and what looks like an oval running track.

"Do you mind if we just walk?" I ask pointing up.

"Whatever you want." He says, smiling down at me. The butterflies in my stomach flutter around like crazed teenagers as my sex throbs letting me know damn well what she wants.

Down girl! We are on a dick hiatus until further notice!

Chase nods his head to the double doors under a sign with an arrow pointing up and I follow him.

"Elevator or stairs?"

I give him a knowing look, that I'm hoping portrays, *boy if you haven't figured me out yet.*

He smiles and presses the button for the elevator.

"I swear I'm not completely allergic to physical exertion. I've spent plenty of days subbing for gym teachers." I say as the double doors close.

I've never in my life battled claustrophobia. I mean growing up in my house, sharing every space with another person is the only life I knew but suddenly these four walls and Chase, take up all the air beside me. It's too much. His scent all around me invades my senses, making my body tingle and it takes everything in me to not close my eyes and moan.

"You're a teacher?" He asks and I appreciate the distraction.

"Mhm. First grade." I say, trying to push through the cloud of lust pulsing through my mind.

"That's amazing." He says as the doors open.

"Eh, I'm not saving the world."

"But you are." He says stopping abruptly as we exit. "For some of those kids you're their second home. I can imagine the level of patience you must have and compassion to handle a classroom full of tiny monsters. Don't sell yourself short on the impact you're leaving."

Well damn.

"Thank you," I say.

Chase nods, walking over to the wall as I follow and take in the indoor track. From downstairs it didn't look that bad but up here now, I realize just how big it really is. It spans the entire circumference of the building with three wide rows taped to the black and red flooring that curves around the metal railing.

Chase drops his bag along the wall and jogs back towards me. A pair of women power walk past me, sharing hushed words as they openly gawk at Chase like he's every single one of their wet dreams.

"Damn Zaddy." One says as they slow their pace and I narrow my eyes at them, hoping they run right the fuck off this track.

Whoa there, killer.

"You ready?" Chase asks, bending down in front of me to tie his shoe.

Right, I should double check these ties and make sure I don't fall in front of him again.

I rush to bend down and check my laces as he leans up and our foreheads knock into each other. We both groan in pain.

"Are you okay?" Chase asks, placing his hand over mine that is currently rubbing my head.

"Shit, you've got a hard head, Thor."

"I could say the same to you." He says. "Are you okay, though?"

"I don't know how much more injury my head can take."

"This poor, pretty head of yours…" He says rubbing the pad of his thumb over last week's yellowing bruise.

Pretty head? He thinks I have a pretty head?

Looking up at him, I suddenly realize how close our bodies are. His tall frame keeps his face an ocean away from me as his piercing gaze makes it feel like it would take nothing at all to close the distance between us.

"Beautiful." He whispers, the sound cascading over me like a cool breeze while burning my skin with nothing but a single word from his lips. A single touch on my skin.

Aw shit. This is bad.

Chase clears his throat and shoves his hand into the pocket of his sweats.

"Shall we?" He says.

———

WE WALK in awkward silence for a few minutes before Chase finally speaks.

"Are you new in town? I've never seen you around before."

"Eh, sort of. I grew up here, just down the street actually, but I've been gone the last few years until recently…"

"It's crazy we've never bumped into each other growing up. I grew up off of Irving street."

"And you're still there?"

"Yea." He says, clearing his throat and turning his gaze to the ground.

"It's the school district cut off. Had you lived just a block closer we would have been the best of friends over at Jefferson."

"Maybe." He says, smirking at me.

We talk a bit more about growing up in the neighborhood. Places we both hung out at and how we still somehow never crossed paths.

"We had to have bumped into each other at least once!"

"I don't know, I'm pretty sure I'd remember you, Dora. Oh, I forgot to roll my r's . Dorrrra."

I ignore the raging butterflies in my stomach and the sound of his tongue rolling over those r's. *Mmm, I know something else that tongue can roll over.*

Tripping over my shoes I catch myself and place my hand over my stomach to steady myself.

"You okay?"

"Yea, too much cardio for me in a day."

"We'll have to work on your endurance, then. Thirty minutes is nothing compared to what I have planned for you."

I swallow down the lump in my throat at his words.

Mind out of the gutter right the fuck now!

"That's two miles." He says raising his hand in a high five.

And for some reason I give him a fist bump instead, cringing at my fucking awkwardness. Seriously, who does that?

"I have to be somewhere in a few, but you have my number. Shoot me a text confirming for tomorrow, maybe same time?" He says as he walks over to his gym bag and slings it over his shoulder.

"Okay." I say following him over to the elevator as he presses the button. We get in alongside a pair of women whose shorts leave so damn little to the imagination they are basically underwear.

I roll my eyes and tuck myself back into the far corner while the itty bitty committee fails miserably at flirting with Chase. Glancing back at him and whispering to each other as they giggle and stick their asses out more than they already are.

Gag!

I shake my head and chance a glance at Chase, expecting him to be ogling them right back but I'm surprised to see his eyes locked on mine.

His heavy gaze takes the breath from my lungs as my pulse thuds in my ears. What is he looking at when there are perfect ass cheeks in front of him?

The elevator doors open and we all shuffle out.

"Tomorrow, we're taking the stairs." He says, walking backwards and smiling wide like taking the stairs is his favorite thing to do before he is out the glass doors. I watch him walk across the sidewalk until he disappears around the building.

"You need me to get you a napkin for all that drool, mama? Damn near panting over Thor like a bitch in heat." Mya's voice comes from beside me as she bumps into my shoulder.

"Leave me alone. This is all your fault. I was perfectly fine donating my gym dues and pretending he was nothing more than a figment of my imagination."

"Liar." She says, hooking her arms with mine as we walk out of the gym. It's late but luckily the parking lot is lit up by bright led light poles. I squeeze Mya's arm tight as a crisp breeze wisps by and we reach our cars parked next to each other.

"How was your session with DC himself?" I ask.

"Great. I'm already sore as shit from the workouts we did. Just a few more months and I'll be back to my snatched self."

"Your ass is still fine and you know it."

"I do." She laughs as she opens her door. "I have to get home and milk these suckers, though. I'm surprised I made it this long." She points to her chest.

"Kisses to EZ from his favorite aunty." I say as I walk over to my door and get in.

"Only because you're his only aunty."

When I get home, after I shower, I do something I haven't done once in the seven months since I moved back home. I don't reach for Estebon's sweater. I don't scroll through hours of posts or even think about him or his new insta-model girlfriend.

Instead, I think of Chase. I let my mind throw caution to the wind, replaying every touch, every look, and every word we shared.

6

CHASE

"Get out of my house you no good-" I don't flinch as the plate in her hand crashes against the wall near my head.

"Nora." I say her name, exhausted with this bullshit and the mess I'll have to clean up.

It's been a shitty night and I just want to get it over with already and go to sleep.

And wait for Izzy to text you.

Why hasn't she texted me yet?

Maybe she's changed her mind about the gym? She clearly hates it, but then why sign up for a gym membership.

Another plate lands at my feet, and I curse myself for not putting those dishes away the day before.

Mental note: get Nora some goddamn paper plates.

"You stay the hell away from me, Keagan! I don't want you here!" She says through gritted teeth. "I hate you!"

She doesn't mean it.

I know she doesn't.

This isn't her, it's just the fucking alcohol and who knows what else raging through her system right now.

But damn it if her words don't make it feel like the hardwood floor might just give out underneath me and swallow me whole.

"Mom." I beg, even though I know it's goddamn pointless; she doesn't see me, not Chase, her only son and the last person in her fucked up world that hasn't given up on her.

No, all she sees when she looks at me is the face of a ghost, a man who did exactly what she is begging me to do right now, but unlike him, I can't. I may be the spitting image of my father, but I am not him.

"It's me, mom. It's Chase. Let's put these down and get you into bed." I say grabbing onto her wrist as she picks up the last plate on the dish rack.

Her blue eyes glare daggers into me.

How can't she see me?

"Mom, please. Put the plate down." I say as softly as possible.

Her eyes flutter as the venom I just saw in them dissipates and she comes back to me.

"Chase? Chasey boy, where have you been?"

"I've been right here, mom." I force out. Savoring this moment and the feel of her cold hands on my cheek as she looks up at me.

"It's a shame how much you look like him." She says and I nod my head in agreement. Maybe if I didn't remind her so much of him, she wouldn't have spent my childhood using alcohol to forget him.

"Let's get you to bed, mom. It's late."

After getting her into bed and cleaning up the floor, I put the dishes away and close her bedroom door behind me. I take the stairs two at a time to my room and let out a sigh of relief as I fall into my bed. My sore limbs and tired eyes finally weigh me down as I sink into the soft bedding. Just then, my phone vibrates in my hands. With one eye open, I peak at the notification on my screen and smile when I read the text I've been waiting for all fucking week.

Unknown Number: You really saved your name in my phone as Thor?

Finally.

Me: It took you long enough. I thought you changed your mind. I mean it's not like you need it.

Isadorrra: Har,har,har. Not funny, Thor.

Me: I'm not being funny. Why did you join the gym if you hate it?

Isadorrra: Part to avoid getting stuck with babysitting my bad ass nephews and the other part because obviously I could stand to lose a few pounds or twenty.

Me: TWENTY! Where?

Isadorrra: Shouldn't you be trying to keep my money and talking to me about the importance of dieting?

Me: I hate diets. Getting healthy should be about changing your lifestyle for a better one that will sustain and nourish you. Balancing all that with indulgences every now and then are key to maintaining goals.

Me: Also, #TacoTuesday counts as a solid and very allowed cheat day in my book.

Isadorrra: You were convincing for all of one message there Thor. And agreed #tacotuesday is LIFE. But I can get down with this lifestyle change if you're telling me I don't have to eat like a rabbit for the next month. Maybe even exercise for longer that thirty minutes.

Me: Stick with me and you might even come to enjoy it.

Isadora: HA! Never!

Me: Never say never, Dorrra

Isadorrra: So, then I'll say never, ever, everrr, Thor. I should get to bed, I've got an early start and a gym sesh I need to prepare for.

Me: Same time okay with you?

Isadora: Yup. See you tomorrow.

Me: Good night, Izzy.

My head falls back against the soft cushion of the sofa.

Goddamn Damon! I dial his number, not even waiting for him to respond before chewing him out.

"Fuck you and your childish games, man."

"She's cute though and you two seemed to hit it off upstairs.."

"I need you to tell me everything I need to know about being her personal trainer."

He chuckles. "It's not as hard as you think and you already are about this life. Practically been living in the gym and treating your body like a temple since high school."

"Yea, but how am I supposed to help this girl lose weight when I think she's perfect the way she is?"

"So, it's not about losing weight rather than her being comfortable in her own skin and seeing what you see."

"Okay, so how do I do that?" I put him on speaker and open the notes app on my phone and jot down everything he says.

———

The next day I walk into the gym surprised to see Izzy already there. She stands up front talking with Damon.

"There he is. The man of the hour."

I shake my head as I reach them.

"Sorry, I got held up at work."

"You have two jobs?" Izzy asks, her eyes narrowing at my navy scrubs and gym bag.

"Um." Shit. Fuck me!

"Yes. I have another job that I work when I'm not here." I internally smack the shit out myself for not forming words stronger than the crap I just spewed out.

"I'm just going to change."

"I'll warm her up for you, *Thor.*" Damon says, winking at me, and I try to bite down the image of him *warming* her up.

I slam the locker door open and change out of my clothes as quickly as possible. Walking out as I pull my t-shirt up over my head when my bare chest smacks right into someone's face.

My arms shoot out and grab her before she falls back.

Izzy.

"Is there any part of you that isn't hard?" She says under her breath. I can't fight the smirk working across my lips as her eyes bounce over the muscles of my chest. My skin heating as she lowers her gaze down my abs.

"Are you okay?"

"Huh," She mutters, her gaze fixed on my naked chest, and I realize my t-shirt is still hanging around my neck.I tug it down and work my arms through the sleeves, breaking Izzy from the spell.

"Sorry-um. Damon was going to get my weight and measurements before he got distracted." She says pointing behind her.

"I'll get your measurements." I say and turn towards his office.

I nod to the scale beside the door as Izzy groans.

"Do we have to?" She says looking like a toddler ready to throw a tantrum.

"We don't have to do anything you don't want to do but these numbers will help in seeing progress and tweaking the training so you can see the results you'll be working towards."

"Fine." She says, kicking off her sneakers.

"You can keep your shoes on."

"Nope, not giving this deceiving square trap of lies any more ammo than it needs." She says holding her breath and squeezing her eyes shut.

"What are you doing?"

"Did you get it?" She asks, keeping one eye closed to look up at me.

"Get what?" I ask, confused.

"My weight."

"Yeah, I got it." I say turning the clipboard over before laying it on the desk.

"Good. Don't tell me. I don't want to know."

"Okay." Clearly this is a touchy subject for her, and I don't want to make her feel any more uncomfortable than she already is.

"Let's just get this over with, what's next?"

"You know you're pretty average compared to other women around the same height as you."

"Just what every girl wants to hear, Thor. Thank you."

"I didn't mean it like that-"

"Chase?"

"Yeah?"

"Can we please just get this over with?"

"Yeah. Can you spread your arms out?"

She huffs, biting her bottom lip as she stretches her arms out for me.

I take the measuring tape and try to remember exactly where Damon had said to place it around before wrapping it around the midpoint of her arm. I jot down the measurements quickly before repeating it again for her other arm.

Her eyes bounce around the entire space, and I notice her deep breathing before squeezing her eyes shut.

When I wrap it around her waist she sucks in a breath, practically jumping out of her skin, and I can't take another second of this torment.

I drop the tape and stand up, placing it on Damon's desk.

"I think we're good here."

"You didn't even finish."

"It's not important if it's going to make you feel uncomfortable. Remember sustainability and enjoyability. This isn't about dropping a quick twenty to just gain it right back because you hated the process. We'll find what works for you, Izzy."

"Thank you." She says, her eyes shining up at me as if I said exactly what she needed to hear, and I allow myself an internal pat on the back.

If she could see how beautiful she is, even with her loose fitted gym wear, what lies underneath is undeniable.

I walk her out and to an empty space on the gym mat where we start the workout Damon planned for me. Now, all I have to do is keep my eyes off of her and my hands to myself as much as possible for the next forty minutes.

I can survive not being a total creep for that long, I think to myself as she pushes her chest out and stretches one foot behind her.

My dick twitches at the swell of her breasts.

Fuck, this is going to be harder than I thought.

7

IZZY

Fuck. This. Shit.

I can't. I just can't fucking do it.

Day five–the end of our first week of training–and my body is spent.

Every single one of my muscles is sore. It hurts to laugh, to breathe, and I have failed miserably at trying to pee standing up because my thighs quiver and threaten to give out any time I attempt to squat down.

Yet, here I am, still putting myself through this miserable agony.

"I can't-" I pant as my arms buckle and I collapse onto the mat on my stomach. My face sticks to the gym mat as sweat trickles down my forehead. The oversized t-shirt I've been wearing for these sessions feels like a hot blanket weighing me down and clinging to me like a second layer of skin.

This is so stupid. I can't do this. I can't. I can't. I can't.

"Yes you can. Get out of your head Izzy."

I shake my head and squeeze my eyes shut.

Why am I even putting myself through this?

"Because you can do hard things, Izzy. Come on, we're almost there." Chase says, and I pop my eyes open as I feel him lean over me. Taking in a deep breath, his woodsy evergreen scent fills my airways. Those honey emerald eyes of his lock on mine before dipping down to my lips, like they have done every single time he looks at me.

"Just one last set." He says, low, his voice wafting over me like a cool breeze in the dead of summer. It gains the attention of every damn cell in my body; my nipples tighten and push through the thick padding of my sports bra.

"Come on, Iz. You didn't get this far to just give up now."

I groan in protest as I will my body to move. Holding myself up by my arms and the tips of my sneakers, I drop down in a half assed attempt of a push up, then bring both my feet forward and jump up in the air, barely managing to swing my arms past my ribs.

"That's it. You've got it. Keep going." Chase says, counting down from five as I force myself back down on the mat as fast as possible so I can get this the hell over with.

"Four."

"Three."

"Keep going, you're almost there!"

"Two."

"One."

"Yes! You did it!" Chase shouts. When I jump up from the ground into my final fucking jumping jack, he immediately wraps an arm around my waist and thank God for that because I'm pretty sure I would have crumbled in a heap on the floor if he hadn't.

"I've got you." He says, peering down at me as I pant like a wild dog. I grip his arms and get lost in him.

"Breathe." He says, inhaling slowly, but I can't think, let alone breathe, with him so close. With his touch burning through the thin layers of fabric between us.

"Izzy?" He says, concerned, and I attempt to shake the lust from my thoughts. Can you tell it's been seven long months since the last time-

"I didn't push you too hard did I?"

Oh God, do I know somewhere he can push hard.

Down, girl!

"No, I'm okay." I force the words out. Placing my hands over his chest, I immediately regret the movement because I don't want to take my hands off. But I need air and definitely need to put some distance between Chase and my horny mind right now.

Reluctantly, I pull away and stumble over to the nearby bench.

"Whoever invented Burpees can burn a slow death in hell for this shit, though." I pant as I sit down and chug from my water bottle.

Chase chuckles as he walks over and joins me on the bench.

"Royal Huddleston Burpee."

"What?" My face crunches in confusion as I swipe the water that dribbles down my chin with the palm of my hand.

"The guy who invented the Burpee." Chase says, raising an eyebrow as if this is common knowledge.

"Why?" I ask before bursting into a fit of laughter. Chase's own laughter erupts with me.

"I might have said the same thing as you a while back, before I started taking my fitness seriously."

"You're telling me you didn't come out of the womb doing Burpees?" I tease.

"Haha. No. They suck. I can't lie about that, but it is a very efficient workout and you killed it, Izzy." He says, wrapping his Hulk-like arms around me and squeezing me to him. God, it takes everything in me not to moan out loud as I let my tired body sink into his warmth.

"I'm proud of you." He says, rubbing the palm of his hand up and down my arm, making my stomach twist in knots.

"Don't you two look cute." My mother says, walking in with a Cheshire smile across her painted pink lips because yes, even at the gym, her makeup, though more subdued than usual, is still on point.

I quickly shrug out of Chase's embrace as he stands and walks over to his water.

Mom's greedy eyes waste no time tracing every sculpted muscle on his back.

"What do you want, ma?"

"Are you almost done? We still have to get ready for ladies night."

I roll my eyes, letting my head fall back against the brick wall behind me.

"*No comience. Don't start.* You're coming. The couch needs a night off and you need to stop acting like a spinster."

"Mom!" I whisper shout, widening my eyes at her in hopes that she stops being so embarrassing. I glance towards Chase, who still has his back towards us, and rush to my mother's side.

"Okay, Ma. We're just wrapping up. I'll meet you in the car."

"Why don't you invite your friend." She says loud, peering over my head.

"Shhh. We're not friends. He's just my trainer."

"I can show him something he can train. Hard." She says clamping her teeth together.

"Mom."

She laughs. "I'm kidding. Besides, he clearly only has eyes for you." She bumps into my shoulder, and I turn around, catching Chase's eyes on mine before he busies himself with his phone.

"Can you go? Please." I beg her.

"Ten minutes." She says, turning around. I don't miss the extra swing in her hips as she passes Chase. A wave of jealousy sinks deep in the pit of my stomach.

"Wild plans tonight?" Chases asks, walking towards me. I walk to the middle of the mat and turn to face the mirrors. Spreading my legs wide, I lower my upper body as I stretch the way he showed me in the beginning of the week.

"Mandatory ladies' night with my mom and her friends which, yes, will be wild as fuck. Please pray for me." I say catching his heavy gaze on my lower body in the mirror. I push my ass out a little further as I switch legs.

God, am I my mother's daughter or am I my mother's daughter?

I shake my head at myself and drop down into a calf stretch. When I look back up to the mirrors, Chase's eyes are on mine, heating my skin.

"Don't bring your knee in front of your hip like that." His voice comes out thick. "Lay down on your side, arm out." I comply instantly. He kneels down behind me, his hands grasping my hip and leg, maneuvering them into the proper stretch I was failing at and I'm a goner. The lust-filled thoughts in my mind scream at the sight of him in the mirror behind me and what he would look like naked just like this, pushing into me and stretching my body past all of its limits.

I'm lost to the image in front of me and the R-rated ones distorting my mind. His lips move, but the only sound I hear is the steady drum of my heart wreaking havoc against my ribcage.

I'm supposed to be coming down from my workout, not feeling like I'm running a 5k.

"Lay back," He demands, and damn if those two words don't make my thighs clench together.

His eyes lock on mine as he places my legs over his shoulder. Gripping my thighs in his large hands, he leans down over me and I suck in a breath as my muscles twist and pull against the pressure of his weight above me. Stretching my tight joints past their limits.

"Is this okay?" He whispers.

I nod my head, biting my bottom lip, too afraid I might just moan–not from the pain, but from the liquid desire coursing through my veins right now.

He doesn't look away as he holds the stretch and that delicious burn spreads from my hamstrings up to my core and the moan I have been trying to suppress finally escapes. My hands rush to cover my mouth.

Chase stills above me, his eyes locking onto mine–golden orbs darkening right before me. My heart thuds loudly in my ears as I stare at him completely mortified.

His nostrils flare as his breaths come out just as ragged as mine. He drags his eyes to my hands, narrowing them as if they've offended him then drops my leg, straddling me as he places his hands over mine, pulling my hands away and up above my head. His tongue sweeps across his bottom lip and he stares at my mouth as if he's dying for a taste.

"Is *this* okay?" He whispers. His mint breath skates across my skin. My breast heaves against his chest and I nod my head again, because there is no way my muddled mind can form words.

"You have to say it, Izzy." He says again, pressing himself against me.

"Oh, God, yes." I push my hips forward, feeling his hard length.

Lost to the burning forest in his eyes as he leans down, I send a silent prayer to Jesus that this man take me right here, right now on this gym mat.

A crash interrupts us and we both tear our gaze away to the commotion as a lanky teenage boy struggles to lift a large weight off of the ground. His cheeks turn red when he glances up as if he didn't want to interrupt, and the realization hits us.

Holy shit!

Chase and I both scramble up off of the gym floor. Chase rushes over to help the kid with the heavy weight, lifting it with ease. I glance around the open gym floor and notice eyes burning into me, clearly enjoying the show they were just about to get.

A wave of embarrassment crashes over me and sends me dashing to grab my phone and water canteen before I rush out of there.

I need air.

I need water.

Fuck me. I need Chase to finish whatever we were about to start back there.

No.

No, I am not fucking my trainer. I am not fucking anyone.

Dick Hiatus, remember!

8

CHASE

I KNEW THIS WAS GOING TO BE HARD.

Not the training part, which thanks to Damon's help has gone off without a hitch. Also, taking Izzy's cues to make changes to the workout plan that wouldn't discourage her. I've actually really enjoyed coming up with ways to help her reach her goals and watching her get stronger and more confident in her workouts.

It's the keeping my goddamn hands to myself part of this that has proved to be the hardest thing I've ever done and I'm failing... miserably at it. What started as completely innocent soft touches here and there to help guide her into proper forms at the beginning of the week have somehow turned into me almost taking her right on the gym floor.

I should have my balls kicked in for the way I came on to Izzy. The way I pushed my erection right up against her hot center. Even through my thin gym shorts and those fucking baggy sweatpants she is always wearing, I know she felt it.

Fuck.

I can't get the sound of that moan out of my head.

The *yes* that fell from her plump lips, giving me the green light to keep going.

Green light for what?

To fuck her right there on the dirty gym floor while everyone else watched.

I am not an exhibitionist, but I am pissed I didn't at least get my lips on her before being interrupted. Before realization set in and she ran off.

I crossed the line. She thinks I'm her goddamn personal trainer for Christ sake!

It was unprofessional for me to lose my shit over a soft moan.

Fuck.

I opened our messages, the last one being hours earlier, when I admitted to her how I had actually never watched an Avenger or Thor movie.

I was, however, into the comics as a kid and still owned a few classics.

I type and delete and type and delete again, unsure of what the fuck I even want to say.

Hey, sorry about pressing my dick against you but you did give the green light. Would it be cool if I kissed you and maybe took you out on a date?

I sound like a prepubescent teenager or a fucking pervert.

Shit.

It's late and she's out on a wild ladies night, probably dancing the night away and forgetting all about our little show. The almost-moment I'm sure she regretted the second she came to her senses.

Suddenly, the small blip with three dots appears in the corner of our text, then disappears. I sit up from my spot on the bed and stare at the screen, willing her to come back and type out whatever she had to say.

The blip returns again and I hold my breath waiting until it disappears again and a picture comes through. A picture of her at the bar with her mom as she sticks her tongue out and holds a drink up in her hands.

She looks so completely diffcrent from what I've seen of her at the gym; it makes my mouth go.

Her long hair falls in soft waves over her shoulders, past her breasts, which are barely contained by the low cut of her top.

Fucking gorgeous.

I stare at the screen for another second before finally tapping out a response.

Me: You're stunning.

Isadorrra: I'm drunk.

I smile and glance at the time. It's not that late, only eleven.

Me: Lightweight

It's another five minutes before she replies.

Isadorrra: You should come and show me a thing or two Papi Thor,

Fuuuucck. I want to hear her say that out loud.

My phone rings in my hand before I can type out a response, and I groan at the name on the screen.

"Yeah," I respond, knowing exactly what the fuck it's about. Annoyance surges through me and kills whatever joy I had just felt.

"Third night this week, O'Rourke."

"I'll be there in ten."

"Make it five. She found out we were watering down her drinks and spit in my face when I tried to pry her from the counter."

Shaking my head I angrily push myself out of bed and shove my feet into my sneakers. Snatching my car keys from the counter I slam the door so fucking hard I'm surprised it doesn't break off of its hinges.

BY THE TIME I crawl back into my apartment, I'm so exhausted with another night of Nora's bullshit I fall asleep on the couch.

She'd sent me on a wild cat and mouse chase all night long, running and dodging me.

By the time I wake up, some time after eleven, I couldn't be more thankful for a Saturday. Nora won't be up for another few hours and I can sit and fucking relax.

I reach for my phone and remember Izzy's invitation last night that I never responded to.

God, she must think I'm such a fucking tool.

I send her an Are you alive gif of Darla from Finding Nemo tapping on the screen.

She responds with an I'm dying gif of Cameron from Ferris Bueller's Day off in bed.

Me: Have you ever had a hangover cure before?

Isadorra: Like the kind of cure that involves more alcohol? No, I think I'll suffer and learn my lesson the hard way.

Me: No, not more alcohol. It's not to be enjoyed but it will cure your hangover so you can at least be somewhat of a human and a little less walking zombie.

I send her the recipe my mother taught me to prepare as a kid and I could make with my eyes closed. 3 ounces gin. 1/4 ounce lemon juice, freshly squeezed. 2 to 3 dashes Tabasco sauce. Chile pepper slice.

Isadorra: Yeah, that looks like I'll have to run to the store, so pass. Just let me learn my lesson the hard way and suffer.

I get up and walk over to my fridge.

Me: What's your address?

Isadorra: Are you sending flowers for my grave when I succumb to this hangover?

Me: No, I'm bringing you Hair of the Dog. I'm making one already and have enough for another.

Isadorra: Ooo, did you have a wild night Thor?

Me: Something like that.

She texts me her address and I downstairs and make her and Nora their hangover cure.

I stop in and place Nora's drink on her nightstand, pausing to tuck the blanket back over her before tiptoeing back into the hallway. Quietly, I close the door behind me.

AFTER A SIX MINUTE DRIVE, I park my truck and search the row of brick homes for her house number.

"YOU LOST?" A guy smoking a cigarette asks me sitting on the steps of the house that matches Izzy's address.

I open my mouth to tell him I'm looking for Izzy when a girl storms out, throwing something at the back of his head. A sandal bounces down the steps and lands at my feet.

"What the fuck, Leslie?" He asks as he rubs the back of his head.

"Who the fuck is Cindy?"

"Cindy? Baby, I don't know who that is. I don't even like that name!"

"Oh really? You want to play stupid with me. Fucking dumbass! I swear you were the worst thing to happen to me."

I turn my head as they bicker, rubbing the back of my neck with my free hand.

"What are you doing here?"

"I'm here to see Izzy." I recognize her from the first night I met Izzy at the gym.

"Why?" She asks as Izzy's mom pushes through the screen door.

"What do you mean why? *Chismosa*, let him in. And keep your fighting off of my front porch," she says, holding the door open for me.

"Thank you," She eyes me up and down before opening the screen door wider for me to squeeze through into a narrow living room.

"I thought Izzy said no gym today?"

"Yeah, I just wanted to bring something to help with her hangover."

"*Ay, que lindo. Aw, how sweet.* It's a shame you couldn't join us last night, Papi Thor."

I swallow hard and clear my throat as heat burns my cheeks red. She takes the tumbler from my hands, opens the lid, and brings it to her nose.

"Hair of the dog." She says making a face. "Good luck trying to get her to drink that." A little boy runs down the stairs and straight into her hip.

"Lulu, I'm hungry." He says, tugging on her shirt. She sucks her teeth and picks him up into her arms.

"Izzy is upstairs, second door to the left." She says walking back out the front door.

"Come take care of the children you two *sinverguenzo's* made." I hear her shout behind me. I take the stairs and follow the framed pictures along the wall. It's not hard at all to spot a young Izzy in the family pictures. I notice all the differences and similarities she shares with her siblings.

I always wanted a brother or sister. Someone to confide in and lessen the burden it was to be the only one taking care of mom and getting the brunt of her insobriety.

I reach the second door to the left like her mom had said and knock twice, hoping I'm not waking her. Worst case I just leave her the drink and head back home, but I would really like to see her and talk about yesterday.

The door opens, and I don't notice the kid who opened it until he speaks.

"Who are you?"

I peer down at him as he cranes his neck to look up at me.

"Hey there, little man." I glance up into the room behind him. "I'm looking for Izzy."

"Why?"

"I brought her some medicine for her headache."

"Are you her boyfriend?" He frowns.

My eyes widen as the words *I wish* flash in my mind.

An off-key female's voice sings at the top of its lungs through the thin walls, belting out words to a song I don't recognize.

"Izzy is obsessed with Encanto." Little man says, rolling his eyes. I smile, staring at the door the singing is coming from. I can't say she sings like an angel but it is cute.

"Is that a movie?" I ask.

"You haven't watched Encanto!" He shouts, his eyes bulging out of his face in shock.

"Liam, your father is here." Izzy's mom calls out.

The kid groans. "I'll be right back. My dad never hangs out for long but we can watch all together later." He says.

"Um-" I start. He waits, looking up at me as his mom calls his name again.

"Sure." I finally respond. That earns me a big dimpled smile that is identical to Izzy's before he's running down the hall.

Great job lying to her little brother now, Chase.

This is stupid.

I bend down and place the tumbler on the floor in front of the bedroom door. I'll just leave before she notices and hopefully the kid isn't too upset I had to leave.

The door beside me swings open and wet creamy bare skin comes into view.

I lean up slowly, taking my time as my eyes trace a path up her smooth thighs and over the thick cotton towel. Her wet hair drapes over her bare shoulders and her red-rimmed eyes widen in surprise.

"Chase?"

"You've been crying." I can't stop myself from reaching over and pressing the pad of my thumb against a tear at the corner of her eye.

"What's wrong?" I ask, needing to know who hurt her.

"I'm fine, really. What are you doing here?" She says, turning away from me.

I reach down and pick up the tumbler for her to see.

"Hair of the Dog, remember?"

"Right. Sorry, my brain has been every way today and this headache isn't helping."

She stares at me for a second longer before speaking.

"I'll just leave you with that then so you can start feeling better." I say, pushing the cup out for her to take.

"Have you ever had an empanada before, Thor?"

"A what?" I ask again.

She smiles. "I'm just going to get dressed, and then I am changing your clean eating life for the better."

If only she knew that the sight of her, dripping wet in nothing but this towel right now, is more than enough to change my life.

9

IZZY

Shutting my bedroom door behind me, I let my head fall back against it and take a deep shuddering breath. The tears I'd been able to keep in check in front of Chase, now prick the corners of my eyes. It took everything in me not to jump into his arms and seek the comfort I so desperately need right now.

The heaviness that has been weighing on my chest since last night returns all at once, along with the memory of Esteban's latest post on his social media account.

Stupid fucking tears. Stupid fucking heart. And stupid fucking Esteban and his new stupid fucking fiancé.

My hands shoot out to cover the sob that rips through me as my already fragmented heart shatters even more. As if it hasn't been seven months since he so gracefully cast our relationship to the side.

He's engaged. After only seven months with some random girl.

He's engaged. We were together for four years and marriage had been nothing more than an afterthought. A *yeah, sure, one day, Izzy.* A one day that would never come and he fucking knew it. Wasting my time while I doted on him like the future fucking wife I thought I would be. Dragging my naive, stupid heart along for so long.

I swipe at the tears staining my cheeks and unwrap the towel from around my chest. I bring it to my face and muffle a needed scream into the damp cotton.

My head throbs painfully behind my eyes, reminding me of the hangover

I'm stupidly nursing. Which reminds me of whatever Chase brought over and the fact that I left him alone... in the hallway... where my family can sink their claws into him.

I drop the towel and get dressed in the only clean clothes I have left—it's laundry day—and fan my face a few times before opening the door. But instead of Chase's smoldering eyes, I'm met with an empty hallway.

Oh no.

"Chase?" I call out. The floor creaks beneath me as I walk down the hallway. Mom's obnoxious laughter carries over the old school reggaeton music she refuses to live without.

I ignore the sinking feeling in my chest at the thought of him just leaving without a goodbye and rush down the stairs into the kitchen, skidding to a stop in the doorway.

Chase in Mom's "Queen of the kitchen" apron makes no sense at all, but damn if he doesn't look good in it. The way his large biceps flex as he rolls the rolling pin over the fresh dough in front of him make my mouth water. Long legs spread wide apart as he leans over the counter which, compared to him, resembles one made for dwarves. Chase seems to be focused on the task in front of him as my mother shakes her hips to the beat of the music beside him, methodically rolling small balls of dough for empanada discs.

I watch for a second longer, leaning my aching head against the doorway. Chase and empanadas are a pleasant and needed distraction from the dark thoughts swirling around in my head.

"Creeper much?" Lydia, the older of the twins, whispers in my ear as she brushes by me to get into the kitchen. I stick my tongue out at her and she pretends to grab Chase's ass when Mom grabs her wrist and twirls her into her arms. Dragging Chase into it next they back him up into the corner of the counter. His flour dusted hands raised in the air as my mother grinds against him and my little sister swings her hips in front of her.

Although everything inside of me still feels like it is splitting in half, I can't help but laugh. The slight fear and amusement in Chase's eyes is adorable.

Esteban would never be caught in this situation. The few times we did happen to come over *together*, he damn sure never stepped foot in the kitchen. He maintained his distance from my family, claiming they were too loud or too ghetto for him. I never pressed it, especially since he and my mom butted heads anytime they shared the same space.

My brain throbs painfully as if just the thought of that *cara de culo* is what is causing this suffering and not the rum, tequila, or vodka running through my bloodstream. I am full of so much regret right now I can't take it.

I squeeze my eyes shut and rub my temple in hopes it could alleviate some of this pressure. Instead, my body sways to the side. I blink a few times trying to break through the tunnel vision threatening to swallow me whole.

"Izzy?" Chase calls out and I somewhat register him squeezing past my mom and rushing to my side. "Are you okay?" He asks, hooking his arm around my waist, steadying me. The warmth from his body mixed with the cool mint from his breath as it skates across my forehead sends a chill up and down my spine.

"Are you okay?" He repeats. His voice etched with concern as he leans down and searches my eyes.

"I told you to watch your liquor." Mom says, pulling a chair out from the dining table and dragging it behind me before checking on the seasoned beef simmering in the pan on the stove.

"Lightweight." Lydia mutters next, earning herself a smack with the large wooden spoon in mom's hand.

"And what would you know about being a lightweight, huh?"

"I was kidding! Damn-ouch, Ma!"

"Language, little girl."

Lydia rubs her hip and sucks her teeth.

"Why don't you sit down." Chase suggests, but I shake my head. I don't want to move from this spot in his arms. At least here, the only thing I can focus on is his hard body and whether it was just body wash or soft cologne wafting off of him.

"I'm okay. I just need a minute."

"Didn't Chase bring you something *dique* a hangover cure?" Mom doesn't turn around as she stirs the meat for the empanada filling.

"I did." He says, guiding me to the chair mom pulled out before taking a few steps to the counter and reaching for a Norriton Vet tumbler. "I forgot that is why I came here in the first place, not empa-" He stops himself short and mom, Lydia, and I finish his sentence for him. Slowly emphasizing the sounds for him.

"Em-pah-nah-das."

"Right." He says, his cheeks growing a shade pink as he hands me the tumbler.

Our fingers touch when I take the cup from him, sending an electric current up my arm. My eyes snap to his.

The look in his eyes tells me he felt it, too, as the amber flecks take hold and swallow the forest shade they had just been.

"Trust me, this will help." He says before pulling his touch from mine, tucking his hands into front jean pockets. The movement tugs his pants down slightly, revealing a sliver of smooth...

Lydia clears her throat, distracting me, and I catch Mom's eyes tracing the same path as she clamps down on her bottom lip.

"Diablo, migente. Busco un mapo para limpiar este baba del piso?" *Damn, my people. Should I get the mop to clean this drool off of the floor?* Mya's wide smile teases us. Baby Z perched on her hip coos along with her and Mom breaks down into Spanish baby talk, tearing the baby from her arms. Mya goes around cheek kissing everyone before stopping in front of Chase.

"Fancy catching you here." She says to him, her eyes playfully bouncing between the two of us.

"He was just bringing me something for this hangover." I say, raising the cup.

"Psh, I know Lulu taught you better than mixing tequila and vodka." Mya says, shaking her head.

"I sure did!" Ma says as she stirs the ground meat around with Baby Z on her hip.

"I fucked up. Trust me, I realize the error of my ways, okay." I say, opening the lid of the hangover cure and eyeing its contents suspiciously.

Ma walks over and takes a seat, shaking her head in disappointment. "You made a lot of mistakes last night, mama. The alcohol was just the brunt of it."

"Oh yeah. Leslie told me about Esteban. Izzy, that's just messed up and wrong. I'm sorry, sis. You know I never liked him, right?" Lydia says, placing a hand on my shoulder.

"Thanks, Lyd." I nod my head at her then turn back to Chase in front of me.

"You spend a lot of mornings having to recover from wild drunken nights, Chase?" Mya asks next.

"Oh, I don't drink." Chase says walking back to the counter, flattening balls into perfect shaped discs.

"Like at all?" Mya asks, unbelieving. I kick her under the table to shut her up and not interrogate the man on his drinking habits.

"Nope. I make these for my mom all of the time, though." Chase says,

"Awwww, how sweet!!" Mom shrieks, as she rocks baby Z back and forth. "Your mother is lucky to have a son like you. How is it that not one of my six children can do that for me?"

"I mean if you're lucky Liam might at least leave the tap on in the bathroom for you." Lydia says as she spoons a bit of ground beef into her mouth.

Mya and I burst out in laughter as mom shoots daggers at Lydia. Chase merely smiles, but it doesn't meet his eyes the way it had before. He stares down at his shoes, lost in thought. The corners of his lips turn down in a frown, his eyes slightly glossed as if he were replaying a distant memory.

"You're lucky I'm holding this baby."

Bringing the metal tumbler to my lips, I take a sip and am surprised by how good it is. Coconut, lime, and something else I can't quite put my finger on. For some reason I was expecting it to taste awful but it's not bad at all.

"What do you think?" Chase asks, the light in his eyes returning.

"Not as bad as I imagined."

"Papi Thor, back to work on the empanada discs."

"Ew, ma please don't call my trainer Papi."

"Like you don't want to call him, Papi." Mya mutters under her breath. Chase takes his spot back in front of the counter and I shamelessly watch the delicious muscles in his upper back.

"I would never call a man Papi." I say, shuddering. I notice Chase's eyebrows pulled tight together as he stares at me in confusion.

Mya takes baby Z from mom, who fries the first set of empanadas; my mouth instantly begins to water.

As soon as they are out of the frying pan and on the cooling rack, I snatch two and wrap them in a napkin leaving Mya and Lydia groaning behind me as I grab Chase's hand and lead him out of the house and to front porch.

"Am I taking this to go?" Chase asks as I hand him his empanada. I sit down on the steps and pat the spot next to me before taking a bite, attempting to both enjoy and cool the steaming piece in my mouth.

Chase chuckles softly as he takes his time to cool his down before bringing it to his mouth. His eyes close as he chews slowly and moans his satisfaction out loud, the sound hitting the spot right in between my legs.

"Fuck, that's good." He groans.

"I know." I say smiling.

We sit in comfortable silence and take a few more bites before he speaks again.

"Are you going to tell me why you were crying?"

I let out a deep heavy sigh as my mind takes me back to the bits and pieces of last night I do remember – when I opened facebook only to have it ask me if I wanted to congratulate the happy couple on their new engagement, followed by a picture of them together and her showing off a stunning engagement ring. "My ex is getting married."

I hate how much it hurts to say those words. The sting feels like rubbing salt into an already bleeding wound.

Chase nods his head. "Esteban." He mutters.

"We were together since sophomore year at Temple."

"What happened?"

"I don't know. We changed. Drifted apart, and I guess in the end I just wasn't enough."

"Don't." He says, shaking his head.

"Don't what?"

"Izzy, you are more than enough. You-You're strong, beautiful, funny as hell. It wasn't you, it was him. *He* wasn't enough for *you*." The look in his eyes as he spoke made my heart melt, but his words, they hit me right at my core. I tear my gaze away from him and back to the quiet street in front of us. The early summer weather taking its time to announce itself pushes a cool breeze between us. I glance back at Chase who is as lost in thought as I am.

"You're kind of perfect, you know that right?" Biting my cheek, I bump my shoulder into his.

"So are you, I-sah-dorra."

I smile wide. "You've been rolling your r's."

"Just for you."

Just for me?

CHASE

I HAVEN'T HAD A SHIT DAY LIKE THIS IN A LONG TIME. MAYBE SINCE IZZY stumbled her way into my life, a sweet distraction from the everyday bullshit it is.

I hate my job. I hate my house. I hate everything I see when I look in the mirror, and no matter how much I run, I can't seem to get anywhere.

"CHASE, get me a blood sample on the Doberman in room three." Dr. Nordone tells me. He doesn't stop to ask if I'm busy before locking himself up in his office like it isn't ten minutes to closing. I'm the only vet tech in the office currently because Christa had an emergency at her kid's school, and I'll bet my last dollar this blood sample will lead to an emergency surgery.

All I want to do is get to the gym, take out my frustration on some weights, and listen to Izzy ramble on about the kids in her class or the latest drama at home. Her family is more entertaining than anything on TV. Between Leslie and her on again off again relationship with her ex, Lulu's dating adventures, and Lydia and Layla's highschool dramatics, I can't get enough. And then there's the boys. Aiden and Alfonso are a handful but evil geniuses for sure with an xbox controller in their hands. No kids their age should be that good at first person shooter games. Then there's Liam. He's sensitive but fiercely protective of his family. I'm convinced he's an old man trapped in a little kid's body.

I've been spending every Saturday at their house since my introduction to empanadas three weeks ago. Even trading Taco Tuesday for whatever is cooking at the Peña household. From Dominican stew, to smashed fried plantains and tamales, if I wasn't at the gym everyday during the week I'd be at least ten pounds heavier with the amount of food Izzy serves on my plate and then packs for me to take home. It takes everything in me to not bend down and kiss her everytime she hands me a plate of food.

I TAP out a quick text to Izzy letting her know I'll have to push training a little late.

Isadorrra: Or we can just skip leg day completely.

I chuckle at her response.

Me: Not a chance. I'll meet you in an hour.

Isadorrra: You're no fun, Thor.

Isadorrra: Also, Lulu wants to know if you like fish. *Bacalao* is on the menu for Saturday.

Me: I like fish but baca-what?

Isadorrra: Trust me, you'll love it.

Two HOURS later I jog into the gym, eager to escape from my life for at least the next hour. I'm running thirty minutes later than I told Izzy. If I hadn't stopped at home for a quick shower and change I would have gotten here on time. But instead, when I walk out of the shower, I catch Nora searching my wallet with my car keys already in one hand. After prying my things from her hands I then spend a whole twenty minutes arguing all the reasons why she can't drive with a suspended license or while already fucking intoxicated.

"I hate you!" She reminds me as I follow her into the kitchen and she throws the nearest object at me. As soon as the roll of paper towels bounced against my chest, I was done.

"Fuck you, too, Mom." I shout before heading up the stairs to get dressed and storming out the front door, slamming it shut behind me. She can tear the whole house up if she wants. I'm done.

THE NOISE and clatter of the gym around me soothes some of this tension that's been knotted in my shoulders, but the thought of seeing Izzy melts the last hour of my life away. I have to bite my lip in an attempt to suppress my wide grin. I can't explain how I feel when I'm around her. Giddy, nervous, excited, and stupid all at once. I'm dying to make a move, ask her out for real, or just give in to the desire swimming in both our eyes. It's written all over her face when she looks at me but for whatever reason, most likely her dickwad ex, she shakes it away.

When I reach the studio room Izzy and I have been using, my heart drops to my feet at the sight of the empty mat. The stupid flutter of hope in my stomach bursts as I scan the room, and disappointment sets in when I don't see her.

She must have gotten tired of waiting. My shoulders drop at the thought of not seeing her tonight. I force myself to turn around, and I pull my phone out to apologize for running so late.

I look up when Damon passes. "Relax, *Thor*." He says, rolling his eyes before nodding his head to the side. "Your girl is on the treadmills."

My eyes snap past him to the last place I would have thought to find her, and my heart skips an actual beat in my chest.

My girl, as Damon just stated, is jogging at a steady pace and I couldn't be prouder of the girl who refused to walk up a flight of stairs a few weeks ago.

I walk towards her. My mouth goes dry as my hungry eyes trail down her backside and I take in the tight pair of shorts hugging her hips. They stop at her mid thigh exposing the pair of delicious bare legs I have been dreaming of since I caught sight of them in her hallway. I still haven't been able to get the image of her wrapped in that towel, dripping wet, out of my head, nor do I want to.

I clear my throat and force my legs and eyes forward.

"I never thought I'd see this day again." I say behind her. My voice comes out deeper than intended. Izzy, of course, jumps in alarm. Her hands reach out and grip the corners of the treadmill. I dash forward and immediately tug on the safety string as my other arm wraps around her waist to catch her.

"This thing is a death trap!" She wails. I chuckle and reluctantly release her.

"I don't think it's the treadmill." I say, giving her a megawatt smile.

"You're right! It's you! At least you had the decency to catch me this time."

"I'll always catch you, Izzy."

Her beautiful brown eyes stare up at me through thick lashes and her lips fall open. It would take nothing at all for me to just lean down and kiss her right now.

Make your fucking move, idiot!

"Izzy." I reach for her hand instead, carefully tracing her delicate fingers and giving her time to move away before interlacing my hand with hers.

She cocks her head to the side, her eyes looking down at our intertwined hands before glancing up. Her moon shaped eyes widen as they search mine. I lick my lips and take a steadying breath.

God, I want her more than I've ever wanted anything.

But of course I forgot to silence my phone and it chooses *that* moment to ring.

"I'll just silence it." I say, reaching into my pocket and pulling out my phone. I hit the side button to mute the ringing when I notice the number on the screen and freeze. I stare at the screen in my hand while the other tightens around Izzy's. Dread fills me in that moment of recognition but Izzy squeezes reassuringly, anchoring me like the life line I never knew I needed.

"Do you need to answer that?" She asks.

"I think so." I say bringing the phone up to my ear. I exhale slowly, locking eyes with hers as I answer.

"Is this Keagan O'Rourke?"

"Keagan Chase O'Rourke, yes." I correct the woman on the phone. Clenching my jaw at hearing my full name out loud.

A cold chill works its way over me as I listen to the dispatcher on the other side of the phone explain to me the stolen car Nora crashed into a police cruiser and the hospital information of where she was taken, unresponsive. My heart locks in my chest as if this isn't anything new. My mind locks on to the one word the dispatcher used. *Unresponsive. Nora is laying on a stretcher unresponsive.* The heaviness I thought I had dropped at the door when I first entered the gym returns. A soul crushing weight that sucks all the hope and joy I have left.

I HANG up and hold the phone in my hand so tight I'm surprised it doesn't shatter in my grip, then I remember Izzy's hand still in mine. I release her, worried I'd hurt her, and shove my beanie off of my head so I can run my hands through my hair.

"I have to go, I'm sorry."

"You have nothing to apologize for." She wraps her arms around my waist, hugging me. My body sinks into her warmth. I ignore the small twinge of pain from the awkward position of my 6'2" frame and her much shorter one. Instead, I tighten my arms around her and wish I could stay right here, for-goddamn-ever."

"Is it your mom?"

I nod my head, squeezing her to me once more.

"She's at Einstein."

"That's just fifteen minutes away." She says pulling back and grabbing her water bottle and keys from the floor beside us. "Come on, I'll drive."

"What? No. You don't have to do that. This isn't anything new, Izzy. I'll be okay." I say scraping my hand over my face.

"Chase, you're shaking."

Shit, am I? My body freezes at her words. With my stomach rolling over, I raise a hand in front of me, watching it wobble uncontrollably in the air.

How didn't I notice I was shaking?

"There is no way you can drive like this, Chase. I've got you. You don't have to be alone. I'm here. Let me be here for you."

Too many emotions all at once clog my throat. Words she couldn't know could mean the world to the lonely kid who still lives inside of me.

I nod my head, too caught up in Isadora Leticia Peña Yotún De La Vega and her beautiful heart, and follow her out of the gym.

The drive to the hospital is excruciatingly long, yet her hand in mine makes it feel not long enough. Izzy's reassuring grip hasn't let up since she started driving, and I haven't been able to keep from staring at her as she whips my Jeep around. The street lights around us sweep into the cab interior making her skin glow. God, she's beautiful and sweet and good and if it wasn't for her shit faced ex she would know these things were true. From the few things she has shared with me about that relationship, I want to drive down to Philly and punch this guy in the face for taking her for granted for so long, or I could thank him for putting her in my path and with me now, even if she's not *with me*, with me.

I release a heavy sigh and close my eyes as my head falls back into the headrest.

We were there, so damn close. A mere few millimeters away from kissing those lips. So fucking close until that phone call reminded me of the slave I am to my drunk of a mother.

"I'm sorry, Chase."

"Don't be. If I'm lucky she's dead. Fuck. I don't mean that." I swipe my beanie off of my head for the umpteenth time and pull on my hair as if that will somehow wake me up from this fucking day.

Izzy stays quiet, her gaze focused on the wet road in front of us–of course it's raining, which makes a fifteen minute drive ten minutes longer. The steady drum of rain drops beat against the windshield.

"I just want her to not drink herself into a damn stupor and then get behind the goddamn wheel. That's it. I'm not asking for mother of the year, just a sober one."

"Maybe this will be the wake up call she needs." She's glancing over at me with all the hope in her beautiful brown eyes. I want to believe her, but whatever hope I had in Nora one day getting the help she needed died a long time ago.

. . .

NORA in the hospital isn't anything new. I'm still paying the medical bills from the alcohol poisoning she gave herself during last year's annual Mummers Parade.

You would think for being the grade A drunk she is, she would have known a little better than doing that to herself, yet here we fucking are.

"I'LL WAIT OUT HERE." Izzy says when I reach the nurse's station. Her fingers pull away from mine but I'm not ready to let go. I tug her into me instead, her sexy as fuck mouth popping open as her eyes grow wide in surprise. I intertwine my fingers into hers, squeezing tight as my other hand tips her head back.

"Thank you." I say, tracing the length of her bottom lip.

"Chase?" She breathes.

"Izzy?" I mutter, not realizing how close I am hanging over the edge as I lean down. This is probably the worst timing for a first kiss, a kiss I've imagined going alot differently than this one but fuck, I just want this one thing for me.

If I jump, will she jump with me or cast me aside?

"Can I kiss you, Izzy?"

She nods and stands on her tiptoes. I slide my other arm around her waist and give in to this feeling, this hope she fills me with.

I kiss her, taking her full bottom lip between mine, savoring this moment I've been craving since the moment I laid eyes on her.

Finally!

"Ahem." A throat clears behind us and I very reluctantly pull back.

"Excuse me?" A very annoyed nurse calls out.

Izzy's cheeks burn bright red in embarrassment before falling into my chest and I place one more kiss to the top of her head before turning around to face the nurse.

"Is there something we can help you with or do you need the address to the motel across the street?" She says, narrowing her eyes between me and Izzy before shaking her head.

"GO, I'LL BE RIGHT HERE." Izzy says.

I nod my head and head over to the nurses' station and ask for my mother. The nurse continues to shake her head as she clicks on her computer before standing and leading me down the hall. I can't help myself from stealing glances at Izzy, waiting *for me.*

The weight around me doesn't feel as suffocating knowing she's here.

11

IZZY

THE RUMBLE OF THE ENGINE STIRS ME AWAKE. I SIT UP IN MY SEAT, MY EYES widening at the numbers flashing on the dashboard in front of me. It's already midnight? The last time I glanced at the time, I was in the waiting room and it was a quarter to ten. Chase must have carried my comatose ass from the hospital chair.

I move my eyes over to Chase, who seems to be lost in thought and frowning at the road in front of him. My body is still buzzing from our kiss earlier. I try to tame it down and focus on the broken man beside me. Those strong shoulders of his are slumped forward and his arm is propped up against his driver side mirror holding his head up as his fingers grip the hair on the top of his head. He looks so defeated it makes my heart hurt.

"How's your mom?" I ask, sitting up in my seat and wiping the sleep from my face.

"She's alive." He croaks, not giving me anything more.

"And you?" I ask, my eyebrow raising as I look him over.

He tilts his head towards me, pulling his lips up in a lopsided smile. "Better now."

I press my lips together as a blush spreads up my cheeks.

He swaps hands with the steering wheel and reaches for mine in my lap. His large palm swallows my hand in his as he brings it up to his lips and presses a warm kiss to the back of my fingers. My body burns at the feel of his soft lips on my skin and I swallow down the thick lump of desire in my throat.

"Do you want me to drop you off at the gym for your car or-"

"Or you can take me home with you." My words are out before my brain has even had time to process what the fuck just came out. "If you don't want to be alone right now, that is."

Chase releases a heavy sigh and shakes his head. "I don't want to be alone anymore, Izzy." He says, squeezing my hand in his.

"Then I'm not going anywhere."

I run my other hand up his arm. "So, what happened?" I ask, trying hard not to focus on his thumb tracing circles against my knee.

His hand stills before he lets out another deep heavy sigh, and I instantly regret asking.

"You don't have to talk about it if you don't want to. I'm here regardless, Chase." I trail my fingers over his knuckles.

"Thank you. That means more to me than you know, Izzy." He squeezes my knee and returns to tracing circles before he continues. "She stole my neighbor's car, crashed into a parked police cruiser as she sped down the street, and never told me about the liver disease diagnosis she got last year."

"Chase." My voice is thick with emotion. I wish I knew the magic words that would take this crushing weight off of him.

"I'm so sorry."

He maneuvers the car into a spot, and removes his hand from mine before slamming the shifter into park. The streetlight he parks under illuminates his face, giving me a front row seat to the stress, anger, and desperation he has been drowning in for so long.

"She's going to jail this time and I can't do anything to help her." His voice cracks as he drops his head back into the headrest and squeezes his eyes shut. "I don't want to fucking help her. I'm done. I'm so done, it's eating me up inside. This emptiness inside of me when I think of her, I can't stand it." I jump in my seat as he throws his fist out and punches the hard roof of his jeep. "And do you want to know the worst part?" He asks, his face crumbling before he shoves the emotion away and continues. "For a minute there, I really thought she was dead, and I fucking reveled in those sixty goddamn seconds. Just sweet fucking relief at the thought of finally not having to worry about her. God, what is wrong with me to think like that! Feel like this for my own mother." He wraps his arms over his face and my heart jumps into action. I climb over the center console and into Chase's lap. He drops his arms and stares at me in confusion as his hands grip my waist.

"Izzy, what are you-" I cut him off and place the palm of my hands around his strong jaw, forcing him to see only me and what I see when I look at him.

"There isn't a thing wrong with you, Chase. I can't speak for your mom, or her demons but you and your beautiful heart are the rarest stone set in imperfection and still you shine. Still you make the world a better place, my world a better place, simply because you are."

Chase stares at me for what feels like an eternity. The pain in his eyes melts away right before me.

"Where have you been all my life, Izzy?"

"I think I've been waiting for *you*." I say biting my bottom lip as the look in his eyes sets my skin ablaze. My heart beats so loud in my chest I know he has to hear it. His thumb reaches up and pulls my bottom lip free before his lips are on mine, pressing a soft kiss against them.

"Let's get inside." He says, turning the car off.

I nod my head and begin climbing back over the center console before Chase pulls me back and swings his driver door open.

I wrap myself around him as he climbs out, holding me up easily in his strong hands. He slides my body down against his until my feet hit the ground and wraps his hand over mine, kicking the door shut behind him. I follow him up a stone path and neatly manicured patch of grass and onto a small front porch.

He unlocks the door and swings it open, letting me walk in first but before I can take in my surroundings I'm spun around and lifted up into his strong arms as he kicks the door shut and crashes his mouth onto mine. I wrap myself around him as our tongues collide. His heavy footsteps echo around us as he blindly moves us through his home. I'm curious about his home, having spent countless nights imagining where he lived, but right now, there is no way I am capable of pulling away from his lips.

Up a set of stairs and a few more steps, my back hits a door and Chase presses into me while he leisurely fucks my mouth with his lips. A low rumbling sound comes from the back of his throat.

"Izzy. You don't know how bad I've wanted you." He mutters and presses himself against me.

"Chase."

"I want you, hell, I need you right now but I can wait. If this is too fast, we can stop right now. I'll go to bed on the couch downstairs and you can have my bed-"

I shake my head. "Don't stop." I push my fingers through his hair, deepening this kiss into something frantic and desperate. The intensity of this kiss threatens to obliterate the one before, hell his mouth alone is capable of destroying me, and being destroyed by this man is exactly what I want. Perhaps more than that, it's what we both need.

He pulls my sweatshirt and top off over my head and latches his mouth over my bra-covered nipple, which is threatening to break right through my sports bra. My head falls back against the door behind me as he moves his lips to the top of my breast then skates up along my collarbone and neck.

"Chase," I beg as I push my sex up against him. He finally opens the door and lays me down onto a soft bed.

I squeeze my thighs around his waist, pulling him down with me. My greedy hands tug at his t-shirt, prying it off over his head before exploring every contour of muscle on his body.

"Take this off." He growls as his hands tug on the hem of my sports bra. I lift myself up on my elbows and pull it off. Then, deciding I don't want to waste anymore time on undressing, I make quick work of my shorts and underwear. My heart beats viciously against my ribcage as I pant heavily and lock my hungry eyes on him.

Oh. My. God.

Standing at the end of the bed, he watches me with hooded eyes.

My vagina aches in anticipation as my mouth falls open at the sight of Chase's flawless naked body and the impressive length standing so fucking tall between us.

This man is going to destroy me and good God am I going to enjoy every sweet, Earth-shattering inch of it.

Chase drops a condom wrapper on the bed beside me and crawls over me as his hands sweep up the sides of my thighs and waist.

"Chase, please." I cry out, arching my naked chest against his face. His hard cock rubs against the inside of my thigh.

"Oh, God, please, Chase."

"Tell me, Izzy. Tell me what you want." He says, burying his face in my breast. I gasp at the feel of his teeth scraping over a hardened nipple. I wrap my hands around his head, reveling in the sensations coursing through my body.

"You. I want you." I don't recognize the sound of my voice.

My nails rake down his back as he moves down instead of up, leaving a trail of tantalizing hot skin in his wake as he kisses and nips his way down my body. My body freezes when his lips reach the softer part of my stomach, my hands automatically shoot out to cover it as I am suddenly reminded of all of my insecurities, but Chase is there, pushing them away.

"Don't hide from me, I want to see you. Every mouth watering inch of you, Izzy." Holding my hands on either side of me, he continues his relentless pursuit down my body with his mouth.

Chase's tongue trails between my folds, igniting a fire between my legs unlike anything else I have ever known. As he sucks and licks over my swollen bud, I melt against his skilled mouth and cry out. My needy hips move of their own accord, trying to keep up with the addictive rhythm on my clit as he devours me like a starved man.

Two thick fingers push inside of me and that's all it takes for my thighs to start shaking. My release is so close I can taste it, or well…Chase can, at least.

"That's it, Izzy." Chase says, his fingers working me over and over. I wrap my hands around his head, holding on for my life as he twists those perfectly skilled fingers in and out, pushing me so far towards the edge I'm not sure which way is up. I cry out and buck my hips against his skilled fingers.

"That's it. Ride my hand like you're going to ride my cock."

The sound of my slick wetness echoes off of the walls as I fuck his hand, chasing the intense wave of sensation until I shatter around him, shuddering his name.

12

CHASE

Fuck me.

Izzy falling apart in front of me is probably the single most beautiful thing I have ever witnessed.

My hard cock nods its head in agreement as it throbs painfully in front of me, begging me to dive into her already.

I tear open the condom in my hands and drag it down over my length, slowly stroking it a few times as my eyes ravage her naked body.

"You're so beautiful." I breathe, leaning down over her and holding myself up on my elbows.

"So, are you." She says, her eyes fluttering closed as I press the head of my cock against her wetness.

"Fuck me, Thor." She sighs, biting down at her bottom limp as her eyes focus on my cock between us as I position myself.

"As flattering as being compared to the Norse God is baby, the only name I want to hear you screaming is mine." I grab onto her hips and slide myself all the way into her. She's so tight, so wet, so fucking perfect.

My body falls forward and I catch myself on my elbows. My mouth meets Izzy's blindly, swallowing her soft moans. I pull out and thrust in again and again.

"Chase." She cries out against my lips, grinding her hips under me.

"Fuck." I groan, knowing fucking well I am not going to last long with the addictive rhythm of her hips meeting my every thrust.

I wrap my arms around her and flip us over, keeping my cock still happily buried inside of her.

"Take it." I tell her, moving her hands and placing them on my chest. She rolls her seductive hips over me.

"Take whatever you need, baby."

She grinds herself against me, rocking into me and throwing her head back.

"That's it, Izzy." I sit up, my cock twitching inside of her as her muscles pulsate around me, squeezing me.

"I'm going to come!"

I tighten my grip around her and pound relentlessly into her. Skin slapping against skin until her orgasm erupts through her, taking me right down with her. I suck in a breath as the intensity of my own release holds me fucking prisoner while it rips out of me.

Izzy tumbles forward, her head resting in the crook of my neck. I can feel her heart pounding against me, matching my own as we both try to catch our breath.

"That really happened, right? I didn't die and make this all up?" She whispers.

My hands slide up and down her back.

"Feels pretty real to me, but just in case, let's not leave this room." Her lips turn up in a smile against my shoulder.

"Only if you promise this is the only cardio you'll be making me do."

"Oh, I promise you, that is definitely getting added to the workout plan." I fall back onto my bed, bringing her down with me.

"Please tell me the gym doesn't have anything prohibiting client trainer relations because I will quit my membership right the fuck now."

Everything inside of me stills. Her words feel like a bucket of ice cold water over me.

"Oh no, there is!" She laughs out, burying her face in my neck. I try to clear the lump lodged in my throat and think of the right words to say.

"It's all good. I don't need a gym membership when I've got you." She says, so fucking sweet it makes my stomach twist.

"I don't know if the gym has rules like that but if it did this kind of makes it all work out for us, anyways." I stumble through my words like an idiot. "I'm not actually a trainer. At all."

She lifts her head up, brows pinched together as her eyes narrow into small slits. "What?"

"Izzy," I reach my hand out to touch her but she jerks back.

"You've been lying to me?" She says jumping out of my arms. "Why? Who even does that, Chase? Who lies about being a personal trainer then goes out of their way to fucking train a random ass person?"

I sit up and rub the palm of my hand over my face, wishing like hell we can go back to where we were just a few minutes ago. "When we first met, you assumed I worked there, and then you asked me for help. I couldn't say no after the way you hurt yourself. I didn't mean to lie, Izzy. I was going to tell you, but then Damon started running his mouth and-"

"Is this some game you two play to pick up women?"

"What? No. What are you talking about?" I stand and take a step towards her, my heart sinking as she takes a step back away from me.

The condom is still wrapped around my cock, so I pull it off and tie it at the end. "Let me take care of this and then I'll explain."

She doesn't respond but the hurt in her eyes is so fucking evident I have to look away, knowing I'm the one who put it there.

I exit my bedroom and stomp over to my bathroom, dropping the used condom in a waste basket before rushing back to Izzy. When I reenter the room, she's fully dressed and is putting her sneakers on.

"You're leaving?"

"It's late. I have an early morning." She doesn't even look up at me.

"You aren't even going to let me explain? You're acting as if I-"

"I'm acting as if you lied to me, Chase, because that's what you did. *Have* been doing every single day for weeks."

"Izzy."

"God, you're all the same!" She pushes past me, her footsteps carrying down the stairs until she slams the front door shut.

"Fuuuck!" I snatch a pair of sweats from my dresser and grab my phone before running down after her. My bare feet hit the sidewalk hard as I search for her shadow in the night. It's late. She shouldn't be out here this late walking around.

I call her phone hoping I'll at least hear it nearby, but it goes straight to her voicemail.

"Izzy, call me. You shouldn't be walking home alone this late. Just call me and I'll pick you up."

I try her again and again as I run down the few blocks to her house. Still no sign of her; even if she ran all the way here, I would have seen her ahead of me. She just disappeared.

What the fuck!

My phone buzzes with a new message.

Isadorrra: I'm fine Chase. Go home.

Me: You shouldn't have walked all this way alone, Izzy.

Isadorrra: I didn't.

Me: Can we please just talk?

Isadorrra: Tomorrow. I'm exhausted.

Me: Technically it already is tomorrow.

Isadorrra: Later Chase.

I STARE at her front door a second longer before tucking my hands into my front pockets and trudging back up the block in darkness. When I walk back into my house, her scent is everywhere. It hangs in the air, up the stairs, and damn near suffocates me when I land back into my bed.

I WAKE up to my phone ringing and jump up out of bed, answering it without even looking.

"Izzy?"

"Pumpkin?" Everything inside of me freezes at the sound of Nora's voice on the other side of the phone.

"Pumpkin, are you there baby? It's mama."

"I'm here." I push the words out of my mouth as my throat tightens. I can't remember the last time she was sober enough to call me by the moniker.

"Oh, it's so good to hear your voice. I've missed you. I want to come home, Pumpkin. Will you come get me?"

"Mom." My voice cracks. "Nora, you're sick. You need help."

"I know. I know but not here. Not like this. Please, I just want to come home, Pumpkin."

I've heard this song a thousand times, and as old as it gets, it doesn't ease the ache in my chest at the sound of her voice. It makes the loneliness in this house echo off of the walls.

"Pumpkin, please, you need to come and get me."

"I'll be there later."

"No, I need you now!"

A second voice sounds on her side of the phone. "Miss Nora what are you— don't pull those out!"

"Mom, just let them do their job. Calm down. Please." I cry out, threading my hands through my hair as I listen helplessly to Nora screaming for help on the other side of the line. The call disconnects.

I know she wasn't calling for me. It's not me she needs. It never has been.

I lower the phone in my hand between my legs and stare at the screen as it jerks in my trembling hands. My last message to Izzy staring me in my face. *For once I just wanted one thing for myself.*

My breaths come fast as my chest pounds in my ears. I rear back, throwing my phone across the room, but it does nothing to relieve the searing pressure inside of me.

This never-ending cycle of push and pull between Nora and her vices is my life. It's the burden I will carry for her because she can't do it herself.

13

IZZY

"G-Ma, she's still on the couch. We want to play!" Adolfo's annoying, high pitched voice rips me from my sleep, followed by stomping which I can bet is my mother's.

"*Carajo*, not again! Isadora Leticia Peña Yotún De La-fucking-Vega, get your ass up." I groan and turn over on the sofa, careful not to fall off and cover my head with my pillow. Lucky for Liam, Leslie and Jimmy worked things out yesterday, so the living room is back to being my bedroom. Unfortunately for me, that means not getting to wallow in fucking peace.

"Come on, come on. Papi Thor should be here any minute." She says, swiping the blanket off of me. I quickly sit up and tug the piece of fabric back from her hands a little too forcefully, causing her to stagger back slightly. Her head jerks back and eyebrows shoot so far up her forehead they touch her hair-line. I can practically see the *Who the fuck do you think you are?* flashing in her mind right now. And if I wasn't a grown ass woman, I would be scared as hell, expecting a full on ass whooping. Who am I kidding–she could reach for the *chancla* on her foot and still whoop my ass with it. I'm just so sick and tired of everything right now.

"He's old enough to be your son, Lordes, not your daddy, and he's not coming." I say, burying myself back under the covers. My heart sinks at just the mention of Chase. The moments we shared just hours ago are all I see. His perfect lips on me, all over me. Heat creeps up my cheeks at the memories burned into my skin.

"Old enough to be my son, my ass." Mom mutters. I feel her sit down on the edge of the couch behind me. "I'm going to ignore your momentary slip because clearly something has happened." She says rubbing my arm.

"Aw shit, I knew I didn't trust his pretty ass. What did he do?" Leslie calls out from the kitchen. Her footsteps are followed by the savory scent of empanada wafting in the air. It penetrates my senses, even through the blanket over my face, and all I see is Chase and the way his eyes lit up when he took his first bite of doughy meat filled goodness.

Ugh, now he's ruined empanadas for me, dammit. Unbidden tears fall down my face and I have to cover my mouth to silence my cries.

"Ay mami, what happened?" Mom pleads.

"Nothing, it doesn't matter." I sniffle, swiping at my cheeks and sitting up. "He's a liar and I should have been more vigilant before letting him in."

"Oooo, *sucia*! You climbed his mountain, didn't you! You let him all up in there, yes! Details, girl!"

"Callate, muchacha. Now is not the time." Ma says, shaking her head, but I catch her mouthing the word *later* to Leslie who nods.

"I'm so stupid. What is wrong with me that I'm so oblivious to a man's bullshit."

"Pretty sure it's hereditary." Leslie mutters, pointing to mom, who turns to her and glares daggers straight into her soul before turning back to me.

"Before you start blaming me for your relationship woes, what happened?"

"Chase has been lying to me from the moment we met. He isn't a personal trainer. He doesn't even work at the gym."

"What?"

"Why?" They both ask. I shrug my shoulders, wracking my brain for the umpteenth time for any other plausible answer other than the only one I've come up with.

"He probably does this all of the time. Offering free training services to helpless women like me just so he can get in between their legs." I grumble crossing my arms in front of me. How easy I opened my legs and wrapped them around him.

"I want you to think about this, okay because I think you're too busy holding on to this one thing and not looking at the entire picture. Does Chase really seem like the kind of person to do something like that?"

"I'm sorry but no. I don't see it." Layla cuts in out of nowhere, walking in and shaking her head. "Hear me out." She pauses in front of us, "You meet a fine ass guy-"

"Hey!" Mom warns.

"My bad, my bad. Hella hot gorgeous specimen of a man at the gym who dotes on you when your clumsy ass-"

"Nena." Mom's voice raises in another warning.

"Sorry, sorry but she is crazy clumsy. So, whatever, you fall over your two left feet and said guy then offers to help you workout so you don't kill yourself because," She pauses and motions over me with her hand. "And then he goes out of his way for five or six days out of the week, practically taking on a whole extra job for the last month. And lets not forget these past weekends of his spent here hanging out, *not* working out, and just chillin with us. Getting to know your family and most importantly *you.*" Layla finishes with a hand on her hip and a pointed look at me.

"That is one mighty long game to be playing just for some *na-na.*" Leslie sing songs, nodding her head in agreement.

Suddenly, the three of them burst into loud cackling laughter around me. Leslie falls to her knees, clutching her stomach with one hand. I quickly snatch the empanada from her other hand and she doesn't even notice as she continues rolling around beside Layla.

"It's not that funny." I mutter under my breath before taking a bite, mulling over the very valid facts I'd chosen to ignore.

Mom fans her face beside me, trying to dry the tears threatening to ruin her makeup. "*Dios mio,* what am I going to do with you girls." She breathes out, finally gaining control of herself.

"But wait, what did Chase have to say?" Lydia speaks up behind us. I roll my eyes and turn around to see her, Liam, Alfonso, and Aiden sitting at the bottom of the stairs.

"How has this turned into a family discussion?" I huff out, tossing my head back into the couch.

"More like an intervention. You're being extra as hell for a guy who is crazy about you, and you can't even see it."

"Girl, you know *extra* is the Peña way."

"I didn't stay long enough to find out his reasoning. I just needed space to process everything.

"Izzy, he's not Esteban."

"Esteban didn't lie to get with me, he just lied about everything else." I groan.

"Chase is crazy about you."

"Mhm." Everyone chimes in.

"I know I have drilled it into your heads about guarding your hearts but that wasn't because I didn't want you to not *ever* experience love. I love love. The heat, the burn, the risk, and the excitement of something new that changes you for the better in ways you had no idea you even needed. Guard your heart, but don't make it a forbidden place."

"You were never happy with Esteban, Izzy, but Chase...he lights you up in a way I have never seen you shine before, mi reina. You deserve more of that. Don't sacrifice that happiness now that you have found it because what, you're scared? You are strong, beautiful inside and out, and I promise you if you fall I will be right there to catch you, reina."

"Me too." Layla says, sitting down next to me and wrapping an arm around my other shoulder.

"Me three!" Lydia wraps her arms behind me.

"And us." The boys all run over, Liam jumping into my lap.

"And even me." Leslie says, smooshing the top of my head with the palm of her hand.

"I'm falling for him hard, but that's insane. It's too much too soon for me to be feeling like this. It scares me."

"You can be in a relationship for years and feel nothing, or be in one for a few weeks and feel everything. It's not about the time put into it, just the love. But if you don't want him and feel nothing at all for him, let a mom know now. I think there's a kid or three here that could use a new Daddy around." Mom says standing.

"Maaaa!" We all cry out together as she walks back into the kitchen laughing out loud, and this time I can't help but laugh with them.

After devouring another empanada, I shower and get dressed, then turn my phone on. Chase's messages are the first thing I see. It makes my stomach sink. I tap out and delete message after message, each one either too long or not enough of what I'm trying to say. I decide to call him instead, but it goes straight to voicemail when Jimmy walks in tossing my keys in my lap.

"Finally!" I say jumping up. I squeeze him.

"I'm sorry I couldn't get it done sooner or cheaper." He shrugs.

"What's another month or two of couch sleeping at this point?"

"I don't know how you sleep on that thing. Felt like I slept on a concrete slab."

"Wait!" Mom comes rushing as I push my feet into my sneakers. "Take this with you." She says pushing a white pastry box into my hands.

"Pastelitos de guava. I picked it up for Chase to try this morning."

"What? I like watching him try new foods. The way he moans in pleasure." She bites her bottom lip and rolls her eyes back.

"You are never allowed alone with him, Ma. Ever, but thank you. He definitely won't close the door in my face with these in my hands."

"God and your momma will always have your back, babe. Now go get our man. Your man, I'm sorry. He's all yours."

———

WHEN I GET to Chase's house and notice his car isn't there, I'm not surprised no one comes to the door. His phone still goes straight to voicemail so I try my luck at the gym.

"Izzy?" Damon asks, surprised to see me.

"Have you seen Chase? He's not answering my calls."

"He's at the hospital, but do you mind if we talk real quick?"

"Um…okay."

"Chase told me about what happened between you guys, and I just want to say I'm sorry. I know technically I lied about him being a trainer here, but I need you to know I didn't mean it in a malicious way." His tone is undoubtedly sincere. "It was wrong and unprofessional. I was thinking like a guy and what I thought was a romantic gesture was clearly not. I didn't think about how you would have taken it as deception, but I need you to know, this was never a game to Chase. Thanks to Nora, he's got a pretty messed up idea of what he does and doesn't deserve."

"Thank you, D. I really appreciate that. Promise you'll never do something like this again?

"Promise."

I smile at D and walk out of the gym towards Chase. Towards the happiness and love we both deserve.

My heart flutters in my chest at the thought of that one word I swore I was done with. Esteban ruined that word for me but Chase took the wreckage of my heart and little by little he restored the ugly pieces into one I could love.

14

CHASE

I'VE BEEN AT THE HOSPITAL SINCE NORA'S CALL THIS MORNING. THEY HAD TO give her something to calm her down earlier, but since then, she awoke like a completely different person. Sitting up in bed, smiling while pleasantly complying with all the nurses' requests.

I stare at her as she finger combs the tangles in her dull blonde hair, waiting to see how long this little act will last. But how much more of this *can I take* before the hollow pit in my stomach swallows me whole? I feel nothing but indifference for this woman and for the first time in my life I don't feel bad or guilty about it. I don't want to be here. She's broken something inside of me, something I wish I could fix but I'll never be able to scratch the surface on the damage she's left on me if I don't start helping myself first and accepting the fact that I can't save my mother.

"Nora, I can't do this anymore."

"Do what, pumpkin?" She asks, so fucking sweet it feels like nails on a chalkboard to my ears. Her blue eyes meet mine and I stare back, wishing I could see more to her than the verbal and physical abuse I've taken because I thought I deserved it.

"You're sick. You need help."

"You've been a good son caring for me the way you have. I know I haven't said it enough, or ever, but thank you, pumpkin. This time is going to be different, you'll see."

"It won't and I can't keep living like this. I can't keep choosing you."

"Oh, so you're going to leave me, then? You're just going to walk out now that I need you the most?"

"When haven't you needed me, Ma? Who else is going to pay your bar tabs, bail you out of jail, pay your medical bills and lawyer fees? Do you know how much debt I'm in because of you?"

She shakes her head. "I'm your mother."

"Well you damn sure haven't ever acted like it."

"You ungrateful bastard. I should have known you'd be just like your father."

"Good!" I shout. "I wish I was more like him. Maybe I would have gotten the sense to leave you a long time ago instead of wasting my entire life chasing you around town! You need fucking help, Nora!."

"I don't need anything, especially from you!" She screams, hurling the bed table in front of her in my direction. I catch it before it slams into me. A nurse opens the door.

"Is everything okay in here?" She asks.

"I want him gone!" Nora says pointing at me. "Get him out of here!" Nora shouts.

"Sir?" The nurse eyes my wearily.

"I'll go." I say nodding my head. "Good luck to you, Nora." I walk past her bed, brushing past the nurse and close the door behind me.

"Wait," I hear her call me back. "Pumpkin, I didn't mean any of that. Keagan?"

KEEPING my eyes down I barrel through the hallway and down the stairs. It isn't until I'm walking out of the lobby that I release the heaviness that's been building inside me. A warm breeze sweeps by carrying it away and I breathe in through my nose. I get a surprising lung full of an intoxicatingly sweet scent that reminds me of Izzy. I shake my head at my delirious mind for conjuring her perfume and scrub the palm of my hands over my face.

"Chase?"

The sound of her voice makes me look up. I had expected her voice to be a figment of my imagination but she's here, in front of me. Another soft breeze sweeps by pushing strands of dark hair into her face. My fingers beg to push the strands back as my heart gets lodged in my throat.

"Izzy." It's only been hours but it feels like so much more time has passed between us since she was in my arms. "What are you doing here?" I ask, tucking my hands into my front pocket to keep from reaching out and touching her.

"I came to bring you these." She says waving a white pastry box in front of her as she walks up to me.

"You brought me food?" I ask, narrowing my eyes.

"Technically, they're from Lulu."

I stare at her searching her eyes for more than just her showing up here to bring me food.

"Can we talk?"

We both say in unison.

I raise my hand in the air between us. "I'm sorry but can I go first?" I ask, my eyebrows pulling together as I take a step towards her. "I need you to know I could never do anything to hurt you, Izzy." I reach out and brush her hair away from her face. "You thinking that I'm that level of douche makes me sick but I-"

She stops me, reaching up and pressing a finger to my lips.

"You don't have to explain, Chase. I know exactly the kind of man you are." She declares. Her eyes hold me still and the finger on my lips moves down over my racing heart. I can't help leaning into her touch, needing her warmth, needing her. "You're a good man, Chase. A thoughtful one who puts others first. You're loyal and kind beyond measure with the biggest heart I have ever known. You are the kind of man that is deserving of all the love this world has to give." She says taking a step closer.

"I'm sorry for how I reacted earlier."

"You have nothing to apologize for." I brush my thumb along the soft skin of her cheek. Relief washing over me when she leans into it.

"You deserve all of that too, you know?" I tip her chin up. "To be cherished, appreciated, and loved. If you'll let me, I want to be the one to give you that, Izzy."

She looks up at me, her eyes shining bright and her lips stretch into a soft smile.

"I want that, too." She says and my heart soars in my chest. I capture her lips with mine and wrap my arms around her.

The box in her hands falls to the ground.

I pull back and press my forehead to hers. "Come home with me?"

Izzy pulls her bottom lip between her teeth and nods her head.

"Wait, how's your mom doing?" She asks.

"Better. I think this time around is going to be different for her."

"That's great, Chase. I really hope that for her."

———

WAKING up to Izzy's terrible singing on a Sunday morning is probably one of my new top favorite ways to start the day. The sight of her naked in my bed and the first thing I see in the morning, being number one. I can't help smiling to myself as I stretch my arms out, the memory of yesterday still fresh in my mind. This is real. She's here and she's all fucking mine.

Grabbing a condom from my nightstand, I walk out into the hallway, not bothering with putting clothes back on since I'm planning on joining Izzy and her shower musical. She's singing in Spanish and besides a couple words here and there I've never really heard her speak it. The song she's singing to makes me wish I understood enough so I can understand the lyrics.

I open the bathroom door, the music from her phone on the sink, mutes my entrance as she continues singing. My eyes trace the curves of her naked silhouette in the shower curtain as she sways back and forth.

"*Y solo por un beso.*" She belts out into a shampoo bottle.

I smile to myself, sneaking in behind her and sliding my hand around her slick waist.

She screams, jumping away from me and nearly slipping. I wrap my arm around her waist and pull her against me.

"You scared me." She says, her head falling back against my chest.

"I'm sorry." I mutter and press a kiss onto the top of her head.

"I've never heard you speak so much Spanish before."

"Memorizing lyrics doesn't count as speaking Spanish." She says. My hands skate up and down her sides enjoying the way she feels in my hands before cupping her breast.

She moans and I lean down peppering her neck with soft kisses.

"What was the name of the song?" I ask.

"*Un beso.*" She says spinning around and standing on her tiptoes. "He sings about a woman who dominates his senses." She says, wrapping her arms around my neck and pulling me down to meet her lips.

"I can relate to that." I say groaning against her mouth. I press myself against her and kiss her. Our tongues collide as I grip her ass in my hands and lift her up into my arms. I turn us around as the shower water streaming over us turns from hot to lukewarm and press her into the shower wall, reveling in the feel of her wrapped around me.

"Chase." She breathes against my lips. I slip my hand in between us and press the pads of my fingers against her clit, swallowing her gasp with my mouth as my fingers work the tight bundle of nerves. Her hips twist and turn and I press my thick cock against her, keeping her still. Leaning down over her chest I take the peaked tip of her dark nipple into my mouth, swirling my tongue around it in slow, languid strokes. Izzy's body trembles all around me as she chants my name like a fucking prayer.

I reach out onto the sink and tear the condom wrapper open with my teeth. The head of my cock pushes into her. We both moan, reveling in this feeling before I pull back and drive back into her again and again and again.

Her cries echo off of the walls until her tight pussy squeezes my cock so tight I explode with her.

"You're insatiable, you know that?"

"Just for you, Isadorrra."

"I could get used to that."

"Good, because I'm not letting you go."

EPILOGUE

IZZY

TEN MONTHS AND THREE WEEKS LATER.

"Keep going, Izzy."

"I can't! It's too big." I grunt.

"You can. Now, open your legs wide, baby." I do as he says, my body burning under his heated stare."

"Wider. There you go. That's it."

Sweat trickles down my forehead as I huff and push the monster truck sized tire down to the ground. My entire body burns from the ache in my muscles but surprisingly I don't hate it…as much as I used to.

"I told you you could do it." Chase says, wrapping his arms around my waist and dragging me up his body.

"Eww, stop, I'm all hot and sweaty."

"You know I like you wet, baby." He whispers into my ear.

"Hey, the gym floor is for working out, not making out. Y'all know this." Damon calls out.

Chase begrudgingly lowers me down, glancing around once more before planting a quick kiss to my lips.

"Feel like a run?" Chase asks.

"Maybe?"

"Come on," He says, pulling me down to the row of treadmills.

I may still not be able to outrun Leslie but I have definitely come a long way since the first time I stepped foot in this gym. I have Chase to thank for that. He's a certified trainer now doing this full time, and I couldn't be more proud of him for finally following his heart.

I stop to tie my sneakers as Chase jumps up on the treadmill and kicks it to life. My eyes roam up his body appreciating the defined muscles in his legs and the ones I know lay underneath the thin material of clothing he's wearing.

"You okay back there?" He asks, glancing back at me as he jogs steadily.

"Yup, just avoiding any unnecessary trauma to my head." I turn and step up onto the treadmill beside his when suddenly Chase's body hits the floor, rolling down onto the gym floor.

"Chase!" I gasp and hop to his side. "Are you okay?" His eyes flutter under his eyelids but other than that he isn't moving. "Chase?" I call out, pressing the palms of my hands to his cheeks. My heart hammers in my chest as I watch, waiting for his hazel eyes to light up.

"Damon!" I call out as one corner of Chase's lips turns up into a smile before he finally breaks out into laughter.

"What is wrong with you! I was so fucking worried." I say smacking his chest feeling both pissed and relieved right now.

Chase wraps a hand around my wrist, still laughing. "I'm sorry." He says and covers my hand with his. My eyebrows scrunch together as he pushes something into the palm of my hands.

Chase moves his hands away. "What are you-" I stop as I stare down at the stunning ring in my hand- a beautiful solitaire ring surrounded by smaller sparkling white diamonds. My eyes snap to Chase who is kneeling down in front of me. My mouth falls open as realization hits me.

"Holy shit." I breathe.

"I think you're supposed to be standing." He says, taking the ring from my hands and helping me up.

"Chase." I breathe as I stare down at him and tears brim my eyes.

He squeezes my right hand in his, smiling up at me with so much love shining through his eyes, I have to cover my mouth to keep from crying.

"Isadora Leticia Peña Yotun De la Vega," He says in a perfect, well prac-ticed accent. "Today marks exactly one year since you fell into my life. All it took was one look at you for me to know you were the home my heart's been searching for. The love I've spent my life begging for. I love you more-"

"Yes." I say, cutting him off as tears spill down my cheeks. "I love you so fucking much." I nod my head and spread my fingers wide for him. "Yes, I'll marry you."

"I wasn't done." He says smiling wide and slips the ring onto my finger.

"I'm sorry." I say, placing my hands over the stubble along his jaw. "I just couldn't wait another second." I kiss him as his strong arms envelope me and he pulls me up as he stands.

Applause breaks out around us and I turn my head to find Damon, the usual evening gym crowd, and my entire family plus Mya's standing around us.

"It doesn't matter." He says, pressing his forehead to mine. "You're all I want."

I find his unwavering eyes on me. I picture the life we'll have. The children I hope will have his eyes and loyal heart. My heart swells in my chest with so much love for this man. "I've never been so happy in all my life, and I have you to thank for that."

"Right back at you, babe. You've made me the happiest man in the world and I'm going to spend the rest of my life treasuring the gift you've given me. I love you, future Mrs. O'Rourke."

I smile so big it hurts my cheeks. "I love you."

ABOUT K. RODRIGUEZ

K. Rodriguez is a sleep-deprived homeschooling mom of three; living in SouthWest Florida with her high school sweetheart and FOUR beloved fur babies. She loves pizza, Aventura, and pretty words that hit her soul. Her favorite kind of self-care is reading, writing, biking, or bingeing Netflix into the wee hours of the night. She writes whole-hearted romance flavored with sazón.
  Caution in Love is her debut novella and first published work.

facebook.com/krodwrites

instagram.com/k.rodriguezwrites

STEEL AND STARLIGHT

KATHRYN TRATTNER

Visit my website at
https://www.kathryntrattner.com

 Created with Vellum

ABOUT STEEL AND STARLIGHT

Subgenre: Fantasy Romance
Trope: Enemies to Lovers

Graphic sexual depictions, open door sex and explicit language

Blurb:

A princess…
When war threatens the borders of her father's kingdom Daphne's life and happiness are exchanged for weapons and soldiers. To seal the deal, she will have to travel to meet her new husband and pray that love and respect can grow out of a marriage contract signed in blood.

A highwayman…
Time is running out for Finian as the war approaches. His men know what it's like to live in the hell that is a battlefield, and they'll do whatever it takes to avoid returning to one. The only way to keep ahead of the looming army is enough money to finance escape. Ransom is the perfect solution.

How much is one princess worth?

How much is one man willing to change?

One kiss can change it all.

1

IN A SKY WITH NO MOON, A GOLDEN STAR BURNED LOW ON THE HORIZON. IT outshone all the constellations in the heavens, pulling the eye, impossible to ignore. There was a legend about this star, a myth about gods and saints wandering the land, holding salvation in one hand and destruction in the other.

A golden star would appear, and the world would change.

Daphne had watched the sky for years, wondering what might be beyond the walls of her father's house, beyond the tiny mountain kingdom that had been home until now. But she had never wanted to leave. Neither happy nor unhappy, she had been content to let it go on as it always had. Content to be ignored, half hoping that it wouldn't change.

But here was the star, and change had come.

The coach rocked, passing over an uneven spot in the road, and she gripped her seat, the view through the small window jumping. It was little more than a dirt track through the mountains, off the main roads, trees and rocks crowding in on either side. There was no one out here, no little towns or villages to pass through, no estates to wander by. Only a wide, unknown wilderness, between her father's castle and Cautes.

Her future home.

Her future husband.

She pushed the thought away, glancing at Olesia and Mae sleeping peacefully on the opposite bench. The questions had finally stopped, each word tentative, barely there, but still managing to crawl beneath her skin, picking at the worry she was fighting to conceal. They weren't wrong to ask. It had all happened so quickly, a matter of days between the envoy and the signed contract. Everything they questioned, she questioned as well.

Do you think the rumors are true?

Do you think things will work out?

Do you think you'll be happy?

She envied them their sleep, wishing it would come for her, take her to a dreamless place. They'd been with her through it all, childhood friends and now handmaidens to the third daughter and most minor princess of King Haran. She was grateful they were with her. She'd given them the option to stay behind, and without hesitation, they'd both chosen to come. It was comfort and worry all wrapped into one package. Their fates were now tied with hers. For better or worse they would all have to find a place in this new court.

Outside she could hear Yaron and Adler, the guards her father had sent with her, talking, soft voices, words indistinct. She wondered briefly what they thought of this journey. For them, it would be over in a few short days, and they'd be returning to their families. Their futures would remain unchanged, to go on and be surrounded by their loved ones. But at the end of this journey, change waited for Daphne.

She would be creating a new family. If you could call what lay ahead the possibility of a new family. Her future husband was less than kind, his reputation for cruelty well-known. There would be no happiness in the days ahead. Her father had known but signed and sealed the documents without hesitation. There was no other option. This was the way to save the kingdom from the war rolling across the continent toward them.

Only a high, narrow pass through the Black Stone Mountains offered protection. The Needle. The only way over or through the sprawling mountain range for hundreds of miles. If they could keep it closed, they would survive. But no one had come, despite countless messengers, and no other help had been offered. King Haran had reached out to their closest neighbor, barely an ally, one final time and a bargain had been made. Her life for his soldiers. It would have to be enough. But if it wasn't, the dark horde of the empire would come through the pass and flood across the plains, destroying everything and everyone.

They'd all heard the stories, and most of the country had begun to flee south and west. But her father was stubborn and refused the messenger who had come from the dark prince, refused to become a minor lord beneath an invader and refused to retreat into exile. He'd even turned away messengers from her distant sisters begging for him to flee. Marius and her father had formed an uneasy alliance, half his troops sealed with a marriage. But she would be a minor wife, one of many, and all had failed to produce an heir. Her father had promised she would the woman to give him what he so desperately searched for.

Daphne leaned back and closed her eyes. Stomach knotting, she resisted the urge to rub her arms or pick at the embroidery on her gown. She focused on each breath, trying to release some of the anxiousness that had filled the last few days. There was no point in being anxious. It wouldn't change anything. What would be, would be.

The coach bounced over another deep rut, lurching sideways but moving slowly, and the horses neighed, the guards shouted, their fearful voices rising above the sounds of the horses. Someone called out, an unknown, strong male voice, a command, and then more shouts. Daphne sat up, pushing back the curtain over the window, searching the night. With a jerk, the coach stopped, the guards louder now, their voices strained. She shook Mae and Olesia awake, both muzzy with sleep, and held a finger to her lips for quiet, pointing to the window.

"What's happening?" Olesia whispered.

"The coach stopped," Daphne said, straining to hear what was happening outside. "There's shouting."

"Adler or Yaren?" Mae's pale eyes were large, brow creasing as she leaned toward the door, listening.

"Someone else."

The coach rocked as Adler jumped down from the driving perch, shouting as he went. The horses whickered uneasily, the coach swaying as they pulled against the traces. The clashing ring of steel on steel filled her ears, swords crossing, another man shouting.

"Soldiers?" Olesia guessed.

"Are they already here?" Mae asked. The women exchanged a look, fear traveling between them as quickly as lightning.

"Impossible," Daphne said, trying to get a better view beyond the window. "Father said they were several weeks out. The emissary traveled far ahead of the empire."

"Bandits then," Olesia said.

"Or the Wolf." Mae put a hand over her mouth, covering the name, eyes wide.

Daphne stared at her, the hair on the back of her neck rising. The Wolf. They said he traveled ahead of the horde, preparing the way for the dark prince, a pack of killers led by a monster. If that's who it was, if these were his men, there would only be one outcome.

"It can't be," Olesia shot Mae a hard look. "Yaren said there has been a lot of bandit activity. If the Wolf had crossed the mountains, the whole forest would be burning by now."

"Would it though? If he were trying to conceal his location?" Mae asked.

Daphne bit her lip, glancing at her, exchanging a look that said more than words could. Bandits or soldiers, it didn't matter who was outside, it meant danger for them.

"What do we do?" Mae asked, going over the interior of the coach as if a weapon might have materialized while they slept.

"Adler and Yaren will take care of it." Daphne was relieved her voice remained steady. Her heart was pounding, stomach now a rock made of fear and dread.

"But if they don't?" Olesia asked.

The coach held only a few things: books, furs to keep the chill off, a basket of food, and another basket full of embroidery materials. There was a deep purple gown with a half-finished pattern around the neckline in a darker shade, handkerchiefs with flowers, a pillowcase edged in gold roses. But in the basket, nestled in a tin, were several pairs of small, sharp scissors. She pulled it toward her, digging through the fabric and floss to find them.

Two pairs, gold handles shaped like graceful birds, the beaks sharp silver. She handed one to each of them, pressing cool metal into their hands, fingers trembling now. Outside the sounds of fighting continued—Alder yelling, a shout from Yaren. Something heavy hit the side of the coach, rocking it, and the women gasped, reaching for each other.

"Hold on to these," Daphne gasped. "Hide them on you somewhere. Don't hesitate to use them and run. Do you understand?"

The two nodded, eyes wide and on the door of the coach, many voices now reaching them, the sounds of fighting ending abruptly.

"What about you?" Mae tried to hand the tiny scissors back.

"No, keep it. A title should be enough protection."

But what if it wasn't? Nothing was a guarantee. But if anything happened, she wanted her companions to have something to defend themselves with, however small. Torchlight flickered beyond the glass, shadows moving, the darkness touched but not truly lessened by the light. Daphne forced herself to breathe steadily, watching the window and waiting. Olesia and Mae moved to sit on the bench beside her, the three of them squeezed into a space meant for two.

Boots crunched on rocks—swift, sure strides—and then paused. Daphne's heart pounded, pulse racing as torchlight filtered through the curtains on the coach windows and door, voices murmuring beyond the glass. Mae squeezed her hand; Olesia drew in a hissing breath between her teeth. They sat frozen together, rabbits holding themselves taut in hope of being overlooked, with the hope that they might escape. The coach smelled like fear, Mae and Olesia staring wide-eyed at the door, the three of them holding on to the moment, drawing out the inevitable.

Someone knocked on the door of the coach, two sharp raps in quick succession. A man spoke, a deep strong voice that reached inside her and twisted, plucking a string within her, thrumming through her. Implication and threat, and beneath that a dark, curling promise.

"We have something to discuss, your highness."

2

THE COACH DOOR REMAINED CLOSED. FINIAN SIGHED AND EXCHANGED A LOOK with Claudius, his second-in-command, who shrugged.

"If I have to come in and get you, you're not going to enjoy it."

He hardened his voice, wanting the woman to come out on her own, dreading the idea of going in after her. That was the last thing he needed. Nothing had gone right up until this point. He didn't want to deal with hauling her out of the carriage, screaming and cursing his name. Did princesses curse? Possibly if a strange man was dragging them out of a coach. He nodded to Rishon standing near the coach door, and the man knocked again, harder this time, the noise echoing.

Finian stepped forward, resigned to the task at hand, but stopped when the coach swayed slightly and the handle on the door moved. *Finally.* He straightened his shoulders and nodded to his men. They shifted, ready to grab the woman if she took off running.

The coach door opened; the interior all in shadows, three figures barely visible. The driver and guard said there were three women—the princess and two handmaidens. He had no idea who would step out first. If it were him, he'd be the first out the door. He would never send one of his men to face something he wouldn't. But he had the vague idea that royalty valued their own skin over that of those around them.

A woman stepped into the torchlight, pausing on the top step of the little stairs that flipped down. She scanned the scene with a flat expression. Green eyes landed on him, intense and full of anger, not the expression he'd been expecting at all.

He was struck by her beauty, his mouth open as he watched this woman step out of the coach with her head high and unafraid. There was a moment of complete silence as she looked around, the men watching her, caught beneath the star-filled sky. Her hair was deep auburn, reminding him of the woods he'd grown up in, how the leaves had gone from green to red, the feeling of it all changing around him. A woman made of autumn, all the promise of winter while summer still held sway.

Rishon held his hand out to steady her as she stepped down. She took it without looking at him, keeping her gaze locked on Finian. He envied their contact, her elegant hand in the other man's grasp. He wanted to be the one touching her. He swallowed, the silence stretching out, the world coming down to her eyes, and the rushing blood in his ears. Claudius coughed, and Finian found his voice.

"I regret to inform you of a slight detour in your traveling plans. Allow me to introduce myself and my men."

Finian put on his best lopsided smile, flashing a dimple, and gave her a slight bow. But beneath the charm and show of manners was the sense of a sword sheathed, danger promised. He'd been caught off guard by her beauty, but he wouldn't let it happen again. She was not a distraction he could afford. She raised an eyebrow, hands clasped together, the other women in the coach now at the door and watching the scene with wide eyes.

Her hard voice cut across his words. "I know who you are."

He raised an eyebrow, a smile touching his face. Beyond the flicking light of the torch, someone chuckled.

"The Wolf."

Behind her another woman gasped, the small noise loud in the ringing silence. Then someone began to laugh, the sound rippling through the men surrounding the coach. The man's face creased, the smile widening, white teeth glinting in the light. He wanted to applaud. Her voice barely shook, and she kept her face hard as rock. Not everyone had such command over their emotions. Over the years he'd faced plenty of people who had pissed themselves or begun to cry before he'd even spoken.

"No, your highness. If I was the Wolf, you would all be dead. Fortunately for you, my name is Finian. And we," he gestured to the men, "are here to ransom you. Not kill you. Now, if you would like to come with me," he said, crossing to her in a few quick strides, "we can begin."

He reached for her with a gloved hand, eyes on her face, a question in them. He was wondering if he was going to have to grab her or if she would come without a fight.

"Come," he said softly, a dimple flashing in one cheek. "This will all be over before you know it. I promise no harm will come to you between now and then."

When she didn't move, the smile fell away.

"Let me tell you how this is going to go, your highness. One guard and one handmaiden will travel to your father and the other two to your future husband. Whoever pays the highest price gets you first. It's easy. In no time at all, you'll be back to sleeping in a feather bed."

"You seem to know a lot about me."

He shrugged. *Not enough.* He hadn't been prepared for the beautiful woman in front of him, the way looking at her would make him feel. "I know enough."

"Because someone gave you the information. Who?"

"They're not important."

"You don't think so? I do."

"I don't plan to kill you, princess."

She opened her mouth, but he held up a hand, stopping her.

"Or hurt you or do anything else you might be worried about. You're no good to us unless you remain just as you are now."

"Betrayal matters. And this person, or group of people, have traded my safety for what? Money?"

Anger touched him then, flashing across his face, catching in his blue eyes. "A war is coming, your highness. Or perhaps you don't know. But a little gold right now could mean the difference between life and death for someone."

Her face reddened. "Why do you think I'm standing here now? Is one person's life worth more than a kingdom?"

"That's war." He brought his smile back, a charming façade. "And besides, your ransom will be paid before you know it. The bargain made will be kept. It will all turn out that you were never in any real danger at all."

"My lady, what choice is there?" Mae asked softly from the door of the coach, worry and fear all over her face.

"We don't seem to have one."

Finian didn't respond. There was no point.

The horses were unhitched from the coach, sidestepping and nervous, aware of the tension in the air. The two guards had been disarmed and gagged, anger on their faces, hands tied together behind their backs. They'd been tied the harnesses with a short rope, one to each horse, and they grumbled at the men through the fabric stuffed in their mouths. The two handmaidens sorted through the trunks tied to the back of the coach, murmuring over the contents, focused, and ignoring the men standing near them.

"Your turn, ladies."

———

THE MAN who spoke was short with dark skin and a stern face. But his voice was kind enough as he explained which group would travel to her father and

Marius. He didn't rush them when Mae and Olesia threw themselves at Daphne. The three women stood together, arms linked, watching as the horses were readied and the guards armed with carefully sealed letters. Daphne wasn't sure where their weapons had gone, and most of their armor had been taken.

"They need their swords," Daphne said, stepping forward.

"They don't," Claudius responded without looking at her.

"What if they run into bandits?"

"Time to say goodbye, your highness." Finian gestured to Mae and Olesia.

Daphne squeezed their hands, pouring as much love as possible into them. Mae was crying, and Oleisa looked as if she might start, both their faces pale, mouths trembling.

"I'll see you again very soon," Daphne said, glancing at Finian, wondering how true it might be. Mae and Olesia stepped closer, the three forming a tight knot, their heads together.

"What would you like me to say to your father?" Mae asked.

"To King Marius?" Olesia asked.

Daphne shook her head. It wouldn't matter. Nothing they could say would change whatever answer would come from either man. "Don't worry about that. Promise me, both of you, that you'll take care of yourselves."

"We'll see you soon," Mae promised.

"Soon," Daphne repeated, closing her eyes.

Another tight hug, swift kisses, and the women were led to where the guards and horses waited. After they'd been helped up on the horses Finian nodded to his men.

"Claudius and Tallis will lead your horses a few miles in the right direction. After that, you're on your own. I trust you will do the right thing and carry my message to the kings."

"We will," Mae said, nodding at Daphne.

"Wonderful. Feel free to untie the guards after my men have left. I'm sure we'll be hearing from one royal highness or another very soon."

"How are we going to untie them?" Olesia asked, irritation coloring her words.

"Use those tiny scissors of yours."

"What scissors?" Mae asked. It was obvious the men had known, and it was even more obvious that Mae was incapable of hiding anything. But maybe they'd guessed and now she'd given it away. Not that it mattered. They didn't seem to care.

"The rope is too thick!" Olesia protested.

"All things are possible with patience and perseverance," Claudius said with a chuckle. He gestured at the women to move, shooting Finian a look that conveyed irritation and humor at the same time. "We'll see you back at camp."

Finian nodded, turning to Daphne. He held out a hand, waiting for her to take it or refuse him. When she didn't move, he gestured to a waiting horse. "Come. We have places to be."

Daphne followed him, aware of the eyes on her, the thoughtfulness behind the gazes, feeling Mae and Oleisa at her back, their worry for her a physical presence. What if she never saw them again? What if she never made it out of these woods? The thought terrified her. The man, Finian, stopped beside a golden-brown horse with white legs. The horse turned her neck to look at Daphne; gaze as curious as everyone else's.

"Turn around."

"What?"

He turned her around, picking her up and placing her on the horse. It happened too quickly for her to react. She went from standing to sitting, clutching desperately to the saddle as the horse stepped sideways, moving beneath the unfamiliar weight. Daphne stared down at the man, surprised at his gentleness. He could have thrown her across the saddle or forced her to walk.

"What kind of man kidnaps a woman?" she asked, studying his face, looking for anything that might help her later; a clue as to what kind of man she was dealing with. "A coward? A killer?

"Someone desperate." He nodded to the saddle. "Hold on, your highness."

Finian grabbed the reins and began to walk the horse away from the coach, away from Olesia and Mae, away from the future she'd been preparing herself for.

3

THE FOREST SWAYED AS A CHILL WIND BLEW THROUGH, TREES RUSTLING, MOVING with the arriving fall in the mountains. Daphne shivered, pulling the velvet cloak tighter, wrapping her hands in the fabric. If it weren't for her friends, she would have gone on without it. Practical Mae. Fierce Olesia. They'd shoved a few things into the hastily emptied embroidery basket: a gown, a tangle of underthings, and this cloak. The basket had been tied to the horse's saddle, a small piece of a past so different from the present.

Again and again, her gaze came back to the man leading the horse deeper into the woods. They'd left the road behind, a single-file line of riders moving deeper into the trees, and no one spoke. She wanted to scream at them, shout, throw things at them. But no one said a thing. She was in a bubble, floating along, her fate tied to the man in front of her.

Finian.

What kind of man became a kidnapper? A thief? And worse, could he be a murderer?

She studied him, his clothes were worn but of good quality, and he carried a short sword at his hip. Blue or green eyes? They were light, but she hadn't been able to see the color clearly in the torchlight. He was attractive, a dimple flashing when he smiled, tall with broad shoulders and a swagger. The kind of man her father might have employed for some nefarious reason. A man who all the court ladies would whisper about behind their fans.

He'd promised this would all seem like a bad dream in no time. In a few days, she would be back in her feather bed, back to her life as expected. But inside, a small voice was stirring, a tiny faint hope, and she was struggling to crush it. *What if.* Not the what-if of fear or pain, danger come home to settle squarely on her shoulders, but the what-if of change.

What if life took her in another direction? One away from Marius?

Daphne shook herself, shoving the thought away. It didn't matter. The important thing was to make sure the treaty was kept. It was a matter of life and death for the people in her father's kingdom, the place that had once been her home. She would do what needed to be done.

She always had.

———

THEY MADE camp an hour or so later. Dawn was still a distant promise, the sky full of glimmering stars. It felt like an age had passed, between the coach jerking to a halt and arriving at this small clearing in the woods. A fire burned cheerfully; the men sat around it, talking and laughing, unconcerned with the strange woman in their midst. She held her hands out, soaking in the warmth, hoping soon her frozen feet would thaw. Daphne would have given anything for a pair of fur-lined slippers and thick socks instead of what she wore now.

She scanned the camp, the horses tied a little distance away, saddles and bedrolls sorted into sleeping areas. A pot bubbled near the fire, something savory filling the air, making her mouth water. She was surprised she was hungry and couldn't remember the last time she'd eaten. There had been dried fruit and nuts in the carriage, a flask of water and another of white wine, but now she couldn't remember if she'd had any. Her stomach rumbled, insisting that whatever was in that pot would be wonderful, no matter what it was.

Claudius caught her eye, his face a blank mask; she couldn't read his gaze, whatever his intentions might be. She'd picked up their names as they'd traveled and made camp, and she'd made an effort to remember them all. Before she could look away, he nodded, recognition and hello in the gesture, and pushed to his feet. She went back to the fire, tension growing as she watched him fill a mug with the contents from the pot. He walked toward her slowly, like a man approaching a wild animal, and held out the mug.

"It's mostly vegetables and not too terrible."

Hunger won over wariness, and she accepted the mug gratefully. She inhaled deeply, grateful for the warmth in her hands, mouth watering. "Thank you."

He crouched down, looking around the camp, before meeting her eyes. She leaned back, away from him, heart beginning to pound. "I know it might not seem like it, but nothing bad will happen to you here. Finian is an honorable man. You can trust what he says."

"Are you all as honorable?"

He smiled at her, the blank expression lifting, kindness touching his eyes. "Believe it or not, yes."

"Honor among thieves then?"

"Honor among brothers." Claudius nodded to the mug in her hand. "If you want more, help yourself."

"Dinner smells wonderful! Who cooked?" Finian strode into camp, back from whatever scouting expedition he'd been on. He looked around the camp, and his gaze came to a halt on Daphne. He smiled, dimple flashing. "Happy to see you eating, your highness. The food won't kill you, I promise."

Claudius leaned toward her a little, whispering, "Don't forget what I said."

Daphne nodded, staring down into the mug, watching the contents and inhaling the steam.

"Esdras cooked," Claudius said, standing and crossing back to his spot among the group.

"I wouldn't call it cooking. It's all sad, dried vegetables and tough mutton," Rishon mumbled.

"And you're eating it anyway," Esdras pointed out.

"Something is always better than nothing," Finian said with a chuckle, crossing to the pot and helping himself. He scanned the small camp, the men talking amongst themselves and Daphne sitting in the same spot where he'd left her.

She sipped the soup, too thin to be a stew, and was grateful for it. It wasn't the best thing she'd ever eaten, but it wasn't the worst. The warmth of it spread out, easing the chill she'd been feeling. The men talked of horses and gambling, someone mentioned a distant city and a distant relation there who owed them money. The conversation centered around it—how much they had and how much they could get. She wondered why they needed it, why they needed whatever her father or Marius would pay.

"How far can we go on that? How far will it take us? How far away do we have to be so he won't find us?"

So that was it. They were running from the dark empire too, working to stay ahead of the Wolf. Why would these men fear him? It didn't make sense to her. Surely a man like that would have better things to do than deal with petty highwaymen.

She felt someone's eyes on her, hot and searching, and she glanced up. Finian looked away. It made her uneasy, the way his gaze made her feel, the way her stomach clenched and heart beat faster. His smile had tugged at her own lips, wanting to return the expression, wondering what he would do with her response. She shook herself, pushing the thought away, and concentrated on keeping her face expressionless and ears open.

———

H<small>E WATCHED HER</small>, fascinated by the play of firelight on her face, the way it revealed and concealed, always in motion while her expression stayed the same. She sat far enough away to seem disinterested in the warmth while still benefiting from it, hands clasped and resting in her lap, face serene. He wanted to reach for her, drag her fully into the light and hold on until she had nowhere else to look, hold her until she finally met his eyes.

She wasn't the woman he'd expected: spoiled and haughty, cold and aloof. There was a sadness about her, a thoughtful observance, that caught at something in his chest. In the area of a heart, if he'd had one. He wondered where that came from, what sorrow could have possibly touched a life as easy as hers. He thought again of her expression when she'd stepped down from the coach, standing in the torchlight, her gaze driving everything else from his mind. She'd left him breathless, mouth open, unable to do or say anything.

"You should keep your eyes to yourself."

Her voice cut through his thoughts, pulling him back, her green eyes just as hard now as they had been before. He wanted to know what it would take to make her gaze soften.

"I wasn't looking at you, your highness."

Her mouth curved, there and gone. "Weren't you?"

"Now that you mention it," he stood and crossed to her, studying her face. "You do look a little worse for the wear."

"Any guess why that might be? Perhaps being waylaid by a highwayman could cause such a look?"

"I promise you that any woman appearing to be so worn out in my presence has a much more pleasurable reason to appear so disheveled."

Her eyes flashed up, reflecting firelight.

"There's a stream down that track, just a few yards. Can you hear it?" He gestured to the trees behind her, the bubbling stream audible even over the sounds of the camp. "Take a moment, go refresh yourself."

Daphne didn't move.

"Go on," he said, turning to camp with a whistle. "The princess is going to the stream. I would like all of you to respect her privacy."

The men barely glanced at her, voicing their agreement and then going back to their conversations and dinner. She turned toward the sound of water, moving beyond the circle of light thrown by the fire and welcoming the solitude.

––––––

T<small>HE WATER STUNG</small>, biting cold and crystal clear. She drank several mouthfuls, teeth aching, not caring that it numbed her fingers and soaked into the silk sleeves of her gown. She was torn between wanting the warmth of the fire back and holding on to the feeling of loneliness a little longer. The sound of rushing water drowned out whatever conversation was happening around the camp and for an instant, she could pretend her reality was unchanged, that this was some kind of detour and she would be back on the road to Marius very soon.

Maybe she would be.

The night was wide and dark with no moon in the sky. A night that belonged to the hunted, to the prey running ahead of the predator. She could sneak away, up the hill and toward the road.

She stood, drying her hands on her skirts, the embroidered fabric bunching in her fingers as she watched the circle of firelight. The men laughed and joked. Out here, watching them from the outside, they appeared to be close, friends and brothers, a force against the world. Whatever image she had of a person in this situation, it didn't include these relaxed happy faces. They reminded her of the men around the castle or in the villages. Ordinary people. Not thieves and highwaymen, kidnappers and possible killers.

She took a step in the direction of the road. How long would it take them to realize she was gone? They'd agreed to give her some privacy, and they wouldn't expect her back right away. She could cross the stream, move in the opposite direction of the road. Thinking about it now, it would be foolish; they'd expect that. There would be someone who could help her eventually. If she went quietly and made sure she left no tracks to follow, she could be gone before they realized it.

"You wouldn't make it very far."

She jumped, a squeak of surprise escaping as she spun, searching for the source of the voice. The men around the campfire paused, glancing toward the stream, and then laughed, going back to their conversations. Finian stepped out from between two trees, a shadow given shape and form.

"What are you doing? You said you'd give me privacy." Her heart pounded, beating in her throat, skin heating as he strolled toward her. So cool and casual, moving easily in the dark, more a part of it than anyone had a right to be.

"I told my men to give you a moment of privacy."

"But here you are. Gentlemen don't lurk in the dark."

"How convenient that I'm no gentleman. Otherwise, you might already be lost in the wilderness, and we'd be forced to find you. And at that point, really, it would be a mission of mercy. Finding the sweet princess and returning her to the care of her future husband would result in a reward, I'm sure. It might be better than anything else that could happen out here."

"I'm surprised you're choosing ransom instead."

Finian chuckled. "Believe it or not, it's the easier of the two. This way no one has to pretend. We all know who we are."

"Yes," she agreed, stepping around him and heading back toward the fire. "We do."

He reached out and stopped her, hand warm around her upper arm. There was gentleness in his touch but also the knowledge that at any moment his fingers would tighten if she tried to pull away. She shivered at the contact, looking up into his face, trying to make out his features. He was so close, and she wondered what he would do if she closed the distance between them.

She was shocked at the thought. The desire to lean into him was so strong she swayed. It was his blue eyes, the way he'd looked at her when she'd stepped out of the coach. No one had ever looked at her that way. She wanted to find out what the look meant.

He didn't speak, night noises creeping up on them, as curious as she was. *Why do you look at me that way?* But she didn't voice the question aloud. The moment was separate from the rest of the day, another time and place, and he was someone else here in the dark alone with her.

She wanted to know this man, explore the heat he brought to her skin, give in to the curiosity and attraction. It was insanity. A handsome face and charming smile didn't change the situation: a princess taken hostage and a kidnapper who saw nothing but gold in her face.

"Let go," Daphne said.

"Maybe I don't want to."

His voice was low and full of promise. She waited, holding her breath. She didn't know what she wanted to happen, for him to kiss her or let her go, for whatever she felt to be answered. He released her, stepping back. She felt his eyes following her, but she refused to look back.

———

THE CAMPFIRE BURNED LOW, deep red embers glowing as the last pieces of wood settled. There was no more to place on it, nothing to keep it going, and she sat quietly, watching it die. Somewhere nearby Finian kept watch while the others slept. The two men that had led Mae and Olesia away had returned and now slept as well. She sat a little distance from them, gaze shifting from one to the other.

Exhaustion tugged at her, sleep at the edges of her mind begging her to give in. But there was too much fear and anxiousness to let sleep take hold. Ransom. Money her father would not pay. Money she was positive her future husband would not pay. He didn't need her; her father didn't want her. Though the contract, the support from King Marius would mean everything for the kingdom, it still would not be worth it to her father.

What would happen then? She didn't know, but she wasn't going to wait to let it happen. If she watched them closely and learned their patterns, something would present itself. Someone who fell asleep on watch. A few stolen moments beside some other stream. Finian couldn't be everywhere at once, and eventually, he'd have to take his eyes off her. She would wait and watch, and when the time came, she would run.

Finian sat beside her, no warning or sound, just there beside her in the blink of an eye. She was too surprised to make a noise, leaning so far away she almost fell backward. He grabbed her, keeping her steady, large hand warm around her wrist.

"I expected you to be asleep by now," he said.

Daphne pulled her arm away, rubbing the spot he'd touched. "No."

"You should sleep. Tomorrow we have a lot of ground to cover."

She didn't respond, moving over on the bedroll he'd given her, putting a little distance between them. "I'm fine."

"Are you waiting for us all to fall asleep so you can sneak away?" he chuckled.

"Not at all. I don't even know where I am."

Tilting his head back Finian gazed at the sky, searching, and then finding what he was looking for. He raised a hand and pointed to a bright star. "There. The Arrow. Always rises in the south. If you know enough about the constellations, they could guide you."

Daphne glanced at the sky, not needing the reminder of where the star fell in the heavens. She knew it. Knew where the others would fall in beside it, how they would wheel across the sky, invisible during the day, sparkling at night. She didn't need him to tell her what or where it was.

"Only in the summer months," she said. "But you're pointing at the wrong star. That one," she pointed in the opposite direction, "is the Arrow."

"Well done," he said, nodding. "Now I know which direction you'll go if you manage to slip past any of us."

Daphne shot him a glare, swift and sharp, before trying to smooth her wrinkled brow and hide her expression. He smiled, enjoying her discomfort. She'd watched him all evening, glancing away when he turned to her, unaware of how much he saw. And now, with his undivided attention, she reddened beneath his gaze. She was angry and maybe a little afraid, but there wasn't as much fear there as he'd expected. She wasn't some pale, wilting flower. Quiet, yes, sheltered and naïve, all of that, but beneath it there was strength.

"Are you going to get some rest now?"

She shook her head.

"Well, if you won't sleep, I will," he said. He stretched out beside her, half on the bedroll he'd given her, and put his hands behind his head. She reddened, eyes furious and glittering in the dying firelight.

"What are you doing," she hissed.

"Going to sleep."

"Not here!"

"Then where? If you aren't going to use it, I will!"

"I will not sleep beside you," she said, tugging at the fabric beneath him, trying to move him.

"You are not sleeping at all."

"I might choose to if you were not here."

He raised an eyebrow, propping himself up on an elbow. "Where else should I sleep?"

"I don't know. Not here. In a tree maybe."

"Hmmm, yes a tree." He tapped his chin thoughtfully. "You know, I think I'd fall out."

"I'm sure you'd be perfectly comfortable. Now please move. I would like to sleep." She nudged him, hoping to ease him farther away, hoping he'd get up and leave.

"Well, if you're so sure, I guess I should give it a try." He stood up and stretched, gaze sweeping over her face thoughtfully. "Good night, your highness."

Daphne didn't look at him, easing down and occupying as much of the blanket as possible to discourage him from changing his mind. Forcing each breath out steadily, pulling the next all the way in, all the way to the bottom of her lungs, she drifted into a kind of half sleep. But it didn't last. The noises of the forest, trees swaying, animals passing in the night, brought her back with a jolt each time. Finally, she gave up, listening and trying not to think about the way Finian had looked at her beside the fire earlier.

———

HE SAT BEYOND THE LIGHT, watching the stars, listening to the quiet of the forest. He glanced at her once, small in the night, with her back to him. She wasn't sleeping. He could tell by the stiffness of her shoulders, the way she breathed. He considered the idea of her, the woman made of gold and rubies, a means to an end—plain and boring, scared, and meek, a woman who would have followed instructions and been out of his sight in a few days without his giving her a second thought.

Daphne was something else.

———

THE NEXT MORNING, she watched as the men broke camp and the horses were saddled. There would be a long day of traveling, though they were careful not to say to where. Maybe they were worried she'd escape and give them away. If she had the chance, she would. She made sure her meager belongings were in the bag, wrapping the cloak tightly around herself as she waited for her fate to be decided.

Finian strode toward her, looking over what was left of the now cold fire and the small clearing. Reaching her, he put his hands on his hips, looking her up and down.

"Is that the dress you plan to ride in?"

"Is that the tone of voice you're choosing to speak to me with?"

He laughed. "Fair enough, your highness. I just wanted to make sure you'll be as comfortable as possible. We've got a lot of distance to cover."

"You didn't leave me many options for traveling attire."

"You're right, of course. My apologies. It's time to go."

He took her arm gently, leading her toward the group of mounted men. There was only one horse without a rider, the same one he'd put her on the night before when he led her from the coach.

"I would prefer not to ride with you," she said, stomach twisting into a knot. She was too aware of his hand on her arm, the warmth that traveled through her with his touch. She couldn't imagine sharing a horse, being so close to him.

"You'd rather walk then?"

"Yes."

He shrugged, smiling at her. "As you wish, your highness. Gentleman, I wish to inform you that our guest would like to stretch her legs this morning. We'll be taking things a little slower than anticipated."

The men turned to her, questions on their faces, a line of worry between Claudius's brows. He dismounted, nodding to Tallis, who shook his head. Esdras dismounted with a shrug, but the others stayed mounted, Rishon urging his horse into the lead. Finian remained beside her, whistling under his breath.

"Aren't you going to ride?" Daphne asked.

"It's a beautiful day for a stroll," he replied, falling in line, Claudius falling in behind them. "Besides, who am I to resist the company of a beautiful woman?"

Daphne bit her tongue, keeping the sharp reply to herself, wondering how long it would be before he decided to ride. He lasted longer than she'd expected. He'd given up trying to make small talk, her silence hard and fast between them.

They moved slowly, winding uphill through the forest, zigzagging up deer trails. Sometimes Finian walked beside her and other times he rode. His men did the same, all of them laughing and joking with each other, sharing stories, and making plans for their futures. The conversation was less bleak in the daylight; beyond the light of the fire, they didn't mention the Wolf or the coming horde.

"Come. Ride with me, your highness. I don't bite."

Daphne hesitated, torn between her pride and the ache in her feet. Finian smiled, eyebrows raised, as if he could read her mind and was laughing at her, and held out a hand in invitation. She took it with a sigh, disappointed with herself over sore feet and tired legs. He pulled her up to sit in front of him, their bodies fitted together as she was forced to share the saddle with him. With a chuckle his arms settled around her and he gripped the reins, hard and warm at her back.

"Not so bad after all?"

He whispered against her ear, a shiver racing across her skin, warmth pooling in her stomach.

"You smell," she said, fighting to keep her voice level.

"Well, maybe I'll have a bath later."

"You need it."

"You should join me. You could use one yourself. Your face is covered in dirt."

She huffed, half turning to him, surprised to find his face so close to her own. "I wouldn't get naked with you if my life depended on it."

He threw back his head and laughed; his men glanced at him, ready to join in the joke.

"Now I know exactly where I stand with you. I'll have to see if I can find such a situation for you." He leaned in, chest to her back, arms tightening. "I would very much enjoy seeing you undressed."

Heat flooded her, warming her cheeks and twisting complicated knots in her stomach.

"You will never see me undressed."

"Want to make a wager?"

She turned, furious. "You have given me your word!"

He chuckled. "And I will never go back on it. I'm not serious. You have nothing to worry about. I have no interest in you. It's just that you turn such a lovely shade of pink when you're upset."

Daphne balled her hands into fists, wanting to pummel him, wanting to knock the laughter out of his voice. He was teasing her, enjoying how uncomfortable it made her. A small part of her, buried deep inside, was a little sad that it was nothing more than that.

———

DAPHNE SLEPT HEAVILY THAT NIGHT, exhausted from walking, trying to untangle the emotions curling inside of her like a nest of snakes. The heat of his body, the way his arms had come around her, the way she'd reacted to his touch. It had taken everything she had to keep from leaning into him. And he knew it.

She could feel it coming off him in waves, his pleasure at her discomfort, the way she reacted to him when they were alone.

What was it? What was it about this man that had gotten beneath her skin, touched some unknown place in her soul? Everything she should never ever want. Everything she would have sworn two days ago she never would.

They traveled for several days like this, passing single file beneath trees and down narrow paths between boulders. She found herself waiting for the moment when he'd grip her tight, pull her into his body, as they both rode the horse. The rest of the time he walked to give his horse a break from carrying both their weight. He wouldn't let her anymore, insisting she ride after her first refusal.

Each time he swung up in the saddle with her, she complained.

"Can't you find your own horse? Can't one of your men share? I'm sure Claudius wouldn't mind."

"Claudius's horse doesn't like me."

"I don't blame him."

He laughed, head back, eyes sparkling. "Come now," he said, leaning into her, a hand light on her waist, voice in her ear. "You don't really mind riding with me, do you?"

Daphne reddened. "I mind very much. I prefer to ride alone."

"It was a terrible oversight on our part. Of course, I should have considered that you would want to have your own horse. I'll remember this for next time. A personal horse for the hostage."

They made camp that night as they had so many times before. Each night blurred together for her, all into one long night full of campfires and thin soup, rides in the day shared with Finian, the closeness of him, the feel of his hands lingering and haunting her each time she closed her eyes. She watched him when he wasn't watching her. She could feel his eyes, the intent gaze that slid away from her just before she turned, just before she caught him.

What would Mae and Olesia say? What were they doing now? Surely, they had made their way to her father and Marius by now. They would be bartering for her life. A man who didn't love her and one who didn't know her. It wasn't much of a choice on their part. But the only thing keeping her safe was the idea that she was valuable. She'd listened enough to the men around her to know they saw her as little else. Despite the small kindnesses, the courtesies they showed her, she was a mission to be accomplished and nothing more.

———

DAPHNE WOKE UP SLOWLY, listening to the sounds of the camp being dismantled, the already familiar voices.

"Rise and shine, princess," Finian said. "I need that bedroll."

She opened her eyes. He stood over her, hands on hips, eyebrows raised. The desire to inconvenience him overtook her, swamping all common sense.

"I'm not done with it yet."

His eyebrows went higher. "No? Well, you don't have much of a choice. It's time to get up."

"What will you do if I don't? You've already said you won't harm me. What can you do if I chose to stay here all day?" A smile touched her mouth, and the men made noises of surprise and delight.

"Yes, Finian! How?"

"Go on then Finian, leave the princess alone. We can always spend another night in the woods," said Tallis.

There was a groan at his words.

Finian crouched down. "Would you rather spend the night in the woods or a feather bed?"

"What?" Daphne propped herself up on an elbow.

"Dirt or feathers, it's your choice."

"Feathers, of course."

"And yet, here you are in the dirt." He spread his hands out, a dimple appearing in one cheek. "I could give you another reason to get up if you'd like?"

Daphne narrowed her eyes, mouth pressed into a firm line.

"It might even change the sour expression on your face." He leaned closer, reaching out to touch a lock of her hair.

Daphne pushed his hand away and stood, dusting her hands off on her skirts, feeling beyond grimy after traveling for days without a decent wash. Finian stayed where he was, crouched at her feet and looking up, a strange expression on his face. She stilled, a breeze whisking through camp, ruffling her hair.

"Look who's back bearing gifts," Tallis said.

Daphne turned as Esdras came into camp leading a horse she hadn't seen before. Finian stood and rolled the bedding up, tucking it neatly together and brushing past her. His arm grazed hers, the contact hot and distracting. She glanced at him, noticing his head down and, catching his thoughtful look before he turned away.

Esdras waved to Daphne, holding out the reins of the horse with a smile. "For you, Daphne."

"Me?" She went to the horse, holding out her palm.

"We're all pretty tired of listening to you complain about sharing a horse with Finian. We thought this would be the best way to get you to stop." He shrugged.

Finian laughed.

"Where did you get her? Did you steal her?"

"We're not all villains. Finian paid for her." Esdras nodded to Finian, the other man grinning down at her from his mount. "She came from a village nearby. The farmer said her name is Clover."

Daphne put her hand out, and the horse snuffled her palm, ears perked forward. She didn't want to thank them, to feel touched by a small gesture, didn't want to feel any kind of gratitude toward these men, but it was there just the same.

"Thank you," she said, voice soft.

Esdras inclined his head, smiling happily, and when Daphne looked to Finian again, he winked.

4

THERE WERE A HANDFUL OF OTHER TRAVELERS ON THE ROAD. A COACH DRIVEN
by a dark-eyed driver who watched them warily. A pair of riders with wide-
brimmed hats concealing their faces, swords strapped to their saddles. A
woman on a plow horse, with a baby in one arm and a haunted expression in
her eyes.

Daphne considered calling out, asking for help, begging, but Finian must
have seen it on her face because he reached toward her, placing a hand over
hers with a slight smile. The ever-charming man. From then on, he'd ridden
beside her, so close that his leg brushed hers, their horses' shoulders bumping.
If any of the travelers they passed thought anything of her at it all, they'd likely
brush her aside as some irritated wife to a doting husband. Though how they
would account for the rest of Finian's men she had no idea.

Her stomach grumbled, but they rode past midday and kept going as the
sun settled lower, the light drawing out and going golden. The air took on an
edge of frost and she tucked the cloak in around herself, wondering when
they'd stop for a fire. The men began to peel away, galloping down other roads,
taking other paths with only a handful of quiet words exchanged before calling
their goodbyes after a little distance, a shouted promise to see each other again
at the inn.

She found herself envying their closeness, the brotherhood of thieves
they'd built. They so obviously relied on each other. It made her miss Olesia
and Mae. Her heart ached with missing them, the women she'd grown up with,
not her father or the kingdom or far-off sisters.

They passed a few homesteads, little places with smoke curling out of chimneys and back gardens with woodpiles, goats and chickens, and barns tucked away into steep hillsides. If there was anyone outside, they watched them from out of sight, on guard against something she could not name. But there were some houses with no smoke, no light in the windows. It was strange to pass those places, abandoned, eerie from a distance.

"Are you hungry?" Finian asked.

His questions cut across her thoughts, drawing her eyes back from a dark and silent cottage. She met his gaze, raising an eyebrow. "Do you plan to feed me then? I thought you'd let me starve."

He laughed, throwing back his head, Tallis chuckling with him. "No, your highness. I do not intend to let you starve. We're very close to an inn. We'll stop there and get you a meal and a bed."

"Such extravagance," she said, tilting her chip up. "A bed. I might die of the unexpected luxury."

They chuckled between themselves, exchanging smiles around her, over her head. She let them laugh. It was better to have them laughing than watching her with sharp eyes. There was still a chance she could get away. If they weren't watching her too closely, she would take it.

———

THEY CAME to a crossroad in the foothills of the mountains, rocky giants rising in the distance, washed in the colors of sunset and early night—snowy peaks violet and glowing white. One road led away, toward a wall of deep green ancient forest, another toward a mountain pass, and the last meandered along the scrubby foothills, following a narrow rushing river. Wet stone and vegetation filled the air, crisp in her lungs, and hinting of the coming winter evenings.

An inn sat back from the road, exposed beams with a freshly thatched roof, built into and between an outcropping of dark stone with a fenced-off yard connected to a barn and a handful of other outbuildings. It rose three stories from the trampled grass, faceted glass windows reflecting the last of the light, a sign above the door—a blacksmith's iron and tongs—painted in bright gold.

The Strong Arm.

Finian led them through the open gate into the yard. There were four of them now. Everyone else had peeled away, off on other errands, leaving Daphne with Finnian, Claudius, and Esdras.

Daphne was exhausted, looking forward to sleeping in a real bed and not on a thin pad on rocky ground. She wanted a bath too. A real one. Not a quick wash in the woods in an icy stream. She wanted hot food and a cup of warm tea to wrap her fingers around. She wondered if the men wanted all of those things too. If they were just as tired as she was or if they were so travel hardened that they'd prefer the freedom of sleeping beneath the stars to whatever comforts this place might have. She hoped not. Maybe they'd stay here for however long it took her father and Marius to respond.

A lanky boy with blond hair and curious hazel eyes came out of the barn to meet them.

"Nathan," Finian said, with a smile and a wave. "A pleasure to see you as always. How is Effie? And yourself?"

"Good as always. It's a full house tonight."

Finian pulled something from a pocket, silver flashing as he pressed it into Nathan's palm. "Everyone the same?"

"Oh yeah, all friends," Nathan said, tucking the coin away and nodding at Daphne. "Who's she?"

"A friend."

"Effie will have won a bet if she's a *close* friend." Nathan grinned at Daphne.

Claudius leaned over to slap Finian on the shoulder. "Effie should know better than to place any bets where Fin is concerned."

"Thank you," Finian said, nodding, a flash of indignation crossing his features. "My thoughts exactly."

"But maybe I need to get in on this wager," Esdras said, winking at Daphne. "I think I might be on the winning side."

"As long as you're betting against him, I think you should do fine," Daphne said, cheeks burning.

They began to laugh again, the stable boy as well, and she was pleased to see Finian's cheeks looking a little rosy.

"Fair enough, fair enough." Finian held up his hands, a good-natured smile back in place. "I realize I might not be everyone's first choice, but I will have you know there is a female who loves me very much. Which proves all of you wrong."

"Your mother?" Nathan cackled.

"Are you kidding? No! My horse!" Finian dropped a kiss on Victory's nose, patting her fondly. "And if you were any kind of a gentleman, Nathan, you wouldn't keep her waiting. Do you have anything special for the horses? We've had a rough few days on the road, and they need a good rest."

"I can find something," Nathan said, stepping forward to take the reins. "She still likes apples?"

"Always."

"I've set some aside for my favorite visitors." The boy ran a hand down Victory's neck, and she nodded at him as he leaned in to whisper, "I'll show you right where they are."

Finian turned to Daphne and held out a hand. "Would you like help down, my lady?"

"No, I'm perfectly capable." She bristled, wanting to accept him and keep him away at the same time.

"I know you're capable. I'm still offering."

She met his eye. "You can keep your hands to yourself."

The Esdras and Claudius chuckled; Nathan watched them all with curiosity. Whatever he saw, or thought he saw, everyone else in the inn would soon know. Finian held out his arms for her anyway. It had been a long day, and she'd been in the saddle a long time.

"She'll fight you all the way," Esdras said, leading his horse toward the barn. He called over his shoulder. "Don't let him win, Daphne. Nathan, my boy, come show me where I can find the oats. Claudius will bring the other three in a moment."

The boy hurried after him, talk about the horses passing between them. Daphne followed him with her eyes, mouth open. *Daphne*. He'd called her by her given name as if he knew her. As if he weren't a part of the reason she was out here on a strange horse with strange men, waiting to be ransomed. But a small part, a deep inner voice, was pleased. It was the same tone the men used amongst themselves, the joking edge, the familiarity that meant time spent together, a certain level of comfort. They'd built something like a family. She'd been envying them the easy connection, the warmth, and with one casual word, Esdras had opened up a small part of it to include her.

But of course, it didn't really, couldn't. She was a princess. A woman about to be married. A prisoner. A captive. Nothing but a warm body waiting to be exchanged for gold and rubies.

She slid off the horse on the opposite side from Finian, taking the moment to compose her face, the emotions she knew would be there. She could never keep a secret, never hold anything back. And she didn't want Finian to see the brief spark of happiness at being included. She needed to hide it, keep it to examine more closely later, and then forget that it had ever come to life at all.

"We'll go in separately. Let me know what you hear. Maybe there's news of some kind from the East." Finian handed the reins of his horse to Claudius and gestured to Daphne's. "Keep an eye out, and only share as much as you need to."

"You don't have to worry," Claudius said.

"Who said I was worried?" Finian smiled, arms outstretched. "I've never worried a day in my life."

Claudius rolled his eyes and took hold of the horse's reins, speaking softly to them. "Come on, girls. I don't want you hearing any more of these terrible lies."

The side door to the inn opened, noise and smoky light and the scent of roast chicken wafting out, spilling across the yard. A man stumbled out, barely looked at them, and headed for the stable, grumbling as he went. The room beyond was full. Crowded tables and too many voices, overwhelming after the last several hours on the quiet ride were a jolt to her senses. Unease threaded through her, careful stitches that became a pattern of doubt, as it swung shut again, cutting it all off from view.

Finian came to stand close, tilting his head to whisper in her ear. He placed a hand at the small of her back, the touch light but possessive. "No one will save you here, your highness. I might be a highwayman, but I'm also your best protection against much worse. You make the choice to say anything, and something unfortunate might happen to you."

"Unfortunate," she repeated, glancing at him and finding his face too near to her own. His blue eyes held both a warning and a promise. A stab of fear shot through her, coupled with anger and frustration.

"Do you understand?"

She nodded.

"Well done," he said in a normal tone, pulling away and extending his arm. "My lady, let me escort you in. I shall find you dinner and a soft bed."

She ignored him, moving forward without him, his laugh following. She was coming to recognize his laughs, and this one was pleasure at her refusal, enjoyment in her rejection and stubbornness. He came up behind her, swooping in to open the door with a mocking bow.

"After you."

Daphne could feel his gaze, the hot pressure of it on her skin, but refused to meet his gaze again. Stepping through into the chaos of the crowded tavern, she sucked in a breath as the room quieted and all eyes turned to inspect the strangers who had just entered. Each face was sharp and focused, equal parts curious and suspicious. Then the room changed as recognition came, jovial greetings arriving as Finian eased around her and waded into the room. Daphne followed closely, watching each response he gave, how familiar he was with each person.

How many were friends? How many mere acquaintances? It was hard to know; she could only guess. Their eyes would slip to her after greeting him, looking her over head to toe, wondering about her place in his life. What would they say if they knew? Some wouldn't care; others might take advantage of the situation. It was on their faces, plain in the hard gazes. These were the men and women moving ahead of the horde, living on the edges and watching for the places where they could use their talents to make a little bit of money; thieves and conmen, women of negotiable affection, murderers for hire. They played a careful game, dancing at the margins, running toward the invading army, hoping to increase their wealth, then running ahead, hoping not to be swallowed whole.

But there might be someone who would help her. So she scanned the room, hopeful, refusing to give in to Finian's wishes simply because he wanted her to.

They made their way to the back of the room, where a bar ran along the wall, people coming and going with flagons of ale, laughing and talking as they went. A woman and a man stood behind the worn counter, talking with each other and everyone else as they served drinks. When the woman saw Finian, she held up a finger, silent instruction for him to wait, as she finished speaking to a young woman with a tray full of glasses.

Finished, she put her hands on her hips and approached Finian, eyes going over his in a careful inspection. She was older, with laugh lines around her wide mouth and sharp brown eyes, curly dark hair shot through with silver. She looked like she laughed a lot, always smiling, happy with whatever might come her way. But she wasn't smiling now. She scowled at Finian.

"I need a room, Effie."

"And what about the bill you didn't pay last time?"

"Paid in full along with tonight."

She gave him a sour look, raising an eyebrow as she took in Daphne.

"It's not what you think," Finian said.

"No? Well, I've got the one room. If you want it, it's yours." She waited until he nodded.

"Second floor, end of the hall. A west-facing window so the sunrise won't bother your hangover."

"I don't have a hangover."

"Yet!" she said with a laugh. "If I know you, it won't take you long."

"And dinner?" he asked.

"Find a seat, and Annie will bring you a couple of plates."

"Do I get a choice?"

"Not tonight," she said, laughing as she moved to help another customer.

Finian turned, scanned the room, and reached for Daphne's hand. The contact startled her, his large hand warm and callused, wrapping around her own. It was such a casual gesture, but it made her stomach drop, warmth fanning across her cheeks.

"Come on," he said, pulling her behind him as he navigated between tables and laughing or bickering groups.

They found a table in the corner near the fireplace; an eddy in the fast moving stream, the spot a little removed from the main area and quieter. Hunting trophies covered the walls, a pair of blacksmith tongs crossed above the mantle. Oil lamps hung from the rafters, a few on the walls, and each table had a little oil lamp flickering in the center, the flame protected by glass. The room managed to be bright and shadowed at once, the corners deeper, figures in hooded cloaks bent close to each other, groups sitting together and laughing loudly. Across the space, a man played guitar, a fast, light tune that managed to rise above the noise.

"Finian! You and I have business." A man with a red beard called out from across the room, waving Finian over. A man next to him raised an eyebrow, nodding to Daphne.

"If I left you alone, would you promise not to run?" He waved to the man, gesturing that he'd be just a moment.

"I'm not making you any kind of promise."

He turned to her, giving her his complete attention, blue eyes piercing. She leaned back, biting the inside of her cheek as he slid a hand around her waist, easing her toward him, bringing them together like a pair of lovers. Anyone watching would think he was going to kiss her. Anyone watching would think she was his. He bent his head, lips brushing her ear, whispering across her skin. She shivered, the hair on the back of her neck rising. They stood together, the room around them fading, as she inhaled sharply.

"You don't have to make me any promises," he said, voice low. "I wasn't really asking."

She turned into him, their cheeks brushing as he pulled away, an emotion that she had no name for flashing in his blue eyes. He focused on her parted lips, a response on the tip of her tongue.

Say something! Say anything!

But the way he'd touched her, his lips so close to her skin, the way she'd warmed all over, had chased all of her sharp responses away. Each time he got close, each time the space between them vanished, he left her breathless and wanting.

What do you want? A small inner voice asked, curious and laughing. But she wasn't going to think about it, wasn't going to follow the thought back to the buried place it came from.

"And look! Here is some roast chicken to keep you company." He turned her to the table, pushing her gently into a seat as a serving woman placed two plates and flagons on the table before her. He leaned down, touching her shoulder, sending a shiver through her. "I'll be back before you've finished."

"I'm Annie. Wave me down if you need anything," the woman said with a smile, already moving to the next table.

"Thank you," Daphne murmured, glancing up to see if Finian still stood beside her.

But he was gone. She half turned in her seat, considering him as he walked away. There was obvious respect and friendliness in each greeting, a well-known and well-liked man. He seemed to cultivate that everywhere he went. She'd seen it firsthand with his men. What was it about him that drew others to him? What was it about him that drew her?

Daphne went back to her meal, mouth watering at the scent of chicken. Anything would have been better than the soup, but this was beyond what she'd imagined. Dinner. She would concentrate on dinner and think of nothing else. She wouldn't think about his hand at the small of her back or his rough cheek brushing against her smooth cheek. Or the way he'd laughed in the yard. Or how blue his eyes were.

She wouldn't think of him at all.

———

FINIAN MADE HIS ROUNDS, settling a few small debts, sharing information. There were one or two subtle questions about the woman traveling with him. Where was she from? Where was she going? Had he gotten desperate and gotten into the bodyguard business? Had he gone soft?

Have I gone soft?

Across the room, Daphne ate dinner, curious and watchful of the surroundings, her eyes occasionally resting on him before darting away. He was just as quick to look away before she caught him watching. What could it possibly be like to sit in a room like this after being served in giant, echoing castle halls, sitting in high rooms away from the dirt and grime of life, served and never going hungry, never wanting for anything? And here she was, having slept out in the open for days, eaten terrible soup, and been handled like a sack of potatoes but still composed and the most beautiful woman in the room.

Beautiful?

Maybe he had gone soft.

"So what about it, Fin?"

He turned back to Kerin, another sword for hire that he'd met since leaving the army. "What?"

"A hand of cards. You won a lot of money off me last time, and I intend to win some of it back." He laughed, holding up his beer in salute. "Maybe we could talk your second into playing as well. He has the worst luck, and I know at least I won't lose to him."

Finian laughed, nodding. "It's true. But as much as I would love to win whatever gold you've got on you at the moment, I won't be able to. I have too much to settle before we move on."

Kerin raised an eyebrow, indicating Daphne across the room. "I've never known you to be so distracted."

He shrugged, wondering if the man was right. Distracted. They knew each other well enough, were almost friends, two men on similar paths, moving in the same circles. He wouldn't have said he trusted his opinion like he did Claudius or Tallis, but even they had watched him more closely the last few days, exchanging a pointed expression when they'd thought he wouldn't see. If this relative stranger had seen it, what must they think?

His duty was to them. He couldn't fail them. He couldn't let anything in this situation sway his original goal. Enough gold to travel further south, enough money to smooth their path, to charter passage across the sea. It would take a princess's ransom to get as far away as they could from the dark horde and the approaching empire.

Daphne's ransom.

"Some other time, yes?" Finian asked, clapping Kerin on the shoulder.

"Of course," the man said amiably. "Before you return to your enchanting companion, though, perhaps you would share any news you might have? I'd hoped to talk to you over a hand of cards, but I'm interested in what you've seen out there. There have been conflicting reports coming in. No one really knows how close the horde is. Someone said they saw the Wolf crossing the mountains."

Finian went cold. "What?"

"Roberts claims he saw a small group coming down from a narrow pass to the south, dressed in all black, a white skull tied to the saddle of the man in front. I told him it couldn't be the Wolf. He's weeks away yet, hundreds of miles. But Roberts insisted. Have you seen him out there?"

"I thought the only way through was The Needle?"

"So did I. Something else he mentioned that was odd. He thought one of the riders might be a woman. If Roberts is right, I'm planning to leave in the morning."

"A woman?"

Kerin nodded. "Have you heard the stories about the saint? I don't believe it. But the empire seems to think it's true."

"I know the stories." Finian shook his head, mind churning. "I didn't think they'd be this close already."

Kerin gulped from the mug in his hand, nodding to himself now, thoughtful. "I'll see what else I can find out. If you hear anything let me know."

"Do the same for me as well."

"We might find ourselves following the same road south."

"If we do, you're welcome to join us." Finian extended a hand, and Kerin took it, the two shaking to seal the deal.

"Won't Claudius mind?"

"Try not to win all his money tonight at cards and he won't mind traveling with you so much tomorrow."

They shared a laugh, Finian turning toward Daphne, a riot of thoughts filling him. *Distracted.* He hated to admit it, even to himself, in the privacy of his mind. Claudius would see it, and he'd have some sharp opinion to share. He'd never been one to hold back, and Finian was surprised he hadn't already said something. Maybe he was waiting for the right moment to remind him that this was a job and their end goal remained unchanged.

Nothing has changed.

A large man he didn't recognize was leaning over Daphne, speaking in a low voice, a smile playing around his lips. Her eyes were hard on his face, but her cheeks were reddening as she listened, one hand gripping the knife that had arrived with her dinner. Finian hesitated, wondering if she would use it and surprise them all. But he wasn't going to give her the chance. His hand itched, wanting his sword, wanting to curl into a fist, but he put a smile on his face as he moved toward the pair. As he approached, he could hear the man's tone if not his words. The words didn't matter. Daphne's expression was all he needed.

"Good evening, friend," Finian said, moving around the man and coming to stand beside Daphne. He brushed her cheek with a finger, a quick touch that brought her eyes up to his face. Relief was there, her features softening, posture relaxing. He almost reached for her again, wanting to cup her face, keep her eyes on him and see if they changed, see if relief became a different emotion.

Distracted.

"Who're you?" The man looked Finian up and down with bloodshot eyes. He straightened, shoulders back, a sneer on his face. He was bigger than Finian, frame large and running to fat but with plenty of muscle underneath it.

"Finian."

"Well, Finian, the woman and I are having a conversation. I'll let you know when we're done."

"I can see that," Finian said, looking from one to the other. "It's over now."

"I don't think so. We're on the verge of an understanding, aren't we love?"

Anger, sharp and hot, shot through Finian, a haze of red clouding everything.

"She's mine."

Two words. That was all it took. Spoken aloud they altered the air in the room, each breath he pulled into his lungs. They touched a place inside him, where a heart might have beat once upon a time, and where nothing would ever be the same. The words came without thought, without hesitation, and the truth of them rang in his ears.

The man leaned forward slightly, getting ready to speak or ball a hand into a fist, getting ready to deny or dispute his words. Finian pulled back and punched him, a quick one-two to the man's torso that sent him stumbling back into a table and a watching group of people. Finian followed, landing another punch on his jaw, the man's eyes glazing. He wanted to hit the man again. He touched his hip, where his sword would be, fingers shaking and ready to grasp it. When had he ever shaken when he pulled his sword? When had there ever been so much emotion behind the gesture?

Never.

"Stop, Finian." Claudius was there, voice calm, evaluating the room. "Be careful what you do next."

Kerin and another man grabbed the stranger and hauled him up, the man stumbling and yelling, a finger pointed at Finian. He tried to shake free, but

Kerin managed to hold on, the two men dragging the stranger toward the door leading to the stable yard. Finian and Claudius remained surrounded by curious faces, some smiling, others scowling.

Finian could feel Daphne there—so aware of her beside him, but unable to look at her. What did she think of his words, issued with so much assurance to the room? To her. For her. She was his hostage, a prisoner, and not the lover they all assumed she was. She wasn't his at all. Not in the way it mattered.

"No fighting in my house, Finian! You know better than that!" Effie yelled, coming around the bar, furious and holding a short club in one hand. Sam and Mac, the bartender and cook, followed closely behind. Mac gripped a cast iron skillet with a calculating expression on his face.

"You saw it, Effie." Finian gestured to the man being escorted through the door. He struggled to smile, to put the humor he always carried into his voice, to ease the tension in the room. He put a hand to his chest. "I gave him a chance. What kind of man would I be if I didn't defend a beautiful woman?"

Several people chuckled, a few voices raised in agreement, the room relaxing as some of the watchers turned away.

Effie sighed, pointing the club at Mac. "Make sure there are no scores to settle here."

Mac nodded, what was left of the crowd parting quickly for him to pass.

"And you," Effie glanced at Sam. "Get the lady drink."

The guitar player began to play again, the notes fast and bright, luring people toward him. Effie waited until the last of the men and women had returned to their small groups and conversations. "A small piece of advice? Call it a night and head to your room." Effie leaned toward Finian, keeping her voice low. "Because if you're trying to keep a low profile you're failing miserably."

"What could I do?" Finian shrugged. "I told him she was mine."

Effie shook her head, turning away from him and heading back to the bar. Finian finally looked at Daphne. Her eyes were full of secrets, whatever she felt concealed in pools of pale green. He didn't know what to say. There was never a time when he'd been at a loss for words but standing here before her, the words he'd spoken still ringing in his ears, he had no idea what he could say.

"Shall we go?" She stood, brushing her skirts off, reaching up to touch her hair, tucking an errant strand into place. "You promised me a bath."

He swallowed. "I did."

"Good."

He offered her his arm, holding his breath, waiting for her to refuse. But she took it, wrapping her fingers around his, following as he led her out of the tavern and up the stairs.

5

Daphne stared at the single bed.

The room was small, the bed smaller, and it was all lit by a cheerful fire jumping in the hearth. The window faced a rocky outcropping wall of the cliff the inn was built into, letting in light during the day. There was a small shelf on the wall with books, a bedside table with a brass candlestick and several tapers, and a worn-out wingback chair. The colors were faded, a mix of muddy florals and solid greens, but everything was well taken care of. The wooden floors were scrubbed clean, and an empty enamel hip tub crowded one corner.

"You can't be serious. There's only one bed."

"Don't worry, princess. You're safe enough with me."

"There has to be another room. An extra bed."

"You heard Effie. Full house. This is it." He waved at the bed, a roughish smile on his face.

Daphne shook her head. "Then you're sleeping on the floor."

"I'm afraid not. You're not the only one who has been sleeping on the hard ground for a week. I intend to sleep in that bed whether you're in it or not."

"No," Daphne said flatly.

He smiled. "There's more than enough room for two."

"I refuse to sleep in that bed with you."

"Then sleep on the floor." Finian gestured to the chair. "Or there."

"You would make a princess sleep on the floor?"

"I did say the chair was an option." Finian glanced around the room as if another option might appear.

"I refuse the chair as well." She turned, inspecting the small room. "I won't change my mind, Finian."

"I understand, Daphne," Finian said, holding out a pacifying hand. "We'll see how it goes."

Daphne opened her mouth, shocked at the use of her name, shocked to realize that she'd used his name.

"Do you still want a bath?" he asked.

She paused, torn between the desire for hot water and the need to make sure he knew her name wasn't for his use. *Your highness. Princess. My lady.* Those were all ways he could address her. Barriers between them, meant to keep him in place, to keep her out of reach. But the need to keep him at a distance, to keep how he made her feel at a distance, was getting harder to hold on to.

Finian. His name had fallen so easily from her lips.

"Yes," she sighed, accepting it. Nothing else made sense, so she wouldn't expect this to either. "A bath would be lovely, thank you."

Finian left to arrange hot water and laundry. She hesitated, almost sitting on the bed, and then decided against it. The books on the shelf turned out to be history collections. She flipped through one, skimming the small type and detailed illustrations before placing it back on the shelf. Moving to the window, she tried to peer through it. But everything beyond the glass was so dark, a deep perfect stillness, that the window became a mirror. It reflected the room, the fire, and her.

She's mine.

The words repeated, swirling around with the last week in her head. His smile. Why did she keep thinking about his smile? Or how blue his eyes were? She shook herself, clearing her mind as Finian swept back into the room, flopping down into the chair.

"Your bath will be ready momentarily, your highness."

She looked from him to the open door and the empty hall beyond.

"By magic?"

"No, of course not. Not magic." He gestured to the bath in the corner.

"That is my bath?"

"There's always the river."

"Yes. Of course, there is. This sounds like the sleeping options." Rubbing her eyes with the heels of her hands, she let out a sigh, a mix of frustration and disappointment, and beneath it, all the great engulfing sea of exhaustion.

He stood and slid around her, taking the enamel tub from the corner, and placing it before the fire. It appeared smaller on the floor. He pushed it with a booted foot, the enamel scraping against the smooth floor until it clicked against the stone hearth. Daphne stared at it. She would fit. It wouldn't be the long deep soak she'd been dreaming about, but of course, it was still a bath. And better than the river.

Two girls appeared with half-full buckets of steaming water from the kitchen. They chattered with each other as they worked. Daphne watched the tub fill slowly as they came and went, watching her out of the corner of their eyes, a swift inspection each time, glancing to Finian and away, whispering and giggling as they worked. He sat in the chair, boots off, arms crossed, and eyes closed.

WHEN THE TUB had been filled and the door closed again, Finian opened his eyes and smiled like he'd been the one doing all the hard work.

"I promised you a bath, and here it is!" He flourished his hand, taking in the large enamel tub of steaming water before the fireplace, the sponge and towel, and a bar of thick white soap. "Never say I don't keep my promises."

Happiness was a bath full of hot water. She could have sunk into it with all her clothes on, content and grateful until the warmth wore off and the cold set it. Even then, as long as she no longer smelled of sweat and horses, she would be pleased.

"Thank you," she said, going to the tub and dipping a finger in to test the temperature. There was a bucket of steaming water near the hearth, ready to warm the water back up, and an extra towel. It was perfect, but she didn't want to tell him that.

"My pleasure, your highness." He moved to the small shelf in the room where a few books were stacked next to an ink well and a pink porcelain pig. He chose a book, blue leather with worn gold leaf, and looked around the room. There was only the bed and a sagging upholstered chair near the one window. With a sigh he fell into the chair, kicking his feet out and opening the book.

"What are you doing?"

He stopped, looked at her, and then back to the book, holding it up for her inspection. "Reading."

"You can't be serious."

"You don't think I know how to read?"

"I can't take a bath with you here."

"You can," he said, going back to his book. "I won't peek, I promise. Your virtue is safe with me."

"I refuse! You must leave. Go downstairs! Go drink ale and swap stories with your friends!"

"I can't."

"Why not?"

"Because being up here with you is part of my cover story this evening."

"What are you talking about?"

"Well," he said, putting a finger in the book to hold his spot. "If I left you

687

up here, people would wonder why such a beautiful woman was alone. They might ask why. Especially after the show I made about you belonging to *me*. I don't want them asking questions."

"Then go somewhere else."

"I'm perfectly comfortable, thank you."

Daphne stood there, gasping, angry, and on the verge of tears. She wanted to throw something at him. She wanted to knock the smug look off his face. But she wanted a bath more; she wanted clean sheets and sleep. She refused to get into the bed dirty, couldn't stand the idea of being in these clothes a moment longer.

"Turn the chair to the wall."

"It's heavy," he protested.

"Move it anyway," she said between clenched teeth.

He sighed, setting the book down and moving the chair with a grunt, muttering under his breath. She watched him, waiting until it faced the window and he had flopped back down into his seat, before turning back to the tub. Her chest felt tight, the hair on the back of her neck standing. She could feel Finian as if he stood beside her. And somewhere in her reaction to him was the desire to step within his reach to see what would happen; here in this room, with no other gaze on them, truly alone together.

It was ridiculous. She shook herself, making the decision and beginning to loosen her clothes. But she struggled to reach the ties along the back of her gown. There was a series of complicated decorative knots that were now like locks. After several days on the road in this gown, and without the help of Olesia or Mae, they had solidified with grime. She would have to cut them to get the gown off. But she hated the idea of it, loathed to destroy one of the few beautiful things she owned.

"Let me help you," Finian said, taking a step toward her.

"Don't you dare!" she said. "I told you to face the window."

"I have been." He held up his hands with a shrug. "But I can see your reflection in the glass."

She groaned, going limp, sinking onto the bed. It was too much. She'd reached her emotional breaking point and could feel the sob boiling inside, half anger, half fear, all of it threatening to come out all at once. Tears filled her eyes, and she brushed them away savagely, refusing to let him have her despair. He could have anger, her frustration, but she refused to give him the satisfaction of her sorrow.

He stopped, watching her, one hand outstretched as if he wanted to touch her. The noise of the tavern below traveled through the floorboards, breaking up the silence between them, a cheerful string of notes from the guitar drowning out the voices for a moment.

She wanted a bath. More than anything. Right now, she wanted to be clean and then sleep. She needed a few moments of thoughtlessness, of routine. With a sigh, she stood and went to him, turning around so he could work at the knots, waiting patiently for him to begin.

———

FINIAN LOOKED DOWN AT HER, the straight shoulders, auburn hair tied into a messy knot at the back of her neck, a few strands had pulled free. He wanted to lose her hair and comb his fingers through the waves, to smooth the tension from her shoulders, slip the mussed silk and cotton from her body. He wanted to touch her, kiss every place on her body that made her blush, kiss her until she writhed beneath him and said his name in a dark, delicious way.

She turned her head slightly, a glance, nothing more. "Will you undo the knots please?"

He trembled, forcing a steadying breath out, and worked at the knots. They came apart easily enough, too quickly to suit his liking, and she was stepping away from him before he'd gotten the chance to run a finger against the sheer blue cotton beneath the outer shell of her silk gown.

"If I asked you to face the window again, would you?"

"Yes."

No, he wanted to say, *no because I want to see you. I want to see everything.* But he turned away, closing his eyes, ignoring the window and the reflection if offered. Behind him, there was the rustle of fabric and a gentle sloshing of water as she stepped into the tub and eased down with a sigh. She sounded pleased, happy with the warmth and comfort it offered. Suddenly he wanted to give her more of that: more comfort, more happiness.

Stop. Stop right now. You're an idiot for even thinking that.

But the thought persisted, and when she spoke, he didn't hear her the first time.

"What?"

"Will you wash my back?"

He didn't move, convinced his brain had betrayed him, his ears deceiving him.

"I don't care anymore. I'm exhausted. I'm dirty. I just want to be clean and go to bed. Will you help me?"

He turned, belly tight with expectation, the sight of her naked in the tub, her face to the fire in the hearth, knees up, with her arms wrapped around them. The water came up to the middle of her back, hiding most of her, offering a hint of modesty. Easing down beside her, he took the sponge she offered, soaking up warm water and drawing it over her shoulders. He held his breath, counting the scattering of freckles on her back. *Ten. Eleven. Twelve.* Any moment she would say it was enough and he would have to figure out how to let go.

"Thank you," she said quietly, resting her chin on her arms. "I miss them. I hate you for sending them away. Mae would wash my back for me sometimes. It seems odd maybe. Once upon a time, my sisters did it for me, when I was little, and when they left, Mae did. I think she wanted me to feel less alone."

"I didn't think the life of a princess would be so lonely."

"I didn't think the life of a highwayman would leave room for much kindness, however small." She sighed, changing the angle of her head, laying it down, and closing her eyes. "You are cruel as well as kind, laughing all the while. Don't you ever get tired of being so terrible?"

"Am I terrible?"

She nodded, voice low, sounding far away and very tired. "What else could you be?"

He didn't respond, hesitating, water dripping from the sponge onto her back. She was thin, the suggestion of bones beneath muscle and skin visible; he wanted to feed her, he wanted to wrap her in the softest thing he could find in the world and carry her around like a shard of crystal. *Terrible.* Yes, he supposed he was. The sponge dropped from his hand, splashing in the water as he stood and turned away, back to the window, focusing on the world beyond this room, on the things he'd always wanted.

"Thank you," she said, water sloshing, as she found the sponge, moving to finish her bath.

"You're welcome."

He didn't say anything else as she finished, closing his eyes and focusing on the things ahead he knew would have to happen. What would happen in a week when this situation was over and his men needed to figure out the next step to take them south. He thought about dinner. He thought about the last time he stood on a battlefield. He thought about his mother and the song she'd sung when he was little. He thought about the last time he'd seen his father.

Any and everything to stop himself from thinking about Daphne.

OUT OF THE corner of his eye Finian caught the pale flash of Daphne lifting the quilt and slipping between the sheets. She sighed, wriggling down into the bed, pulling the quilt up to her chin. Her pleasure and contentment with the soft, smooth cotton and softness of the mattress was palpable.

He stared at the pages of the book in his hands, painfully aware of her, the flash of skin he'd caught from the corner of his eye as she'd slipped beneath the sheets naked. He'd left her traveling clothes in a bundle on the door handle for Effie to collect and wash. She was feet away, inches, and he could cross them and kiss her; he could pull her into his arms, cover her body with his own, and explore her soft curves. He shifted in the chair, the old leather creaking, as he listened to the noise from the tavern below.

She'd sleep and, in the morning, they'd hear from her father or future husband. Her fate would be decided. It had already been, it was already out of his hands, the deal was waiting to be finalized. He had no doubt they wanted her back, whole and untouched, the woman they'd bartered with and made promises over. If it was a choice he had to make, if her life were in his hands, he wouldn't barter her away, trade her smile for soldiers, her flesh for peace.

She was worth more than all of those things.

If he could, he would fall to his knees and swear undying loyalty.

"Finian," Daphne whispered.

He dropped the book, turning toward her in surprise. The candle was almost gone, flickering low, shadows dancing as the flame stretched and spat. She was propped up on one elbow, the quilt pulled up to her shoulders, the pale curve of her neck exposed, hair tumbling across the pillows. He swallowed, unable to speak as his mouth went dry.

"Do you plan to sleep in the chair?"

"What?"

She glanced down, cheeks reddening. "I don't mind sharing the bed."

His mouth fell open.

She held up a hand. "To sleep. And you have to sleep on top of the quilt."

His mind raced as he moved toward her. He gave her his most charming smile. "What if I get cold?"

"Then you freeze to death in this overly warm room." She shrugged, laying back and pulling the quilt up to her chin.

He laughed, easing onto the bed beside her, every nerve in his body screaming. *Kiss her! Touch her!* The mattress sank beneath his weight, the old bed creaking. It was soft and warm, dipping in the middle from years of use, bringing Daphne and Finian closer together.

"You keep your hands to yourself," she said as he settled in.

Finian smiled, putting his hands behind his head and closing his eyes. "You don't have to worry about my hands. I'm exhausted and plan to spend the whole night snoring. Go to sleep, your highness."

———

DAPHNE WATCHED the candle burn low, dipping and wavering, mind racing. She kept her eyes closed tight, listening to his steady breathing and the noise still coming up from the tavern below. Maybe they planned to sing all night, maybe they'd still be singing when the sun rose, and she'd still be here, heart racing, too aware of the man beside her to even think about sleeping.

She glanced at him, ready to meet his gaze, but his eyes were closed, arms crossed over his chest. Had he already fallen asleep? How could he sleep if she couldn't? Maybe he spent enough time in bed with women to not be distracted by one sharing his bed now. Maybe all his flirting was meaningless, and she had no effect on him. Maybe he was exhausted. She studied him, the sharp planes of his face, a faded scar along his jaw she had not seen before. He was tanned from being out in the sun all the time, hair longer than most men kept it. Though it looked as if someone had cut it in the not-too-distant past with a dull knife and little skill. Possibly he had done it himself.

Without thinking about it, doing it before she could stop herself, she reached out and traced the line of his nose. The touch was feather-light, her heart stopping at the contact; she held her breath, afraid that she would wake him up but wanting him to wake up and look at her with those piercing blue eyes; an impossible blue, a blue that was starting to color her dreams.

"If you don't have to keep your hands to yourself princess, neither do I."

6

DAPHNE JERKED BACK, PULLING THE QUILT WITH HER, AND ALMOST FELL OFF the bed. Finian laughed in surprise, turning toward her slightly, a dimple flashing in his cheek.

"I can't sleep," she admitted, meeting his gaze, daring him to ask why.

"What would you like to do instead?" he grinned and raised an eyebrow.

"I want to ask you something. Will you answer honestly?"

"Depends on the question."

She sucked in a breath, surprised to find herself wanting to know more about him, to discover anything about him beyond the careful façade he kept up. "How did you get here?"

"Oh, well. You've met Victory. The horse?"

A smile crept across her face. "Not what I meant."

He chuckled, low and warm, making her toes curl against the soft linen sheets. "It's connected, I promise you. Have you heard the stories of the dead saint?"

"Yes," she nodded. "A myth used to frighten children. A monster in the night, under the bed."

"There is always a little bit of truth in every story, in the fear a person holds on to in their heart."

"Maybe," she said, voice soft, watching the subtle slide of expressions cross his features. "I've heard stories about a cult, people who worship a saint. They claim he's a dead god."

"The dead don't always stay dead. The empire is hoping the stories are true."

The candle flickered, shadows jumping with his words, as he blew out a deep breath.

"What do they want?"

"They're looking for relics of the saint."

"How do you know?"

"Because I was one of them." He looked at her and away. "Once upon a time I was a soldier."

"How long ago?"

"Some days it feels as if it were a lifetime ago. Others?" He shrugged. "I've woken up some mornings not knowing where I was, expecting to face another battle. Claudius and Esdras have had the same experiences. So at least I know it's a common thing."

Daphne studied his face, the far-off expression in his eyes. He was seeing something else, surrounded by other people, standing in a different place. She waited for him to continue, feeling the pressure in the room around them, knowing there was more.

"Foolishly I thought I'd run far enough. I thought the mountains might stop them. I thought the prince would be satisfied with all that he had already conquered. But they will never stop."

"How do you know?"

He turned, studying her face, his own partly in shadow. "In another life, I was a captain in the prince's personal army."

Daphne's brow wrinkled, a curl of fear stretching out, pulling her back. "You were one of them?"

"Not just one of them, a valued soldier, a leader. The Wolf was my commander. I fought under his banner, with his men." His voice trailed off, weighted down. "I was his man."

Daphne held her breath. The Wolf's men were brutal, monsters, killers feared even by the rest of their army. People spoke of them in whispers, rumors, and stories reaching even her, protected in a castle hundreds of miles away. Even she knew.

"You asked if I was a coward before."

She opened her mouth to respond but he continued without pausing.

"Maybe I am. Do you know much about the empire and prince?" When she shook her head he continued. "They call the Wolf the prince's monster there. The City Killer. He's infamous everywhere he goes. But you know that part of it.

"The court is deadly and my father died there. By fair or foul means, nothing is ever what it seems there. But with him gone, I had no other reason to stay. I'd never wanted to be there in the first place. There's more to this story but it's enough, for now, to know that the prince enjoys taking hostages.

"After the city of Satya fell, I asked the Wolf if I could go. I don't even know why I asked. No one leaves. No one gets out. But I had to. It would be better than running, that is certain death, you don't walk away from the Wolf and live."

He closed his eyes, sucking in a deep breath, letting it out slowly.

"But I did," Finian said.

"How," she whispered.

"I made a bargain with a monster."

"And the monster let you go?"

He nodded.

"Why?"

Fininan opened his mouth and then shut it before continuing, thoughtful and hesitant. "I don't know. If he had a heart I'd say sympathy or any kind of emotion really. But he doesn't. Maybe he's playing a long game and knows he'll have the chance to kill me later."

"What did you give up?"

"Well, my life if he ever sees me again. If I ever see him again. If we ever cross paths in this miserable world at some future point. My life is his. That was the deal."

"It doesn't seem like much of a deal."

"For most people, it wouldn't seem that way. But for that man, in that place," he paused, a dark chuckle escaping. "It's everything. I took it. Claudius and Esdras came with me. They'd been under my command. Though they don't have the same deal. They deserted. They'll be dead too if the horde catches up with us."

"But why? Why would it matter?"

Finian shrugged. "I don't think it matters to him, but it matters to the prince. And what matters to the prince informs Wolf's choices. He doesn't breathe unless the prince tells him to. But the only thing the prince asks him to do is kill, and he's happy enough to do that."

Silence sat between them for a moment.

"When the next city fell, and while the prince celebrated yet another conquered land, we packed what little we had and rode south."

She wondered what it would be like to ride away from the only life you'd ever known. If she would have the courage to do such a thing. She could understand, a little maybe. Going to Marius was life-changing. Things would never be the same while remaining exactly as before in so many ways. But she didn't want to think about Marius right now.

"Where did you go?" she asked.

"South. Always south. I thought I'd buy a farm and raise cows. But I know nothing about cows or crops. And when it came down to it, I realized I didn't have whatever it took to love the land. The thing that makes someone stay in one spot all of their lives. It was a mistake to think I could ever be happy in one place and never travel again. Then the money began to run out."

"What about Claudius and Esdras?"

"Oh, they'd gone their own way and discovered the same things. It turns out the only skills I've ever possessed were the ones I'd picked up in the army. Then I discovered those skills could be useful in other areas."

"So you took up the life of a highwayman?"

He held up a finger. "Not exactly."

"Just thieving then?"

"Some of that, yes." He shrugged. "Mostly that actually."

"When did you start holding people for ransom?"

The question was sharp between them; her mouth tasted bitter with it, the words, the implications, the situation. He glanced at her, that half smile of his in place, eyes dancing.

"Congratulations, your highness. You are the very first."

She laughed. It bubbled up, bursting out before she could stop it, cutting between them and easing some of the tension. He put his hands in the air, a question on his face.

"You're laughing?"

"I'm the only person you've ever kidnapped for money?"

"And it turns out I'm not very good at it. Here we are after all." He indicated the bed, their closeness. The air changed, a new tension slipping in, the room drawing in around them.

She nodded. "Yes, here we are. So, tell me, what do you do now? After all of this is settled."

"Head south, cross the sea, and see what kind of highwaymanning we can do across the water. Try to stay ahead of the empire."

The empire. The Wolf. Marius. He would be able to run from it all while she stood in a tower to watch it all come for her like a tide—inescapable, relentless. *Wash over me. Take me.*

"Is that even possible?"

He didn't respond right away. She watched him consider the question, watching some inner thing, his past come to life and now a part of his future. He turned to her, coming to her out of memory, this man who had killed and conquered and then walked away from it all. He shook his head.

"No. I don't think it is. They won't stop. Not until the prince finds what he's looking for and once he gets it, everything else will fall."

"What is it he wants?"

"He's looking for the pieces of legend. Holy relics scattered across the continent that will come together and become a living myth. A creature or monster. The people who believe in it, a pack of death worshippers, are convinced it can resurrect the dead. The prince believes it."

"Do you?"

He glanced at her, searching for disbelief or judgment and finding nothing but honest curiosity. "I didn't at first. But the farther we traveled, the more cities he took, I began to believe the stories. I saw things I can't explain. Belief is a powerful force."

"What will you do? If there is no escape, nowhere you can go that's far enough?"

Finian shrugged.

"Could you go back?"

"Who would want to go back to hell?" he glanced at her, a smile hovering around his mouth, black humor, darkness stretching his lips, tugging at his cheeks.

"Could you?" she pressed.

"No, I wouldn't. Not even if the Wolf offered me a place. Not even at the prince's right hand."

"And you think they'll come here?"

He studied her face, his answer there without words. But even then, he'd already told her. There was no chance that this place, small and out of the way, would escape the all-encompassing empire in its search for deathless relics.

They would come. It was only a matter of time. When they arrived, she would be behind castle walls. King Marius's castle walls.

"What if I don't want to be ransomed?"

His voice came softly, matching her own. "What other life is there for a princess?"

She lifted a shoulder in a halfhearted shrug. "What life is there for a soldier who's no longer a soldier?"

He chuckled. "Where would you go, your highness?"

"I have a sister in the south. She married a merchant. I have a nephew I've never met."

"How far south?"

"The city of Mare Testa."

"That's easily several weeks of travel."

Daphne nodded, holding her breath. He turned to her, thoughtful, eyes narrowing.

"So, you'd give it all up? Everything? Pretty dresses, title, the way people bow and scrape. Money. Respect. You'd walk away from it all?"

"There's not much to walk away from."

"No?"

"No love, no respect. The people who love me are my sisters. They're beyond my reach at the moment. Though even when we all lived together, we were never very close. They were married and gone before I was ten. My father doesn't love me. King Marius has never met me. All I have left in the world are Olesia and Mae." Her voice trailed off, thinking of her friends. "And you sent them away."

He started to speak, but she cut him off.

"If I go to Marius, I will be nothing more than an animal in a cage. I would rather live without fine clothes and a title than live like that." She closed her eyes. Nothing but the truth. A harsh truth, an unwanted truth. But it couldn't be ignored. She would have to face it; she would be living it very soon. She sighed a huge heavy sigh that rocked her body, moving through her and out like a ripple in water. It broke against the walls and returned, a loop of impending grief and fear.

This is what I have to look forward to.

She'd accepted it a few days ago, nodded when her father gave her the news, and knew it was what would be best for her people. She hadn't even questioned it. But now? Now, everything had changed. A stranger had given her a glimpse of another kind of life, beyond the stone walls and rules that had defined her place for so long. She would trade all of the known things about her life for the unknown in this moment. Each security, each promise, on the hope that tomorrow she would wake up and be a different person.

Finian's fingers brushed across her cheek, a gentle touch, and she opened her eyes. He was there, studying her face, deep-blue gaze filled with an unknowable emotion. She wanted him to say something, to offer an apology or beg forgiveness. She wanted anything from him other than his blank expression that might look a little like pity in another light. His hand cupped her cheek, heavy and warm, the bed creaking as he leaned toward her.

Daphne opened her mouth, a thousand words on her tongue, but none of them were the right words. What she wanted from this man right now had nothing to do with words. She leaned forward, bridging the distance between them, pressing her lips to his in a swift kiss. He grabbed her, stopping her from escaping, keeping her close enough to count the freckles on her cheeks, to see the emotion in her eyes.

"I knew it! You've been dying to kiss me this whole time," Finian said with a smile.

"No. Not until recently."

"Then kiss me again to make up for it."

He pulled her to him, kissing her fiercely, the tension between their bodies breaking as they came together. Daphne clung to him, holding tight, unable to think of anything other than his mouth. With her heart pounding in her ears, blood thrumming, everything else faded away.

Until she realized it wasn't just her heart pounding.

Someone was knocking on the door.

7

Daphne stared at the wall, not even bothering to listen. Their voices were too low. She'd caught a glimpse of Esdras when Finian had opened the door, a shoulder, a slice of his profile, but nothing else. The pair spoke, the minutes drawing out, long enough for Daphne to slip out of bed and pull on the wrinkled gown from the bag she'd carried. It smelled like horses too. But maybe everything of hers would now after this.

For a moment she struggled to fasten the gown, the row of buttons, the ribbons at her waist, then she gave up. It was on; that was enough. She swung the velvet cloak over her shoulders, pulling it around herself, hiding the gown. The moment in the bed had passed, flown away like a startled bird, and what was left felt cold—the answered and unanswered questions, the desire between them, opposites tugging in separate directions.

The door opened, and Finian stepped back into the room. Behind him the door remained open, the hall beyond him empty, watchful and waiting. His tone when he spoke was subdued. "Your father has responded."

"What did he say?" she asked. But she knew; he didn't have to say it. He might be surprised by whatever the response was, but she would not be.

"Your guard is waiting downstairs."

"And Mae?"

Finian shook his head and motioned for her to follow him. Daphne nodded, not really expecting her friend to be there, but she'd been hopeful all the same. It would have been a great comfort to be able to hug Mae and Olesia now. She needed someone to talk to, to be able to confide in about the last hour and how her world had changed. She went with Finian down the stairs, heart racing, skin tingling still from his touch.

Stop. Stop and kiss me again. Kiss me, and maybe I'll know how to feel about your lips on mine, the warmth spreading through me, the fire you've kindled in my soul.

But she didn't speak. Couldn't bring herself to speak the words she didn't quite understand herself. She wasn't sure of her own heart, emotions coursing through her, a mixture of plain want and something tenuous, delicate.

Then she saw Adler flanked by Claudius and Esdras. They waited in the crowded tavern, a quiet group near the back.

"Come," Finian said. "Let's sit down and hear what he has to say."

When they reached the table, Adler studied her carefully, taking an inventory, making sure nothing had happened to her. But the most important differences in the before and after he would be unable to detect.

"Where is Mae?" she asked, sitting in a chair and clasping her hands in her lap.

Adler shook his head, glancing at the men on either side of him. Claudius motioned for him to sit, and Finian joined them. The other two took up casual positions, blocking the small group and ready to keep anyone from interrupting. "She's been sent on to King Marius."

"And father?"

Adler shifted his gaze away from her face, uncomfortable with the question and slight edge of hope in her voice. She eased back in her seat, clasping her hands in her lap, waiting. The man was obviously uneasy, gaze darting around, coming to rest on her again and again. Maybe he was afraid too. She couldn't tell. But she could guess. If she didn't know the other men, if she hadn't experienced their kindness and rough charm, she would be afraid too.

It was an odd feeling to sit here across from a man that she'd been familiar with, someone who had ridden behind her when she'd traveled, who she'd seen in the great hall near her father, and think of him as a stranger. She was surprised to find herself more at ease with Finian than with Adler.

"How did you know we were here?" Finian asked, watching Adler carefully.

"I didn't. There was a man you bought a horse from. He gave me the general direction. I stopped here in the hopes of finding someone else who would be willing to talk to me."

"And no one else is with you?"

Adler shook his head.

"What's the response from King Haran?"

Slowly, painfully, Adler opened a clenched fist, anguish painted across his features. On his palm, a single gold coin caught the light, rough and worn, a piece that had been passed from many hands, bought many things. Now, it was intended to ransom a princess. Too little, not enough, and yet all her father deemed worthy of his child. He had always blamed her for her mother's death, for not being the boy he so desperately wanted. Even now, when he needed her for a contract that was signed and sealed, he cared nothing for her fate. This was a rebuke, a knife twisted in her heart just for the sake of fostered and fed malice on her father's part.

Adler placed it on the rough wooden surface and slid it across to Finian. He didn't speak, staring at the coin. It sat on the table between them.

"No message?" Finian asked with steel in his voice, winter in his eyes.

Adler looked up, catching Daphne's eyes, and spoke softly. "I'm sorry."

She stood, tears pressing, and forced a curt nod. It hurt. It shouldn't, it was exactly what she expected, but it hurt all the same. Turning her back on the table, heading for the door leading into the yard, she caught Finian's words.

"We'll see what Marius has to say."

———

THE STABLES HAD BEEN peaceful until the men had followed her out. She stood with her face buried in Clover's neck, the horse's ears tipped toward the conversation happening a few stalls away. Daphne listened. They didn't bother to whisper, not concerned with hiding anything. When Adler returned, her father would know where they were, and soon after Marius would know. None of that had been part of their plan. The goal had been to remain hidden, otherwise the idea of ransom was worthless. If they knew where she was, they could come and take her without handing over any gold or rubies or whatever it was that Finian had demanded.

Emotions swirled through her, a confusion of wants. To go home, to have life the way it had been, to see her friends, to never marry the man she'd been promised to, to change her fate, to kiss the man in front of her—a stranger with a pair of piercing blue eyes and a mouth she wanted.

Crazy. It's all crazy.

"We can't stay here," Esdras said.

"I know," Finian said. "We need to split up. Make it harder for them to track us."

"Where will you go?" Claudius asked.

"The Silvas. No one will look there."

Silence greeted his words, and Daphne shivered. *Silvas.* It was ancient and primordial, a forest as deep and dark as any hidden mountain pass or rocky ocean shore. It was a place from fairytales, full of old myths and legends. It was the place where some of the creatures from those stories were said to survive.

"You can't be serious."

"Why not?" asked Finian.

"Because no one ever comes out."

"I have." Finian spoke confidently, with no hesitation or doubt.

"And when have you been inside the Silvas?"

"After I left the Wolf."

A long silence and Daphne could almost see their skeptical expressions.

"You think you'd be as lucky a second time?"

"It's worth the chance," Finian said.

"We need the money. We need to keep moving south, and this is the way to do it. We all agreed." Finian's voice was hard, decisive.

"Things change, Finian," Claudius said.

"What I want hasn't."

Again, there was no doubt in Finian's response. Daphne bit her lip, wondering if this was the same man she'd been with earlier. The man from the dimly lit room who had kissed her so softly.

"Hasn't it?" Claudius's voice was lowered, gentle with the question but unrelenting.

"What do you want from me?" Finian sounded tired. "I promised you an opportunity for a fresh start. A new life. Any life at all beyond the empire."

"And you have given us that a thousand times over. I haven't stood on a battlefield in three years, Finian. Three glorious, bloodless years." Claudius sounded tired, as if this was a point often visited between them.

"Not bloodless," Esdras corrected.

"Relatively bloodless," Finian offered.

"Compared to killing cities alongside the Wolf? Our lives have been full of sunshine and daisies."

"Do you even know what a daisy is?" Esdras asked.

"A flower," Claudius guessed.

"What color?"

"Yellow."

"No." Esdras sounded truly offended. "They're white."

"They have yellow on them, in the center, the petals go around it."

"But the petals aren't yellow."

"I never said they were."

Esdras snorted. "I don't believe for a minute you really know what a daisy looks like."

Daphne put a hand over her mouth to keep from laughing.

"Gentlemen," Finian said, sounding exasperated. "Next time I happen to see a daisy I'll point it out. They're very pretty. Yellow with black centers."

"You have no idea either!" Esdras accused.

"It doesn't matter. We aren't going to stand here bickering about flowers." Claudius cut across Finian's outraged snort. "When do you leave for the Silvas, Finian? What happens after that?"

"Tomorrow morning before dawn. I want you to split up, two groups, and make your way around the forest to the south and west. Travel separately, watch the roads. If you see anyone suspicious, I want you to just head south and keep going. I'll meet you in Mare Testa."

"And Daphne?"

Not the girl or woman, not *her highness* or *princess*. Esdras said her name as easily as Finian did. They all did. She was just a person to them, another human being they'd met out in the world they all traveled through, lived through. Except that they were thieves and robbers and retired soldiers, and she was royalty. And they'd kidnapped her.

She thought about that less and less. The farther away she got from her father, from Marius, the more she'd begun to consider what might be out there beyond the life she'd expected. Could Finian change his mind? Would he? Claudius seemed to think things had changed.

"Marius will pay for her return. She'll go on to live the life she's been raised for. She'll be a queen."

"Is that what you want for her?"

Finian sighed. "It's what she deserves. Go. It's late. Dawn will be here before you know it, and we all have many miles to travel before we can put this behind us."

Daphne concentrated on the feel of straw in her hand, the coarseness, the way it shredded between her fingertips so quickly. There and gone. Already nothing more than dust. She listened to them walk away, leaving the stable behind, going back to the tavern, the room above with the single bed. She could never go back to that room now.

"Daphne."

She jumped, a noise of surprise escaping her. Finian was there, more shadow than man in the light thrown by the distant lantern. Clover shuffled, snorting at him. She couldn't see his expression and wondered what the dark hid. Would she have seen disappointment? Wistfulness? Apology?

"Get your things ready," he said, pushing the gold coin from her father into her hand. "We're leaving before dawn."

8

THEY LEFT THE INN TOGETHER IN THE EARLY HOURS OF THE MORNING, THE SUN beneath the horizon, crickets singing their night songs. Daphne pulled her cloak tight against the chill. The gold coin from her father was heavy in her pocket. A physical reminder of her value to him, of her worth in this life. It left a sour taste in her mouth, bitterness lingering on her tongue.

Finian led her off the road, back toward the mountains and the way they'd come, deep forest on one side and a swift stream on the other. At a large boulder in the middle of the stream they turned and headed directly for the trees. As they neared, a kind of arch appeared, a point where two giant trunks had come together, crossing high above their heads, a narrow path just visible in the dawn.

"What is this place?"

Finian stared into the trees, seeing something she could not. "Do you know anything about the Silvas?"

Daphne shrugged, shaking her head. She knew a little, not enough, and the scraps of knowledge she did have came from fairy tales. More myths, more legends. She'd left the sensible confines of her father's house for a world full of stories.

"It covered everything that wasn't rock or water at one point. A great sea of swaying green without an end. But little by little it was broken up, edges created and gnawed away at, bare patches peeking through. But the trees remember. They know where they came from, who they belong to." He glanced at her, eyes touching her briefly and then moving on. "Each other."

He stopped talking, watching the way the tops of the trees moved in the breeze, the rustle of small things in the shadows. She felt watched, as if the woods had eyes, as if they could see her as clearly as she saw them. A great mass of forest, deep and dark, a place that people went into and never came out of.

"Are you familiar with the idea that all woods are the same?"

"No," she said softly.

"I think they're all connected still. Even though all that's left are these pockets in remote places. Really, it's just bits and pieces of the Silvas that are left. But all over the continent, these pockets, no matter the distance, are connected."

"Connected how?"

"In the way that you could go in one area and but exit in another."

"Have you tried it?"

"No."

"Then how do you know?"

He shrugged. "I don't. It's a guess, that's all."

"And you expect me to follow you in there?"

"Don't worry, princess." He flashed a dimple at her. "I'll protect you from all the monsters."

It had grown quiet beneath the trees, the shadows deep, the night that had been a few hours away before was here now, waiting for them in the wood. Trees grew close together, branches intertwined, trunks mossy, everything smelling of old growth and rotting evergreen needles. There was almost a path, a narrow track, that the horses followed, picking their way carefully forward, snorting and shaking their heads.

Daphne ducked, avoiding a low branch, only to be caught by another, hair snagging and then pulling free with a jerk. It stung, sharp and hot, making her hiss. Another branch caught at her sleeve and she pulled away, something snapping in the trees, breaking and falling away. They seemed to want her, branches reaching for her, pulling at her hair and clothes.

She felt watched. The silence was unnatural, the kind that came from intense observation. Finian seemed unmoved. He rode a little ahead of her, humming softly to himself. Nothing snagged his clothes or hair. He went forward untouched, unafraid. It irritated her. How could he be so casual? For her, the feeling of watchfulness was oppressive.

There were stories about this place. The Silvas. A place outside of time, where the things from the old world had retreated, hidden away from the ever-modernizing world. Fairies. Monsters. Wild magic. These trees held onto it all, the myths and legends, and never let anything go. People went in but never came out.

But Finian said he had.

———

When Daphne realized they were being followed, not only observed and noted, but hunted, her heart began to pound. *Pound.* She hated the term, the sound, the way it made her hands clammy and stomach jump, the feel of it all so familiar now. She'd never known her heart could race and lunge this way, beat so hard it might break free of her chest.

And now it seemed that it happened all the time.

"Finian." She spoke, stumbling over his name. She cleared her throat and tried again. "Finian."

He remained ahead of her, as calm as he'd been before, though his humming had stopped. The horses whinnied softly, uneasy, ears going back and forth. Daphne blew out a breath, fighting to calm her heart. The horses could feel her fear. It would only make them more afraid and the situation would get worse.

"Finian, do you—"

"There." Finian cut across her voice and indicated a darker place between the trees and off the path. "We can camp for the night there."

"Where?"

Daphne scanned the trees, trying to see through the shadows. They'd entered the wood in the early morning, the sky gray and tinged with gold and pink. But once inside, they'd moved through a late afternoon place, the sky deepening, the shade and shadows between the trunks permanent. There had never been a full morning or midday. And now it was almost fully dark.

"There's a temple here. We'll stop and camp for the night."

"Is it safe? I've heard something in the woods." She lowered her voice, leaning toward him, wishing they were closer. "Something following us."

He nodded, meeting the question in her gaze. "The temple will be a good place for the night. Nothing will bother us there."

"How can you be so sure?"

"I guess at some point princess, you're just going to have to trust me." Finian shot her a smile, one eyebrow raised, waiting for her to take the bait he offered.

Trust me.

She shook her head, dropping her gaze and looking anywhere but at him. She didn't want to admit it to him, or even herself, but she *was* beginning to trust him. It was annoying. With a grimace she followed him through the trees, moving farther away from the path, wondering if knew it already.

Thousands of years ago the temple might have stood alone, tall pillars and arches, pale rock and shallow steps, but the Forrest had crowded in. Stones and trees had come together, fusing over time, to create a living temple. It was in ruins, murals cracked and frescos peeling, the floors covered in leaf mold and fallen branches.

"Who is this temple for?" Her words were hushed, the barest rustle beneath fallen leaves, the sigh in a fold of fabric; so faint and almost not there.

"No one we need to worry about," Finian said, hands on hips, looking it over as if he'd seen it a dozen times in the last year and it no longer held any surprises for him. "A guardian of the forest and friend of the saint."

"The saint? Here?"

"Why do you think the dark prince is coming? Because the weather is nice?"

She shook her head. "I didn't think this would be so close to where I've lived my whole life. Until the empire, I'd never heard any of these stories."

"Lucky you," he muttered.

"Maybe," she conceded, wondering what else might be lurking beneath the surface of the place she'd considered home all of her life. Not only home, but kingdom, she belonged to the land and its people as much as they belonged to her. What other secrets could there be? What else might surprise her?

"We'll lead the horses in as far as they'll go. I don't want to leave them outside the temple tonight." He looked over his shoulder, watching the forest, thoughtful and calculating. "Then we'll light a fire and get some rest."

They went up the stairs together. The horses moved hesitantly behind them, shuffling and snorting uneasily but moving forward all the same.

DAPHNE HELD THE LANTERN HIGH, warm light sliding along the walls and dipping into alcoves, illuminating color. Murals covered the walls, half-hidden in places by layers of moss and small ferns, tendrils of creeping mold. Beneath the growth bucolic landscapes seemed to glow when the light touched them, perfect moments captured in plaster and paint.

In mural after mural, a gold skeleton moved through the world. It loomed over buildings and filled horizons, the way before it sunny days and summer skies, the way behind it velvet black with painted stars.

The light-bringer. A savior. The Saint.

She stopped, transfixed, and reached out to press a gentle fingertip to the golden figure striding through a perfect village. How much truth was here, in this place? The weight of it all pressed on her, a sense of impending doom beginning to tickle the back of her mind. Tiny flecks of gold glittered on her finger when she held it up to the light, turning it back and forth, transfixed and horrified by the idea of such a monster walking the world.

"Through here," Finian said, nodding toward an arch leading deeper into the temple.

Daphne hesitated, torn between the fear beyond the arch and the fear at her back. Neither one she knew; nothing was for sure. Finian laughed, holding out his hand, waiting for her to take it.

"What if what we find inside is worse?"

"Than what? Whoever wants to eat us out here? I'll take my chances."

"And the horses?"

"Safe enough. We're inside the temple for the night. Nothing is coming through those arches." He nodded toward the entrance, the dark trees beyond, the expectation lurking there. He held out his hand, eyes on her face. "Shall we?"

She took his hand, allowing him to lead her further into the ruins. It had been a huge temple ages ago, more years than she could count, the stones worn smooth first by tools and hands and later by air and water. The air was full of whispering trees and the scent of fresh springs—cold, clear water—and dead stone.

They stepped through an arch and out into an open space. A wide star-filled sky stretched over their heads, sparkling and vibrant. The trees had not taken over yet, the walls of the temple holding against nature's siege. But here and there the walls had begun to buckle, on the verge of giving in, piles of stone collecting at the base with a few small saplings growing in corners. In the light thrown by the oil lamp, Daphne could see patches of tiled floor, a flowing muted pattern of red and gold, moving throughout the space. Debris collected against the edges of the room, leaves and small branches, a flash of stark-white animal bone.

"Did you know this was here?" she asked.

Finian shook his head, lifting the lantern higher.

He pointed to a shallow alcove across the room; a little of the ceiling remained there, leaves swirled into a heap, patches of painted plaster. It took a moment to clear most of it, leaving behind dirt and leaf fragments. She hugged herself, standing close to the wall and watching the sky. The golden star wasn't visible here, it sat lower on the horizon, blocked by the forest. But she could feel its influence over the last few days.

"Are you cold?" he asked.

"A little," she admitted.

He set the lantern at her feet, the glow touching the lines of his face, shadows jumping behind him. She was grateful he left her the light as he stepped away, beyond the warm circle, collecting fallen branches and twigs from around the room and coming back with an armful. He dumped them in a heap by the alcove and dusted his hands off.

"You aren't going to sit?"

She made a face. "It's dirty."

"So?"

"I'm dirty enough as it is. I'd like to avoid getting dirtier."

"So, you're just going to stand all night?"

"Or you could get a blanket from the horses."

"Or you could have thought of that before we tied them up for the night."

She made a face, gesturing to the door they'd come through, to where the horses had been tied up. She could hear them, the soft rustle of sound they made from the bottom of the shallow steps. They'd brought them inside the building, but nothing would get them up the steps leading into this room. It worried her that they were out of sight, beyond their immediate help. He'd seemed so sure nothing would come inside, but what if he was wrong? They'd be stranded, forced to walk the narrow paths crisscrossing the forest, slow and vulnerable. Things were waiting for them, watchful in the darkness. *Hungry.*

He snorted and turned away, going to fetch a blanket. She inspected the alcove, kicking a small stone out, picking up a twig, and tossing it into the pile Finian had collected. It took a moment before he was back with a bedroll and a blanket, whistling cheerfully.

"Your blanket, your highness," he said with a bow.

"I might be inclined to thank you if you weren't also going to benefit and if that bow of yours were more sincere."

"You don't think I'm sincere?" He arched a brow at her, smile catching in the lantern light.

"You're never serious," she said with a laugh.

He dropped the blanket and bedroll, crossing to her in a few quick strides, wrapping her in his arms. She gasped, surprised, their bodies pressed close, the nearness of him everything she'd wanted since their interrupted kiss. Her stomach fluttered, skin tingling, as she tilted her head, looking up at him, breathless, expectant. The kiss from the night before was a thing between them, an almost physical presence, a creature to be coaxed nearer or chased away.

"I can be very serious," he murmured, searching her face.

What was he searching for? She didn't know. Everything she wanted in the world was right here, right now, and she would stop the world to feel his breath on her skin, his mouth on hers. Daphne swallowed, placing her hands on his chest, curling into the fabric of his shirt.

"Are you being serious now?" she asked softly.

"What would you like my answer to be?"

The expectant feeling faded, and she pushed away. He let her go, his warmth vanishing, the closeness she'd craved gone. She didn't want to tell him what his answer should be. What she wanted it to be and knew it could never be. A wish. A pointless, worthless wish. To have the undivided attention of a man who could give her nothing. No, that wasn't true. He could give her many things, but nothing permanent, nothing that she needed in the long run of her life. She had no illusions about Finian.

There were other promises to keep. Her fate lay ahead, tied to another man. Marius's answer had yet to arrive. She'd begun to wonder if she'd been wrong about him. Maybe he wouldn't refuse outright; maybe he had some interest in her after all.

"You should light the fire," she said, reaching for the bedroll.

"Yes, your highness."

The humor was back, returned and sounding bitter, and she knew it now for what it was. A defense against pain, a deflecting blow, the refusal to present a target large enough hit. How much did old wounds pain him now? How much pain did he continue to carry? Enough. More than enough for one man.

She watched his hands as he shook the bedroll out and lit a small fire, cataloging each scar, faint and faded, old but not forgotten. He'd stood beside one of the most hated and feared men on the continent. Done the bidding of a monster. And then turned his back on it all, running, still moving in the hopes of getting away, but never getting far enough.

She was surprised to find that she didn't hold it against him, the ransom, the exchange of gold and life. He'd promised not to hurt her, promised a return to feather beds and normality. And here she was, in the middle of a mythical forest, not wanting to go back to the world, all the while knowing there could be no other future.

He was exactly as he said he was. Highwayman. Thief. Kidnapper. A desperate man in desperate times, trying to keep the people he loved going, trying to keep them safe. She understood that better than anyone. The want had grown despite all of this, the desire burning through her with each touch, each glance.

In all of this, she wanted his mouth. She wanted his hands on her body, the heat he brought, the delicate brush of his fingertips against her skin. The slightly awed look in his eyes, as if he were touching something fragile, something beautiful he wanted to keep. *Keep me.* Nothing but her heart had changed. The world around them was the same, all of it falling apart and falling down. But her heart was different now.

"Coming or going, princess?" he asked, glancing up at her, the firelight catching the edges of his face.

She eased down onto the blanket beside him, hands in her lap, fighting to keep them still. It would be her choice, hers alone, in a way that nothing might ever be again. She made it, wrapping her skirts in one hand, covering the small distance between them so that nothing could be left to the unknown, all of herself offered. She sucked in a breath, holding herself so tight, waiting to be accepted. On her knees before him, everything inside focused on the blackness of his pupils expanding, going wide to take her all in, his hands coming up to cup her face.

———

EVERYTHING HE HAD NEVER KNOWN he wanted, the sense of coming home he'd hoped to discover when he'd left the army behind and then discovered he was unworthy of receiving. But here she was, offering him the very thing he wanted more than all the gold, the freedom, in the world.

"Daphne," he whispered her name, part prayer, part plea. A request, not a demand, this man who took everything he wanted with a smile, but not her. He would come to her without expectation, without demand. He would take only what she offered, what she gave freely, but he would take it all, all of her, heart and soul, lungs and panting breaths, his name on her lips. He would take her body and press his mark into her skin, claiming every inch and leaving behind all the warmth of his soul, the scorching heat of his desire.

She pulled him toward her without hesitation, pulling him into a kiss that drove everything from his mind. He groaned against her mouth, wrapping his arms around her, fitting their bodies together. He kissed her the way he'd wanted to on the road as she'd stepped down from the coach, head held high. He'd almost slid from his horse to throw himself at her feet, face upturned, expectant and willing to take whatever she gave. Now her hands tangled in his hair, mouth soft against his, as hungry as he was. Daphne arched into him, pressing closer, as his hand moved over her breast, tracing her hard nipple.

"Yes," she murmured against his mouth, between desperate breaths.

Finian pressed a kiss on her jaw, trailing down her neck, and tugged the bodice of her gown lower, easing her breasts free and covering them with his hands. He sucked a nipple into his mouth, smiling as she whimpered, clutching him tighter. After a moment he pulled the hem of her dress up, smoothing a palm up her thigh until he came to her most secret self.

His hand dipped between her legs, finding her inner heat, parting her gently to run a fingertip over the bud of her sex. She shivered and hot pleasure tightened low in his belly. He could feel her want, the hot desire for his hands to be everywhere; to scorch her, to mark her. He kissed her, sucking on her bottom lip, as he traced the slick entrance of her body.

"Here?" he asked, pausing, giving her a moment to change her mind.

She nodded, pressing her mouth to his, touching her tongue to his lip, and opening wide as he engulfed her in a hard kiss. He eased one finger inside her body, groaning against her mouth as he penetrated her slick heat, cock twitching and aching to be inside of her. He stroked her gently, drawing out each sensation, whole body tingling as she gasped and moved with him.

"Finian," she gasped, breaking the kiss to tug at his shirt. "Take everything off."

"Only if you do," he said with a smile.

They fumbled to remove her dress and his underthings, desperate now to see each other all at once. She helped him, hands steadier than his, a half-smile curling one corner of her lush mouth. He pressed kisses to her collarbone and throat, tongue following the curve of her breasts and peaked nipples.

"You're so beautiful."

Shyly she pulled him back to her, tilting her mouth to meet his, swallowing his whispered words, giving her own back. He came to rest in the cradle of her hips, hard length burning against her thigh. He continued to stroke her, fingers sliding in and out of her slick body, the palm of his hand pressed against the tight bud of her sex as she rolled her hips to meet each gentle thrust.

He couldn't wait any longer. He needed to be inside of her, he wanted to feel her all around him, stretched and aching, and gasping his name. He groaned as he rubbed the head of his cock against her, eyes locked on where their bodies met.

———

Daphne gasped as he pressed the head of his cock against her entrance, her slick body easing for him, inner muscles trembling as he moved into her, filling her. An exquisite mix of pleasure and pain washed over her and she buried her face against his shoulder; the warmth between them a mix of heated skin and woodsmoke.

He began to move and she moaned, clutching him tightly as they found a rhythm. Finian cradled her head in one arm, propped up on an elbow, and gripped her hip with the other. He kept her tilted and pressed against him, the friction between them building, her body tightening.

"Finian," she gasped, squeezing her eyes shut, tensing as the pleasure built, spiraling up. "Don't let go."

"I've got you," he whispered hoarsely, fingers digging into her hip.

His breathing was ragged as he drove her, pushing her to the edge, waiting to tumble over it with her. The orgasm hit, a tidal wave of pleasure bursting behind her eyes, flooding her limbs as her inner muscles clenched around the hard length of his cock. Crying out, fingers digging into his shoulders, she rode the wave, gasping as his pace increased and holding tight. With a groan he pulled out, cock jerking against her stomach, warm liquid spilling across her skin. He groaned, shuddering with release, holding on to her so tightly she gasped.

They lay together tangled in the firelight, breathing heavily, pounding hearts beginning to calm. Finally, he pressed a kiss to her breast, propping himself up on an elbow to search her eyes.

"What would you like, my princess?"

She inhaled sharply, the soft endearment making her eyes prickle; her thighs were tender and sweat was beginning to dry in places, the wet patch on her belly was sticky. *Be honest.*

"A bath," she said aloud.

"I can do that."

She laughed. "How?"

He stood, leaving her cold and exposed to the star-filled sky overhead. But she didn't move to cover herself. She studied him as he rummaged through one of the saddlebags, enjoying the curve of his bare backside. He returned with a rag and canteen, pupils wide and dark as he took in her nakedness again.

Pouring cool water from the canteen he gently cleaned her, wiping away his seed and rinsing the rag again before pressing it to her swollen mound. He pushed her legs apart gently, lowering his head to press a kiss on her inner flesh. She twitched, laughing at the faint tickle of beard stubble rasping her skin, and ran a hand through his thick dark hair. He finished washing and then helped her to dress, adjusting the fabric, easing it down over her breasts, and running a finger over her areole before settling her beside him again.

"Come here," he said, pulling her into his arms, her head coming to rest against his shoulder. He stroked her hair, tracing the edge of her face, the line of her brow. Sleep gathered between them, coaxing and then demanding.

"What comes next?" she asked.

Finian stared up at the stars. It had changed for him, his heart, the desire he'd held so close for years wealth and freedom. Beside him lay an unexpected future. He turned to Daphne, running a hand down her arm, enjoying the softness of her, bare beneath his hungry gaze. Already he wanted her, wanted to roll her on top of him, watch her, study her face as she came, learn how to repeat it and drive her there over and over. He was desperate to learn her secrets, her desires, and give them to her again and again.

The want, beyond desire, beyond need, was so fierce it made him catch his breath.

"What do you want to happen next?" he asked.

"I don't know," she said quietly, eyes focused on some internal scene.

"Tell me when you do."

He felt everything, all of it, the things he'd tried so hard to avoid for so many years. Now a piece of his heart was moving around outside of his body, and he needed to protect it. He had to protect her. He held her as she slept, counting each gentle breath as the fire crackled and popped, and thought about the ocean.

———

"WE'RE GOING BACK the way we came," Finian spoke quickly, collecting all the little pieces of their camp from the night before.

"What?"

Daphne rubbed the sleep from her eyes, sore in places, and still exhausted. She couldn't keep up with what Finian was saying. He spoke quickly.

"We're not going to wait to hear from Marius. That's done. We're going to Mare Testa."

"You can't be serious."

"Why can't I?"

"You've made promises. Your men."

"You heard the conversation in the barn. You heard Claudius. Besides, Esdras likes you. The others like you."

"But the money," Daphne began, hating the words even as she spoke them. Money. No amount of rubies or gold could touch the worth of a person. But she understood their desire to get as far away from the Wolf as they could. She understood that it took money to do that. She hated the choices they'd made that brought them all together. But without those choices, without this twist of fate, she would have never known Finian.

He dropped the bundled bedroll and saddlebag he carried, coming to her with his arms out, pulling her to him. She listened to his heart, thudding against her ear, crushed to him in an embrace that could bend bones. Finian mumbled into her hair, the words starting low, running together, until finally she caught the edge of what he was saying, the rest of it falling into place.

"Daphne, I'm so sorry. Please forgive me. I don't know if you can. Or if you will. I've been an idiot. Of course, I have. I'm an idiot. But you've changed everything, all of it. I will do everything I can for the rest of my life, our lives, if you come to Mare Testa with me. Just say you'll come. If you want to. I won't force you. I will make sure you make it anywhere you want to go."

He pushed her gently away, studying her face, drinking in the sight of her.

"Finian," she began, hesitant to begin and not sure where to start.

He shook his head, holding up a hand. "Wait. Don't say it yet. Give me your decision when we reach the road. We'll choose our direction from there."

———

DAPHNE HELD UP A HAND, shading her eyes in the early morning light. The difference between the twilight of the forest and the new day was startling, as if they had crossed from one world to another. Beside her, the horse shook its head and sidestepped, uneasy, and she patted her, making a soothing sound.

Movement caught her eye, men stepping from behind trees, standing in the road.

"Stop."

Soldiers stood in a loose circle around them. They were waiting for Daphne and Finian, swords drawn and wary faces grim. With a sinking realization, she recognized the colors they wore. These were King Marius's men. He'd refused to pay a ransom, but he'd come to collect her anyway.

There would be no city in the south, no journey across the sea, no more nights beneath a wide sky filled with stars. Part of her had never expected it to happen, a half dream, not even a whole one, something so impossible she had not let herself take hold of it. But even knowing all of that, not really believing it would happen, seeing the king's men here now was crushing.

"Good morning gentlemen," Finian said, tone light and cheerful. "How may I be of assistance?"

The man who had spoken urged his horse forward a few steps. He was middle-aged, hair going gray at the temples, face weather worn, brown eyes tired and wary. When he spoke, his tone was hard and clipped. "Princess Daphne, I am Captain Tarver and here to carry out King Marius's orders. We will escort you to the castle."

There was no word of rescue, no mention of a future husband. She was a contract, a bargain, a price paid. The king had sent his men to collect. She opened her mouth, to agree or refuse, she didn't know. But Finian spoke first.

"She won't be going to the castle."

The captain looked from Daphne to Finian, a question on his face, then it passed. He nodded to his men, and they began to advance, swords raised. Finian reached for the sword stored with the saddle, the horse shying away, nervous with the energy surrounding them. He drew it and faced the advancing men.

"Wait," Daphne said, holding up a hand. "If I go with you, do you promise not to hurt him?"

The men glanced at their captain, unsure.

"It doesn't matter," Finian said.

Daphne ignored him, focused on Captain Tarver. "If I go with you willingly, without a fight, do you promise not to hurt him?"

Tarver nodded, motioning to his men. One by one they sheathed their swords, some looking unhappy, others with a shrug. It didn't matter to them either way, she thought. But Finian kept his sword ready, eyeing the nearest man.

"Mount your horse and come with me," the captain said. "We have many miles to cover, and time is pressing."

Daphne turned to her horse, gripping the saddle, unable to bring herself to look at Finian. She could feel his eyes on her. But she pulled herself up, the horse settling with her weight.

"Don't," he said, wrapping a warm hand around her ankle, gentle pressure, gentle want. She stared down at him, speechless in the face of his pleading, the need in his voice.

"Goodbye, Finian," she said, voice barely above a whisper.

He didn't respond, but he didn't have to. His face, always laughing, always a mask held up to the world to keep his emotions secret, was open, exposed. She wanted to change the situation, for there to be a different outcome. But this was what she had been expected all along. A trade, an exchange, a woman for a bag of gold and rubies. The only difference was that he wasn't receiving any ransom. He'd been cheated of that. But maybe he'd consider keeping his life reward enough.

Daphne urged her horse forward. Finian's hand fell away, leaving her cold.

Captain Tarver met her, leaning across to take the reins of her horse. She avoided the muted curiosity, curious but not enough to pursue it, and she wondered what he would tell the king. He gestured to his men, and they drew their swords.

"Wait!" Daphne turned in her saddle, watching as they closed in around Finian. "You promised!"

Tarver didn't respond, urging his horse into a trot, her horse moving to keep up.

"Wait!"

But the horses were moving faster now, picking up speed, and as she watched Finian was surrounded, his face grim. As the distance between them widened, she caught one last glimpse and heard the clash of steel on steel.

9

THE MIRAGE OF A CITY FILLED THE DISTANCE, A PROMISE, AND A THREAT. IT rose over the landscape, glimpsed between hills and across rivers as they traveled. Cautes. It meant "the scar." Home to Marius, death of her future.

No. The death of her future had happened back there, at the edge of the woods, in the dirt. She'd made her choice, and Finian had paid the price. Her ankle was still cold where he'd touched her, skin crying out for contact, wanting him.

As the small group traveled, they passed villages and farms, land cleared for summer wheat now ready to harvest, orchards heavy with fruit, fields of flowers, bees buzzing through them. But there were no people, no one else on the road. No one in the houses they passed.

It was an empty and quiet world.

Daphne moved through it silently beside Captain Tarver. The others exchanged a few words, always quickly silenced, and the horses seemed as subdued as the men. Dread sat on her shoulders, a creature made of fear and darkness, stroking her neck, whispering in her ear, *Something is wrong here.*

Before they entered the cobbled streets of Cautes, she knew it was empty. Every door and window was shut, shutters closed, the signs over doors taken down. The city had been carefully abandoned, all the laughing, living, yelling people moved on having taken what they could with them.

Now it waited.

Their progress through the streets echoed back at them, giving the illusion of others, of more life beyond their small group. But with each winding turn through the city and nearer the castle, it changed. She watched it, catching movement on the high walls, a few lit windows in the higher reaches of the main building. Two towers rose into the sky, one higher than the other, and from the highest, a banner flapped in the breeze.

At the very heart of Cautes, there was life.

As they neared, Daphne noticed other things. From the walls facing the city, dark shapes hung; she stared, brow coming together. Bodies. There were bodies hanging from the walls. She noticed more shapes on the ramparts. Decapitated heads on pikes.

"It's best not to look, your highness." Tarver's voice came to her softly, low enough that she almost didn't catch it.

She nodded, turning away, refusing to look back and wishing he'd warned her. Fear and chaos clung to the place like a fog, tainting the air she breathed, coating her throat. Her stomach hurt. Finian circled in her mind, the last glimpse she'd had of him there on the road. But her future was here. She needed to push him away, focus on the present and pay attention, if she planned to survive it.

The city was built right up against the castle walls, the gate to the inner kingdom kept closed at all times, but torches burned brightly. A thin sort of welcome in the growing dusk. Tarver called out to someone on the battlements above, and somewhere unseen gears ground together, wood groaning as it shifted inch by inch.

The courtyard came into view, and with it came noise and movement. After all the nothingness they'd passed, the deep quiet and stillness, the franticness and chaos beyond the doors terrified her. Men in armor lit by flickering torches crossed back and forth, shouting, weighed down with ropes and iron chains, bags of gear, and sharpened weapons. Everyone moved with purpose, faces set in hard lines, tight mouths.

A man came down the wide steps of the entrance hall, which had a tall, smooth face rising out of the dirty cobbles, several stories tall, carved arched windows staring out at the empty city. Stables and other buildings opened onto the courtyard as well, a garrison, a smith, with more carved arches. It was elegant and spoke of wealth, nothing like the small castle she'd come from high in the mountains.

She turned her attention back to the man striding toward them—tall with broad shoulders, close-cropped hair, and flat black eyes. She couldn't imagine a more imposing figure, his eyes unreadable. Tarver dismounted to meet him, the two exchanging greetings, speaking in low tones.

This had to be Marius. Her future husband. No one had been able to tell her what he looked like; everyone had spoken of his personality, his deeds. But his man did not seem to be cruel. His mouth was set, but when he glanced at her, there was something almost kind in his eyes. When he saw her watching, he raised his voice so she could hear the conversation.

"Where did you find her?"

"Near the Silvas. The contact was correct. The highwayman was there."

"What happened to him?"

"I left some of my men to deal with him."

"Good. Marius will be pleased."

Not Marius then. Where was her future husband? She'd expected to be met here, despite the circumstances, being greeted was the bare minimum. No one else stood near them. Men glanced at the small group and away, uninterested in their conversation, preoccupied with whatever drove them forward.

"Your highness, I am Thomas, King Marius's castellan." The man approached her, bowing deeply, a hand to his chest. "I am thankful we were able to recover you from this horrible ordeal. I pray that the rest of your journey was much more peaceful than the first half. If you would like to follow me, I can show you to your room."

"Thank you," she said, swallowing. Her throat felt dry. "Are Mae and Olesia waiting?"

The man's eyes shifted, mouth pinching around something bitter before speaking. "The king sent them away, your highness. He was unsure that we would be able to recover you. He had no wish to keep them here, separated from their families and waiting. They were sent home."

"I see," she said. Tears stung, and she struggled to maintain her composure. She refused to cry here in the courtyard of her new home, in front of these men who she didn't know and wasn't sure she could trust. She glanced back the way they'd come, the gates were scraping shut, cutting off the view of the deserted city.

"My apologies, your highness. We can send a messenger to fetch them as soon as one can be spared. At the moment there is no one who can go."

"I understand. Have you received any word that they arrived safely?"

"No, your highness. But if we do, I will alert you immediately." He stepped closer, holding out a hand. "Please let me help you dismount, and I'll show you to your room."

"Thank you, but I don't need help." Daphne shook her head, dismounting before he could respond. She kept her back to him, gripping the saddle as she touched the earth, smoothing out her features and hoping the fear and sadness wouldn't be visible.

But when she turned, meeting his gaze, she knew he could see it.

"This way, your highness." He indicated the huge doors leading inside. "If you desire anything at all, please let me know. Her Highness Constance has made her lady-in-waiting available to you."

Constance. With everything that had happened, with Mea and Olesia gone, she hadn't even considered the other women. The wives she would be joining. There was no way to know what kind of relationship she could build with them, what would be wanted or encouraged. But if Constance had offered the help of her personal maid, that was a good sign.

Daphne followed Thomas through the doors, expecting candles and torches, expecting to walk into light and warmth. But it was dark in the hall. Looking up, she could make out the shapes of the high ceiling, rafters and banners, unlit chandeliers and torches. There was a dais at the end of the room, a single throne on it. All around the room were arches leading to other parts of the castle. Most of these were dark as well but a handful glowed dimly, light coming from distant and unseeable sources.

The silence here was like the city: an abandoned silence, an emptiness that spoke of many voices having just vanished, many people never returning.

Thomas led her down one corridor and then another, taking several sets of stairs up, oil lamps burning in alcoves. They passed no one else as they moved deeper into the castle, the sounds of the courtyard receding.

A thousand questions swirled through her. Where was everyone? What had happened? Why was the place empty? What were they preparing for? Where was Marius? There was something about Thomas that made her think he dreaded her asking these things. But she needed answers, even if it made him uncomfortable.

"When will I meet the king?"

He cleared his throat, glancing at her without meeting her eyes. "Your highness, I don't know how much news you've heard while you traveled. And it's not my place." He paused, clearing his throat again. "Did Captain Tarver speak with you at all? Or did you overhear the men talking?"

She shook her head, following as they began to climb another set of stairs. These were smaller, the walls covered with tapestries depicting battles and hunt scenes, the oil lamps placed closer together. When Thomas did not speak right away, she prompted him.

"What's been happening? Where is everyone?"

Thomas stopped, half turning to her, brow furrowed, voice low. "They've left. Gone. All of them. Only a few remain, even the army has begun deserting."

"Why?"

But she knew the answer. The horde had arrived, and the Wolf must be very close. There had been a game she'd played as a child, with her sisters; one of them would be a wolf and try to catch the others. She'd hidden in a cupboard once, stuffed into a lavender-scented darkness with a pile of folded linen, and her sister had knocked on the door, whispering between the crack, *The wolf is knocking on your door!*

"The dark empire is here. The horde will reach us soon."

Fear shot through her, and she grabbed his arm. "How soon?"

"I don't know. I don't think anyone does. But *he* will reach us before they do."

He.

"The Wolf," she whispered, thinking about the things Finian had shared. She'd feared the man before; the bloody stories that had reached them had been so awful she thought they couldn't be true. Not all of them. But Finian knew the man; he'd confirmed the stories, shared his small part in them all.

She'd agreed to come quietly in an effort to spare Finian any pain. But Captain Tarver's men had attacked anyway. And Finian had believed a princess should live a protected life surrounded by luxury. He'd wanted her to go to Marius because he thought it would be best. He'd changed his mind in the end; he'd chosen her, her as a person and not some idea of who he thought she was. And she'd ended up here, in a castle with a wolf about to knock at the door.

"Yes, your highness." Thomas began moving again, beckoning her to follow. "I cannot say more. I will let the king tell you everything we know."

Daphne laughed bitterly. "What is there to tell me that you haven't already shared? The horde is coming. The Wolf will be here soon. That's all that matters."

"Yes, your highness."

He didn't speak for a long time, leading her up, always up, and turning in toward the deepest part of the castle. When they came to a stop, it was before a wide door painted deep blue. He pushed the door open, bowing as he spoke, ushering her inside.

"These are the queen's quarters, your highness."

Oil lamps and candles burned all around the room, lighting the small sitting area, warming the space. Deep carpets covered the stone floor, the walls covered with tapestries of mythical creatures. There were full bookshelves and several low sofas, and on the far wall, a writing desk. A tall, sleek gray dog rose from its bed in the corner, a silver bell on its collar tinkling.

"That's Sara," Thomas said, gesturing to the dog, who began to wag her tail. He pointed to one of four closed doors leading out of the sitting area. "These will be your rooms."

He opened the door to reveal a beautiful bedchamber, fire crackling in the hearth, then he moved farther inside to open the water closet door, before coming back to where she stood. "Please let me know if there is anything at all that I can do. If there is anything you want."

"Thank you, Thomas," she said, taking in the space, the elegant fabrics and cool-toned colors, the window facing out over the valley. "I might have been happy in these rooms."

Might have been.

She could see it in his face, knew it must be reflected in her eyes. They both knew she would not be using this space for very long. It was a waypoint in a longer journey, one which was very close to coming to an end.

"I will inform the king of your arrival."

"Thank you," she said.

With a nod, he stepped from the room, pulling the door shut behind him, the sound of the latch clicking in place filling the space. She waited for two heartbeats before turning back to it and twisting the knob. The door opened onto the empty sitting room, and Sara lifted her head.

"Hello, Sara," she whispered, wondering where the other women were. Should she knock on the other doors? Should she wait?

Daphne closed the door again, relieved that it hadn't been locked. For a cold moment, she'd thought he'd locked it and that she was trapped in this room.

But you are trapped.

You're in a half-empty castle, in an abandoned city.

And the horde is coming.

She blew out a shaky breath, glancing around the room again. Her room. A room that her future husband would soon visit. She didn't want to think about that right now. She didn't want to think about anything at all.

There was an ewer of water and a clean basin in the water closet, and she poured some out, concentrated on the liquid, clearing her mind of anything else. It was cold, but she was grateful for it, taking a small cloth from the shelf nearby and washing her face and hands. Slowly she removed several days' worth of travel, pushing back her sleeves and pulling at her neckline. The gown was ruined.

After she finished washing, she went to the wardrobe, hoping it would have something fresh she could wear, not daring to hope that anything she'd packed from her father's house might have ended up here. Whatever fit, she would wear. It didn't matter what it was. She just wanted clean clothes.

She was going through the contents of the wardrobe when someone knocked on the door. It creaked open, and she turned, steeling herself for the king's face, to speak with the man who had refused to greet her in the court-yard. But it wasn't him. A small, fine-boned woman stood in the doorway; pale hair hung loosely around shoulders draped in a simple green gown several years out of fashion.

"Hello," she said, voice soft, a smile touching her lips. "I wanted to welcome you. I wanted to have my maid help you unpack, but I can't seem to find her."

Daphne dropped into a curtsy. "Your majesty, I want to thank you for all the kindness you've shown me."

"No, no." The woman stepped into the room, waving her hands. "Please don't. Not here, between us. My name is Constance. And you are Daphne? King Haran's youngest daughter?"

"Yes," she replied, stepping forward. "It's wonderful to meet you. I was wondering when I would get the chance. Can you tell me anything at all about what's happening? Have you had any news?"

"News?" Constance touched her cheek, tracing the line of bone, eyes darting around the room.

"Yes, are there any kinds of evacuation plans in place? Are you, are *we* being sent away?"

"Marius will want to visit you this evening, I'm sure he will. I'll let you get settled." Constance reached out, giving her hand a quick squeeze. She was so cold, icy, and still she refused to meet Daphne's gaze. "You're not alone here."

"Thank you," Daphne said, reaching for the woman to return the gesture. But she was already beyond her reach, moving swiftly through the door, skirts rustling like an uneasy flock of birds.

10

DAPHNE RAN A HAND OVER THE BEAUTIFULLY EMBROIDERED DUVET—FLOWERS and vines, a riot of rich greens and deep reds—hours of work, days and weeks in each petal. She wondered who had done it, each stitch, sitting in this room or another like it, sharing stories with someone as colored threads were laid down, laughing as seasons changed. It was old, impossible to tell for sure, but much older than her. Something created in another woman's time—love, and memory carrying over to touch Daphne here, now, in what would be her marriage bed.

The thought was a stone in her stomach. She would do what was necessary, keep the treaty, provide an heir. She was glad she hadn't eaten earlier. The tray sat beside the fire, untouched, the food cold now. She might never want to eat again.

The door to the bedroom opened. She took a step back, startled and apprehensive, fighting to keep her face in a calm mask. But it wasn't Marius. Captain Tarver stood in the doorway, in leather armor with a sword at his hip, gaze emotionless.

"The king is waiting for you."

"He's not coming here?" Daphne gestured to the room, the empty bed.

"No, your highness," Tarver said. "I will take you to him."

Daphne wrapped the dressing gown more firmly around her, feeling exposed even with it on, wishing she had more than just the thin nightgown on beneath it. She hesitated, wondering if she should put a gown on, if she should find her slippers; her feet were bare, the carpet warm enough. Captain Tarver came into the room, leather creaking, bringing the scent of cold with him, that sharp smell of the first frost. He took her arm in one large hand, a flash of pity in his eyes.

"We must go right now."

"But—" Daphne began, looking around for her slippers.

"Now."

The Captain took her from the room as she protested, shocked and more than a little afraid. In the sitting room, they passed Constance and another woman with haunted eyes. Isadora, one of the other wives. The women watched with pale faces, hands clasped, mouths in matching thin lines, eyes large and dark.

"What's going on?" Daphne demanded, speaking more to Constance than anyone else. But no one responded, and soon the two women were out of sight as Tarver led her out of the Queen's chambers and into the rest of the castle.

The stone floors were cold beneath her feet, and she clutched the robe to her neck, almost skipping to keep up with Tarver as he led her through the halls. She saw no one else but could hear the preparations for a siege continuing. In the Queen's quarters, she hadn't been able to hear it so clearly; the rooms had seemed so removed from it all, but there was more urgency in the air now, a frantic edge that alarmed her.

"What's happening? Where are you taking me?"

Tarver kept his gaze straight ahead, moving her forward, across the great hall, and toward a set of stairs. "To the king, my lady."

They went up the stairs, winding the circular stairs until she gasped for breath. Above her, she could see a small platform and a door, the inside of the tower hollow aside from the stairs winding up and up. The captain did not appear to be out of breath or even bothered by the climb. At the door he paused, letting her regain her breath, he looked at her then, a hard look.

"Be careful what you say."

Before she could respond, he opened the door, fierce wind rushing past her, cold and biting. Tarver led her through the door and out into the night. Fires burned nearby, smoke and ash filling the air. And on the horizon, a golden burning eye, the star that heralds change and war.

A large man stood overlooking the castle below him, the small city huddled at the castle walls. Several fires burned, spreading slowly, moving from house to house beyond the castle walls. Daphne studied him, the fine armor and sword in his hand, hair shorn close to the scalp, a beard trimmed close to his jaw. This man could only be Marius, King of Cautes, and her husband. Or her soon-to-be husband, on this, their marriage night.

Daphne trembled with cold and fear. She was grateful for Tarver's grip on her arm, he kept her upright and in place as the wind worked to push her off the tower. There was no barricade between herself and the fall, simply the edge of the tower and then the drop several stories to the courtyard. The ramparts below were manned, figures running back and forth, voices raised but words meaningless.

Something was happening beyond the castle walls.

Marius spoke, voice hard and clipped, focused on the kingdom before him. "How will the Wolf approach?"

Daphne looked to the captain, waiting for his answer. But his mouth remained closed, his gaze fixed on a point beyond Marius. The wind blew her nightgown tight against her body, hair tangling around her face; she pushed it out of the way and looked back to Marius. He had turned to face her, lit by the burning fires, and she saw for the first time the insanity in his gaze.

In two steps he had grabbed her, pulling her free of the captain's hold, and swung her toward the edge of the tower. She gasped, clutching at his arm, but he held her straight out from his body, walking her toward the edge until there was nothing but the drop. She was too shocked to speak, feeling the worn edge of the stone beneath her feet, searching Marius's face for anything beyond the fury.

"How. Will. The. Wolf. Approach?"

He spoke each word carefully, inching her closer to the edge, as she clutched at his arm with both hands. His eyes glittered madly, focused hotly on her face, mouth in a tight grimace. He shook her; for an instant she lost contact with the stones beneath her feet, pure terror slicing through her as the wind caught her and she thought she was falling. But Marius kept his grip on her.

"I don't know the Wolf," she gasped.

He shook her again, and she screamed.

"Tell me what you know!"

"Nothing! I know nothing!"

"Your father is dead. The messenger arrived a day ago. Did you think they'd show mercy? Or that I'm so blind I wouldn't see your deception for what it was?"

Dead. The truth of it cut through her. He hadn't even looked at her when she'd left, focused on the papers before him, hands moving over the stacks, that familiar sour twist to his mouth. Dead. The whole kingdom must have fallen as well, the place she'd been born and raised now truly beyond her reach, in a much more final way than she'd expected. What had happened to Mae? And Olesia? They were beyond her reach now too.

Marius shook her again, spit flying from his mouth. "You have all betrayed me! I know you're a spy!"

"My king," Tarver spoke softly. "I have spoken with the men who tracked the group that captured her, and I do not believe she has been sent as a spy. We found her with the highwayman, as the informant said we would. They were not anywhere near the other raiding party we discovered."

Marius stared into Daphne's wide eyes. She could see it all passing across his face, a horrible mix of fear and indecision, paranoia and madness. If she spoke, would it matter? Would he hear the truth or assume she'd lied? She watched Tarver, his face a careful mask, waiting for his words to touch Marius.

"Take her then," Marius spat, shoving her toward the stairs.

Daphne stumbled, gasping and grateful, desperate to leave. Tarver gently took her arm, steadying and guiding her through the tower door and out of Marius's presence. She continued to shiver, even out of the cold wind, the threat of it clinging to her, the dark space behind each blink filled with the possible fall.

They made their way slowly down the stairs, he let her set the pace, not speaking when she paused, hand pressed flat against the wall, feeling the rough texture, reminding herself she stood on solid ground.

"Do you know what happened to Mae and Olesia?" she asked when they reached the bottom of the stairs.

"No, your highness."

"When did you receive the news about my father?"

"I'm told a messenger arrived yesterday. He was struck with a poison arrow and died in the hall after delivering his message."

"I don't understand how Marius could believe it was a betrayal on our part."

The captain remained silent, but she caught a flicker of emotion on his face, almost a grimace, there and gone before she could be sure. They walked on a few more steps, down an empty hall, and toward the queen's chambers. Hesitantly, voice soft, Tarver spoke.

"This last year has been hard on us all. I do not believe the king is thinking clearly."

"It's been a hard few years for many people," she replied, careful to keep her tone smooth.

"For him more than others, I think. If the others," he paused, glancing at her and away. "If they share anything at all, I would pay attention."

Daphne nodded, biting her lip, saving her questions for Constance.

A deep throbbing call of a horn broke across their silence—long and low, vibrating through the stones and into the back of her teeth. It brought fear with it, the hair on the back of her neck rising, stomach clenching.

"What was that?"

Tarver was pale, terror-filled eyes turning to her.

"They're here."

11

HIGH IN A TOWER, A BELL RANG—SONOROUS, ECHOING THROUGH THE CASTLE, in his bones. An alert. Horns came next, the two sounds blending, becoming one terrible warning.

Finian slipped through the side door between the courtyard and the guardhouse, edging along the courtyard, alert and ready to draw his sword. Beyond the castle walls had been silence, the streets eerily quiet, doors and windows shuttered, not even the sound of a dog barking. But here, inside the castle, it was loud and chaotic. Nothing was organized, and they only seemed partially ready.

Fools. Not that being more prepared would have helped them. Finian had seen it up close for too many years. The Wolf always found a way. He'd been guided and driven by a kind of sixth sense. Maybe it had been magic. Finian had never been sure. The result, every time, was death.

The guardhouse door should have been locked. He shouldn't have been able to even get this far. But the castle seemed half empty already despite the men running from one building to another, soldiers moving uneasily on the ramparts. Everywhere there was the jingle of chainmail and shouts.

If the people had been smart, they would have fled long before now.

The Wolf was here. A mix of fear and anger churned in his gut. If he faced the man again, he knew it would mean his end. There would be no way of avoiding it. A promise made, a promise kept. If nothing else, the Wolf was a man of honor. He always kept his word. It was a strange feeling to be so near him again after all these years. Someone he had counted as a friend at one point, in their youth, in another life. Someone who had promised to kill him.

They were here together in this small valley after all these years. He'd gotten comfortable, lazy, and assumed he'd run far enough. He wouldn't make that mistake again.

Tonight his past and present collided. But he wouldn't run, wouldn't leave Daphne behind. He would find her, escape the castle, and they'd move beyond the reach of the Wolf and the horde.

Cutting across the courtyard, he made his way into the castle. He expected someone to stop him, to say something, but no one did. Each man he passed wore a preoccupied expression, half fear, half determination. They were all focused on what the next few hours would bring. They whispered of the horde, the Wolf, and what his killers would bring to them—the gift of blood and death, the endless sleep that would come at the end of their swords.

For years he had been on the other side of that blade, following orders, pushing down each protest, each moment of horror with himself. He pitied the men around him. There would be no escape from what was coming. From the man who was already here.

It all circled through his head, driving the desperation to find Daphne. The women's quarters would be in some inner part of the main building—protected, secluded. He would have to stop someone and ask, alert them to the stranger in their midst. But it was a chance he would have to take.

He passed through one inner door and another, following a curving hall. The sounds were fainter here, the commotion and preparation for invasion something like the distant sound of waves breaking against rocks. This must be closer to where the court lived, the fine lords and ladies who didn't want to know what it took to keep a castle running or know what the cost of a siege would be.

A servant came hurrying around the corner, clutching a bag to his chest and muttering. When he saw Finian, he stopped, face going white.

"Who are you?"

"No one," Finian said, holding out a hand, keeping his voice steady. "I'm looking for the princess that just arrived. Have you seen her?"

"King Haran's daughter." It was a statement, not a question, the man's eyes large and round with fear. "Why do you want her?"

"Can you tell me where she is?"

The man shook his head, eyes darting away, beyond where Finian stood and the empty hall behind him. He would break out in a run any moment; Finian could see it in how he held himself, muscles bunched, poised to spring.

"Please. I have to find her."

"Who are you?"

"You might make it if you go up into the mountains and then south. Don't go through the town. They'll be checking. You have to keep moving, even at night." Finian spoke quickly, hoping that this would be enough to prompt the man to share Daphne's location. "I need to find the princess before they breach the walls. It won't take them very long."

"The mountains?"

Finian nodded. "Do you know where the princess is?"

"There's a great hall behind me and a grand staircase leading up. The queens' chambers are through several more halls and rooms. A man is guarding the door that will take you up to their rooms."

"Thank you."

But the man was already past him and hurrying away, disappearing beyond the curve of the wall and out of sight. Finian wished him well. Maybe he'd make it. No one had ever escaped before, but if that man could, if he did, then Finian and Daphne would.

Someone else was coming. He adjusted the grip on his sword, breathing out, clearing his mind. Two guards came into view, chain metal rattling, faces set in grim lines, fear in their eyes.

They drew their weapons, rushing toward him without questions, recognizing him for the stranger he was. He met them, blocking the first blow, grunting with the heavy contact, pivoting to stop another and lunging forward. They moved frantically, sloppy in their terror, determined but distracted. They kept looking beyond him, ready for the other men they feared would arrive to overrun them. Finian used it, finding the hole in their defense, thrusting his blade between a joint into the soft and yielding body it protected.

The killing came easily. It shouldn't have. He hated that it did. His muscles remembered; his mind would never forget. But he knew this would be the first of many tonight.

He would cut through them all to find Daphne.

12

"Please, Constance," Daphne leaned her forehead against the door, gripping the handle tight. "You have to let me in."

She could hear the two women whispering beyond the locked door, a rustle of movement as one of them approached. The door remained closed, Constance whispering through wood, her voice so low Daphne almost couldn't hear it. A low mournful thread wove through the words, inevitable and resigned.

"No, Daphne. No. Go away. There isn't enough for three."

"Enough of what, Constance?" Daphne pulled the handle, hoping that it had unlocked itself. It remained frozen in place. She slapped a hand against the wood, wishing for splitters, for any small amount of pain to pull her back from this moment. "Enough of what?"

Constance stepped away from the door, two low voices mingling, fading. Daphne knew; she didn't have to be told what would happen within those walls. A mercy killing, choosing to meet death on their own terms instead of at the end of the Wolf's blade. If Daphne had been in her father's house something similar might have been offered to her. Would she have taken it? She didn't know. Fear, hot and panic inducing, filled her. Her hands trembled, her breathing growing unsteady.

What should I do? Where can I go?

The women had locked her out of what might have been her rooms had she stayed, if the life that had been expected had come to be. She hadn't wanted to be here, to live in those rooms, and now they were truly gone and beyond her reach.

She stepped away from the women and the queens' quarters, stumbling and reaching out to steady herself on the cold stone wall, the smooth texture beneath her fingers, the feel of it as she slid her palm across it. She kept her hand there as she walked, following the wall, turning with it, continuing until she reached the great hall. Banners hung from banners overhead, vibrant colors and snarling beasts, a crown with a dagger through it. Huge tapestries covered the walls, scenes from victories of past kings, a portrait of Marius.

The man himself stood on the dais. His captain at his right hand, an advisor on his left, and a handful of knights scattered around the room. They were silent, eyes trained on the huge, closed doors at the end of the hall. The sounds of battle came from beyond them, muffled but growing, approaching with horrifying certainty.

This is where I'm going to die.

Daphne crept into the room, back against the wall, moving away from Marius. Under different circumstances, she would have run in the opposite direction after what had happened on the tower. But not now. There was no escape.

There were other arches branching off the great hall, filled with silence, the sucking emptiness of death from the rest of the castle. How many had already made the choice Constance had? How far had the Wolf's men gotten?

On the dais, the advisor's voice rose, high-pitched, begging for the king to leave. But Marius shook his head, eyes wild, one hand balled into a fist and the other gripping his sword. The men in armor scattered around the hall shared his expression, faces set in stone, etched and weathered like the mountains. But not even the mountains could keep these attackers out, and she knew these mountains, these men, would fail as well. They would fall and so would the king. So would she.

A terrible cry rolled out from one of the arches, the words indistinguishable, the voice swallowed up, consumed, in battle. Daphne twisted her hands into the fabric of her skirt, simple cotton, a color recalling evergreen forests and moss. She studied it, listening to the room, to the noises beyond the room. She should run. But run where? There was nowhere else to go. She was alone in a room full of strangers brought together by death. The pressure of a gaze touched her, and she looked up to meet the king's eyes.

"This is your fault," he shouted, gesturing to her with his sword. He spit and turned to his knights. "Kill the woman."

Several of them glanced at her, seeing her for the first time, but their attention didn't linger. They were focused on the door, the open arches that would soon contain a more serious enemy.

"Daphne!"

Finian.

His voice came echoing down the stone halls, over the clash of steel and screams of pain. Her name, repeated, drawing closer. He had come for her. Fierce joy filled her, hot and righteous, vindication and affirmation. Passion or love, obsession, confirmation. He had come for her. The man who wanted nothing and no one, he had come for *her*.

Finian rushed into the room, a sword in one hand and dagger in the other, covered in blood, face set and determined. But his expression changed, softening when he saw her, light touching him, joy shattering into a million iridescent pieces between them.

She ran to him, his name on her tongue, eyes stinging with tears. He met her with open arms, dropping his sword, metal on stone ringing out. His kiss was fierce, possessive, and she welcomed it, wanting more, even here and now. She wanted the safety he offered, love here at the end of it all.

"You came for me," she said against his mouth, hands tangled in his hair. "You came for me."

"Always, Daphne." He pulled away, cupping her face in his hand, pressing one more hard kiss to her swollen lips. "I will always come for you."

"The Wolf!" Marius was screaming the name over and over, face red with fury. "Kill him!"

Men rushed Finian, swords drawn, silent in their concentration as their king screamed. He swept up his sword, pushing Daphne away, prepared to meet them. She moved along the wall, unable to look away, terrified that if she did, he would die. But a noise drew her attention, reluctantly she pulled her gaze away, scanning the room. Marius was charging toward her, mad, glittering eyes fixed on her face, her death written across every plane of his body.

Desperately Daphne looked around, searching for anything to defend herself, moving quickly away from Marius. She picked up a discarded sword; the hall was full of weapons, stacked and piled for the final stand. It was heavy, making her arm ache, and she looked around for something small, easier to wield. But he was fast, covering the distance quickly, raising his weapon over his head and bringing it down, teeth bared and gritted, hatred and fury in his unblinking stare.

By some miracle, she blocked the blow, stumbling back beneath his weight. He came at her again, and she brought the sword up, trembling, jaw clenched, expecting the blow and knowing she could only hold him off for so long. She wasn't a fighter. She'd had no lessons and possessed no skill. The only thing she had was desperation and the determination to kiss Finian once more. Just once. It was the one thing in the world she wanted most.

Tripping backward over something, fumbling her grip on the weapon, Daphne hit the wall. Marius pressed his advantage, closing in, blade whipping out. Daphne ducked beneath it, feeling the air sing as it passed, too close to her head. But in his confidence, he'd come too close as well, and she thrust out her

733

blade, screaming with the motion, shuddering as it parted skin and muscle, sinking deep into the king's gut.

His eyes widened. He dropped his sword, hand reaching out to touch the blade buried in his middle. He swiped at her, grasping, hissing profanities under his breath, through yellowed teeth. She leaned away, moving out of reach, the sword pulling free, blood coming with it. Marius crumpled to the floor, gasping and going pale as he bled out onto the floor. The sword was heavy in her hand and a tremble crept up her arms, the weight of it pulling her down.

Then Finian was there, meeting her gaze over the dying king, his look of surprise becoming fierce joy. She dropped the sword, the weapon clattering to the flagstones and ringing in her ears, as she stumbled toward Finian.

"You never mentioned you were good with a sword, Daphne." He smiled taking her hand to pull her away, relief coming off him in waves. "If you still need rescuing, I'm here to do it."

"It took you long enough," she gasped, wrapping her fingers around his and holding tight.

They moved toward an arch, out of the great hall, away from the dying men they left behind. She shook, unable to control it, wanting more than anything to stop it. She needed a moment, needed his reassurance, needed to offer her own to him when she realized he was shaking too.

"Finian, wait," Daphne said, stopping him, reaching out to touch him and know he was real. "I know what I want. You asked me in the woods to tell you. When I knew. I know now."

He smiled, the answer between them before she could speak, the shimmer of it in her eyes. "What would you like, your highness?"

"Stop it," she whispered.

"What?"

"Calling me your highness. I'm not that, not anymore."

"You can't change the fact that you're a princess."

"Yes, I can," she said, taking a step toward him. "You can help me."

"Daphne, Princess of the Highwaymen? Ransomed turned ransomer?" His smile was back, light dancing in his eyes.

"Something like that."

"Tell me what you want, Daphne."

"You."

"And what if that isn't enough?" The sudden thought, a pang of anxiety.

In two swift steps, she was in his arms, kissing him fiercely. "How could you ever be anything more to me than my whole world?" She searched his face, kissing him again, pressing all of her heart into his hands.

Break me. Love me. I am yours for a thousand years and a thousand more.

"We'll go south," he said, pressing his forehead to hers, their breath mingling, hearts pounding, a lover's tattoo. "We'll keep going until we're out of the horde's path, beyond the empire. I don't know what's out there. I can make no promises about what we'll come across."

"I will go anywhere with you."

He kissed her, hungry, hands desperate on her body. She clung to him, holding on to a dream given flesh and bone, the man in her arms the only person she had hoped for, dreamed for.

"But there's no way out," she said, fighting the tears that threatened, their reality breaking across the dream, shattering the happiness blooming in her chest. "The Wolf is here. You know that no one escapes."

"But we will," he said, taking her hand and reaching for the blade he'd dropped.

THE SOUNDS of fighting came from all directions, echoing down corridors, coming to meet the crashing metal in the rooms around them. They were everywhere; it was impossible to know how or where the walls had been breached or where the inhabitants of the castle were making their last stand.

Finian hurried them along the narrow halls of the servants and soldiers, ready at any moment to face an attacker down. But luck was on their side, fate conspiring to keep them alive and clear a path. Daphne held tight to his hand, matching his pace, whispering prayers.

The outer buildings and courtyards were burning, flames shooting out from upper windows in the castle, screams bouncing off stones. Daphne wanted to cover her ears, block it all out, but she needed her hands and her eyes. Later it would haunt her, later she would wake up in the middle of the night in a cold sweat, positive that the Wolf was at their door. But right now, now, she had to face it and make it through.

The courtyard was chaos, a mix of attackers and defenders, the battle for the castle not yet won but the outcome already apparent. A horse, blood on his flanks, the whites of his eyes showing, stood stamping in a corner, already saddled and bridled, someone else's escape. But there was no rider, and there were several dead nearby. There was no one to claim him now. She raised her arm, pointing, trying to still the tremble in her arm.

"Finian," she said, voice soft. "There."

"Good eye," he said, pleasure in his voice as he tucked her under the eaves of an outbuilding. "Don't move. I'll be right back."

She almost went after him, terrified to be left alone, watching the fighting, knowing she would be noticed at any moment. Finian approached the horse, hands out, speaking soft reassurances, promises of escape and sweet apples, sugar lumps, and green fields. She edged toward him, hugging the wall.

Movement at the castle gate caught her attention, the courtyard quieting as a figure came into view. A huge man on a black horse, dressed all in black, a white wolf skull tied to his saddle. She was struck by his beauty, cruel black eyes, dark hair framing the unusual face. He radiated power, a physical force that made her want to pull back and hide in the shadows.

The Wolf.

Daphne knew him at once. They all did. How she ever could have mistaken Finian for this man was a mystery. The fear the Wolf brought was palpable, certain death sweeping them with a cold gaze, taking it all in, knowing how each of them would die. His eyes settled on Finian as he dismounted, unsheathing his weapon with a smooth motion.

She ran to Finian. If he died, they would go together, no matter how horrible a death it might be. After everything, having discovered him, found him in an unexpected place, she would not lose him again. He shook his head when he saw her coming, motioning for her to stay away.

But she didn't stop, not until she was beside him and his hand was in hers. They stood together, facing the monster, staring down the man who had sworn nothing less than death if their paths crossed again. Beside her, Finian adjusted his grip on his weapon, moving in front of her, ready to block a blow.

The Wolf looked between them, down to their clasped hands, something flickering in his eyes. The sounds in the castle seemed to fade, the world constricting around them.

"I made you a promise, Finian."

Finian inclined his head. "You did."

The Wolf took in the courtyard, surveying the ruin he'd brought. Daphne couldn't tell if he was pleased or disappointed. Then his eyes came back to her, dark and intense, searching her face. He was everything they said he was, a monster and killer, and his scrutiny raised the hair at the back of her neck.

"The pieces of the saint are coming together," The Wolf said, moving his attention to Finian. "In a matter of weeks, the continent will belong to him."

"To the prince or the saint?" Finian asked, his tone cool and unconcerned.

"Does it matter?"

Finian shook his head and Daphne wondered what was happening between them here. She'd expected the Wolf to charge with sword raised, to make good on the promise given. Instead, they spoke calmly about the death of countries and the rise of monsters like old friends.

"He hasn't forgotten you," the Wolf said.

"I'm a very memorable person," Finian replied. "Is that why you're here?"

"No, I'm not here for you."

The Wolf turned away without another word, dismissing them. Daphne could feel Finian shaking beside her, their hands trembling together, the tension in their shoulders hard as stone. They watched him cross the courtyard, striding through the men who had yet to resume their fight, who still watched him with horror. He passed through the castle door, into the darkness, without looking back.

"What was that?" Daphne breathed out, willing the tightness in her chest to ease.

"Doesn't matter," Finian said, hustling her to the horse, patting the animal with one hand and her with the other.

"I thought he was going to kill you," she whispered.

"I thought he was too. Something's changed."

"What?"

"Doesn't matter." Finian helped her into the saddle and scrambled up behind her, tucking her tight against him. "Right now, we go south, and we don't stop until we reach the sea."

"Will that be far enough?" she asked.

A thousand questions flowed through her, and she couldn't help but glance to where the golden star burned on the horizon. *Change.* A visible sign and signal to it, calling it and creating it. A thousand things were possible beneath that star. The future was unknown with that star in the sky, the world a stranger place. Finian urged the horse into a trot, passing through the castle gates, and into the deserted city beyond.

"I don't know." He pressed a kiss into her hair. "But we're going to find out."

ABOUT KATHRYN TRATTNER

Kathryn Trattner has loved fairy tales, folk stories, and mythology all of her life. Her hands-down favorites have always been East of the Sun, West of the Moon and the story of Persephone and Hades. When not writing or reading she's traveling as much as possible and taking thousands of photos that probably won't get edited later. She lives in Oklahoma with her wonderful partner, two very busy children, one of the friendliest dogs ever, and the ghost of an extremely grumpy cat who doesn't like anyone at all.

Signup for her newsletter here:
https://www.subscribepage.com/kathryntrattner

facebook.com/kathryntrattner

twitter.com/k_trattner

instagram.com/k.trattner.author

pinterest.com/kathryntrattner

amazon.com/Kathryn-Trattner/e/B083YS4T8Q

bookbub.com/authors/kathryn-trattner

THRONE FOR IT

MELISSA WILLIAMS

A Royal Love Lines Prequel Novella

ABOUT THRONE FOR IT

Tropes: Secret Identity, Royalty, Opposites Attract, One-Bed

Graphic sexual depictions, open door sex and explicit language

Blurb:

Henry
I've been mistaken for a prince before. Never like this, however.

When I walk into my hotel suite, needing to prepare for my niece's birthday party, I'm accosted by a woman in a fairy-tale princess costume. And she thinks I'm her Prince Charming.

Stunned at her beauty and direct manner, I instantly follow her every command until a phone call ruins it all.

As I watch my princess flee, I know this won't be the last time I see her. I'm determined to win her affections, even if time isn't on my side.

Ellie

After making a complete fool of myself as a party princess, I'm thankful to turn in my heels for my hiking boots. As a wilderness experience guide and expert hiker, being out in nature brings me absolute joy. Yet even losing myself in the beauty and majesty of the mountains doesn't help me forget about a certain finely dressed man with piercing blue eyes.

Dear Reader,
This novella, which is a prequel for an upcoming series launching this summer, contains explicit language, talk of family estrangement and briefly touches on the topics of anxiety and stress burnout. Please be kind to yourself and determine if this hidden identity royal romance is right for you.

1

ELLIE

I KNEW THEY WERE DESPERATE WHEN THEY CALLED ME. I WASN'T ANYONE'S definition of a princess. No matter how much makeup I applied or which wig I was forced to wear, I could never get it right. It was a part I struggled to play.

So to be here, hustling down the long hotel hallway with my arms full of tulle, bags of fabric and fake hair, was really saying something. Blowing a fluffy scarf away from my sweaty face, I strained to see over my collection of stuff. I was hoping to hear the chaos of the other party princesses, but the floor was absurdly quiet.

Maybe I was the first one to arrive? Seemed a bit strange, but I did like to be punctual.

This party was a big deal—or so I had been told repeatedly by my friend Tallie. This was a princess party for an *actual* princess. It was mind-blowing… and a little weird.

When I thought of a princess having a birthday party, I didn't imagine them surrounded by happy, singsong, cartoon-inspired, pastel-wearing women. But then again, kids are kids, and they're going to like whatever the heck they like.

I'm beyond thrilled that singing isn't part of my role here today. I was called in only because half of Tallie's staff had come down with a spring flu thanks to a Moana-themed party last weekend.

Turning the last corner, I give a sigh of relief when I see a man in a black suit standing at the end of the hallway. I've finally arrived. Thank goodness. My arms were about to give out under the weight of this costume.

I was under strict instructions from Tallie to get to the suite that had been booked for us, get dressed and wait for my prince to show up. Well, not *my* prince per se. But the prince who was hired for today's birthday. I would be one of three (fake) princesses at the party but there would be only one charming prince.

This is not my first stint at being a fake princess—Tallie has blackmailed me in to two previous parties last year. Her confidence in me is nice, but misplaced.

"Hey. Hi. Hello," I say to the man-statue by the door as I approach. "I'm Ellie. I'm here for the prince and to get ready for the party."

His eyes flick to me. I get the oddest sensation from the slight incline of his brow that I've somehow surprised this man, but the feeling quickly passes. We stand, staring at each other, neither one of us backing down or blinking.

Unsure if I'm waiting for him to grant me approval or if he's waiting for me to carry on, I continue to stare up at him. When our silence goes from funny to awkward, and I'm about to burst, the man puts me out of my misery and nods.

I'm a sweaty mess by this point, and he continues to take pity on me by turning and opening the door. I give him a strained smile and a little curtsy— I'm getting into character!—before throwing myself across the threshold and dumping everything onto a huge armchair.

Oh sweet relief!

That's when I see it. The bed.

Giving in to a childish urge, I take off in a flash, running and diving onto the semifirm mattress of my dreams. The oh-so-soft sheets flutter around me and I starfish, taking up as much room as possible on this dreamlike cloud.

I really, really wished I had enough time to nap. Or even just chill here for a little while. This was nice. But, a princess's duties were never done. I needed every spare minute before the party started to get ready.

Reluctantly, I pushed up from the bed with a dramatic sigh. Rolling my head from side to side, I took in my surroundings. It was a pretty sweet setup. The suite was huge.

Due to the high-caliber guest list, security was over-the-top. I'd had to complete a background check last night even to be allowed within a mile of the hotel. The checkpoints just to get in here had been extreme, yet I understood why they were necessary.

The only part of the hotel that didn't have security measures was the elevator. I was able to hop right in without anyone stopping me.

But, like, yeesh. It was a lot.

Even this suite was part of the security measures. We had to get ready at the hotel and not at home so that the media *wouldn't catch on.* Tallie's words, not mine.

Catch on to what I had no idea. Was it a surprise eight-year-old's birthday? Was that a thing?

Shaking my head to dislodge all my weird thoughts, I drag my feet back to the armchair and start sorting through the costume pieces. Every time I temped for Tallie, I thanked my lucky stars that I wasn't cast as one of the core four classic princesses.

There's no way I would be able to pull off Belle's huge ball gown or Cinderella's grace and melodic laugh. Instead, I was happy to put a five-pound wig on my head and twirl barefoot as Rapunzel.

I also didn't have to layer loads of makeup on my face to play the part since I was naturally tanned from the sun and had a smattering of freckles across my nose and cheekbones. I only had to accentuate my green eyes with liner and add some sparkle before I was ready to party.

"One layer, two layer, three layer, four," I sing off-key to myself as I begin laying out the stages of my costume. I hated long silences. Needing something to distract me, I dig my phone out of one of my bags and hit my "Mood Boosting" playlist.

As Dwayne Johnson's voice begins to sing to me, telling me "You're Welcome," I serenade him back. I wasn't a good singer, in any sense of the word, but that didn't mean I didn't sing. I loved to sing. I just kept all my concerts within the privacy of my room or the shower.

When the rap verse hits, I go all out. While undressing, I moonwalk over to the first layer of my dress, grab it and begin to use it as a floppy microphone. When the song draws to an end I dramatically throw my arms out wide and belt out the last word, holding the off-key note until there wasn't any more breath in my lungs.

A slow clap sounds behind me.

My eyes shoot open. I spin around so fast I briefly feel the sweet heat of the carpet burn my foot.

A pair of shocking blue eyes lock with mine.

I give a gasp of surprise.

And immediately start choking on my own spit.

747

2

HENRY

IT WAS THE WAILING THAT ALERTED MY GUARDS THAT SOMETHING WAS WRONG. It sounded like a cat was dying somewhere on this floor.

And it was coming from my suite of rooms.

One of my men ran ahead, hand already clutching the gun hidden under his suit jacket as he cautiously approached the door. A young man I didn't recognize, no doubt one of my cousin's hired security people, raised his hands to stop us. An odd look was on his face.

"Stand down!" he called out, taking a step in our direction. "It's not a threat."

Neither Toby nor Jonas believed him, instead they silently communicated with one another before drawing their guns and stealthily opening the doors.

Toby went in first as Jonas covered him from behind. Ignoring both of them, I continued into my suite of rooms. Whoever or whatever was making all this noise was not a threat. I was sure of it.

Until I got a look at her.

My heart jumps into my throat, causing me to lose my breath for a moment. The sight before me is one of the strangest things I've ever seen but also the most beautiful.

A woman with long dirty brown hair and a strong lean body is jerking her body to the music. Her movements aren't on beat, and I don't know if I would call what she's doing singing, but there's such passion in her voice.

I can't take my eyes off her.

Jonas and Toby only lower their guns slightly. Giving them a signal not to interfere, I let the woman finish her song. And she does, in a big way. I have to press my lips together to hold in my laugh.

When her arms extend wide and she finishes the song, I can't stop myself from applauding her.

Which was probably the last thing I should have done.

Her eyes pop open in fright. She gasps, a scream seconds away.

Then she starts coughing. Violently coughing.

Fumbling backward, she trips and falls to the side, clutching the bedsheets. Her choke-coughing continues as she tries to say something, face getting red from the strain.

"It's okay. Breathe. Breathe," I gently coo to her, holding up my hands to show I mean no harm.

Her eyes are watering now, tears threatening to fall. I cup both hands to the sides of her shoulders and direct her to sit on the edge of the bed.

A shimmer of something catches my eye behind her, and I quickly look over my shoulder to see a pile of clothes. The colors of the fabric look familiar but I don't know why.

I start to sit down beside her but she makes a frantic squeaking between chocking coughs and reaches for something.

"Oh my God," I shout, pushing myself up to standing. She's grabbed a ball of hair that freaks me out. For a second I thought it was alive.

Torn between concern for her and utter confusion as to why she has a large ball of hair with her, I give my guards a wide-eyed look before carefully sitting on the bed again. I was completely dumbfounded as to who this woman was and why she was here.

After what feels like an hour her cough dies down, leaving her with hiccups. The room lapses into silence.

Her face is still a rosy hue, but I think that's more from embarrassment now than lack of oxygen.

I'm about to speak when I notice she's taking all of me in. Her eyes lock on my suit and the medals I have pinned on my lapel. I'm not a huge fan of the sash I have to wear at formal events, but with the way her eyes trail down, following the red fabric, I could have a change of heart.

I watch as the muscles in her arms contract and release the ball of hair she's holding, fascinated by the power I see there. She's petite, but strong. Slowly she straightens, her startling green eyes dancing around the room, noting my security team.

I'm surprised again when her arms fall to her sides and she throws her head back to burst out in laughter. I can feel my guards looking at me for direction on what to do, but I can't seem to tear my eyes off of her.

"Oh my goodness! You scared the bejesus out of me." She continues to laugh through her words. "That was a good one." Her mossy orbs pin me in place, her smile doing something to my stomach that I hadn't felt in years.

"I'm sorry?" I start to say, not understanding what she's referring to or why she's in my suite.

Waving a hand at me, she stands and quickly places the hair down and grabs another shinny fabric, shoving the material over her head, finishing dressing. "Nah, don't worry about it. I get it. I'm the newb. It was a pretty cool entrance though."

Well that didn't clear up anything.

"Tallie told me there might be a bit of fun teasing or whatever since I was new. Well, I'm a temp—you know that. It's all in good fun."

Slipping on what looks like the fourth and final layer of her...dress, I think, she turns back to me with a small smirk that twists up only one side of her lips. "I was told there was going to be a Charming joining us for the party but you're more an Eric. Though your prince costume is on point. Can you get that last button for me?"

Something is wrong with me. I can't seem to form words, too awestruck by the woman in front of me. I stand at her command, helping secure her dress. The faint scent of oranges and pine hit me. My fingers linger on her neck, already addicted to her soft skin.

"You okay back there?"

I step back, feeling sheepish. When have I ever been at a loss for words? For the appropriate and trained response to any situation?

"Can you help me with this monster?" She doesn't wait for my answer. Instead, she drops the giant hair ball into my hands and turns her back to me again.

"It's a wig," murmur dumbly.

She snorts. "Duh."

Yes, duh indeed.

"How," my voice breaks and I pause to clear it, feeling hot all of a sudden. "How do I do this?"

Gathering her hair with a tie at the base of her neck, the woman shakes her head.

"Raise it high, yes like that, then place it down over my head. Good—no, wait! Ready." She guides me through the process of putting the heavy wig on. She's a bossy and direct woman who doesn't pull her punches. I like that she's not holding back with me.

"There. How's that?" My arms are wide, as if I'm presenting her.

"Excellent. Now I just have to survive the afternoon with this mini bowling ball on my head." Her small laugh has me smiling.

"Damn, look at this sash. It looks like real silk." Her hand extends to my chest, her soft pink painted nails glittering in the light. Instinctually knowing what's about to happen, I'm too slow to stop it.

Toby and Jonas jump into action, going for the woman and stopping her from touching me. I need that touch though. I can't explain why.

She gives a little bark of fright when both men spring into action but it's quickly cut off as I reach for her hand and pull her to me.

"Are"—she swallows, confusion and a bit of apprehension in her gaze— "are they with you? I was told that there would only be one party prince today since the others were out sick."

Party prince? I knew she wasn't talking about me or hinting toward a party reputation. Yet what else…

"You're here to perform for the party." It's a statement. An epiphany.

"Yeah, Tallie called in a favor, well, it was more like blackmail if I'm being honest, because I do not fit the princess bill if you know what I mean." I didn't, but I let her continue rambling. "But here I am, a party princess for a day because I have trouble saying no to the people I love. What are the chances that some kid will barf on me today? Do royal kids do that, you think?"

Instead of answering any of her questions, I place two fingers under her chin and lift her head. Her lashes flutter as she looks up at me.

"What is your name?"

"Oh, duh. Sorry about that. You helped put a wig on me and we haven't even introduced ourselves." She extends her hand. "I'm Ellie. I'll be princessing with you today."

"Nice to make your acquaintance, Ellie. I'm…Henry."

"Are you in character or is this just how you talk?"

"This is me," I simply say, hoping that's enough for her. I know my slight accent can throw people off.

"Very nice," she sighs, more to herself than me. A comfortable silence stretches between us. Ellie is gazing at me, lost in her thoughts. I find this utterly charming. A smile breaks across my face, the first honest grin I've given in months.

Something shifts in the air.

Realizing that she's been staring at me, Ellie blinks rapidly and takes a step back. "Oh, umm, sorry. I was…never mind. I just"—she holds up a hand, something I'm noticing she does a lot of—talking with her hands—"I just," she draws the word out again, "need to finish getting ready. Yes, that's it. I was told I needed sparkles on cheekbones and eyelids."

"I think you look perfect." The words are out before I know I'm going to say them. I can feel the apples of my cheeks getting red, but I mean them.

"Thank you. I was worried I wouldn't do this Rapunzel costume justice but I think I'm pulling it off. It's this wig. It's magic, even if it is like five pounds of synthetic hair."

Now I understood why the dress looked so familiar. My niece was obsessed with *Tangled*.

Yet now I was dying to know what she looked like with her real hair down and free. Would her hair be as wild as her laugh? The need to stay around her until the very end of the day so I could discover this was strong.

I have to make that happen. Somehow.

Wanting some time alone with Ellie, I motion to my guards for them to leave us. They both hesitate, giving me a stern look and arched eyebrows that silently questioned *Are you sure?* I give them a slight nod before turning back to Ellie.

I hear them leave but don't turn to make sure. Carefully moving to the other side of the room so I could sit down, I straighten my cufflinks. Ellie wasn't wrong in her assumption that I was dressed in costume—however this attire was the dress uniform I was expected to wear to all royal family events. I felt like a fraud and a fake every time I wore this finery.

I also wasn't a prince.

Just a mere earl.

I would keep that little piece of information to myself. No need to freak her out just yet.

"So, Ellie, you're a temporary princess for a day, what will you do with all that royal power?"

She snorts a laugh, twisting from her place in front of the mirror where she's dabbing on something shimmery.

"This is trick question, right? Aren't I obligated to say world peace?"

"I think that is more aligned to pageant winners."

"Right, right," she mumbles. I watch in fascination as she puckers her lips in thought. "Then I would definitely have to say climate change. I would add my royal voice and influence to that fight."

Her answer impresses me. A sensation that feels like pride bursts through my chest.

"That's a very noble cause."

Ellie shrugs like it's nothing, but I can see the glow of happiness in her eyes.

"Well"—she clears her throat, tilting her head just a little so her newly applied makeup catches the light—"my 'regular job'"—she uses air quotes—"is as an adventure guide. Without the lush forests, rivers and wildlife I'd kinda be screwed."

I take a step toward her and drape my arm over the back of the love seat that's to the side of where Ellie is sitting, needing to be closer. There's a pull here that I can't deny.

I want to know more about her. I want to know everything. Her voice is soothing a part of me I didn't realize was hurting.

"I'm sorry," I speak up, meeting her eyes in the mirror. "What's an adventure guide? Like a tour guide?"

"Kind of, but for nature. I lead hiking groups of different experience levels through the mountain trails to the north of here. Most groups are only day trips, about seven hours of hiking, but sometimes we get overnight groups."

"I've never heard of such a thing."

Her smile is almost blinding as she turns around, placing an arm across the back of her chair. "You're not from around here, are you?"

I pause for a moment, considering my next words.

"No, but I'm thinking of extending my stay."

"You definitely shouldn't leave without doing a hike and exploring the mountains. The company I work for does all kinds of outdoor activities."

She turns back to the mirror where she adjusts her wig and nods in approval, and then Ellie stands and makes her way over to me. Fingering the sash that is across my chest, she makes a quiet humming noise.

"If you don't live here, how did Tallie find you? Were you working with another party company?"

"The opportunity magically appeared before me," I tell her, not wanting to lie but not ready to reveal my true identity yet.

"Huh." Her hand drops from my chest. "Well, I guess you're one lucky prince then." Ellie laughs, shrugging her shoulders. "So, tell me, what's the secret to being a good princess out there? Tallie already promised I don't have to sing, but I don't want to ruin the illusion for the kids."

"The secret to being a good princess?" I ask, a little taken aback.

"Yeah, to being a good party princess. What have the women you've performed with in the past done that the kids have loved?"

Oh. The *party* princess. My heart rate begins to calm when I understand her meaning. She's not asking about being *my* princess, she's asking about the role. The line between what was pretend and what was my real life was very thin.

"Just be yourself. Smile. Laugh. Engage with them. They may be children but they are smart and observant." I grin, thinking about my niece. "They're going to try to trip you up with question after question but keep cool."

"And twirl."

"Pardon?"

"Keep cool and twirl on. It's like Rapunzel's thing. Or, like, a princess thing, right? Twirling in your dress so that it flares out."

"Sure." I was assuming that was a party princess thing. I had never seen my cousin twirl in my life. I think her mother, the queen, would have a conniption if she ever saw such a thing.

"Do you—" She stops talking when the melodic jingle of her cell phone goes off. Looking over, she must recognize the number because she instantly reaches for the phone.

"Hey! I'm all ready to…what?"

The instant her eyes dart to me, I know my ruse is up.

"What do you mean? I'm in the suite…the room? No, you texted 1405… Then who is in this suite with me, looking like a prince?"

The person on the other end of the conversation says something, but I can't make it out, not able to take my eyes off Ellie. She's looking a little pale all of a sudden.

The phone falls from her hand, landing with a thud on the carpeted floor.

"Perhaps now is a good time to tell you I'm here for the party, but not as a performer."

She doesn't move, doesn't say anything as we continue to stare at one another.

"Wh-who are you?" she finally whispers, eyes growing larger. I believe she knows the answer before I even speak it.

"My name *is* Henry," I begin, hoping that will reassure her. "I just left off all the fancy bits."

"And the fancy bits are?"

"His Royal Excellence Lord Henry Cragnoor, 12th Earl of Caledonia."

Ellie's eye close. Taking a deep breath, she slowly begins to nod her head. I feel knot of tension in my gut easing slightly, believing that's she processing this new information and coming to terms with it.

The relief that she doesn't care about my title is refreshing, I want to shout my excitement. I want to…oh no.

I barely register what's happening she moves so fast. From one elated blink to the next disbelieving one, Ellie has grabbed her phone and made a dash for the suite doors.

"Wait! Ellie, please let me explain—" But she's gone before I finish my sentence. My guards enter the room, blocking my way and slamming the door behind them as they look for threats around me. The only threat to my sanity and my heart ran out of the room seconds before.

"Lord Cragnoor, are you all right?"

My resolve finally breaks with that, frustration buzzing through every vein in my body.

"Damn it, Jonas, I told you to call me Henry. None of this Lord crap."

I can feel rather than see both my guards giving each other a look of shock. I rarely lose my cool. But Ellie, my God, in the brief time I've known her, been around her, she's thrown me off my axis.

She's thrown me right off the cliff and left me free-falling with the knowledge that she's the something special I've been looking for.

Running a hand through my hair, I turn back to my men.

"I need all the information you can get on that woman." When neither of them makes a move I let out an exasperated breath. "Now, please," I state, waving my hand.

They both grab their phones and get to work.

3

ELLIE

Keep smiling. Just keep smiling.

I repeated this mantra in my head, trying not to break character.

On one hand, smiles were easy since I was surrounded by a bunch of kids who were twirling with me. On the other hand, I had zero doubts that Henry was watching me.

Was I even allowed to call him Henry in my head? Or did it always have to start with Lord? Or Earl?

Crap, it didn't matter. After the complete mess up on my part upstairs, there was no way we'd find each other alone in another room. We'd probably never exchange another word.

Urg, why did that make me feel awful?

My traitorous eyes flick up and over the kids' heads to the far side of the lawn. Henry was standing with three other men. All of them where in similar suits. All of them were stupid good looking but none of them looked as handsome as Henry did. And his eyes were on me, like I predicted.

I quickly look away, only to gaze back at him seconds later. I couldn't help myself. He had me mesmerized.

While I was still completely embarrassed that I had waltzed into a royal's suite like I owned the place and peppered Henry with questions, wanting a professional's help to prepare for the party, he hadn't made me feel dumb. At no point did he try to correct me or make me feel like the help I was asking for was a bother.

Should I have picked up on more of his confusion at the beginning? Absolutely. Yet, I couldn't be blamed for that. No man should be blessed with looks like Henry—and with a kind heart to boot.

I had this insane urge to run my hands through his hair and grab one of his curls, pulling and releasing to see if it's just as bouncy and silky as it looks.

I'd never seen a man pull of a sash as well as Henry was rocking his today. Damn, that just should not be legal. Royalty bending the rules again.

"Yo, Rapunzel. Earth to Rapunzel," a voice calls softly.

Shaking out of my man-trance, I jump back into action, slapping a huge smile on my face and joining my hands together in a gentle clasp. My eyes land on a chicken standing beside me.

What the—

"I know. I know. I'm the lucky costume winner today. Dressed as a fricken' chicken."

"Umm," I begin, not really sure how to phrase my next question. "Are you, ah, sure you're at the right party?"

"Unfortunately, yes."

"But I thought this was a princess party."

"And I'm a princess's sidekick. A special request by the birthday girl. Or, er, can we call her a girl? Should she always be called princess?"

"I was just thinking the same thing about—" I catch myself. Waving that line of thought off, I focus back. Scanning the costume of the woman beside me, I try to figure out what character she is. What princess had a chicken sidekick?

"Wait, are you supposed to be Heihei? From *Moana*?"

"Ding-ding-ding."

The laugh that bursts out of me felt good. All the tension I was holding from my earlier encounter with Henry dissipates in a fit of glee.

"Oh my goodness. That's amazing and yet so cruel at the same time. How did Tallie get you to agree to this?"

"Blackmail."

I'm expecting her to go into more detail but she leaves it at that. I nod, my smile falling just slightly. She's scowling, yet I can see some humor behind her eyes.

"Yeah, Tallie does have a way with getting friends to help her against their will."

"Well, just be glad she made you a princess for a day and not a punchline."

My eyes flare. Yeah, there was that.

Instinctually, my attention is drawn back across the lawn to where Henry is standing, now with a drink in his hand. One of the men is also looking in my direction, but his eyes appear to be on the chicken beside me.

My elbow prods the woman/chicken but she doesn't say a word. The padding of her suit is too thick for her to feel my poke.

"God, this thing is hot," I hear her say a second before a small girl runs up to her and grabs her wing/arm, demanding she dance. Then my newish friend is gone.

I think for a moment about joining them but decide against it. I've had my time in the sun. My princess character was liked at the beginning, but as soon as I declined singing any songs, the kids lost interest in me.

Which, fair. The woman who was playing Moana was absolutely killing it. She was even taking other movie song requests. That level of commitment to a character was admirable.

Sweat pebbled along my hairline as I discreetly made my way to the edge of the lawn. As soon as I stepped into the shade, a little out of sight of the party guests, I let out a deep breath and adjusted the bodice of my costume.

Oh man, layers of polyester and a heavy wig did not mix well with the unexpected heat of the day. I had no idea how my chicken friend was surviving under her feathers. I was shaking my head at the thought of roasting alive in that thing when my gaze landed on Henry. Again.

Why did I keep singling him out of the crowd? After the embarrassing case of mistaken identity, I should be trying to avoid meeting his eyes. But no. I can't seem to stop searching for him.

There's a look of concentration on his face. It's not outwardly grumpy, but his brows are drawn together slightly. I can't help the little giggle that escapes me when he places his hands on his hips, his stance turning stern.

Could he...? No, that's too crazy to...but maybe. Could he be looking for me?

A wave of heat that has nothing to do with the weather rolls through my body, making me very aware of certain body parts.

Did I dare approach him? Talk to him again and apologize for the mistake? Maybe he'd confess why he didn't reveal himself to me right away too.

Take the chance.

The words dance across my mind, repeating over and over, getting louder.

Gathering all my courage, I take a step toward the sun, intending to make my way to Henry.

Someone grabs my arm and I wince at the small sting of pain.

"There you are. I need your help. We have a costume emergency."

My mouth opens, but no words come out. Before I know it, I've been dragged back into the hotel. I give Henry one last look over my shoulder, committing him to memory.

At least our meeting was a memorable one. A good story to tell in the future. Once I got over my embarrassment.

I knew I'd never see him again—besides all the Googling and social media stalking I was going to do once I got home—and I tried to be okay with that. But the deep ache in my chest told me otherwise.

And not even cutting open a chicken costume to rescue a performer from heat exhaustion distracted me enough from my feelings.

4

HENRY

"Have you requested a background check yet?"

My hand tightens on the glass of iced tea I'm holding. It's a miracle the glass doesn't slip through my fingers and fall to the ground with all the condensation. The clouds that threatened to darken the afternoon disappeared as soon as the party started and the sun was now beating down.

"What are you talking about?" I ask my cousin, not bothering to turn to him. We're both doing the same thing—staring across the lawn.

However, I'm confused as to why he's looking at the chicken. I, on the other hand, can't seem to tear my eyes away from Ellie.

"You know exactly what I'm talking about," Simon scoffs. And he's right. I do. "That's the move."

"The move?"

"Yes, when someone sparks our attention, good or bad, that's our move. Our indicator that we're interested."

My lips press together in a concerned frown. He was right again. That was our move. As a member of the Caledonia royal family and a minor celebrity of sorts, we always had to be careful about who we let near us. Especially within our inner circle.

"So…" Simon draws out the word, turning to me with a knowing smile on his face. I wait until my cousin has taken a drink before I decide to respond.

"Yes."

A brow lifts in delight but he doesn't say anything.

Clenching my jaw, I give in and tell him what he wants to know.

"Eleanor Lyn Bailey. Twenty-six, youngest of two children from parents Craig and Mary-Lyn. Master's degree in environmental engineering, with no priors or criminal record. Will that suffice? Or do you want to know her social security number and allergies?"

"It will do for now," Simon jokes. "I'm sure by the end of the week I'll be getting a packet informing me about your new relationship."

Or engagement.

The thought pops into my mind. The idea doesn't shock me, I realize, my lips twisting in a small grin. I really like that idea.

I'm getting ahead of myself, however.

"I hate to say you're right," I begin and stop, leaving Simon hanging. I don't want to give him the satisfaction.

"Bastard," he mumbles quietly, but there's humor in his voice.

"Have you done the same with the"—I pause, not sure how to end my sentence without insulting my cousin or the performer—"the, umm, chicken?"

"Firstly, she's a rooster."

"I'm sure the distinction is very important to her."

"And secondly," Simon continues like I didn't say anything, "no, I haven't. We had a brief encounter on the way here but…" He lets out a long, tired sigh. "She's not…I mean I can't. Shit. Look, things are a little complicated right now."

There's something in his voice that has me giving him my full attention. Placing a hand on his shoulder, I meet my cousin's eyes. I don't know how I missed it. The tiredness and strain on his features.

"What's happening? Is it your brother?" I ask, remembering the family issues we'd talked about months ago.

"No. No. It's nothing really. Jasper is good, I promise. My father has… thrown down the gauntlet, in a manner of speaking, and my carefree days are coming to an end."

Well, that was shocking. King Hector, Simon's father, was a stern but fair man who loved his three sons fiercely. To hear of him speaking to them in such a harsh way was surprising.

My curiosity was piqued.

What could he have possibly been telling them to do? To correct?

Even though King Hector was my uncle, lines were often drawn between what was family knowledge and what were royal secrets.

Words are on the tip of my tongue, my curiosity getting the better of me, when Simon gives me a tight smile and excuses himself. I watch him make his way up the stone patio before disappearing inside the hotel. Something was definitely up with my cousin.

Left to my own devices, I take one last sip of my watered-down iced tea

761

before placing the glass down and beginning a slow walk around the lawn. I say hello to a few people and smile at the delighted squeals of the children. My niece has a huge smile on her face as she dances around with a performer who is dressed like a chameleon.

It's then I notice that Ellie wasn't a part of the party anymore. She wasn't even outside on the lawn. Stopping my slow walk around the perimeter of the party, I anchor my hands on my hips and scan the area again. Where the heck was she?

Swirls of different emotions wash through me. Disappointment at not being in her immediate presence. Confusion as to why she would have left the party. Fear.

The fear that I wouldn't see her again.

I'd never felt so out of control and yet centered at the same time. She was grounding me, making me more aware of the world outside my royal duty while also causing my entire world to upend. It was madness.

These feelings, this strong reaction, was utter madness. But I didn't care.

"Sir, we have to get moving." Jonas appears out of nowhere.

Still scanning the lawn for any sign of Ellie, I give a small nod. As much as I would love to stay and celebrate more with my niece and find Ellie, I have a commitment I have to keep.

In sync, we leave the sunny lawn and make our way through the hotel. Sliding into the back of the dark SUV, I see a folder waiting for me on the seat.

Elation spreads through me. I can't help but smile as I grab the folder and start reading through the pages. Armed with even more information about Ellie, an idea forms in my head. One that is a bit over-the-top but worth the risk.

The papers fall to my lap as I tell my men, "You know what, boys? I think a little break is in order."

5

ELLIE

THERE'S NOTHING A LITTLE SUNSHINE AND A DAY OUTSIDE CAN'T FIX. TURNING my face up to the bright sun, I let out a sigh, releasing all my anxiety from the past day.

Since leaving the real-life princess party, I've been a ball of tension, thinking that the royal guard or secret police would be kicking in my door, putting a sack over my head and throwing me in a dark prison cell. Dramatic? Totally. But it had been a real fear.

I'd only just let my overactive imagination calm a bit when I left my apartment for the first time this morning and made it to work without incident. My huge mistake in bossing around an earl and treating him like a commoner had gone unpunished.

If the rational side of my brain had bothered to speak up this weekend, it would have mentioned that at no point did Henry act like a pretentious royal. In fact, he'd been quite charming. Kind and funny in a way that had made my foolish little heart beat a bit faster.

Not that it mattered now. Obviously that mistake and our embarrassing but I-can-look-back-at-it-now-and-laugh meet-cute was all we'd ever share. It was a good story. I'd just keep it to myself for a couple years until the sting wore off.

Focusing back on the earth around me, I spin around and smile wide, taking in the group of people walking behind me. Their happy faces, tinged with hints of red in the cheeks from exertion, shine back at me.

"All right." I clap my hands, gaining everyone's attention. "Congratulations, everyone! You've just completed the Larkingdom Trail. I'm so proud of all of you, and thank you on behalf of Elevated Adventures for choosing us as your partner in adventure today. We're at the end of the hike now, and the main cabin is just past the upcoming bend. Thank you again for joining me this morning and have a great evening."

Murmurs of thanks and grunts of relief meet my ears as my hikers make their way past me. I count everyone and check their names off my list, confirming that I had everyone who left with me this morning. The hike hadn't been a strenuous one, but four hours of walking was a lot if you weren't used to it. Or if walking wasn't your actual job—like mine was.

Giving Judy, a regular of this hike, a nod of thanks, I check her name off and give the list a second and final scan. Everyone was accounted for and no injuries were sustained. An excellent day indeed.

Tucking the clipboard under my arm, I spin on the toe of my boot and head for Elevated Adventures' main cabin, or Adventure HQ as I like to call it. The large A-frame cabin was my home away from home. Heck, I was here almost as much as I was in my apartment downtown.

The high-beamed ceiling and wall of windows at the back is a comforting sight. There are five of us working today including me, two in the café, one on the floor helping customers with merchandise and one behind the counter.

I wave to all my coworkers as I make my way to the counter. Everyone is all smiles. After logging in to the trail leaders' program we had set up long ago, I enter in all the information from today's hike and mark everyone as safe.

"How was it today?" My boss, Shirley, slides her upper body across the counter, coming to stop beside me.

"Good." I unclip my hiker list and slip the paper into the folder where we keep our hard-copy files for the week. "There was a couple who definitely fibbed on their experience level, and another person who didn't wear the correct clothing for the elevation, but it was fun overall. The peak was gorgeous."

"The colors right now are stunning."

I nodded, thinking of all the flowers in bloom and the sea of green I'd looked out at when we hit the trail's peak.

Resting my upper body on the counter, I grin over at my boss. While Shirley and her late husband did open Elevated Adventures because of their love of nature, Shirley was not a guide. She preferred to run operations from the A-frame and not have to deal with hikers one-on-one for long periods of time.

"How have things been here?" I ask, running my hands over the smooth, dark oak surface of the counter. I listen to Shirley tell me about a humorous interaction with a camper looking for bear spray and get updated about two upcoming hiking expeditions.

I'm scheduled to lead another hike tomorrow that will have me camping out overnight on the mountain. The muscles in my shoulders relax at knowing I'll have something else to distract me tomorrow. It had helped today to be outside and get out of my head, showing others the beauty of the area instead of obsessing about a man I would never see again except for in gossip magazines.

I'm just about to ask Shirley if she could add me to a couple more outings this week when she curses and rounds the counter, leaving me in the blink of an eye. Trying to follow her flurry of movement, my eyes scan past the front door and across—

I double back.

It takes me a stupid amount of time to believe what I'm seeing. At first, I think it's a trick of the light. That I've conjured him here thanks to my overactive imagination.

But that smile. Damn, I would know that smile anywhere.

Holy shit.

Henry Cragnoor, 12th Earl of Caledonia, was at my place of work. An honest-to-God royal had walked in the door. He was standing at the front doors, grinning at me like he didn't have a care in the world.

Holy shit.

Still not truly believing what I was seeing, I slowly straighten from my hunched-over position. With every step he takes toward me, I feel a new flutter in my stomach.

He's almost unrecognizable in a dark green plaid button-down and dark jeans, artfully torn at the knees. I'd thought in a full suit he couldn't be any more good-looking but I was very wrong. There was something about a man in plaid that made my heart beat into overdrive. Maybe it's just a Canadian thing.

His eyes were focused on me as he sauntered his way over. A shine to them had me fighting not to bite my lip. Being the sole focus of Henry Cragnoor was thrilling—and probably one of the scariest things to ever happen to me.

Coming to a stop and interlacing his hands on the counter, he continues to give me a knowing grin. My mouth opens but no words come out. What is happening right now?

"Hello, Ellie." The low tone of his voice sends shivers throughout my body. It both delights and terrifies me.

I know my eyes are wide with shock as I continue to gaze at him without a word. My body seems to have lost all function. *Oh my God, Ellie, what are you doing?*

"Hey." The word is quiet, but drawn out. My brain is still glitching, trying to get back online after this second shock of a lifetime. This man keeps sneaking up on me!

"Did you have a good hike today?" he asks, all innocence and ease.

My vocabulary comes back, slow and a little hesitant, but at least I'm able to form full sentences.

"Yeah, it was a great hike. Spring days like this are the best weather for long trails."

Oh, good one, Ellie. Yes, let's talk about the weather with a freakin' earl. That's a baller move.

Shaking off my total lack of game with this man, I press my body closer to the counter until I feel a sting of pressure and I'm bending over a bit. Lowering my voice, I ask, "Why are you here?"

Following my lead, he leans forward too. I know immediately initiating intimacy like this, getting closer and whispering back and forth, was a mistake. His lean, muscular frame blocks out the store and his fresh scent, something earthy and pure temptation, engulfs me.

If the counter wasn't nailed to the ground and separating us, my face would be pressed into his neck, taking long pulls of his scent, like an addict.

In an equally soft voice he replies, "I would think my reason is obvious."

His words hang between us.

Distracted by how plump and juicy his lips look this close, I don't immediately catch his meaning.

Wait. What? He wasn't saying I was the reason, was he?

"I think I know the reason but I'm not one hundred percent sure. Why don't you tell me?"

God Almighty, he licks his lips. He licks his lips and my body bursts into flames I'm so hot for him. It's such a simple everyday move, an innocent wetting of the lips, but I swear the way Henry does it is full-out seduction. I'm ready to either throw my panties at him or change into a fresh pair. Holy moly.

"I came to see you, sunshine."

It was official, this man was trying to kill me. I had a nickname. He was too handsome and too sweet for his own good.

"Me? Really? Why?"

Chuckling a little, he rocks back on his heels and straightens. "Let me answer those questions in order," he teases. "Yes, I came to see you, Ellie Bailey. And yes, really. Because you made an impression on me yesterday and I would like to spend more time getting to know you."

My eyes must be comically wide, because they're feeling dry. Or maybe it's because I haven't blinked in a while. I'm that stunned. He wants to spend time with *me*? Getting to know *me*?

"You know I'm not a real princess, right? Because if that's why you're here, to secure my father's secret dowry by tricking me into marriage, I'm afraid you have the wrong girl. I come from a long line of engineers, that's it."

"Oh, my plans are foiled!" he cries, throwing his hands up and then smacking them back on the counter. There's no helping it, I laugh with him. It was an absurd thing to suggest. He walks the fingers of one hand over to my side and grabs my hand.

"In all seriousness, I really would like to spend more time with you."

That sounded nice, really nice. There was just one problem.

"I'm booked to lead an overnight camping group tomorrow. It starts pretty early in the morning." I grimace at how lame that sounds, but it's the truth.

Staying up late isn't hard for me, but when it comes to the safety of my hikers, I like to be as rested and alert as possible.

"And after the hike you're here? At the headquarters?"

"Yeah," I say sheepishly. I feel horrible. "Will you be here on Wednesday?"

"No, that's the date I'm to depart."

Silent disappointment hangs between us.

"I'm sorry," I offer, hating that I'm missing this opportunity.

Looking at something over my shoulder, he tilts his head, as if he's thought of something and needs to concentrate.

"If we were to find a magic time to meet and spend time together, is that something you would like?"

"Yes," I blurt out, not needing a second to think about it. I would definitely like to spend more time with him. While Henry was gorgeous on the outside, I also felt that there were more layers to him. He was so much more than an earl with a great face.

And body.

And oh my God his hair.

"Good." He smiles, letting go of my hand and nodding. "Very good."

He turns away. Confused that he's leaving after that declaration, I call after him.

"That's it? You're leaving?"

He begins walking slowly backward. "This is not the last you'll see of me, sunshine. You can count on that." Then, with those last words ringing out across the store, he exits into the setting sun.

That night, as I'm debating on watching one more episode of *Agents of S.H.I.E.L.D.*, my cell rings with Shirley's name. I've been taken off the camping trip. Instead, I'll be leading a private hike.

Well, I'll be damned. He did it.

6

ELLIE

I'M STANDING ON THE EDGE OF THE DIRT PARKING LOT WHEN A BLACK SUV rolls to a stop. My stomach begins to flutter with nerves.

I can't believe this is happening. Henry really did it.

One of the back doors open and a second later Henry hops out. Shooting a quick smile my way, he reaches back in and drags out a large backpack.

The low murmur of his voice reaches me, and I feel a shiver dance its way down my spine.

Oh man, it's already begun. I needed to get myself under control. We were going to be alone together for a six-hour hike, so I needed to at least begin the day on a professional footing.

As Henry approaches, the slamming of his door echoing through the trees, I take in the slight flush on his cheeks from the cold spring air.

His hair is a little wild today, the curls looking unruly and full. I like it. He even looks adorably eager to begin the day.

No, I can't think like that. Crap, what have I've gotten myself into? There was no way I was making it out of this day-long hike without some kind of damage—most likely to my heart.

The sky was clear, the weather brisk and invigorating, and yet, I knew a rocky path was ahead of me. I had to walk that weird line of personal hike tour guide and woman on the edge of total lust. A forbidden civilian to this royal heir.

Or, like, whatever he lorded over.

Henry's words about wanting to spend time with me play over in my head as he stands before me. I wasn't sure if this was something new he was doing or if I truly was special, yet either way, I was looking forward to our time together. That wasn't to say I wasn't a damn catch, but the chances of me ending up with a member of a royal family were super slim. Like, almost nonexistent.

We'd spend a lovely day hiking together, share some personal stories and take in some amazing views, but then we would also part as friends. That's the way it had to be.

Then why does the thought depress me? I was making the emotional rules after all.

"Good morning, sunshine," he says, coming to a stop.

"Good morning, Henry," I say back, quickly losing my train of thought when I see what he's wearing. Oh no, I'm done for. When I'd agreed to do this hike last night, I forgot to take into account one thing: the vest paradox.

It was a proven fact, entirely science-driven really, that when an attractive man put on a moisture-wicking outdoorsy vest, he got twenty times hotter. Thirty if he was wearing a plaid shirt. And God help you if the sleeves were rolled up to expose forearms. There was no coming back for your ovaries if that was the case.

Henry was wearing a damn vest…over a burgundy plaid shirt. A color that brought out the rich texture of his skin.

I was totally screwed.

The clearing of a throat brings me out of my thoughts. I realize my eyeline was…just below his beltline. My cheeks heat and turn an embarrassing red. I'm going to blame it on the vest paradox. It was throwing me off my game.

A strained smile spreads across my face while I give him a little wave. The amusement of how awkward I'm being is written all over Henry's face.

It wasn't just the vest and plaid combo that was grabbing my attention, it was also how…normal Henry looked right now. With his outdoor gear on and a backpack thrown over his shoulder, he looked like your average, run-of-the-mill outdoor enthusiast. Not an earl. Not someone royal.

And wasn't that just shitty of me.

I needed to get over his title or rank or whatever it was that seemed to be glued in my head. I was categorizing him. Holding him hostage in this little box when he was so much more than a title.

I needed to get over my damn self. Henry had done nothing but be a kind and considerate man. He'd also been refreshingly honest about his attraction to me. Who booked a private hike at double the rate just to spend time with them? Henry—that's who.

I promised myself right then that I would give him a chance. We had this opportunity, just us, to get to know one another while seeing some of the most breathtaking sights in Calgary. I was going to take it.

With my mind made up I instantly felt the tension in my shoulders melt and the stress in my smile ebb. As if sensing the change, Henry paused in clipping together the restraints of his backpack across his broad chest and eyed me.

"Need any help?" I asked him, following suit and picking up my backpack, which was resting by my feet.

"No, I think I'm all good."

My head tilts back as I look up at him. The light dizzying flutters that began in my stomach the moment he arrived burst into full butterflies.

He brings a hand up to the side of my face, cradling my cheek. The instant his warm palm touches my skin, I feel electric.

"How are you today, sunshine?"

God, that nickname. I don't care how many times I hear him say it, each time feels special. He makes me feel special.

"I'm good," I whisper back, hypnotized by the sky blue of his eyes. "Are you good?"

One side of his grin tips higher than the other. "Better than good. I'm here with you."

I unintentionally stop breathing, the answer taking my breath away.

On a whoosh of air, disguising my sigh, I step back.

"Good. Great. Fantastic," I ramble, not sure what the hell I'm doing. "How about...we get going? Yes! Let's get going."

Oh my God, Ellie, nice cover. It's not like leading this hike is your job or anything. I internally shake my head at my idiocy.

"Lead the way," Henry says with a sweep of his hand.

So I do. Giving my backpack one little hoist on my back, I turn and head to the trail's opening. There's no going back now. We're really doing this.

Fingering the walkie-talkie that's hooked on the side of my belt, I reassure myself that everything will be okay. Even though Henry and I are the only ones scheduled to hike this particular trail today from Elevated Adventures, I still have a team of people who are looking out for me. Plus, this was a public trail. I'm sure we'd run into other hikers too along the way.

A couple minutes into the hike, surrounded by the quiet of nature with only the crunch of our boots to disturb the peace, my equilibrium returns. I always feel my best when surrounded by nature, out in the sunshine.

"How long have you been leading hikes like this?" Henry's voice floats to me from behind.

"About three years now. I used to live in Toronto—do you know where that is?" His grunt sounds affirmative, so I continue. "With an engineering job. I was supposed to step in and join the family firm. I thought I liked it in the city, you know? But all it took was a visit out here to meet up with college friends and I knew this was where I was meant to be. And then the obsession with hiking took over." I laughed at my own words.

Obsession was putting it mildly. As soon as I discovered Elevated Adventures and found out they were hiring, I applied nonstop until I got the job.

"I can understand that. There's something so humbling, yet so powerful about being out in nature. Back in my country, we have mountains and trails similar to this, and I try to get out and explore them as often as I can."

His words hit me like nothing else ever has. That's exactly how I feel when I'm outside, getting lost in these hills: powerful but humble. I've never felt so small surrounded by these tall trees, decades in the making and yet so strong. They inspire me, making me believe I can tackle any challenge that comes my way.

Licking my lips, I eye him over my shoulder. "And do you? Get out often?"

"No." He shakes his head slightly, eyes turned down to watch his step. "Unfortunately a lot of my duties have me behind a desk. But I'm hoping to change that soon."

That has my curiosity piqued. I'm not able to ask him what he means, instead he asks me a question.

"So is all your family back in Toronto?"

Dread falls like a brick in my stomach. Family was always a sensitive topic for me.

"Umm, I actually don't know."

"What does that mean? How do you not know where they are?"

Usually, this is the point I change the subject. Hell, when someone asks me about my family I often pretend like I don't hear them and continue talking like the question was never brought up.

Yet, I find myself clearing my throat and confiding in Henry. I trust him.

"Well, I know my sister still lives out there, but when I gave up my engineering job and moved out here, my parents didn't...well, they didn't approve. They didn't understand why I would throw away the privileged life I had worked so hard to achieve just to walk in nature all day. Their words, not mine."

He's quiet, taking in what I've said. Turning my head, I see he's looking at me with that little tilt to his head again. There's something in his eyes I can't make out. Is it admiration?

The trail opens up and he catches up to walk beside me.

"That must have been very hard," he finally says, his hand brushing mine. I think it's an accident, a wayward swing of his arm, but when his pinky intertwines with mine my heart skips a beat. He's done it on purpose.

"I know the pressure you speak of. I love my family and the good change my title allows me to create in the world and for my country. But sometimes..." His voice goes soft, almost wishful. "Sometimes I think about what else I could be doing. What my life would have been like if I hadn't been born into my title."

That was…a lot to take in. And he was sharing this with me? That thought alone made me glow from the inside out.

He trusted me.

"That does sound like a lot. But you said you were taking more time now for the things that were important to you. I'm sure you'll find the balance between duty and what sparks joy."

"And is that what this job is for you? Your spark of joy?"

"The job is definitely awesome," I laugh, skipping over the bumpy ground of a tight corner. "But I think it's more about being outside for me. I could do a job like this anywhere in the world and be happy."

He gives a little grunt. I can't tell if it's a grunt of acceptance or if he's concentrating on his footwork.

For the next hour and a half, we steadily climb the mountain, sharing pieces of our lives and our innermost feelings like it's the most natural thing in the world. With Henry, the words tumble out of my mouth, like we've been friends forever.

There's no hesitation as I tell him more about my family and my reasons for needing a break from the city. I feel no shame when I admit that after days of back-to-back group hikes, I need to time to recover and hide out on my apartment balcony.

Henry opens up to me too, sharing with me the side of his family that the public isn't privy to. He tells me wild stories about the mischief he and his cousins—actual princes!—got up to when they were young and how they're like brothers to him.

I learn that although the title of earl comes with many responsibilities and high stress, he doesn't take his privilege for granted.

He has such a big heart. And the higher we climb, the more my heart fills with admiration for him. I won't dare call it anything else.

I can't let myself dream like that.

As we make it to the first peak, stopping to bask in the breath-taking view, a gentle mist of rain begins to fall. The spring shower comes out of nowhere—it definitely wasn't in the weather report I looked at early this morning.

It's not enough precipitation to have us running for cover and grabbing the tarp from my backpack, but it dampens my hair. My gaze turns to Henry and I lose all logic.

His head is tipped up to the sun, arms open with his palms facing the sky. The serene grin on his face makes my stomach flip. He looks so happy. So at peace.

He must feel my eyes on him because Henry extends his hand to me, his head rolling to the side to encourage at me. Without hesitation, I take his hand and go willingly.

With his arm wrapped tight around me, we stand like that, basking in the warm sun and the cool rain. It's a perfect moment.

My heart takes a running leap off the cliff and begins its fall. There's no stopping my growing feelings for Henry now.

7

HENRY

I NEVER CONTEMPLATED THAT A SIMPLE HIKE COULD BE SO LIFE CHANGING.

But that's what this is. A day that I will never forget. With a woman who I never saw coming.

It was funny, really, to think that when we met she was a fake princess, thinking I was her prince. Because in reality, it was the reverse. I had been a royal, faking his way through the day-to-day until she charged into my life. Saving me.

When I came up with this plan to have her lead me on a private hike, my hope was that we would get to know each other and see if what I was feeling was real. If there was a possibility of more with her.

I never expected that minutes into the hike I would know she was it for me. The one. Whatever you wanted to call it. She just made me feel…more. Feel everything.

Like the rain that was gently misting around us, this knowledge didn't wash over me all at once. It was a gradual buildup. With every step we took up this mountain, with every word and thought and feeling we shared, the sentiment grew. Until it burst and I realized I was in deep.

Head-over-heels in love with this woman.

The scariest part was that I wasn't afraid of my feelings at all. It was like every step I had ever taken, every decision and move I'd ever made was to lead me to her.

And the first moment I saw her, ridiculous wig and all, it clicked into place.

Squeezing her tighter into my side, I let out a long exhale. The view is miraculous. Every shade of green and the bright blooms that signalled the start of spring. But it was nothing to the beauty that I held in my arms.

I turn her so that she's facing me, and my eyes meet Ellie's. Her moss-green orbs shine back at me, her lashes dark and wet from the mist. They told me everything I needed, and yet, I had to make sure.

"Ellie," I whisper, my voice low and husky. "I'm going to kiss you. I'm going to kiss you and never stop unless you tell me no right now."

Her eyes flare with surprise at my words. I told her my intentions yesterday, but even I had no idea that I would take this step so soon.

Instead of answering me, Ellie takes matters into her own hands, revving up my desire for her. Grabbing the edges of my open vest, she fists the material and pulls me down at the same time she rises on her tiptoes.

Our lips crash together.

She pushes her tongue into my mouth, kissing me like a starved woman. The thought has me growing hard, thinking about her needing me so desperately. Only me.

My touch turns possessive. I grip her neck a little tighter, pulling her deeper into me so that I can feel all her curves, then I drag my hand down her back.

Ellie's leg lifts, wrapping around me. When she starts to grind on me, I almost lose all reason. I want her, need her with a fierceness I've never experienced before, but I didn't want our first time to be out in the open. Exposed to the elements.

Reluctantly, and with more willpower than I thought myself capable of, I slow our kiss until it turns into gentle pecks.

"We—" She clears her throat, a charming blush reddening her cheeks. "We should keep going. We still have a couple more hours until we hit our destination."

Both my hands come up, each tucking her hair behind her ears before trailing down to cup her neck. With a gentle squeeze, I silently demand her eyes come back to me. She swallows and I know the emotions she's fighting. I'm fighting them too.

"Okay," I tell her, hoping she understands my hidden meaning. If she needs a little more time to get used to the idea of us, I'll give it to her. But I won't back down. When the time was right, I'd show her that our heated kiss was just the beginning.

Releasing her, I take a step back but offer her my bent arm. "M'lady," I joke with her, giving her a slight bow. Her nervous energy instantly vanishes, and she loosens up again. With an exaggerated eye roll and a small smile, she loops her arm in mine.

"M'lord. Shall we?"

"We shall! Lead on."

We both chuckle at our absurd back-and-forth.

Our arms stay linked for only a couple minutes until the trail path grows thinner. Ellie takes the lead, telling me this is the most challenging part of the hike but that the end view will be worth it. From where I'm standing behind her, I already agree the view is spectacular.

My legs begin to burn as we ascend the rocky path and my heart rate kicks up. Splashes of mud begin to cake my shins, and I have to catch myself a few times when I lose my footing. My attention darts back and forth between watching Ellie in front of me and down to where I'm stepping. It might not have rained hard where Ellie and I were resting only minutes ago, but I had the feeling the same couldn't be said for higher up the mountain.

Concerned that this might be getting too dangerous, I open my mouth to ask Ellie if we should stop and consider our options, when I see her teeter to one side. The scene that plays out before me happens in slow motion.

Ellie's upper body sways to the right the exact moment her foot slips off a wet rock. She catches herself, but not before her ankle rolls unnaturally in the opposite direction. There's a ringing in my ears. I don't hear her cry of pain, but I watch helplessly as her face contorts and her body falls to the muddy ground.

"Ellie!" I shout, fumbling toward her as fast as I can. The mud is thick and causes me to slip as I try to get to her. Ellie's hands are clutching her left ankle, her face pale as what's just happened dawns on her. "It's okay. You're okay," I repeat to her, praying my words are true.

I've never felt more helpless in my life. What the hell do I do in a situation like this? I'm unprepared. A pampered fool who has never had to deal with any sickness or injury other than my own. Shit.

Shit.

Shit.

Still holding her ankle, Ellie tips her head back to the sky and lets out a long hissing breath. She's trying to fight through the pain. Hiding it from me. And that's the last thing I want.

"Sunshine, let it out. It's okay. I'm here. I'll help, however you tell me to."

Her face keeps that smooshed grimace of pain for a second longer before it breaks and she cries out.

"Oh fuck. Fuck me that hurts. Ohhh my God."

"That's it. Let it all out."

Tears begin to fall down her face. She starts to rock back and forth.

And I start to really panic.

Trying to play the part of a calm and collected partner, I continue to mutter nonsensical words to her, keeping a reassuring tone. But I can feel bile rising in my throat. What else am I supposed to do here?

"Henry? Henry!" She has to repeat my name in increasing volume before I snap out of my thoughts. Shit, I'm being selfish. Worrying about how to take care of her. "Why do you look like that?"

"Like what?" I try to joke. "Devilishly handsome?"

"No, like I have bone sticking out of my body and you're about to barf."

"THERE'S A BONE—"

"No, you idiot. It's probably a bad sprain. But you look like you've just discovered a dismembered body in a serial killer's kill room. I'm okay, just a bit hurt."

Her words are said with humor, but I know I'm letting her down. I'm the one who should be comforting her, not the other way around.

Fisting my hands and mentally getting myself together, I duck my head. Okay, I could do this. There was no blood, no critical damage other than my pride. I could help.

"Sorry," I tell her softly, shifting closer to her in the mud. "I—I'm not good in situations like this."

"It's okay," she grits out through her teeth.

"It's not, but tell me how I can help you. I'm here for you."

Her pain-filled eyes dart over to mine. I hope she sees my sincerity. I do want to help her. No, I need to. Seeing her hurt and hurting is killing me.

Finally, with her teeth imprinting on her bottom lip, she nods.

"Yeah, okay."

Pushing a strand of wet hair out of her face, I smile, feeling the fist around my heart unclench. "Okay," I repeat. "Tell me what to do."

"Umm, we need to radio for help. There's no way I'm walking back to base headquarters."

Right. We need to end our hike, obviously. My mood takes another dip before I remind myself that this doesn't mean our time together would end.

Awkwardly pulling my backpack off, I start searching the pockets for my cell phone. "Give me the number."

Her giggle catches my attention. "Use this." A moment later a hard, square object is placed in my hand. A radio.

"Wow. I can't believe how horrendous I am at taking care of you," I say, more to myself than Ellie.

Still laughing she agrees with a smirk on her face. "It's cute though, the way you're fumbling. I would have expected you to be an expert when it comes to damsels in distress."

I snort, surprised by the sound but also by how at ease she's making me as I try to help. "Damsels are for princes, sunshine. I prefer woodsy warriors."

Her face softens at my words. The shine of pain leaves her eyes for a minute and is replaced with a sparkle of joy. Holding her gaze for a little longer, I then focus back on the radio. Something pricks my hand.

The small antenna is cracked near the base, making the thick stick wobble.

Gently, I finger the area and hear Ellie gasp when the antenna falls to the ground.

"That's not supposed to happen." Her voice is low; she's shocked at what just happened. "Press the button and see if the radio still works."

I do as instructed, but all that comes through is static.

Dropping her head into her hands, Ellie curses. Unsure what to do now that our only way of communicating with her colleagues is lost, I fall to the side and sit next to her. I place a hand gently on her good leg and give her knee a reassuring squeeze.

I grab my cell phone again and see that I have no signal. I try to send a message through to Jonas, but I repeatedly get an error message. Well, there goes that idea.

Running her hands over her hair and down to the base of her neck, Ellie looks up to the sky. A crack of thunder rumbles overhead.

"I can carry you back," I hear myself saying, trying to offer up solutions.

"I have no doubt you can carry me, Henry, but not for over four hours safely. And not with a storm coming."

"Rain wasn't in the forecast," I say dumbly.

"Mother Nature is a wily and unexpected bitch sometimes. Looks like she's not going easy on us today," she says, pointing up to the darkening sky.

"So what's our next best option? Stay here and wait out the storm?"

Ellie looks around, taking in our surroundings. Her body goes stiff when she spots something. I try to follow her line of sight, and the only thing that looks out of place to me is a green ribbon around one of the far trees.

"Grab the map in my backpack." Her voice shakes me out of my perusal. I do as she asks, not questioning the demand.

When the map is in her hands, she opens it up and starts tracing a line across the paper.

"Fuck," she whispers. "It's far but it may be our best option."

"What is?" I interject into her thoughts.

"There's a ranger's cabin about three miles from here. Which will take about an hour to get to with me on your back." She looks to the sky again. "And if the rain holds."

"Shouldn't we wrap your ankle or something?"

Shaking her head, she responds, "There's no time. We can tend to my ankle when we're safe in the cabin. But we need to go now."

"Then let's go." I wasn't going to question her again. With each second that passed, the sky seemed to grow more ominous.

Standing, I swung my backpack to the front of my chest and put it on backward. After tightening the straps, I extended both arms down to Ellie.

Taking a deep breath to steel herself, she reaches for my hands and I lift her up slowly, making sure she's putting weight on only one leg. She wobbles when she's at a full stand, but I'm right beside her and I won't let her fall.

With a steadying hand on my shoulder, I give her a nod and turn my back to her.

"Do you think you can jump on?" I ask, adjusting my backpack one more time.

She doesn't answer me. Instead she jumps without any warning. I think that's her subtle way of telling me to shut up.

I stagger forward with the abrupt movement and weight. Panic flares in my stomach at the thought of dropping her. With that in mind, I focus on getting my feet stable.

"Jesus," I grunt, finally steady. "A little warning next time, sunshine." Her legs squeeze me tight around the middle.

"We need to go, Henry," she grunts back, her voice filled with urgency.

Doing a little jump so that I can move her up my back a little more for balance and adjusting her legs so they're not poking into my ribs, I take a tentative step forward. All right, everything feels…okay.

I'm not going to say that this will be a walk in the park—because it definitely won't be. It'll be a walk up a mountain during a rainstorm with precious cargo on my back.

But I couldn't think about the journey right now. It was the destination that was important. I needed to get Ellie to safety.

"Point the way," I grunt out at the same moment her legs squeeze me again. It's the sweetest kind of torture, honestly. Having her wrapped around me so tightly and yet not being able to enjoy it. To run my fingers down her strong legs and feel her softness.

"Follow the trail for a little longer. We should come to a fork in the path."

With that instruction, I start out.

Ten minutes later, the sky opens up and everything goes to Hell from there.

8

ELLIE

Pressing my face into the crook of his neck, I fight the urge to cry.

I'm not in overwhelming pain. I'm fighting back all my emotions because Henry is a damn hero. I have no idea how he's doing this.

We're both shivering from the cold rain that hasn't stopped since we started out for the ranger's cabin. From where I'm gripping Henry around his neck, I can see the blue hue of my fingers.

Henry hasn't said a word since the rain began to fall other than to ask me directions and to ensure I'm okay. He's been moving up the mountain like a man on a mission. Like he's lived in these hills all his life.

I sniffle, hoping that he thinks the noise is because of the rain and not because I'm on the brink of tears. This man is too damn good and so damn sweet.

If my heart hadn't already been his, this moment would have clinched it. He was kind and selfless. Stoic but curious about everything around him.

He was too good for me. That much was clear. Even if I took his royal blood out of the equation. But damn did I like him. *Like* like him. A lot.

It was hard to picture a future for us. If that was even something he'd want. I knew he liked me, but I wasn't sure what this was for him. For all I knew, it could just be curiosity on his part. Slumming it with a normal.

I cringed, knowing that's not what this was at all for him. The rain and my throbbing ankle was making me dumb. Henry wasn't the kind of man to play games and lead someone on. He went after what he wanted with single-minded focus.

And right now all that focus was on me.

A shiver of delight, not cold, cascades through my body.

His voice breaks through my thoughts, causing me to lift my head and scan the area.

"There it is."

It takes me a moment to see the cabin through the trees, but as soon as I do, relief hits me. We made it!

Henry's feet slip and slide through the thick mud path that leads to the front door of the cabin. His hold on me tightens as he slows his pace. I can feel his frustration at being so close but having to slow down to make sure he doesn't fall as we near the finish line.

And then, he's done it. He's gotten us to shelter and safety.

The creak of the old wood steps is music to my ears. The pitter-patter of rain hitting my clothes ceases, and Henry comes to a stop.

"You did it," I whisper into his ear, giving his chest a squeeze and then another longer one. I'm so proud.

"*We* made it," he corrects me, his hand coming up to grab my wrist and give it a similar squeeze.

Slowly, he helps me down. My muscles protest as I stretch out my legs and arms. Henry does the same, dropping his backpack and rolling his shoulders to ease the tension that surely built up there from carrying so much.

And wow, he really had carried a lot. There has to be a couple pounds of mud caked on his boots and jeans. He'd had to negotiate uneven ground and hilly terrain all while physically holding me and my backpack and his backpack. Plus the psychological burdens he held on to as well. The pressure to get us here safely. Fear about my injury.

I couldn't imagine everything else he was shouldering for others. Surely the fact that he couldn't get in contact with his team either made him worry about them. He was caring like that.

A thank-you is on the tip of my tongue, ready to burst out along with a few tears. My mouth opens, but no words come out. Sensing my emotions, Henry turns to me and steps into my space. His arms wrap around me, holding me tight against his hard body.

His clothes are wet, we're both caked in mud and slightly shivering. Yet this hug is warming me from the inside out. The simple gesture of needing me close, needing the reassurance that we're here and okay.

Tilting his head down so that his face is buried in my damp hair, he inhales. I do something similar, rubbing my nose against the material of his vest.

With one last lingering hold, Henry releases me in small increments until we're far enough apart that our eyes connect. Pools of dark ocean blue stare back at me, crinkling in the corners and making my heart skip a beat.

The rumble of thunder overhead breaks me out of my trance and brings me back to reality.

"Umm, can you test the door? See if it's open."

Henry doesn't move or say anything for a long moment, continuing to look at me. I take a deep gulp of air when he finally turns around. My God, what was that?

When the knob turns in his grip and the door opens with a long, creepy groan, I tip my head back to the sky and send up a silent thank-you. After all we'd endured today, a B&E wasn't something I wanted to add to my list of new experiences.

Leaving the door wide open, Henry turns back to me. Before I know what's happening he's picking me up and carrying me through the entrance, bridal style.

"Henry!" I cry, surprised. "Let me down. I'm okay to walk."

"No way, I'm not chancing you hurting yourself further. It's only a few more steps, no big deal."

I stop flailing, instead wrapping my arms around his neck. His face is dangerously close to mine, my gaze locking on his full lips. I want to kiss him again. No, I desperately need to, but I couldn't. I wasn't sure if his feelings for me had changed thanks to this disastrous turn of events.

I was more trouble than I was worth now probably.

Tearing my eyes away from temptation, I focus on the cabin. The place was a mess.

Dust everywhere. Knickknacks and other random objects are scattered all over the floor and it looks like the back window has a pane of glass missing.

"An animal must have gotten in and trashed the place." Henry's voice is lined with amusement.

"Why is that funny?" I ask, honestly curious.

"After the day we've had, of course this cabin had an unwanted furry guest." Gently placing me down and making sure I was steady on my own, Henry rights a fallen chair and indicates for me to sit. "I'm going to do a quick walk-through."

I scan the small space. The cabin is literally one room.

"Umm, you realize this is it, right? There's no hidden wings or secret doors that lead to a five-star luxury hotel."

With a quirk of his lips, he nods. "I thought by now you'd stop thinking of me as a spoiled royal. I do realize this is the entirety of the cabin, thank you. I've been in worse."

"No you haven't," I snort in disbelief. My eyes flick up to him when Henry doesn't make a noise. He has an eyebrow raised. "Wait. Really?"

"Yes really," he says, turning his back to me and beginning his search around the cabin. "In my youth I joined my country's military and went through basic training. I vividly remember having to sleep in dirt ditches and waking up so cold I feared I would never be able to wiggle my toes again."

"You were in the military?"

"For about two years. I had to resign when my great uncle passed and more royal duties fell to my family."

The cabin goes silent, the only sounds Henry's steps as he continues to wander the space.

"Do you miss it?"

He stops to contemplate my question, staring out the window. "Yes and no. I miss working with others, being a part of something that was bigger than myself, and the friendships I made. But I know that wasn't the path for me, even while I was a part of it. I loved it," he almost whispers, his head turning to me so that the weight of his words hit me right in the solar plexus, "but it didn't fulfill me."

I understand. I've felt the same way too. The career I had in the city didn't bring me an ounce of fulfillment. It was only when I came here to Calgary and surrounded myself with nature that that spark finally consumed me.

To know that Henry had also felt this need, this desire to discover more from life just anchored me to him further.

He claps his hands together to break the tension in the room and opens his arms wide. "Looks like the furry invader is no longer here. I say we start to settle in for the night and get cleaned up."

"Oh man, yes. I feel like the mud on my clothes is turning to ice. I'm so cold."

Henry laughs his agreement, grabbing his backpack from the floor and placing it on the bed.

It hits me then. We're going to be spending the night here. Together. Alone.

I turn my head to look at the far corner of the room. And there was only one bed.

9

HENRY

I KNOW THE EXACT MOMENT SHE PUTS IT TOGETHER. THE FACT THAT THERE IS only one bed.

One very small bed and two of us.

It goes against my gentlemanly instincts not to ease her mind and offer to sleep on the floor or somewhere else in the cabin. I know that's what I should do. Yet I don't.

There really is no other place to sleep in here. The floor is definitely not an option. The dust alone would probably kill me or cause a kind of lung illness that I did not want to sign up for.

From the corner of my eye, I watch as Ellie pauses in untying her boot laces. Her body stiffens and she jerks her head to the side, focusing her attention to the area of the room I'm in. On the bed.

She stays like that, staring at the bed, for what I believe is a full minute. I struggle to keep my expression neutral as I go about pulling out the extra clothing I packed. When I have the extra pair of socks out of my bag along with the baggies of food I had packed for lunch, I finally break the silence.

"Do you need help? You haven't moved in a while." Her mouth opens but her gaze never wavers. "Are you in pain?"

That has her expression clearing. "No. No, sorry. I just—" She clears her throat. "I just realized a couple of things."

"And those would be..." My voice trails off, but I can no longer hide my amusement from her.

"That there's one bed and we both only have the clothes on our backs."

I hadn't factored in a full change of clothes. It wouldn't be smart to stay in our wet clothes. While the thought of losing items of clothing with Ellie was appealing, this was not the time.

"And the bed's a problem?"

"No, not a problem just…inconvenient maybe? But really, it matches the luck we're having today." She rubs the back of her neck, brow bunched.

I feel like an asshole. Here I am delighting in the fact that our circumstances are going to help me get to know her better while they only cause Ellie stress. Her face is pale and her shivering has intensified.

In four quick strides I'm by her side, crouching down and reaching for her hand.

"Is the bed thing really that bad?"

"No, it's not that. It just all hit me. This clusterfuck of a day. And now we're trapped here until the storm lets up with barely any food and no change of clothes." She lets out a long sigh, running a hand down her face. "Sorry," she mumbles. "I'm being—"

I cut her off, not wanting to hear her brush off her valid concerns.

"You're right. It has been a clusterfuck of a day. But you know what? I wouldn't have wanted anyone else by my side but you. In between the moments of chaos you've shown me absolute beauty, shown me the value of quiet, and you've become one of the best people I know. You got us out of that storm and here to safety."

"I'm the one that got hurt and broke our only means of calling for help."

I wave that away. Placing a hand under her chin, I gently tilt her head up so that she can see the sincerity in my eyes.

"None of that was your fault. Shit happens. And we're here now. I for one couldn't be more grateful for the extra time I get with you."

Her lashes flutter, and a nice rosy stain fills her cheeks, making something unclench from around my heart. With bated breath, I watch as her hand lifts and comes to the side of my face. Thumb scraping along my stubble, she nods, giving me a small grin.

"The extra time is nice," she whispers.

Having her hands on me feels electrifying. I never want it to end.

But I need to take care of her first. Get her cleaned up and warm.

Covering the hand that is on my face, I beam at her and bring her palm down to my mouth. I gently kiss the center of her hand. She lets out a shaky exhale.

"Good. I'm glad you feel the same, sunshine." Reluctantly, I place her hand back down in her lap and stand. "Now, let's see if I can find any extra clothes or blankets that we can use. You need to get warm and staying in those clothes is not an option."

"What about you?"

I give her a cocky grin, wanting to hear the magic of her laugh again. "I'm sure you'll enjoy the view."

My words have the desired effect. She rolls her eyes playfully as a small giggle rings through the cabin.

It takes more time than I care to admit to spot the small closet that holds shelves of linens and bulky sweaters. Everything is packed in sealed bags and seemingly clean.

We both let out little cheers of relief and the tension I was unknowingly holding in my shoulders disappears. We'll make it through the night without turning into human popsicles now.

Helping Ellie into the small bathroom, I hand her a change of clothes along with two towels. There's a shower but we're both unsure of the water situation.

While she's in there, I make myself useful and begin lighting candles and lamps around the room. The storm is casting a dark shadow through the cabin and soon we'll lose all light as evening creeps closer.

Needing to get rid of some extra pent-up energy, I go about cleaning up the cabin as I wait for Ellie to appear again. I find a roll of duct tape in a kitchen drawer and cover up the hole in the window. It solves the draft problem for tonight but definitely isn't a permanent fix.

The small squeak of the bathroom door has me turning to see a refreshed Ellie hopping out.

"Careful, sunshine," I say, going to her side. She looks insanely hot and ridiculous in the oversize sweater and large sweatpants. Both items are so big on her that she's rolled them at the wrists and ankles.

"I'm fine, Henry, honestly."

I give her a grunt, not agreeing. She'll be better once her ankle is wrapped and I can assure myself it's not a break like I initially feared. I think I'll play back her falling down for years to come and still lose my breath every time.

She laughs at me as she twists and sits on the bed.

"I see you've made the bed." Her voice has gone a little husky.

"Figured you'd rather lie in bed than sit in that uncomfortable wooden chair for the rest of the night. Now, let's see that ankle," I say as a way to distract her from realizing that I'll be joining her in this bed shortly too.

Scooting back on the mattress until her back is leaning against the headboard, she pulls up the leg of the sweatpants.

I hiss. Her ankle is swollen and colored with bruises.

"Ellie," I whisper. "You should have told me it was bad."

Her tone matches mine, quiet and low. "It's not bad, I promise. It looks worse than it is."

"On a scale of one to ten, how bad is the pain?"

She bites her lips, a contrite look coming over her face.

"On the way here, it was a solid eight. But after resting and sitting down for bit, I'm sure it will go down to a four now."

A four gutted me. Hell, I would probably feel like an asshole for not taking better care of her if she was at a two. I hated that she was in any kind of pain.

I needed to push that aside though. Grabbing the first aid kit I had found with the duct tape, I pulled the kitchen chair over and angled myself so that I could easily reach her bad ankle.

"You should have said something earlier."

"Well, a lot was happening earlier."

Upon opening the kit, the first item I went for was the bottle of ibuprofen. I shook two pills out and handed them to her before grabbing my water bottle. Without protesting Ellie threw back the pills with a gulp of water.

I give her a nod of approval. She gives me a glare.

Loving the attitude she's throwing at me, I shake my head with a satisfied smirk.

Next, I go for the hot-cold pack. I snap it in half to activate the liquid inside and place the quickly heating pack on her ankle.

"Go get cleaned up." She waves me away once I get the pack balanced on her leg.

I think about it and decide she's right. I am uncomfortable in these wet clothes, and I can't do much for her while the pack is heating her ankle.

With a quick "Fine," I grab the extra clothes that I thought would fit my frame and head to the bathroom.

By the time I'm changed and as clean as I can get, the hot-cold pack has lost its effect. Ellie doesn't say anything, just gives me a knowing smile when I pull out the roll of gauze next. Unrolling the end, I meet Ellie's eyes and she takes a deep breath before silently giving me her consent.

As carefully as I can, I lift her foot just enough so I can get under it and begin wrapping her ankle. I go a bit overboard, using the whole roll, but I don't care. I'd rather her ankle be overly supported than have her be in any discomfort.

I'll unwrap and help her ice the area again later with the last hot-cold pack, but for now, we'll rest and wait for her pain meds to kick in.

"Thank you."

Running two fingers gently down her shin and hovering along her ankle, I then unroll the leg of her sweatpants again so that she doesn't catch a chill.

"No problem, sunshine."

"Are, um, you going to join me up here?"

"Definitely." I grin at her, closing the first aid kit. "Just going to put this away and grab us some snacks. That sound good to you?"

"Yeah, real good."

I like her answer. It gives me hope that the bond we began developing the first time we met and throughout today was still there and going strong. This may not be how I saw the day ending, but I was being given more time with the woman who fascinated me.

I grab the snacks I had packed for the day and the half-dozen granola bars that I found buried at the bottom of Ellie's backpack. There's a crate of water bottles at the far end of the cabin and some canned goods, but I'm going to try to go through our stuff first before eating the ranger's food.

I pass over her refilled water bottle with the small filtered nozzle and throw all my snack bags plus the sandwich container up onto the bed.

"Did you really pack gummy bears?" Ellie asks, trying to claw for the bag but not able to reach it.

"Absolutely. Gummy bears are the best. I'm addicted."

"Addicted?" she snorts. "There's no way you can be addicted to gummy bears and still look like you do."

"There's a compliment in there somewhere," I tease back, failing to act offended.

"I mean," she begins as I crawl onto the bed and work my way up to the headboard. I expect her to continue but the silence continues.

Flipping myself over, I sit back and twist my head to her. She's staring at me in a strange way.

"Are you going to finish that sentence?" She shakes her head, eyes lingering down my body. "Are you okay?"

"Did...did you pick those sweatpants on purpose?"

Confused I peek down at the gray sweatpants I grabbed to change into earlier. "Is something on them? Do they say 'assman' or something on the butt?"

"N-no." She pauses, finally making eye contact with me. "Don't you know that gray sweatpants are a woman's ultimate weakness?"

"Sweatpants?" I respond, thinking she's pulling my leg. "That's a joke, right?" Pinching the material, I try to think back on if I've ever heard anything like this. I thought a man in a tux was the ultimate fantasy.

"You've never heard that? Or seen, like, memes or whatever about gray sweatpants."

I shake my head. "I guess I've been living under a rock."

"A royal rock," she murmurs with a smile.

"The mouth on you," I tease, turning my upper body fully toward her and giving her side a little tickle. She squirms away just enough to escape my fingers but not upset her injured foot.

"I'm serious!" she cries, laughter filling every corner of the cabin. "If my phone was working right now I would totally prove it. It's a thing!"

"Fine. I believe you, but it seems like a weird thing to be turned on by."

Her eyebrows rise and her eyes flare, mocking me and my disbelief. "Eat your granola bar." I laugh with her, tossing the snack in her direction.

For a couple minutes we eat in silence, opening baggies and sampling each other's snacks.

"I guess this isn't how you thought the day would end, huh?" Ellie tries to make light of the situation, but I can hear the note of insecurity in her voice.

Finishing my bite of pretzel, I look across the room and watch rain drip down the window. There's barely any light outside now and the storm rages on. The candles flicker, casting long shadows around the room.

I've taken too long to reply to her, and Ellie flicks the baggie that's in her lap and begins to fidget uncomfortably.

Stopping her hands from wringing over and over, I grasp one and hold it tight, intertwining our fingers and setting my hand down on her upper thigh.

"Actually"—I take a deep breath, drawing on my courage to tell her the truth—"this *is* what I had imagined."

Her head jerks to me, brow quirked. She definitely doesn't believe me.

"I had hoped that after our hike today that I could convince you to have dinner with me. I knew that only a day with you wouldn't be enough. I knew that the first time we met and I knew it the moment we headed out today. There was this moment when you turned back to look at me, with this wide smile on your face and your eyes sparkling with joy and I knew. Knew I'd have to drum up my courage to ask you for more time."

Her expression of disbelief has fallen into one of shock. Ellie's lips are softly parted, her eyes shimmering.

"And honestly, I never thought we'd end the day in bed together so I have to say, all in all, it's been an exceptional day."

"You really mean that, don't you?"

"Mean what? That it's been a great day?"

"No, that you never expected to end the day in bed with me."

Licking my lips, I try to think of the best way to answer.

"I, ah, would never presume anything like that. I won't lie and say it didn't cross my mind, but I wanted to take my time."

She makes a thoughtful noise.

"This surprises you?"

"Yes," she says before quickly changing her answer. "I mean no." Covering her face with her hands, Ellie takes a deep breath then turns to me. "I just mean, I'm sure you're used to women throwing themselves at you and moving a little…faster."

It's my turn to make a thoughtful noise.

"Maybe. But women do not throw themselves at royals. That's what we pay our security guards the big bucks for. I'm generally more accustomed to the long con."

"How the heck did I slip by your guards then?"

"I guess I got really lucky that day."

Her lips twist up in a small smile, her head dipping a little. "I did too," she says on a whisper.

The cabin lights up with a flash of lightning. A rumble of thunder rolls through the sky next, making us jump. Her hand shoots out to me, clutching the fabric of my sweatshirt and twisting.

I place my hand over where she's holding me, reassuring her with a touch.

"God, this storm is nasty." Her voice is a little shaky. It hits me then that maybe I haven't asked the right question yet.

"Do storms make you uncomfortable?"

She doesn't hesitate. "A little. It's more the lightning than anything." Her hand slowly untwists from my shirt but I don't let her pull away. Instead I bring her hand up to my lips and give her a light kiss.

The move is innocent at first. Wanting to calm her as the storm rages on outside. But at her quick inhale and the slight tremor that worked its way through her body, I couldn't stop there. One kiss to the back of her hand, another to her palm, then wrist.

A low moan comes from her parted lips, and I can feel myself getting turned on by the tempting noise. I want to hear more. I want to cause more little sounds of pleasure from her.

"Henry," Ellie sighs, twisting closer to me. "I want—I want more."

"What do you want?" I demand softly. I need her to say the words.

"I want you to—to kiss me again."

Conscious of her ankle, I pull away from her for a moment. She makes a sound of protest but it's quickly cut off when I scoop her from her side of the bed and drape her over my lap. I grab one of the pillows that was supporting her back and place it under her bad foot.

Then I get back to taking care of my girl.

10

ELLIE

HE LEANS IN, CLOSER AND CLOSER UNTIL I CAN FEEL THE HEAT OF HIS BREATH. Then, finally, he gives me the sweet relief of contact. Our lips meet in a soft kiss, parting on a content sigh.

His lips feel perfect on mine. So worth the anticipation.

The kiss turns devious when his tongue sneaks past his teeth and gently licks along the seam of my mouth, then, when he slips his tongue in to dance with mine, I moan.

One of my hands tangles in his hair as the other one twists in his large sweatshirt. His kisses are addicting, teasing softly one minute and pressing deep the next. I could do this all night.

Evidently, Henry had other plans. He starts to slow the kiss down, his hand working its way beneath my top. The feel of his cool hands on my skin has me jumping at the sensation.

"I've got you," he says, voice low and husky as he drags his nose down my hairline.

My mew of disappointment turns into a high-pitched squeal when his hand pulls my sweater up and over my head. His shirt goes next. Laughing, I reach for his face and bring him back to me.

"God, you're so beautiful, sunshine."

My hands slip up his chest to wrap around his neck. The hair on his chest tickles my palms but I love the feeling. His rough to my soft. I nip at his bottom lip, and he growls at the action.

The ache that has slowly been building in my abdomen turns into a full-fledged fire. I'm so turned on by Henry's kisses, his touch and grumbly voice that I can feel the slickness between my legs. I'm wet for him, embarrassingly so.

I open my mouth, wanting to demand more. Wanting to demand everything, when Henry anticipates my needs. Carefully but rapidly, he rolls us down onto the bed, this time with me under him.

My lust-heavy eyes scan down his body, landing on the bulge that's straining against his gray sweatpants. If I didn't like gray sweatpants before, I love them now. Trailing my hand lower, rubbing the edge of the material before dipping my hand inside, I flick my eyes up to Henry's.

The blue eyes that so easily hypnotize me are a deep blue now, full of hunger. And it's all for me.

Wrapping my fingers around his hard shaft, I feel a surge of power when he curses out my name. He guides my hand up and down his thick cock, and I explore every inch of him. His skin is smooth and silky, hot to the touch and throbbing.

"Sunshine," he grunts, pumping into my hand once, twice, before grabbing my wrist and pulling me away.

His hands are pulling at my sweats next. They come off easily, but we're both conscious of my ankle even as we hurry to take our clothes off. Henry nuzzles my neck as he lays me back down on the bed then presses a trail of kisses down to my breasts.

My back arches off the bed when his tongue flicks my nipple, which has turned into a hard peak at his touch. I try to reach for his cock again but lose all train of thought when he turns his attention to my other breast, nipping the bud.

"Shit," I cry, the sensations rippling through me. My hands clutch at his shoulders. "What are you doing to me?" I ask, shocked by how well he's reading my body.

"I'm loving you," he whispers back, capturing my mouth again. "Are you ready for me, sunshine?"

"Yes." I nod.

"Do I need to get the condoms I saw in the first aid kit? I haven't been with anyone in quite some time."

"Me neither. And no." I swallow, having told him a secret. "I have an IUD. I want to feel all of you. Every inch."

Running both hands down my shin, taking care not to press on my ankle, he lifts my leg. Placing it over his shoulder so that my knee is bent at the top, he eyes my core.

"You will keep your leg here. Do you understand, sunshine? I don't want you hurting yourself more."

"Yes, I understand. But I'm hurting now, Henry," I whine, giving him a little pout. "I need you."

"I'll be careful," he says, adjusting himself closer to my wet core. "But I have to be inside you."

"Yes. Please, Henry." I nod again eagerly.

With my good leg propped up gently to the side, he begins to push into my tight opening. There's a slight burn as he begins to pump, working his way inside me. It's a delicious sting, making me feel alive and so desirable.

The throb between my legs intensifies with each of his slow thrusts. I try to be patient, but I need more. I lift my hips, encouraging him to move faster. The pain in my ankle is gone now, all there is now is him. And so much pleasure.

"Henr—" I cry, only to get out a part of his name.

He shifts, his hand slipping between us. His fingers go to my clit. A groan leaves him as my sex starts to flutter around his cock as he strums my clit. I'm close. So, so close.

I sink my nails into his back as erotic delight explodes through my body unlike anything I've ever felt in my entire life. My hands claw at the sheets. I can feel my whole body shaking, quaking as my orgasm builds up and up, until I burst. Pleasure crashes over me.

He keeps pumping in and out of me, making me moan his name over and over. His body jerks as he comes along with me, his warmth spilling deep inside of me.

He collapses on top of me, being careful of my ankle. He buries his face in my neck, and his warm breath tickles my skin, making me smile.

He nips my neck. My sex contracts again around his cock that's still inside me.

"That," he says against my skin before pulling back to meet my eyes, "was incredible. You're incredible." His voice has gone soft, his eyes reverent. The emotion I see twinkling in his eyes takes my breath away.

"It was," I sigh, skimming my hand down his back. "And it's a good thing we're alone, stranded in the middle of the woods."

"Why is that?" he asks, placing a finger under my chin so that I look back at him.

"Because you're loud."

He's stunned at my words, his face going slack for a moment before he ducks his head and laughs.

"I'm loud? You're the one who was chanting my name."

I smack his shoulder, faking being insulted. Before I can say anything more he covers my mouth with his, drawing me into a long, sweet kiss.

It was a life-changing kiss. A toe-curling, full-body shiver kind of kiss. And at that moment, I knew I loved Henry with every fiber of my being.

It was too bad happily ever after wasn't a path we could take.

11

ELLIE

It's not the chirping of birds that stirs me from sleep. No, it's an unnatural sound. A hum but with no melody.

Squinting an eye open, I instantly regret my decision. The room is too bright, beams of sunlight coming in through every uncovered window. Groaning, I turn away from the offending light.

And hit a wall of warmth.

An arm snakes its way around my waist, pulling me in closer until I'm pressed against a hard, hot chest. Lips skim along my hairline, peppering kisses. A grin spreads across my face as I snuggle just an inch closer.

What a way to wake up.

Henry continues to kiss down my face and neck, causing shivers of delight and a low laugh from me. Then the low hum sounds again.

We both freeze. I angle my head back so I can meet his eyes, and we listen, both confused and trying to make out the sound.

"Shit. That's my cell," Henry huffs as he tries to untangle himself from the sheets.

I'm no help at all, too stunned to move as I process his words. My eyes follow a naked Henry as he rushes across the room to his discarded backpack. It takes only a second of searching before he has his cell in his hand and answers.

As he speaks quietly to whoever, his eyes never leave me. I glow under his admiration but there's a sick feeling building in my stomach. Our time together is coming to an end. It's time to get back to reality.

Sitting up, I fix the sheets around me and force myself to keep the happy smile on my face. Even though my mind is whirling with what this call means. Realistically, I knew our time here in this cabin would be short.

Even if the storm had continued today, I had no doubt Henry's team and my boss would have called in more help to retrieve us. And I knew that the private time Henry and I were able to enjoy as we got to really know one another was finite too.

Yet, knowing and hoping we could steal another day were two very different things.

I wasn't ready to go back. I wasn't ready to say goodbye to Henry or lose this connection we'd forged. But the real world was calling.

The real world where an earl and a wilderness guide couldn't be together.

Right?

"That was the head of my security," Henry says, stopping my thoughts from catastrophizing any further. "Your boss and the local ranger will be here with my guys within the hour."

I know not to question how they'll get here or if the area is safe. If Henry's team says they're coming, they're coming by any means necessary.

"Okay," I reply on autopilot. What else is there to say? "Can you check to see if our clothes are dry?"

Henry doesn't acknowledge my question, instead coming to the side of the bed and sitting so he can easily reach me. With a firm grip to the back of my neck, he crashes his lips against mine.

I'm so stunned it takes me a moment to kiss him back. The kiss is hard, possessive. I can feel his claim all over my body and give him the same passion back.

The kiss slows, then ends with a series of small pecks before he rests his forehead against mine.

"Stay with me," he whispers to the air between us. "Don't leave me yet."

His words are full with so much meaning, my heart breaks a little. He saw the look of unease in my eyes, he must have. He knew I was starting to pull back. Yet he's asking for more time.

And I'll gladly give it to him.

Because I love him.

This may be the last time we'll ever have alone. And this may be the last time we'll ever see each other. But even so, I won't let this moment slip away. I'll show him how much I love him and how much our time together meant to me.

And then I'll let him go.

As he slips back into bed, his hard, gorgeous body sliding over mine, I cata- logue every feeling, every emotion, every touch to memory. We make love slowly, but the sensations are stronger than ever before.

When we come together, I know I've been changed for the better. Gripping his hands tight, I hold his stare as my orgasm crashes over me.

We linger in bed as long as we can but with only a handful of minutes left before the others arrive, we reluctantly begin to get dressed. Our clothes are damp but they'll be good enough to get us down the mountain. Plus, I don't mind at all how Henry's shirt clings to his chest.

My ankle is still tender, but the swelling has gone down and there doesn't seem to be more bruising. That's a good sign at least. I still can't put a lot of weight on it, but at least no one else will have to piggyback me around.

When we've both finished dressing and packing our things, we silently move toward each other. My arms go around him and I take a deep breath.

Then, before I'm ready, our time is up. Half a dozen people enter the cabin in a flurry of movement and questions. We're swarmed by medical professionals, men in dark suits and ranger uniforms.

I try to protest as I'm being helped out of the cabin and toward a large vehicle with tires that are almost as big as me. Turning my head side to side, I search out Henry. When our eyes meet, I can see he's surrounded by people too but being led in the opposite direction.

He calls my name.

I smile at him, giving the last piece of my heart to him as we say our silent goodbyes. My smile is genuine. I'm sure he can see everything I'm directing at him. My eyes pool with tears and my smile turns shaky but I incline my head by the tiniest degree.

I can't read Henry's expression as I'm led away. There's no time to figure it out either. In the next second, I'm being hoisted into the vehicle, buckled in and driven away.

I stare at Henry through the tinted glass for as long as I can before he disappears from sight.

And, most definitely, from my life.

12

ELLIE

AN UNKNOWN NUMBER HAS CALLED ME TWICE TODAY. AND FOUR TIMES yesterday.

And a dozen times the day before that.

I know it's Henry, but I can't allow myself to pick up.

What's the point?

Our adventure in the Calgary mountains made the national news. While I hadn't been hounded by the media—good luck finding me holed up in my apartment, eating my feelings—my cell had blown up with calls and messages.

On the first day that Henry had started calling me, I had memorized the number. So it wasn't hard to reject the other numbers that called. It had been half a week since Henry and I had been together, lost in the mountains and blissfully happy.

It was tempting to pick up the call. It would be so easy to fall back into Henry, get swept away by him, with his charming smile and his caring nature, but I couldn't let myself. One syllable of his sexy accent and I would be goo in his hands.

I was already too big of a mess after falling in love with him after knowing him only three days. How much more of a heartbroken disaster would I be if I spent more time with him?

The room goes silent when my cell stops vibrating on the coffee table. I stare at the stupid thing, willing it to ring again. Maybe if it does I'll pick up this time.

Who am I kidding? His calls are coming less and less each day that passes. I know he's still in the city, I've been watching the news and stalking him on social media, but tomorrow he's leaving. Heading back to Caledonia and away from me for good.

And that was fine.

I was fine.

Everything. Was. Great.

The prickle of impending tears tickles the backs of my eyes and I fight it. I can't believe there's enough water in my body to even make tears. I've been crying so much over the last few days and not really taking care of myself. I don't remember the last time I had a non-chip bag meal or a sip of water.

With my sprained ankle and emotions all over the place, Shirley gave me a week off from Elevated Adventures and then allowed me to work from home until I was fully healed. Sitting in front of a screen and doing paperwork wasn't my idea of fun, but it allowed me to feel a little useful and got my mind off a certain someone for a bit of time.

With a long, dramatic sigh, I tear my eyes away from my cell and focus back on updating EA's website. I've just clicked save on the upcoming hike schedule when there's a loud pounding on my front door.

My body instantly freezes while my brain goes into hyperdrive. Who could that be? Why were they here? Could it be Henry? I didn't let myself think about how that last question made my heart rate pick up.

My laptop falls of my lap and onto the sofa when I realize the person at the door is actually jiggling the handle. Shit. Had I locked it when I staggered in days ago?

The answer to that was no. A huge fucking no.

My front door swings open and the person who steps through has me sitting up at attention.

"What are you doing here?"

Hands swiftly going to her hips, Shirley gives me a look that's a mixture of annoyed and fed up.

"What the hell do you think I'm doing here? I'm checking in on you." She grimaces as she looks around my apartment. "And from the look of things"— she pauses—"ew."

I roll my eyes at her. "It's not that bad," I say in defense, giving myself a moment to take in my place through another's eyes.

Okay, sure. There were a lot of containers on my kitchen counter and yeah, I had about half a dozen mugs lined up on my coffee table, but the place wasn't smelly or anything. I didn't have food on the floor or stains on my shirt.

I discreetly looked down at my chest. Yup, no food stains.

"Oh honey," she said sarcastically, "it's cute that you think that. But this is level four heartbreak."

"How many levels are there?" I pray for more than ten.

"Five."

Shit.

"I'm fine, Shirley."

She makes her way through the apartment and after rounding the sofa, she sits beside me. Or tries to. She has to flick multiple peanut butter cup wrappers to the ground before she can comfortably glare at me.

"No, you're not, Ellie."

My mouth opens, ready to tell her again that everything is fine and I'm healing, but I stop. There's legitimate concern on her face. Shirley is a hard shell to crack and a very blunt woman, but once you're in her circle, she's as protective as a mama bear.

I can't lie to her. And I can't keep lying to myself.

Pressing my lips tight together, I let the emotions I was holding back come to the surface.

"I'm not okay," I whisper seconds before the floodgates open. Awkwardly, Shirley opens her arms and I fall right into them. Clinging to the soft fabric of her blouse, I tell her everything.

While it feels good to get the story out, it's also bittersweet to relive the memories. I can so vividly recall the feel of Henry's stubble across my fingertips. The deep timbre of his laugh. By the time I'm finished, I'm more exhausted than I've ever felt in my life.

"You love him," she says simply, letting her words hang in the silence of the apartment.

Lifting my head from the tissue I was wiping my tear-streaked face with, I scowl at her. That's all she got from the story? That I loved him? Captain Obvious much?

"So what are you going to do about it?" she continues, like the answer is simple.

Sniffling, I scrunch up my face and blink at her. Wasn't she supposed to be a supporting shoulder to cry on? Someone to nod and agree with every decision I've made and top up my glass of wine? If I was drinking wine, that is.

"Ex-excuse me?" I ask her through hiccups.

"I asked what you were going to do about it. This whole sad act is kind of pathetic."

Straightening from my slouched position, I gasp at her. "I am not!"

She leans back, slowly and purposefully raising one eyebrow. Goddamn her.

"I'm not," I say again at a more reasonable volume. "I had my moment in the sun with Henry but there was no future for us."

"He said that?"

"No, but—"

"And you believe it?"

"Well, it wouldn't be easy so I—"

"Honey, I love you. You've been like a daughter to me over these last three years. A true godsend. But right now, you're being incredibly stupid."

Shocked at what she's saying and completely insulted, I jump up from the sofa and begin pacing. My ankle protests at the sharp movement and I slow down, going from a stomp to an agitated slow walk. I round the sofa once, twice, my fingers lost in my wild hair as I squeeze my temples with the palm of my hands.

I'm sputtering, trying to find the right words to defend myself. But the longer I pace, the more sense Shirley makes. I don't like thinking that I'm a coward, yet that might be exactly what I am.

Did I make up my mind without weighing all the options?

Had I imagined words in Henry's mouth? Tearing us apart before he got the chance to tell me what he wanted? What he was feeling?

I'd run away before the real fight began. I *was* a coward.

My hands drop to my sides and a new wave of tears takes me. I topple back on the sofa, my impact causing Shirley to bounce on her side.

"What have I done?" I moan into a pillow, squeezing it tight to my face.

Shirley curses beside me. A moment later, the pillow is yanked from my arms and I watch it soar across the room.

"Get your ass up and go."

"Shirley, I love you, but you're being really mean to me today," I whine to her.

"Stop your complaining. You'll thank me later for this tough love once you've gotten your man back."

Rolling my eyes and silently asking for divine intervention, I take a long, shaky breath and try to reason with Shirley.

"It's too—"

"Goddamn it, Ellie! When did you become this sad sack of whiny bones? Where did the fierce woman I hired three years ago go? The one who was scared shitless but still moved across the country to follow her heart? The one who started from scratch but showed up every day ready to learn? Where's that woman? Huh?"

Eyes wide in disbelief, I stare at Shirley as she gathers herself. I'm not sure if I should be insulted (again) or flattered by her impassioned speech. I'm still processing her words when she speaks again.

"Don't let fear stop you this time, Ellie. If you love him, isn't he worth fighting for?"

He was. The words echo across my mind and shoot directly into my heart, causing a burning sensation to spread through my chest. He was worth fighting for.

With a new determination, I stand, ready to go get my man.

"For the love of God, please shower first," Shirley yells at my back as I march into the bedroom. I pivot quickly, one hand on the door, and glare back at her before slamming the thing in her face. I can hear her laughter, and it does lighten my mood again, but I can't stop now.

I have an earl to win back.

13

HENRY

"Is this where all the grumpy men meet now?"

I hear my cousin's comment but don't look away from the spot on the wall I've been staring at for the last...however long. The only outward sign I give that I heard Ambrose's stupid joke is a low grunt.

"Fuck off," my other cousin, Simon, snaps from his wingback chair near the balcony doors. The glass of whiskey he had been staring into a while ago is now a glass of ice he's frowning at. We've both really progressed over the last hour.

My mood is in the gutter. And my heart...shit, it's hanging on by a thread.

"Wow. What a warm welcome to the club."

From the corner of my eye I see Ambrose take a seat on the sofa across from me. At first, I don't acknowledge him, but I can feel his stare. Something is eating at him.

Interlocking my fingers and letting them hang in the center of my chest, I turn my attention from the fascinating spot on the wall to him. There's an annoying smirk on his stupid face that I instantly want to smack off. He may be the future king, but as one of my best friends who I think of as a brother, I had no problem bringing him down a peg or two.

"What is wrong with you? Why do you look like that?" Simon demands at his brother from across the room. Not one to be left out, my other cousin flings himself from his chair and makes his way over to us, passing the beverage cart without stopping. He doesn't sit, instead bracing a hand on the fireplace and staring down into the low flames.

"I don't look like anything but what I am." Ambrose smiles. "A handsome prince with a secret."

"You're a gossip whore is what you are. Such an unbefitting trait for a royal."

"Shut it, Simon. The gossip is for Henry."

"Me? What could you possibly have to tell me?"

The room falls into silence as I wait for Ambrose to tell me what he knows. Just as the gleam in his eye turns into a manic twinkle, the door of the hotel study bursts open. Ambrose and I are sitting with our backs to the entrance, so we don't immediately see who's entered. Simon must think nothing of it because he doesn't move a muscle.

Then I hear it. Her. The melodic sound of her sweet voice.

I'm stunned, frozen in place, not believing that she's really here. I was going to give her one more day and then I was going to go get her. There was no way I was leaving without her knowing how I felt.

Yet, as she begins talking, I realize one thing. She's addressing me but not talking *to me*. She's directing her attention to Simon's hunched over form.

What the hell?

14

ELLIE

THIS HOTEL REALLY NEEDED TO DO A BETTER JOB WITH SECURITY. THIS IS THE second time in over a week that I've been able to get up to the top floor and make my way toward the royal suites without anyone stopping me.

At one point I thought I had been made. A man in an all-black suit had murmured something with suspicion into his sleeve, and I had prepared myself to be swarmed, but nothing happened. I got on the elevator without any incident.

Now, here I was, standing outside the room where Henry and I had first met. I knew he was in there. I could feel him. Or maybe it was indigestion from eating too much junk and this was a bad idea.

Yeah, this was a bad idea.

I turn to leave but instead just turn in a full circle, coming back to face the door.

No, I had to do this. I needed to do this and let Henry know how I felt. Then I could scamper back to my junk food cave and eating my emotions for the millionth time this week.

You got this. You got this. You got this.

I repeated the mantra, shaking out my limbs to hype myself up. Then, with one last deep breath for courage, I tore through the doors.

I see a dark figure across the room and come to sudden standstill. He looks so sad. I couldn't see his face, but Henry's posture was unusual for him. Almost like he was defeated.

"Henry," I begin, my voice coming out louder than I wanted in the large room. "I'm so sorry."

My words hang in the air, unwelcome. Henry doesn't say anything, he doesn't even move from his spot. That alone crushes me.

Not because he doesn't acknowledge me, but because I've reduced him to this state. I've broken his trust to the point where he can't look at me.

I needed to fix that ASAP.

"I shouldn't have left," I continue, not really sure what I'm saying but trusting my heart to help me. "I was afraid. Terrified, really, of what you had come to mean to me." I wring my hands, growing more anxious the longer he doesn't turn to me.

"From the moment we met you've thrown me. At first it was because of your kindness toward a fake, nervous princess. And then I found out who you really were." I laugh a little at that, our first meeting playing out in my mind's eye. "That was a real shock. But then you threw me again and again as we kept meeting and you kept wanting to know more about me. Which is crazy, because...well, look at me. I'm a mess."

I laugh again but still Henry doesn't move. I'm becoming desperate.

"I get why you're angry at me. Hell, I'm angry at myself too. I ran from you and didn't answer your calls because I was afraid." I ready myself, trying to stay calm as I pour my heart out. "And because it's the first time I've ever loved someone. When I realized that, how much I'd come to love you, I didn't know how to deal with those emotions. It's a big feeling, really overwhelming."

Finally Henry moves. His head lifts, but still he doesn't turn to me. Here I am, being vulnerable and laying my heart at his feet and he stands there unmoved. Son of a bitch.

"The least you could do, Henry, is look at me while I'm telling you I love you."

"Sorry, sunshine. Didn't want to interrupt."

I scream when a head pops out from around one of the highbacked chairs. I take a few steps backward, almost tripping. The man who I had assumed was Henry is now looking at me too. In fact, there are three pairs of eyes staring at me.

"Holy Hell. There are three of you."

Standing, Henry rounds the chair and comes to me. Placing his hands on my shoulders, he smiles down at me. The two men behind him have similar coloring and height, but neither of them have my Henry's stunning eyes.

His hands glide up from their hold on my shoulders to my neck and on to frame my face. It's only been a week but I've missed him so much. Seeing him now, having him touch me lets me know just how much. The ache in my heart melts away under his sky-blue gaze.

"You were saying?" Henry grins down at me.

I shake my head at him a little, laughing with him. I'm not afraid now. Not with Henry here.

"I love you, Henry. I love you so much. And I know that our path to a happily ever after won't be smooth. There'll be a lot of rocky moments and challenges and people in our way. But I want you. I love you so much that from this moment forward, I'll fight for you, for us, always."

"You were never one to shy away from a hard trail."

"As long as you're by my side, I'm prepared for anything."

Taking a step closer to me so that are bodies are pressed together, Henry bends down, his lips hovering over mine.

"I love you too, sunshine. Thank you for saving me."

"Saving you?" I whisper back, confused and a bit distracted.

"You weren't the only one who was thrown when we met. You've helped me find joy again and given me a love I'd never dared to chase."

"Well then, you're very welcome. But, Henry——"

"Yes, my love?"

"If you don't kiss me in the next two seconds, I'm going to lose my ever-loving mind."

"We can't have that, can we?"

His lips capture mine in the sweetest kiss. Relief, love and immense happiness burst from my chest and travel through my whole body. I'm home again in Henry's arms.

Our kiss turns heated, and I can't wait to get more of Henry, but a sound has us both freezing.

It's a slow clap, growing faster after every beat.

Shit. I forgot we're not alone.

Turning toward the sound, I feel my cheeks heat when I see both men giving us a standing ovation.

"Okay, assholes, get out of my room."

"I guess the grumpy man club is officially over," one of the men says, standing from the highbacked chair. He goes to the man by the fireplace and swings an arm around his shoulder, giving him a hard pat. "Don't worry, brother. We'll get you sorted." With that, they leave.

"Those two are royal pains."

I laugh at his words before it hits me.

"Oh shit. Are those your prince cousins? Did I just declare my love to you in front of a future king?" I have no idea if I'm horrified or impressed with myself.

"Don't pay them any mind," Henry says, placing a finger under my chin and directing my attention back to him. "Now, where were we?"

"I think we were at the part where I ravish you," I tease.

The biggest grin spreads across his face. I let out a squeal of shock and delight as Henry scoops me up and begins to carry me into the adjoining room.

"Then we'll live happily after."

Brushing a stray piece of hair back off his forehead, I cup his cheek and nod, so full of happiness and love I could burst. Our future may be unknown at this point, our path unmarked, but I know, without a shadow of a doubt, that Henry is my North Star. He'll always point me home.

Together we could conquer anything.

THE END

Ellie and Henry's story is over, but this isn't the last time you'll see them. Look out for ROYALLY PLUCKED, Simon's love story, this summer.
What happens when a chicken crosses the path of a royal on the road? Find out in ROYALLY PLUCKED, a fake-dating royal romance, coming soon.

Join my newsletter and be the first to know about cover reveals, new releases, giveaways and more!
Or follow me on all my socials and laugh with me:
Facebook
Instagram
TikTok
Amazon Author Page

ABOUT MELISSA WILLIAMS

Melissa Williams lives and works in Toronto, Ontario and loves to surround herself in the random and ridiculous. When not writing steamy romances, she enjoys watching bad reality TV, drinking wine and basking in the sun. But more often than not she can be found reading in her favorite comfy chair with a coffee by her side.

For the latest updates follow Melissa.

 instagram.com/melissawilliamswrites